Blood Awakening

by Tessa Dawn

A Blood Curse Novel
Book Two
In the Blood Curse Series

Published by Ghost Pines Publishing, LLC
www.ghostpinespublishing.com

Volume II of the Blood Curse Series by Tessa Dawn
First Edition Trade Paperback: July 4, 2011
10 9 8 7 6 5 4 3 2

ISBN 978-1-937223-00-7
Printed in the United States of America

Author may be contacted at: www.tessadawn.com

Ghost Pines Publishing, LLC

Acknowledgments

To my family and friends with love ~ thank you for your endless support.

To Reba (the world's greatest editor) ~ thanks for making the "hard part" easy! And to Miriam, for another wonderful cover.

To all the fans and readers who have taken the time to write ~ you have truly made the series a shared experience of joy and appreciation.

Finally, a special shout-out to Megan R for being such a dedicated supporter (just how many contests can one fan win???)

The Blood Curse

In 800 BC, Prince Jadon and Prince Jaegar Demir were banished from their Romanian homeland after being cursed by a ghostly apparition: *the reincarnated Blood of their numerous female victims.* The princes belonged to an ancient society that had sacrificed its females to the point of extinction, and the punishment was severe.

They were forced to roam the earth in darkness as creatures of the night. They were condemned to feed on the blood of the innocent and stripped of their ability to produce female offspring. They were damned to father twin sons by human hosts, who would die wretchedly upon giving birth; and the first-born of the first set would forever be required as a sacrifice of atonement for the sins of their forefathers.

Staggered by the enormity of *the Curse*, Prince Jadon, whose own hands had never shed blood, begged his accuser for leniency and received *four small mercies*—four exceptions to the curse that would apply to his house and his descendants, alone.

Ψ Though still creatures of the night, they would be allowed to walk in the sun.

Ψ Though still required to live on blood, they would not be forced to take the lives of the innocent.

Ψ While still incapable of producing female offspring, they would be given *one opportunity and thirty-days* to obtain a mate—a human female chosen by the gods—following a sign that appeared in the heavens.

Ψ While still required to sacrifice a first-born son, their twins would be born as one child of darkness and one child of light, allowing them to sacrifice the former while keeping the latter to carry on their race.

Tessa Dawn

And so...forever banished from their homeland in the Transylvanian mountains of Eastern Europe, the descendants of Jaegar and the descendants of Jadon became the Vampyr of legend: roaming the earth, ruling the elements, living on the blood of others...forever bound by an ancient curse. They were brothers of the same species, separated only by degrees of light and shadow.

Prologue

Marquis Silivasi stood silently in the shadows. He watched as the last of the humans made their way from the graveside ceremony following Joelle Parker's funeral. He had come to pay his respects but was unable to face the human family whose lineage he had known for centuries. Having to tell Kevin Parker the news of his daughter's death had been one of the worst moments of Marquis's life, and he had lived a very, very long time. His regret was insufferable, his shame for being unable to save her...almost unbearable.

Shimmering out of view, he materialized deep within the Dark Moon Forest at yet another recent grave site—that of his little brother, Shelby. It was the first time he had visited the final resting place since the tragic loss. The first time he had seen the simple white granite marker lying over the desolate plot: *Shelby Silivasi. Honored Brother and Beloved Twin.*

Marquis ran a trembling hand through his thick black hair. The pressing moisture of tears stung his deeply troubled eyes. Shelby had only been five-hundred years old when he died, the same age as his twin, Nachari, but the difference was, Nachari had lived to graduate the Romanian University. Nachari had lived to reach the status of Master Vampire.

Shelby, on the other hand, had stopped just short of receiving such an honored distinction because he had found his *blood destiny*: the one human woman chosen by the gods to be his mate, Dalia Montano.

His one opportunity to avoid the ultimate curse of his kind.

Fulfilling the demands of the Blood Curse and securing his future with the human female had been far more important to Shelby than completing his studies. He had planned to return to Romania as soon as the blood sacrifice was made, yet the young fledgling had failed at both tasks.

Marquis knew he was the one to blame.

He should have been more vigilant.

He should never have let down his guard.

BLOOD AWAKENING

Things had just gone so smoothly—so unbelievably seamlessly—between Shelby and Dalia that no one had foreseen Valentine Nistor's wicked scheme.

It wasn't an excuse.

Marquis was an Ancient. He should have known better.

Marquis balled his hands into two tight fists, struggling to contain the rage—the gut-wrenching heartache—that threatened to consume him. The sky above him had already turned as black as night, and the wind was picking up into a fierce howl. He had to keep his emotions in check.

He kicked at the cold forest ground, causing a not-so-subtle tremor in the earth beneath him in an effort not to cry out. The vengeance he had finally exacted on Valentine was nothing against the breadth of this loss.

Celestial gods, how could this have happened!

And it wasn't just that Shelby would have been a Master, an achievement borne of *four-hundred years* of studies; he would have been a *Master Warrior*, like Marquis. And that meant Marquis would have been in charge of his little brother's ongoing training: It would have been the first time in four-hundred and seventy-nine years—since their father's death—that Marquis would have shared his day-to-day existence with another being.

The first time in four-hundred and seventy-nine years that Marquis Silivasi would not have been alone.

Marquis knelt before the simple white slab of granite and bowed his head in reverence. So much loss.

He had seen so many warriors needlessly slain over his lifetime as a result of the wretched curse—a pronouncement made upon generations of males for a sin committed so long ago that the fallen warriors didn't even remember the crime. They only knew that when the Blood Moon came, they had thirty days....

One opportunity in an otherwise eternal existence to claim the one human woman who could save them from the ultimate fate of their kind. One month to obtain a chance at life, create the possibility for love, and acquire the blessing of a family.

Thirty days to live or die.

Marquis shook his head. What was the purpose of being a warrior...of being an Ancient...if he couldn't even protect the ones he loved? What was the purpose of surviving this long when his life had been nothing but time, education, endless battles, and loss? And why hadn't that one opportunity to love—to share such a barren existence—ever been given to him?

He was so very weary of living.

Like a slowly boiling cauldron of water, Marquis's body began to tremble with the depth of his anguish. His lungs labored, and his heart pounded from so much rage and injustice, until finally, he could no longer contain his grief, and the pain of a lifetime spilled over.

Hands pressed tightly against his temples, Marquis Silivasi threw back his head and shouted his rage, his grief, in one gut-wrenching cry: a lion's roar that shook the heavens, sending balls of fire the color of blood crashing down upon the earth, hail the size of baseballs battering the valley floor.

As the Ancient Master Warrior's crimson tears fell like raindrops, the rivers overflowed and the heavens shook. Giant boulders perched atop nearby canyons crashed to the earth's floor in violent rockslides, even as the sides of the mountains split open.

And then all was silent.

The anguished cry of the male reverberated through the Rocky Mountains. It echoed through the rising hills, rose to the blackened sky, and stirred deep beneath the cavernous valley, until it finally settled as nothing more than a subtle tremor buried deep within the earth's crust.

Ciopori Demir stirred.

III

BLOOD AWAKENING

Her resting place disturbed.

Deep golden eyes, dotted with amber-sparkles like sun-drenched diamonds, blinked once...twice...a third time. Heavy, dark lashes fanned ancient cheeks as eyes that had been closed for centuries fluttered open. A sleeping mind awakened. A soul became aware.

The echo of the male's call stirred Ciopori's heart as she slowly sat up. His anguish penetrated her soul. The cadence of his cry restored her eternal heartbeat. Somehow, his rage reanimated her pure, royal blood...primordial, innocent, and unblemished...even as his grief broke the ancient spell.

Ciopori rubbed her eyes, trying to clear her mind. She pushed a heavy lock of her hair from her face and struggled to remember: Where was she?

Who was she?

The memories came back slowly, one scattered piece at a time: She was the daughter of greatness, the first-born female-child of the Great King Sakarias and his beautiful wife, Jade. She was the caretaker of her youngest sibling, Vanya, and the sister of the royal twins, Jaegar and Jadon. So what was she doing buried deep within the earth? Surrounded by so many layers of rich minerals, crusted soil, and clammy moisture?

The ancient princess suddenly felt entombed in the endless layers of evolution. Trapped in a timeless grave. *Think, Ciopori,* she urged herself, as the dirt walls of her grave seemed to close in on her. *How is it that you find yourself in this predicament? And what must you do to get out of it?* The memories began to creep in incrementally, like water through a leaky dam: all the killings, the endless sacrifices, the loss of so many females.

The last of their great kind, the Celestial Beings, had been reduced to ashes by the moral depravity of their men, their ravenous hunger for power. Their culture had been decimated by a wicked, insatiable thirst for blood that had become unquenchable.

Ciopori sat up and hugged her knees to her chest, rocking in a smooth, rhythmic motion, trying to calm her mind. Who was the last person she remembered seeing? Ah, of course, *Jadon*, her beloved older brother. Now she remembered.

Jadon had whisked them away—herself and Vanya—at great risk to his own life. In the midst of a violent storm, he had come into their castle bedchamber like a thief in the night, imploring them to flee Romania at once, explaining that they had to get out of the castle immediately if they hoped to live: Jaegar and his warriors were coming for them.

The men had finally crossed the last and final boundary: They had gone mad from their endless blood-lust, and were ready to make the ultimate sacrifice, the virgin daughters of the great king himself, Jaegar's very own sisters.

Determined to see his siblings live and his society survive, Jadon had whisked them across the vast, open countryside, taking them deep into the heart of the Transylvanian Alps, where he had met up with a convoy of traveling warriors, a secret group of mercenaries led by the infamous wizard, Fabian. Eventually, Fabian had secured passage on a ship across the great sea, taking himself, Ciopori, and Vanya to a foreign land far across the ocean, an uninhabited refuge where they would finally be given sanctuary from their own kind.

Sanctuary in the form of a living death.

A deep, dreamless slumber where their bodies would remain alive—immortal, yet asleep—until such time as it was finally safe to awaken them again.

Until Jadon came back to get them.

Ciopori wondered what time it was. *What year it was.* She began to thrash around, frantically searching for her sleeping sister in the darkness of the shallow chamber. She must find and awaken Vanya! How long had it been? How many years had they slept? Had Jadon finally come back for them?

And whose anguished cry was that?

Her heart felt heavy from the torment in his voice. Had his sorrow awakened her? Ciopori didn't know why, but she had to

V

find that male.

She had to go to him!

Desperately, she began to claw at the ground, digging in frenzied circles as her body scraped against the walls of the earthen tomb.

"Vanya! Vanya!"

She cried out until her voice grew hoarse, digging...turning...clawing...twisting her body this way and that in a frenzied effort to uncover her baby sister. "Vanya, where are you!"

After what seemed like hours, Ciopori dropped her head in her hands and started to weep. The earth was suffocating her. She was about to panic. She had to get out of the ground. Now that she was awake, she could no longer stomach the shallow grave: The smell of damp earth was all around her, the blanket of rich soil encasing her like the burial shroud of a mummy.

Ciopori took a long, slow, deep breath and worked to calm her mind. She was a Celestial Being. *Picture the earth. See the sky above you.*

She shifted until she was on her knees.

"Ancestors, Great Ones, I humbly beseech you: *From deep within the earth I pray, my tomb as dark as night; for freedom from this lowly grave...awaken heaven's light.*

Place my feet along earth's path, the sky above my head—where flowers bloom and children laugh; release me from earth's bed."

All at once, Ciopori was standing in a clearing, her feet on solid ground. Towering pines and fir trees surrounded her, and the sky transformed right before her eyes from a darkened gray to a brilliant aqua blue. Her eyes swept over the land, taking note of the simple granite markers. It was a circular, hallowed clearing.

This was sacred earth.

A burial ground.

Ciopori stepped backward, removing her shoes reverently from her feet as she paid silent homage to the dead. She

wondered who they were. Were these her father's soldiers?
And then she saw him.
The powerful, stunning warrior.
The one whose cries had awakened her.

He was an enormous male, clearly a fighter, with long, thick hair the color of midnight: the color of hers.

His eyes were like the depths of the ocean, so black they gleamed blue. And his remarkably handsome face was stricken with sorrow as he knelt before a simple white stone marker. Ciopori knew immediately that he was a warrior of some standing. It was in the proud set of his shoulders, the way he crouched above the ground with both stealth and purpose, the arrogant slant of his chin. There was a hard certainty in his demeanor...in spite of his sorrow.

Ciopori had spent very little time with her father's guard growing up, but she knew enough etiquette to approach the warrior with respect.

She padded silently around the periphery of the grounds, stopping roughly four feet behind him. As was proper when addressing a male of authority, she averted her eyes, cleared her throat, and awaited his attention.

The male sprang to his feet like a predator, rising and whirling to face her in one smooth motion. He looked startled to find her standing there, as if no one had ever snuck up on him before. His face was a hard line of menace as he stared her down with those hauntingly beautiful eyes.

"Greetings, warrior," Ciopori whispered in the old language.

one

Startled by the impostor, Marquis sprang to his feet and crouched into a warrior's attack stance. *Great gods*, he must be losing his mind. No one had ever caught him unaware before.

As soon as he realized the intruder was a female—a strikingly beautiful, very unusual female—he began to relax. Her hair was the color of the Vampyr, a deep raven black that shone with highlights of midnight blue. Her eyes were like nuggets of pure gold with amber diamonds in the centers, sparkling like the noonday sun. They were clearly *not human*, and her countenance was positively regal: The woman stood before him like an Egyptian queen, drunk with nobility, as if she owned the entire world. Yet at the same time, she bowed her head and averted her eyes with great deference. She had obviously been raised to behave in such a manner.

Marquis took a step back. He wasn't at all sure who *or what* he was dealing with.

The female squared her shoulders and declined her head once again in the slightest gesture. "I have startled you, warrior. Forgive me. Once again, I bid you greetings."

Marquis blinked several times. He had been so taken aback that he hadn't even noticed—*she was speaking in the Old Language.* But unlike himself—or his brothers for that matter—her accent was pure. Her tongue, absolutely flawless. The cadence was hypnotic.

He cleared his throat. "Be at ease, milady. Should it please you, this warrior would know your name...*and your lineage.*" Whoa, where did that come from? He knew, intuitively, that it was the proper response, although he had no idea how.

The female raised her head then, and her smile was positively radiant. "I find your inquiry satisfactory, warrior. My name is Ciopori Demir, begotten of the goddess Cygnus and the human ancestor Mateo Demir. Daughter of our noble King Sakarias and his gracious wife, Queen Jade."

BLOOD AWAKENING

Marquis cleared his throat and stared at the female like she was an alien from another planet. He opened his mouth to respond, but when no sound came out, he simply cleared his throat a second time and continued staring. He was positively dumbfounded.

The female looked momentarily confused. "'Tis I who would hear your lineage now, warrior. Do you belong to my father's guard?"

Marquis shook his head, trying to clear the cobwebs. His grief had finally consumed him. He was hallucinating. "Let me get this straight," he said. "You claim to be the *daughter* of King Sakarias? *The* King Sakarias? As in the father of Prince Jaegar and Prince Jadon: the ruler of the Celestial Beings before the Blood Curse?"

Ciopori's shoulders stiffened and she raised her chin. "I make no such *claim;* 'tis an assertion of fact, warrior. And I am beginning to find your attitude almost as wanting as your command of our native tongue, far too relaxed for my liking. Do you not have more respect for your kingship? Do you or do you not serve my father's guard?"

Marquis licked his bottom lip and stifled a laugh, although the situation was hardly amusing. "No, milady; I can assure you that I do not serve your father's guard…as King Sakarias died *twenty-eight hundred years ago*—thirteen-hundred years before I was even born. And even if he hadn't, *serving* is not my thing."

Ciopori staggered backward. Her eyes grew big, and she cried out before abruptly catching herself. She brought her hands to her mouth to stifle the sound. It was as if such a display of emotion would be undignified in front of a…commoner. Despite her gallant effort, her face became gaunt and her body started to sway back and forth as if she were about to faint. The female was shocked…terrified…and clearly grief-stricken.

Marquis felt as overwhelmed as she looked. Surely, she wasn't…she couldn't be…

She did appear to be of their race, though, and she spoke

2

their native tongue—obviously better than he did, as she found his dialect offensive. But there were no female Vampyr, only human *destinies* who were sired by their mates. So what else could she be...if not a Celestial Being? Marquis delved gently into her mind, quickly scanning her thoughts, unraveling her memories. He followed the pathways back...back...to—

Holy mother of Cygnus!

As tears began to pour down the beautiful woman's face— *Princess Ciopori's face!*—Marquis glanced around the forest. He wasn't at all sure what he was looking for, but given the impossible turn of events, he half expected to see a god or goddess saunter out of the trees, perhaps someone better suited to handle the astonishing revelation than he. Gods knew, he was anything but tactful on a good day, and today was a very bad one.

And then Ciopori fainted.

Marquis moved with all the fluid, supernatural speed of the Vampyr race, catching her just before her elegant form hit the ground. As his hand slid beneath her waiste, a bolt of awareness shot through him like a sudden surge of electricity. Memories— *no, dreams*—began to flood his mind at record speed...

They were memories of his own dreams, ancient pictures that had come to him again and again over the centuries. Dreams that had sustained him through battles and losses. A face that had haunted him with eternal loneliness...

They were fantastical visions he had almost forgotten over the endless years: images of a woman with raven black hair and golden eyes with amber irises, dreams of a woman he had always known...

And loved.

Marquis looked down at the frail body slumped peacefully beneath him. Was he really holding a living, breathing *female* of his race in his arms? After all these centuries—his people believing not one had survived? And was the angel from his dreams—the raven-haired beauty who had come to him so many times in the night—actually a real woman?

Or was he just going mad?

His arms tightened around her waist, and he pulled her closer to his chest, deeply inhaling her scent.

It was familiar.

Dear gods, it was her.

And she felt exactly as he...*remembered*...exactly as she had felt in his dreams.

Marquis stared down at Ciopori's face, studying every detail, not knowing whether to laugh or cry. He wanted to awaken her, but it had been so long...so many years since he had touched a woman, held a woman in his arms...or his heart. So many years since he believed he even had a heart. Her beauty stole his breath away, and he knew the moment she awakened, he would have to let her go.

Marquis thought about calling out to his brothers telepathically. He had to tell someone what was happening. After all, this had monumental implications for their race. But not yet.

Not yet.

Right now, he would hold this angel from his dreams safely in his arms and remain in whatever fantasy-world he had drifted into. Right now, he would imagine she was his.

Time seemed to stand still. It was as if the sun had simply ceased its journey across the sky and all of heaven was holding its breath, while Marquis basked in the glow of Ciopori's exquisiteness...gloried in the feel of her slight frame tucked so reverently beneath his own. Felt alive for the first time in centuries.

And then the princess slowly opened her eyes.

Dear gods, she was breathtaking.

She looked up at him but did not appear afraid. And then she lifted her elegant hand and placed the palm ever so gently against his cheek.

"Marquis?"

Marquis froze. Her voice was like a robin's song as she

spoke his—

Dear gods in the heavens, she knew his name!

Marquis's lips curved into a tentative smile. "Yes."

She blinked several times. "You are the warrior...from my dreams."

Marquis began to tremble as he slowly let his forehead rest against hers. He had never met this woman, yet he knew her intimately: everything about her. The way she moved. The way she talked. The sparkling sound of her laughter. The elegant fall of her hair against her bare shoulders when she...undressed before bed.

Marquis closed his eyes, afraid to hope. He had been alone...forever. Born alone with a Dark One for a twin; cast into solitary existence following his father's disappearance; cursed as a male who had never been given a female destiny...in fifteen hundred years. The only peace he had ever known had been in his dreams—loving a woman he could never possess—throughout the endless centuries of his life. Yet, here she was...

When he opened his eyes, his gaze locked with hers. Her own recognition was reflected in their light: She knew him, too.

Marquis exhaled slowly. "I have waited over a thousand years for you." His voice was not his own.

Ciopori studied his face. She softly traced the hard slant of his jaw to the masculine angles of his cheeks, her fingers gently brushing the chiseled lines as she traced the outline. All at once, she drew back her hand and smiled. "And I, you, warrior. *And I, you.*"

Marquis drew her close to his heart, and held her like she was the very air he breathed—the most precious thing on earth—because she was. When he finally released her, there were tears rolling down her cheeks. He gently brushed them away. "Where did you come from, angel of my dreams?"

Ciopori shook her head. "I...I'm not sure. What year is this? What is this...Blood Curse...you speak of? And where am I?"

Marquis shook his head. *Wow.* Where to begin? Perhaps the

less traumatic information should come first. "You are in Dark Moon Vale."

"Dark Moon...what? Is this place in Romania?" Her eyes swept the forest floor, the distant canyons, and the high mountain peaks. "We are yet in the Transylvanian Alps, then?"

Marquis blanched. "No, Ciopori; you are in North America. The Rocky Mountains."

Ciopori sat up then, and Marquis helped her to her feet. She slowly turned around. "Then we did cross the great sea as I remembered." She rubbed her eyes as if awakening from a dream. "And the strange, uninhabited land, it is called...*North America?* Yes, of course, that's right. Fabian brought us here. Myself and Van— Oh dear gods, Vanya!" Her tone became frantic. "You must help me find my sister. At once!"

Ciopori explained how she and Vanya had escaped Romania prior to the Curse—how Fabian had placed them both in an enchanted sleep to await the return of their brother Jadon. The story was almost impossible to believe.

Marquis followed Ciopori to the site of her awakening and scanned the earth's crust for anomalies. Fortunately, it was early autumn, and the ground was growing cold. While he couldn't see beneath the surface, he could easily detect the slightest variation in temperature. It was a lot like having a built-in, infrared heat detector. Wherever Vanya was, her body would put out a clear, recognizable signal.

Sure enough, the undisturbed sleeping chamber was directly ten feet beneath them, about five feet to the east of where Ciopori had lain...*for twenty-eight hundred years.* As the original Celestial Beings were neither gods nor humans, but the prodigy of the two species intermixing, they had very long life spans. But they were not immortal.

No, immortality had been a cruel punishment enacted upon the males when they were turned Vampyr at the time of the Curse. It had been done to prolong their suffering—to make sure they experienced it...indefinitely. Consequently, Fabian's feat had been nothing less than astounding: keeping two females suspended in animation—alive yet not aging—for this many years. Casting a spell that could only be broken by the return of their beloved brother, Jadon.

Marquis shuddered at the thought. Jadon would have never returned. What if Marquis's own cry had not awakened her? He refused to allow the thought.

"She is here," he said matter-of-factly, indicating the ground with his foot.

Ciopori turned toward him. "How will we get her out?" Her face paled. "Dear gods, what if she's—"

"She's alive; just as you were."

"How can you be sure?"

"Because I can hear her heart beat."

Ciopori shook her head in disbelief. "Whatever did my sisters turn you into?"

Marquis ran his tongue over the tips of his fangs, wondering if she knew—from the dreams, that is. He studied the ground intently. "The fastest way to reach her is to dig in a straight line."

Ciopori nodded. "Very well. Where shall we find a spade?"

Marquis smiled then. "A shovel? We don't need one."

"You intend to use a digging fork or some other lesser tool?" She scoffed.

Marquis chuckled. "I'm going to use my mind."

Ciopori frowned.

"I can move matter with my mind," he explained.

"Matter?" Ciopori raised a brow.

"Yes: objects, things...materials." He eyed her sideways. "Never mind."

Ciopori sighed. "Even if one could do such a thing, it would take forever."

Marquis shook his head. "No. Not with enough speed behind it."

Ciopori cocked her head to the side, like a canine studying a confusing human, lost somewhere in the translation between species. "Marquis, this curse that was wrought upon the males...what did it do to them? You say you are still related to our people, the Celestial Beings, yet you are a separate race altogether: *Vampyr*. What all can a *vampyr* do?"

"A vampire," Marquis supplied.

Ciopori nodded. "What all can a *vampire* do? What powers do you possess, warrior?"

Marquis rubbed the bridge of his nose, thinking. "We have heightened senses: sight, hearing, taste, smell. We can fly or simply move through time and space at will. We can read the thoughts and memories of others, or change them if we choose. We can control the actions of others, speak to one another telepathically, and harness fire or electricity in our hands." He paused, trying to think of anything else. "Our strength is tremendous, and our speed is...well, beyond anything you have witnessed, I'm certain."

Ciopori blinked several times. "Wow, is that it?"

Missing most attempts at wit or humor as Marquis often did, he shrugged. "No, we can also walk through walls and self-regenerate...heal ourselves of almost any injury. We're more or less just better at everything."

Ciopori cleared her throat. "Humble as well, I see."

"No, not really."

When Ciopori stifled a laugh, Marquis stood quietly, not sure if he should go on.

"Well, I can do magic," she offered playfully.

Marquis shifted uncomfortably. "Yes...so can my younger brother, Nachari."

Ciopori laughed heartily then. "Were vampires not given a sense of humor, warrior?"

Marquis frowned. So that was the source of her amusement. "I guess one man's humor is another vampire's...headache. If vampires got headaches, that is. Which we don't. Get headaches."

Ciopori wrinkled her forehead. "Pardon me?"

Marquis shook his head, irritated. "Nothing. It was just something stupid my brother Nathaniel said not long ago. Uh...no...we have humor. I mean, they have humor—other vampires—apparently, it's just me." He turned away and began studying the ground in earnest. Princess or no, he would not continue to make a fool of himself for a female. "I'm going to lift the dirt from here." He made a circle with his hands. "And move it over there." He gestured toward a small grove of birch trees. "The circumference should probably be...at least ten feet around, so that nothing falls in on her." He glanced up then, to see if she was still laughing.

Ciopori sauntered closer, her eyes sparkling like rare jewels, and he could have sworn his heart literally skipped a beat when she cupped his face in his hands. "Know this, warrior: I have not traveled across oceans—and survived for centuries—in order to enjoy your brothers' humor. You are the one I have dreamed of."

Marquis sighed and drew her to him. His hands fell down to the small of her waist. His grip was strong and possessive. "You will come to understand me, Ciopori." He cupped her chin in his hand and raised her head to meet his gaze. "And I will come to understand you...if such a thing would please you."

Before she could answer, he bent his head, his mouth suspended just above hers. "Vampires are extremely passionate," he drawled. "Some of us are better with our bodies than our words." He brushed her lips with his, kissing her ever so gently. "And all of us are enormously protective." He pulled her tightly against him, overwhelming her body beneath his own until she was forced to arch her back. When he looked down at her seductive curves, he groaned. "And fiercely possessive." He

9

fisted his hands in her hair, carefully tilting her head until she gasped, and her lips unwittingly parted.

It was then that he kissed her: the full hunger of fifteen-hundred years unleashed in one erotic brush of passion. He flirted with her mouth, tasted every texture of her tongue, nibbled on her lips, and drank in her taste. He loved her with the hunger of one who had never before been sated. Yes, he had experienced a few romantic affairs with human women before, but such couplings had never satisfied his deeper longings. Not to mention, they were always so dangerous. Vampires were primarily animals—powerful, instinctual predators—and a passionate interlude could easily turn deadly for a mortal woman. Males had to exercise extreme restraint.

In his loneliness, Marquis had imagined his *destiny* many times over the centuries, until he had finally given up believing she would ever come. But this woman—this angel he had loved in dreams long since forgotten—she was his every erotic fantasy, and his body craved hers like his species craved blood: to sustain, quench, and regenerate until he was replete.

His hands rose to cup the weight of her breasts, his thumbs instinctively finding her nipples. "I know how to protect what is mine." His mouth found the hollow of her throat, and he teased her pulse with his tongue until she shivered. "I know how to defend and avenge that which I hold dear to my heart." And then he pressed the hard length of his arousal against her quivering stomach. "And make no mistake; I know how to please a woman."

Ciopori went limp in his arms before stuttering an incomprehensible reply. And then she cupped his face in her hands and returned his kiss, matching him passion-for-passion, desire-for-desire, need-for-need.

When Marquis finally pulled away, his eyes were burning, and they must have been glowing red because Ciopori looked startled. "Your sisters gave us these feral eyes, but the heat you see—that is your doing." His fangs elongated against his will, and he scraped them gently along her carotid artery. "We use these to feed...but I will use them to bring you to your knees *with pleasure.*"

Ciopori groaned as he nicked her skin, then swirled his tongue over the wound, creating the dual sensation of pain and pleasure. "This is who *and what* I am, Ciopori. Can you accept me?"

Ciopori took a step back and rubbed the small wounds on her neck. She stared at him then...taking in everything.

Her eyes missed nothing.

After what seemed far too long for his comfort, she smiled a mischievous grin. "Only if I am to be the one to please you...*and feed you*...warrior." She stepped forward and laid her head against his chest, just above his heart. "And love you...if you will have me."

Marquis bit down on his lower lip and closed his eyes. He didn't dare breathe. Warriors did not shed tears. *Marquis Silivasi did not shed tears.* Yet, for the first time in his life, his heart wept with joy and gratitude. "The gods themselves could not take you from me now, Ciopori."

Stroking her long raven hair, he motioned toward a tall quaking aspen that still had its summer leaves. "Stand over there, my lost angel. Let us find and awaken your sister."

two

Marquis and Nachari stared at the ancient sovereign king of their people with more than a little concern in their eyes. In all their years of living, they had never seen the powerful ruler so rattled. The male could hardly pull himself together.

He paced a quick lap around the formal receiving room of his four-story manse—for the fifth time. He glanced down the hallway toward the bathroom, where the females had retreated to bathe before dinner, and then he glared at Marquis and Nachari as if he had half a mind to throttle them both. For what, they had no idea.

"Jadon and Jaegar's sisters," Napolean rambled. "Alive after all this time." He wrung his hands together and sat back down on the sofa. "Remarkable, don't you think?"

Just as Marquis started to speak, the sovereign lord jumped back up.

Lap six.

"Nachari," Napolean spoke gravely, "you are a wizard now, are you not?"

Nachari glanced at Marquis. "Yep, last time I checked."

Marquis shifted uncomfortably and shook his head, regarding his little brother harshly. *Do not be so arrogant,* he admonished telepathically, wondering where the question was headed. After all, Napolean had already posed the same query. *Twice.*

Sharing Marquis's sentiment, Napolean spun around, the silver slashes in his deep onyx eyes growing harsh: "Watch yourself, son. Do not think to be that informal with me, even under circumstances such as these."

Nachari paled. His strong shoulders drew back as he bowed his head. "Forgive me, milord; I meant no offense."

Napolean turned to look out the window then. His waist-length, black-and-silver hair shifted along his back. His proud frame became rigid. "You know, Marquis…" He didn't turn around to look at the Ancient Warrior. "The county fire department is still extinguishing several blazes as we speak; public service has been pumping water back into the rivers all afternoon; and there are several cleanup crews removing boulders and debris from the roadways."

Marquis was too old and too hardened to placate the sovereign lord, although he knew exactly what he was referring to: his earlier outburst at Shelby's grave. The dangerous results of his unchecked emotions. Marquis remained quiet, waiting to hear what the king had to say.

"If it was anyone else, there might be consequences." Napolean turned around to regard the warrior then. "But I know the weight of what you carry, and how long you have carried it. *Marquis*,"—he said his name with veneration—"there were several humans injured."

Marquis frowned. "Were there any deaths?"

Napolean sighed and turned back toward the window. "No...*fortunately*."

Marquis remained quiet. There was nothing to say. *Don't let it happen again* was implied, and Marquis already knew the gravity of his actions. He also knew that their king had far too much respect for him to reprimand an Ancient Master in front of his younger brother of lesser status. He and Napolean were two of the oldest males in the house of Jadon. Though Marquis understood clearly who his Sovereign was, the two were more like equals than king and subject.

Realizing that Napolean had said all he was going to say, Marquis distracted himself by looking around the room. As many times as he had stood in the foyer or entered the Hall of Justice, this was the first time he had ever sat in the king's private living quarters: Napolean kept his personal life primarily hidden from his subjects, and seeing the interior of the house for the first time was fascinating.

The sovereign lord's manse was certainly a home befitting a king: dignified, formal, and reflective of all twenty-eight hundred years of the Original Male's life. There were four levels to the private rectory, which was linked to the public Hall of Justice by a sealed tunnel that gave the king easy access to the three, ceremonial chambers: the chamber that held the tomes of the Vampyr race, containing the laws, histories, births, and deaths of their people; the chamber where the first-born sons were *relinquished* to atone for the sins of their forefathers; and the chamber containing the insufferable circular hall, where the sons of Jadon—those who failed to satisfy the Blood Curse—spent their last, agonizing hours.

The chamber where Marquis's beloved younger brother Shelby had so recently spent his last unthinkable hours.

Marquis shifted once more on the sofa, forcing the memory from his mind: That was not a safe place to go. Looking up at the ceiling, he gazed at the artistry, his eyes taking in the intricate detail of the hand-painted mural at the top of the dome: It was a scene from the ancient Greek myth about the god Zeus and his son Apollo. Now that was certainly fitting, Marquis thought. Glancing at Napolean, he could envision the king in the exact same pose, a lightning bolt shooting from his royal hand. Hell, he'd actually seen that vision a time or two in battle, already.

As his gaze drifted from the ceiling to the walls, he noticed that every corner—every window, niche, and archway—was encased in hand-carved white moldings, and the actual windows themselves were made of frosted glass, adorned with scenes of battlements and pictures of the gods etched skillfully into the iced canvases.

While the walls were painted in soft hues of grayish blue, the furniture was far bolder, displaying deep royal blues with red and green accents.

There were art-niches and custom inlays everywhere, each one containing a timeless treasure, items dating back as far as the Barbarian Migrations to the east Roman Empire…when it was still ruled by Constantinople. And the mementos were as eclectic as they were valuable: reflecting the varied cultures of Greece,

Tessa Dawn

Persia, and Egypt, as well as North America. Marquis shook his head: The place was equal parts museum and monastery, which just meant that Napolean lived as he ruled—always a king first, an individual second. It was a good thing their king was so private: If a human being ever got wind of these treasures...

Marquis smiled. Now that would be a sight to see: Napolean versus an army of humans. Just as Marquis began to play out the scene in his mind, the ancient lord began to speak.

"I asked you here for a purpose, Nachari." He placed his hand on the glass window and declined his head with a seriousness of purpose.

Nachari sat up straight. "As always, I am at your service, milord."

Napolean nodded. "Good...because there is a great deal we need to do in a short amount of time."

Nachari raised his eyebrows but remained, respectfully, silent.

"As a wizard, you are one of the few among us who might be able to make sense of what Fabian did to the women." He rubbed his jaw. "We do not yet know if they share our immortality, whether or not they are impervious to human disease, what strengths and vulnerabilities they possess. There is much to be learned in a little amount of time if we are to adequately protect them." With that, the king turned back to the window and became absorbed, once again, in his own thoughts.

Nachari waited to be certain Napolean was done speaking before he replied. "I am honored, milord, and I will do my best to serve you and the daughters of our ancient king."

Marquis glanced sideways at his polished younger sibling. King or no, Napolean Mondragon was the greatest warrior among them, and his knowledge of magic was legendary...frightening. Indeed, it was a great honor for him to request Nachari's assistance. And, of course, Marquis could not have agreed more: The safety of the two original females was paramount.

BLOOD AWAKENING

Nachari smiled, and his eyes seemed to twinkle. *You seem to have taken a rather...personal...interest in all of this, my brother.*

Marquis snorted: *I'm glad you're so amused, Nachari; I see no humor in the situation.*

Nachari leaned back, crossed his legs, and chuckled. *Of course you don't, Marquis.*

Stay out of my business, boy, Marquis warned.

Nachari patted him on the knee and sighed with satisfaction. *Oh, I'm afraid I just can't do that, Master Warrior. I have waited over four-hundred years for this: You have no idea.*

Waited for what? Marquis scowled.

Before Nachari could answer, a door at the end of the hall opened, and a single set of footsteps advanced along the polished marble floors. It was the princess Vanya, and she was wearing a garden motif dress with a draped bodice and a flowing sash in the center: one of several garments Napolean had requested delivery of earlier that afternoon. She looked like a walking Monet painting: both stunning and timeless.

Nachari leaned forward on the sofa, and Napolean turned away from the window. Both males were unmistakably breathless. And despite his best resolve, Marquis exhaled slowly. No offense to human women, but the Celestial gods certainly knew how to perfect a female.

Vanya Demir was a princess in every sense of the word. Her body was slender with sleek, regal lines and she sashayed as she moved, her head held at a slight upward angle, her shoulders pulled back and straight. Her soft, sculpted lips were set in a gentle but stern line, and her keen, attentive eyes took in everything around her with noble acuity.

The young celestial female had long, flaxen hair with light blond highlights that fell well below her waist, and her eyes were an unusual pale rose: as stunning as they were unique. She knew she was beautiful. She knew she was royalty. And she knew she commanded the moon and the stars. It was in her every movement, her every breath.

Tessa Dawn

The princess stopped at the entrance to the hall and gracefully curtsied as Marquis and Nachari stood. Napolean quickly advanced across the room, and then all at once, he stumbled over an antique coffee table—nearly falling over.

Nachari swallowed a gasp and shot a bewildered glance at Marquis. *What the—*

Not a word, Marquis growled. *Not a single word.*

Napolean shot them both a harsh, reprimanding glare, and Nachari took a step back. *Tell me we are not broadcasting our thoughts on a public bandwidth, Marquis. Please...*

Marquis frowned. *Of course not, brother. I do not believe he can hear us speak to one another—but he can certainly perceive our visual images and read our emotions.*

All at once, Marquis sensed a powerful shift in his younger brother's energy, and then he caught the deliberate, fixed image of *the ocean* planted in Nachari's mind. *Four hundred years at the Romanian University to become a Master of Wizardry, and you conjure an image of the ocean to conceal your thoughts? Well, that makes sense—coming from a male who lives in the Rocky Mountains.*

Nachari rolled his perfect eyes.

"Good evening, princess." Napolean spoke in the Old Language, motioning toward a cushioned, high-back chair. "Are you feeling any better?"

Vanya took a seat, her elegant back arched with imperial posture. "A bit."

Despite her response, her eyes were swollen, and her words came out hollow: Marquis knew that she had been crying off and on ever since they had awoken her. Ever since she had learned that all she once knew was gone. That she had outlived her brothers, her parents, her people...and her civilization. It was an enormous amount of grief to carry, and Vanya was clearly still in shock.

Napolean took a seat beside her and gestured toward Nachari. "You have already met the Ancient Master Warrior Marquis, but this is his youngest brother, the Master Wizard

17

Nachari. He is here to help us sort through this...situation."

Vanya looked up at Nachari and smiled faintly. "'Tis an honor to meet you, wizard. How do you and thy brother fare this evening?"

Nachari gulped. "Very well, thank you."

Marquis took a seat. "Is Ciopori...is your sister...okay?"

"Indeed," Vanya replied. "She will be joining us soon, warrior."

Nachari sat back down as well, and put his hands in his lap.

As the king cleared his throat to speak, his severe silver-pupils were fixed on Vanya's face like lasers. "I took the liberty of bringing in a temporary chef to cook for you and your sister until we figure out something more permanent. You will both be staying here for the immediate future."

And no doubt, the security will be greatly increased, Nachari commented absently to Marquis.

Vanya nodded. "Thank you. I'm sure the accommodations will be lovely. You did not yet have a chef to your liking, I take it?"

Napolean wrung his powerful hands together like a teenage boy fidgeting, and then he promptly...*stuttered*: "We...uh...we...we don't eat...food." He swallowed an obvious lump in his throat.

"I see," Vanya responded cordially, pretending not to notice.

Nachari put his arm along the ridge of the sofa and leaned back as if taking in a very interesting show. *I believe our king is...drooling...Marquis: I swear, in all my years, I have never seen Napolean react like this...*to anything.

Marquis didn't respond.

Although, I can hardly blame him; she is breathtaking, is she not? I don't think I've ever seen a more beautiful creature in all of my life.

All at once, Napolean's head snapped to the side in a wicked, serpentine movement. His eyes flashed from onyx to red—then back again—the warning so swift it was almost imperceptible. His top lip twitched in the same rapid manner, displaying a lightning quick flash of fangs.

Nachari shot back on the sofa and looked down. *I don't care what you say, Marquis; he can hear us!*

Well, perhaps you should shut-up then, little—

Of course I can hear you! Napolean's eyes never veered from Nachari's. *I have the blood of every male in the house of Jadon in my veins, including your own: I know where each one of you is and what each one of you is doing...at all times. Trust me: I can do far more than intercept your private communication at will. I am your Sovereign, and I can reach into places you do not even know exist, youngster.* There was a clear note of warning in his voice.

Oh gods—Nachari shrank down on the sofa—*I'm sorry...milord.*

Napolean smiled then. *You are young and proud, wizard. There is no offense taken...yet.*

Just then, Nachari's cell phone went off, and he reached into his back pocket so fast one would have thought the thing was on fire. "Excuse me," he said, opening a screen to read a text. He immediately turned to Marquis. "Brother, Chad has been trying to reach you for the last hour; is your cell phone off?"

Marquis shrugged. "I don't know...maybe." He checked all of his pockets. "I must have left it in the truck."

Having the ability to either fly or materialize at will, vampires rarely drove their vehicles. Unfortunately, Marquis had needed a way to transport Ciopori and Vanya to Napolean's, and it wasn't possible for a vampire to materialize carrying anything more than fifty-pounds at one time. As for flying, he could have easily carried them both, even cloaked their appearances for safety; however, soaring through the air at supernatural speed might have been a bit much for Vanya at the time. Of course, learning about the automobile had been an adventure in its own right for both females.

"Well, it looks like there's a *situation* at the casino," Nachari explained, showing Marquis the text.

Marquis took the phone from Nachari. Chad Baxter, his security chief at the Dark Moon Casino, rarely, if ever, tried to get a hold of Marquis at home, unless there was something really pressing going on. "Do you mind if I step outside and make a call?" Marquis asked, addressing his Sovereign.

"Not at all," Napolean answered.

"Thank you." Marquis headed for the door. On his way out, he heard Vanya whisper to Napolean—

"What's a...call?"

Marquis just shook his head. Communication was going to be a major challenge between himself and Ciopori for a while. He was hoping like hell he could simply transfer huge blocks of information to her at one time: the same way he could with his Vampyr brothers. Otherwise, she was looking at relearning everything—including a new language.

Marquis dialed the casino and smiled at the thought of spending that much time with Ciopori.

"That you, boss?" The voice on the other end of the phone sounded anxious.

"You texted Nachari: What is it?"

Chad sighed like he had something to say but was afraid to say it.

"I haven't the time, Chad," Marquis warned his employee.

"It's Kristina...and Dirk."

"Again?"

"Yeah..."

"How bad?" Marquis asked.

"Well, she certainly can't work her shift tonight, and I'm afraid if she goes back home...he's gonna kill her this time."

Marquis frowned. Kristina Riley was more than just the casino's most productive cocktail waitress; she was a close friend and ally to the Silivasi family: Only eight years earlier, the human female had been a homeless runaway when Kagen Silivasi had brought her into the house of Jadon. He had been flying over the outskirts of Silverton Park one night when he heard a woman cry out from the back end of a dark alley. Though vampires rarely got involved in human affairs, the unmistakable scent of a Dark One had permeated the air, and Kagen had known, instinctively, that one of two things was about to happen: Either a Dark One was about to feed on a human—draining her of every drop of blood she had—or worse, he was going to take her back to his lair, impregnate her, and force her to undergo a gruesome ritual which would end in her agonizing death and the birth of his twin sons.

Marquis shook his head. He didn't want to think about that. He didn't want to remember his youngest brother's recent death at the hands of Valentine Nistor—a son of Jaegar who had done the exact same thing with Shelby's *destiny*, leaving the youngest Silivasi brother to die at the hands of the Blood Curse.

Fortunately for Kristina, Kagen had slain the son of Jaegar and brought her back to the Dark Moon Health Center before the Dark One could carry out his plan. After learning of her circumstances, he had given her a temporary place to stay and worked with Marquis to find her a job at the casino.

Kristina had worked out beautifully.

And over time, she had become an ally if not a friend.

Due to her deep gratitude and absolute ability to keep a confidence, Kagen had not erased her memories. He had allowed her, instead, to retain full knowledge of who and what the sons of Jadon were, knowing that every now and then, having a human who could go human places, do human things, and move undetected in the deepest arenas of the human world came in handy. Having a second set of eyes at the casino had proved to be especially useful.

Marquis scowled, thinking about Kristina's idiot boyfriend, Dirk. The man was a human menace, or at least he wanted to be. He rode around on a purple Harley with a tattoo of a scorpion on the side of his neck, another of a python on his steroid-enhanced left bicep. He smoke, drank, cursed like a sailor, and tried way too hard to convince the world that he was the scariest thing next to Satan. Marquis scoffed. He could have squashed the human like a bug on several occasions, drained the blood right from underneath that ridiculous scorpion, but Kristina had strictly forbidden it. In fact, she had begged Marquis to stay away from him. What she saw in the imbecile, Marquis would never know. Still, he had always respected her wishes—

Until now.

Enough was enough.

"Where is Kristina now?" he asked.

Chad sighed. "She's in your office. We cleaned her up, but she needs to see a doctor."

Marquis restrained an instinctive snarl. Chad had no idea he was a vampire. "Where's Dirk?"

"Don't know—probably down at the bar getting drunk. He's not in the casino, but that's just a matter of time, especially if she doesn't come home after her shift."

"Well, keep her in my office; I'll be right there."

"Will do. Oh, and boss—"

"What?"

"Sorry to bother you away from work."

"I'll be there in a minute." Marquis hung up. He placed the phone in the inner pocket of the light-weight jacket he wore over a well-fitted, black muscle-tee and turned around just in time to catch the beautiful sight of Princess Ciopori stepping out onto the front veranda.

Her hair was twisted to one side, the ends collected in a thick, looped braid that hung enticingly over her bare shoulder, and she was wearing a sleeveless, ruffled dress that hugged her curves like it had been made just for her—another thoughtful contribution from Napolean.

Marquis placed his hand over his heart. There were no words.

Ciopori instantly brightened. "Do you see something you

like, warrior?"

Marquis stepped toward her and purred, a deep throaty growl rising from his broad, muscular chest. As he bent to taste her lips, his hands found their way to the small of her back and he pulled her tightly against him. "Mmm," he moaned, his tongue sweeping over hers. "Yes, I do."

Ciopori smiled, and then she took a step back. "Something troubles you, warrior, and it is more than the concern you share for myself and Vanya."

Marquis shook his head, not wanting to let go. "It's nothing—just business...work. Just something I need to take care of. Believe me, I will handle it as quickly as possible and return to you this night...I promise."

Ciopori's eyes positively sparkled. "And I will hold you to your word." She rested her hand on her stomach and became all at once serious. "I must confess, I am fearful of falling asleep again. After twenty-eight hundred years in the ground, I am terrified that the spell might—"

Marquis pressed his finger against her lips. "Shhh. None of us will let you slip away, Ciopori. Don't worry about such things."

The princess smoothed out her dress then. "I'll try." She looked off into the distance, took a deep breath, and turned back once more to look at him. "Now then, as for your proprietary affairs. Be it known, warrior, that I do understand a man's obligations. Do not forget that my father was the king"—she stumbled over the word *father*, her losses too great to comprehend, and then, she simply collected herself with an ingrained dignity and continued—"but if you do not wish to share the details of your business, that is acceptable as well."

Marquis reached out to take her hand, still enamored by the way she spoke. He gently pulled her back into his arms. "It's not that, Ciopori. It's just that it's ugly business...nothing you need to concern yourself with right now. Trust me: You will see more of my life than you care to, soon." He gently nipped at her throat, nibbled just beneath her ear, and kissed his way forward from her jaw to the corners of her mouth. *Blessed gods*, he couldn't help himself. The door suddenly opened, and they quickly broke apart.

Nachari poked his head out. His deep, forest green eyes appeared darker in the natural light, and his thick mane of hair fell forward as he glanced around. "Did you get a hold of Chad?"

Marquis shot him an annoyed glance. "*Yes.* What do you need, brother?"

Nachari looked at Marquis, glanced over at the princess, and then stared at Marquis again....smiling a huge cat-that-ate-the-canary smile.

Marquis sighed. "Do you have a purpose, Nachari?"

Nachari blanched, feigning insult at Marquis's blunt dismissal. "Do you mean right now—or as in life in general?"

Ciopori cleared her throat.

Marquis turned to regard the princess then. "Forgive me; have you met my youngest brother?"

"No, I have not yet had the pleasure." Her voice was deliberately kind. "I believe he was speaking with Napolean when I passed through the room."

Marquis gestured in Nachari's general direction. "This is my brother, the Master Wizard Nachari. He was born of the last set of my mother's twins."

"'Tis a pleasure to meet you, wizard," Ciopori said.

"The pleasure is all mine, princess. And I have to tell you, it is a gift from the gods to have you and your sister back where you belong."

Ciopori nodded and smiled, her manner gracious.

And Marquis waited...while the angel of his dreams took her first real, in-depth look at his little brother.

There was no question: All of the Silivasi brothers were handsome to a fault, and Marquis's harsh beauty had a powerful effect on females, but Nachari Silivasi was in a class all to himself. And unfortunately, he knew it. Whenever he flashed that radiant, flawless smile—and his ridiculously perfect features lit up like he was more god than man—women lost their composure. They swooned. Stuttered. And sometimes just stood dazed with their mouths gaping open, until eventually, they got used to the sight of him. His masculine beauty was arresting.

Ciopori looked back and forth between the two brothers. "While the adjustment is overwhelming, we are fortunate to have been found by my brother's descendants." She quickly turned her gaze back to Marquis, her eyes glistening with adoration...for only him.

Marquis glared at Nachari. "Well?"

"My phone," Nachari said.

"What?"

"*My phone.* You asked me, *what do I need*—I need my phone back."

"Oh." Marquis retrieved the phone from his jacket and tossed the thing so hard it became a missile, the casing shattering upon impact with Nachari's hand.

Nachari cursed and glowered at Marquis, incredulous. Fortunately for the Master Warrior, all vampires had lightning quick reflexes, or the phone might have entered the house and struck the king—or worse, Vanya.

"I'm sorry," Marquis quipped. "I—"

"Yes, I know," Nachari snarled, "you underestimated your own strength."

Marquis peered at the hundreds of little pieces of metal in Nachari's palm. "Did the SIM card make it?"

Nachari frowned. "You need therapy, my brother; you really do."

Marquis waved a dismissive hand. "Our kind does not...do therapy. Why do you always say such...inconsequential things?"

Nachari rubbed the bridge of his nose with his free hand. "Why, indeed, Marquis."

Marquis pulled back. "You are angry now, wizard? I can buy

you another phone."

Nachari just shook his head and turned to face Ciopori. "Good luck with him," he mused. And then he pulled his head back inside and shut the door.

When Marquis looked over at the princess, she was standing several feet away with one hand on her hip, the corner of her mouth turned up in a scolding smile. "So, I take it vampires are not only passionate...and protective...but they are also extremely jealous and territorial. Is that not right, warrior?"

Marquis bared his fangs and stalked over to the beautiful female, moving very, very slowly, his gait the easy shift of a predator, his large, muscular frame expanding and contracting with every step. "*Extremely territorial*," he snarled.

Ciopori laughed and covered her mouth with one hand. "You mustn't be concerned about other men, Marquis." And then she eyed the strong warrior from the tip of his head to the bottom of his toes and let out a long, drawn-out sigh. "You have absolutely nothing to be jealous of, my love. *Trust me*."

three

Marquis threw open the door to his office at the end of the main foyer on the top, executive floor of the Dark Moon Casino. The elegant suite took up both sides of the hall, the center facing outward toward the eight remaining offices. It was decorated in rich, dark colors and sparsely fitted with refined cherry-wood furniture.

Marquis's desk faced the entry, overlooking a black leather sofa, which was flanked by two, matching high-backed chairs with dual cherry-wood end tables. The east and west walls were made of floor-to-ceiling windows—the back wall, a series of floor-to-ceiling bookshelves.

Kristina Riley sat on a burgundy chaise in front of the window, her small frame slumped over, her knees tucked tightly to her chest. Her face was shielded behind her shoulder-length, naturally-curly red hair, but Marquis could smell the bruises...as well as her fear.

As was typical for Kristina, she was wearing a suede mini-skirt with a fitted top and a pair of three-inch heels; her legs were scratched and bleeding as if she had tried to crawl away from her attacker across a rough patch of ground. There were fingerprints marring her throat and a cigarette burn on her left arm.

Chad Baxter immediately jumped up when his boss entered the room: The stalwart employee went through the same series of adjustments each time Marquis showed up for work. There was an initial scent of fear, an instinctive reaction to the presence of such a powerful creature—whether Chad knew what Marquis was or not—then his adrenaline would level off as he remembered the trust between them; and finally, he would shift from his natural dominant personality to a more appropriate submissive one.

It all took place lightning-quick, on an unconscious level, yet none of it escaped Marquis's awareness. It was simple, really. Marquis Silivasi was an intimidating male, even to other vampires. To humans, his presence was like having a wild animal in their midst: His predatory nature seeped through his pores, the threat of aggression simmered just below the surface, and his calm, sculpted exterior did very little to hide the unconscious projection of what he was.

To her credit, Kristina displayed no fear. Her reaction to Marquis was always the same—one of casual acceptance and absolute safety.

"Evening, boss," Chad greeted.

Marquis looked in the male's direction and inclined his head before stalking over to Kristina. "What happened?"

Kristina slowly looked up beneath a black-eye and brushed a trickle of blood away from her busted lip. And then she simply shook her head.

"Where is he?" Marquis demanded.

Kristina shook her head more adamantly this time. "Don't, Marquis...please. It'll only make things worse."

"Not this time." Marquis scowled. "This time, when I am through with Dirk, he will never touch you again."

Kristina looked up and studied her boss with scrutinizing, deep blue eyes. Her heart-shaped lips quivered as she recognized the truth of what he said. "Do you mind if I talk to Marquis alone?" she asked Chad.

Chad took a step toward the door. "Not at all." He regarded Marquis. "I'll be right outside if either of you need me for anything."

Marquis nodded. "Thank you."

Once the door was closed behind Chad, Kristina stood up and tried to walk to the other side of the room, but Marquis caught her by her arm and turned her to face him. He raised her chin with his hand. "If I don't put an end to this, Kristina, he is going to kill you. Is that what you want?"

Kristina frowned. "No...no, of course I don't. But I don't want him dead, either."

Marquis remained silent.

Kristina sighed then, her bright eyes becoming dim. "Marquis, we both know you can't deal with Dirk—after everything he's done—and not kill him. What are you gonna do? Warn him? Break an arm or a leg? He'll say something smart. I know he will...and that'll be the end of it." She reached out and took his hand. "Please, boss...let me handle it: I'll figure somethin' out. I swear."

Marquis surveyed the bruises on her neck, Dirk's fingerprints. "Kristina, you know that I respect you, that my family cares for you, and that it is not our way to interfere in the affairs of...mortals. But this thing with Dirk...it's over. Your relationship with him is over."

Kristina put her head down in her hands and sighed with frustration. She was fighting to hold back tears. "What do you mean by *over*?"

Marquis refused to be more specific. "Just...*over*."

Kristina began to shake. "Oh, God, Marquis, this is way out of hand. You can't just—Marquis, if you took Dirk outta the picture, you'd have to erase all my memories, or I'd go insane. So, what then? You're just gonna wipe-out the last five years of my life? No way! Please...don't. *Please*. I'm asking you not to— just let me call the police."

"Again?" Marquis asked.

Kristina nodded. "They'll lock him up this time. I swear, they will."

"For how long?" Marquis scowled. "How many restraining orders has he violated already, Kristina?"

Kristina shook her head. "That was my fault...I took them all back."

"Yes...so you could go back to him."

Kristina nodded and averted her eyes. "I know."

"Kristina," he said sternly, "it really doesn't matter if it's Dirk's inability to stop hurting you or your inability to stop letting him, the end result is the same. And I don't see either one of you stopping."

Kristina started to protest, but Marquis held up his hand. "The thing of it is this: When you came into our world, when you were given the choice to keep or relinquish your memories—your knowledge of Dark Moon Vale—you made a covenant to honor and serve the house of Jadon in exchange for our shelter, protection, and care. We are not as you are. *I* am not as you are. I have tried to view this from a human point of view, but Dirk has crossed an irreversible line: As a male who is bound by a covenant to protect you, I no longer have a choice in the matter. *These are the laws of my kind.*"

Marquis walked over to his desk and sat down in the large burgundy chair. He placed his elbows on the desktop and folded his hands; his chin rested on his fingers while he considered his next move.

Kristina waited quietly, her body visibly trembling.

After several minutes had passed, Marquis raised his head and regarded Kristina with resolve. He knew his eyes were cold, like two hollow coals, as they always appeared vacant when he made up his mind to enact final-retribution. "I will allow you to keep all of your memories, as long as you show me that you can handle them. But Dirk's time with you has—how shall I say?—come to an end."

Kristina gasped. "No, Marquis! *No!* Please, just listen. I have this—"

Marquis raised his hand again, this time taking abrupt control over Kristina's body. For a fleeting moment, her vocal cords no longer worked, and her tongue was paralyzed. It was just long enough to halt her speech—like flipping an *off-switch* on her protest—while still forceful enough to show her the discussion was over.

Marquis meant business.

Kristina sat down in one of the high-backed chairs across the desk and began to cry, her face growing white as a sheet.

Marquis hit the intercom and asked Chad to return.

When Chad came in, he took one look at Kristina, glanced

over at Marquis, and winced, his soft, hazel eyes narrowing with compassion. "It'll be all right, Kristina," he offered.

"No, it won't," Kristina sobbed.

When Marquis didn't bother responding, Chad's face turned the same shade as hers. Only, he wasn't about to question his boss.

"So, has her schedule been taken care of?" Marquis asked, abruptly changing the subject.

Chad cleared his throat and ran his hand through his short, dirty-blond hair. "Uh...yeah, Lacy is covering her shift for tonight, and José was able to get Emily to cover for the rest of the week."

Marquis nodded. "Good. And security? How are you handling that?"

Chad sat down in the remaining chair across from his boss. "Well, you said you wanted us to allow Dirk to come in if he showed up; so right now, we'll know the minute he breaches the perimeter, and at least two guards will stay tight. But no one's gonna confront him or call the police...not without your go-ahead. Unless of course, he acts like the ass he is, and we have to deal with him in the interest of our other patrons." He immediately turned to Kristina and shrugged. "Sorry."

Kristina began to sob all over again.

"Good. That's fine." *My brother...*

Kagen Silivasi answered the telepathic call immediately. *Greetings, Marquis: How are you?*

I am well, Kagen, and you?

Very well.

Kagen simply waited then.

Marquis didn't call out to his brothers often. Usually, if he wanted something, he just demanded it, or took it, or put the command directly in their minds. If Marquis was calling him now, Kagen had to know it was important.

I am at the casino with Chad and Kristina, Marquis explained. *Dirk has made a real mess of her this time. I would like to bring her by the health center.*

Kagen sounded puzzled. *You want* me *to treat her? Why not just use a human doctor, as usual?*

Not this time, Marquis argued. *As soon as Dirk shows his face, I'm going to remove the problem once and for all; the less contact we have with humans, the less potential drama...or mess.*

Kagen cleared his throat. *I see.* He paused for a moment. *Well, I must say, I'm glad you're going to finally put a stop to this.*

It is long overdue, and I have neither the time nor the inclination to deal with it anymore—which is why I have an additional favor to ask of you.

'Ask?' Kagen sounded surprised.

Marquis sighed telepathically. *Yes...ask...unless and until you say no, of course.* There was no hint of humor in his voice...because he meant none.

Kagen laughed anyway, although his laughter sounded primitive, both amused and irritated. But then, that was Kagen: the kindest and the meanest of the Silivasi brothers at the same time. Luckily for the rest of them, the easy-going persona took up ninety-five percent of his character; however, when that five percent came out, even Marquis knew enough to clear a path...although not because he feared him. Marquis feared absolutely no one and nothing—save, perhaps, Napolean Mondragon—but when Kagen got that damn-mean, it just wasn't worth all the energy it took to try and calm him down.

I'm listening, Kagen drawled, Mr. Nice Guy spilling over.

I want you to keep Kristina for the next week or so. I don't want her staying anyplace where Dirk might find her, and if for some reason, he does happen to track her to the clinic, then you are to...take care of him...for me, long before he gets anywhere near her. No human involvement.

I have no problems with Kristina—or handling Dirk—I'll keep her.

Good. Be well, then, Kagen.

And you as well, my brother.

Marquis looked across his desk at Chad, who was still waiting patiently for his boss's directions. "I'm going to take Kristina to the health center, where she'll be staying for a few days."

Kristina looked up, startled. Her eyes grew wide, and her face hardened like stone. If there was any doubt that Marquis meant to kill Dirk, it was gone now. She was being placed under the supervision of a Master vampire until her boyfriend was in the ground. By the look on her face, she knew it was final. The situation had been removed from human hands.

"Absolutely no one is to know where she is," Marquis admonished, staring at Chad. "And the moment you see Dirk, you call me. Are we clear?"

"Crystal, boss."

"Good."

Kristina dropped her face in her quivering hands, defeated.

It was dark when Marquis pulled his H3T Hummer onto the private dirt road that led to Kagen's health clinic and private residence. The graphite metallic truck—with its eighteen-inch chrome wheels and ebony leather seats, encased with cashmere inserts—made easy work of the rough terrain, and it took them less than ten minutes to pull into the front lot of the clinic once they made the final turn.

Kagen Silivasi was a true loner—preferring to live as far back into the mountain as possible. The high-tech clinic was virtually hidden within a dense forest of pine and spruce trees, anchored into the base of a steep mountain. Kagen's own personal residence was about one mile west of the center, also built half-in, half-out of the steep, rocky crevice.

Both properties were accessed by a single dirt parking-lot that bordered the southern branch of the winding Snake River. To get to either one, visitors had to go forward on foot, crossing an archaic stone bridge that arched across the deepest branch of the white-water tributary; then follow a steep, inclining path that finally took them to the structures. In the event of a severely injured patient, there were stretchers and wheelchairs available, but the difficult environment served a purpose: Vampires could materialize, and humans weren't welcome.

Like every other structure in the house of Jadon, the clinic was on private property. With human hunting societies, Dark Ones, and lycans always posing a threat, it was important that the community remain well-hidden.

Marquis parked the Hummer just to the right of the bridge and got out of the truck, leaving the keys in the ignition. He never worried about such things; after all, gods help the soul who decided to steal from him. Although...it might make interesting sport: fun to track, easy to dispose of. He opened Kristina's door and waited while she slowly climbed out of the vehicle, her eyes bloodshot and swollen from crying.

Marquis frowned. He was good with his fists and his guns— and his trident, stilettos, and sling—but words were simply not his forte, which was ironic considering he spoke twenty-one languages.

"Do you need a minute before we go in?" he asked. It was all he could think of.

Kristina looked up at him, incredulous. "What difference would that make?"

"None at all," Marquis answered factually.

"Well, why not take one then," Kristina quipped sarcastically. She crossed her arms in defiance and leaned back against the graphite, metallic truck, wincing from the pain of moving her battered muscles. And then she stared straight ahead at the bridge as if it were the final walkway to the gallows—the last journey of a condemned woman. She said nothing, so Marquis peered into her mind...

It was more or less blank. She was listening to the roaring sound of the rushing water, trying her best not to think or feel anything.

Marquis crossed his heavily muscled arms and leaned back

against the truck next to her; he figured he'd give this whole reflective-silence thing about three minutes, and then he was taking her inside.

As the two of them stood side-by-side, waiting for time to slowly tick by, the air around them began to fill with strange electricity. The night suddenly became eerily dark, almost as if someone had turned out a light in the sky. Instinctively, they both looked up, and their mouths dropped open in unison.

The sky above them was transforming. From a clear, solid blue to a deep, infinite black. It was as if the moon and the stars had simply burned out—as if light no longer existed—and then, just as unexpectedly, the celestial lights began to come back on. One after the other, the most brilliant, iridescent stars shone in the sky like a thousand torches in the hands of the gods. The heavens were positively...and unequivocally...breathtaking.

And then the moon reappeared, shifting along its lunar path, dipping down until it hovered behind the stars, beaming like a spotlight trained on the most magnificent constellation. The spotlight began to change color. From grayish white, to pinkish rose, to a deepening shade of wine...until it finally emerged the color of *fresh blood*.

A crimson moon beckoned in a backlit sky, shining its haunting light on a single constellation.

Draco...the Dragon.

If Marquis had not been leaning against his truck, he would have fallen over. Awestruck by the incredible sight. Fascinated by its beauty. Stunned by its meaning.

After *fifteen-hundred years*—living alone, walking alone, sleeping alone...existing alone—he had all but given up on the idea that the gods even remembered who he was. Yet now, his princess had awakened after so many centuries, and in the blink of an eye, they had rediscovered a love beyond the confines of this world.

Marquis drew in a deep breath and almost...smiled.

He had to get back to Ciopori right away. He had already explained the Blood Curse to her, but he had failed to tell her his own constellation. She would be thrilled to know that the gods had blessed them—that they had made it possible for them to truly be together.

Marquis ran his hands through his thick raven hair and looked at Kristina. "We need to get you inside right away; there is someplace else that I need to be."

Kristina's deep blue eyes blinked several times, and she swallowed a lump in her throat. She looked up at the sky, over at Marquis, and then back at the sky a second time.

And then she repeated the whole process again.

She nodded quickly, tucked her injured arm behind her back, and began walking at a strange angle so that she continued to face him even as she attempted to walk beside him.

Halfway over the stone bridge, Marquis stopped. Cold spray from the rushing river misted his face. "Why are you walking like that?" he asked—straight to the point as usual.

Kristina shook her head way too rapidly. "Oh...was I? I didn't realize. Yeah...I think my injuries are just...yeah. I didn't realize that I was...walking strange."

Marquis frowned. He noticed that her left arm was still tucked behind her back—the arm Dirk had burned with a cigarette. "Is that burn still causing you pain?"

Kristina visibly trembled. "No, not anymore...I mean...yeah, but not if I hold it like this." She tried to smile. The warmth didn't reach her eyes.

Marquis took a step back then. There was a pungent odor in the air. One he had never scented around Kristina before: *fear*. More specifically, *fear of him*.

He wrinkled his forehead. "What is wrong with you?"

Kristina shook her head and looked toward the clinic. "The

pain is just…we should hurry and get inside so you can go on and get to…wherever you need to be."

Marquis's stomach lurched. All at once, a powerful sense of dread swept over him. "Show me your arm, Kristina."

Kristina showed him her right arm.

"The other one," he barked, holding his breath.

Kristina blanched and took a step back.

Marquis heart did a back-flip in his chest. "Kristina, you will show me your left arm *now*." He pitched his voice an octave lower, the tone as smooth as velvet, making the command impossible to refuse.

Like a puppet on a string, Kristina's left arm came out from behind her back and dangled in front of him as if he were working her limbs from above.

Marquis took one glance and staggered back, catching himself against the solid stone railing. His head spun in circles like he had just stepped off a carnival ride.

It was right there in front of him. As clear as the sky. Every marking, every line, every unmistakable contour—creating one inevitable image: *on Kristina Riley's inner wrist.* Draco, the Dragon. Marquis's own birth constellation.

The woman was terrified now, and frankly, Marquis could not have cared less. His mind was in a free-fall, as if he had just been in a terrible accident and was still trying to regain his equilibrium, figure out where he was—what had just happened—whether or not he was going to survive.

Marquis shook his head adamantly. "No, this is not possible." He looked at Kristina's arm again, and then he stared into her petrified eyes. "Do you know what this means?"

The petite redhead croaked out an incoherent sound.

Marquis spun around and stared at the river, his powerful hands closing into two hard fists...

And then just like that, an iron gate closed in his mind.

It closed in his heart, shut out all thought, and locked out emotion. It allowed only instinct and obedience. He couldn't afford anything else right now.

Marquis looked up at the sky, then at the parking lot behind them, and finally, at the shadows among the trees. "It is not safe for you to be outside anymore, Kristina." His voice was monotone.

The skinny red-head visibly wilted, too afraid to speak.

Just then, Kagen Silivasi shimmered into view, standing on the bridge directly in front of them. His glorious dark brown hair rustled in the wind like fine spun silk. His commanding brown eyes, with their unusual silver reflections of light, stared straight through the Ancient Master Warrior with wonder and concern. As he took a step forward, Kagen's muscles shifted like the powerful haunches of a black panther stalking toward prey. It was the signature walk of a male vampire. "My brother..." His raspy voice trailed off.

Marquis met the healer's gaze but said nothing.

Kagen looked up at the moon then. "I just saw the sky."

Marquis's mouth was set in a hard line as he refused to respond.

Kagen looked completely taken aback. "*It's Draco.*"

"I know this!"

Kagen frowned. "Who is she, Marquis? Do you know yet? Do you think the princess—"

Marquis held up his hand and just shook his head.

Kagen looked at Kristina then...and all the pieces fell into place. There was a moment of stunned silence while the three of them stood on the bridge, desperately trying to process the enormous turn of events.

Finally, Kagen spoke to Marquis telepathically, his worry readily apparent. *My brother, are you okay?*

Marquis scowled then. *You and Nachari—you both ask such inconsequential questions!*

Kagen didn't respond to the derisive remark. More than likely, he understood.

All of Marquis's brothers understood him—even if they

Tessa Dawn

didn't always appreciate his personality—and they were smart enough to know when to back off, that there was nothing they could do when he didn't want their help. Marquis prayed Kagen would just leave it alone.

Kagen turned to Kristina then. "Welcome...*little sister*...it is nice to see you again; we need to get you inside so we can attend to your wounds."

Kristina looked like a deer caught in the headlights as she slowly nodded and began to follow Kagen inside.

"I'll be there in a while," Marquis whispered.

Kagen stopped walking then. He squared his shoulders to Marquis and just glared at him...speechless.

Though it was very poor manners—if not downright disrespectful—Marquis didn't have the time...or the ability...to deal with Kagen's confusion right now. Desperate to head any inquiry off at the pass, he delved into his brother's thoughts, hoping to put the healer's concerns to rest before an uncomfortable conversation ensued.

Kagen was thinking about the one—and only—opportunity a male vampire had in a lifetime to start a family. To find a mate. To atone for the sins of his forefathers and once and for all live free of the Curse. Following the Blood Moon, a male had only thirty days to secure his female...to live or die...and consequently, the territorial instincts of a male who had just discovered his *destiny* were as powerful as they were overwhelming. It was simply unheard of for such a male to leave the female's side so soon after the Omen. And as for leaving her alone in an enclosed space with another male? Whether that male was a friend or a brother, it just wasn't done.

Ever.

As far as Kagen was concerned, Marquis should have been edgy, defensive, and overbearing right now. If anything, he expected Marquis to shackle his *destiny* to his wrist, to drag her indoors, cursing and fighting every step of the way, especially considering the warrior's complete lack of tact. Kagen knew

39

something was wrong.

Terribly...terribly...wrong.

And because it was such a volatile time, he was worried to death about his eldest brother.

Do not waste your energy concerning yourself with such things, Kagen, Marquis advised. *Please, just take my* destiny *inside and see to her wounds. I will be there shortly: I promise.*

Kagen looked surprised, and then he nodded. *Very well, Marquis...but hear this: You are the most honored amongst our family, and I understand that this is a very pivotal...and difficult...night for you. And I also know that you have a habit of checking up on all of your brothers by brushing our minds from time to time. That is simply your way, and we all accept it. However, should you ever retrieve my thoughts again without my permission, you and I will have a very serious problem.*

Marquis snorted and frowned. Kagen was right, of course. Etiquette amongst the males in the house of Jadon was paramount. *Sacred.*

Oh well, his silence was the only acknowledgment Kagen was going to get and as close to an apology as Marquis would go.

Understanding, Kagen turned to Kristina and gestured toward the clinic. "Shall we?"

As they began to walk away, Kristina looked over her shoulder at Marquis, her deep blue eyes wide with shock. When their gazes finally met, a deep sorrow passed between them.

Marquis quickly looked away. This was all wrong. *This was all so absolutely, positively...inexcusably...wrong!*

After all this time—serving his people honorably, living for his brothers, enduring century after century alone; after watching his beloved mother, Serena, die; his best friend and father, Keitaro, disappear; and the joy of his heart—his youngest brother, Shelby—slain by the Blood Curse; this was simply...

Wrong.

And it was cruel.

In his mind's eye, he saw the princess in her beautiful summer dress. He heard her infectious laughter and remembered the tantalizing sway of her hips—the way that she looked at him with so much love in her eyes—and his heart wept at the enormity of what the gods had just done. Why now? Why to him?

Marquis watched as Kagen and Kristina made their way up the path toward the clinic, and he couldn't help but think...for just one day...

Out of hundreds of thousands...

He had actually been—happy.

four

Ciopori spun around on the back terrace of Napolean's majestic home, marveling at the beauty of the sky. As one of the original Celestial Beings, observing such an event was the equivalent of witnessing a miracle, a rare blessing bestowed upon them by the divine god, Draco, and her emotions varied from reverence to awe...to disbelief. Despite their ultimate extermination, the females of her race had once been very powerful, indeed. Powerful enough to fashion a curse that was still carried out by the gods twenty-eight hundred years later.

A soft breeze blew through her hair, rustling a wall of towering aspens that flanked the back porch, and Ciopori closed her eyes, taking in the magic of the moment. Her last memories, before Marquis had found her, had been of a dark ship taking port in a strange land, her brothers being left behind in the Old World, her culture being decimated...her life forever changed. When Fabian placed the two remaining females under the spell, Ciopori knew she would awaken to a completely different life, but in her wildest dreams, she could have never imagined this. She could never have imagined Marquis.

The warrior from her dreams had been real all along. And he had found her.

Ciopori felt a chill shoot up her spine, even as goose bumps appeared on her arms. Marquis was such a proud and sure warrior, a leader by both nature and birth, as passionate as he was intense...the celestial epitome of a wild animal. Yet there was a rare, indefinable beauty beneath his harsh exterior, a spiritual quality that hinted of something much deeper. He had a soul that had been honed through fire, a wisdom that had been refined through experience, a strength that was deeply anchored in primordial law, and yes, a love for his brothers that surpassed all else. A love that now included her.

Ciopori smiled, lost in her daydream, swimming in the memory of Marquis's impossibly beautiful blue-black eyes...and that gorgeous, thick raven hair. She could still hear the velvet tenor of his voice as it played again and again in her mind, a haunting melody, pure and hypnotic. When she concentrated, she could still see the hard cut of his jaw, the sculpted perfection of his lips, the perfect angles of his face, and the rock-hard lines of his body—a body that appeared to have been chiseled out of granite by the hands of a master artisan. Truly, her sisters had created a magnificent, unparalleled species...even as they had sought to curse them.

Ciopori laughed aloud then, as she also remembered the warrior's complete lack of social grace, and his cerebral analysis of simple wit: The male didn't have a clue when it came to humor or subtle nuances; yet oddly enough, Ciopori found those traits adorable. In fact, they were the qualities she admired most because they softened what might otherwise be a far too overwhelming male.

She regarded the sky once more. What an amazing night. She had found the mate of her soul, the man of her dreams. And now, another warrior in the house of Jadon—her beloved brother's direct line of ancestry—was being given the same chance to find eternal love. She was so caught up in her musing that she didn't realize Napolean Mondragon had joined her on the veranda until he spoke.

"Greetings, Princess." Napolean remained formal, as usual, speaking to her in the Old Language. "It is an incredible sight to behold, is it not?"

Ciopori turned toward the monarch and bowed her head ever so slightly. "Milord." She turned back to the sky. "Indeed, it is magnificent. I don't believe I have ever seen anything more spectacular in all of my life."

Napolean smiled, his shimmering silver irises casting light like crystals against the moon; his gorgeous, waist length hair swaying with his regal movements. "I've seen the Blood Moon sky a thousand times over my long life, yet every time it appears, it is as if I am viewing it for the first time. I am pleased that you are able to see it."

Ciopori gave him a curious glance. "Why wouldn't I?"

Napolean shrugged his broad shoulders. "The Blood Moon is an omen—a sign which only appears to the male descendants of both Jadon and Jaegar—"

"My brothers," Ciopori clarified.

"A sign which only appears to the male descendants of *your brothers*," Napolean corrected, still clearly in awe of her lineage. "Yet, it was a *mercy* given to the descendants of Jadon, alone, following the Curse. And for that reason, humans have never been able to observe the phenomenon: The sky looks perfectly normal to them right now. The moon looks the same as always."

He came to stand beside her and paused, as if searching for the right words. "As you are not...a product of the Curse...I wasn't sure if you would be able to behold it or not."

Ciopori sighed and gazed toward the forest, both of them now leaning against the banister. "I can see your point, milord. However, I am a Celestial Being of pure blood, one of the remaining descendants of the goddess Cygnus and her human mate, Mateo; so of course I can view the Omen: All that occurs in the heavens occurs in my ancestral home."

Napolean looked at her wistfully—clearly studying her face. "You know, I remember you, Princess Ciopori...from before."

"Pardon me?" She looked surprised.

Napolean's smile was exquisite. "I remember you from Romania."

Ciopori turned to face him then, her hands clasped together in front of her. "I'm afraid I don't share this memory, Sir Mondragon; please, elaborate."

Napolean laughed, his voice a rich baritone. "You wouldn't, Princess—being that I was only ten-years old when the Blood Curse occurred." He sighed. "I saw you only once. It was right before...the sacrifices began...when our world was still a fair and just place to be...

"It was after a particularly successful harvest—at one of the honoring ceremonies: You were there with your father, the king, although I don't recall seeing your sister or your mother. But you—you were standing behind your father on the platform, wearing one of the most exquisite gowns I had ever seen. Well, for a five-year-old." He chuckled lightly. "It was lavender—like the lilies of the field—and I remember staring at all that silk as it swayed in the wind. The sun cast a shadow beneath you, causing the effect of a halo above you. I was but a child then, and I believed our king to be a god. Gazing at you on that platform, I was certain you were a goddess as well."

Ciopori laughed. "Well, that is quite a compliment coming from one who grew up to be such a powerful leader himself. I'm sure many of the children here think the same of you now." After a moment of silence, she ventured, "If you don't mind me asking: What house are you from? I mean your lineage *before the Curse*."

Napolean looked off into the distance. He raised his eyebrows and sighed as if he rarely thought of such things anymore. "I am the only one of my family that has survived—the last remaining pure-blood Celestial Being of our people." He glanced at her and smiled. "At least until now."

Ciopori nodded.

"My direct descendants were begotten of the goddess Andromeda and her human mate, Demetrius Mondragon."

Ciopori caught her breath. "You come from a very powerful house of magic, milord: I did not realize..."

"That's quite all right," Napolean replied." There is little time for practicing enchantment anymore, ruling the house of—leading your brother's house is a full-time job."

Ciopori crossed her arms in front of her. "Then I must say, as difficult as all of this is, I am glad we are here with you, Lord Mondragon of the house of Andromeda. It is not a good feeling to be all alone."

Napolean declined his head but didn't answer.

"Speaking of which"—Ciopori gestured toward the sky—"I

am quite curious about the male who is being honored tonight by the gods. Who does our Lord Draco smile upon? Do you already know his mate?"

Napolean cleared his throat, and then his face became a blank slate, completely devoid of emotion. "Ciopori...how shall I say this?" He turned around to face her. "The duty of my kingship is this: I see everything that happens in the house of Jadon, both good and bad. I know the thoughts, intentions, and fears of all the males, and all of the choices they make the moment they make them, but I am not permitted by the gods to act upon—or even reveal—such information. To interfere in the lives of my subjects would be to...*tamper with the future*...or alter the hands of fate. To change destiny or obstruct free will.

"Not to mention, it would be a severe violation of the privacy of our males—certainly unworthy of the respect each one has earned. Verily, I may act only upon a direct request, a matter of law and order, in the interest of our survival, or the earth's protection...but my reach ends there."

Ciopori declined her head in deference; perhaps she had violated some sort of tenet. "Forgive me, milord: Was I wrong to inquire about this matter?"

Napolean smiled and shook his head. "No, Princess—not at all. A male's constellation is common knowledge in the house of Jadon; however, the identity of his mate is not. Therefore, I can answer your first question but not your last." He drew in a deep breath. "It is the warrior Marquis whose constellation illuminates our sky this night. He is the chosen one of Draco."

Ciopori hesitated. "You don't mean Marquis *Silivasi*?" As if she knew more than one vampire named Marquis.

Napolean nodded, his face serene. "Yes, the Ancient Master Warrior, Marquis Silivasi."

Ciopori caught at the rail, her knees buckling beneath her. She froze as she turned away from Napolean, dumbfounded. He had repeated the name twice, yet she still could not believe she'd heard him correctly. "You mean...the male who was here earlier

Tessa Dawn

today…Nachari's brother…*that Marquis Silivasi?*"

Napolean's calm demeanor appeared deliberate. "Yes, the constellation is his."

Ciopori's hand flew to her mouth in a desperate attempt to restrain from asking a third time. It took every ounce of composure she had to stand on the deck and look at the king…as if the entire world had not just collapsed around her. "If you would be so kind, I would require a moment alone." Her voice sounded hollow and far away, as if the words were coming from someone else's mouth.

Napolean bowed ever so slightly, his expression betraying nothing. "Of course."

Ciopori held up her hand. "I would, however, like to have a word with the wizard, Nachari, if you wouldn't mind. Please send him out as soon as possible." She swallowed a lump in her throat and fought to keep from trembling.

Napolean placed a comforting hand on the small of her back but refrained from speaking. And Ciopori knew it was just as he had said: The sovereign leader of the house of Jadon already knew everything, and he would ask no further questions because providence had to play itself out—good, bad, or indifferent. The wizened king was faultlessly neutral, an observer at best.

"I will go fetch Nachari now," he said in a soothing tone of voice.

Ciopori waited restlessly, pacing back and forth across the veranda. Although it had been less than five minutes since she had asked to see Nachari, it felt like an eternity. Finally, the wizard appeared, and like a swan gliding across a lake, his proud gait carried him effortlessly to her side.

"You asked for me?" His voice was deep with concern.

Ciopori tried to hold his gaze, but her own eyes glazed over with tears, and she had to turn away. It was written all over his face—Nachari knew everything—but then, of course he would: Marquis was his brother, after all, and he had seen the two of them together. Ciopori searched for words but found none.

47

"I am so sorry," he finally whispered, "not just for you—but for my brother as well."

Ciopori drew in a deep breath and forced herself to face him. "Then you know who the...female...is then?" She nearly choked over the words.

Nachari nodded, the soft lines of his face hardening. "Yes, when I reached out to my brother just moments ago, I felt her energy in the air around him. As she is someone well known to our family, I recognized her right away."

Ciopori began to cry, and she brought her hands up to cover her face, ashamed.

"Please do not be embarrassed." Nachari sighed. "Whatever you are feeling, I'm sure my brother is as well..."

Ciopori wiped her eyes. "Nachari, does he have to—"

"He does, Ciopori."

She sniffled and tried to regain her composure. "But why? Why can't it be changed? Has anyone ever tried?" She knew she sounded desperate, but she no longer cared. "Surely, I am not bound by this curse. There must be some kind of exception, some way for Napolean to intercede with the gods. He is from the house of Andromeda; if anyone can do it, he can."

Nachari looked out toward the forest, carefully considering his next words. "Honestly, Ciopori...I wish it were so." He shook his head and ran his hand through his silky mane of dark hair. "It is true that there are a lot of *unknowns* in this situation, but, Princess, the Blood Curse—that just isn't one of them. Nor is the sacrifice my brother *must* make at the end of the Blood Moon." He paused then and took a deep breath before going on. "Kristina Riley—the *destiny* the gods have chosen for him—is the only female who can give him what he *must* have right now."

Ciopori felt his words like a knife slicing through her gut. Although she knew he meant no offense, no words had ever wounded her more deeply. Unwilling to give up so easily, she gathered her courage once again and defiantly squared her shoulders to the handsome wizard. "Forgive my insistence,

Nachari, but you simply do not know that. From what Marquis had already told me, there is only one woman who can bear your children...without suffering a horrible fate...and that is your chosen *destiny*. But there are things you don't know, reasons why Marquis and I believe we are meant to be together..."

Her voice trailed off. There was no point in trying to convince Nachari of the rightness of her union with Marquis. She needed to stick to the facts, the logical argument. "Is it not true that the woman who ultimately bears the imprint of a male's constellation on her wrist actually has small traces of celestial blood in her veins? And is it not true that it is the *celestial blood* that makes them compatible...in terms of having children?"

"Yes, that's part of it," Nachari conceded, "but—"

"Then do I not possess more celestial blood than any *destiny* the gods have ever chosen?"

Nachari hung his head. The compassion in his eyes was as maddening as it was painful. "You have *pure* celestial blood, Ciopori. No one would argue such a thing. But your blood is that of the goddess Cygnus, is it not? Marquis's *destiny* was chosen at birth by Lord Draco, and it is Draco's blood his mate will have running through her veins. The blood of the dragon god is the only blood that is compatible with Marquis's."

Ciopori stared at the wooden planks on the veranda for quite some time before regaining her courage. She lifted her head and tried one last time. "Again, wizard, with all due respect: You just don't know if it can be done...because your males have never tried any other way. Until now, there has never been any other possibility." She sighed and held up her hand. "But for the sake of argument, let us assume that what you say is true, and I cannot give Marquis...children.

"I can still argue for him—at the end of the Blood Moon— when the curse comes to claim him." Her voice was beginning to waver. "Nachari, surely those who have cursed you would not punish me. *I am one of them.* One of the original females—*the very reason the curse was enacted in the first place.* Even the gods would have to concede to that point."

Nachari glanced at the sky. "Ciopori, being who you are, you must be a woman of great faith, are you not?"

"Of course I am. That's just my point—"

"Do you believe that the gods know all and see all?"

"Of course I do. *Of course they do.* Yes."

Nachari looked her in the eyes. "Then they know you are here, don't they? They know that Marquis...loves you...and you, him. They know exactly who you are and where you are from, yet they do this anyway." He gestured at the heavens. "Forgive me for being so blunt, but after fifteen-hundred years of making him wait, why did the gods choose now? It is almost as if they acted in haste to *prevent* the two of you from joining. If you believe in divinity, then there is no coincidence."

Ciopori blanched at his reasoning. *He was right.*

She shut her eyes and clutched her arms tight to her stomach. If the gods truly knew all, then they had to know she couldn't possibly let go of Marquis now that she'd found him: They had to know that she would fight for this warrior to the bitter end. She would never let such a punishment stand.

Ciopori Demir was willing to enter the Valley of Death and Shadows with him if necessary.

five

As if Nachari had read Ciopori's mind, he held out his hand. "Will you walk with me, Ciopori? There is something I need to show you."

Ciopori took Nachari's hand and followed him back into the house. They passed through the receiving room, entered a main hall, and eventually made their way to the rear of a large mudroom that sat just beyond the kitchen. The door to the mudroom opened up to a dark, circular tunnel with a hand-laid cobblestone floor.

"What I'd like to show you is just on the other end of this hall," Nachari said, ushering Ciopori in front of him. And then with the sweep of his hand, he lit a long row of torches, each one anchored in rows at the top of the arched wall.

Ciopori drew in a deep breath as she followed the wizard through the long, damp tunnel.

When they finally got to the end, there were two heavy, wooden, arched doors—like one might find in an ancient castle. Nachari gestured to the one on the left. "This entrance opens up to the Hall of Justice as well as the Ceremonial Hall of our people." He placed his hand on the thick iron handle of the door on the right. "And this one leads to the Chambers of Sacrifice and Atonement." He cleared his throat. "You should prepare yourself for the...energy.... It is a place of great mourning and death."

Ciopori took a slight step back, braced herself, and then nodded. "I'll be fine."

Nachari was the one to pause then—lost in a frozen moment in time. It was as if the weight of the entire world were sitting on his shoulders, and he couldn't bring himself to open the doors. As if his hands were frozen in place.

When he finally summoned his courage, he swung the heavy door open so hard that it slammed against the wall behind it, sending a resounding echo through the already creepy room. He swallowed a lump in his throat. "Come on."

The moment Ciopori entered the chamber, she felt a sudden drop in temperature. The room resembled a small, 1800s church: There were several rows of pews, all lined up, each one facing a single platform where a pulpit would have been, and the energy of the place was indeed heavy with sorrow. On the solitary platform was a small altar made of multi-colored granite. It had a smooth, hollow surface at the top, and an extremely dark energy swirled around the base.

Nachari pointed to the altar. "At the end of the Blood Moon, each male has two sons: one child of light to carry on the race, and one child of darkness—the soulless one—who is brought here as demanded by the Curse." He pointed toward the hollow groove at the top of the structure. "The child is placed on the altar by his father or Napolean, depending upon the circumstances. Sometimes the mother attends, as do other family members, but more often than not, Napolean performs the ceremonies himself."

Ciopori felt sick to her stomach, but she didn't question the gods. The universe was a place of balance: Light cast a shadow. Day gave way to night. Birth and death mirrored one another. The good could not exist without the contrast of the bad to make it so. However difficult, the disparity of two sons—one good, one evil—was a balanced punishment, and she understood her ancient sisters' reasoning...even if she didn't agree with it.

Nachari and Ciopori walked silently through the space. When they got to the other side, they were met by yet another door. This one had crossbones on the front and an ancient warning written in the Old Language: *Behold the portal to the Corridor of the Dead.*

Nachari bit his bottom lip, opened the door, and ushered the princess inside. "Don't worry; that doesn't apply to us."

Princess Ciopori took a quick step back. "And you are absolutely certain of this, wizard?"

Nachari's expression was deathly serious. "Yes, *absolutely.* I am not ready to leave this earth quite yet, Princess."

Ciopori followed him through the macabre door into what she realized was a confined entry-way: Just beyond the cramped space were two steps leading up to a hatch, the final entrance to the death chamber, and the hatch was covered with an enormous iron bolt that locked it in place. It was obviously meant to keep whoever was inside the cavity from escaping.

The lingering energy of torture and agony was almost tangible as Nachari reached up, took a large iron key from a rusted hook, and unlocked the hatch.

Ciopori recoiled.

The interior was shaped like a cylinder—about twelve feet tall, twenty-feet in circumference—and it reeked of the smell of death...

And vengeance.

And malevolence.

Without a doubt, she knew that the souls of her slain sisters had become the very evil they had sought to punish. As all energy only multiplied and attracted unto itself, every act of hatred and revenge—every death meant to atone for their extinction—had simply added to their own darkness and depravity. What happened here in this chamber was not justice, and it was not penance.

It was unholy.

For the first time since she'd met him, Nachari's proud swagger faltered, and he stumbled back as if he could barely stand. His hands and arms trembled uncontrollably.

Ciopori followed his eyes as he took in the contents of the room: There were dozens of oval shower-heads perched around the upper perimeter of the ceiling, and they were clearly positioned to wash the sterile-looking walls. But...of what?

"Blood," Nachari answered, easily reading her mind. "The shower-heads are needed to wash away all of the blood."

He pointed to a large drain in the middle of the floor, which dipped down at the center. "It has been said by our people that when the souls of our female ancestors are done punishing some of the males, there is nothing left of them to bury or incinerate. What little that remains flows down that drain like liquid. Others are left intact as a reminder to those who must bury them...as was the case with my twin."

Ciopori caught her breath and shrank back from the door. *His twin?*

Nachari forced himself to continue. "The male enters the chamber on the last night of the Blood Moon: the night he failed to provide the sacrifice of the Dark Child." He shivered. "It is also said that the walls are sound-proof because the cries are too agonizing to bear by those outside. The punishment is too cruel. The death too prolonged." He took a slow, deep breath and steadied his voice. "The death curse has been known to take up to twenty-four hours when the male is incredibly strong—never less than twelve."

He turned away and placed his hand over his stomach. His perfect face grew pale. His voice quivered despite his effort. "My...twin"—he stopped and clutched at the wall—"and Marquis's brother...died in here...less than two months ago. For no other reason than he did not have a son to hand over at the end of the Blood Moon."

Ciopori winced. She had no idea what to say. Dear gods...what were these males being put through? "Why didn't he have a...sacrifice?" she finally asked.

Nachari glanced at his trembling hands. "One of the Dark Ones, a descendant of your brother Jaegar..." He exhaled. "Wow...this is harder than I thought...his name was Valentine Nistor, and he stole Shelby's *destiny* before they could complete the ritual."

Ciopori's hand went up to her mouth and a tear escaped her eye. "Dearest gods..."

Nachari slowly backed away from the chamber. "Ciopori, you may be right about arguing with the gods. You may even be right about there being some possibility—some way—for you

54

and Marquis to conceive children together that does not end so…badly. But if you are wrong—if there is even the slightest chance that you are wrong—then this is where Marquis will end up at the end of this moon. This is what he will endure if your argument fails."

He turned to meet her gaze, and she saw everything he couldn't say in his eyes.

Bringing her here had been one of the hardest things he had ever done. The grief and pain he was shouldering were beyond imagination. Standing so close to the place where his twin had died was taking something good, *something elemental*, out of him, but he was pleading for his living brother's life.

"Ciopori," he whispered, "I do not often make requests. In fact, I am forever chastised for my pride and arrogance, my inability to humble myself before others…but with the gods as my witness, I am begging you right now—do not interfere with Marquis's destiny. I know that you love him, and that my plea is purely selfish, but I cannot survive the loss of another brother."

Nachari turned away, locked the hatch, and rushed out of the chamber.

Nachari Silivasi was in the tunnel retching when Ciopori finally caught up to him. He hated that he had left her like that, but she was in no immediate danger—and he couldn't bear for her to see him fall apart.

As most vampires rarely ate food, there was nothing for him to throw up, so his stomach just heaved painfully, convulsing until he truly believed his ribs might crack.

Why had he done such a thing?

What had made him believe he was strong enough to see Shelby's last destination? Dear gods, the males in the house of Jadon never had to witness the punishment—or see the death chamber. Napolean had always sheltered them from the worst of the Blood Curse, and for good reason.

Try as he might, Nachari could not get the image of his adventurous, good-natured brother—kneeling and screaming, flailing or fighting, ultimately being murdered—in that cold, sterile chamber out of his mind. And for what reason had he been so brutally slain?

His stomach started a new round of dry-heaves, and he doubled over.

It was then that the princess approached him. She placed her hands on his trembling shoulders, bowed her head, and began to chant in a slow, repetitive cadence...her voice a haunting echo of the Old World. The song was unfamiliar but beautiful, and even though it contained words Nachari could not understand, as a wizard, he knew the presence of power when he felt it. Ciopori was commanding the energy around him, and he felt her healing compassion seep into his soul, relax his stomach...and ease his burden.

When the princess was done singing, Nachari stood up and wiped his mouth with the back of his hand. "Thank you," he whispered. "I apologize for my...reaction."

"You have nothing to be sorry for," she insisted. "I have been so selfish in all of this..." After a long, pregnant pause, she added, "If I might, I would ask you one more question."

Nachari raised his eyebrows and waited.

"Why in the name of all that is holy would a male willingly submit to such an *evil* punishment? Why would he come here—turn himself over—even if he had failed to make the sacrifice?"

Nachari leaned back against the tunnel wall. "The punishment is not escapable, Ciopori: The only thing a male can control is where he spends eternity. If he gives his life up with honor, then his soul remains intact, and he will live on in the Valley of Spirit and Light. However, if he runs and hides from the punishment, his soul is lost as well, and he will spend eternity in the Valley of Death and Shadows. It is not a matter of dying or not dying—the execution is inevitable. It is a question of where he will spend the afterlife."

Ciopori brushed a tear from her eye and took Nachari's hand. "Look at me, wizard."

Nachari smiled as graciously as he could and stared into Ciopori's amazing golden eyes; it was easy to see why Marquis had fallen so hard, so quickly. Although he had the feeling that there was far more to the story than he knew.

Ciopori stroked his arm. "You have asked me not to interfere with Marquis's destiny, and I give you my word as a princess: I will do nothing that might endanger your brother's life. But in return, I must ask something of you."

"What?" Nachari held his breath.

"Please do not deny me the opportunity to speak with him once more...to know his heart...to say good-bye. Nachari, take me to Marquis now, wherever he is. I have no way of finding him without you."

Nachari closed his eyes and considered Ciopori's words. The last thing Marquis needed right now was to have Ciopori show up while he was with Kristina, but there was simply no way he could deny her this one request. For whatever reason, the princess clearly loved his brother, and the two of them deserved a chance to say good-bye.

Nachari opened his eyes, squeezed her hand, and managed a faint smile. "If we can get past Napolean, I will take you."

Ciopori shrugged. "Oh, the king will object, but it is of no consequence. I am not bound by his rule." She paused then. "If anything, he is bound by mine."

six

"Why is that infant still crying!"

Salvatore Nistor glared at the worthless human nanny he had captured to care for his newborn nephew, Derrian. Ever since his youngest brother, Valentine, had disappeared five days ago, the eight-day-old infant had done nothing but scream. Vampire infants grew at a much more rapid rate than humans, at least psychologically. They knew their parents right away and were aware of even the smallest change in their environment; unfortunately, this one wanted his father.

Salvatore was seething as he stared at the trembling human female he had abducted from a daycare parking-lot four nights ago on her way home from work. Snatching, cloaking, and transporting the human had been as easy as walking and breathing for the twelve-hundred-year-old male, and he knew deep inside that it wasn't truly her inability to calm the baby that was causing him such rage: What really had his blood boiling was the ever-increasing realization that Valentine wasn't coming home...

Not ever.

True, Salvatore had expected the sons of Jadon to seek vengeance for his brother's crimes, and the heart of the matter was—Valentine had never really known when to say *when*. His arrogance and love of the game had always preceded his better judgment, and the Dark One had simply gone too far when he used Shelby Silivasi's *destiny* to father his son, ultimately murdering both Dalia and Shelby.

And as if that hadn't been enough, he had impregnated Marquis's housekeeper by pretending to be Marquis in the hopes of achieving the same result. Unfortunately, it hadn't worked out quite like Valentine planned.

Salvatore rubbed the bridge of his nose, still fuming. Joelle Parker had been laid to rest earlier that day, which meant her body had been returned to her family, and that meant she hadn't given birth to Valentine's sons. It was simply impossible to go on believing Valentine was off having a good time somewhere—perhaps feeding or enjoying human women—celebrating the birth of two more offspring. The cocky son of Jaegar would have incinerated Joelle's body immediately after the birth, leaving no trace of her demise for her loved ones to bury.

No, someone had gotten to Joelle first—and someone had gotten to Valentine. Most likely, *Nathaniel or Marquis Silivasi*, one of the detestable Ancient Master Warriors in the house of Jadon. Salvatore refused to believe that the wizard, Nachari, could have managed such a feat, and Kagen, the healer, was kept as far away from battles as possible because of his value to his people. No, the warriors had sought blood-vengeance. And in doing so, they had started a feud that Salvatore intended to finish.

Salvatore raised his arm and backhanded the stupid female the moment she lay Derrian down in his crib, sending her flying sideways into the cavern wall. As her head cracked against the limestone, she put both hands up in front of her defensively. "*Please...*" she groveled, her high-pitched voice only irritating him more.

Salvatore stalked over to where he had thrown the five-foot-six wisp of a human. Her dirty auburn hair had become a tangled mass over the last week, and her long bangs partially shielded her eyes from view. "Please what!" he thundered, towering over her—his own feral eyes burning with rage. His fangs exploded from his mouth, and he ran his tongue over them slowly, moaning as his eyes swept over her body.

Her knees came up in a defensive posture, and she folded her arms around them, hugging both legs tightly to her chest.

Salvatore snarled and snatched her by the hair. He had left her clothed in her raggedy blue jeans and rock-band tee, not because he cared about her dignity, but because if she had been naked, the temptation to take her would have been too strong to resist. And there were several good reasons Salvatore did not want to rape the female...yet.

BLOOD AWAKENING

First, she would get pregnant, and after taking care of Derrian for twenty-four hours, he knew he was not ready to be a father; besides, he had matters of vengeance to attend to which took precedence over all else. And last but not least, the birth would kill her, and he would just be forced to search for another nanny—which also meant he would have to take care of his nephew by himself in the interim.

Salvatore let go of her hair and stepped back, not trusting his own rage. "What did you say your name was again?"

The human shook so hard her teeth rattled. "S…S…Susan."

Oh, to hell with it. Her weakness irritated him. Maybe she wasn't worth keeping, after all. Salvatore crouched down, his feet floating just inches above the ground, and grasped her by the back of her neck, fisting another handful of hair—this time hard enough to rip some out.

She cried out in pain and clutched at his hands, trying to wrench free.

"Why can't you make my nephew content, *Susan*?" he hissed.

She struggled to speak through her fearful sobs. "Pl…please…he…he doesn't want me…I…I think he misses his mother."

Salvatore threw back his head and laughed. His thunderous voice shook the walls of the lair and rattled the heavy antique chandelier looming above their heads. "Oh, I can assure you, Susan, he does not miss his *mother*!" He leaned in closer, so that his hot breath brushed against her ear. "He killed his mother the day he was born."

He licked the side of her jugular, and she fainted.

Salvatore moved away from the woman then, taking a perch on the platform just in front of his heavy iron bed. He paused and looked around the room: The lair was one of hundreds in the underground fortress, a limestone and granite masterpiece carved out of rock and clay, built far beneath the earth, revealing centuries of brilliant architecture. The ancestral females of his race might have cursed the vampires' souls, but they had not taken away their minds, their talents, or their brilliance. And make no mistake, the Vampyr race as a whole was brilliant.

While the Light Vampires lived and thrived above the surface, walking in the sun and interacting with humans in their precious Dark Moon Vale, the Dark Ones had built an entire colony deep underground, utilizing thousands of acres just to the west of the Red Canyons, creating an elaborate system of tunnels, lairs, and structures that stretched all the way beneath Dark Moon Vale itself.

It had been both a necessary and defensive plan: Should the Light Ones ever discover the true scope of their civilization, the sons of Jadon would be forced to destroy their own empire, economy, and way of life in order to eradicate the colony of the sons of Jaegar. The two were intrinsically connected.

No, unbeknownst to their arrogant brothers of light, the Dark Ones lived—and thrived—miles underground, right beneath their own domain. And they had for over two-thousand years.

Salvatore watched as Susan woke up, scampered to the crib, and gently began to rub Derrian's back. Her trembling hand jerked back every time the babe hissed, as if the child might bite her. It only took a few minutes for the boy to fall asleep, after which time, Salvatore relaxed and sat down on his bed. The female was anchored to the wall by a thick length of chain, manacled to her ankle. She had enough room to move around, but couldn't possibly escape; therefore, Salvatore didn't have to watch her that closely. She moved to the small stone-bench that sat just a few feet beyond Derrian's crib, wrapped the thin blanket Salvatore had given her around her shoulders, and nervously rubbed her tired arms.

Salvatore swung his legs onto the bed, stretched back, and closed his eyes—just as the door to his lair swung open so hard a piece of the wood splintered against the wall.

"*What the*—"

"You're not going to believe this," Zarek Nistor—

BLOOD AWAKENING

Valentine's twin and Salvatore's only remaining brother—
snorted as he stalked into the room.

A narrow bolt of blue lightning shot across the lair, hurtling
from Salvatore's hand to Zarek's, clipping the tips of two of his
fingers right off.

Zarek grabbed his injured hand and howled in indignation.
"What the hell did you do that for?"

Salvatore snarled. "Next time, knock!"

Zarek shot him an evil glare and raised his hand to his
mouth. He released his incisors and dripped healing venom over
the cauterized fingers, a process that would quickly grow the
digits back.

"Now what was it you came to tell me?" Salvatore barked.

Zarek turned his head as if he had just noticed Susan for the
first time, and a low, demonic hiss escaped his throat. He turned
back to Salvatore. "The Blood Moon—have you seen it?"

Salvatore nodded. He'd seen it, all right, even though he
hadn't been outside when the phenomenon occurred.

Salvatore's command of Black Magic had become so
powerful over the centuries that the Omens now presented
themselves to him in a crystal cube he kept on a night-stand
beside his bed: Whenever the cube glowed, Salvatore examined
it for information. Why the cube could not reveal what had
happened to Valentine, he wasn't sure. Unfortunately, the
information it had relayed on the subject was spotty at best: *fire.*
Whatever that meant…

Valentine had been headed toward the Dark Moon Lodge on
the night of his disappearance; that much, Salvatore had
discerned. But shortly after that, the energy field had become
static, as if someone had intentionally caused a rift in the
quantum waves. In fact, the entire thing reeked of the presence
of another sorcerer; well, in the case of the Lighter Vampires,
the male would be viewed as a wizard…

No matter. *Their time would come.*

Salvatore glanced back at his brother and sat up on the bed.

He folded his hands in front of him. *If Zarek only knew...*

"Draco—the dragon?" he drawled.

"Yes, brother. Not only do they have the two, original females now, but the warrior Marquis will soon be permanently immortal."

Salvatore waved his hand in dismissal. "No more immortal than Valentine was—"

"Is!" Zarek corrected.

Salvatore shook his head. Zarek was having a really hard time accepting that his twin was not coming back, and it was beginning to border on delusional.

"Was...or...is," Salvatore said, "you and I both know that immortality is the natural order for a vampire...unless that order is *severely* interfered with. Trust me, brother; I intend to run interference with Marquis Silivasi. As far as I'm concerned, he is the one responsible for Valentine's dea—*disappearance*—and I have no intention of letting it go."

Zarek glared at Salvatore, his own rage building. His dark eyes narrowed into two tiny red slits of hatred. He undoubtedly knew what Salvatore was about to say, and for a minute, it looked like he was going to challenge the older vampire. Luckily, he thought better of it.

Just the same, seeing Zarek so worked up was extremely unsettling.

Salvatore sighed. While the vast majority of vampire twins were fraternal, every now and then, two identical sons were born—and such was the case with Zarek and Valentine. They both had identical black eyes and the same wavy hair; their straight noses were sculpted in the exact same shape; and even the way their thick lips turned up in a snarl when they smiled was the same. But that was just it, unlike Zarek, Valentine had rarely smiled. Unless, of course, he had been hurting someone, plotting to hurt someone, or celebrating the fact that he had just succeeded in hurting someone. Seeing Zarek with such a cold, empty look in his eyes only made the loss of Valentine more real to the ancient vampire. It was like looking into the face of his lost brother.

Salvatore looked away. "Regardless...believe me when I tell you, Zarek; I am intimately aware of what is happening with Marquis Silivasi." He absently stroked the hard leather cover of an ancient tome lying on the top of his bed, and a wicked laugh rumbled in his throat. "Is that all you came to tell me?"

Zarek frowned. "No, brother—I also sensed your hunger: Do you need to feed?"

The question was asked without emotion or intent—just a simple *yes or no* inquiry.

Salvatore threw back his head and shook out his long black-and-red banded hair, the signature crown of a Dark One. While cut in different styles and lengths—some wavy, some straight—all of the sons of Jaegar had it. His fangs began to throb, and his gut ached. Ah, Zarek had been diligent after all, just as a youngest sibling should. Indeed, he was extremely hungry; he had just been too wrapped up in Valentine...and Derrian...to notice.

"Your sense of duty pleases me, little brother. Come." He motioned his hand forward.

Zarek's gait was proud and unafraid as he sauntered over to his eldest brother, his shoulders back, his head held high—whatever differences they had, unimportant.

Although all vampires needed to feed every five to eight weeks, unlike the sons of Jadon, the Dark Ones preferred to kill their human prey, innocent or not. And the tendency to always give into blood-lust had created serious problems with the humans over the centuries: Wherever they chose to hunt, dead bodies were left in their wake like carnage behind a plague of locusts, often riling up humans into hunting parties. Eventually, the house of Jaegar had found a suitable remedy:

The youngest male of every family would join with his brethren to hunt together in packs—sometimes traveling hundreds of miles away to find new prey—and then they would return to the colony and feed their elder brothers and fathers. Not only did it keep the body count down, but it taught the youth how to fight...and how to submit to the natural hierarchy of the Vampyr world.

Over time, it had become a significant rite of passage: Upon a male's twenty-first birthday, the Dark One would hunt alone for the first time ever, consuming as much blood as he possibly could, and then he would return to feed *all* of his brothers, including his father. Although none was allowed to drain the male dry in blood lust, each feeder was required to take his full measure—the normal amount he would consume if feeding alone. If the male had not hunted enough, killed enough, or fed enough, he would come close to death in the process and be shunned by his brothers, who would be forced to save him. However, if the male fed them all—without weakening or flinching—he was officially inducted into the house of Jaegar.

As the second born of the last set of twins, Zarek Nistor had been feeding both Valentine and Salvatore for the past eight-hundred, seventy-nine years, so the process was as routine as sleeping or walking.

Zarek stopped just short of touching his brother, chest-to-chest, their eyes locked in an inevitable gaze of predator and prey, neither one blinking or turning away. Satisfied, Salvatore nodded, and Zarek spun around, presenting his back to his respected elder while kneeling down on one knee.

Salvatore crouched down slowly, his hands going to each of Zarek's shoulders. His dagger-like fangs elongated to their full length, and a slow, sultry hiss escaped his lips. With a gentle hand, he brushed Zarek's hair out of the way and tilted his head to the side until it sat at an angle he liked. The moment he released him, Zarek held the position, his muscles completely relaxed—his heart-rate never increasing.

And then Salvatore struck. The bite was clean and hard, inflicting the kind of pain that would honor a warrior. Zarek's muscular body began to convulse for about fifteen seconds as

BLOOD AWAKENING

Salvatore took his first deep pulls of the rich, heady substance, and then he went limp, falling back against Salvatore's chest.

Salvatore's hands remained on Zarek's shoulders, yet for some reason, the act was unusually pleasurable this time: perhaps because Salvatore needed so desperately to feel the presence of his one remaining brother so close—*and safe*—in such a dangerous time. Whatever the reason, a deep moan of ecstasy escaped his lips, and his hands tightened on Zarek's shoulders.

Salvatore felt Zarek's body instantly stiffen, and he knew it wasn't just his chest, arms, and legs that were turning hard in response to his deep groans of pleasure: No matter how one turned it, feeding was a highly erotic act for a vampire—as was the pleasure of being struck by a piercing set of fangs—and arousal was a natural, physiological response.

Sexual orientation had absolutely nothing to do with it.

However aroused a vampire became during the process of feeding, the males in the house of Jaegar *never* acted on their sexual impulses with each other. While it wasn't unheard of for one or the other to climax during the ritual—sometimes both, and sometimes more than once—the release was understood. And accepted. And never, *ever* mentioned.

Because of the Blood Curse, the innate need for a male to reproduce with a female in order to provide the required blood sacrifice—*to live and remain immortal*—heterosexuality was deeply ingrained in the Vampyr DNA. The drive to reproduce was overwhelming and irresistible. Yet over time, feeding had become an altogether different erotic need. It was the pinnacle of uninhibited ecstasy, sexual or otherwise, the one time when males were allowed to simply let their bodies fully enjoy the exchange of blood.

Salvatore held back his release, although it was difficult: The blood Zarek had recently consumed was especially sweet, and it lit him up like a fire burning from the inside out. Reluctantly, he released the seal he had made over his baby brother's vein and slowly removed his fangs.

The moment Zarek stirred, Salvatore knew precisely where he was going next: to the Chamber of Cobras. To the one place where he could take pleasure in as many venomous bites as he desired, invite as many strikes to his body as he craved.

Release his pent-up sex in private.

Or maybe not.

As Zarek rose from the floor, sporting the same proud gait in his retreat, the male turned directly toward Derrian's crib—and his new nanny.

Susan.

Oh, shit! Salvatore swore to himself. *Now that was an inexcusable oversight.*

Salvatore rubbed his eyes. His grief over Valentine was worse than he thought: He was missing things he would have never missed before. Females didn't stay alive very long around the sons of Jaegar, not unless they were sired vamps who had willingly relinquished their souls for the promise of immortality. And even then, the moment they became pregnant, the relationship was over. Well, technically, forty-eight hours after they became pregnant, but why split hairs?

Thinking he could feed from Zarek in the presence of a female *and still keep her alive afterward* was...well, unworthy of an ancient. Salvatore shook his head in frustration, but he made no attempt to stop his younger brother. It wasn't worth the battle. Rather, he simply sat down on the bed and prepared to watch. No doubt, Zarek's performance would be better than the movie of the week.

The sexed-up vampire stalked toward the human female like an African lion approaching a zebra. He snatched her up from the bench by the waiste and threw her face-first into the stone wall, securing her there with a callous forearm across her back.

BLOOD AWAKENING

The nanny wailed a blood-curdling scream and turned her head toward the bed, her eyes desperately pleading with Salvatore—for what, he had no idea. If anything, her terror only aroused Zarek more—which meant, at this point, trying to remove the female from Zarek's grasp would be like trying to wrench a piece of meat out of the mouth of a pit bull. Not something an intelligent being did.

As she begged and pleaded—reminded Zarek of his nephew's need for a nanny—the vampire ripped her tattered clothes from her body in one harsh movement and shredded them to pieces with his talons, watching as they curiously drifted to the ground like snow.

The female was practically hyperventilating.

Damn, could that girl scream or what?

And struggle.

Oh, bad move!

In desperation, the nanny tried to head-butt Zarek, cracking the tip of his nose with the base of her skull. Salvatore winced before laughing.

Zarek growled in anger...and ecstasy...at the female's unexpected assault, and then he fisted her hair, jerked her neck back, and sank his fangs so deep into her jugular that Salvatore heard his fangs scrape against her bones.

Salvatore grimaced as an unnatural howl of pain echoed through the lair, and the female's body began to convulse, making her a rather difficult target to nail. With a guttural snarl, Zarek wrenched her hips away from the wall, kicked her jerking legs apart, and speared her so hard with his shaft that the air left her body.

And then he groaned...as his eyes rolled back in his head.

Salvatore was positively enthralled, watching Zarek ride the nanny with such brutal force and primal desperation, drowning out her pain-filled cries with his own raspy groans of pleasure, turning her heart-wrenching pleas into metrical grunts, and clamping down even harder on her neck as he pounded her body against the wall with violent thrusts.

Salvatore had to give credit where credit was due.

Zarek had quite the rhythm.

His powerful, muscular physique was truly something to behold as it drove in and out of the female, going deeper and deeper with each plunge. And considering all of the grief they had been dealing with lately, Zarek certainly deserved the distraction.

Salvatore lay back on the bed, turning away from the side-show long enough to consider the blood war Valentine had started with the Silivasis. He had barely begun to replay the events when he heard a hoarse shout, and the floor shook beneath him. When he looked up, Zarek was moaning against the female's neck and—damn it all to Hades—releasing every bit of the powerful orgasm into the worthless nanny's body.

For the love of the Dark Lords.

"You really want kids right now, my brother?" he barked across the room.

Zarek rested his head on Susan's back, panting, while holding her up with one arm. He slowly withdrew from her body. "What?" he groaned. He was clearly still feeling the effects of the orgasm.

Salvatore cleared his throat. "*A son?* Now? Is that what you want?"

Zarek met his brother's gaze, and his body shook one last time. "Not really." He moaned and closed his eyes. "Although I have to admit, it would be nice to be safe from the Blood Curse once and for all." He slowly exhaled, and when he opened his eyes again, they were glossed over.

Salvatore shrugged his shoulders. The Blood Curse was hardly something to worry about, not for the sons of Jaegar, anyway. For the sons of Jadon? *Yes.* They had to find—and keep—one woman over an entire lifetime, and the mating had to be accomplished in a single moon, or they were doomed. But the sons of Jaegar could use any female to reproduce, and it didn't matter one lick whether or not she wanted what was about to happen to her. Time was of no consequence. As long as an immediate sacrifice was made from the male's first set of twins, it was acceptable. For the Dark Ones, fulfilling the demands of the Blood Curse was as easy as counting to three.

As if Zarek had read his mind, he grunted, "You're right. It is enough that we have Derrian to take care of right now." He glanced toward his nephew's crib. "It's important that we give him the same attention Valentine"—he swallowed hard—"*would have* given him."

With that said, Zarek turned to Susan, kissed her thoroughly on the mouth, then placed one hand on top of her head, the other on her chin, and twisted in opposite directions. There was a quick snap before her lifeless body slumped to the ground. As he zipped up his pants, he sighed. "You know, brother, I think I love that kid like he's my own."

Salvatore smiled. "As do I, Zarek." He frowned then. "However, I am sorry for your grief. I do know how hard this is, but I give you my word: Even if it takes an eternity, Valentine will be avenged."

Zarek nodded. "Be well, my brother."

Salvatore watched as Zarek sauntered out the door.

All in all, he was such a good kid.

"Be well, Zarek."

seven

Nachari pulled his vintage Calypso Coral 1970 Ford Mustang—*which was in mint condition*—into the parking lot of Kagen's clinic and slowly turned off the roaring engine. Ciopori had absolutely no idea what all those words meant, but Nachari had mentioned them several times on the way to the clinic. Apparently, he liked to collect the Ford Mustang automobiles and was extremely passionate about all the special features of the machines as well. Especially the mint condition.

"Stay put," he said, exiting the driver's side door.

Ciopori cocked her eyebrows. "Pardon me?"

Nachari smiled then—that breathtaking smile he undoubtedly used to charm females of the human race into letting him feed. "Sorry. Please, don't go anywhere. Remember, you agreed—I have to clear it with Marquis first."

Ciopori took a deep breath and nodded. Her chest felt like the weight of the entire world was sitting upon it. She had given the wizard her word, and she never broke it. "I will wait, but you must convey how desperately I need to see him."

"Of course." Nachari held up the keys and pointed to the dark panel he called a dashboard. "Would you like the radio?"

"The what?"

Nachari shook his head. "Never mind. I'll be right back."

Marquis stood in the back of treatment room number three, watching as Kagen meticulously attended to Kristina's wounds. His mind was still in a fog when he heard a gentle knock on the door.

"What is it?" Kagen sounded irritated. "I've told the staff a dozen times not to interrupt me when I'm with a patient."

The door slowly opened, and Nachari stuck his head around the corner.

BLOOD AWAKENING

"Brother," Kagen greeted, his concentration remaining on Kristina.

"Greetings, Kagen," Nachari responded, and then he turned to Marquis. "May I have a word with you?"

Marquis blinked several times as if coming out of a trance and snorted. "We're busy right now, Nachari." He had no intention of answering his baby brother's inquiries about what had happened.

Nachari immediately switched to telepathic communication: *I realize that, Marquis, but there's someone with me who desperately needs to see you.*

Marquis eyed the doorway. *Who?*

She's in the car, Nachari explained.

She?

Yes...Princess Ciopori. She insisted, Marquis, and frankly, if you don't agree to see her, I think she might just have the nerve to walk right into this room—even with Kristina sitting right over there. Nachari glanced at Kristina for the first time, and her responding blush revealed more than a little *appreciation* for the wizard's beauty.

Marquis looked back and forth between the two. Unlike Ciopori, Kristina didn't have the grace to hide her reaction: She saw a stunning male, and she looked momentarily stunned. How many times had she seen Nachari before? Hundreds?

Marquis cleared his throat, and Nachari lowered his eyes respectfully. "Greetings, sister," he said, as was proper in addressing one's brother's *destiny*.

Kristina blanched and quickly looked away, not bothering to respond.

She's taking this well, I see, Nachari commented.

Kagen looked up at him then. *Why don't you bring the princess around back to the patio, just outside of my office; my door is unlocked, so Marquis can meet her there.* He looked up at Marquis. *Take as long as you need; I'll make sure Kristina doesn't go anywhere.*

Marquis hesitated, while both of his brothers stared, waiting for a response. He turned to Kristina, more out of courtesy than

72

need: "I'll be back."

She jolted at the sound of his voice but never looked up.

Nachari let out a low whistle as he held the door for Marquis, clearly realizing how bad things really were. As soon as the door closed behind them, he whispered, "Wow, you two have quite a ways to go."

Marquis shot his youngest brother a heated glare that would have melted ice, and Nachari quickly dropped the subject.

"Bring her up the outside steps to the second-floor deck. I'll cut through Kagen's office and meet you there." Marquis ran his hands through his hair, feeling suddenly weary.

Nachari frowned. "Uh...yeah, I think we already established where—" His voice abruptly cut off. "No problem." He headed out the clinic front doors, and Marquis dropped his head in his hands.

He was not prepared for this. For any of it. Seeing the princess right now was the last thing he really wanted...because he wasn't at all sure he could go back to Kristina afterward. Maybe death was preferable. He wondered: Could he exchange a lifetime with someone he didn't love for thirty-days with someone he did? Could he refuse the demands of the Blood Curse and spend his last remaining days with Ciopori instead? He sighed, headed up the stairs, and then shot through Kagen's office to the deck, where he waited for Nachari to bring the princess.

The moment Ciopori came into view, his heart skipped a beat, and he had to steady himself with the railing. *Don't get caught up,* he warned himself, knowing it was already too late.

Nachari gracefully averted his eyes and shimmered out of view, leaving the two alone to talk. As soon as he was gone, Ciopori melted into a pool of tears.

Marquis held out his arms, struggling for breath. "Do not cry, Princess. *Please*, do not cry. I don't think I can bear it."

Ciopori fell into his arms and clung to him so tightly her body trembled. She clutched at his back as if she would never let go, sobbing uncontrollably into his shoulder. "I'm sorry. Gods, I didn't intend to do this."

Marquis rested his chin gently on the top of her head and brushed back her hair. His own hand trembled. "You have no idea how sorry I am," he whispered. "When I first saw the moon, I thought it was...for us."

"I saw it as well, but I never imagined it was you." Ciopori sniffled and pulled back to look him in the eyes.

"Who told you?" Marquis was already lost in the golden amber of her eyes, even though the sparkle was clearly gone.

"Napolean." She brushed away a tear.

Marquis nodded and pulled her close once again. He didn't know what to say...or do. Like her, he just wanted to hold on. Forever.

He had no idea how much time had passed, the two of them locked in each other's arms—thinking, feeling, grieving—trying to come to grips with what had happened. And what was yet to come.

Ciopori finally broke the silence. "I understand the blood sacrifice." She steadied herself. "And I know what will happen if you and your new..." Her words trailed off. She simply couldn't say the word *destiny* aloud.

Marquis cupped her chin in his hands and lifted her head to meet his gaze. "At risk of offending the gods, I have turned this over in my head a dozen times, Ciopori, searching for a way out, but there isn't one. Outside of my own death in thirty days—"

"No!" Ciopori sounded horrified. "Absolutely not! That is not an option!" Her entire body began to quiver.

Marquis sighed and looked away. "Okay," he whispered, holding her head to his heart and stroking her hair. "Okay, my love. I will not speak of it again."

Ciopori slowly calmed down. "What I was trying to say is that I understand what you have to do—what you and Kristina have to do." Her voice faltered. "And I came to tell you that *you must*." Her voice grew stronger, and she took a step back in order to face him squarely. *"You must make the sacrifice, Marquis. You must be with your* destiny—*and you must live."* She lowered her voice. "I would rather love you from afar than try to live in a world without you. Do you understand?"

Marquis felt moisture swell in his eyes, and he blinked it away. He instinctively glanced at the sky, noting how it was becoming ominously dark. Rain clouds were forming in response to his tumultuous emotions; he had to hold it together.

Napolean had already warned him about his last outburst— too many humans had been injured as it was. He reached deep inside, drawing on the seasoned warrior within, and a familiar strength answered. "If that is your decision, then I will abide by it, but know this: If it were up to me, I would choose thirty days with you."

Ciopori turned as pale as a ghost. "'Tis not an option warrior; 'tis never an option!"

Marquis shook his head and regarded the sky once again. "The gods are cruel," he whispered. "I never questioned why they allowed the Curse...*but this?*" He took a slow, deep breath. He kissed the princess on the forehead and clasped her by both shoulders. "Ciopori, I cannot see you again after today. There's just no way..."

Ciopori's courage dissolved like an icicle on a summer's day, all the air suddenly leaving her body. The look in her eyes was one of both shock and desperation, and she seemed on the verge of panic. Trembling, she reached up, cupped his face in her hand, and shook her head aggressively. Stretching to the tips of her toes in order to reach him, she pressed her lips to his.

Marquis told himself to stop.

To just pull away.

To honor Lord Draco's choice and Kristina, the woman he was expected to turn Vampyr, the *destiny* who would soon bear him twin sons. But his ageless soul could not. In that moment there was only her: *Ciopori.* The sweet taste of her mouth, the intoxicating scent of her skin, the soft curves that molded so perfectly against him as he pulled her closer. There was only an aching, empty void, and his heart was so bereft—so filled with grief and loneliness—that it overpowered his every sense of duty. Good and bad no longer existed. Right and wrong were abstract concepts.

No...all that was good was in his arms. All that was right had been taken from him. Marquis Silivasi owed the gods *nothing*.

Never again.

He had paid his dues. *For fifteen-hundred years.* And this was his reward?

As the earth fell out of focus, all other life drifting away into the ether, Ciopori opened her love-filled eyes and whispered, "We don't have thirty-days, but we have right now, warrior. Give me this one moment—before you and Kristina come together. Let me have this one memory to hold onto before you are mated."

As her enchanting eyes pled with his, Marquis could hardly believe she was real. Where had this woman come from? When had their love become so strong? And why did he feel it—trust it, know it—all the way down to his soul?

His mind said, *No.*

His discipline said, *Absolutely not.*

His sense of loyalty and duty said, *Go inside and find Kristina.*

Marquis tried to push Ciopori away, desperately willing his legs to move, urgently commanding his body to dematerialize...

And then his fangs extended as if they had a mind of their own. He traced the alluring pulse along the side of her neck with his finger, up and down...once, twice, three times. Marquis shivered as the last vestige of his control slipped away, and his fangs sank deep into the soft hollow above Ciopori's shoulder.

She shuddered beneath him, and he drank like a man possessed.

He would take everything she wanted to give—her blood, her heart, her body—before he walked away. And when he finally did, he would leave all that he was with her.

His heart. His body. His seed...
His soul.
And as for the gods? *Well, they could just be damned.*

Ciopori looked deep into Marquis's eyes, certain he was going to leave her—that he would simply melt away right then and there—without responding to her plea. And then she felt a sharp, stabbing pain in her neck followed by a pleasure so intense that it robbed her of breath.

Her body shook for about fifteen seconds as Marquis took long, greedy pulls of her blood, and then she simply melted into a pool of liquid heat in his arms. *Dear gods, the man felt like silk, power, and perfection at her throat, and she prayed it would never end.*

When Marquis finally withdrew his fangs, he moaned deep in his throat as if the adjustment were painful, and then Ciopori felt two thick-drops of liquid closing the puncture wounds...and the pleasure was gone. She slowly lifted her head to protest, but when she parted her lips to speak, he caught her words with his mouth, devouring her protest with his tongue—seeking with fevered urgency.

His taste was hot and exotic, and Ciopori met him kiss for kiss, passion for passion, as their lips explored and their tongues tangoed in a powerful dance of love. Her breasts began to feel heavy, and her nipples ached in a way she had never experienced before. And even deeper...lower...at the junction between her legs, a pulsing warmth began to build into a slow fire that caused her womb to contract and her body to move against his.

She cried out from the unexpected intensity and grasped at his shoulders, his hair, anything that might hold her up as her knees gave way.

Marquis caught her effortlessly, lifting her gently into his arms as if she were weightless. And then just like that, they were in Kagen's office, and he was laying her down, ever so softly, against a wide, velvet chaise.

She had no memory of Marquis walking—or even flying, for that matter—but as his lips descended once again to claim hers, she forgot all about the miraculous change of scenery. She felt and knew only one thing: Marquis.

"Marquis…"

His name escaped on a throaty groan, wrapped in a voice far too seductive to be her own, yet his reaction was immediate. He moaned in response, and his warrior's body blanketed her own.

Propping himself up by his powerful arms, he gazed down into her eyes, his own changing pupils glazed over with desire. "You are the most beautiful woman I have ever seen," he whispered. His eyes drank her in like a man dying of thirst. He sat up then, his deep, heavy breaths increasing as he eyed her from head to toe. "Undress for me, Ciopori. Let me watch you…slowly. I want to remember every part of you. Do this for me…now."

Ciopori felt suddenly self-conscious. Having been raised a princess, modesty had been part of her required decorum. Few females had ever seen her body nude, let alone a male, yet the look in Marquis's eyes drew her like a magnet. His blatant desire made her want to please him more than she had ever wanted anything in her life.

Ciopori sat up and leaned toward the arm of the chaise, slowly unzipping the back of her sleeveless dress. Her eyes remained locked with his, and she smiled when a deep, almost indiscernible growl escaped his slightly parted lips. Oh yes, he was going to enjoy her as much as she was going to enjoy him.

Emboldened, she unfastened the remaining clasps and slowly let the top fall away, knowing there were no undergarments between her smooth skin and the fabric. And just like that, her breasts were exposed to his hungry gaze.

Marquis's breath hitched, and he shuddered. "Ciopori…"

His husky voice poured over her like liquid silk, his eyelids growing heavy with carnal need. She knew he couldn't stay away.

He grasped her by the narrow of her waist and pulled her to him, simply drinking in the sight of her for what seemed a lifetime, his eyes leaving a trail of fire in their wake. His hands cupped the weight of her breasts with a lover's tenderness, slowly kneading the sensitive flesh as his thumbs swept up to brush the peaks in taunting, exhilarating circles.

He traced her areola with his forefinger and hissed when the nipple hardened in response to a quick, hard pinch, a gentle tug, and release. Ciopori cried out at the brief pain and then sighed as his thumb gently massaged it away. His eyes were like lasers locked to hers, his mouth turned up in a wickedly sinful smile.

"You like that?" he whispered, his voice no more than a deep, raspy purr.

He caressed her other nipple in the exact same manner and watched as she squirmed, moaning his approval, and then he bent his head and took the first aching peak into his mouth.

Ciopori felt the jolt all the way down to her toes, an electric stream of energy pooling in her core. Unable to control it, she began to roll her hips beneath him like waves following a commanding tide, and she instinctively arched her back, offering more of herself to his seeking tongue.

Marquis began to suckle in earnest as she cried out with pleasure, his lips exploring one nipple while his fingers explored the other. And then she grabbed him by his glorious mane of hair and held him to her.

Dear gods, she wanted this man inside of her...

Marquis snarled a low, approving growl as he remained deftly lodged in her mind, obviously reading her thoughts, as well as her reactions, for the sake of increasing her pleasure.

He seemed to know everything she craved the moment she craved it, and as his hands began to explore the rest of her body, he adjusted the pressure...the motion...the intensity in accordance with her every whim. He was creating a whirlwind of passion, a growing storm of need that was driving her out of her mind.

BLOOD AWAKENING

And then a large, commanding hand gently stroked the base of her ankle and slowly began to slide up the inside of her leg, his fingers tracing the contours of her calf as it approached her inner thigh, where he began to knead the flesh with increasing pressure. She gasped at the unexpected advance when he caught at her legs and eased them apart.

He smiled and dropped his head, blowing warm air over the lace panties that lightly covered her core, and then he licked right through the thin material. Ciopori moaned and shifted on the chaise. Her body slid down, and her legs eased apart.

Marquis sat back then, all at once leaving her bereft. "The rest of your dress," he instructed as his eyes swept over the apex between her legs.

Ciopori held her breath as she awkwardly removed what remained of the garment, leaving only her panties between them.

Marquis smiled and cupped her, rotating the heel of his hand against her cleft, groaning as she raised her hips and pushed back against him. "*Da, dragostea mea—danseaza pentru mine.*"

Ciopori's heart skipped a beat, and her womb clenched as the familiar Romanian words rolled off his tongue: *Yes, my love—dance for me.* She was as aroused as she was startled by her own powerful responses.

In her relatively young life, she had never thought of herself as sexual, erotic. As the king's daughter, her virginity had been guarded like the castle treasure; to even think of a male in such a way was to endanger his life. But lying here now, beneath Marquis, every carnal desire she had ever buried awakened beneath his hands, stirred in response to his words, trembled at the sight of his smoky eyes and smooth skin. The heat he was generating was almost painful, and she found herself wanting him...*wanting things*...that were as shocking as they were exciting.

Marquis purred like a jungle cat. "What is it you want, my love?"

Ciopori inhaled sharply, unable to speak, and Marquis shook his head back and forth. "No. That is not an answer." He slipped two fingers beneath her panties and began to massage the heat of her desire. "Tell me what you want, Ciopori."

Ciopori arched her back and writhed beneath him. She tried to talk—she really did—but the sound was trapped beneath a growing inferno of heat and sensation and swirling colors. Her mind was engulfed in pleasure.

Marquis stared down at her through heavy-lidded eyes as he slowly removed her panties. His fingers traced every curve and angle of her long, sexy legs as he went along.

When he finally knelt on the chaise above her, she felt so incredibly vulnerable and exposed. He was still completely dressed, while she was laid out before him like a banquet on a palace table. Before she could ask him to undress, he slipped two fingers inside of her and probed in a sweet, thrusting motion, pressing against her with his hand, even as he teased the same spot with his thumb.

"Do you want this?"

Ciopori whimpered like a child.

"Or this?" He replaced his fingers with his tongue.

Marquis groaned into her core, sending shuddering vibrations deep into her womb as he slowly tasted her essence. And then, his tongue took on a life of its own. "Dear gods," he moaned, "you taste like…the moon and the stars, themselves…a goddess." His body shuddered. "I could love you forever."

His tongue dove back in, this time bringing his lips, his fangs, and his sweet, sensual mouth with it, as he ravaged her like a hungry animal: grazing, tasting, suckling…drinking.

Ciopori cried out, her harsh scream filling the room. Oh gods, she had to be quiet...but how? When Marquis stopped abruptly, she almost cried out again—only this time, with need. She couldn't have stopped now if she wanted to. Was he angry?

She opened her drowsy eyes to peek at him and saw nothing but love—and desperate need—dripping from his chiseled, handsome face. "I am afraid you still haven't told me what you want," he admonished, "so I have no idea what to do next." He laughed a wicked, sinful laugh.

Ciopori was breathing in short, rapid breaths as she forced her mind to focus. "I want..." She panted some more. "I...oh gods...I want...I don't know." She clutched at him, but he moved out of reach. "*I want you*," she whimpered. It was all she could think of.

Marquis's eyes burned into hers. "How, *prinţesa mea?*"

Ciopori shivered as her eyes involuntarily swept down to the center of his trousers and the thick, straining sex that pressed against them, now jerking in response to her gaze. He slowly licked his full bottom lip and stroked the enormous shaft through the silky material with his hand. "Is this what you want, Ciopori?"

She writhed beneath him in response and groaned.

Marquis smiled then, his perfect white teeth gleaming beneath his full, sculpted lips. "I didn't hear you."

Ciopori sighed. "Yes." It was a mere whisper, but it seemed to please him.

"Where?"

Ciopori's eyes grew big.

"*Where?*"

Ciopori held his gaze, knowing her eyes were pleading. "I want you inside of me," she capitulated. "Dear gods, I've never wanted anything so badly."

Marquis bent over and slowly kissed her, his passion so intense she felt like her heart might stop beating. His desire was only eclipsed by his tenderness as he massaged and tasted her breasts, swept his hands down and around the flat of her stomach, and finally drew his fingers up over her core...again and again...until she was nearly weeping.

"Why are you teasing me?" she uttered, breathless. Her voice hitched from the torture.

Marquis shook his head. "Not teasing you, Princess. *Preparing you.*"

He leaned back then and removed his shirt, exposing

muscles like a granite statue, a stomach made of layered bricks. And then, in a slow, languid movement, he began to unzip his pants. As he dropped the black silk slacks along with his boxers to the floor, his magnificent erection sprang into view, and Ciopori froze beneath him.

The male was positively *enormous* and oh-so-incredibly beautiful. His sex was like a steel rod sheathed in pure velvet: hard and invincible, yet smooth and refined. The blunt, curved head was only slightly smaller than her fist, and the sight of it gave her pause. She wanted him, but...

Her eyes moved down to the thick shaft itself—at least the width of her forearm—and she shuddered. Marquis shook his head and slowly traced her bottom lip with his fingers before gently inserting his thumb in her mouth. Instinctively, she began to suckle.

"I would *never* hurt you, Ciopori," he murmured. "I need you to trust me—completely—to give yourself fully over to my control."

Ciopori stared into the eyes of her timeless lover, and her heart filled with him even as her body grew warmer. Whatever hesitation she had felt melted into absolute assurance as she relinquished her concerns, and her body became fully, irrevocably, his. "I do trust you completely, warrior."

Marquis smiled then and gently blanketed her, his powerful erection pressing tight against her stomach as he continued to kiss her and explore her body. As Ciopori groaned, his sex jerked and expanded, small drops of arousal leaking out of the tip to coat her belly. Reaching down, Marquis caught one of the pearls on his forefinger and placed it on her tongue, grinding his thigh into her sex at the same time...

And she fractured.

Unsure of what was happening, Ciopori clung to his broad shoulders, her nails digging in for support, as her body spun out of control, contracting and releasing in shocking waves of ecstasy. From her thighs to her womb, she became a spiraling comet, the vibrations in her inner and outer core causing her to cry out like she was mad, her mouth buried in the thick of his arm.

Taking full advantage of the moment, Marquis repositioned his hips and gently pushed her legs aside with his thigh. In one fluid motion, he thrust his heavy sex into her, sheathing himself halfway.

Ciopori cried out as the enormous shaft broke through her maiden's barrier and began to stretch her impossibly from the inside out, but the powerful waves of the orgasm carried her through the pain on an inexorable peak of pleasure. Before she could lose one to the other, Marquis began to rock back and forth, gently at first—stretching, opening, seeking deeper and deeper with each careful thrust—until he was finally surging in and out of her with total abandon.

His head was thrown back, his glorious, wild hair spilling out around him. And in his primal nature, he grunted and growled...and groaned...as he took her with such primal power.

With absolute control.

Ciopori thought that she might die from the pleasure.

This was where she belonged: lying beneath Marquis, existing only for his pleasure...while drowning in the same. The intensity was overwhelming, and she began to weep.

Marquis brushed away her tears and dipped down to kiss her lips even as his hips kept up their furious thrusting, taking her higher and higher with each passionate stroke. He understood her tears to be exactly what they were, and they seemed to only heighten his response. His need.

Marquis's eyes were half-open, half-closed, his handsome face stamped with a look of such pleasure that it almost appeared pained. "I want to come inside of you," he groaned into her ear. "I want to fill you, and I want you to take all of me...to keep inside of you even when I'm gone."

Ciopori cupped his face in her hands. "Will I be in danger of getting pre—"

"No," he assured her, his thrusts becoming shorter and faster, his pounding harder. "Not unless I command it. You can't—" His voice cut off in midsentence as he suddenly inhaled and shuddered. His back stiffened; his body froze; and his face became *harshly beautiful* in a way Ciopori had never imagined a male could be.

Marquis shouted his release, his body trembling as stream after stream of his essence spilled into her core. He plunged deeper and deeper even as he climaxed, almost as if he wanted to crawl inside her and hold her there forever.

Ciopori clung to the magnificent warrior as her own body came apart a second time. She held on for dear life, riding out the waves of pleasure with him until they slowly came down together.

Finally spent, Marquis fought to catch his breath, his head falling forward against her chest. Careful to shoulder the bulk of his weight with the strength of his arms, he slowly withdrew and rolled to his side, gathering Ciopori close to his heart.

The moment was too delicate.

Too sacred.

Too timeless to interrupt with words.

Everything and nothing was said at the same time, both of them knowing this was their final good-bye.

After at least an hour had passed, lying in each other's arms, Marquis moved. "I have to go, my love; I'm surprised my brothers have not come for me yet."

Ciopori exhaled and sat up. "And Kristina, she's probably wondering—"

Marquis held up his hand to cut her off. "She's probably resting. Please...don't go there, Ciopori."

Ciopori sniffled and climbed off of the chaise. They both dressed side-by-side in silence. When finally, there was no more excuse to linger, Marquis opened his arms one last time and bid her into them.

Ciopori fought to maintain her dignity, struggled to preserve her composure.

While she should have felt guilty over what they had just done, she could not. The female downstairs had no feelings for Marquis whatsoever.

Ciopori had pressed Nachari for information on the way to the clinic, and according to him, there was no existing relationship between the two of them. While Marquis's future was dependent upon them building one quickly, that process had not yet started. For all intents and purposes, Ciopori was his past. And this new woman...*Kristina*...would be his future. The two points were linear, and never would their destinies intersect. No, Ciopori would not taint the only part of Marquis she would ever have—her memories—with guilt.

Marquis's arms tightened around her as if he had read her thoughts. And truth be told, he probably had. She felt his throat constrict against her forehead as she nuzzled into the hollow of his neck. He, too, was swallowing his pain.

"I will miss you always, warrior."

Marquis stood as still as a statue. "And I, you, Princess." He stepped back swiftly and caught her by the shoulders. "Look at me."

Their eyes met, and an unspoken grief passed between them.

"*I love you, Ciopori.*" He stroked the side of her jaw, allowing his fingers to linger over her chin before his arm fell back to his side.

"I love you too, Marquis." She choked over the words, unable to stop her tears. When she reached out for his hand, he backed away...swiftly, defiantly.

Resolutely.

Ciopori felt the blood rush out of her face the moment she looked into his eyes. Her stomach turned queasy, and her heart sank in her chest. Marquis looked like a granite statue: dark, cold, and lifeless.

Hardened to the core.

Whatever passion or life had been in the warrior just

moments ago—just an hour ago—was irretrievably gone.

Ciopori reached out to him once more in an effort to take his hand, but he pulled it away, his eyes completely devoid of emotion. "From now on, *stay away*."

The arctic words caught her off-guard, sending shivers of ice down her spine. She tried to force his gaze, but it was as if she wasn't even there. Her warrior—*her lover*—was no longer standing before her. There was only a vampire. A creature with ghostly, obsidian eyes. A male who was cold and cruel...and empty.

Her heart beat a mile a minute. She had to reach him. "Marquis," she whispered, "don't do this to yourself—to us—*to me*. To never see you again would be a fate..." Her words trailed off. He was looking straight through her as if he didn't even see her now.

Dear gods, she was as dead to him as his little brother.

"Be well, Princess." His words drifted into the empty space, and then he simply disappeared, vanishing from her view before she could respond.

Ciopori stumbled back to the chaise and sat down, her mind a cauldron of jumbled thoughts, her stomach tied in knots.

Her heart irreparably broken.

She stared at the space where Marquis had been—where the empty shell that had briefly been her world had just stood—and shuddered.

Dearest virgin goddess, how will I go on?
She had lost him forever.

eight

"You can stay in the guest room tonight. I'll retrieve your things tomorrow." Marquis spared Kristina a sideways glance as they pulled up to his house on the northern edge of the Dark Moon Forest.

Kristina blinked several times but said nothing as the rugged Hummer came to a complete stop in front of the old-fashioned, three-story home. She stared at the wide wraparound porch, thinking it reminded her of something one might find on a farm, absently imagining it filled with dogs and cats. She tried to make sense of the fact that this was now her new home, but she just couldn't grasp it.

"Did you hear me?" Marquis asked.

"Huh?" She turned her gaze to the huge, intimidating vampire who had been her boss for the last eight years.

"I said you can stay in the guest room tonight, and we'll go get your things tomorrow."

Kristina nodded like an obedient child. "Yeah…okay." *Boss.*

Marquis came around to the other side of the truck and opened the door for her. Well, wasn't that just all gentlemanly and stuff. At first, she tried to fold in on herself, making her body as small as possible, and then she quickly ducked by him, putting several paces between them. *Please, God, don't let him touch me.*

Marquis didn't appear to notice…or care.

Good.

Kristina followed the angry-looking vampire to the front door and stopped just short of the threshold. She didn't want to go in. She didn't want to be anywhere near Marquis Silivasi right now. She knew exactly what the Blood Curse was—what it required of her—and frankly, she wanted no part of it.

Kristina shivered at the mere thought of having sex with Marquis Silivasi, wishing her mind would quit wandering like that.

Tessa Dawn

It wasn't that he wasn't good-looking or anything: The man was fine as hell, actually, but he was a *vampire*, after all! And he was three times her size. And ten times meaner than the meanest man she'd ever met...Dirk.

Marquis frowned and held the door open: *the door to his lair.* "Come inside, Kristina. I'm not going to bite you."

Kristina blanched and took a step back. She hadn't thought of that possibility...yet. Oh, hell, was she going to have to start drinking blood now too? "I...I think I left my purse in the car." While it sounded like a pitiful excuse to get away, it was actually true.

"I'll get it," Marquis barked. He sounded more like a bloodhound than a man, and apparently, she was his new bone.

"No! I can get it myself. *I'm not helpless.*"

Marquis's frown deepened, his freaky blue-black eyes turning as dark as the night. "I will not have you arguing with me at every turn, Kristina. I am entrusted with your safety now, and I will retrieve your—"

"Look, *Mr. Silivasi...*" Kristina held up her hand to shut him up, clearly catching her boss by surprise—well, her former boss, anyhow. *What was she supposed to call him now, anyway?* She cleared her throat and continued: "In the last three hours, you told me my relationship with Dirk was over—all but admitted you were going to kill him..." Her voice began to falter, so she quickly changed the subject. "And now you're forcing me to give up my life completely and come live"—she pointed at the house—"here in this Victorian mausoleum."

"It's not Victorian," Marquis said matter-of-factly.

Kristina rolled her eyes. "Well, *whatever!* The point is, forgive me if I need a few seconds alone right now without you hovering over me like...like Freddy Kruger or Jason Voorhees or something." She gestured toward the thick surrounding trees and mountains. "This place is already creepy enough, don't you think?"

Marquis shook his head, clearly annoyed. "I can assure you,

Kristina; I haven't the faintest idea what—or who—you're talking about." He waved a cocky hand through the air like a king dismissing a slave. "And frankly, I don't care to know." He leaned back in the doorway and stared at her, looking totally like the big bad wolf in that story about the girl who liked to wear red.

Hmm, did the wolf actually eat Red Riding Hood? Or—

Kristina's heart sank into her stomach. *Blessed Mary, mother of God*, the guy was scary. Even as her boss, he always had been. But at least then, their interactions had been limited to *Hi—yes, boss—are the paychecks here yet?*—and *good-bye*. Now that she thought about it, he acted like he wanted to keep it that way: the boss-employee power structure. Well, maybe except for the paying her thing, 'cause that would make her a prostitute, wouldn't it?

She forced herself to meet his scary gaze and tried not to show her fear. Damn, but the man was fine, though. His body was cut...like iron...like some kind of sex god decided to reproduce himself as a vampire. And his face was freakin'...well, *perfect*.

Except he was just too harsh.

All those sculpted features were just like the man: rough, cold, and hard as stone. There was no give or take in Marquis Silivasi, just absolute command and control.

Kristina stared at the ancient vampire like she had never seen him before as he stood in the doorway with his rock-hard arms crossed over his chest and his dark, demon eyes boring into her skull. And then it suddenly occurred to her, Marquis didn't just look like a demon; he had all the powers of one too.

Oh, shit!

The man was dangerous as hell...

Maybe she needed to chill—just a bit.

She cleared her throat. "*Please*," she said as nicely as possible. "Just five minutes? Then I'll be right in."

Marquis pointed at the truck. "Fine. Take ten if you like, but

I'll be right here watching."

Kristina was just about to argue when his land-line rang inside the house. She closed her eyes and threw out a quick Hail Mary—*who the hell still had a land-line?*—praying he would just go and get it. She could hardly breathe with the old geezer hovering over her like that.

Marquis looked back and forth between the truck and the kitchen, and then he growled deep in his throat like a tiger. "To the truck and straight back," he snarled. And then he leaned in so close she could feel his breath on her cheek. "Don't even think about running, Kristina; it would only serve to irritate me."

Kristina restrained herself from rolling her eyes and nodded. *Yeah, that's what I'm gonna do—outrun a vamp—and in high heels, no less.* She forced a smile. "To the truck and back."

Marquis didn't return the smile—not that she was surprised. The moment he turned his back and headed down the hall she swore beneath her breath…

And then the cursing really got good to her.

Apparently, she was channeling her inner sailor.

She kicked at the ground on her way to the truck, blinking back a fresh onslaught of tears. How in the hell had this happened? *Her. Kristina Riley! Marquis Silivasi's destiny?* The vampire gods had to be smoking crack or something.

As she got closer to the truck, she tried to calm down. She took a few deep breaths, noticing how cold the mountain air had become with the changing seasons. She tried to collect her thoughts.

Steady as a drum, Kristina. Just breathe.

She had all of eternity to get ticked-off and freaked out. Right now, she just needed to take it one minute at a time.

She opened the heavy door to the H3T—damn, her boss had a sweet ride, though. She leaned over to pick up her purse, when all at once, a big hand snatched a handful of her hair and yanked like there was no tomorrow.

Kristina started to scream, but the other hand clasped over

her mouth before any sound could escape. "So, you're sleeping with your *boss* now, Kristi?" The fist in her hair tightened. "How long?"

Kristina froze at the sound of Dirk's voice. How in the world had he found her so quickly? How could he possibly know that she was with Marquis?

Oh, shit...Marquis!

"Dirk. *Dirk!* Listen to me," she cried against his hand. "You gotta let go and get out of here." The words came out muffled: Why she was trying to save his sorry-butt in that moment, she had no idea.

Dirk hauled her out of the car, slammed the door shut, and started to drag her across the lawn toward a grove of trees. Her head splintered from the pain. She kicked with her legs—trying to regain her footing in order to ease the pressure—all the while, thrashing her arms wildly in a wasted effort to break free.

"I asked you a question!" Dirk shouted. *"How long!"*

He stopped dragging her and threw her carelessly to the ground. He knelt over her and slapped her crisply across the face. "How long have you been screwin' your boss, Kristi?"

Kristina was too stunned—and too scared—to speak. She was scared for herself, scared for Dirk, and scared what would happen if Marquis found them. "I'm not," she whimpered.

Dirk frowned and put his hand to her throat. "Don't lie to me, bitch! Tell me now, or I swear I'm gonna kill you this time." He leaned over until his nose touched hers. The smell of alcohol was thick on his breath as he whispered, "And then I'm gonna kill that arrogant bastard you work for."

A deep, sinister laugh rumbled behind them. *"Really?* Well, this should be interesting." Marquis's voice was dark and deadly. His eyes glowed feral red. "By all means, Dirk, kill me if you can."

The human piece of trash released Kristina's throat and spun around like a madman. He was violently enraged and completely...off balance. Marquis was just about to strike when he pulled back. This was just too easy. The fool couldn't even stand up straight. Besides, he preferred to play with his prey a little longer.

Taking his time, Marquis stepped back and allowed Dirk to regain his footing, and then he reached out with supernatural speed and slapped him so hard he flew back five-feet before slamming into the tree behind him.

The foolish human never even saw it coming.

"Get up," Marquis drawled calmly. "We're not through." He turned to Kristina. "Are you okay?"

Kristina slowly sat up and grasped her throat. She rubbed her head at the scalp. "Yeah, I think so."

"Can you walk?"

Kristina tried to stand up and weaved. Marquis caught her, holding her upright, while she fought her disorientation. She steadied herself on his arm and then took a step back. "Yeah...yes...I can walk."

Marquis nodded, keeping one eye on the tattooed idiot by the tree. For the love of Perseus, how long did it take to get up? "Then you need to go inside, Kristina. Go inside and stay there."

Kristina glanced at Dirk, who was kneeling on the ground, on all fours now. When she looked back at Marquis, her face was pale. "Mr. Silivasi," she pleaded, "please."

Marquis spared her a glance. "Please what?"

"P-p-p-please don't..." She cleared her throat. "*Please don't.* Just send him on his way and come inside with me, please." She looked back and forth between the two men and cringed when she saw the same thing Marquis did—Dirk pulling a huge, serrated hunting knife out of the inner pocket of his leather jacket. She swore under her breath. "Better yet, let's just go in and call the police."

Marquis seared a powerful command directly into Kristina's mind, leaving no room for error: *As long as you live, Kristina, you will never think to bring a human into our affairs again. Do we understand one another?* Vampires never involved humans in their affairs. *Never.* And Kristina should have known this.

Kristina blinked at the psychic intrusion and nodded her head.

"Are we clear?" Marquis repeated aloud, just to be sure.

Kristina started to cry. "Don't do that, Marquis," she whimpered. She was obviously referring to the power he had just exerted over her mind, knowing she was helpless to defy him. Still, her desire to save the human cretin was strong. She looked up into his eyes. "Yes, we're clear. No police...*ever.* But please, just let him go."

Marquis frowned. "Get inside, Kristina."

She hesitated.

"Now."

Kristina took a healthy step back, but she held her own. "Marquis, look—"

"Now!"

She took a long, deep breath and fidgeted with her hands. The smell of fear permeated the air. "I'll trade...okay? *I'll trade.*"

Marquis suddenly had a very bad taste in his mouth. "You'll trade what, Kristina?"

She swallowed hard.

"*Trade what?*"

"Myself."

Marquis stared right through her.

Her hands trembled, but she stood her ground. "Me...*my body*...okay?" She looked away then, embarrassed. "I won't fight you on this whole...curse thing. You can have whatever you need from me. Just let him—"

Before she could finish speaking, Dirk let out a crazed war cry and lunged at Marquis with his knife in hand. Marquis welcomed the battle—well, the annoyance—but he was equally sick to his stomach, Kristina's words still swimming around in his head.

Freezing the human in suspended animation, he turned to face his *destiny*. "Words are funny things, Kristina. Once spoken, they're very hard to take back."

Kristina blanched. "I...I just meant that—"

"I know exactly what you meant, you foolish child," he hissed and grabbed her by the arm, trying not to squeeze too hard in his anger. "You are my *destiny—my mate*—yet you offer yourself to me like a common street-walker...and for this human?"

Kristina shook her head. "No, I—"

"Be quiet!" Marquis was about to lose it.

Not only had he found—and lost—the only woman he had ever really wanted in all of his life, but he was now stuck with a virtual child, a female who had little education, even fewer manners, and no formal upbringing whatsoever in how to behave like a lady. On top of that, she was under the protection of the house of Jadon yet repeatedly insisted upon letting some pitiful excuse for a human being—he checked to see that Dirk was still suspended in midair—beat her like a punching bag.

His voice dropped to a low growl. "Know this, Kristina: If Dirk had never laid a hand on you before tonight, he would still be a dead man for trying to take what belongs to me. He would be a dead man because of his arrogance. And he would be a dead man because you dared to defend him—to offer your body—in exchange for his life."

Kristina caught her breath and then quickly squared her shoulders. She raised her chin in defiance, even as she trembled. "If you kill him, Marquis, I will never let you touch me." She swallowed, as if gathering all of the courage she could. "You will have to rape me to have your sons."

Marquis took a step back then, not at all certain if he was impressed by her courage or floored by her stupidity. He drew back his lips in derision, the tips of his canines now showing. "Is that what you think, Kristina? That I would have to rape you to get you pregnant?"

Kristina's eyes dimmed, and her face turned gaunt.

Marquis laughed. "Woman..." He shook his head. "*You truly are a silly human female...*" He felt his eyes heat up and his fangs begin to elongate. "If I wanted you to crawl across the ground like an animal, weep at my feet, and beg me to take you, I could make it happen with the wave of my hand." A deep, feral growl emanated from his throat. "Woman, I could make you need me so badly that the only time you were *not* in pain was when I was inside of you."

Kristina recoiled, stunned by his words.

"Oh, trust me, Kristina: I could make you beg for it...sob for it. Luckily for you, I may be a lot of things, but I have never been a rapist—nor have I ever taken a woman who offered her body to me in barter."

His voice dropped an octave lower and all but dripped with venom. "And as for what you will or will not do: You will do whatever I tell you to do, Kristina Riley *Silivasi*. Now. Get. Inside."

Kristina took off like she had seen a ghost. Her eyes were as big as saucers, and her mouth hung open in stunned horror as she kicked off her heels and ran toward the house.

Marquis was just about to release Dirk when he heard the loud pop of a gunshot in the distance. As he whirled around in the direction of the high-pitched drone, his eyes narrowed into two tiny slits that could perceive heat, motion, and light in infrared. The world began to move in slow motion as he listened for the trajectory of the bullet, his hand coming up automatically to shield his face from impact.

He ducked with preternatural speed as the blazing red metal soared right at his head, the missile searing straight through his hand instead. He looked down at the hole in his palm and hissed like a snake, his lips turning up in a smile: Dirk's biker gang was approaching his house on their Harleys, all leathered up and loaded with weapons. As they rode in like the cavalry, some fool had caught Marquis off guard and shot him.

So, that's what Dirk had been doing under the tree for so long—calling his biker buddies for help before he got up. The stupid...cowardly...fool.

He had just led seven uninvolved men to their deaths.

The moment Marquis released Dirk—so that the dim-witted human could watch what he had wrought—the short, muscle-bound cretin flew at him with his knife still over-head. He was almost like an ancient, Apache warrior; well, except for the strength, skill, courage, or element of surprise. Marquis chuckled, thinking that if anything, the idiot should have approached him thrusting upward, coming in low from the ground.

No matter.

Marquis caught Dirk by his wrist and then snapped his arm like a chicken bone, easily breaking the radius in half. He lifted him by the collar of his dirty leather jacket and paused to read the lapel. "Scorpion, huh?"

Dirk howled in pain.

Marquis extracted one of his razor-sharp claws and slowly traced the matching tattoo of the insect on Dirk's neck, being sure to cut deep into his skin as he went along. "You did not feel as if the artistic representation of the scorpion on your throat was enough of a statement?" He shrugged. "You felt the additional need to have the name sewn into your jacket, huh? Hmm. Interesting."

Dirk kicked his legs wildly in an attempt to break free, his eyes dilated and fixed on the three-inch talon shooting out of Marquis's hand. "What are you?"

Marquis smiled, and his fangs exploded from the roof of his mouth. A deep, feral growl rose from his throat even as his eyes began to heat like molten lava, undoubtedly glowing crimson red. "I'll give you three guesses...before I kill you." He snarled for added effect.

"Ohhhhh...shiiiittttt!"

Dirk squealed like a pig.

He kicked his legs, twisted his body, and flailed his arms frantically in a desperate attempt to break loose. Somehow, he managed to slide right out of his jacket, although Marquis had no idea how—considering Dirk's ample size. And then he hit the ground running, sprinting toward his buddies like a banshee out of hell, waving his one good arm in the air as he went.

"Run! Run! Runnnn!"

A filthy-looking mortal with a blue bandanna wrapped around his head and a goatee that flowed into a five-inch beard stepped off his bike and stomped his steel-toed boot into the ground. "What's that you say, Scorpion?" he spat, looking annoyed at his friend's sudden lack of manliness.

"*I said run*, Spider!"

Marquis smiled: *spider...scorpion...*a few more insects and he'd have enough for a Discovery documentary.

Apparently Spider couldn't hear Dirk over the seven—well, now six—roaring engines behind the men. "I can't hear you, buddy."

Marquis waited until Dirk was about twenty-yards away from the men. He launched himself in the air—allowing his six-foot wings to unfurl for added effect—flew across the yard, and hovered just above Dirk's head. Through five-inch fangs, he snarled, "I believe he said *run!*"

He snatched Dirk up by the waist before he could react—twirling him around until he folded in on himself in a fetal position—at which point, he tossed him at the row of bikes like a bowling ball speeding down a lane. The men dove from the bikes as they fell over and crashed into one another, and then they stared up at Marquis—and froze—almost in unison.

All then all hell broke loose.

Grown men stuttered and yelped like baby seals. They ran

into each other, kicked at their bikes like they were stomping divots in a wild frenzy, and reached for weapons they no longer believed would work. They cursed and screamed, and a few even threw up. It was a hell of a thing to watch, really.

Marquis let his wings recede.

Like the magical quality of his fangs—or his claws—they simply retreated into the powerful, sculpted muscle of his back, leaving no visible sign that they were ever there, unless and until he needed them again.

He stalked slowly toward the men, breathing in the acrid stench of fear and desperation, which only grew stronger as he approached. A dagger came hurling through the air at his heart, but he simply stopped it in mid-flight and reversed it. Unfortunately, his heart-level was the other man's eye-level: The clean pierce to the skull made the death instant and painless.

And then he heard the tell-tale sound of two rifles being cocked and looked up just in time to see Spider simultaneously level two sawed-off shotguns, one in each hand, right at Marquis's torso.

Whoa...Spider was serious.

Not a bad decision, really. The body made a much better target than the head. Marquis smiled and tilted his head to the side. "Now, Spider: Why would you want to do that?"

The man actually snarled, "Go back to hell, vampire!" He aimed both rifles and pulled the triggers.

Marquis threw up both hands at the same time, the tips of his fingers pointing toward the guns as he unleashed two powerful bolts of electricity in the oncoming path of the bullets. Both missiles exploded in the air, and the sizzling arcs of fire burned the shotguns right out of Spider's hands. "What the—"

Marquis leapt the remaining distance, lifting Spider off the ground by his throat.

"I don't come from hell, Spider. In fact, my people are actually from the heavens. Now, pick your poison, Wyatt Earp." He unsheathed his four remaining claws. "Would you prefer that

I dislodge your heart? It is horribly painful, but relatively quick." He ran his tongue over the tips of his fangs. "Or I could rip out your throat—extremely nasty business." And then he shot two narrow beams of light—two glowing red lasers—out of his eyes, pulling them back just before they made contact with Spider's skin. "Or I could simply burn out your brain: clean and effective."

Spider started to jerk like a man having a seizure, and Marquis heard a curious, unsteady rhythm coming from his chest like the erratic beat of a drum. It sped up, paused, and then quit altogether. The man was having a heart attack.

Marquis shrugged. "Very well then, the heart it is."

He dropped him to the ground, allowing nature to take its course.

Just as Spider fell, a tall, lanky, bald guy with a curved mustache, two-inches long on either side of his mouth, came at Marquis with a pair of spinning nunchucks in his hands. He shouted as he swung a high, powerful round-kick right over his head.

Ah, martial arts.

Marquis sighed and weaved backward, avoiding the well-placed kick and catching the man with a clenched fist right between the legs. And then he twisted as the biker squealed like a soprano. Doc Holiday disguised as Bruce Lee released the nunchucks, and Marquis caught them effortlessly with his free hand. He spun the center chain around the biker's neck, releasing his grip on his groin, and catching—then pulling—each wooden handle in an opposite direction with a quick, hard snap. The man's head shot up in the air like a rocket being launched into space before tumbling back to the ground, absent of his body.

Marquis grunted and spun around to face the remaining five men.

And then he stood in quiet curiosity.

They were huddled together like a small herd of cattle, the

smallest one—a kid with spiked blond hair—standing in the front. The kid held up his arms in a gesture of surrender and then promptly...wet himself.

Marquis frowned. "Is this your representative?" He snarled and snatched the kid's jacket right off his chest without removing the sleeves, ripping the leather like it was mere paper, and then he read the center emblem aloud: "The Pagan Brotherhood. Is that the name of your club?" he asked. "Can just anyone join, or do they all have to be cowards?"

The blond kid was shaking from head to toe now. "N...n-n...no," he quivered. "I mean...I...I...I mean...we're not really that organized."

Marquis sighed in annoyance. He was just about to strike when the kid started talking a mile a minute, rambling like his life depended on it—because, well, it did. "L...l-l...look..." he stuttered, "we...we...we...we...we've been talking it over, and you don't have to kill us because we're willing to serve you." He gestured toward the other men. "All of us."

Marquis shifted his weight from one leg to the other, and the kid immediately hit the deck like a grenade had just been launched. Marquis scowled, growing impatient.

"S...s-s...sorry," he squeaked, once he had collected himself.

When Marquis leaned over to look at him, the man flinched and covered his head. "I'm listening." Marquis crossed his arms and waited while the kid slowly stood back up.

"L...l-l...like I've been saying...we...we...we would like to be your...puppets...or minions...or whatever it is you call human servants"—the boy knelt down on the ground then—"and I swear to you, we would never tell anybody." He looked over his shoulder, and the other men bobbed their heads up and down, encouraging him to keep on talking. "We can bring you things, lots of things. Anything you want. Whatever you need."

"Women," one of the other cattle whispered.

"Y...y-y...yeah...women," Blondie offered.

"Or blood," a slovenly male urged, poking the kid in the

back.

"Or...or...or blood...or...women to drink blood...I mean so you...you can drink the women's blood." He scratched his nose. "When we bring them to you."

When Marquis didn't answer, the kid became desperate, and his voice raised an octave higher. "We could do things for you...you know...in the day. Like whatever you can't do for yourself. Like go to the bank maybe...or even pick up your dry cleaning."

The short, bald guy beside him slugged him in the arm. "Damnit, Donnie, don't adlib!"

"What?" Donnie snapped, his nerves clearly frayed. "He might have dry cleaning...maybe for his cape or something."

"Shut up already, Donnie," the male who had reminded him of the women shouted. And then they pushed him forward. "Go with the coffin."

"What?" Blondie whispered.

"Cleaning his coffin."

Donnie turned back around to fully face Marquis. "Oh yeah..." He swallowed hard, his Adam's-apple protruding from his throat. "And we can clean your coffin at night—and guard it when you sleep." He ran a trembling hand through his ruffled hair, now damp from perspiration. "And if you're afraid to let us go, then that's cool too. Yeah, we don't mind living...you know...in your lair...or wherever. Just let us know—whatever you want, man..." He ducked then, waiting for the blow he was sure was coming.

"Master," his sidekick whispered.

"Huh?"

"Say master!"

"Oh yeah...yeah...just let us know, *master.*" Donnie knelt down then and bowed his head.

Marquis exhaled before he slowly bent over, drew back his hand, and slapped the kid across the face, cuffing him so hard that his eyes bulged out for a second before snapping back into his skull.

Donnie looked up and began to wail like a three-year-old girl, groveling in his own puddle of urine. "Wh...wh...what did you do that for?" he sobbed. And then he whispered, "master" again.

Marquis snarled, "That was for your horrible taste in movies...or books." He stood up straight. "Great gods, where do you humans get this crap?"

He stepped back and viewed the herd as all of the men quickly fell down into a kneeling position next to Donnie, their heads bowed so low that they rested in the dirt. Marquis began to probe their minds, one at a time, and just as he suspected, these weren't the hard-core members: These were the followers, the rejects, and the wannabes—none of them willing to die for their girlfriend-beating buddy, Dirk.

"Will you sing me to sleep?" Marquis asked, suddenly amused.

Donnie looked up from the ground. Surprised, he quit crying. A faint light of hope illuminated his gray eyes. "Oh...yeah...yes! *Absolutely.* Anything you want!"

Marquis took a step back. "The Star-Spangled Banner?"

Donnie eyed the other men; they were all bobbing their heads up and down like a chorus of synchronized yo-yos. "Yes!" he exclaimed, pleading with his eyes.

Marquis cleared his throat. "Well, stand up and show me then."

The men stood up slowly, clearly afraid that it was some kind of trick, that the vampire was going to play with them before he ate them.

"Turn your backs to me," Marquis ordered, unable to stomach their pitiful expressions a moment longer.

The men slowly turned around and began to quake, a couple of them outright crying. And then Donnie led the charge: *'Oh, say can you see, by the dawn's early light...'*

The male who had offered the brilliant coffin idea joined in then, even though he was clearly tone-deaf. *"What so proudly we hailed at the twilight's last gleaming..."*

Reluctantly, the last two got on board. *"Whose broad stripes and bright stars through the perilous fight, O'er the ramparts we watched—"*

Marquis swept his hand over the tops of their heads, silencing the obnoxious noise and wiping out their short-term memories at the same time. As far as any of the idiots knew, they had gone to a wild party, had way too much to drink, and left the next morning a few buddies short. As they would not remember where they had gone, they could not come back to search for their missing comrades. When Dirk, Spider, and Doc Holiday—aka Bruce Lee—never returned, they would just assume they had left the gang.

Glad to be rid of them, Marquis watched as one by one, they returned to their banged-up Harleys, searched for bikes that still worked, and started to ride off. The four of them had to ride double as there were only two working bikes left.

As the last of the Pagan Brotherhood rounded the bend, Marquis turned his attention back to Dirk, wondering if the pitiful excuse for a man was still alive. He rustled through the remaining heap of metal, bikes, and corpses until he found Dirk's mangled body and then pulled the gasping imbecile from beneath a dark purple Sportster.

He was still breathing.

Snarling, Marquis knelt over Dirk, grabbed him by the shirt-collar, and forced him to meet his angry gaze. "You will never touch another woman again, Dirk. You made your last mistake when you touched mine." Hissing with disgust, he added, "I hope your god has mercy on your pathetic soul."

With that, he drew back his arm, struck through the chest cavity, and grasped the feeble human heart—

Just as a series of jacketed, hollow-point bullets sliced painfully into his arm—three, to be exact. Marquis winced as one of the bullets went straight through its target, and the other two lodged painfully in the muscle.

"What the hell—"

"Let him go!"

He turned his head just in time to see Kristina standing on the porch like a crazed lunatic, holding a gun in her hand.

She raised it a second time. "Don't do it, Marquis! Let him go. Take your hand out of his chest, *now!*" She aimed the gun right at him, and then, holy hell, she pulled the trigger *again.*

Marquis reacted with preternatural speed, his predatory instincts kicking into high gear. In one fluid motion, he ripped the heart out of Dirk's body, hefted the corpse up like a shield, and caught the next round of bullets with the carcass.

Kristina cried out in horror. "No!"

Marquis was flabbergasted.

Was it even possible for a male's *destiny* to try and kill him, let alone love another male—*a human man*—so much that she would actually prefer him? Never in his fifteen-hundred years had he seen anything like this. What in all of Hades was going on?

Marquis squatted down, staring at the bullet-ridden body beneath him. His anger boiled over in a fevered haze. His powerful shoulders trembled with rage.

How dare she defy him like this!

After all the Silivasis had done for her over the years: the job, the apartment, the ridiculously high salary—*rescuing her from the Dark One who would have ripped her throat out and bled her dry.* Even allowing Dirk to live when they should have killed him long ago...

He threw his head back and roared like an enraged lion, leaping to his feet with equal stealth and grace. Like it or not, this female *belonged to him.* And if she couldn't love him, then she would most certainly obey him.

Marquis's muscles rippled and his joints popped as he turned to face his *destiny.* She had tried to kill him.

Kill him!

His predatory eyes narrowed on the female's terrified face as he embraced his iron resolve. Well, didn't this make things easy?

BLOOD AWAKENING

Etiquette and words were simply no longer necessary. All the playing nice-nice was over.

Kristina Riley was his to do with as he pleased, and he intended to make that crystal clear. A feral hiss escaped his lips as his tongue swept over his fangs.

She had tried to kill him...

nine

The Ancient Master Warrior stalked across the front yard of his remote mountain home like a native cougar homing in on its prey. The pain in his arm spurred him on. He glared at the wisp of a woman standing on the porch, still holding the gun she had used *to shoot him three times* in her hands. She was shaking like a jackhammer as she watched his approach.

Good!

She needed to be afraid.

Maybe she was finally starting to get it.

This wasn't a game. His life was on the line. Her life was on the line. That piece of trash she had just shot him over had fully intended to kill her.

Marquis had read Dirk's mind as easily as a billboard on the side of the freeway, and his intentions had been crystal clear. But then, she knew that, didn't she? She just didn't care. She would rather kill Marquis than the fool that had wanted her dead.

Kristina stepped to the side as he came closer, her deep blue eyes as wide as saucers, but Marquis adjusted his position accordingly, keeping the defiant female directly in front of him. She quickly stepped in the opposite direction. He just as quickly made another adjustment.

Back and forth they went, his stealthy approach becoming a slow waltz of madness between the two of them. Yet Marquis had no intention of dancing with Kristina. He had tolerated more than enough of their dancing.

The Ancient Warrior was resolute.

They were never going to love each other. Hell, they probably wouldn't even like each other after this night. So that just left the basics: thirty-days to convert her. One full moon to produce twin sons and provide the required sacrifice.

That was it.

That was all.

And the process was going to begin right here and now.

BLOOD AWAKENING

Marquis leapt onto the porch from ten feet away, easily wrenching the gun from Kristina's hand. By the way she screamed, one would have sworn he had just tried to wrench her head off her shoulders. Marquis could not have cared less.

Let her scream.

He snatched her up by the waist, turned her around, and sat down hard on the porch. Her slight form flopped into his lap like a rag doll, and she fell back against him, her back instantly molding to his powerful chest. As her derriere sunk into the cradle of his hips, he encircled her upper body with his injured arm and locked her to him like an iron vice.

And then he did the same with his legs. Sweeping two powerful thighs over her weaker, lean ones, he anchored her down in an unbreakable hold. Involuntarily, her head fell back against his shoulder, and she began to struggle, her voice shrill with panic.

"Marquis! *Marquis!* Please—"

The sound of his long, snake-like hiss cut her off midsentence. Marquis could have heard a pin drop as he smoothed her wild red hair away from her neck with his free hand, and slowly tilted her head to the side in pursuit of a more favorable angle.

The pulsing artery taunted him beneath her creamy white skin as the vein rose and fell with her frantic gasps of hysteria. The beat of her heart rose to a thundering crescendo like the bass of a rock song that had just hit the chorus. "No!" she wailed. "Oh God, Marquis—don't. I'm sorry. I'm sorry! I swear it, I'm so sorry…"

Marquis may as well have been deaf.

He lowered his head and licked her jugular…once…twice…as he slowly released his incisors, the razor-sharp teeth vampires used to inject their powerful venom—the teeth the sons of Jadon used to convert human *destinies* to their species.

And then, without hesitation or apology, he sank the twin ivory fangs deep into Kristina's neck and began to inject the poison that would change her forever.

Nathaniel Silivasi materialized on the front lawn of his eldest brother's home about ten seconds before Nachari joined him.

"You felt it too?" Nachari asked.

Nathaniel frowned, his dark eyes scanning his surroundings. "Absolutely, and it wasn't his typical *I just mopped the floor with someone who crossed me* energy. Something is really wrong with—"

His voice cut off abruptly as his eyes swept the front porch. Marquis was perched in deadly silence, bent over the limp body of Kristina as she lay across his lap like a flimsy doll. The feral vampire's jaw was locked on her throat, and his eyes were glowing crimson red.

Nathaniel cleared his throat. Releasing a low whistle, he inclined his head in Marquis's direction, urging Nachari to take a look.

Nachari eyed the scene on the porch and blanched. He took a few tentative steps toward Marquis and then stopped abruptly in his tracks as the warrior's head snapped up ever so slightly, his eyes darting back and forth between his brothers in warning. A low, territorial growl rumbled in Marquis's throat, and his top lip twitched several times. Instinctively, he tightened his arms around his female and scooted further back on the porch.

Kristina appeared to be either unconscious...or dead.

Nathaniel listened for a heartbeat and sighed in relief when he heard two distinct sets: the vampire's and his mate's. Slowly nodding at the Ancient Warrior, he put his arm out to motion Nachari back. "Whoa there, little brother; you need to step away."

Nachari swallowed a lump in his throat and did as Nathaniel suggested.

It was obvious that Marquis was in no state of mind to deal with his family right now. In fact, the male didn't appear to be in *any* conscious state of mind at all. He was pure instinct. Wholly predator. And he would perceive any move in his direction as a threat against himself and the female he wasn't about to relinquish.

In reality, he couldn't.

Once a male began the process of converting his *destiny*, it was too dangerous to stop before the procedure was finished: Short of completion, the female would have too much venom inside of her to survive as a human, but not enough to sustain her as a vampire. And during the process, the male couldn't speak—not verbally or telepathically. He couldn't let up, and he couldn't give in to the female's pleas for mercy.

Conversion was an incredibly painful event. Nathaniel ought to know.

As if on cue, Nathaniel's mate entered his mind, her psychic voice heavy with concern. *Is everything all right, Nathaniel? Is Marquis okay?*

Jocelyn's steady, loving presence soothed him as always. He had only had his *destiny* for a couple of weeks now, yet he could hardly remember life without her or their new baby son, Storm.

It depends on how you define 'all right,' my love.

Jocelyn sighed. *What's going on?*

Nathaniel knew the water was frigid, but he dove in anyway. *He's converting Kristina—*

No way! Tell me you're lying, Nathaniel. Already?

He cringed. *Yes, already—and on the front porch.*

Jocelyn gasped, no doubt remembering the extreme pain of her own recent conversion: Even when one's mate was gentle and had his partner's full love and devotion, it was a traumatic event.

I can't believe she consented so quickly, Jocelyn quipped. *I mean...maybe she's a helluva lot stronger than me, but there is no way I would've come willingly into your arms less than twelve hours after meeting you, let alone given you control over my heart, life, and body...accepted what was going on as my true destiny.*

Nathaniel knew that Jocelyn was referring to the sacred siring ceremony that took place between mates before conversion, the reverent words that were spoken to one another, as well as the gods, as part of the sacred mating. He sighed. *I can assure you,* Iubirea mea, *there was no consent or ceremony between these two.*

Jocelyn became deathly quiet.

Darling?

He wouldn't!

Nathaniel knew better than to respond.

He didn't!

Again...nothing.

Oh God...that poor girl! Is she hurt?

Nathaniel glanced over at the porch and frowned, choosing once again to say nothing.

Nathaniel, please tell me he hasn't hurt her. I mean, I know he's a bit...severe...but even I didn't think—

She'll be fine, Jocelyn. I don't think Marquis is going to let anything happen to Kristina—

Anything but him! Jocelyn snapped, her tone daring him to argue.

Jocelyn...darling...I did no such thing to you, remember? He is my brother.

She took a slow, deep breath. *I'm sorry, Nathaniel: You have enough to think about without adding me to the mix. I just...wow...honestly, I feel sorry for both of them.*

Nathaniel sighed, searching for a way to change the subject. *Is our son still awake?*

Jocelyn's voice eased then. *Is that a trick question? Bright-eyed and bushy-tailed! This kid isn't going back to sleep for hours.*

Nathaniel snarled. *He is beginning to disrupt our...private time...together. That kid.*

Jocelyn laughed. *Good grief, Nathaniel; we made love three times today, already. What more do you need?*

A deep, sultry growl rumbled in Nathaniel's throat.

BLOOD AWAKENING

Jocelyn cleared hers. *I see*, she murmured. *Well, I'll tell you what—you take care of your brother, and I'll go make some warm milk, see if I can't get this boy back to sleep.*

Nathaniel hissed and sent a visual image of him sinking his fangs into the smooth shelf between Jocelyn's neck and shoulder, his hands slowly roaming lower and lower... *Try hard, my love.*

Jocelyn purred a soft invitation to her aroused mate and closed the communication.

When Nathaniel turned around, Nachari was standing there with his arms crossed over his chest, a look of disinterest in his eyes. "Not the time or the place, brother."

Nathaniel grunted.

Nachari rolled his eyes and gestured toward the porch. "What are we going to do about *that*?"

Nathaniel gave him a stern glare and shrugged. "Stay the hell out of it, that's what." He turned his back and started to walk the boundary of the yard, pointing out the large pile of metal, rubble, and bodies strewn about at the apex of the looped, gravel driveway. "This must have been a lot of what we felt."

"No doubt."

When Nathaniel squatted down over a mangled body, Nachari simply materialized at his side and crouched down beside him. The young wizard frowned. "Is that Dirk Warner?"

Nathaniel lifted the head by the back of the neck, careful to keep the blood off his hands. Jocelyn didn't need to know the full extent of what had taken place at Marquis's estate earlier that night, and even if he tried to wash the blood off, with her new and improved vampire skills, his mate would smell it on him. "Looks like it."

"Damn." Nachari stared at the gaping chest cavity, which was clearly missing a heart. He stood up and walked toward the pile of metal. Then he bent over and picked up a bald, severed head by the two-inch mustache hanging off the mouth. He held it up in the air. "You know this guy?"

Nathaniel shrugged and tilted his head to get a better look. "Never seen him before."

"Hmm." Nachari gave the head a good once-over himself.

"Maybe you can try and read Marquis's energy...*wizard*," Nathaniel said, emphasizing the last word with mock contempt.

Nachari sneered. "I've just about had it with this *warriors-are-superior* crap, *brother*."

"Yeah, well, by the looks of this yard, we are."

"Oh, please," Nachari jeered. "Storm is what? Four or five days old now? Given another year or two, he could've taken care of these humans himself."

Nathaniel laughed.

"Hell, even Braden—"

Nathaniel raised his eyebrows and just stared at his baby brother.

"Yeah...you're probably right," Nachari conceded.

They both knew that Braden Bratianu—bless his little human-turned-vampire heart—would have been strung up in a tree somewhere. And that would have been the best possible outcome.

Nachari dropped the head, held his hands out level to the ground, and closed his eyes...then frowned. "Unless his mother named him Bruce Lee, aka, Doc Holiday, Marquis didn't know him, either."

Nathaniel chuckled then. "Marquis always did enjoy his battles." Although clearly, this had been more of a slaughter.

Nachari kicked at some metal. "He ruined some really nice bikes, though. My guess is that Dirk's riding buddies decided to come lend a hand."

Nathaniel winced. "Poor souls. Are you getting anything else?"

Nachari closed his eyes again, held out his hands, and made a funny face.

"What?" Nathaniel asked.

"Nothing."

"Tell me."

Nachari looked annoyed then. "Trust me, it's nothing."

"*Nachari...*"

Nathaniel pulled rank with the mere tone of his voice, eliciting a harsh glare from the young wizard. Even though Nachari had recently earned the title of Master for his four-hundred years of study at the Romanian University, Nathaniel was both a Master and an Ancient. And he was also Nachari's elder—which meant that if Nathaniel decided to exercise his rights by hierarchy, Nachari had to answer, whether he wanted to or not.

Nachari threw up his hands. "You are so completely inappropriate, brother. You know that?"

Nathaniel chuckled. "Perhaps. Never-the-less, I'm waiting?"

"The Star-Spangled Banner," Nachari snapped. "That's what I'm getting."

"What?"

"You heard me."

Nathaniel growled then. "I think you need to go back to school for a while, little brother. Your divination could use some work."

Nachari flipped him off. After several minutes had passed, he swept his hand over the yard and asked, "So, what do you want to do with all of this, *elder?*"

Nathaniel stood up and eyed the mess. Then he turned to look at the porch again. "Ah, hell...Marquis is going to have his hands full for a while. Let's incinerate the bodies and move the remaining garbage back to the shed until we can send someone to haul it off."

Nachari nodded, and then he hefted up two mangled Harleys, one in each hand. He released his spectacular black-and-emerald wings and flew to the shed with such amazing speed that the metal in his arms left a buzz in the air like a small jet flying overhead.

Nathaniel made quick work of incinerating the bodies.

Although he couldn't gather molten red fireballs the size of boulders in his hands like Marquis, he had no problem generating fire or lightning from his fingers, and the scalding heat left nothing behind, not even teeth.

Closing his eyes, he began to concentrate on the connection all Vampyr—whether light or dark—had with the earth: the power of union through emotion. He concentrated on a light rainstorm, just enough to wash away the smoke and ash, to cleanse the scent of death from the air, and tried to visualize the feelings connected to the phenomenon: gray ...wet... contentment. Cleansing.

He pictured Jocelyn giving Storm a bath and allowed the simple emotion to swell within him until the earth responded to the focused intention and began to create matching clouds and moisture, at last, letting loose a gentle rain.

Nachari materialized at his side. "The rest of the yard is clean."

Nathaniel nodded. "Good."

He turned to look at the *couple* on the porch. Kristina was awake now, her eyes as wide as saucers, a look of pain so intense etched on her face that Nathaniel had to turn away, stunned that she wasn't crying out. He cloaked his appearance so that she wouldn't see him, not wanting her to believe that he could be so callous as to refuse to help her when, in actuality, there was nothing he could do. Not without endangering both her and Marquis's lives.

"What must she have done to provoke him like that?" Nachari asked. "To make him go that far?" The wizard immediately cloaked his own appearance as well.

Nathaniel just shook his head. "I'm not sure, but something is really wrong here."

Nachari nodded. "I agree."

Kagen Silivasi's voice resounded loud and clear on a common family bandwidth that both brothers could hear: *Are you two going to stay and watch over him through the night—at least until he finishes the conversion?*

We could, Nathaniel offered, responding quickly to his twin.

Kagen's voice was congenial. *Go home to your wife, brother; I will come and stay with Nachari in your stead. Nachari, is that all right with you?*

Before either of them could answer, Marquis drew back his lips and let out a snarl so menacing that it shook the leaves on the trees and hung in the air like electricity. His next growl was even louder and more feral.

I don't think he wants us here, Nachari said, pointing out the obvious.

Agreed, Nathaniel retorted. *And the last thing we need to do is rile him up with Kristina lying in his arms.*

Kagen sighed. *Wow...this has been one crazy night, hasn't it? What in the hell were the gods thinking...to do this to him?*

A third growl ripped through the night, and the earth beneath them began to shake.

I'm out, Nachari said, unwilling to ignore any further warnings. He bowed his head slightly to Nathaniel. *Be well, my brother. Catch you later, Kagen.* And then he dematerialized.

Kagen sighed as he addressed Nathaniel. *Call me if you need me, my twin.*

Nathaniel didn't respond, although he knew his silence was easily understood.

He turned one last time to regard his Ancient brother and just shook his head: Indeed, why had the gods been so cruel? It wasn't just that Kristina was a mere child, or that the two of them were about as compatible as oil and water; it was the fact that no one had served the house of Jadon more valiantly over the centuries than Marquis. The warrior had lived for his family, for his people, and for the earth. Yes, he was rigid, and even difficult to get along with sometimes, but underneath all of it was a fierce love and protectiveness.

A love that had only been returned with loss.

His feelings for the princess, Ciopori, were no secret. Hell, the energy between them was palpable, and the Silivasi brothers were far too close to evade one another in matters of such deep emotion.

It just didn't make sense.

And after all that had happened with Shelby and Dalia...

With Joelle...

So much loss.

Nathaniel was not at all sure that Marquis was going to make it through this with his usually impenetrable grit and endurance. He had lived so long. He had waited so long. He had seen so much tragedy.

His brother deserved more: He deserved better.

Heck, Kristina deserved better than this union as well.

Letting out a deep breath of frustration, Nathaniel placed a shield of comforting energy around the two beings on the porch and said a silent prayer to the gods, beseeching them to bless and watch over his beloved older brother.

Be well, Marquis, he whispered in his mind, and then just like Nachari, he faded away.

ten

Ciopori woke up in a cold sweat, the image in her mind too incredible to be real.

Marquis was sitting on the front porch of his beautiful, farm-style home with both of his arms and legs wrapped tightly around Kristina, his mouth latched firmly on her throat. His eyes were the color of dark rubies, and his brow was etched with exhaustion. The look on Kristina's face was one of shock and agony. Utter despair. And they had been like that for hours.

Marquis was converting Kristina. Bringing her into his world against her will. And what was done could never be reversed.

Ciopori sank back into a large, fluffy pillow in the lavish, guest bedchamber at Napolean's manse. She rubbed her eyes, trying to erase the disturbing image from her mind, her heart still racing like it wanted to leap out of her chest.

Was this to be her fate, then?

To continue to see Marquis in her dreams for the remainder of her life...with another woman? If so, then she couldn't bear the thought of falling back asleep.

Ciopori threw back the covers and sat up once again; this time, tears ran down her cheeks. How could the gods be so cruel? For over two-thousand years she had lain in a suspended state of animation—neither dead nor alive—with nothing to sustain her outside of her dreams. Dreams of a dark, handsome lover who had worshipped her, waited for her, *existed for her* from the moment he was born.

The instant she had looked into Marquis's dark eyes, she had *remembered* everything about him: his masculine scent, the timbre of his voice, the feel of his touch...the familiar, steady beat of his heart. They had already shared eternities together, and great celestial gods, when they had made love, the earth had stood still as if no one and nothing existed outside of the two of them.

Ciopori stood up and shrugged into the long, silk robe that was lying on the edge of the bed. She had to get out of there.

Tessa Dawn

Quietly opening the door to the veranda, she stepped into the brisk night air and looked down at the ground. She might not be able to materialize and dematerialize like the Vampyr, but she could move herself small distances with magic. "Ancestors, Great Ones, I humbly beseech you...

Beneath the stars and moonlit sky,
the gentle breeze that passes by—
Beyond the threshold of this door,
place now my feet on nature's floor."

All at once her feet touched down on the cool damp earth, and she sighed. It wasn't as if she was tired anyhow. She had only gone to bed as a means of escape: to quiet her thoughts of Marquis and Kristina. It was a pitiful attempt at buying a moment's peace.

Peace.

What was peace anyway?

Ciopori began to wander into the forest, hoping to get lost in the giant pines. Did she really believe she would ever know peace again? Without her parents, her brothers, her familiar civilization? *Without Marquis?* Why had the gods even allowed her to awaken?

She wiped her eyes as she continued to wander, flashing back to that fateful night that had changed everything, when her brother Jadon had shaken her awake in the middle of the night.

"Sister! Sister! You must wake up; we haven't much time!"

Ciopori shot up from her sleep, her heart racing in her chest. "What troubles you, brother? Why are you here?" She looked around the large, stone chamber searching for her sister. "Where is Vanya?" The panic in her voice rose quickly. "Vanya!"

"Shh!" Jadon placed a firm hand over her mouth. "You mustn't make a sound, Ciopori. Vanya is just outside in the hall with my men. We must make haste. Please, heed my warning. You must leave Romania at once!"

Ciopori climbed out of bed, disoriented and confused, reaching out to accept the simple blue gown Jadon extended to her.

"Dress quickly." He turned around, his pitch-black hair shimmering

119

in the reflection of torchlight from the walls. His body shook with urgency...and fear.

"What has happened, Jadon?" she asked, as her fingers fumbled to clasp the dozens of buttons on her bodice.

Jadon hung his head, and the chamber became deathly quiet.

"Jadon?"

"Please...just hurry, sister."

"Jadon, what has happened?"

He cleared his throat, obviously gathering courage. "You and Vanya are no longer safe."

*Ciopori inhaled sharply, her throat suddenly constricting. "What do you mean—*no longer safe? How...how *is that possible? We are...the monarchy."*

Jadon turned around then and simply shook his head. "No, you are the only remaining females. Virgin daughters of the King. The most valued sacrifice of all."

Ciopori clasped her hand over her heart and tried to ease her trembling. "Yes..." She swallowed hard. "But...you and Jaegar...the men respect you; they obey you. They dare not take us without your consent."

Jadon's eyes bored into hers, the truth revealed before he could speak it.

"No!" Ciopori cried, taking a step back. "Jadon!" Her voice was racked with sobs. "Tell me it isn't so."

Jadon shut his eyes. "It is Jaegar who leads the men to the castle." He shook his head. "My loyalists are few, but they would die for me. They are willing to die for you, but we must get you out of Romania if we are to have any chance at all—there are not enough of us to fight Jaegar's men. He commands the whole of our father's army."

Ciopori staggered back. Dear gods, she and Vanya were to be sacrificed along with the others! *Captured like common criminals—murderers and thieves—made to kneel before the executioner's stone with their hands manacled to the sides, their heads turned to face the east, the direction of newness and rebirth. They would be held down against the cold, rough surface as the men chanted and cursed—and slit their jugulars—causing them to bleed out over the stone, spilling rivers of torment onto the barren ground.*

Tessa Dawn

And as they lay there dying, the remaining vestiges of their lives pouring out upon the crimson earth, the high-priest and her brother Jaegar *would drink the first of their spilled blood.*

Ciopori clutched Jadon's arms, finding it hard to breathe. "Oh gods, Jadon! Do not let us die like that."

Jadon's eyes glazed over, but he squared his chin with defiance, his shoulders held firm with resolve. "Never, Ciopori. You have my solemn vow."

Ciopori caught her brother by his strong, angular chin and turned his head to meet her gaze. By all the gods, her brother was as handsome as he was kind. "Tell me, do you carry your blade?"

Jadon declined his head in the proud manner of the aristocracy.

"Then promise me: Should Jaegar find us before we reach safety, you will take our lives, yourself, with honor."

Jadon recoiled. Then he grabbed his sister by the arm and gave it a hard tug. "It won't come to that, Ciopori. Come now. We must hurry!"

All at once the chamber lit up with an eerie glow from a powerful bolt of lightning. A piercing clash of thunder shook the castle walls. The whole world seemed to be coming apart. "Promise me, Jadon. Swear it. Now!"

Jadon looked incredulous.

Lost.

Horrified.

His deep, sad eyes dimmed before her gaze, and his words were a mere whisper. "I promise."

She watched him finger the hilt of his blade and knew that he was imagining the act he would have to perform, making certain he could carry out his vow. Retrieving a torch from a sconce on the wall, he ushered her out of the chamber.

Ciopori stood quietly, staring up at the moon from beneath the small clearing she had wandered to in the forest. The memory of that night would never leave her. The sting of Jaegar's betrayal would always be fresh. The grief never far behind.

She had thought that nothing under the sun could ever hurt her worse, but she had been wrong. The gods were crueler than

Jaegar had ever been. At least with Jaegar, there would have been an end to her suffering.

With Marquis now bound to Kristina, her anguish had only just begun.

Ciopori put her face in her hands and wept.

Salvatore could not believe his good fortune. He had to blink several times to convince himself that he was actually seeing what he thought he was: *the princess Ciopori*—one of the original celestial females—standing all alone under the night sky, less than a mile from Napolean's compound, with absolutely no escort or protection.

Incredible!

A wicked laugh rose up from his throat and echoed through the night. His appearance already cloaked, he landed noiselessly just beyond the clearing in a thick grove of trees and crouched low into the stance of a predator.

His taut, lean muscles rippled as he moved, the thrill of the hunt rising with every step he took toward his unsuspecting prey. His feet glided over the ground with graceful ease, his eyes never straying from his quarry. She was weeping. And completely unaware of her surroundings.

Completely unaware of him.

Now, less than ten feet away, he crouched even lower, shifting his weight to the balls of his feet, his powerful arms dropping to his side. His body twitched as he readied himself to spring.

Dark Lords, what a prize she would be.

As a princess and a woman.

His shaft hardened at the mere thought of touching her, taking her, the sweet taste of her royal blood. But he would have to be careful: This woman was a rare artifact, and one of great significance to the sons of Jaegar. The possibilities were endless. Too much was unknown to simply use her to feed...or breed...to risk killing her prematurely in the process.

No, he would need to consult the Darkness. Study the *Blood Canon*—the ancient book of black magic. Princess Ciopori might very well be the bridge to a new future for his kind. *Lord Jaegar's very own sister!*

Not wanting to waste another fortuitous second, Salvatore sprang into action like the dark predator he was, grasping the princess by the waist, covering her mouth with his hand, and pulling her tight against his chest before she even registered his presence. His body shook from arousal—the scent and feel of a celestial female in his arms—and his fangs exploded in his mouth as he took to the skies, hefting her like she was no more than a feather in his arms.

A golden celestial feather from the time of antiquity.

Ciopori shook from head to toe. Her mind spun with confusion. As she soared across the sky at unbelievable speeds, her stomach turned over, and she fought the urge to vomit. She looked beneath her and eyed the distant ground. *Dear gods,* she was going to die.

Instinctively, she clutched at the neck of the male that held her, her arms encircling his broad shoulders in a death grip, and then a feeling of unbelievable darkness swept through her. The feel of his cold flesh against her hands made her skin crawl, and the air suddenly became dense. It was hard to breathe. Something was missing in his soul. She was in the presence of...evil.

Without thought or deliberation, Ciopori recoiled from the

darkness, drawing back her arms and pushing hard against his chest. Caught off-guard by her reaction, he loosened his grip, and she tumbled out of his arms.

Ciopori let out a blood-curdling scream as she plummeted toward the ground, her death imminent, the air sucked out of her body. She wanted to pray, but she was too afraid. She was paralyzed with fear. And then out of nowhere, the vampire reappeared beneath her, moving at unimaginable speed: a dark blur shooting across the sky.

He snatched her back up with a grip so unyielding that his hands felt like shackles on her arms. His hard body pressed so tightly against hers that she could feel every contour of his erection straining against her quivering stomach as they flew across the sky like a shooting star.

"Do not do that again!" he warned.

The chilling, demonic voice vibrated against her ear, and Ciopori shuddered. *What was he?* What male in the house of Jadon would dare to treat her so harshly? Who would defy Napolean so openly? And why did he positively reek of malevolence, death, and sin?

Ciopori quivered in his arms as awareness flooded her consciousness: *He wasn't from the house of Jadon.* He was a descendant of her brother Jaegar.

Fear seized her heart like an iron vice.

And then the world went suddenly black.

eleven

When Ciopori opened her eyes, she was in an underground chamber—a large stone master bedroom—and she was chained by the wrists and ankles to a four poster bed, her torn silk robe barely covering her thighs.

She tried to lift her head and look around the room, but it was too dark to make out details. With the exception of one lit torch in the far corner and a few black candles scattered about the marble floor, the space had the quality of a tomb.

She heard the sound of an infant whimpering and strained her neck to get a look at a small bassinette just to the right of the bed, up against the cavern wall. As she turned away, her eyes began to adjust to the light, and then she saw him for the first time: the vampire who had taken her from the forest.

The creature looked jarringly similar to the males she had met from the house of Jadon, yet terrifyingly different at the same time.

His banded black and red hair fell in thick, wavy locks past his enormous shoulders, and his dark sapphire eyes seared into her like he was staring straight through her. He had a high widow's peak at the juncture of his hairline and thin arched brows that were perpetually curved into a frown. His features were chiseled in a sharp, unnatural manner, and he would have almost seemed handsome—stunning, in fact—if an aura of evil didn't hover about him like a swarm of bees to a honeycomb.

Ciopori struggled against the chains. "Where am I?"

The male sauntered to the foot of the bed, practically gliding above the ground as he walked. And then he stopped and smiled a wicked, soul-piercing grin. "Allow me to introduce myself, Princess Ciopori." He stretched out his arm and bowed low at the waist in an Old World gesture. "I am Salvatore Rafael Nistor. And you are my guest."

Ciopori's eyes grew wide. The male was mad. "Do you always chain your guests to your bed?"

BLOOD AWAKENING

Salvatore lowered his head and briefly shut his eyes. "I apologize for the inconvenience, but I needed to be sure you would behave." He stalked around the length of the bed then, reaching down to drag the back of his hand along her body as he went. He brushed her toes, traced her lower legs, and kneaded her inner thigh, a primal groan of pleasure escaping his throat as his fingers swept over her stomach, through the valley between her breasts, and stopped to grip her throat. "You are most exquisite, Princess. I must admit, in all my years on earth, I have never seen anything quite so...delicious."

"Don't touch me!" Ciopori trembled and tried to pull away.

Salvatore laughed a low, evil hiss. "Spoken like a true aristocrat." His hand tightened around her throat, pressing down until it sealed off her airway, and then he sat beside her on the bed and leaned over, glaring into her eyes. "Unfortunately, you are in my castle now, and I am the only king in this room." He relaxed his hand, nicked her jugular with the nail of his right thumb, and licked his lips at the sight of her blood.

Ciopori stifled a scream. She would not give him the satisfaction. "What do you want with me?"

Salvatore sat back. His eyes swept over her body, his nostrils flaring as he deeply inhaled her feminine scent. "Ah, but that is the question of the millennium, is it not?" He laughed again. And then he stood and paced around the room, his hands clasped tightly behind his back.

"At first glance, I would have to say to drink your celestial blood until I become drunk with it. And then, of course, to screw you to death when I'm finished...or perhaps at the same time." He sighed. "Mmm, do you think I could break your pelvis with my groin, Princess?" His hand traced his lower belly and then he spun around and eyed her again with his head cocked to the side. "Yes, I'm certain that I could. A most exquisite death, no?"

Ciopori winced and looked away.

"But then, that would be such a waste of a precious jewel.

You are the sister of our Dark Lord, Jaegar, himself—are you not?" He rubbed his chin as if deep in thought. "There is, of course, the more pressing temptation: to sire children with an original female, to watch my young tear their way out of your glorious body, knowing they will grow to be powerful beyond measure, but again, that would most certainly kill you. And you are far too precious to exterminate...yet."

He glided over to a nightstand beside the bed and rubbed his hand in soft, sensuous circles over an old tattered tome, stroking the leather like a long-lost lover. "But here's the thing: I believe that with the proper magic, you might be made immune to the curse of your sisters. You might be able to live through a live birth. You might even be able to conceive female offspring." He bent over and kissed the cover of the book. "You are part goddess and part human, are you not? And I can feel the ancient wizard's—*Fabien's*—magic all around you. He changed you somehow, and I intend to find out exactly what he did."

He leaned over the bed and gave her a slow, lingering kiss on the mouth, his tongue piercing so deep that she gagged.

She spat when he pulled away.

"No, Ciopori; you are not going to die right away, and unfortunately, I dare not risk getting you pregnant...at this juncture. It is my hope that in time—and with enough experimentation—you might be used to breed the most powerful vampires ever born for the whole of the sons of Jaegar. Perhaps you will be the queen ant of our civilization." His laughter echoed off the walls, making Ciopori sick to her stomach.

"In the meantime, however..." He gestured toward the small red crib at the side of the room. "There is the immediate matter of my nephew, Derrian. His nanny recently—how shall I say?—passed away. And I am in need of a caretaker to provide for him until I can find a replacement."

Ciopori raised her chin in defiance. "I'd be happy to watch the little monster. Bring him to me, Salvatore, so I can snap his little neck!"

Salvatore shot backward like a reptilian bird of prey. He ascended into the air and hovered directly above her on the ceiling, his eyes glowing red, the tips of his fangs gleaming in the candlelight. "Will you, now?" he growled, trembling from head to toe.

Oh goddess… Ciopori held her breath.

He descended so quickly, his motion was a blur. Then, one by one, he reached for her chains and tore them free with his bare hands, placing his arm around her waist so she couldn't escape. Hefting her over his shoulder like an insignificant sack of potatoes, he walked right through the chamber wall into a long, dark hallway.

Ciopori gasped, terror beginning to seize her, as Salvatore stormed down the endless tunnel—half walking, half flying—growling like an angry lion the entire way.

"We will see about that, Princess. We will see about that!"

He took her through an endless maze of tunnels, weaving this way and that, walking right through walls, passing straight through heavy wooden doors, with her body in his arms as if the obstacles weren't even there.

Dear gods, what kind of magic does this male possess?

As they moved through the underground fortress, she heard male voices and shrill laughter, grunts, and groans—sounds that were as disturbing as they were animalistic—coming from behind doorways, down distant hallways, both above and below. There were many, *many* more males just like him inhabiting the space, but somehow, he managed to avoid coming in contact with any of them as he whisked her through the tunnels.

When they finally reached a set of pitch-black, double-arched doorways, Salvatore set her down roughly and seized the back of her neck in an iron grasp. "Open the door!"

Ciopori clenched her robe at the sides, her hands balled into two stubborn fists. "No."

He slapped her in the back of the head so hard that her face hit the heavy door and bounced off, causing her to bite her own tongue. "Open it!"

Ciopori glared at the handles and frowned. They were made of interwoven cast iron and ivory, each one bent into the shape of a coiled snake, with several of the ivory bands painted red to give the appearance of cobras guarding the entryway. Their eyes were inlaid with dark rubies, and their tails were coated in solid gold. She cringed as she gripped the reptilian handles and slowly opened the door.

Salvatore shoved her inside, remaining close behind, and then he waved his hand to light the twelve candelabras placed evenly around the room.

Ciopori stared at her surroundings. There were two man-sized granite beds situated in the center of the space with large hand-sculpted statues of gargoyles at the head and foot of each, the creatures glaring down over the benches. The hideous monsters resembled a cross between an angry lion and a mythical lizard, with large, bulging eyes framing their faces and huge upper and lower canines distending from their mouths. Along the walls were rows of tunnels—like miniature caves carved into the limestone—and the ceiling was painted marble with ghastly renditions of snake-heads covering every square inch, all of the eye-sockets inlaid with gemstones.

Ciopori grimaced and tried to hide her fear. "What is this place?"

Salvatore crept up behind her and bent to her ear. "It is a chamber of exquisite pleasure, Princess. However, for you, I do not believe that will be the case." He snarled, causing the hair on the back of her neck to stand up. "Come," he ushered, dragging her toward one of the beds.

Ciopori tried to resist, but the male possessed ungodly strength, forcing her compliance with casual ease. Attached to the wings of the gargoyles were chains with manacles on each end, and the moment she saw them, she broke away in a sudden burst of terror, fleeing toward the doors.

BLOOD AWAKENING

The vampire merely waved his hand, and her body froze, midstride. "Where do you think you're going?"

Ciopori stifled a scream and fought back her tears. She raised her chin, summoning as much dignity as she could. "Take me out of here at once, Salvatore." The command came out far weaker than she intended.

Salvatore shook his head slowly, his sapphire eyes glowing with intensity. "You still do not understand your place, do you?" He sauntered over to her, snatched her by the arm, and dragged her back to the granite bed. "But you will."

As if she were nothing more than a limp doll, he shackled her arms above her head to one gargoyle and her feet, crossed at the ankles, to the other—laying her out on the bed like a pagan sacrifice. And then he cruelly removed her robe with one hard tug, ripping it to shreds.

Ciopori shrieked as she eyed the salivating creature above her, her thin silk nightgown all that remained between herself and the cold stone beneath her.

"Relax," Salvatore hissed, "I said I wouldn't kill you—*or rape you*—yet." He took a seat on the bench opposite her, and with the wave of his hand, removed his own clothes.

Ciopori gasped. "What are you doing?" Her voice was thick with disgust.

Salvatore lay down on the stone parallel to her. "You shall see soon enough."

With that, he took a deep breath and waved his hand. A strange ethereal music began to play in the chamber, and a dense black smoke began to rise from the floor, swirling around the gargoyles and the beds in a sultry, serpentine motion.

Ciopori blanched and blinked her eyes. The feel of evil was so thick in the darkness that her throat was constricting.

"You will want to regulate your breathing, Princess...to slow down the venom."

Ciopori's eyes shot open. *Venom? What venom?*

Before she could ask Salvatore what he meant, the room

130

began to come alive: The walls began to undulate like the hips of a male making love to a woman, thrusting back and forth in slow, seductive gyrations, and the flames in the candelabras danced, swaying from side to side, the tips of the flames burning crimson red.

And then the cobras appeared.

One after the other.

Slithering from the entrances, the hollows in the walls, dozens upon dozens of gliding black-and-red serpents slinking out of the tunnels and dropping to the floor. Gliding toward the benches.

Ciopori screamed so loud her vocal cords burned. Her chest heaved up and down beneath her erratic heartbeat. "Salvatore!"

Oh, dear gods, please make him—

"Salvatore! Stop this! At once…" At this point, pride was a wasted emotion. "I'm sorry, Salvatore. *Please*, just make them stop."

The languid vampire simply chuckled low in his throat and groaned in anticipation of what was to come.

Ciopori shook from head to toe, eyeing the floor as a large flat-headed snake slithered toward her. "Please…" Her voice was a hollow plea.

Salvatore snarled then. "You were going to do what to my nephew, Princess?"

Princess Ciopori shook her head vigorously. "Nothing. *Nothing!* Unchain me, Salvatore. Get me out of here." Her cries rose in direct proportion to the approach of the snake.

And then she heard a deep, guttural groan, and her eyes flew open in shock.

Salvatore was lying on the stone, his back arched, his head tilted back, panting in ecstasy as a half-dozen cobras slithered up his naked belly and found their way to his chest, arms, and throat.

Ciopori watched in stunned horror as the first snake struck him hard, sinking long, pointed fangs into his chest right above

131

his heart, releasing venom on a hiss. And then, as if the first snake had cued the others, they began to strike one after the other, causing a frenzied reaction in the other snakes in the room. Like a sea of red and black, the snakes began to descend upon the vampire's quivering body, striking wildly, latching on with death grips to release their poisonous venom.

"The first strike incites the demons," he moaned, gyrating beneath the slithering creatures, his enormous sex jutting upward with fevered arousal. He bent his head back as far as it could go, offering his throat to a giant beast that had wrapped around his arm, his own tongue practically hanging out of his mouth, swiping back and forth over the tips of his fangs.

Ciopori looked away, horrified.

She tried to pray, to chant, to remember her magic—how to push the snakes away—but she couldn't concentrate. *Oh goddess, help me!* She couldn't remember the incantations.

As a large reptile meandered up the side of the gargoyle and slithered across her shackled feet, Ciopori began to panic. *Oh gods!* "Salvatore! Please. *Please.* Stop this! I'm begging you."

She watched in revulsion as Salvatore began to climax, shouting his release even as his body began to seize in reaction to the enormous amount of poison attacking his system. He was having multiple orgasms while enduring excruciating pain.

How is he living through it? she wondered. Sweet Cygnus, how would she?

Waiting a couple of seconds to come down from the high, Salvatore struggled to speak. "My own venom is stronger." He hissed and moaned like a love-slave being taken by his master. "Over centuries, we have built up antibodies—"

His voice dropped off suddenly. On a sharp inhale, his sex jerked several times with another release.

Ciopori recoiled as warm tears rushed down her face. *Marquis.* Where was Marquis? Did he even know she was missing? Would he come for her? Dear gods, what would happen when he found her like this, dead and mutilated from a hundred snake bites?

She whimpered in frustration—and terror—as the snake made its way down the gargoyle, slithered up her belly, drew back its iconic, flared neck, and stared at her with dark, piercing eyes, its tongue darting in and out. "No," she pleaded beneath her breath, trembling like she was about to come apart. "No, no, no...please..." She struggled frantically against the chains.

And then it struck right above her collar bone, its fangs sinking deep.

Ciopori cried out in horror and mind-numbing pain as the venom passed through the bite, and her heart immediately constricted in her chest. Then just like they had with Salvatore, the remaining snakes descended upon the stone. A hard strike to her inner thigh made her jerk even as a third set of fangs entered her stomach. Her cries were primal and unrelenting; her terror hovered on the edge of madness; her soul pleaded for a merciful, swift death.

And then a deep male voice thundered through the chaos. "Retreat!"

The snakes swayed back and forth, hissing their displeasure, their hypnotic heads weaving back and forth with the threat of another strike, yet slowly...one by one...they began to draw back, even as the three already attached withdrew their fangs.

Ciopori sobbed in pain and desperation.

And then Salvatore held up his hand, and the snakes turned back toward Ciopori, renewed hope gleaming in their demonic eyes. He leaned over her trembling body until she could feel his rancid breath against her face. "Will you take care of my nephew, Princess?"

"Yes," Ciopori sobbed. "*Yes!*"

"*Good care?*" Salvatore asked.

Ciopori gasped for air as her tongue swelled and her throat began to close in reaction to the venom. "Yes...oh, gods...please..."

Salvatore smiled then and bent over to press a soft kiss

against her lips. "You do realize you are dying? Rather quickly, I might add."

She stared at him in abject horror, unable to speak, unable to think, her body convulsing as a pain unlike any she'd ever known seized her muscles, and her organs began to shut down.

Salvatore cupped her face in his hands and nuzzled her neck. "Would you like my assistance, sweet princess?"

She pleaded with her eyes.

And then he knelt softly beside her, lifted her head in his palms—allowing it to fall back, and struck her jugular quick and hard with his own razor-sharp fangs. Venom a thousand times more painful than that of the cobras' assaulted her blood stream.

Ciopori prayed for death.

But it didn't come.

It felt like hours—though it was probably only seconds—before Salvatore withdrew his fangs and her voice slowly returned, the swelling in her throat receding. Her body began to heal as Salvatore's venom overpowered the cobras'. "Will I become a vampire?"

Salvatore laughed. "No. Only the *destinies* of the lighter vampires can be so easily converted. You would have to willingly relinquish your soul first. The unfortunate word being *willingly*."

Ciopori swallowed hard and tugged at the chains. "Release me, Salvatore"—she paused—"Please."

Salvatore looked around the room and eyed the waiting snakes. "You will do as I say, or there will be no mercy."

"Yes."

"You will come willingly into my arms. You will acknowledge that I—*not you*—am the master of this domain. And you will obey me from this moment forward, or I will keep you here all night, allowing every snake in this pit to strike you, providing you with just enough venom to keep you alive so that you cannot escape the torture. Do you understand me, Princess? *Your insolence will not be tolerated.*"

Ciopori looked up at the wicked being now standing above

her, his hard, muscular body naked and soiled with his own pleasure. Reluctantly, she nodded.

Salvatore unchained her hands first, still allowing the snakes to hover.

"Please," she begged, hugging her arms to her chest. "Get rid of them."

He unchained her feet, and she stood up on the bench as if she could avoid the vile creatures by stepping out of their range. They slithered around her feet.

"Salvatore!"

He held out his arms. "I'm waiting."

Ciopori swallowed hard and leaned toward the repugnant son of Jaegar. He moved his body even closer to hers. As a large snake began to climb her leg, she kicked it off, threw her arms around his neck, and crawled into his arms.

"And?"

Ciopori squirmed, trying to keep her body out of the reach of the snakes. She clung to Salvatore's gigantic frame like a thrashing boat tethered to a buoy in a storm. "And you are..." She struggled to say the words.

As Salvatore lowered her slowly toward the serpents, she dug her nails into his shoulders, grasping for sanctuary.

"You are the master of this domain."

Salvatore bent his head. He sniffed her fear and moaned. "Whose master?"

Ciopori brushed away a burning tear and buried her head in the crook of his neck. It was of no use. She was terrified...defeated.

Humiliated.

"Whose master!" he thundered.

"Mine," she whispered, unwilling to die for pride. "You are my master, Salvatore."

Salvatore waved his hand at the snakes. "Leave us."

One by one, the cobras slowly retreated, slithering away from the bed, up the walls, and back into their hell-holes.

BLOOD AWAKENING

Trembling like a child awakened from a nightmare, Ciopori relished the safety of Salvatore's arms. Her body still suffered the effects of the snake and vampire venoms. Her heart still pounded erratically in her chest. The slick, viscous substance of Salvatore's pleasure clung to her tattered gown and skin.

Salvatore purred deep in his throat. "You are mine, Ciopori."

With the wave of his hand, he clothed himself. And then he gently stroked her hair and headed back to his lair.

twelve

Marquis stood outside of the guest bedroom early Monday morning, gathering all of the courage he could muster. He had fought in countless battles over the centuries, defeated formidable enemies, and led respectable armies, but he knew that he was in for the fight of his life now.

He knocked gently on the bedroom door. For the third time.

"Go away!"

Another large object smashed against the wall and splintered into pieces: This one sounded like the Renaissance vase he kept on the armoire.

Marquis cringed.

Well, at least there was nothing left of value for Kristina to destroy. Anything else she got her hands on was at least from the current century, and thus, possibly replaceable.

"Kristina," he grumbled, even though he tried to whisper. At least he didn't growl. "I'm coming in...okay?"

"Don't you dare open that door, you cretin son of a..."

The string of words was as long as his arm, and he winced. "*Kristina*, please—"

"Please what!"

Please what, indeed.

What had he expected after that primitive demonstration he had put on the night before? A Hallmark card and breakfast in bed? Marquis leaned back against the wall and shut his eyes. *Dearest Lord Draco, what had he done?*

As a male vampire, even in the house of Jadon, his nature was both civilized and untamed. He possessed equal parts light and shadow, and like any primitive being, there was a breaking point, a threshold beyond which caution and reason gave way to pure primal instinct. Where judgment became impulse, and the animal became too feral to restrain.

He chided himself on his complete lack of control. Never— well, rarely—in his great expanse of life had he allowed himself to go that far over the edge, and now he was paying the price. Converting her like that? On the porch? Without her consent? The pain and suffering she had endured...

It was extreme, even for him.

He took a deep breath and steadied himself. She had tried to *kill him*, after all.

Twice.

He knocked again. "Kristina, *îmi pare rău*." He leaned his forehead against the door. "I had a...very bad day." *I'm sorry.*

"What!" she squealed as another heavy thump resounded, this time against the door: definitely a shoe this time. "*You* had a bad day? Go to hell, Marquis!"

Marquis shook his head. He'd had more than enough. They had been at this for hours. This standoff had to end. Using the supernatural speed of his kind, he flung the door open, entered the room, and quickly waved his hand, paralyzing her arms.

To his surprise, as he started toward his mate, a large, heavy object launched off the bed and barely missed his head. He ducked back out of the room and slammed the door. Wow, she had *kicked* an old Webster's dictionary with her foot. He hadn't seen that coming. Perhaps the woman had missed her calling; she should have played soccer.

"Kristina!" Marquis snarled, slowly reopening the door, this time immobilizing her legs as well. "That is quite enough." When he looked over at the bed, her face was beet red, and her bottom lip was quivering like a toddler's, just moments away from a god-awful wail. He held up his hand. "Please, don't."

Her eyes bored into his skull like daggers as she sucked back air, too proud to cry in front of him. "Yeah, those words sound familiar, don't they?"

Marquis shook his head and slowly approached the bed. She was just a human and a small one at that—paralyzed—but for the love of Perseus, the female looked scary. "Can I release you now? Will you behave?"

Kristina blanched at the word *behave* and glowered at him

with pure, unadulterated hatred in her eyes. "Will *you?*" she retorted.

Marquis shrugged his shoulders. "Yes."

Kristina rolled her bright blue eyes. "Well then come on in, *honey dumpling, sweetheart, baby.* Let's get this marriage rolling!"

Marquis blinked several times, absolutely lost. Under normal circumstances, he had absolutely no idea what to do with a woman—outside of making love—and these circumstances were *strained* at best.

Kristina laughed aloud. "You should see the look on your face, *boss.* Damn, and I always thought you controlled the universe. You're clueless, aren't you?"

Marquis huffed, indignant.

"Yeah, well, let me give you a hint. What you did last night? First, to Dirk…" Her voice trailed off as tears welled up in her eyes. She fought them back. "And then to *me?* You may as well save the rest! This it-shay is too broke to fix. *Ever.*"

Marquis took a few steps toward the bed, then stopped. He dropped his head in his hands and smoothed back his hair, pushing it away from his face. "Kristina, I regret the way things…unfolded last night."

She chuckled. "Oh, well then, what was I thinking? Being so angry and all?" If looks could kill, he would have been six feet under.

He sighed. "How are you feeling this morning?"

She reached for a glass paper-weight beside the bed, but Marquis was too quick. Using only his mind, he whisked it out of her hand and gently floated it across the room, lowering it smoothly onto an antique dresser before she could launch it at his head. "We need to talk, Kristina. There is much—"

"Oh, shut up, Marquis!" Her voice was sharp with anger. "Just. Shut. Up."

Marquis felt his top lip begin to twitch and quickly closed his eyes, willing his fangs to stay where they were. *Do not kill the human, Marquis. Do not kill the human, Marquis. Do not kill the human…*

"Kristina—"

"I agree," she interrupted a second time. "There are some things that need to be said, but it's your turn to listen *while I talk*."

Grateful for the reprieve—and because he had absolutely no idea what he was going to say next, anyway—Marquis took a seat in a high-backed, upholstered arm-chair adjacent to the bed and waited. This was a far better strategy anyhow. Learn your enemy's position and then counter with—

Enemy?

Had he just said *enemy*?

The reality struck him. Dear gods, this woman was not supposed to be his enemy; she was his *destiny*. His *eternal* life mate.

As quickly as the thought entered his mind, the princess's beautiful face flashed through his memory; he rubbed the bridge of his nose and looked away. "I'm listening, Kristina."

Kristina sat up and pulled the covers all the way up to her chin. "So, here's the deal: Have you ever heard of IVF?"

"IVF?" Marquis asked.

"Yeah, IVF! *In vitro fertilization*. It's when—"

"I know what it is, Kristina." Marquis scowled.

"Good. Because—"

"And if I know where you're going with this"—it was his turn to interrupt—"then I think what you mean to say is *artificial insemination*. Unless of course, there is some reason you are unable to become pregnant, which"—he took a deep sniff of the air—"there isn't."

Kristina gasped, incredulous. "OMG! You are disgusting! Damn! You are way too much for me, Marquis!"

"Too much what?" he asked, contemplating. "Oh…is this what you fear?"

Kristina's hand shot up in the air. "Stop! Don't even go there. *Holy shit!*" She took a deep breath. "Remember, you're supposed to be *listening*. Just listen, Marquis!"

Marquis leaned back in the chair, stretched out his legs, crossed them at the ankles, and folded his hands in his lap. "Very well. Have I ever heard of artificial insemination? Yes, I have."

"Well, good," Kristina snapped, trying to regain her composure, "because that's the closest you're ever going to get to me. And that's assuming I agree to do this whole...baby thing...because let's just both be honest, that's the only reason I'm here. You sure as hell don't love me or want me. And I sure as hell don't love or want you! And I never will."

Marquis was surprised at how badly her words stung.

They were true, but after so many years of waiting for one's *destiny*—imagining, believing, hoping—the whole situation was like a horrible nightmare, too awful to be true. "Go on," he mumbled.

"If I have to live here"—she waved her arms around the room—"then there are going to be some changes...some additions."

"Like what?" Marquis snarled.

Kristina sat up straight and glared at him. "Like any damn thing I want! A home theatre! A sauna! A covered swimming pool out back—anything I want!"

Marquis stared at her, swallowed hard, and bit his lip. "Continue."

"And that's just the house," she stormed. "There are a whole lot of other things...like my own Hummer to drive in the winter, and maybe a pink Corvette for the summertime: a convertible. And clothes. Jewelry. A new iPod. A few gold cards to spend at my leisure—"

"Is that what you wished to tell me?" Marquis growled in frustration, his temper growing short. "Make a list and write it down, Kristina. I haven't the time for this nonsense."

"Excuse me?" She sounded mildly surprised.

He sat up and leaned forward. "Will all of those *things* shut you up? Make you cooperative? *Get you out of my hair?*" To heck with trying to be cordial. The female was right—they had nothing in common, and they never would.

Not to mention, this was the second time she had tried to trade her body for favors; and frankly, it disgusted him. It was the second time she had treated something as sacred as bringing life into the world as an abomination to be bartered over—and the second time she had acted as if whether he lived or died was of no consequence whatsoever. Very well, then. Forging an understanding up front would make life a lot easier on both of them.

"Money is of no consequence to me," he quipped. "Go on."

Kristina cleared her throat, suddenly a little less cocky. "And I don't want children," she whispered, straightening her spine as she delivered the words.

Why was he not surprised?

"So that means a nanny twenty-four-seven ...maybe several...whatever it takes to keep the kid out of my hair. I won't raise our son, Marquis. And trust me, the one we *have to have* is the only one we're ever going to have."

A low growl escaped his throat as he tried counting backward from ten to one. "Go on," he spat through gritted teeth.

"I don't work unless I want to, and you let me go wherever I want and do whatever I feel like, even if I have to have a bodyguard—one of those *sentinel dudes* with me all the time." She crossed her arms in front of her.

"Is that it?"

"No," she sighed. "We sleep in separate rooms, and if I want..." She took a deep breath. "If I wanna...*get with*...someone else, another guy, then you've got nothin' to say about it, so just turn the other way." Feeling emboldened, she added, "It's none of your biz, feel me?"

"Are you through?"

Kristina looked down then. "Maybe, but if I come up with

something else, I'll let you know."

Marquis rose slowly from the chair. His heart-beat was eerily steady, his demeanor far too calm. As he stalked to the edge of the bed, his fangs began to elongate on their own accord, and he felt the primal heat of rage burning in his eyes. But he made no attempt to soften their intensity: Let them burn the color of blood. It was better than spilling hers.

Kristina scooted as far back against the headboard as she could, her throat working in anxious swallows, her hands now clutching the covers like a drowning man grasping a life jacket.

Marquis didn't blink.

He stopped with his face a few inches from hers and then knelt with one knee on the mattress, his powerful frame towering over her miniscule one. Slowly and evenly, he began to speak: "Kristina, you will take the remainder of this day and tomorrow to recover from the conversion, and then you will go to Kagen's clinic tomorrow night for the insemination. I will command the pregnancy, and we will get it over with."

He shifted his weight, his muscles rolling in silent waves of contempt as his warrior's body contracted. "You may have your swimming pool, theatre, and sauna—and whatever else you desire—once my own contractors have seen to the plans: You will not make a pretentious eyesore out of this home…or this land…and you will not obstruct the natural views or compromise the architectural integrity in any way."

He stopped to lick the tips of his fangs, drawing a single drop of blood from his tongue and swallowing it. "Drive whatever you wish, Kristina, and I will see to it that you have a credit card with an inexhaustible balance—but not because you have extorted it out of me. As I said before, I can make you want…*and do*…whatever I wish. No, you will have your precious possessions because as my mate, there is nothing I would have denied you anyhow."

Kristina's face paled, and she didn't dare speak.

Marquis cleared his throat. "You may also travel with a

sentinel escort and seek your own entertainment, within reason, but I will not have you demean the honor of our house—or the house of Jadon—so choose your activities wisely, lest you lose all freedom *forever*."

He leaned closer then, their noses touching, and then he chuckled, though the laughter did not come from humor. "As for your sexual desires and what is or is not my business: Should you *ever* avail yourself of the pleasures of another man, I will rip his throat out while you watch, and then I will force you to kneel in his blood and feed from his dying heart. So, again, I say—choose wisely."

He backed away then, stalked to the door, reached for the handle, and turned around. "Oh, and Kristina..."

Her eyes opened wide.

"You will have your nanny, and the less you have to do with our child, the better. But know this: Should you ever do anything to compromise our son in any way, *I will put you in the ground myself! Feel me?*"

He didn't wait for an answer. He simply walked out the door and shut it behind him.

thirteen

Marquis leaned forward on the back stoop and stared out at the river. It was so peaceful, so unassuming.

So unconcerned.

How could there be so much turmoil going on all around it? He sighed. But that was the way of nature, was it not.

He walked down the short set of stairs and meandered toward the bank, wanting to draw closer to the water. Hell, with Kristina living here, he might not ever go inside again. He shook his head, trying not to think about it, wishing he could control the constant images of Ciopori that flashed through his mind like an incessant stream, disrupting his thoughts with its ceaseless interruption.

Ciopori.

The regal daughter of King Sakarias and Queen Jade. The hauntingly beautiful sister of Jadon and Jaegar—one of the last remaining females from a people thought to be extinct.

Every time he closed his eyes, he saw her lying beneath him, her stunning golden eyes gazing up at him with such innocence and love, her beautiful, pouty mouth slightly parted, swollen with pleasure, moist with arousal.

The way she had opened her heart to him. Her mind. Her body. So completely. So willingly. Marquis closed his eyes, reveling in the memory, the scent of all that luscious black hair, the feel of her breasts in his hands…

What the heck was he doing?

He had pushed her away—warned her to stay away—and he needed to close his mind to her as well.

He looked back toward the house and frowned. Kristina might not be his first choice—oh, hell, she wouldn't even be his last choice—but she was his only choice; and Marquis was a male of honor. Now that he had claimed her and converted her, they were as good as mated. He would not cheat on her, even if it meant a lifetime of celibacy.

BLOOD AWAKENING

Even if it meant staying away from the princess.

Against his better judgment, Marquis sought to reach out to Ciopori one last time, to simply brush her mind with his, unnoticed. He just wanted to know that she was all right. Having taken her blood the night they made love, he would forever have access to her whereabouts, to her state of mind.

Marquis closed his eyes and began to follow the DNA backward, reaching out beyond the physical structure of the molecules now circulating within his own blood stream in order to trace their deeper energetic footprint: the quantum waves themselves. As he projected further and further out, allowing the energy that was Ciopori to gather unto itself, an image began to form in his mind. Ah, yes, she was lying down, her wavy, waist-length hair cascading all around her, her arms stretched high above her head in—

Manacles.

As if he had been stunned by a bolt of electricity, Marquis jolted, instantly losing the image. Pushing down his panic, he quickly quieted his mind and followed the waves once more to the vision. And then his heart began to beat with a fierce urgency. There were, indeed, manacles around her wrists. *And she was chained to a bed.* A large, four-poster monstrosity in some sort of cold, dark room—no, a cavern—an underground chamber.

Marquis swallowed hard, his heart now racing in his chest as he projected his own essence forward in an attempt to see through Ciopori's eyes. Damnit, nothing else was coming through!

Ciopori wasn't telepathic, and the two of them had not established a common bandwidth as life mates would do, so aligning to her exact frequency in order to see through her eyes just wasn't happening.

But he could feel her.

Their tactile connection was strong.

Marquis relaxed his muscles and tuned in to the feel of

Ciopori's body beneath him, the softness of her skin, the contours and curves of her form...

As the image became stronger, he was finally able to pick up on the palpable signals being sent through her blood. As if they were one, he was suddenly there: lying on a hard mattress, his arms stretched above him in manacles, his legs chained as well. Dear gods, the thin silk covering her body was shredded, leaving her practically naked.

Marquis swallowed his rage and held onto the signal.

What else could he feel?

It was damp, cool, and his skin was chilled. There was a peculiar throbbing just above his collarbone, in the center of his stomach, and another over his right inner thigh. *Holy deities, it was painful.* Like the sting of a scorpion or worse. There was definitely venom surrounding the bites, yet there was something familiar occurring in his body as well...

Regeneration.

The wounds were healing themselves. Poison attacking poison.

Vampire venom attacking...snake venom.

Marquis startled. Where in the name of Lord Draco was she? What in the hell had happened? And then all of a sudden he felt a clammy hand—a rough, heavy male hand—brush against his stomach, and a jolt of malevolence shot through him. Marquis broke the connection at once, his body recoiling from the touch. The unmistakable energy of evil.

The sons of Jaegar.

Marquis ran his palms down his face, then folded them behind his back. *Nachari!* He almost came unglued when thirty-seconds passed without a response. *Nachari! Answer me, now!*

Brother, what is it?

Marquis fought to remain calm. *Are you still at Napolean's?*

Yes, I am. Why, what's going—

Where is Napolean?

Sleeping. He—

BLOOD AWAKENING

Why the hell is he sleeping! Marquis's psychic voice rose to a thundering crescendo, and he felt Nachari blanch.

Our Sovereign fed last night, Marquis. It had been almost eight-weeks, and with the women here, he knew he couldn't risk getting sick or weak. Brother, what is going on?

Marquis spat a string of curse words. Could this get any worse? The sons of Jadon only fed every six to eight weeks, but when they did, they slept—and they slept hard—for at least twelve hours, almost impossible to wake up. Damnit, how could Napolean compromise himself like that with the females there?

Picking up on Marquis's powerful thoughts, even though he had not purposely projected them, Nachari argued, *On the contrary, Marquis; he was far too compromised before he fed. That's why he couldn't put it off.*

Check on Ciopori! Marquis demanded without explanation.

Ciopori?

Now!

Hold on...

Time seemed to stand still. *Nachari?*

Hold on...

Where are you now?

Silence met him. Seconds felt like hours, minutes like days. *Nachari!*

I'm in her room. I just knocked on the door, but there was no answer. She was supposed to be sleeping...hold on...

Marquis paced up and down the river-bank, waiting for his brother to tell him what he already knew: Ciopori was gone. *Dear gods!* His hands began to tremble.

When Nachari returned, his demeanor had changed from curious to deathly serious. *She's not in her room, Marquis. Vanya is searching with me now. Are you going to tell me what happened?*

Marquis cleared his throat and spat. *She's gone, Nachari! That's what happened.*

What do you mean 'gone?' Nathaniel Silivasi entered the conversation, no doubt having sensed his brothers' distress. *You guys are both sending out powerful waves of alarm. Marquis, what's happened to Ciopori?*

Marquis shook his head. *Ciopori is still alive, Nathaniel, but she's with…* He could hardly bring himself to speak the words. *She's with one of the Dark Ones, and whoever has her, he's an extremely powerful entity. In fact, based on the strength of his energy, I would almost venture to say that she's with Salvatore Nistor.*

How can you possibly know this? Kagen Silivasi asked, joining his brothers on the shared family bandwidth.

Last night, at your clinic, Marquis explained, *I took her blood.*

Silence filled the airwaves for a moment while the brothers processed the full meaning of what Marquis had said. Finally, Nathaniel asked: *What exactly did you see, Marquis?*

She's in a cave somewhere. Underground. He let out a slow sigh, trying to keep his temper from erupting. *Brothers, he has her manacled to his bed.*

If someone had dropped a pin, it would have sounded like a boulder.

After a prolonged, uncomfortable silence, Nachari swore in Romanian. *She went to bed late last night, right before Napolean left to hunt. I stayed in the hall the entire night, Marquis, just outside her and Vanya's doors. So I know she never came out. Gods, she's on the third floor, and there are no stairs leading down from her balcony.* He took a deep breath. *I would have felt the energy immediately if a dark presence had entered this house; in fact, I don't think it's even possible: There are too many powerful wards surrounding this mansion.*

Well, Salvatore had to have entered the room somehow, Kagen said.

No, I'm telling you, Nachari insisted, *our Lord's orders were to stay in the hall; not to disturb the women; allow them to sleep unless they requested assistance. But no dark entity entered this house on my watch! And there's no way out of this bedroom except—*

She can project herself short distances, Marquis interrupted.

What do you mean? Nathaniel asked. *How is that possible? She's not Vampyr; she's human.*

She's celestial, and she doesn't use dematerialization; she uses some sort of magic. I'm not sure how she does it, but she could definitely get down from a balcony.

Son of a bitch! Nachari snarled. *Hold on...*

All three of the males waited in tense silence for what seemed like eternity.

When Nachari finally reconnected, an aura of rage permeated his energy. *That's exactly what she did, brothers. Her footprints appear just below her balcony and lead into the forest. I tracked her about a mile and a half into a clearing and—*

And what? Kagen demanded.

And Marquis is right. There was a second energy in the clearing before her trail went cold, and it was definitely dark.

Salvatore? Nathaniel asked.

Nachari paused. *I'm not sure. He studies black magic, right?*

Yes...absolutely, Marquis answered. *Why?*

Because the energy here is beyond darkness, my brother. There's a demonic feel to it. The evil here isn't just individual—it's collective. So, yeah, whoever it was, he's heavily into the dark arts.

Marquis shut his eyes, and Nathaniel sighed before speaking as the voice of reason. *Okay, so it's most likely Salvatore who has her; frankly, that's probably a good thing.*

How so? Kagen asked, clearly as curious as the others to see where his form of logic was taking him.

Valentine was both arrogant and impulsive, Nathaniel explained. *And Zarek is like a child, beholden to his every dark impulse, as many of the Dark Ones are—completely instinctual—driven only by their base nature and immediate desires. But Salvatore is a sorcerer, one who values learning and thinking...one who employs strategy. He will not act in haste and must have a dozen questions about the princess—just as we do: Is she immortal? Can she bear children with the Vampyr race? Could she give birth to a female?*

Nathaniel has a good point, Kagen said. *Salvatore will keep her alive until he discovers her...highest use. And because the others fear his magic, he just might be able to keep her safe from them, for the time being. At any rate, he won't rape her right away because that would kill her within forty-*

eight hours, and Salvatore is not that stupid.

Agreed, Marquis grumbled, beginning to view the situation as a tactician. *But you should each know that he's already tortured her. There is no time to waste.*

Nachari swore again beneath his breath.

The twins remained silent.

And then Marquis simply shifted gears and became who and what he was—an Ancient Master Warrior. *Nachari, wake Napolean. Nathaniel, bring Jocelyn and Storm to the mansion; I will bring Kristina. Kagen, my brother, I am sorry, but I am going to have to ask you to sit this one out. We must take Nachari because of his knowledge of magic, and we also have to take the sentinels for tracking. Nathaniel's mastery as a warrior is as essential as mine; but the truth is, that leaves only one person I trust enough to guard Princess Vanya, our mates, and Storm: my own blood.*

Kagen was incensed. *There are plenty of males to watch the women, Marquis!*

Kagen—

You know damn well that I can fight every bit as well as the sentinels, and I am far older and more experienced than Nachari. You will be compromised with your attention on Ciopori—which is as it should be—but someone needs to have Nachari's back. He is a gallant fighter, but he is a wizard first. And if he's concentrating on divination... I would like to be there to see after our youngest brother.

Nachari grumbled. *I'm a wizard—not an invalid—Kagen. How many battles have we fought together? I think I can hold my own!*

Yes, Nathaniel said, *but we're talking about entering the lairs of our enemy, fighting on their turf—while using you for second sight. You are a new Master, Nachari.*

There was simply no objectivity: The loss of Nachari's twin, Shelby, was just too recent, too raw, and it made all of the brothers over-protective.

And you are a real ass sometimes, Nathaniel! Nachari retorted, knowing darn well what the discussion was really about.

Marquis didn't have time for this. *Enough! Nathaniel will come as a warrior; Nachari will come as an advisor; and Kagen, you will stay at the mansion with the women and children. The matter is closed.*

Kagen's anger was palpable, but Marquis had pulled rank and that was the end of it. *As you wish, brother.*

Kagen, Marquis added, uncharacteristically sympathetic. *Ciopori has been...abused... There is vampire venom as well as snake venom in her bloodstream. She is not Vampyr. She cannot regenerate. You are the most gifted healer I know. If we bring her out alive, I must know that you are somewhere safe waiting to attend to her. I need you...unharmed.*

Kagen sighed. *Your praise is an honor, warrior.* It was clearly the best he could do.

Very well. Nachari, summon the Olaru brothers and Julian, our tracker; then go home and retrieve your weapons. I want everyone to meet at Napolean's in full battle armament—we have no idea what we're walking into, so leave no weapon behind. We will meet at the mansion in one hour.

fourteen

Napolean slammed his fist straight through the white brick wall of the library. For the love of Andromeda, the females had only been with him for two days, and already, Ciopori was in the hands of a Dark One.

And not just any son of Jaegar, but Salvatore Nistor: a twelve-hundred-year-old sorcerer, a vampire as evil as the night was dark and as cunning as a fox. Salvatore was no fledgling to be easily out-maneuvered. And his capacity to hurt the princess was limitless.

Napolean gathered his composure and reined in his emotions. Now was not the time for outbursts. The Silivasi brothers, along with the sentinels and the valley's best tracker, would be arriving within the hour: Strategic plans had to be made to retrieve the princess.

He ran his hands through his waist-length hair and grasped the holy amulet he always wore around his neck, sending up a fervent prayer to Perseus, the victorious hero, asking for strength and triumph in battle.

"Milord?" Vanya's soft, musical voice interrupted his thoughts as she peered in through the library doors. "Are you all right?"

Napolean spun around, his hard features cast in a stern line. "I'll be fine, Princess. Thank you." He wanted to say more, but somehow, he always found himself tongue-tied around the flaxen-haired beauty, his behavior certainly unbecoming of a king.

She reached up and dabbed at her eyes, brushing away a fresh set of tears, and his heart jolted in his chest. The pain she was trying to hide was astronomical, and he had no idea how to comfort her, how to reassure her that all would be well. She had lost her entire world, and now, this thing with Ciopori, too?

"Your English is coming along well," he pointed out, wanting to kick himself the moment he said it. Who the hell cared about dialect at a time like this? He bit his lip, waiting for a response. Gods, he was a complete imbecile in the woman's presence.

"Uh…yes…yes, it is," she muttered. "It would seem the information-transfer went very well." She wandered into the library and began looking over titles on the floor-to- ceiling book-shelves as a distraction, no doubt feeling as awkward as he did.

"I…I wasn't sure how you and your sister would respond to the conveyance, considering that you are not…" His voice trailed off.

"Vampires?" Vanya smiled that lovely regal smile she had that lit up her unique rose-colored eyes. "It would seem that much of what your species considers to be a gift of your Vampyr nature is indeed a remnant of your celestial ancestry. Perhaps we are closer to one another than you think."

Napolean nodded. It was true. So many centuries had passed since the Curse was handed down; the males had almost forgotten the power they wielded, long before they had been changed into creatures of the night. *Nosferatu*.

While the ability to speak telepathically and transmit enormous amounts of information through visual images was a distinctly Vampyr trait, Napolean had been able to transfer the language of this time—as well as the history of its devices and modern conveniences—to both Ciopori and Vanya as easily as one might download a new software program into a computer.

He had simply flooded their minds with enormous blocks of information, transferring his own command of language and his knowledge of the world around them into their consciousness, and the females had absorbed the information like sponges.

Vanya had even heated something up in the microwave earlier without asking a single question, and while Napolean knew how to use the microwave, he couldn't remember ever having done so himself. It was truly remarkable. And it had bridged an enormous cultural gap between them, enabling free-flowing communication.

The princess turned her back to him, and he heard her sniffle, no doubt trying to conceal her fear. Napolean cleared his throat and took a step in her direction, careful to check for poorly placed furniture. "Vanya…I am truly sorry. We will get her back."

Vanya's slender shoulders began to tremble then, though she continued to hold them back in her familiar, proud way. She nodded, but she didn't turn around.

Napolean lifted a tissue from a box on his desk, lightly tapped her on the shoulder, and handed it to her. "Here. It's a—"

"Kleenex? Yes, of course: a disposable handkerchief." She accepted the tissue and turned back around.

Napolean tried to swallow his awkwardness. Hell, nothing in the last thousand years had rattled the monarch, yet this female made him forget his own name. He placed his hand on her shoulder and gently stroked her arm, the feel of her soft, warm skin sending chills down his spine. "Marquis is certain she is still alive."

Vanya shattered then. Her head fell into her hands, and her tears began to pour out like a river breaking through a rickety dam. "Oh gods, but what is that monster doing to her, Napolean?"

Napolean thought about the other information Marquis had conveyed—the bites, the venom, the manacles, and her shredded clothing—but he knew better than to share any of it with Vanya. "I don't know," he whispered, grasping her by a thin shoulder. He nestled his forehead against her thick wealth of hair and pressed his body closer to hers.

And then he cringed.

Dear goddess of propriety, not now!

How completely inappropriate. What was he, a teenage boy? For the love of Andromeda, her sister was in mortal danger and he was…aroused. What in the galaxy was wrong with him?

He quickly took a step back, separating their bodies before

his very male reaction to their closeness grew any stronger. It took all the composure he had not to drop his hand from her shoulder and just walk out of the room.

Too late.

Vanya's spine stiffened ever so slightly, and Napolean cringed. She must think him an absolute cretin: What a poor excuse for a king.

She cleared her throat and stepped away from his touch.

Oh, hell!

"I'm sorry," he whispered. "Honestly, I wasn't thinking anything...inappropriate. I...it just...happened." Could this get any more humiliating? He sighed. "I'll go."

As he turned to walk out of the library, Vanya reached out and caught his hand, pulling him toward her so hard that they almost collided. To her credit, her eyes never drifted below his shoulders: She was far too refined to point out his shame.

Napolean winced, but he managed to hold her gaze. "I meant no disrespect, Vanya." He shrugged. "Perhaps it has been too many millennia since I have stood in the presence of a true female of worth." Her eyes softened, and to his dismay, his mouth just kept going. "It's just that when I look at you, Princess, I see the beauty of the gods themselves reflected back to me in a mortal's eyes. I am truly sorry for my inappropriate...reaction."

Vanya's breath hitched, and she clutched her hand to her chest. "*Napolean.*" His name was a gentle whisper.

He looked away. "Again, I apologize; it won't happen again." He drew in a deep breath and waited for her reprimand.

But the reprisal never came.

She took a tentative step forward and cupped his face in her hands. "Look at me, milord."

He slowly glanced up.

"It has been twenty-eight hundred years since I have witnessed a man of such power and grace, bearing the weight of his people on his shoulders with nary a protest or complaint.

Not since my father have I known a more proud or gentle warrior. Yet, even he had my mother to temper the weight of the world which he carried. You have stood, alone, for centuries, milord; and even now, you bear the full weight of responsibility for my sister's abduction. You are the heart and soul of the house of Jadon, yet you will risk your own life to find her as opposed to sending soldiers in your place."

She brushed his jaw with the back of her fingers, the softness of her touch lingering against his skin. "You do not offend me, my gallant king. You flatter me beyond words."

Napolean stood as still as a statue, trying to remember how to speak. He started to open his mouth but chose to keep it shut instead, not wanting to stand there like a drooling dolt.

She smiled then and reached out to stroke his hair. "By all the gods in heaven, you are the most beautiful male I have ever seen, Sir Napolean Mondragon, descendant of the goddess Andromeda."

Napolean took a step back then, not so much to move away from her but to keep from swaying as her words sunk in. Despite his best attempt at restraint, a primal growl escaped his throat. He reached out and drew her to him, gathering her tightly in his arms. He buried his face in her hair and deeply inhaled her sweet lilac scent. As she melted against him—like she had been made to fit his body, alone—he closed his eyes and shivered.

Stop! he urged himself. The king of the noble Vampyr did not indulge in emotion, or touch, with his subjects. There were boundaries.

As the Sovereign of the house of Jadon, his males treated him with great deference, never reaching out to touch him, rarely holding eye contact for more than a second, and their female *destinies* observed the same decorum. Over the endless centuries, he had stopped waiting for his *destiny*, figuring that he probably didn't have one. After all, his responsibilities were enormous, and they grew as the house of Jadon grew—leaving very little room for anything other than governing.

BLOOD AWAKENING

Napolean had become hardened by the endless wars and sacrifices: placing the dark twins on the altar of atonement to spare their parents the horror of their deaths, reading last rites to the males who were claimed—and brutally murdered—by the ghost of the Curse, possessing omniscient knowledge of the thoughts and actions of every male who served him, and always maintaining the safety of the valley and the tradition of sacred ceremony.

No, the only time Napolean acted like a male was when he fed in order to survive, or on the few occasions when he sought the warmth of a human female's arms in order to dull the endless, barren ache of eternal existence.

Yet even that had never been satisfying.

The descendants of Jadon had to be extremely careful with human relationships, especially sexual ones. As they had one and only one *destiny*—a female preordained by the gods—there could be no emotional attachments made with any other. And since no other female could be converted to their species without relinquishing her soul, there was no potential future with anyone else.

Beyond the emotional ramifications, an accidental pregnancy was unthinkable: Even though a male had to actually command a pregnancy—speak it into being within seventy-two hours of planting his seed—the threat to the woman was so grave that it was hardly worth taking the risk. What if the male dreamed it? Wished it? Gods forbid, his primal instincts demanded it? What if the thought came to his mind, unbidden? The female would die a hideous death giving birth to his twins. The danger was simply too great.

And then there was the matter of becoming feral.

As Vampyr, the sons of Jadon were both light and shadow. Unlike their dark counterparts, they still had their souls; but make no mistake, they were vampires just the same—predators by nature. They were instinctual creatures that lusted for blood and warred with the ever present desire to siphon their prey until

158

the weaker species fell lifeless at their feet, to conquer with their overwhelming power and superior strength. To establish themselves as dominant. A male was at his most vulnerable when caught up in the throes of passion, and the potential to seriously hurt a human female was very real.

Napolean nuzzled Vanya's neck, absorbing the exquisite rhythm of her celestial heart-beat through her jugular. Dear gods, he wanted this female like he had never wanted anything in all of his incarnation.

But she was not Vampyr.

And she was not his chosen *destiny*.

And even the gods had to know that once he took her, he could never let her go. Unlike the Ancient Warrior Marquis, he could never make love to a celestial princess and then return to his duty without her. Moreover, he was the king, the heart of the house of Jadon, as Vanya had put it: His soul was not...negotiable.

Napolean slowly pulled away, his mouth lingering over Vanya's indefinitely, their lips lightly brushing each other's before he forced himself away. "I cannot take you, Vanya," he sighed. "You are worthy of so much more."

Vanya nodded and stepped back. "There is much to consider, I know."

Napolean was blown away by her dignity and grace.

She took his hands in hers once more. "But know this, great king, you are not alone anymore. You need not shoulder the burdens of the entire world by yourself. I am here if you need me."

Napolean dropped her hands, desperately trying to resist now. Her words were too much. Her presence was too much. The temptation was too great. He grasped the small of her back with one hand and fisted her hair with the other, arching her beneath him as he claimed her mouth, ravaged her lips, and tasted her tongue with his own, exploring with such urgent passion that he feared he would explode right then and there.

BLOOD AWAKENING

And she returned it all: passion for passion, kiss for kiss, bite for bite, taste for taste.

When her left leg bent at the knee and her thigh began to ride up his own—her pelvis rocking in a hypnotic motion against his, involuntarily—he gasped. If his body became any harder, it would be a spear...and he would have to claim her right now. Right here. Taking them both down to the library floor like a savage, uncaring about the warriors on their way to the mansion—plummeting over the edge again and again as he filled her with his seed.

His canines exploded in his mouth, and he groaned, scraping them gently against her neck.

Vanya tightened her arms around his shoulders and let her head fall back completely unabashed, exposing her vein. "Take what you need, Napolean." Her breath was a series of shallow pants.

Napolean fought the primal urge with everything he had. Thank the gods, he had fed last night, or he would have drained her. She was far too innocent, and he was—exactly what he was—the sovereign lord over a house of vampires. He pulled back and gazed at her, knowing his eyes were glowing red, feeling his fangs grow sharper at her request.

"This is what I am, Vanya!" he hissed, allowing her to see the transformation. "You are better than this."

Vanya didn't yell or cry out, but the shock registered in her eyes just the same, and the sweet smell of fear, mixed with adrenaline, permeated the room. Her heart was racing—and not just from passion. He dropped his head, allowing his long black-and-silver banded hair to conceal his face.

Vanya challenged him then. "Do I, Napolean? Do I deserve better than the human *destinies* that you join to your males? Better than the sons that you revere and take hundreds of years to train as masters? Better than the warriors that you lead...and love? Why is your species beneath mine, dear lord? How could anyone be *better* than you?"

Napolean shook his head. "You forget, *I was there*, Vanya. *Before*. Before all of this. Before the Curse. I know what we once were."

"And still are, Napolean."

Napolean shook his head. "You are the daughter of our *true king*; you are pure and untainted. Vanya, I have the blood of a thousand men on my hands. I do not even remember the names of the human women I have taken to my bed, regardless of how seldom I may have done so. I carry newborn infants to their death, evil or not. I clean up the remains of our healers…and our warriors…and our wizards after the Curse has claimed them. I drink the blood of every member of the house of Jadon, and I absorb their every emotion—their hate, their fear, their lust…even their love. You were placed in an enchanted sleep at the tender age of *twenty*. My angel, I have *lived* for over twenty-eight hundred years. Oh Vanya, you are innocence incarnate compared to me."

All at once, the serious discussion was interrupted by a heavy set of footsteps approaching from the hall.

Vanya smiled knowingly. "We will continue this discussion later, my dear king."

When an ensuing loud knock resounded against the library door, Napolean frowned with frustration. "I apologize for the interruption, Princess."

"Milord?" The deep resonant voice belonged to Nachari Silivasi.

Vanya placed both hands on Napolean's shoulders, stood up on the tips of her toes, and kissed him on the cheek. "Do not let this matter distract you, Napolean. Go now, and bring back my sister."

Napolean kissed her forehead and stepped back. "I will do all that I can under the sun to make it so, Vanya. You have my solemn vow."

Vanya nodded. "I know this, Napolean." She brushed his cheek once more. "And as for you…come back to me unharmed."

Napolean laughed a little then. "I am very hard to kill, Princess. Believe me, there is little chance of that happening."

Vanya declined her head and gestured toward the door. "Go meet with your subjects, milord. And may the gods grant you victory and guide you with a steady hand."

Napolean bowed slightly at the waist and turned toward the door. She was right; the matter at hand required his full, undivided attention. Yet the woman he was leaving had rattled him beyond any danger he had ever faced.

"Her scent disappears in the clearing." Marquis Silivasi regarded his brothers as well as the menacing-looking warriors who sat quietly in Napolean's dining room, each one tightly situated in a circle around the table, all staring at a map of the local terrain. "Once he takes her into the air, it is very hard to follow a set trail."

"Can you not triangulate her position using the blood that runs in your veins?" Napolean asked.

The twins, Ramsey and Saxson Olaru, exchanged an inquisitive glance. "*You fed from the princess?*" Ramsey asked, staring at Marquis with a faint hint of disbelief. "What the hell, Marquis?"

Marquis growled and turned back to the map. *None of your business, my friend.*

Ramsey's light hazel eyes darkened for a moment, the scattered specks of gold flashing crimson before they returned to their normal hue. "I meant no disrespect, warrior."

Even as a ruthless—and rightfully feared—Master Warrior and sentinel of Dark Moon Vale, Ramsey Olaru had only seven-hundred years to Marquis's fifteen-hundred: less than half.

Marquis severely outranked him, and consequently, did not have to explain a thing to the younger warrior, even under circumstances such as these.

Ignoring Ramsey's apology, as was proper etiquette meant to imply that no offense was taken, Marquis shook his head. "I can pinpoint her whereabouts within a couple of miles: The problem I'm having is her depth. She's miles underground, Napolean. So deep that I'm losing her signal."

Nachari rapped his knuckles on the table, releasing nervous energy. "There is an anomaly in the position of the stars." His tone was thoughtful and deliberate.

"What do you mean?" Marquis raised an eyebrow.

Nachari pulled out a small iron device that resembled a protractor and laid a transparent map of the heavens directly over the map of the valley. The two maps matched each other perfectly in coordinates and dimensions. Turning to Napolean, he began to point out various abnormalities in the constellations, abnormalities that could never be seen by human eyes, but were easily detected by a Master Wizard descended of Celestial Beings.

"She is descended of the goddess Cygnus; is she not, milord?"

Napolean nodded hastily.

Nachari placed the stationary edge of the iron device on the tail of the divine constellation and moved the point toward the beak. "Cygnus is known as the Northern Cross or the Swan, but if you look closely, the beak has moved. *Albireo* is pointing further south." He drew a small dot at the new coordinate.

All of the males leaned in closer to see what Nachari was showing them.

Napolean viewed the map quietly for a few minutes. "Nachari, trace Marquis's constellation: Draco."

Nachari smiled. "You see it, too?" He lifted the iron device and set it back down over the celestial dragon with the base at the dragon's head, the point at its tail. "The tail has dropped toward Polaris." He drew another small dot to indicate the change.

"Hmm." Santos Olaru leaned in closer, his crystal blue eyes focused on the second point. "The gods are moving the stars. That's amazing."

Saxson cleared his voice. "I bet there are a few scientists at NASA having a coronary about now."

"No doubt," Nachari agreed. And then he drew a line straight through the North Celestial Pole.

Napolean sat back. "It's an arrow."

"Yes, it is." Nachari lifted the top map. "Marquis, circle the region where you believe the princess to be."

Marquis picked up a red pencil and drew a circle equal to about two miles in diameter. Nachari laid the second map back on top of it. The arrow pointed directly to the center of the region Marquis had circled.

"Holy Serpens," Santos whispered.

"She's right there," Nachari said. "The gods are showing us her position."

Marquis grunted. "Good work, little brother."

Interesting work, Nachari responded telepathically.

What do you mean?

Why is your constellation connected to hers? Nachari asked. *Why does the goddess Cygnus work with our Lord Draco on this?*

Excellent question, Nathaniel interjected, sharing the private bandwidth.

Napolean turned to Julien Lacusta, the valley's best tracker. "So the question is: If she's several miles underground—at that location—how in the world did Salvatore get her there? There are no abandoned mine shafts in that area."

Julien ran his hand over his short mahogany hair and stared down at the map, his moonstone-gray eyes surveying every mile one quadrant at a time. "I'm getting a terrible feeling about this," he said, squinting. "There's no way she could be that deep underground...unless...." His gravelly voice trailed off.

"Unless?" Napolean prodded.

"Unless there's already some sort of tunnel system or underground structure there, and we're talking about a big one."

Ramsey Olaru exhaled and stared at the tracker. "Are you suggesting that our dark brothers have some sort of cavern system built underground, directly under Dark Moon Vale?"

Saxson caught his breath, and Santos shifted nervously in his chair.

Nathaniel looked at Marquis. *Do you know what that would mean?*

Marquis frowned. "What are you saying, Julien?"

Julien shook his head, looking perplexed. "I'm saying that the nearest underground tunnel is about five miles away in the Red Canyons, the steep cliffs in the old sacrificial chamber."

"I know the tunnel you speak of," Marquis said. "It's in the cavern we destroyed in our short battle with the Nistor brothers not so long ago." Marquis's lip turned up in a snarl as he remembered the night he had tracked Valentine to the sacrificial chamber.

It had been shortly after Nathaniel had discovered what had happened to Dalia, their youngest brother's *destiny*. Nathaniel had searched the memories of his new mate, Jocelyn, only to discover the full extent of what Valentine had done to their family: He had kidnapped the *destiny* of Nachari's twin and impregnated her. He had forced her to give birth to his own evil sons in a hideous ritual that caused her untimely death, ultimately causing Shelby's death as well when the young vampire could no longer fulfill the demands of the Blood Curse.

Marquis had cornered Valentine in the chamber the same night, but before he could finish him off, Salvatore had shown up to save him, and then Nathaniel had joined in the battle, which only encouraged Zarek and Kagen to show up as well. The standoff had almost turned into a full-fledged vampire war, but luckily, Napolean had put an end to the skirmish before the entire valley could be destroyed, along with most of its human inhabitants. In any event, the sacrificial chamber had been all but destroyed in the process.

Valentine got what was coming to him, Nachari reminded Marquis.

Marquis shrugged. Yes, they had killed the evil scourge, but not before Shelby, Dalia, and even his innocent housekeeper, Joelle, had fallen victim to the maniacal vampire's schemes.

Nathaniel placed a hand on Marquis's shoulder, which Marquis abruptly shrugged off, a typical reaction that didn't seem to insult Nathaniel one bit.

"Has anyone here ever explored the cliffs?" Julien asked, bringing Marquis back to the subject at hand.

One by one, the males shook their heads.

"Those corridors go down for miles," Ramsey snorted.

"I always thought they were meant as safeguards, to trap and kill any females who tried to escape the chamber," Santos added, standing up, his crystal blue eyes turning cloudy.

Julien shrugged. "But what if they're not just straight, vertical corridors? What if they connect to—or lead to—somewhere else?" He picked up the pencil and began to trace a line across the map connecting the Red Canyons to the area Marquis had circled. "What if they lead to an underground passage?"

Napolean's canines began to lengthen, and the males instinctively moved away from their fearsome leader, whose legendary power was enough to incinerate any of them right where they stood simply if he lost his temper and glared at them.

No one spoke a word for the next five minutes.

Finally, Julien continued: "To go from there"—he pointed to the Red Canyons—"all the way to here"—he pointed to the area circled by Marquis—"would require a virtual *colony* of tunnels."

Nathaniel inhaled sharply.

"*Holy. Shit.*" Santos sat back down.

"Their lairs are right beneath us?" Ramsey asked, indignant. "How could they hide such a thing?"

Nachari frowned. "With enough diamond and crystal built

into the walls—enough steel to enforce the chambers—they could completely block their energy. And that far underground? They could mask their presence from any of us."

Napolean slammed his fist into the table, and all the males, save Marquis, literally leapt backward, exiting the room. "And our valley has more than enough of those resources." He looked around the empty table and grumbled, "I'm fine." He sighed. "Get back in here."

Ramsey approached slowly and cleared his throat. "You okay, milord?"

Napolean frowned.

"Whatever gems we don't have, they could manufacture," Santos added.

Napolean pushed the map away and nodded. "And if they've been using diamonds to mask their presence, then we really have a problem."

Ramsey nodded. "We can't materialize down there."

"If we really are going into an underground...colony"—he practically choked over the words, his eyes cloudy with skepticism—"we'll have to go in through the tunnels, and only the gods know what we might be walking into. They'll have security. Surveillance. And there could be—"

"Hundreds of them?" Nathaniel spoke the common fear aloud.

"Perhaps thousands," Julien added, causing the entire room to blanch. "Think about it: Do you know how easy it would be for them to reproduce if they've been existing right under our noses, unchecked, for gods know how long?"

"Damn." Nachari shifted uncomfortably in his seat. "Do we need a larger army?"

Napolean frowned. "Absolutely not. The larger the team, the more likely we are to be detected, to have to engage the enemy. We don't want an underground war, not in their territory or on their terms. They would pick us off like flies. No, this is reconnaissance only: Get in undetected; get to the princess; and get her out. And then, we can regroup, start thinking of ways to deal with this new threat. If, indeed, there is one."

Marquis snarled. "We're not going to get her away from Salvatore without a fight."

"Of course not," Napolean agreed. "We'll have to make a few kills, but, warriors, we do not want to start a battle, understood?" He steadied his gaze at Marquis and then glanced at his watch. "It's about ten-thirty now. It'll be at least noon before we reach the target area, now that we know we're going in on foot—"

"Blind," Ramsey reminded him.

"One way or the other, we have to be out of there by sunset," Napolean continued. "As it stands, we have the advantage: The vast majority of our dark brothers will be sleeping, and they cannot follow us out of the tunnels into the sunlight. But should the sun go down…"

Nachari rested his chin on his folded hands. "Then we're all dead…and the princess is lost."

Napolean nodded, and the room became silent, each male processing the new information.

Holy Pegasus, Marquis, Nathaniel said angrily. *I'm not so sure I want Nachari going on this mission, after all.*

Kagen chimed in from the other room, where he waited with the females; clearly, he had been listening to the entire discussion: *Let me trade places with our youngest brother.*

Nachari spun around and glared at Nathaniel. *There's no way in hell I'm staying here now! And Kagen, if you're going to listen to everything, then why not just join us in the room?*

Kagen materialized at Nachari's side with a smirk on his face, and Marquis held up his hand to silence them both. *Nachari is right; we need him. We're walking into a den of Dark Ones, countless unknown traps, and a host of black magic. The first two threats we can combat; the last one…we need a wizard.*

Napolean has powerful magic, Kagen insisted.

If the Dark Ones are living right beneath us and discover that our

Tessa Dawn

sentinels are in their territory—leaving Dark Moon Vale unprotected—then our females will be in more jeopardy than ever before, Kagen. We need a seasoned fighter with the women! Marquis was losing his patience. *We have already lost one princess; I don't want to have to go after another.*

Nathaniel sighed then. *Kagen, there is no one else I would leave Jocelyn and Storm with, especially knowing what we now know. Please, brother...*

Marquis waved his hand to indicate that the discussion was over. His words were his brother's law, and that was that.

Napolean turned to the sentinels, his countenance lacking his usual patience. "Let's get working on a strategy." He glanced at the window. "Because as it stands, brothers, we're burning daylight."

fifteen

The males surveyed the oddly-shaped underground cavity in silence. Having entered the mountain beneath a thin, arched doorway at the back of the Red Canyon cliffs, just beyond a waterfall, they had followed the familiar limestone tunnels to their destination: the ruined sacrificial chamber of the Dark Ones.

Marquis watched as Nachari moved about the cavern, gathering and reading energy. When his little brother's eyes scanned the ancient limestone birth-slab, he knew exactly what he was thinking of: Shelby and Dalia. The last place his twin's *destiny* had lain before her brutal death. To his credit, he betrayed no emotion. His deep jade eyes simply regarded all of the damage to the gigantic chamber with cool objectivity.

While several of the white limestone columns still stood like statues, randomly erected about the chamber, the ceiling of the cave had collapsed in on itself, scattering jagged pieces of stalactites about in hazardous piles of debris. The smell of blood still mixed with the musty scent of sulfur in the stagnant pond at the back of the cave, and two of the three, low-lying ledges that led to the steep cliffs remained intact.

Napolean gathered the males at the rim of the eastern-most ledge. "Marquis, Julien, Ramsey, and Nachari: I want you to split up into one team and take the eastern tunnel. You are to proceed in the order I have called you, and as the senior warrior of the team, Marquis will be in command." He glanced at the remaining vampires. "Myself, Nathaniel, Santos, and Saxson will descend the western cliff and proceed parallel to the first team." It went without saying that Napolean would lead the western charge. "From this point on, maintain cloaked appearances and speak only with telepathy."

The males nodded in unison. *So be it.*

With that, Napolean and the second team dematerialized.

Marquis waved his warriors close, carefully eyeing the males on his team. They were each dressed in black fire-retardant leather with diamond-inset collars around their necks, wrists, and ankles to help maintain their invisibility as they approached the Dark Ones. While vampires could easily cloak their personas from humans, other *Nosferatu*—especially those who were ancient—could easily pick up on subtle shifts in the energy field around them, or measure slight variations of temperature in a cold room to detect the presence of a warm body. The diamond collars would block infrared detection and provide a secondary barrier from energetic projection.

Julien shifted his taut, muscular frame, twitching in anticipation as he fingered the edge of his M4-carbine and deftly slid the handle of a time-worn battle ax into the palm of his hand. The others followed suit, adjusting sickles, spiked bolas, nine millimeters, and one AK-47, along with numerous hidden daggers for hand-to-hand combat. While guns were virtually useless when used by humans against vampires—the species was simply too fast to hit—all bets were off when they fought each other: Bullets had their use as a tactical decoy, and fired in rapid enough succession, they could stun an enemy long enough for another vampire to step in and take the head or heart.

Marquis balled his right hand into a fist, testing the perfect fit of his ancient cestus, the gladiator version of brass knuckles, which employed sharp iron spikes as opposed to hard brass for impact. The leather was dyed a dark inky brown, from all of the blood that had seeped into it over the years, and the fit had become like a second hand. His steel-toed boots had matching spikes along the toe and heel, and there was hardly a square inch of his body that didn't conceal an easily accessible stiletto or throwing star.

When Ramsey pulled out a three-pronged, barbed trident, Marquis blanched and stepped back. *What the hell, Ramsey!*

Ramsey smiled and shrugged, his golden eyes lighting with mischief. The weapon was too large and cumbersome for Marquis's taste, but Ramsey could wield the thing like a switchblade, and one good stab from a trident could tear an enemy's torso in half, extracting the vital organs in one blow. The sentinel was known for his ruthlessness and strength.

Do you have something special, too? Marquis asked sarcastically, eyeing Nachari.

Nachari opened his long, flowing trench coat to reveal a simple medieval scabbard sheathing a perilously-sharpened sword, always good for beheading. Not to mention, Nachari had taken a special interest in fencing while at the Romanian University. That and a curved sickle, which he deftly maneuvered like an extension of his own hand, were typically his weapons of choice.

Marquis rolled his eyes. *Wizards!*

The other males chuckled, releasing some nervous energy as they stepped off the ledge and began floating downward, a slow descent into the pitch-black precipice. While their eyes adjusted instantly to the darkness, the going was slow because they had no idea what they were heading into. The smell of sulfur and wet earth grew stronger as they went deeper, and the air grew colder as they passed several clusters of bats and other strange troglophiles.

Nachari winced as he flicked a strange insect off his jacket only to come face to face with an albino-looking reptile with no eyes. *What the hell—*

Welcome to subterranean life, Julien teased.

As they passed the one-mile mark in depth, Julien's light-hearted countenance became all at once serious. *This isn't natural,* he commented to no one in particular.

Marquis slowed to a halt and ran his hands against the shaft wall. *Julien, come feel this.*

The tracker shook his head in disgust as he ran his hand against the smooth, precise surface. *Man-made.*

Vampyr-made to be precise, Ramsey countered. *Those sons-of-hyenas built this place. It must have taken—*

Centuries, Julien supplied.

Tessa Dawn

Nachari held up his hand. *Yes, they did, and the deeper we go, the more I'm beginning to feel the influence of magic in the architecture.*

Meaning what? Marquis asked.

Meaning there are energetic booby-traps in the cave walls.

Napolean's psychic voice joined the conversation from the western shaft. *There are kinetic trip-wires, if you will, all around us. In other words, don't touch anything as we descend further.*

Marquis nodded. *Understood.* He gave his little brother a separate nod of approval.

The next two miles went painstakingly slow as the shaft occasionally narrowed into a tube so small only one male could fit at a time. As they slowly passed mile number three, they began to hear a distant clip-clop, clip-clop coming from several different directions.

Footsteps? Julien asked.

Marquis nodded and held up his hand to still the warriors. *Napolean, what do you see over there?*

We're approaching an entrance. It looks like an arched doorway, leading off into a westerly direction.

Marquis looked off to the east and noticed the same thing— a horizontal corridor leading into the mountain.

Sentinels at two-o'clock! Napolean's harsh voice snapped them all to attention.

I've got them in my sights, Nathaniel assured his Sovereign from the westerly tunnel, no doubt referring to the sight on his favorite semi-automatic weapon, a polished, nine-millimeter Beretta.

Good, Napolean said. *Fire only at my command.* He turned his attention back to the males in the eastern tunnel. *Marquis, these entry points will lead us in opposite directions. Where do you sense the princess?*

Marquis stilled his mind and began to concentrate, using his finely-honed senses. He followed the essence of Ciopori's life as it ran through his own veins. The pulse grew steadily stronger and stronger, like a radio wave, a central beacon leading into the

173

mountain. *She's definitely east,* he said.

Napolean sighed. *Very well. We are going to take out these guards, enter from the western vantage, and as soon as possible, try to make our way over to your team. Keep going. We'll catch up to you as soon as we can.*

Very well. Marquis waved his warriors forward. *Stay in tight formation.*

Julien palmed his battle ax as they made their way into the vertical shaft. And then all at once, the warriors heard distinct voices:

"With Valentine gone, both Demitri Zeclos and Milano Marandici are battling for his seat on the council," a deep male voice echoed from inside the corridor.

"Yeah, so I hear," a younger male answered. "If you ask me, Valentine never belonged on the council to begin with. He was only there because of his brother."

"Salvatore."

"Exactly." The younger male laughed. "Don't get me wrong, Valentine was definitely twisted enough to do the whole political office gig, but he was straight-up incapable of leading, know what I'm sayin'?"

The older male cleared his throat, hawked, and spat. "Didn't have the patience for it."

The second male snarled, "Who the hell would? I sure wouldn't want to spend all my nights locked up in some freaky council room with a bunch of pissed-off ancients. Good way to lose your head, if you ask me."

Sneaking up behind the younger male, Marquis swung one arm around the vampire's chest and held his head steady, using the other arm as a vise. He swiftly slit his throat from ear to ear. "And this is also an excellent way," he whispered.

The older male lunged at Marquis, his jagged canines exploding from his mouth, but not before Ramsey caught him dead-center with the trident—plunging, twisting, and retracting in one smooth motion. The male's innards fell to the floor as the top half of his body severed from the bottom.

Tessa Dawn

Bleed them out, Marquis commanded, knowing full well that both males were still alive and could still regenerate with a powerful injection of vampire venom. Who knew how many of their brothers were just around the corner.

Nachari slit both wrists of the older male vertically before turning his attention to the popliteal artery next. With cool precision, he sliced a lethal gash in both of the vampire's thighs. Just as quickly, Julien crouched down and sliced the jugular of the male Ramsey had taken down.

Marquis probed the Dark Ones' minds, searching for information about Ciopori. Gossip, innuendo; that was all he could find, a quickly spreading rumor that Salvatore Nistor had captured one of the original females and was keeping her in his private lair. Marquis withdrew enormous blocks of information from each male's mind, one at a time; then he swiftly sorted through the knowledge in order to acquire a firsthand blue-print of the colony. He needed a mental map of the halls leading to Salvatore's private chamber.

Good gods, he exclaimed as the information unraveled. *There is an entire ...organized... civilization down here!*

The colony was built in a huge three-story circle, the east quadrants flowing under Dark Moon Vale, the centers existing directly beneath the Red Canyons, the remaining quadrants extending to the west—where the sons of Jadon had believed, all of this time, that the Dark Ones kept their lairs: haphazardly carved out of caves or empty mine shafts.

Not hardly.

In the center of the circle, on the middle level—the level which they were now on—there was a series of four intersecting chambers, all four linked like Olympic rings: the council hall, a *snake pit*, a breeding and birthing room, and a torture chamber that also served as a courthouse. *What the hell? Did these bastards follow some rule of law amongst themselves?* Marquis found it hard to fathom as the Dark Ones didn't possess a soul or a conscience, but apparently, they possessed a powerful need for organization.

175

He continued to study the colony.

There were hundreds of halls leading out from the center four chambers like the spokes of a wheel, each spoke ultimately leading to a private lair before breaking off into a suite of ten rooms, five on each side, as they went along. Families lived in "spoked" clusters, in *thousands* of lairs.

Linked to Marquis's mind, Ramsey, Julien, and Nachari gasped: One-hundred halls bearing five rooms along either side, with one large lair at the end, meant there were at least eleven-hundred lairs on the main floor of the colony. Surely, they couldn't all be filled.

Holy hell! Ramsey exclaimed.

Marquis let out a deep breath and tried to concentrate. No, they weren't all lairs. Two of the ten rooms in each hall—or along each spoke—were set aside for other purposes. Some were used for storage. Others were wood shops, weapons caches, or *nurseries*. You name it, they had it. Marquis recoiled at the sight of human slave quarters, both sex-slaves and blood-slaves. As he looked closer, he saw that, under special circumstances, they even restrained and punished each other in ritualistic stations.

He cleared his mind and studied the second level. There were no lairs up there, but the evil ones had built a congregational hall, several teaching and sports facilities, sparring quarters, a library, and several laboratories for the practice of black magic.

He had never felt so foolish in all of his life.

Why had they just assumed that the descendants of Jaegar were less intelligent, less driven—*less sophisticated*—than the descendants of Jadon? Just because they were evil?

He dipped down to the lower levels. The nerve center of the colony was held below: surveillances centers, security equipment, generators, electrical grids, and anything else needed to keep the colony functioning smoothly. With a newfound respect, he analyzed the flow of the entire structure, calculating what they would have to do to move around undetected.

He noted that the inner, outer, and center cross-sections of the wheel were dissected by circular hallways, passages that wound around the entire circumference of the colony. And there were exit-entrance points on all three levels at the outer and inner four-directions. As they had entered from the south—on the main level at the inner-most cross-section of the wheel—they would find Salvatore's lair at the far end of a hall just to the east, along the farthest, outer cross-section.

Marquis nodded, satisfied, and then he gave the command to finish the guards. Ramsey stepped forward, grasped the older male by a fistful of his black-and-crimson hair, and proceeded to slowly slice off his head with a serrated dagger.

Nachari stepped back to avoid the spurting blood and held out his sickle, frowning. *One swipe, my friend. Is all that really necessary?*

Ramsey cocked his head to the side and shrugged, waving off the sickle. He stood up, now holding the dislodged head in his hand.

We need to incinerate that, Julien pointed out to Marquis, *or he could still come back...albeit, only with some serious assistance.*

Very *serious assistance,* Nachari added.

Marquis shook his head. *We can't risk making fire or drawing the amount of energy needed to incinerate it with electricity.* He started to look around for an alternative, but he was brought up short by a splintering crack, the Dark One's head exploding against the limestone wall. Ramsey drew the head back a second time and flung it twice as hard, splintering what little remained into a thousand pieces of cranial...slop.

If they can put that back together, the ruthless vampire spat, *the male deserves to live.* He brushed a piece of bloody cartilage off his shoulder and snorted.

Nachari looked down at his filthy, slop-spattered cloak. *Thanks, Ramsey.*

The sentinel proceeded to dispatch and destroy the head of the second guard in the same manner, as well as removing both

BLOOD AWAKENING

hearts from their chests, before they continued on. *That's about as good as I can do without risking detection*, he said, frowning. No doubt, he would have preferred to leave nothing but a pile of ash in his wake.

What about the bodies...the remains? Julien asked. *We've got quite a ways to go; I would hate to get caught this early.*

Marquis nodded and gestured toward a door just inside an intersecting hall. *Put them in there.*

Julien and Ramsey nodded, each hefting a corpse as if it weighed no more than a sack of potatoes, Ramsey carrying the younger male's corpse in two pieces while Nachari carefully placed his hands on the hilt of his sword and stood just outside the door. Marquis took Julien's M4-carbine from the inside of the sentinel's jacket and pointed it toward the door, giving Nachari a brisk nod.

With his sword drawn and in hand, Nachari kicked open the door. As it swung fully open, he and Marquis flew inside first, their eyes quickly sweeping the room for enemies.

Holy mother of Lyra.

Marquis barely managed to pull back on his trigger finger—to keep from lighting up the chamber—as his eyes took inventory of the room. Julien and Ramsey snarled as they dropped the headless, heartless bodies in a heap on the floor.

Their collective mouths fell open.

They were standing in the middle of a nursery, surrounded by at least fifty-cribs, each one filled with a living infant: an infant with crimson-and-black banded hair.

A human female was standing in the center of the cribs, shaking like a leaf. She appeared to be only hours away from death's door. Along the far side of the room was another female—younger, healthier—but she was manacled to the wall with thick, heavy chains attached to her feet and arms.

Marquis motioned for Ramsey to shut the door behind them while he checked for security cameras. Although the warriors were still technically invisible, the sight of a door suddenly splintering open—followed by a couple of mutilated bodies magically appearing, then piling on the floor—wasn't exactly business as usual.

Marquis noticed one eye-cam in each corner and quickly sent a blast of blue electricity into all four devices, short-circuiting the wires, hopefully, before anyone had a chance to see them.

What do you want us to do? Nachari asked.

Marquis frowned. He had come for Ciopori, and he wasn't leaving without her. These humans were an unwanted *complication.* He sighed. *Check the females.*

As Nachari approached the sickly woman standing in the middle of the room, she began to shake so badly she threw up. Her feet were stationary, frozen to the floor in terror, and she was gazing, stupefied, at the pile of dead vampire parts the warriors had dragged in from the hall. Undoubtedly, her spirit could sense the presence of the living males around her, but her eyes saw nothing. Nachari waved his hand, paralyzing the vocal cords of both females to keep them from crying out, and then he slowly shimmered into view, projecting his appearance to the terrified woman.

She staggered back, releasing a silent cry.

"Are you okay?" Nachari whispered as she once again spilled her guts onto the floor. He released her vocal cords so she could answer.

Well now, that was a stupid question, Marquis quipped, quickly growing impatient with his little brother's empathy.

The female shook her head furiously, and Nachari held up both hands. He put his fingers over his mouth as he stepped closer. "Shhh. I'm not going to hurt you."

She shook her head even more vigorously and began to cry. Frustrated, she finally opened her mouth.

Nachari grimaced. *Marquis, they've cut out her tongue.*

Marquis shut his eyes. This wasn't good. This woman was too far gone to save without Kagen's help, and too sickly to bring with them.

BLOOD AWAKENING

Blanching, the female placed her hand over her womb and glared at Nachari.

"You're pregnant?" he asked.

Marquis held his breath, knowing exactly what that would mean, remembering Dalia and Joelle...

The woman shook her head. *Look.*

She was trying to communicate telepathically.

Marquis leaned forward. Nachari stepped back.

You can read my thoughts, right? The woman's psychic voice was quivering but clear.

Marquis watched as Nachari nodded in the affirmative, all of the males listening intently.

Weeping, the woman repeated, *Look inside of me.*

While vampires did possess extraordinary talents, x-ray vision wasn't one of them. However, they could scan a body for health or disease, much like an ultra-sound used sonar waves to create images. In addition, all of the males possessed the innate ability to read the exact phases of a female's reproductive cycle.

Marquis nodded his consent, and Nachari began to scan the woman's womb, projecting the information to the other warriors as he examined her internal structure.

He stopped suddenly and dropped his head, out of propriety or pity, Marquis wasn't sure: The human's insides were a virtual wasteland, littered with maggots, cancer, and worms. In fact, the only reason she was still alive was because the Dark Ones were using repeated injections of venom to keep her that way—no doubt, a desperately cruel attempt to keep themselves from raping her. If her womb was ruined, it could hardly be used to create life, which meant the female could take care of the babies a little longer.

The human slowly nodded as if she understood what the males were thinking. *Kill me,* she pleaded, forcing herself to take a step toward Nachari. *Please, don't leave me here like this...with them.*

Nachari looked over his shoulder to measure Marquis's eyes.

Marquis slowly exhaled, then nodded. *Do it.*

The female was beyond human medicine, and the amount of venom she would require to repair her rotting organs was too great a risk: They would have to turn her Vampyr, which meant she would have to willingly relinquish her soul. No one but one's *destiny* could safely be converted without jeopardizing their eternal being.

Nachari turned back to face her and slowly inclined his head. He mouthed the word, *Yes.*

Despite her resolve, her courage faltered, and her body began to sway.

"It won't hurt," Nachari whispered, reaching out to steady her by her elbow.

Wait. She held up her hand. *Maryann.*

"Who?" Nachari asked.

She pointed to the young female shackled to the wall at the back of the room. *They just brought her in last night. She hasn't been raped or...ruined yet. Take her with you, please. Or kill her, too.*

Marquis snarled, but he gestured toward Ramsey, who immediately went to work on the girl's chains as Nachari stepped up to the dying female. "I'm sorry," he whispered.

She nodded, trying desperately to stop her trembling. *The Lord is my shepherd, I shall not want...*

Nachari winced as he pulled her to him. His six-foot, two-inch frame towered above her. He cupped her face in his hands with exquisite gentleness.

He maketh me to lie down in green pastures; he leadeth me beside the still waters... She was almost in a full-fledged panic now.

Those cursed bastards! Marquis knew this was not easy for Nachari, but to his little brother's credit, the wizard showed no visible signs of emotion as he released one of his hands from beneath her chin and placed it on the top of her head.

He restoreth my soul...

Nachari twisted—quick and hard—in opposite directions, instantly snapping the woman's neck, gently lowering her body to the floor.

BLOOD AWAKENING

Marquis pointed to a closet in the back of the room. *Put her in there with the other bodies, and let's go! I had to use a substantial surge of energy to take out the cameras; we have no time to waste. Ramsey, do you have the other female?*

Ramsey turned around and held up the chains, indicating that the female was free. Her eyes were as wide as saucers, and she, too, was frozen in place like a statue, clearly in a state of shock.

Marquis shook his head. *I can't afford to have you carry her, Ramsey. You must be free to fight.* He frowned. *The woman will unnecessarily slow us down, and as for placing her in a trance, Zombies don't travel well.* He snorted. *Leave her.* His decision was pragmatic. *Gag her so she doesn't scream and—*

Wait, Nachari said.

He walked across the room and took her face in his hands, staring deep into her terrified eyes. And then he began to softly chant a rhythmic series of words in Latin. As his eyes dimmed to a subtle shade of green, his voice took on a sultry lilt, like water trickling down a river. All at once, the female stood up straight, flashed a serene smile, and gently took the wizard's hand.

Enchantment spell, he explained. *She's fully alert. She'll follow on her own, and she'll obey willingly.*

Marquis nodded. *Very well.* He paused to survey the room one more time and frowned.

Are you thinking what I'm thinking? Ramsey asked.

I'm thinking I wish like hell we could use fire, Marquis grumbled.

To take out the infants?

Yes.

There's always the old fashioned way...

Do it, Marquis ordered. *Quickly.*

Ramsey turned to the other males. *Snap the necks, remove the heads, and stake the hearts.* He broke off a piece of wood from one of the crib spindles and demonstrated with the infant closest to him.

The warriors nodded and immediately went to work,

destroying the children of their enemies. Although the babies howled and hissed, flailed their arms and legs in protest and desperation, there was no sympathy to play upon. Evil was evil, at any age, and the sons of Jadon were ruthless.

Marquis tucked Julien's M4-carbine away for safe keeping and went to work with the rest of them. *Keep it quiet and make it quick,* he reiterated.

In a sudden blur of movement, the vampires picked up the pace, traveling from crib to crib with preternatural speed. The vulgar pop of snapping spines and splintering wood echoed like drum-beats—a gruesome lullaby—as one by one, the dark sons of Jaegar died at their hands.

In less than two minutes, they had slaughtered the entire room and were standing once again by the door, weapons in hand.

Marquis gestured forward. *Let's move out.* He looked back at the room. *And pray to the gods that our dark brothers don't find this insult before we find Ciopori.*

Ciopori lay perfectly still, not wanting to awaken Salvatore again. She was chained at his side in his large, four-poster bed, her arms shackled above her head, her left ankle shackled to his right, so that she couldn't even adjust her position without rousing the sinister vampire. She had learned that the hard way—almost getting raped the last time she stirred the monster from his sleep.

It had taken a great deal of pleading and reasoning to get the male to back off, but not before he had siphoned at least a pint of her blood from her carotid artery. Ciopori winced as she recalled the pain; it was nothing like the gentle, erotic pleasure she had felt with Marquis....

Dear gods. Marquis.

BLOOD AWAKENING

How would he ever find her?

She fought back the urge to cry. It certainly wouldn't help the situation any.

Looking around the room, she continued to scan for something she could use as a weapon. She continued to brainstorm ways to escape. If she could only get to the hallway, she might be able to call out to the gods for assistance...without setting off that cursed orb Salvatore kept beside the bed. The damnable cube was as evil as he was, sensing her every prayer, glowing bright orange every time she even thought to use her magic. She was completely crippled without the ability to call upon the heavens for assistance.

Salvatore stirred, and Ciopori held her breath, remaining perfectly still. *Oh, please, go back to sleep,* she willed. The cube flashed once. *And you, too!* she snarled in her mind, glaring at the abominable thing. She quickly looked away before it tried to vaporize her or something.

Great Cygnus, why had she chosen to go for a leisurely stroll through a dark forest without taking Nachari or one of Napolean's guards with her? It wasn't like she didn't have experience with danger or understand the need to be careful. For the love of heaven, before Jadon had whisked her and Vanya away from their home in Romania, danger was all she had known.

Ciopori sighed and glanced up at the ceiling. She forced her mind back to the present, contemplating how she was going to escape. A subtle breeze brushed her cheek, and she instinctively turned her head in the direction of the cool air.

Salvatore's lair was air-tight.

There were no windows to welcome the sun, no fresh source of air to break up the damp, musty smell that mixed with the strong scent of incense, constantly burning from the base of a hideous demon statue. Each statue was erected in one of the four directions, an aberration of the original religion.

The liquid blood that ran from each demon's eyes

represented the element of water. The unnatural flames that burnt beneath the stone urns, heating the incense, represented the sacred element of fire. There were ashes—from burned human corpses—scattered about the demons' clawed feet: a deviant tribute to earth. And the unholy breath that coursed like smoke in and out of the demons' mouths, as if the statues were actually breathing, paid homage to the element of wind.

The gentle breeze brushed her cheek again, and she blinked, still trying to identify its origin. There was something different about the element: a kind, if not gentle, spirit creating the phenomenon. Whatever it was, it was a sharp contrast to the energy Salvatore Nistor projected, even in his sleep.

The breeze began to take form.

The fingertips of a strong hand brushed her cheek and then traced her arms upward toward the manacles that kept her bound to the head of the bed. Her breath caught as the outline of two mystical hands began to fill in. She watched them grasp the chains in an unyielding grip, tightening until the thick steel simply crumbled into dust beneath their enormous strength.

Ciopori exhaled her relief as her taut muscles relaxed, and she slowly brought her arms down to her side. And then his face flashed before her—so quickly she wasn't even sure she had seen it with her eyes. She was almost afraid to hope....

Marquis.

She started to reach out to touch him but quickly caught herself. He was slowly peeling back the covers, gently sliding his hands beneath her waist so that he could lift her quickly, removing her from Salvatore's reach before the evil male awakened. *And awaken, he would.*

"*No!*" Ciopori mouthed, praying that Marquis could see her face. "*No, you can't!*"

His hands froze beneath her. He bent to her ear. "Why not?"

His words were barely audible, yet she heard them clearly, his deep, sultry voice breathing life back into her terrified heart.

"My ankle is—"

Marquis pressed his finger to her lips to quiet her. "I can read your mind. Do not speak aloud," he cautioned.

Ciopori nodded. *My ankle is shackled to his.*

She felt the air around her bristle with anger, but he removed his hands from beneath her and slowly peeled back the covers from around her feet.

Still unable to view Marquis's physical form, she watched in fearful anticipation as a sharp twelve-inch dagger appeared in the air, wielded by the warrior's semi-transparent hand, and slowly rose above Salvatore's ankle. In a harsh sweep downward, the blade caught the male's foot and sliced deep through bone and tendon, effortlessly hacking the limb from his leg. Marquis leapt nimbly onto the bed in a crouch, the dagger sliding up his sleeve as he released his claws and plunged at the sorcerer's heart.

Ciopori scrambled out of the way. She leapt to the side of the bed and inadvertently glanced upward. As her eyes focused on the horror above her, a blood-curdling wail filled the room.

Whatever it was that Marquis was fighting, it wasn't Salvatore Nistor.

The dark son of Jaegar hovered beneath the ceiling like a black widow spider, dangling from an evil web. His pointed fangs extended at least seven inches in length, and his body twisted into an angry funnel—about to touch down as a tornado of wrath.

His own claws were extended into hideous talons as his arm shot forward in a mad thrust to puncture his enemy's back...to extract Marquis's heart from behind.

sixteen

The moment Marquis heard Ciopori scream, he instinctively reached into her mind and leapt to the side. The image of Salvatore hovering just beneath the ceiling and reaching out to take his heart had transmitted not only to him but to the other four warriors as well.

What the hell is on the bed? Marquis demanded as he spun around to face his opponent, who was now crouched low in front of him.

Astral travel, Nachari answered. *The body on the bed is Salvatore's, but he removed his soul in order to strike you.*

Marquis took a step back, confused. What the hell was he up against? *Then this is a spirit standing before me?* He sounded incredulous as he and the ancient Dark One began to slowly circle each other, claws retracted into fists. *How can a spirit attack a physical body, and what the hell do I kill? The soul or the body on the bed? Speak quickly, brother!*

Marquis could feel Nachari's energy expanding as the Master Wizard worked furiously to interpret the spell Salvatore was using to position himself in two places at once.

Salvatore laughed then, a harsh, wicked sound reverberating from deep within his chest. "Perhaps you are out of your league, warrior."

Marquis snarled, a full set of fangs flashing in warning. "Not from the likes of you, Salvatore."

I don't know how he did it, Nachari interjected, *but he switched the essence of his soul and his body. The solid form on the bed is actually ethereal, yet his foot has already grown back. The spirit in front of you is solid and can kill you as sure as if it had a body. I'm honestly not sure....*

Marquis would have to accept that.

Salvatore was an ancient, and he had dabbled in black magic his entire incarnation: Who knew what forces he was calling upon to achieve such a feat. *Very well, brother, then we will have to learn as we go. Seal this room now! Do not allow any thought transmissions to go out from Salvatore—spirit or body!*

Nachari hesitated. *Perhaps I should contact Napolean first. Perhaps he has knowledge of Salvatore's spell.*

Marquis shook his head. *We don't have time.*

Very well—as long as you understand that no thought will go out or in. *Napolean and his crew will not be able to locate us or hear what's going on if I do so, brother. Is this still your command?*

Marquis nodded. *If Salvatore calls for reinforcements, we will have the whole damn colony down on our heads, and all the knowledge of magic in the world won't save us. Yes, I'm sure. Seal the lair. Now!*

Marquis immediately felt the energy in the room grow dense, and the presence of his brother became stronger and stronger as the wizard became one with the elements in order to alter the kinetic grid.

Salvatore's head snapped to the side in a sharp, serpentine movement, and he glared at Nachari, who he had obviously detected in spite of the wizard's invisibility. "So, you bring this pitiful excuse for magic into *my lair*, Silivasi?" He spat on the floor, and the spittle began to coagulate, take form, until the body of a snake arose and slithered across the floor toward Nachari.

Nachari shimmered into full view then, no longer having reason to hide.

"Julien!" Marquis motioned toward Ciopori, no longer bothering to speak telepathically. It no longer mattered if the ancient sorcerer knew of the other warriors: He could no longer call for help.

The tracker flew across the room, materializing into view even as his image was blurred by his speed. He grasped the princess by the waist and flew back toward the door of the lair, moving her far away from both Salvatore and the serpentine apparition.

As the snake approached, Nachari held out his hand, palm facing up. It was almost as if he was encouraging it to strike. His dark green eyes transformed into glowing white as he shot twin beams of pure energy into the snake's eyes. All at once, the cobra reared back and struck at the wizard's hand, but before the strike could land, Nachari opened his fist and a large python swallowed the cobra whole. The python retracted back into Nachari's hand. The hand retracted back into a clenched fist, and Salvatore Nistor suddenly grasped at his throat, struggling for air.

Marquis didn't hesitate. He swiped at the dark vampire's jugular, missing the artery by less than an inch as Salvatore leapt away. Still struggling for breath, the vampire flew backward toward the bed and landed in his own body. And then, like mist from the sea, the fully combined figure rose, hovering once again in the air as an orange and red glow surrounded him, and his eyes blazed like fire. He was a fully embodied sorcerer now, drawing infinite power from the universal forces of darkness.

The son of Jaegar drew in a deep breath, filling his once constricted lungs with fresh air. Then he hurled two balls of fire across the room in quick succession: one at Nachari, the other at Marquis.

While the brothers dodged the lethal missiles, the last invisible warrior struck the Dark One from behind. Ramsey Olaru drove a clawed fist through Salvatore's back, penetrating deep into the chest cavity, barely missing the heart. He quickly retracted his arm and prepared to strike again, but Salvatore spun around before the warrior could take action, sending two scorching beams of fire from his blazing eyes into Ramsey's flesh, even as he howled in agony from the gaping chest wound.

The sentinel's flesh began to burn, but he didn't cry out. He launched himself at Salvatore's front just as Marquis launched himself at his back, pinning the wounded Dark One between them like a vise. Marquis quickly spun the sorcerer around, drew back his fist—still coated with the spiked cestus—and blasted the arrogant prick in the jaw, splintering the bone into pieces, sending several teeth flying from his mouth. The sorcerer flew back against the wall, where Ramsey then rushed him with a dagger, his arms still smoldering from the burns Salvatore had inflicted upon him earlier.

"Go to hell, Dark One," Ramsey bit out as he plunged the dagger into Salvatore's chest.

"Not quite yet, Ramsey!" Salvatore snarled.

He dissolved his body into molecular form, causing the dagger to pass right through him, and then he solidified with his hand around the dagger's grip, wrenching it away from Ramsey and counter swiping in one smooth motion.

Ramsey drew deftly away from the blade, taking only a nick to his stomach as Salvatore spun the handle, crouched down into an attack stance, and began to circle the two warriors counterclockwise.

Marquis retrieved his own black-handled, silver-tipped dagger from its scabbard and matched the Dark One's stance. "He's mine!" he growled.

Salvatore's blood-red eyes lit up with a feral glow, and his lips twitched incessantly as his fangs grew longer and longer. "Tell me what happened to my brother, warrior." He swiped at Marquis's arm, but Marquis spun out of the dagger's path before it could strike.

Marquis laughed. "What didn't happen to your brother, Salvatore?"

The vampire snorted viciously. "Tell me!"

"We cut out his eyes, his ears, and his tongue," Marquis taunted. "We skinned him alive and removed his limbs. We wrapped his intestines around his neck—after we sliced off his manhood. And then we set him out for the sun to take him. Oh, but not before we scalped him…just for the fun of it. Would you like to view the memories?"

Salvatore howled, shaking violently from head to toe. Crackling whips of blue lightning danced from his fingers into his blade and shot out the tip.

Marquis matched the feat, his own dagger spitting red fire in response. "Shall we end this today, Salvatore?" he hissed. "Or just continue showing off?"

A slow smile replaced Salvatore's scowl. "No weapons," he whispered. "No magic. No fire. Just you and me, hand to hand. The strongest male wins."

Marquis threw back his head and laughed. "You would fight me vampire-to-vampire, Dark One?"

"Why not!"

Marquis shook his head. "Why not, indeed. It's your funeral."

He tossed his dagger aside, careful to watch for a trap. This would be the perfect time for Salvatore to lunge, but the sorcerer tossed his dagger as well and motioned Marquis forward with his hands.

Marquis shut his eyes for a split second. The primal pleasure of what was about to take place—what the fool was about to do—made him heady. It felt almost erotic. They slowly danced around each other, stepping sideways in perfect harmony, gliding frontward and backward in a lethal tango, until at the same exact moment, both vampires lunged forward, grasping each other in a death lock.

The ground opened up beneath them, and the granite walls crumbled as the two powerful beings smashed around, each taking a turn flipping the other onto his back. Violent blows landed to jaws and ribs. Arms twisted. Claws slashed skin, and puncture wounds bled out. The lair echoed with guttural grunts and snarls like the roars of ravenous lions feasting on a kill as the two ancient males sought to destroy each other.

And then Salvatore made a mistake.

He plunged his clawed fist at Marquis's heart in a desperate attempt to end the brutal battle, leaving his throat exposed. Moving with the same preternatural speed as his enemy, Marquis blocked the fist with his forearm and lunged at the vampire's throat. He locked his canines onto his jugular and wrenched like a rabid animal. As blood began to spurt from the wound, he went after the heart—and not to rip it from the chest with his bare hands but to gnaw his way through it—to extract the organ with his teeth. This male had protected Valentine: the evil rogue who had killed his baby brother. This male had taken Ciopori and subjected her to gods knew what. He had burned Ramsey and sent a mystical snake after Nachari. And even if all of that were not true, Marquis was just generally ticked off. He would gorge on this demon's heart as the evil one lay dying.

"Marquis, no!" Ciopori cried from across the room, her voice heavy with revulsion. "His heart is evil. Do not consume it!"

Marquis raised his head and turned in the direction of her voice, but he was too far gone to process the princess's words. He was too immersed in blood-lust to stop. He sensed nothing but the powerful taste and feel of the organ pumping blood through the Dark One's body: a vampire's champagne. Snarling, he dipped his head back down and began to tear away the layers of flesh.

And then the door to the lair exploded from the hinges, thick pieces of wood scattering everywhere like haphazard missiles.

Zarek Nistor, along with three other enormous males, flew into the room with glowing red eyes, spittle spraying from their twisted mouths, fangs gnashing back and forth in unbridled fury. The three soldiers let out a primal war cry and attacked, each one leaping at one of the sons of Jadon, claws swiping as they connected.

As Nachari, Julien, and Ramsey tussled with their dark brothers, Marquis let go of Salvatore and went for Zarek. Ciopori was no longer guarded, and he knew the Dark One could take her life in a matter of seconds if he chose to.

Sure enough, Zarek went straight for the princess.

He grabbed her from behind, placed one arm around her waist, and seized her throat with his free hand, razor-sharp claws pressed tightly against her jugular like a knife. He was ready to slice her throat at the smallest provocation.

"Back off!" Zarek commanded, turning to face the room. "Back off, or I'll slit her throat and rip out her heart before you can call her name." He glared at Nachari. "You might be able to block transmissions, wizard, but did it ever occur to you that I would wonder what was up when my brother refused to answer my psychic calls?"

Marquis stood up and tried to catch his breath. He had to calm down.

And fast.

Every muscle in his body twitched, aching to attack. He knew he could move five times faster than the young son of Jaegar, just as he knew he could take Zarek's head in the blink of an eye—but Ciopori might not make it.

He spit out a piece of Salvatore's flesh and snarled, "Let her go, Zarek, and your death will be quick and painless. Hurt her, and you will suffer far worse than your brother Valentine suffered."

Zarek's eyes registered his surprise before returning to a solid, smoldering red, and Marquis saw it clearly then: The stupid son of Jaegar still held out hope that Valentine was alive. He shook his head in disbelief. Just how arrogant were these demons to think that such crimes would go unpunished by the sons of Jadon—their superior *cousins*, as it were. "Did you really think that Valentine could take my brother's wife and live?"

Zarek hissed and drew a sharp line in Ciopori's throat, careful not to cut her artery just yet. He bent down and licked the blood, his free hand tracing the contours of her waist before groping her breast. "Did you really think you could waltz into my brother's lair, take his bride, and still walk away with your life?"

"*Bride?*" Marquis growled low in his throat, his enormous muscles bulging and contracting with such fury that Zarek instinctively removed his hand from Ciopori's breast and took a step back, still holding the princess firmly against him. He glanced across the room. "Tell your boys to stand down."

BLOOD AWAKENING

"Boys?" Marquis hissed.

Zarek scraped a fang against the princess's shoulder, drawing both blood and a whimper. "Now!"

Marquis held up his hand, signaling his warriors to back off. The fighting stopped abruptly as all eyes in the chamber remained fixed on their respective leaders.

Nachari, Marquis muttered, using their private family bandwidth just to be absolutely certain no Dark One could hear. *Can you do what Salvatore did on the bed? Separate your body and your soul into two different places so that it appears as if you're still standing where you are?*

Nachari sounded uncertain. *I don't know, brother. I was able to unravel the spell he used, so I might be able to duplicate it, but even my training does not approach such power. Can you buy me some time?*

Marquis grunted and turned to Zarek. "Salvatore is dying." He gestured toward the bloodied, broken vampire on the floor. "He is too badly wounded to use his venom to regenerate."

Zarek snorted and assessed his older brother. "Don't play games with me, vampire. His heart and head are still intact. We can bring him back no matter how much blood he loses."

Marquis smiled a wicked grin. "Perhaps, but you cannot take the princess's life and save your brother faster than I can kill either him...*or you.*" He looked at the other Dark Ones, each soldier glaring at him from behind a set of soulless eyes. "Not even with your warriors."

Julien, Ramsey, and Nachari remained as ready as ever.

Although they may have momentarily stood down, the heat in their eyes told him everything he needed to know: They were not only ready to react at the drop of a dime, but each male had already planned an offensive against their dark counterpart.

Zarek's arm tightened around Ciopori's waist, but he didn't speak. He was obviously considering his options.

"Just how did you think this scenario was going to play out, Zarek?" Marquis pressed, refusing to give him a moment to regain his bearing. "Think about it: Whose life are you willing to relinquish today? Yours? Or Salvatore's? Because there is simply no way you both walk out of here alive."

Zarek exhaled a long, slow hiss, sounding more like a snake than a man. He nodded at one of the dark soldiers. "Go to Salvatore and give him your venom."

The male hesitated, looking a little annoyed, like it either wasn't his job or he didn't care that much about the dying vampire. "He's *your brother*. Why don't—"

"Do not forget that he sits on the council!" Zarek snarled. "You would be wise to extend your service now...while you can."

Marquis watched as the two males eyed each other with a bit of disdain. *Interesting.* The discord was certainly worth keeping in mind, but then again, it was to be expected. The Dark Ones were without souls or conscience; ultimately, their loyalty to each other was tied to family—blood—and an obvious adherence to hierarchy in order to survive as a group. As these males were clearly not family, hierarchy was Zarek's only leverage.

And apparently it worked.

The male soldier reluctantly turned away from the visual stand-off and went to Salvatore's side. Marquis adjusted his own body, careful to keep the soldier in front of him at all times, seething as he watched the male release his incisors and inject Salvatore's wounds, one by one, with healing venom. The ancient sorcerer would regenerate quickly.

I've got it! Nachari exclaimed, careful to keep his gaze focused ahead. *I cannot create two entities that are both solid enough to interact with matter, but I can leave the illusion of one body in one place, while using astral travel to go to another.*

Marquis considered his brother's words. *Yes, but can you leave the ethereal body where you stand and take the corporeal body across the room?*

Nachari sighed. *That would be difficult. Why? Do you want me to try and take Zarek down while he still holds Ciopori? If that's the case, wouldn't it be easier to just dematerialize?*

BLOOD AWAKENING

Marquis grunted. *No, that's far too risky. Our dark brothers are as fast as we are. I was thinking about the crib.*

Nachari scanned the room with his energy rather than his eyes, careful not to alert his enemy. *Oh...wow.*

Marquis nodded, faintly. There was a raised temperature in the crib, which meant there was an infant sleeping inside.

Nachari bristled. He bit his bottom lip so hard he drew blood, and his expression turned to stone.

Yes, Marquis thought, *Nachari gets it now.* The infant sleeping in the crib was the child sired by Valentine—with their brother's wife, the child Valentine had raped Dalia, and ultimately killed Shelby, to father.

Nachari's psychic voice betrayed his barely-restrained fury. *I can maintain my image here for about two or three seconds after I dematerialize. By then, I will already have the infant in my arms.*

Marquis looked over at Salvatore, who was already struggling to his feet. *Do it!*

Just as Nachari promised, he maintained a solid image beside his dark counterpart as his body dematerialized across the room. Before anyone could register his ruse, he reached into the crib, seized the baby, and locked his jaw around the infant's neck, his four-hundred years of discipline the only thing keeping him from destroying the evil spawn right then and there.

The child squealed, and both Zarek and Salvatore spun around to face the crib. "Stop!" they cried in unison, the ancient sorcerer's sudden vulnerability exposed in his faltering voice: "Nachari, stop!"

"Move and my brother will rip that little demon's head off," Marquis snarled.

Nachari hissed, fangs trembling, as he clearly fought the

196

impulse to slay the child, holding it instead like a mother cat transporting a kitten.

Now standing fully upright, Salvatore held up his hands in a plea for caution. "Do not be impulsive, wizard. We may all leave this situation with what we desire, yet."

Good. Marquis shifted his weight. The child meant as much as he believed he would. Marquis spun around in one fluid motion, struggling to restrain his own rage as his smoldering eyes met Salvatore's once again. "Perhaps we make a trade then? The princess for the demon?"

"You touch him, and I will rip her heart out!" Zarek roared, unable to keep his cool. "Or worse!" He ripped at the thin material that was covering the princess from the waist down and unbuttoned the fly of his jeans with one hard tug. "How fast do you think I can enter her and release?" He laughed and glared at Marquis. "Will you be the one to put her down, warrior, when she's pregnant?"

Marquis understood the threat for what it was: severe.

The sons of Jaegar were not given the *four mercies* allotted the sons of Jadon when the Blood Curse had been handed down so many centuries ago. The Dark Ones did not have *destinies.* They could not love or father children with eternal mates. And the women they did impregnate died a horrendous death in the process of giving birth. Pregnancy was a torturous death sentence.

Provoked by Zarek's threat, Nachari grasped the baby's ankle and twisted, leaving a broken foot hanging off the leg by a tendon. The child shrieked an ear-piercing howl that echoed throughout the room.

Zarek threw back his head and roared. He bit down hard against Ciopori's shoulder, and the princess cried out in turn.

Nachari crushed the baby's leg and snarled in response, his teeth bearing down hard against the kid's throat. The situation was quickly escalating out of control, yet Marquis resisted the urge to censure his brother. He knew the standoff was necessary.

Zarek had to understand: If he raped the princess, the child was as good as dead.

Nachari pushed the envelope a step further by biting down on the infant's neck until he drew blood.

"Derrian!" Zarek shouted, kicking Ciopori's legs apart with his knee.

Ciopori choked on her outrage. She was fighting to hold back tears.

"Enough!" Salvatore thundered, glaring at his little brother. "Button your pants!" He snapped his head to the side and glared at Nachari. "Relax on the baby's neck, my friend. My brother is temperamental. Let's not get hasty."

Nachari relaxed his jaw but continued to glare at Zarek, the threat crystal-clear in his eyes.

Marquis looked at Salvatore then and an understanding passed between them.

Salvatore was not willing to trade Derrian's life, not even for Ciopori. And Marquis would not risk the life of the princess he loved for a vengeance that could always come tomorrow.

"Can you control your males?" Marquis growled, needing to know what he was dealing with.

Salvatore sneered. "Of course. Can you?"

Marquis refused to dignify the question with an answer. Rather, he surveyed the room and rapidly weighed potential tactics: As it was, Zarek was positioned toward the door with Ciopori, whereas, the crib was toward the back of the lair to the right of the bed. "Move your males to the back of the room, but keep a safe distance from Nachari. I want their backs against the wall," Marquis snorted. "And in return, I will move mine toward the door, but a safe distance away from Zarek."

Salvatore surveyed the room, his eyes missing nothing. After a short pause, he nodded. "Do it."

The three dark males slinked noiselessly to the back of the lair like a pride of angry lions, their tense muscles twitching in grudging retreat.

"Ramsey! Julien!" Marquis ordered.

The tracker and the sentinel took perches by the busted door, their hands still fingering their weapons.

Salvatore smiled then, a thinly veiled smirk of contempt. "Now, how shall we exchange our...loved ones?"

Marquis took a calming breath. He knew the moment they left the lair with Ciopori, all hell was going to break loose in the colony, so they not only had to make a clean exchange, but buy some time as well. As a warrior, there was nothing he wanted more than to go to his death slaughtering as many Dark Ones as he could, but that wasn't his objective.

Ciopori's safety was.

Salvatore shrugged his shoulders. "Surely you do not expect me to trust this wizard"—he gestured toward Nachari—"anymore than I can expect you to trust Zarek."

"No," Marquis grumbled. "Trust is not something the two of us share; however, strategy is another matter. As you must realize, we will require a head start to get Ciopori safely out of the colony. That means we cannot allow any of you to call directly for help—or to pursue us. In addition, we must have some assurance that Zarek will not renege on our agreement and hurt the princess during the exchange—"

"Nor will Nachari hurt my nephew!" Salvatore growled.

Marquis nodded impatiently, trying to contain his contempt. "I will have my warriors exit the lair before we make the exchange. This way, they pose you no threat. They will notify me when they are free of the colony so that I know they made it out safely—"

"There's no way in hell we're leaving you and Nachari in here," Ramsey bit out, indignant.

Marquis waved his hand to silence the male. "You will do as you are ordered *under my command.*" Without pausing to look at the sentinel, he continued speaking to Salvatore: "This should be acceptable as you realize my objective is to get out safely with the princess, not to come back and fight with you and Zarek.

This removes two threats to you and two concerns for me."

Salvatore regarded him warily, and Marquis sighed. He looked at Ciopori and swallowed his pride, wondering if the princess had any idea how much he loved her. Did she have any idea what a sacrifice it was for a warrior to make such concessions? Under any other circumstances, he would have rather died here in the lair—and allowed his men to die as well—before submitting *anything* to the likes of Salvatore Nistor.

"Search my mind, Dark One," Marquis bit out, "and know that I speak the truth."

Salvatore's shock was palpable, and Marquis winced as the evil sorcerer penetrated his psyche and stripped his thoughts.

"Satisfied?"

Salvatore grunted. "You may do the same."

Marquis shook his head. Unbeknownst to the ancient son of Jaegar, he had already pierced his mind to read his intent. Despite all of Salvatore's years of black magic, the fool was still no match for Marquis's cunning...or skill. "No need. You will not let Derrian die." He gestured his confidence with his hands. "I have seen your *affection* for your family."

"Very well, then. What is your plan?"

Marquis studied the Dark One's eyes. The whole scenario was killing him, too. "First, you will have your soldiers slash their wrists and bleed out to the point of weakness before sealing the wounds, so they pose no threat to me and Nachari. With all of our soldiers removed from the equation, you and I will take positions—at the same time—behind Nachari and Zarek, each of us behind our own brother."

Salvatore made a tent with his hands, then linked his fingers, listening intently.

"I will then take the infant from Nachari," Marquis continued, "and you will take Ciopori from Zarek so that the final exchange is left between us: cooler heads."

You? Cooler than me? Nachari mocked. *Dearest virgin goddess, you might be the best warrior here, but emotionally speaking—you are the least stable among us!*

Be quiet, Nachari! Marquis warned, giving him a hard look of reprimand. He returned his gaze to Salvatore. "Then our brothers will step away." His eyes swept over Nachari, gauging the wizard for signs of resistance—the potential for disobedience. He knew how badly Nachari wanted the infant dead, and what an affront submission was to any male in the house of Jadon. "Nachari will leave the colony and notify me when he is back on solid earth, just as Julien and Ramsey did ahead of him. He will pose no threat to you at the time of the exchange, and we will each have one less thing to worry about."

Brother, please don't ask such a thing, Nachari pleaded, all jest and humor gone from his psychic voice.

You know this is the only way, Nachari. I haven't time to barter…consider it my Spoken Word.

Nachari briefly shut his eyes, and Marquis's heart skipped a beat. Was he asking too much of the wizard? As Shelby's twin, would Nachari at last choose to disobey a senior command? *Great Perseus, Victorious Hero,* Marquis prayed, *you are the guardian of my brother's soul. I beseech you: Make him compliant in this command.* He turned his attention back to Salvatore and awaited an answer.

Salvatore frowned. "And with all your warriors and your brother gone, you would leave me and Zarek—alive and well—to pursue you and the princess the moment the exchange is made? Why is it I'm having trouble believing you, warrior?"

Marquis shook his head. "Because you haven't let me finish."

Salvatore bit his bottom lip. "By all means, continue."

Marquis dug deep inside, searching for a calm he wasn't sure he possessed. *Gods, this was a bunch of horse shit.* "Once Nachari is gone, Zarek will slice his carotid artery and bleed out"—he took a deep breath—"*until he flat-lines.*"

"Are you insane, son of Jadon!" Salvatore's curses shook what remained of the chamber walls, and fire shot out from the tips of his fingers as he gestured wildly with his hands.

Marquis held steady. All lives depended on this barter. "How else do I insure our safe exit, Salvatore? Be reasonable. You know as well as I do that Zarek does not have the self-control to abide by our agreement, or to keep from coming after the princess the moment we walk out the door. And once you have your nephew, there will be no reason for either of you to honor our bargain." He held up his hands. "Consider this: You have a two-minute window to bring Zarek back to life once his heart stops beating—all it requires is enough of your venom and a great deal of blood." He raised his eyebrows. "You can hardly pursue us and save Zarek at the same time: I am quite certain that you will choose Zarek. Whereas, we will have two minutes to leave this colony."

Salvatore snarled and began pacing in a tight circle, his breath wafting in and out in hard, angry pants. "And what if you don't make the exchange, huh? Then what, warrior? What if you kill the child, instead, or try to take Zarek's head while he is helpless? I cannot defend them both at the same time. What if you force me to choose between Derrian and Zarek's life?"

Marquis shook his head. "There is still the matter of Ciopori, Dark One. Do you think I would go through all of this just to let her die at your hands in order to double-cross you? If I attack your nephew or your brother, I will lose the princess, and I will have to fight you to the death as well; of that, I am quite certain." He waved his hand around the room. "However, should *you* choose to double-cross *me*—considering where we are—remaining behind without my warriors would be suicide. You are not the only one taking a risk, Salvatore. This is a reasonable solution to a difficult problem. Do not be foolish. We all wish to walk away alive." He sighed. "Again, search my mind if you must, but let's get on with it."

Salvatore waved his arm through the air and growled a low, angry rumble. "Give me your word as a warrior—on the life of your king—you will not delay the exchange. The instant Zarek flat-lines, you will place Derrian safely in his crib and leave with the princess."

Tessa Dawn

"On the life of my king, *I will*."

Salvatore pulled at his own hair, taking a large chunk out in sheer frustration, and then he spun around to square off with Marquis. "Know this, son of Jadon: If you fail to keep your promise, I will not allow you an easy death. You will be captured in this colony and restrained. And you will be forced to watch while every male in the house of Jaegar takes his turn with your princess. You will witness her death, birthing my offspring. Do I make myself clear?"

Marquis bit a literal hole through his tongue, meditated on the pain, and struggled to restrain himself. *Salvatore Nistor was the walking dead.* He had sealed his own coffin with that threat. *Tomorrow,* he reminded himself. *Today, just get the princess out of here.* With a strength he didn't know he had, he growled the word *yes.*

"Very well then," Salvatore spat. "Send your warriors away, and let's do this. My nephew is injured." He turned to face the three blistering Dark Ones. They were leaning against the wall, their harsh faces contorted with disgust. "Slit your wrists, brothers. And don't seal the wounds until I tell you to."

The males eyed one another warily, and then glared at their councilman with stunned fury.

"Do it!" Salvatore barked. "And don't bleed all over my bed."

Incredulous, the closest male removed a dagger from the back of his jeans and sliced his wrist all the way to the bone, glowering at Salvatore as the blood shot forth. The remaining two released their canines and tore the veins open with their teeth.

As they sank down to the floor, arms rested against bent knees, the blood began to pool, and Marquis became deathly quiet: He would not trust Salvatore to make such an important determination. Summoning his extra-sensory hearing, he monitored each soldier's heartbeats as his blood pressure fell.

He then turned to Julien and Ramsey. "Go swiftly, my friends. And transmit to me the moment you are back above

203

ground."

As Julien and Ramsey turned to leave, Marquis addressed them privately, telepathically: *And call Napolean at once. Alert him to our position. Explain what is happening. Tell him to prepare an ambush!*

The sentinel cleared his throat. The tracker nodded almost imperceptibly.

And then they sauntered out of the room.

seventeen

"You know this is not over, this thing between you and me," Salvatore snarled in Ciopori's ear, a deep threat reverberating in his voice. He nodded at Zarek. "Release her and take your place across the room so the wizard can walk out unscathed."

Zarek's eyes were two gleaming balls of hatred as they bore into Salvatore's, his entire body trembling with contempt. "You risk my life for this worthless son of Jadon?"

Salvatore reached out and cuffed him, knocking his head so far to the side that his neck popped before snapping back in place, and then he grasped a fistful of Zarek's black and red hair. "Do not speak to me of the choice I've been forced to make when Valentine has already perished at this warrior's hands. Should you and Derrian fall this day, I would gladly follow you into the Corridor of the Dead: How can you doubt my loyalty?"

Zarek wrenched his hair free and stalked across the room, still seething. "You are not the one about to die on the floor!"

Salvatore's claws bit into Ciopori's waist, and she fought not to cry out. The last thing she needed was Marquis losing his cool and having to fight the entire colony because he went after Salvatore without any back-up.

"See what you've caused," Salvatore hissed.

Ciopori didn't respond. She simply watched Marquis and Nachari exchange the baby—the evil little fiend—and held her breath as Nachari left the lair, slowly walking backward, his eyes never leaving Zarek or Salvatore.

The minutes seemed like hours as they waited quietly for word from Nachari that he had made it out of the colony safely. Dear gods, what if something went wrong? Ciopori quickly pushed the thought from her mind. No. Nothing would go wrong. The plan had to work.

Aware that she was wearing what amounted to no more than the remaining lace of a camisole and panties—thanks to Zarek's obscene display earlier—she shivered, keeping a straight face as the enormous erection behind her jerked repeatedly against her lower back. This was definitely not the thing to bring to Marquis's attention, and vomiting wasn't a much better idea. She swallowed her bile and squared her chin. She could endure the foul being for a little longer. *Mother of Aries,* where was Nachari?

When it seemed like time had literally stood still, and both males had become dangerously antsy, Marquis finally waved his hand at Salvatore. "He is back in the valley."

"Show me," Salvatore spat.

Marquis must have projected a powerful image into the Dark One's mind because Ciopori felt Salvatore tense and then relax behind her as a sudden surge of energy flowed through him. His gaze turned back to Zarek. "You know what must be done, my brother. Do not waste time. Let us get this over with."

Zarek crouched down like a wounded animal, and his eyes shot back and forth between Marquis—whose fangs were scraping softly against the infant's neck in lethal warning—and Salvatore, who now had Ciopori's neck in both of his powerful hands, ready to snap it at a moment's notice.

"Easy, Zarek," Salvatore warned, indicating the baby with a nod. "He is all we have left of our brother."

Marquis visibly bristled, and Ciopori's heart ached for him. He had nothing left of his brother Shelby, and now, he would be forced to release the child, born of Dalia's rape, to the rapist's brother. Her soul wept knowing that he did it for her.

"Zarek," Salvatore repeated, his stare fixed on the anxious vampire. "Just do it."

Zarek took a deep breath. He reached behind his back and drew a long silver stiletto, with crossbones engraved in the pommel. He placed the tip against his carotid artery and hastily slit his own throat, his eyes never leaving his brother's.

As the blood began to spurt out, he staggered backward, bent over, and braced his hands against his knees, remaining in that position until at last he began to choke on his own blood. With one final impassioned plea from his eyes, he toppled over onto the floor and sank into the crimson puddle.

Ciopori glanced back at Salvatore as he became eerily still. His heart raced beneath his massive chest, and his eyes remained glued like two hot coals on the crimson pool of blood expanding beneath his brother's unconscious body. "That is close enough," he snarled at Marquis, pressing a sharp claw against Ciopori's own artery.

Marquis didn't flinch as he shook his head. "*Flat-lined,* Salvatore. *Deceased.* That was our agreement."

Salvatore began to sweat as both warriors waited, listening for the sound of *silence.* The complete absence of a heart-beat.

And then just like that, it happened.

Zarek died.

Salvatore spun to face Marquis, his heart pounding so furiously Ciopori could see the rise and fall of his chest. "Put Derrian in the crib, take your witch, and go!" He was shouting, his voice frantic. "*Now!*"

Marquis did not waste time. "Step away from Ciopori, and I will place Derrian in the crib."

Salvatore looked like a crazed madman as he sidestepped a yard to the right of the princess, finally releasing her neck.

Marquis nodded and placed the baby in the crib. "Go to your brother, and we will take our leave."

Salvatore started to rush to Zarek's side but apparently thought better of it. Turning to face the warrior, he slowly stepped backward, circling in the opposite direction of Marquis as the son of Jadon approached Ciopori.

At last, he was at her side.

Marquis reached out and clutched her to him like she was the last remaining soul on earth. His arms trembled as he cradled her against his chest, his hands sweeping over her body all the while to check for broken bones and injuries. As she allowed herself to go limp in his arms, tears began to stream down her face for the first time. She couldn't believe he was there, holding her…that he had actually come for her.

Marquis nestled his head in the crook of her neck and inhaled deeply. "Oh, my love, I thought I had lost you."

She fisted his thick, silky hair and drew him even closer, afraid to let go.

"What the hell did he do to you?" His hand swept over one of the bite marks on her stomach.

"Nothing, my love." She stroked his cheek. "Nothing I couldn't withstand. I'm fine. Believe me."

Marquis growled deep in his throat, his canines emerging even longer. "It doesn't look like nothing." He steadied his voice. "Did he…did Salvatore—"

"No!" Ciopori insisted, pulling away from him in order to look him in the eyes. She cupped his face in her hands. "Look at me, Marquis!"

His eyes bored into hers.

"*No.*"

Breath he didn't seem to know he was holding released from his body, and he pulled her, again, to his chest. "I swear to you on my honor, I'm going to rip his bowels from his body. He will die for this insult."

Ciopori raised her chin. "Do not lose your focus, warrior. I am counting on you to get me out of here. Understood?"

Marquis closed his eyes momentarily, and then a pair of snarls passed between him and Salvatore as he hastily led Ciopori to the busted door, carrying her over the threshold to prevent her from cutting her feet on the rubble.

Thank the gods, she murmured to herself.

She was finally leaving the lair.

She was just about to lay her head on his chest when she heard a loud, explosive boom, the sound of Marquis punching a hole in the cavern wall, his fist penetrating at least twelve inches deep.

"What is it, warrior?" she asked, taken aback. The limestone exploded, sending bits of stone flying in every direction.

Marquis pointed back to the lair.

Salvatore had retrieved Derrian, draaged Zarek to the bed, and pulled a small brass lever on the headboard, causing a solid diamond enclosure to descend from the ceiling, fully encasing the three of them. It was the vampire equivalent of a *safe room*: a diamond fortress that could not be breached.

"We can't touch him now!" Marquis spat. He cursed in an unrecognizable language.

"We?" Ciopori asked.

Before Marquis could answer, the sovereign lord of the house of Jadon approached from the end of the hall: There were three warriors flanking him, two at his sides, and one at his back. Ciopori instinctively drew into herself, feeling suddenly self-conscious. She was acutely aware of her miniscule clothing.

Marquis shook his head with disgust as he met Napolean's gaze. "Don't bother," he snarled. "Salvatore has managed to place himself and his family inside a diamond cell. We don't have time to deconstruct it."

Napolean's eyes flashed deep amber, but he showed no further emotion. "Very well." He gave a hand signal to his men.

As the males fell into formation, a shrill alarm began to ring overhead; the entire colony filled with a painful, pulsating drone.

Marquis clutched Ciopori by the arm. "Son of a bitch! He already set off the alarms."

Napolean remained calm, motioning the males in front of him. "Move out quickly."

"Milord?" A perilous-looking male, with eyes much like Marquis's, glanced inquisitively at the king. "You wish to take the rear? Forgive me, but your life is far too important. Please, allow me in your—"

"Move out, Nathaniel!" Napolean ordered. "Santos, you take the lead. Marquis, you keep the princess in the middle. Saxson, you get Marquis's back. *I* will take the rear."

There was a moment of uncomfortable silence before the king growled low in his throat. "*I said move out!*"

BLOOD AWAKENING

The warriors sped through the underground tunnels like comets racing through a night sky. They were headed in the direction of the eastern-most elevators, the ones that would take them to the surface, when all of a sudden they heard a loud whooshing drone behind them, like an enormous body of water rushing toward them.

"What is that?" Santos eyed Marquis nervously. "You think they're gonna try to flood us out?"

Marquis frowned and began searching the tunnel for signs of an indoor irrigation system. *Gods, he hoped not.* Vampires could slow down their breathing, even hold their breath for long periods of time if necessary, but Ciopori would drown under such an assault. He carefully assessed the limestone wall, analyzing how long it would take him if he had to barrel through it, using only his body as a rotary to dig their way to the surface.

As the men slowed down, each one evaluating the danger, Napolean shouted from the end of the line. "It's not water! It's an army."

Marquis spun around, mystified: The Dark Ones were flying through the tunnels at such enormous speeds that their collective wings gave off the sound of rushing water. And *holy hell*, if they didn't look like an approaching swarm of black and red locusts. Hate-filled, glowing eyes pierced through the darkness even as wild banded hair flapped in the furious wind.

Marquis released Ciopori. He shoved her toward the nearest warrior and withdrew his nine-millimeter. "Santos, take the princess and go!" The remaining warriors would just have to do their best to buy the princess and Santos time.

They could shoot at the eyes of their enemies to slow them down, but they would eventually have to engage in hand-to-hand combat if they wanted to give the two any real chance of escape.

Saxson pulled out an AK-47, and Nathaniel reached for a

pair of grenades. "We're with you, brother." His eyes lit up with harnessed fire.

Napolean held up his hand, a commanding gesture. "Do not fight! Get to sunlight!" He eyed Marquis intently. "*You* take the princess out of here, warrior."

Marquis shook his head. "I am the oldest, most experienced fighter here, Napolean. You know I will not leave you."

Nathaniel snarled, "Each warrior here is worth a hundred Dark Ones. Not to impugn, milord, but we will stand with you." His blue-black hair fell forward, partially concealing his glowing eyes. Death radiated around him. A red haze of intensity framed his face, giving him the ominous appearance of a dark angel.

Napolean held out his arms and threw back his head, his own feral eyes ablaze with fury. His body trembled as it rose off the ground, and then he began to glow, his surrounding orbit emanating such intense heat that the limestone around them began to melt.

The warriors stepped back, retreating with caution, as their Sovereign's head pivoted to the side, and his ghostly black-and-silver hair caught fire.

The male was a blazing inferno, yet he neither smoldered nor burned.

A hint of madness filled his dark eyes as unchecked rage dilated his pupils. "There are *thousands* coming." His voice echoed through the hall like thunder, sparks ricocheting off the walls as the space around him vibrated with electricity. "You will go into the sun, as I command, my warriors"—his fangs descended beyond his jaw, casting the startling appearance of a saber-toothed tiger—"and then I shall command the sun to come to me. *Now go!*"

Marquis cleared his throat and glanced at Nathaniel. *Holy hell.*

Nathaniel whistled low beneath his breath as a swarm of males approached less than fifty-feet away. *Time to go.*

Marquis reached out for Ciopori, held her tight to his chest, and released his own magnificent wings. The rest of the males were already soaring furiously through the hall, rapidly approaching warp speed. As he turned back one last time to view their Sovereign, his mouth fell open in awe.

Napolean had indeed harnessed the sun.

In fact, for all intents and purposes, *Napolean Mondragon had become the sun.*

The ancient vampire was a luminous ball of fire, his aura so intense it hurt Marquis's eyes to gaze directly at him.

Glowing beams of orange and blue light shot out like missiles from every cell of the ancient's body as he hurled UV radiation in circular waves, slinging death from a nuclear hand.

The hallway filled with howls of agony.

The air grew dense with the odor of burning flesh.

The rushing sound of water had all but vanished as no one else dared to approach the burning mass of fire that was Napolean Mondragon—the awesome king of the house of Jadon.

All those who had dared to enter the tunnel were now making their way through the Corridor of the Dead.

Marquis stood breathless.

Transfixed.

Unable to take his eyes off the king.

Although the two of them had been in many battles together, throughout the ages—and the ancient lord's prowess in war was legendary—Marquis had never seen anything like what he gazed upon now. And he knew, instinctively, there would be a heavy price to pay: Such a huge conversion of energy would surely make Napolean sick, and if he didn't stop soon, he would die.

Marquis bowed his head in reverence, stamping the vision of the magnificent king into his memory. As he turned away, he covered Ciopori's eyes. "Do not look back, angel. You will most certainly go blind."

eighteen

Marquis stood in silence as Ciopori entered Napolean's kitchen. His breath caught in his throat. His heart skipped a beat.

Upon returning from Salvatore's lair, the princess had excused herself to shower. She had been exhausted and shaken up, desperate to scrub the filth of both Salvatore and Zarek from her body. It had been just as well. Marquis had needed a moment to collect his thoughts.

Now, staring at the regal female before him, he was at a complete loss for words.

She seemed to understand.

Her damp, raven locks fell about her shoulders like a cascading waterfall, and though her golden eyes were sad, she managed a faint smile. "You waited for me?"

Marquis cleared his throat. "Of course."

"Thank you." She wrung her hands together nervously and took a step in his direction, careful to keep a respectful distance between them. "So, have you seen Kristina yet?"

Marquis looked away. "Ciopori, *don't.*"

She shrugged and threaded her fingers together. "All right, warrior. I was just trying—"

"Come here." He reached out and pulled her to him, wrapping his heavy arms around her slender frame, careful not to crush her. "Tell me what happened to you, Ciopori. Please."

She buried her head in his chest. "You don't want to know, Marquis. Honestly, you don't."

"I need to know," he whispered. "Napolean needs to know—in case there's something that needs to be done for you."

Ciopori sighed and took his hands in hers. "Then take the information from my mind, Marquis, because I don't care to remember it all right now."

Marquis closed his eyes and rested his forehead against hers. He held his breath as the images flooded his mind: Salvatore snatching her from the forest; cruel, insidious torture in the chamber of snakes; the precise moment Marquis had come into Salvatore's lair to free her...

"Gods," he whispered, trembling. "I'm so sorry."

She stepped back then. "No, I'm the one who chose to take a stroll through the forest at three-o'clock in the morning. It was careless, and I am so grateful you came for me."

Marquis shook his head. "In all my centuries of living, I have never been so frightened." She regarded him with compassion and he felt his stomach turn over with pain...and desire.

With longing.

The amber sparkles in her bright eyes warmed him like rays of sunlight, slicing through the pain of such a long, tedious existence, wrenching his thoughts from the future that awaited him, anchoring him to the moment. Gods forgive him; he couldn't help but replay their time together in Kagen's study, the feel of her soft skin beneath his hands, the sound of her heated voice when she cried out in ecstasy, the touch of her—

"Marquis..." Seeming to sense his thoughts, she leaned into him and rose to the tips of her toes. Her beautiful lips parted ever so slightly to receive his kiss...and she waited.

Marquis shuddered.

He bent down, grasped her face in his hands, and lingered— his mouth just a breath away from her own—and then he turned his head to the side and gently kissed her on the cheek.

Crushed, she exhaled slowly and turned away. "I'm sorry."

Marquis wanted to punch a hole in the wall as the frustration burned inside him—the injustice of it all—but he struggled, instead, to remain calm. "No, Ciopori. Don't ever be sorry. I shouldn't be here."

Ciopori swallowed and took a step back, wringing her delicate hands together once again. "You're right. I know...it's not like anything has changed." She hesitated then. "Has it?"

Marquis hung his head. "Who can undo what the gods have done?"

Tessa Dawn

Ciopori nodded and ambled across the kitchen to absently pour a cup of tea from a brass kettle on the stove. "Indeed."

Uncomfortable silence settled around them as each waited for the other to say something—anything—that might make the insufferable tolerable. Neither could bear to leave the other's side, yet they both knew they couldn't be together.

"Vanya was very happy to see Napolean return," Ciopori finally said in a clumsy attempt to change the subject. "Even though he was very weak and in need of blood."

"Of course," he murmured.

"No," she said, shaking her head, "I mean Vanya was *very* happy to see Napolean return."

Marquis raised his eyebrows. "Napolean?"

"He is a male, is he not?" Ciopori managed a faint laugh.

Marquis shook his head. "After what I saw earlier, I'm not sure what he is." He hoped their leader would not make the same mistake he had—falling in love with a woman who was not his *destiny*. The consequence was sheer agony.

Ciopori set her mug down on the counter. "Truly, that was the most terrifying yet spectacular thing I have ever seen: Napolean, I mean."

Despite his good intentions, Marquis growled low in his throat, his territorial instincts getting the best of him.

Ciopori rolled her eyes. "It is good to know that at least you still care, warrior."

Marquis felt utterly powerless. "*Ciopori*...I will always care."

She nodded and began to fiddle with a stack of silk napkins, carefully unfolding and refolding each one before replacing them in their stainless-steel holder. She held one up in her hand. "Funny, isn't it? How a male that doesn't eat keeps so many unnecessary things around."

Marquis walked over to her side, removed the cloth from her delicate fingers, and placed a gentle hand on her shoulder. He bent to her ear. "You will always be the *only* woman I love. Never forget that. *Never.*"

Her eyes filled with tears, and she turned away. "I know I should feel guilty, Marquis, especially now that you are married—"

"*Mated.*"

She sighed. "Now that you are *mated*, yet even knowing…I pray that your words of love are true. And my heart breaks to know that there will come a day when you will also…love your wife."

"My *destiny.*"

"Oh hell, Marquis!" Ciopori spun back around to face him. "Who cares what you call her. *She's yours.* And I'm not!"

Marquis leaned forward then. He placed both hands palms-down on the counter and stared out the window. What more was there to say? "I will stay away from you, Princess…I promise."

Much to his surprise, Ciopori punched him in the arm. "Is that what you think I want?"

He shrugged. *Gods, what more could he do? Did she desire to watch him bleed before her?*

"And how will that make things better, warrior?" she continued. "To never see your eyes again? To never hear your laughter…well, your piteous attempts at laughter." She smiled despite herself, yet the warmth never reached her eyes. "I don't know which would be worse: seeing you, while knowing I could never have you, or trying to exist in a world without you."

"I understand." His words were a mere whisper.

"No," she argued, "I really don't think you do. My heart is *sick*, Marquis. *It's breaking.* And for the life of me, I can't understand it." She paled. "Yes, I realize that you were the one that was there with me all those years, *all those long centuries,* lying in the ground, waiting for a brother that was never coming to awaken me—all those years when your voice was the only sound I heard, your face the only escape I had…in my dreams." She sat down on a high bar-stool and stared at him with such deep sorrow in her eyes he feared his heart would break in two. "But this"—she placed both hands over her heart—"this is something else entirely. It is almost as if I can't breathe without you, Marquis." She looked away. "Almost as if I don't want to."

Marquis stared at the inconsolable woman before him, wishing he had a gift for words. Hell, wishing he knew how to speak to a female at all. He understood her pain. More than she knew. But, unlike her, he hadn't spent the last fifteen centuries asleep in the ground with only dreams to sustain him. He had spent the last fifteen-hundred years living what had been a hard life, fighting in countless wars, killing, and feeding, and protecting his brothers...watching his parents die. He had spent the last fifteen-hundred years waiting on a *destiny* that never came—and learning how to harden his heart.

Marquis had spent a lifetime perfecting the art of shutting down all but the breath that sustained him. "You will not die, Ciopori." It was all he could think to say.

Ciopori cupped her hands over her face and said nothing.

"Brother." A deep, rich voice reverberated from the kitchen entrance. "Can I speak with you for a moment?"

Marquis turned to find Kagen standing beneath the arched door-frame. He was glancing back and forth between him and the princess, trying to hide his concern.

"Can this wait, brother?" Marquis asked.

Ciopori blinked and brushed away her tears, plainly embarrassed.

Kagen regarded the princess with a kind glance, his eyes soft with compassion, and then he quickly looked away out of respect. He cleared his throat. "No, Marquis, I'm afraid it can't."

Marquis turned to face his brother squarely, switching to telepathic communication. *It has been a trying day, healer. I will seek you out when I am finished here.*

I'm afraid it really can't wait, Kagen insisted, the silver centers of his dark brown eyes deepening with intensity.

"What is so important?" Marquis demanded, forgetting to speak privately.

BLOOD AWAKENING

Kagen indicated Ciopori with a nod, looked back at Marquis, and then shifted his weight from foot to foot uncomfortably.

"Well?" Marquis prodded.

Kagen sighed in frustration. "*It's Kristina.*"

Marquis frowned. "What about her?"

Kagen hesitated for a moment. "She's very ill."

"Ill? What do you mean, *ill?*" Marquis had already converted Kristina to their species, and vampires simply did not get sick.

"This morning, right after you departed with the other warriors, she retreated to one of Napolean's guest rooms." He paused, seeming uncertain as to how much to say in front of the princess.

"Go on," Marquis prodded.

"At first, I thought she just needed some time alone. You know, considering the *nature* of your mission."

Ciopori glanced down at the floor. Her tousled hair fell forward, intentionally shielding her face from Kagen's view.

Kagen frowned. "But when I went to check on her, she had a fever—"

"A fever?"

Kagen nodded. "Yes, brother. And as the day progressed, she began having severe muscle pains and cramps, weakness and nausea. It almost appears as if—"

Marquis held up his hand to stay his brother's words. Despite the situation with Ciopori, he felt like a complete jerk for not checking on his *destiny* the moment he arrived at the mansion. Like it or not, she was his first responsibility now. "Where is she?" he asked hastily. The concern in his voice was genuine, and Ciopori lifted her head to regard them both. Her face was stricken with grief, though she tried desperately to hide it.

Kagen sighed. "Last door on the left. Front hall." He turned his attention to Ciopori. "I'm...sorry."

Marquis waved a dismissive hand. Whatever was happening between him and the princess was a private matter. "Thank you

218

for bringing this to my attention, Kagen. I will attend to her shortly."

Clearly in a hurry to leave, Kagen declined his head and instantly dematerialized.

Regretting what he was about to say, Marquis turned to Ciopori. "Princess—"

"*Don't*." She held up her hand and nodded, a tear of sorrow escaping her eye. "I know...but I'd rather not hear you say it."

Marquis couldn't help himself. He came around the counter, lifted her from the barstool, and gathered her in his arms. "Gods forgive me; I have so much to atone for."

"No," Ciopori insisted. She shoved against his chest to gain her freedom but refused to back away. "You cannot help what you feel for me, and still, you remain a male of honor." The resignation was plain in her eyes. "Marquis, we both know you must do what is right. Go to your *mate*, warrior...where you belong."

Marquis held her gaze, wishing he could stay there forever, wishing the two of them could just disappear, but he did not challenge her words. "You will always be in my heart—"

"No." Ciopori pressed her fingers to his mouth. "Words have far too much power, Marquis. Do not damn your future with Kristina, not for me. You must find a way to love her. And I must find a way to move on."

As true as they might be, her words cut him like a knife.

She forced a smile. "In spite of everything, I do want you to be happy, Marquis. Please, if you can do nothing else for me, at least be happy."

Marquis allowed himself one last indulgence as his head fell forward and he nuzzled her neck. He reveled in the feel of her thick, silky hair and deeply inhaled her scent, hoping to store it in his memory until the end of time. And then, drawing on every ounce of strength he possessed, he stepped away. "And I pray for your happiness as well."

Ciopori caught at the edge of the counter as if it were all that was holding her up; she was trying so desperately to be brave. When Marquis reached out to steady her, she drew away. "Go, Marquis. This has to end now. Just go."

Marquis turned and left the kitchen, refusing to look back.

With the quiet resolve of an ancient warrior, he forced his thoughts to the back of his mind, buried his emotions behind an iron wall, and closed the door to his heart.

Propelled by duty alone, his feet carried him through the mansion toward the guest bedroom.

Where his *destiny* was waiting.

nineteen

Marquis threw open the heavy bedroom door. His eyes immediately searched out Kristina, and what he saw sickened his stomach. The pint-size female was lying on the enormous cherry-wood bed, doubled over into a fetal position. Her wild, curly hair was damp with perspiration. Her body trembled with fever.

"Dear gods," Marquis exclaimed, rushing to the bed.

Kagen glanced up from Kristina's side and nodded his greeting. He leaned over the frail wisp of a female and began taking her blood pressure. "She's getting worse."

Marquis blanched. Instinctively, his hand went to her forehead, and he pulled it away when it burned his skin. "She's burning up. Kagen, *what is this?*"

Kagen smiled warmly at the quivering female and whispered in her ear. "We'll be right back." He gestured at Marquis and walked over to the window.

"Is she dying?" Marquis's voice revealed his alarm.

"Yes and no," Kagen answered.

His temper flared. "*Yes and no?* What the hell is that supposed—"

"If you don't take care of her immediately, she will die. But if you see to her needs, she will be just fine."

Marquis's lips drew back in a snarl. "I'm not a healer, brother. Speak plainly."

"She needs to feed, Marquis. And right away."

Marquis took an inadvertent step back. "*Feed?* Are you kidding me?" He glanced at Kristina, suddenly recognizing all of the signs of his species' severe hunger, but still not understanding: Newly converted *destinies* did not have to feed for at least six months following their conversions. Even then, the female would have to endure months of neglect to become this ill. "How is this possible?" he asked.

Kagen looked down, his eyes solemn. "Normally, that is

true, but Kristina wasn't well when you converted her."

Marquis slumped against the wall, a sudden wave of guilt washing over him. "What do you mean, she wasn't well?"

Kagen placed his hand on Marquis's forearm and gave him a firm grasp before releasing it. "Do not take it so hard, brother. I didn't catch it either—that day at the clinic. And I was her doctor."

Marquis snarled, "Enough of the riddles! Tell me what is wrong with her, Kagen!"

Kagen squared his chin and raised his shoulders in a cocky shrug as if to point out that Marquis's words were water rolling off his back. He shifted his weight from one foot to the other and waited patiently...for Marquis to show some respect.

Marquis appraised his little brother then. The healer had always been the epitome of kindness and good manners—until he wasn't. And now was not the time to rub him the wrong way. With everything that had gone on that day, Marquis was in no mood for a heated brotherly argument. There wasn't a doubt in his mind that he would throw the arrogant ass right out the stained-glass window if Kagen pushed him too far. And then Kagen would turn into *Mr. Hyde.*

And then...

He exhaled slowly through his nose. "What happened during the conversion, Kagen?"

Kagen crossed his arms over his chest leisurely, a point of emphasis that he would not be intimidated. "When Dirk...*hurt her*...he caused several internal injuries that I didn't catch in my exam. She was bleeding internally the entire day."

Marquis stepped back. "Good gods. And I converted her in that state?" He glanced at the bed, feeling deep regret for the first time over how he had turned her.

Kagen's eyes grew serious. "You saved her life, actually." He stared at his brother, refusing to blink. "Marquis, if you had waited to convert her, she would've died from her internal injuries, perhaps the same night."

A deep, feral growl escaped Marquis's throat. If he could raise the dead he would bring Dirk back just to kill him again.

"Your venom has been sustaining her," Kagen continued, "and she did convert successfully, but she needs to feed right away. At least a couple of pints."

Wonderful, Marquis thought. *She's going to love that.*

Marquis nodded and visually assessed the tiny, suffering female in the too-large bed. "Leave now, Kagen."

Kagen smirked. "You're welcome, brother." He ambled over to the bed, retrieved his bag, and headed toward the door. "Marquis," he whispered on his way out, "all pettiness aside, do not forget your life is tied to hers." He smoothed his hair away from his eyes. "Please, don't wait."

Marquis nodded. While his own life didn't seem all that important right now, there was absolutely no way he was going to let this female—*his female*—die as a result of being claimed by him. "Do I have time to take her home?"

"Honestly?" Kagen stared at Kristina for an intense moment and then turned back to Marquis. "No."

He turned and left the room.

Marquis approached the bed slowly, understanding just how much the sickly woman hated and feared him. "How are you feeling, Kristina?" His voice was deliberately matter-of-fact.

"I think I'm dying," she muttered. Her deep blue eyes fluttered upward, and she shivered. "Good thing for you, huh?"

Marquis frowned. "Kristina, this is no time to amuse yourself. Did Kagen explain to you what was wrong?"

Kristina doubled over in pain and grimaced. "Sort of. He said I need to feed, but I can't eat anything. I swear; I'd just throw up if I tried."

Marquis placed his hand on her shoulder and gently rubbed the back of her neck. "You are no longer human, Kristina. While you can eat food if you wish, your body does not require it anymore. You do not need to *eat.* You need to *feed.*"

"*Feed?* What the heck does that mean?" Her voice held a hint of fear in it.

"It means—"

"You mean blood? *Drink blood?* Oh, hell no, Marquis. No! I can't."

"You can," Marquis argued, "and you must."

Kristina sat up; her body rocked with spasms at the sudden movement. She clenched her stomach as she shook her head adamantly. "Are you crazy? What am I supposed to do? Go *hunt* like some little vampire warrior or something? Have you seen me, Marquis? I'm not big enough to kill anything. And I couldn't even if I was." She ducked her head under the pillow. "*No!*" The sound was muffled.

Marquis almost smiled. *Almost.* "Kristina, you *are* a vampire now, but our females do not hunt. And you're right, you couldn't kill a fly... Unless—"

He stopped himself.

"Unless what?" she demanded, lifting the pillow.

He offered a lopsided smile. "Unless you did it with your mouth."

Kristina glared at him. "To hell with you, vampire! I bet I could bite you if you made me mad enough, you jackass."

Marquis smiled broadly then. "Now that's the Kristina Riley I know. And that is precisely what I am going to let you do."

Kristina positively recoiled, jerking away so violently she slammed her head into the headboard. "Ouch!" She sneered at him. "Are you insane?"

Marquis took a slow, deep breath. "Kristina, this is no joking matter."

"Do I sound like I'm joking?"

"*You're dying.*"

Now that got her attention.

"I'm dying? Just because I'm not out murdering humans and

sucking their blood?"

Marquis frowned. "I repeat, our females do not hunt, nor do we expect them to *murder humans*. You are dying because Dirk hurt you far worse than we realized, and for that, I apologize. We should have caught your injuries sooner."

Kristina's eyes flashed with anger. "Kind of hard to do with those saber-tooth fangs lodged in my throat, huh?"

Marquis didn't blink. "I am not proud of my behavior, Kristina, although it did ultimately save your life. But think of it this way: This is your chance for revenge." He knew he would have sounded more convincing if he could have smiled—or even put an air of teasing into his voice—but Marquis Silivasi just didn't do lighthearted. And he was hardly going to pick up the nuances of humor now.

The two of them sat in utter silence for an interminable amount of time before Kristina finally looked up at him beneath slightly hooded—and extremely frightened—eyes. "Marquis," she whispered in a tone that sounded far too much like defeat, "I can't. I mean...I really *can't*."

Marquis took her hand in his and forced himself to hold on solidly. "Kristina, you must. You know I will not allow you to die."

Kristina shook her head and rolled her eyes. "No, I mean, *I can't*. Let's say, even if I wanted to drink someone's blood, which I don't, then no offense, but it probably wouldn't be yours. And even if there was someone else more *my type*—like really young and sexy—like maybe Nachari or something...I still wouldn't know how. *I can't*."

Marquis blinked several times, trying to process that his *destiny* had just referred to his little brother as *young and sexy*. And preferable to him. Despite his utter lack of affection for the female, his haunches stood up, and a deep, territorial growl rumbled in his throat. "Be careful, *floricica mea*. I will not have you speak that way of other males, especially not my own brother."

BLOOD AWAKENING

Kristina rolled her eyes again. "Oh yeah, 'cause that would be like...rude or something...as opposed to pawning your mate off on your brother, the doctor, in order to run off and save the woman you *really* love? And then not even coming to check on her when you get back. Yeah, Marquis, I'll have to keep that in mind. Whatever!"

Marquis blanched.

Kristina held his gaze. "I might not be all educated or anything, but I'm not stupid either, *boss*."

Marquis frowned then. "I never said you were. Then again, I'm not the one who just referred to a five-hundred-year-old male as young."

"And sexy," Kristina added, sneering.

Marquis's lips twitched, but he held back his fangs.

Kristina crossed her arms over her laboring chest. "That really does irritate you, doesn't it?" She laughed between coughs. "I will have to keep that in mind." And then, once again, she doubled over in pain.

Marquis scowled. "Kristina, look at you. You need to feed." He reached out and stroked her arm. "As in *right now*."

She shook her head again, all at once becoming frightened. "I can't! Besides, I don't even know how."

Marquis leaned forward and caught her face in his hands. "You do know how."

She glared at him then, her blue eyes boring an *are-you-really-that-stupid* look into his, and then she turned away. "*As if.*"

Marquis cleared his throat. "When you were born—as a human—you went from an environment where you did not breathe oxygen to one that immediately required it, yet no one taught you how to breathe. You simply opened your mouth and began to take in air. So it is with your rebirth as a vampire. Feeding is essential to life. You need not be taught. Trust me, Kristina, the moment you smell my blood, you will know how to feed."

Kristina winced. "That is *so* gross, Marquis. You have no

idea how gross that is." She started to make a face but was racked by a series of painful cramps.

"Enough!" Marquis took her by the hand. He brushed his hair to the side and pulled her forward. "Come to me, Kristina. Take what you need."

Weighing less than one-hundred ten pounds, Kristina flew effortlessly into Marquis's arms. Her head fell into the hollow between his shoulder and neck, and she began to cry. "I can't." She pushed at his chest like a distressed child, desperate to be free of his restraining arms.

Marquis exhaled. "*Kristina...*"

She shook her head and wiped her nose on the sleeve of his shirt. "Wait! Don't force me!" She struggled to catch her breath. "If you're going to make me do this, then at least let me...do your wrist. Your neck is way too...*eww*. No offense."

Marquis shut his eyes and cursed beneath his breath. "None taken, but Kristina, my wrist won't be enough for you. Your need is too great."

It was then that she truly started to panic.

She swung at him wildly, breaking his grasp in surprise, and then she jumped from the bed in a desperate attempt to flee from the room.

Marquis rose fluidly, heading her off before she could reach the door. He lifted her like a sack of weightless potatoes and carried her back to the bed. She punched and kicked the entire way.

"Stop, Kristina. *Stop!*" He restrained her arms to keep her from hurting herself.

"No!" she cried, hysterical.

"Kristina!"

"I won't eat your neck," she squealed, continuing to struggle.

"*Feed* from my neck, Kristina. And fine, we will try it your way."

Her arms stopped flailing, and she caught her breath. "You will?"

BLOOD AWAKENING

"Yes, *I will*."

"Don't restrain me," she bit out, suddenly racked by a fit of coughs.

He smoothed her hair back with his hand as gently as possible. "No restraint—I'm just going to move you, *okay?*"

She eyed him warily, and then she slowly nodded, relaxing.

Marquis moved cautiously, cradling her in his lap like an infant. As her head fell back against his huge bicep, he extended his fangs, tore open a gash in his wrist, and placed the wound to her mouth. "Drink, Kristina," he whispered, "take what you need."

Kristina blanched and reflexively turned away...until the scent of his blood drew her back like a moth to a flame. She grasped his forearm in both hands, tentatively brought it to her mouth, and slowly let the blood-soaked wrist touch her lips.

Her reaction was immediate.

Instinctive.

Her strike like that of a scorpion: swift, hard, and deep.

Marquis jerked, caught off-guard by the power of her bite. And then he relaxed as she began to take hard, drugging pulls from his wrist, her body clearly starving for the life giving fluid pouring down her throat. The more she took, the more she wanted. And the more she wanted, the more frustrating his wrist became.

Kristina twisted his arm this way and that, trying to get a better angle. Three times, she withdrew her fangs and struck him again, grinding her teeth as she attempted to get a better hold. Twice more, she lost her grip and missed the vein altogether, having to strike him repeatedly before she found it again.

She squirmed in his lap, tightened her grip like a vise, clamped down with her molars in aggravation, and snarled. Finally, she sat up and threw his arm aside, weeping in frustration, heavy sobs that wracked her chest.

Marquis leaned over her trembling body and buried his face in her hair. "*Kristina*"—he pitched his voice as gently as he could—"you are torturing yourself." He held up his arm, displaying his raw, mutilated wrist. "And me as well, I might add." He lightly stroked her hair. "Come, little one. Take from my neck. Drink as you were meant to."

When Kristina met his gaze, her eyes were a strange mixture of need, desperation, and *humiliation*. She must have hated herself for needing him so badly, resented him for creating such a primal need within her.

Marquis sighed. There was so little trust between them. No love or respect. Only a raw, animal instinct to survive that drew them both to this moment. Yet, that was something Marquis understood. He knew as well as she did what it was like to desperately need the one person in the world you didn't want. To need them in order to live.

Hefting her from his lap, he moved to the head of the bed, reclined against a stiff pillow, and swung his legs onto the mattress. He clutched her by her narrow waist, lifted her gently above him so that her knees straddled his hips on either side, and then quickly let go, allowing her full control in a dominant position. As he swept his heavy hair behind his ear and tilted his head to the side, he was careful to avoid eye contact, wanting to spare her some dignity.

And then he simply waited.

He remained perfectly still while Kristina climbed up his massive warrior's body, trembling from the intimacy of the act. He held his breath as her pulse betrayed her fear, knowing she needed it too desperately to turn away. She reminded him of Little Red Riding Hood, reluctantly entrusting her well-being to the big bad wolf as she nuzzled his neck, tears streaming down her face the entire time. Then gradually, warily, she scraped her teeth against the pulsing artery, slowly gathering the courage to strike.

And strike she did.

Sinking her teeth so deep that she struck bone.

Marquis suppressed a deep, erotic moan that had nothing to

do with the female above him. He couldn't help it. He was what he was. As she began to take long, ravenous pulls of his blood, he gently cradled her back and held her tightly against him, flooding her with security as she fed to her contentment and her body began to heal.

Although it was not the kind of love a man felt for a woman, a small glimmer of affection stirred in his heart. Perhaps what a brother felt for a sister—or an uncle for a niece. Thanks to the Blood Curse, Marquis had no experience with either of those relationships.

But of one thing he was certain. He had sired this female. He had brought her into his world. He had made her what she was, and it was his obligation to take care of her.

It was his duty to see to her needs.

Holding her close in his arms, her body and mind so fragile, her vulnerability so complete, he knew that he would always take care of her...protect her.

Instinctively, he knew that he would kill anyone—human or vampire—that ever threatened to harm her.

twenty

Nachari sank back into the soft cushions of his leather sectional and put his feet up on the matching Raleigh coffee table. Home was all about class and comfort for the five-hundred year-old Master Wizard, whose four-story bachelor pad sat in isolation at the end of a dirt road, backing up to the northern face of the forest cliffs.

There was nothing country or rustic about it.

Built in the style of a 1920s Park Avenue brownstone, the forty-six-hundred square-foot retreat had a traditional brick face, four-levels of front and back terraces, and a rooftop patio that was to die for: perfect for a wizard who studied the stars through a high-powered telescope.

Glancing up at the fourteen-foot ceiling, Nachari sighed and propped a loose pillow behind his head. He placed the palm of his hand over the leather binding of the antique tome lying in his lap and whispered a prayer to Perseus, the god of his own divine constellation, to protect him from the malevolence embodied in the book he was about to open: *the Ancient Book of Black Magic.* The carnal text, said to have been written by the dark lords of the Abyss, themselves. It was hard to believe the evil artifact had been in the hands of Salvatore Nistor all this time....

Nachari let out a deep, resonate sigh. He had taken an incredible gamble. It had been all he could do to hide his surprise when he had first seen the ancient tome hidden beneath the mattress of Derrian's crib, and it had required enormous concentration to show no emotion while removing the book from the lair.

He absently stroked the leather, regarding the text with awe. There was no way the ancient sorcerer would have allowed Nachari to walk away with the hallowed artifact if he had suspected his intent. In fact, for this treasure, Salvatore may very well have traded both Zarek and Derrian's lives.

Nachari chuckled softly. No matter. He had used his magic

BLOOD AWAKENING

to render the object invisible, and then strapped it to the inside of his cloak, maintaining the threat to the infant the entire time. Nobody had known. Not even Marquis. And Nachari had walked out of the lair completely undetected.

Whew! he thought, brushing his hair away from his brow. *That could've turned out much, much worse.* Just how much worse, he refused to imagine. He turned his attention to a more immediate subject: his brother's recent behavior, the primal instinct Marquis had displayed when rescuing Ciopori from the colony....

While Marquis was renowned for his calm, strategic focus in battle, when it came to personal matters, such as those affecting himself or his family, he was the single most impulsive, hot-headed vampire in the house of Jadon: quick to act and slow to consider personal consequences, which half the time he didn't get anyhow, considering his social...challenges.

Nachari stirred uncomfortably. *Something wasn't right.* Marquis had allowed Valentine's infant son to live in order to save Ciopori. He had bartered with Salvatore Nistor, a mortal enemy, in order to protect the princess. He had checked his own temper at the door and swallowed his pride in order to put her safety first.

Not that Marquis wasn't noble—or wouldn't readily die for any member of the house of Jadon, let alone one of the original females—but not like that. The Marquis he knew would have lit up the whole colony, taken as many Dark Ones out as he could, risked all of their lives if necessary, relying upon his superior fighting skills to prevail in the end. Was he reckless? No. Was he stubborn to a fault and utterly sure of himself? Absolutely.

But not this time—*not this time.*

This time, quite frankly, Marquis had acted like a mated-male protecting his *destiny.* Sure, Marquis and Ciopori had clearly been *involved*—that day he took her to Kagen's clinic had said it all, but this was...more. Marquis's desire to save the female had surpassed all other instincts.

Tessa Dawn

Nachari thought about the way his brother looked at Ciopori, the deep pain etched in his otherwise stoic face, and the complete indifference he seemed to have for Kristina, despite the fact that such indifference went against every strand of DNA in a male vampire's body. He shuddered to think about the crazed look on Marquis's face the night he sat on his porch, Kristina plopped in his lap like a rag doll, his fangs buried deep in her throat. Marquis hadn't shown the slightest hint of compassion or tenderness: He had taken Kristina the way he would take a stranger off the street to feed, all business, no emotion.

Granted, it was not like Marquis was all that connected to his emotions to begin with, but even a hardened warrior such as he, one who had seen too much and lived too long, had a heart when it came to his *destiny*. No. *Something wasn't right.*

"Wassup, homey!" A familiar voice interrupted Nachari's thoughts, and he glanced up from the couch as young Braden Bratianu entered the living room. The kid's shoulders were held back so far he looked rigid, and his chin was tilted upward in an awkward angle as he did his best to strut across the floor.

"What's up, Braden."

"Nata," the youngster replied.

"Nata?" Nachari repeated.

"Not-a-damn thing." Braden laughed.

Nachari resisted rolling his eyes. *Ah, hell*, so the kid was going through yet another phase. He sighed. The handsome fifteen-year-old boy had been placed in Nachari's care less than one month ago by the esteemed fellowship of wizards at the Romanian University as part of Nachari's final task for graduation. The wizards considered the relationship an opportunity for Nachari to gain patience: *through repeated trials and endless tests.* And Braden Bratianu had never failed to deliver. The boy was one ordeal after another.

As the son of a divorced human, Braden had been raised by his mortal mother until Dario Bratianu had found and claimed her as his *destiny*. Having completed the Blood Moon ritual, Braden's mom had given birth to Conrad, their new Vampyr son, leaving Braden as the odd man out—a human in a family of vampires.

Prior to Braden's mom, there had never been a *destiny* claimed who already had a human child: Lily Bratianu was the first, and since she and Braden shared the same celestial blood, Dario had been able to convert him without incident.

And what an experiment that had been—a kid with human memories, impulses, and tendencies suddenly turned into a supernatural creature with abilities beyond his comprehension. Trying to merge the two histories remained quite the challenge.

Nachari eyed the boy from head to toe, assessing his new *warrior's* outfit: Dark military fatigues hung loosely over a pair of heavy black combat boots. A tight muscle shirt stretched over a body that was still in need of a few more muscles, and a long black trench coat flowed to the floor. Nachari's eyes traveled up to the boy's spiked hair—*all eight inches of it*—and he tilted his head to the side, wondering how the child was keeping it up.

"Aren't you hot?" Nachari finally asked, gesturing toward the coat.

Braden slipped his partially-gloved hands into his pockets. "Nah, I'm good."

Nachari smiled. "Braden, your hair is too long to spike like that. If you'd like to have it cut, that's one thing, but—"

"Hell no, I ain't cuttin' my hair!"

Nachari sat forward then. "Since when did you start cursing, Braden?"

Braden shrugged his shoulders and held out his hands. "Just a little nothin'-nothin' that I picked up."

Nachari chuckled. "I believe the vernacular is *somethin'-somethin'*, and where did you pick it up?"

Braden huffed, indignant. "Man, why you always sweatin' me?"

Nachari shook his head. "No one is sweatin' you, Braden,

but you do tend to be a little *over the top* with your changes. I'm just trying to figure out who you are today."

Braden's burnt sienna eyes flashed a sort of…dusty rose…as if they were on their way to turning red but couldn't quite make it. They settled back into their natural hue, and his inherent golden pupils darkened with frustration. "I'm a warrior, and you know that! Like Marquis!"

Nachari held up both hands in apology. "Of course," he conceded, "I just hadn't realized you were such an *urban* warrior of late."

Braden rolled his eyes, but more than likely, he had no idea what *urban* meant.

"Anyhow," Nachari continued, dismissing the argument—*patience indeed*—"I want you to go wash all that gel, or mousse, or whatever it is out of your hair, unless you want me to cut it."

Braden threw back his head in theatrical disgust. "A warrior needs the spikes, man."

He drew a dagger out of his coat pocket, considered flipping it in the air but thought better of it, and then started pacing the room. "It's part of the package."

"Whoa, my man…" Nachari set the book aside and jumped up from the couch. "Where did you get the knife?"

Braden flashed a broad smile, a mischievous look in his eyes. "I found your collection." He paused, unable to conceal his excitement. "I know I wasn't supposed to, but *dayuum*, Nachari, that shit is off the chain!"

Still across the room, Nachari quickly wrenched the blade from Braden's hand, using telekinesis. He laid it down gently on an end table. "What have I told you about weapons?"

Braden rolled his eyes. "No weapons without proper training. I know, I know, but dude, it's just a knife."

"Yeah, well, a knife is a weapon, and that particular weapon belongs to me, *dude*." Nachari sat back down. "And lay off the cursing."

Braden threw up his hands. "*Damn*—I mean, *dag*, you are

such a buzz kill."

"And no more MTV, either." Nachari let out a slow, deep breath. Patience. *Patience.* He possessed an endless reservoir of patience.

Yeah, right.

Vampyr males just did not experience adolescence the same way this human-turned-vampire did. They were a lot more stable and self-controlled. This kid was the flightiest thing Nachari had ever seen; although he had to admit, all and all, Braden was a really good kid. He just tried too hard.

Taking a step back from his frustration, Nachari offered a compromise: "I tell you what, if the spiked hair is the look, then why don't we go into town—get a professional hair cut—so you can wear it spiked...with class."

Braden shook his head adamantly. "That's just it, Nachari. No way am I cutting my hair." He started to run a smooth hand through his locks, got stuck on a stiff patch of gel, and quickly placed it in his pocket, instead. Playing it off, he shrugged. "A brotha's gotta be able to play it both ways, *cool and classy.* Feel me?"

Nachari counted backward from ten to one. How in the world did the fellowship consider *this* an important skill of wizardry? *Whatever.* "Braden, I can assure you of one thing: you are *not* a brother. And why can't one hair-style accomplish both?"

Braden chuckled then, trying to sound older than he was. "The truth?"

"By all means."

"Because, man, I need the spikes to be like Marquis—you know, a warrior. But I also need the waves to be like you—pull the women. 'Cause *that*, my brotha, oh man..."—he let out a deep, wistful sigh—"that's da shizzle for da rizzle." All at once, his body jerked unnaturally, and his right leg swung out from underneath him, causing him to lose his balance.

Nachari jumped up, alarmed. "What's wrong with your leg?"

Vampires did not get muscle cramps, and they certainly did not have seizures.

Braden righted himself, frowned, and looked away. "Uh, nothing. Nothing. It's all good."

"Braden?" Nachari raised his eyebrows.

Braden gazed at the floor and shook his head, exasperated. "Just a little dance move I've been working on, ah'ight?" He paused, and then looked up sheepishly. "Guess it needs a little more work."

Nachari bit his lower lip. *Don't laugh at the boy. Do-not-laugh. Do. Not—* "I'll tell you what: If you want to keep your hair long, then lose the spikes. If you want to keep the spikes, then you have to get it cut. End of discussion. As for *da shizzle for da rizzle* and *the new dance moves*, tone it down. *Way down.* Understand me?"

Braden moped and bobbed his head in reluctant agreement. "Yeah...okay."

"*Way down*," Nachari repeated.

Braden nodded again and then folded his hands in front of him, looking suddenly lost.

Nachari sat back down on the sofa and held out his left arm. "Now then, when was the last time you fed?"

While most males in the house of Jadon only needed to feed every six to eight weeks, Braden's body could only consume small amounts at a time—not because his system wasn't fully converted, but because his once-human brain still resisted the notion of living off blood. Consequently, he had to feed a lot more often.

"See, that's exactly what I'm talking about!" Braden huffed. "Fine, you don't want me to have spiked hair, I won't. And fine! You don't want me to talk like I'm cool, *whatever*, but dang, Nachari, why do you have to treat me like a girl?"

Nachari stared at him, utterly perplexed. "What are we talking about now, Braden?"

The kid sighed and began waving his arms emphatically as he spoke. "No self-respecting vampire feeds off his step-dad and his *guardian*. Off other males! That's just embarrassing. All the other vampires my age hunt already."

Nachari considered the child's words. "I understand your frustration, Braden, but do you really think you're ready to hunt?"

"Yes!" the kid exclaimed, his face flushing red.

Nachari sighed. "Okay, then tell me this: How well can you discern a human spirit?"

Braden's top lip curled up in question. *"What?"*

Nachari held his gaze. "Can you tell evil from good?"

"Yeah, of course. I mean...I think so."

"You think so?"

"Yeah, I think so! Why?"

"Because it's against our laws to take the life of an *innocent*, Braden. And even if you could identify a completely corrupt soul—verify that he or she is a predator against other humans—you would have to be able to isolate the person without being seen, attack so swiftly that they go down without a struggle, siphon enough blood to insure the kill, and then harness the necessary energy to incinerate the body. You think you're ready for that?"

Braden looked down, dejected, and shook his head. "No, but I was thinking more like...maybe I could hunt like you."

"Like me?"

"Yeah, you know, forget the bad guys, just lure the pretty females."

Nachari sank back into the cushions and smiled. "Braden—"

"Why not? I mean, you should see when some of us guys from the academy go into town—man, the human girls flip out!" He reached into his pocket and pulled out a handful of crumpled-up pieces of paper. "See this? They're *phone numbers*, Nachari. Chicks giving *me* their phone numbers! And I don't even have to ask."

Nachari sighed. "Braden, there is no question that you are a handsome young man." Far more striking than the child realized, actually: *thank the gods.* "And even if you weren't, your vampire DNA would still attract women to you. It's a powerful magnet, but the danger is far too great, especially for someone as inexperienced as you."

"Oh, 'cause now you think I'm gonna try and have sex with the female."

"No," Nachari argued, "I was speaking in terms of manipulating kinetic energy and honing your hunting skills, not of having sex—even dogs can do that. But since you're bringing it up, do we need to go back over the consequences of having sex with humans? The fact that pregnancy would *kill* your partner?"

Braden rolled his eyes, clearly irritated. "Have vampires ever heard of *condoms?*"

Nachari snarled a deep warning. "And if the condom breaks, she dies. Are you really that reckless—"

"First of all, I'm not like a Dark One. I would never *speak* a pregnancy into being, knowing what could happen."

"What *would* happen! And you could kill her with just your strength alone, Braden! The power of a vampire, unleashed...unrestrained...you have no idea. Not to mention, you would most assuredly drain her of every last drop of blood even if you didn't command a pregnancy. *I repeat: you have no idea*—the impulse to bite, the need to feed, how integral it is to the sex act."

Braden rolled his eyes.

"Braden?"

The kid huffed.

"*Braden?*"

"What!"

"Are you listening to me?"

He stomped his foot, his lips pursed together in aggravation. "Yeah...I'm listening."

"Good, then let's just say, for the sake of argument, you go ahead and take one of those phone numbers out of your pocket—give a human girl a call. The next thing you know, the two of you are sitting on a bench somewhere, maybe side-by-side at the movies, and she whispers in your ear…or rubs up against you…or has a few too many buttons undone on her blouse: As sure as the sun sets in the west, every cell in your body will ache to drain her, right then and there, and we're not even talking about being in some bedroom half-undressed. Trust me, Braden, you are not ready."

"Nachari," Braden sighed, throwing up his hands, "I'm not—"

"You're damn straight you're not!" Nachari snapped, his fangs beginning to advance in his mouth. "You're fifteen years old, Braden. And while our species might mature faster than humans, you have had less than one year to adapt. Not to mention, a human female? Fifteen years old? That's a child! With great power comes great responsibility—"

"Damn!" The kid was practically jumping up and down now. "*Nachari!*"

Nachari stared a hole right through him. "What?"

"I'm not even thinking about having sex. *Sheesh!* I wasn't even gonna call anyone."

Nachari looked at him warily. "Then why are you holding onto those numbers?"

Tears of frustration welled up in the boy's eyes, which clearly made him even more upset. "Because it makes me feel good"— he crossed his arms and hunched his shoulders—"about myself. Okay?"

Nachari met his gaze.

Braden sighed and turned away. "Did it ever occur to you that it might be kind of nice to think that—*maybe somewhere*—someone sees me as better at something? Here, everything I do sucks. I'm like the worst vampire ever, no matter how hard I try. But to humans, I'm like a god. So yeah, I hang out with them sometimes, and yeah, I like it when the girls flirt with me. But I'm not stupid enough to try and have sex. Geez. You think I don't know that I would probably suck at that, too? How much humiliation is one guy supposed to take? I just wish I could feed from human females instead of always having to take from you and my dad...*that's all.* Forget it, already." He sat down on the floor and crossed his legs, fighting to keep his tears at bay.

Nachari felt like an idiot. He ran his hands through his thick mane of hair and took a deep breath. "Hey...Braden...I'm sorry, all right? I didn't know you felt that way."

Braden shrugged. "Forget it."

Nachari shook his head. "You know, the last time I checked, you and Marquis were getting along pretty well, and if I recall, he said he was going to help you start working out—teach you a few weapons."

"Yeah, so."

"And if I recall, you were also feeling pretty good about everything you did to help save Jocelyn from Tristan and Willie—which means saving Nathaniel and Storm, too." He looked at Braden and smiled. "And I must admit: You *have* been dressing like a righteous warrior instead of a... throw-back from the Dracula era. *Major improvement.*"

Braden laughed then.

"...which we've all been pleased with. So when did all that change?"

Braden shook his head. "I guess it hasn't. I mean, I can't wait to hang out with Marquis sometime—although I'm kind of scared he's gonna try and fry me with some lightning again if I mess up. *When I mess up.* But I do like my new wardrobe." He smiled and raised his chin. "It is righteous, isn't it?"

"Absolutely," Nachari replied.

"I just...it's just...man, you feed from like five or six females at once when you hunt, and you don't kill any of them. I just wish I could do that, too."

Nachari smiled then. "You will one day, Braden, just not right now. You forget, I've been a vampire four-hundred ninety-nine years longer than you, and I spent four-hundred of those years at the Romanian University studying to become a Master. I feed from females because I prefer the softer taste of their blood. And I use so many because I don't want to hurt any one individual by taking too much. And you're right: I'd rather seduce pretty women than kill evil men—just my preference— but it takes a lot of concentration to put someone under a trance, bite a female and not take her...or kill her, know when to stop siphoning, and replace her memories with something else. I wouldn't do it if I wasn't absolutely sure of my control."

Braden cocked his head to the side. "So, are you telling me that you *never* go all the way with any of the females?" He smirked.

Nachari shrugged. "All the way where, Braden?" He waved his hand, dismissing the question. "Gentlemen don't kiss and tell, son." He patted the sofa next to him. "Now then, I think part of the reason you're getting so upset is, truly, because you need to feed." He pointed at the leather-bound tome sitting on the couch next to him and picked it up. "Do you see this book?"

Braden's eyes grew wide as he leaned forward to take a closer look. "What is it?"

"It's the *Blood Canon: the Ancient Book of Black Magic.* It's the Bible for those who practice Dark Magic. I took it from Salvatore's lair."

Braden's mouth flew open.

"Do you know how important that secret is, Braden? In fact, you are the only person I've told so far."

Braden's entire countenance changed. His features came alive. His shoulders, once again, fell back, and he held his head up high. "Cool!"

"Yes, *very cool.* And I'm going to look a few things up right now...in absolute silence...because I need to concentrate. And I have a hunch or two." He pointed at the sofa beside him. "And you, my young warrior, are going to come feed without any embarrassment whatsoever. Think about it this way: Our power is in the blood we consume, right?"

"Yeah, so?"

"Then you are not consuming the substance of a weak human but of a Master Wizard. So take advantage of the opportunity while you have it. I am never too ashamed to take from my brothers if I need it, nor are they ashamed to take from me. Do you understand?"

Braden nodded, and Nachari could see the wheels turning in his head as he weighed the possibilities. He walked over to the couch with as much stealth as he could—for a boy who was a bit challenged when it came to being smooth—and knelt down on the floor in front of Nachari.

Nachari avoided eye contact in an attempt to preserve the young man's dignity. He pulled the book onto his lap, cradled it with his right arm, and laid his left hand, palm facing up, on the couch for the kid. "Go for it, buddy," he murmured, opening the book with his free hand.

Braden took Nachari's forearm in both hands and struck a deep, clean blow. He was getting much better at biting, leaving far less of a mess to clean up. Nachari feigned a wince. "Ouch!"

Braden snarled with satisfaction and began taking long, drugging pulls from the wizard's arm.

He switched them.

Braden's telepathic voice was barely a whisper in Nachari's mind, his mouth still firmly attached to the wizard's arm.

Excuse me? Nachari asked.

He switched them, Braden repeated. *Salvatore: He switched the women.*

Nachari looked up from the passage he was reading in the dark text, and his heart skipped a beat. He stared at the young kid next to him and regarded his keen eyes. What Braden had just said surpassed the insight of a typical vampire. To divine such a thing was...well, unheard of...especially from a fifteen-year-old, use-to-be-human novice.

Nachari's curiosity piqued.

He had already come to the same conclusion, but he was curious to know how Braden had determined such a thing. *Explain yourself*, he coaxed.

Braden slowed his siphoning, released the suction-hold he had made with his mouth, and slowly withdrew his fangs from Nachari's arm. His body swayed gently to the left as he tried to stand, still a tad bit drunk from the heady substance.

Nachari caught him by the arm and eased him down onto the couch. As a stream of bright red blood trickled down his forearm, he realized the boy had forgotten to seal the wounds: Okay, so Braden's brilliance was case-specific. Releasing his own incisors, he raised his arm to his mouth and dripped venom over the puncture wounds to seal them closed.

"My bad," Braden slurred.

Nachari smiled and steered him right back to the previous subject. "What you just said, Braden, about Salvatore—explain."

Braden wiped his mouth with the back of his hand and leaned toward the book.

"Do not touch it," Nachari warned.

Braden nodded and pointed to a circled stanza. "Read this."

Nachari read it aloud in its original Romanian form: *"Lumina lui Dumnezeu atunci când apare în ceruri pentru a apela mai departe de sânge luna, umbra lui se stârni în abis."*

And then, as if he had been born to the language, Braden interpreted the passage: "When the light god arises in the heavens to call forth the Blood Moon, his shadow shall stir in the Abyss."

Nachari was impressed as he continued: *"În cazul în care lumină şi întuneric, împreună fi turnat, sânge torturaţi în nevinovăţie, sigilat, prin oferirea de ars; numele Sfintei se stornează."*

"Should the light and the dark be poured out together, blood tortured in innocence, sealed through burnt offering; the name of the holy shall be reversed," Braden repeated in English.

"*Lumina devine întuneric, și întuneric devine lumina.*"

"Light shall become dark, and dark shall become light."

"*Sigiliul de lumina se aplice la un suflet torturat și de suflet, au obligația de a respecta întuneric se sigilează cu tortura.*"

"The seal of the light shall affix to a tortured soul, and the soul bound by darkness shall be sealed with torture."

Nachari looked at Braden like he had been born on another planet. "You were able to interpret all of that just by residing in my mind?"

Braden shrugged. "Yep. You're not that hard to read...*wizard.*"

Nachari chuckled, impressed. "Very well then, explain to me how you came to your conclusion."

Braden rubbed the peach fuzz on his chin as if he was deep in thought, searching for the right words: "Well, for every Celestial Being in the heavens—every god or goddess in the galaxy—there's a dark shadow twin in the Abyss, right? Down below in the Valley of Death and Shadows?"

Nachari nodded. "Yes, there is. A dark lord or lady who can be called upon through the use of Black Magic, the shadow essence or deity of the original god or goddess."

"Right," Braden said, "like when I was human, my dad believed in heaven and hell; so it's like, for every angel in heaven there's a matching demon in hell, only we're dealing with gods and goddesses, and the heavens are *literally* the heavens."

Nachari shifted uncomfortably on the sofa. The youngster beside him no longer sounded like a confused little boy. "Very well said, Braden. Go on."

"Well, *when the light god arises in the heavens to call forth the Blood Moon* refers to one of the good celestial gods; in this case, Draco, right? Since that's the god of Marquis's constellation?"

Nachari nodded.

"Okay, so Draco, *the light god*, calls *forth the Blood Moon* for

Marquis to finally give him his woman: his *destiny*."

"Go on."

"*His shadow shall stir in the Abyss* just means that Draco's evil twin, down in the Valley of Death and Shadows, got all stirred up when Draco started to make things happen for Marquis. Like it woke him up or something."

"Hmm," Nachari said, "I think you might actually have the gift of knowledge; you certainly have a talent for explaining things."

The kid's eyes positively beamed beneath his broad smile, and he became even more energetic as he went forward with his theory. "Okay, so Draco made the Blood Moon for Marquis—to show him his *destiny*—and his evil twin in the Abyss sat up and started paying attention. Well, *should the light and the dark be poured out together: blood tortured in innocence; sealed through burnt offering* just means that if some assho—" He caught himself in time. "Some *jerk*, like Salvatore, wanted to mess things up, then he could do it as long as he used the right ingredients, sort-of-like making a witches brew with the things connected to Marquis's life: *blood tortured in innocence* and *blood sealed through burnt offering*."

Nachari winced and took a deep breath.

Braden looked away. "Do you want me to stop?"

Nachari shook his head. "No, Braden: I know where you're going with this, and it's okay. I need to hear your theory."

Braden frowned and nodded. "The *blood tortured in innocence* was your twin's—Shelby's. Marquis's little brother was innocent, yet his blood was spilled through torture anyway."

Nachari closed his eyes and concentrated on a neutral image—the sunset—trying to shift his focus away from the picture the young vampire had just painted. The truth hurt way too much, yet this was too important to avoid. "Go on," he muttered, his eyes blinking back open.

Braden swallowed. "Sorry."

Nachari put his hand on his shoulder. "Go on."

"The *blood sealed through burnt offering* was the dude you and

Marquis killed—Valentine." He shrugged. "Sorry, I picked it out of your mind when you were reading the stanza because you were thinking about it. Wow, you guys messed him up bad and then left him to burn in the sun...cool. Yeah, that's definitely a *burnt* offering."

Nachari shook his head, contemplating Salvatore's intelligence. The sorcerer could not have possibly known what they did to Valentine at the time he crafted the spell. But apparently, he didn't have to: If he had divined even the hint of fire or smoke—Valentine's last moments being taken by the sun—it would have been enough to add to the curse. The thought gave him chills. Salvatore was, indeed, a powerful adversary. "*Then the name of the holy shall be reversed* means what to you?" Nachari asked, urging Braden on.

"The reverse of the holy god, Draco, is Ocard—his unholy, dark twin in the Abyss."

Nachari held out his hand and placed it over Braden's heart. He spoke three quick incantations, and a flow of golden light leapt from his fingertips into the boy's chest, radiating outward in a seal of protection. "Braden, you are correct. The reverse name of a god or goddess is the name of their dark twin, but such names should never be spoken aloud. Speaking them invokes them."

Braden's skin turned ghostly white, and his heart began to race.

Nachari smiled reassuringly. "Do not worry; I have placed you in a seal of protection that will remain until the energy of the name you spoke is no longer drawn to you. If I would've known you had the ability to discern all of this, I would've warned you ahead of time, but you're fine now. Trust me. Go on."

Braden swallowed a huge lump in his throat and eyed the white aura around him. "You sure?"

"I'm positive."

Braden nodded slowly. "Okay. So anyway, when the name of a god is reversed, then *light shall become dark and dark shall become light.*" He looked around the room warily.

Nachari gripped his shoulder. "Braden, *you're fine.* Hey, think of it this way—you also invoked the name of Draco, right? The good god. The powerful one."

Braden nodded and looked up toward the sky. "Draco, Draco, Draco," he repeated quickly.

Nachari laughed. "There you go."

Braden smiled, feeling instantly better. "Okay, so if light is dark and dark is light, that just means that everything is reversed. Everything is backward."

"And *the seal of the light shall affix to a tortured soul?*" Nachari asked.

"Well, the way my dad explained it, the male's constellation appears on the arm of his *destiny* at the same time the Blood Moon is in the sky so that the male is absolutely sure he's got the right woman. 'Cause that would really suck...getting that wrong."

"You're not kidding," Nachari agreed.

"And the woman is always within his sight at the time it appears—no matter what."

Nachari nodded. "That's correct."

"So if Marquis's constellation is Draco, then *the seal of the light* would be the seal of Draco—the markings of Draco on his woman's arm."

"I agree."

Braden beamed with self-satisfaction. "I don't know the whole story about what happened the other night, but I do know what torture is: hurting someone real bad to make them do or say what you want. Kristina's boyfriend beat her up a lot, didn't he?"

Nachari nodded, solemn. "Yes, he did."

"Well then, she was definitely a tortured soul, and she was obviously in Marquis's sight at the time of the Blood Moon. So the seal of Draco was affixed to Kristina instead of Marquis's real *destiny.*"

"And *the soul bound by darkness shall be sealed with torture?*"

"Well, I think the soul bound by darkness would have to be Marquis's real *destiny* because she was supposed to be bound to him, bound by the light of Draco. Instead, she's walking around in darkness, and from what my dad said, being separated from one's life mate—their true destiny—is torture. They could even die. So if Salvatore switched it all up, his true *destiny* would have to be hurting really bad."

Nachari sank back into the sofa and crossed his arms over his chest. "Yes, Braden, I believe she is."

The kid cracked his knuckles then. "So, how did Salvatore do it?"

Nachari shrugged his shoulders. Although he knew exactly what Salvatore had done, there was no need to share such gruesome details with the youngster. Salvatore had taken advantage of the spell the moment he saw Marquis's Blood Moon. He had probably read the stanza aloud three times while offering a sacrifice to Ocard—more than likely the blood of some innocent female whose throat he had slit. *Wow*. Well, no wonder things had been so crazy lately.

Glancing at his young protégé, he couldn't help but feel an enormous sense of pride. How in the world had the kid deciphered so much, so easily? He laughed aloud then, considering the *fellowship of wizards* back in Romania. They had given him the kid as a test of patience, knowing that he would come across as a bumbling young boy, awkward and insecure.

But the real test had been something altogether different.

Braden Bratianu was a *seer*.

And a powerful one at that.

A natural who didn't have a clue about the scope of his abilities. He was a diamond in the rough, and the old guys had placed him with Nachari to determine whether or not the wizard could see past the clumsiness. Could Nachari see beyond all the theatrics, spiked hair, and pouting, and still recognize the genius inside?

Amazing. A lot of things were beginning to make sense all of a sudden, and Nachari shuddered to think what could have happened if Braden had not been feeding at his wrist at the precise moment Nachari had been reading the dark book. But then again, wizards didn't believe in coincidence. The gods revealed what they wanted to reveal for a reason. In this case, not just for Braden, but also for Marquis.

Nachari jumped up from the couch and headed toward the stairs, his heart lighter than it had been in days.

"Where are you going?" Braden asked.

"To the roof, my friend. To check my telescopes."

Braden raised his eyebrows in question, his body quivering with excitement.

"Now that we know," Nachari explained, "it should be right there in the sky—as plain as day."

"What should?"

"Draco *reversed*. The other night, I noticed that the tip of the constellation was in the wrong position, pointing to the place where we would find Ciopori, but I never bothered to measure *all* of our Lord's stars. At the time, Draco just looked like Draco—still intact. But what do you bet, our dragon lord was reversed?"

Braden's eyes grew to the size of quarters. "Can I come?" He quickly looked away, trying to appear cool, afraid to sound too eager.

Nachari regarded the young seer appreciatively, his wisdom well beyond his years.

"Absolutely, Braden. *Absolutely.*"

twenty-one

Marquis was sitting on the bank of the river, just beyond his back porch, when he heard Kristina approach from behind, her soft footsteps padding quietly along the deck. As he turned to watch her approach, he assessed her color and the fluid way she moved. It had been mere hours since he had fed her at Napolean's manse, yet she was already healed.

"How are you feeling?"

Kristina shrugged. "All right, I guess."

Marquis recognized the long, heavy robe she was wearing, dark blue, swallowing her frame whole—it was his. He made a mental note that he would have to do something about it immediately, either take her shopping or stop by her apartment to retrieve the remainder of her things. So much had happened in such a short time, he hadn't had an opportunity to properly attend to his *destiny*. Like it or not, that had to change.

"So, whatcha doing?" she asked, looking around and scrunching up her face as if she couldn't figure out why in the world anyone would sit on the bank of a river.

Marquis sighed. "You should be sleeping."

Kristina frowned. "So should you."

"Is the guest room not comfortable?"

She shrugged once again, her bouncy red hair falling slightly forward from the motion. "It's cool, I guess. You know, kind of uptight for my taste, but then considering the source..." She stopped her own ranting. "Sorry."

Marquis just shook his head. "I didn't know rooms could be uptight." He quickly waved his hand to dismiss the comment before a sparring-match ensued. He was exhausted and not at all in the mood for twelve-rounds with Kristina. Ciopori's earlier rescue had disrupted his normal daytime sleep-schedule, and it was much too late to go to bed now. He knew if he slept through the night, it would just make things worse—kind of a hazard of being a nocturnal creature.

"So..." Kristina shrugged and clutched her arms to her stomach. She took a deep breath, held it, and then exhaled slowly. "So...you wanna do it, or what?"

Marquis shut his eyes.

"Well?" she asked.

"Do what, Kristina?"

She rolled her eyes. "You know what. Do *it.*"

Marquis fought not to blanch. *Do it? Gods, what had been his crime? And was there no other worthy penance?* He raised his head to meet her eyes just to see if she was serious.

Apparently, she was.

He was just about to give her a tongue-lashing when he thought better of it, curiosity getting the best of him. "Why the sudden change of heart?"

Kristina plopped down beside him, nearly tripping on the long hem of the robe. Her dainty arms disappeared in the sleeves as if she had none. She blew a piece of curly hair away from her eyes and sighed. "The way I figure it, we should just go ahead and do it like normal people, and the sooner we get it over with the better."

Marquis resisted the urge to get up and walk away. "And why would that be?"

"Lots of reasons." She forced a missing arm down through a massive sleeve and began to chew nervously on her fingernail. "First of all, you promised me my own pink Corvette, clothes, jewelry, an iPod. And I'm pretty sure you're not gonna let me out of this house until everything's squared away and you're safe—you know, from the whole curse thing. So, a month being cooped up? Yeah, that doesn't really do it for me. Plus, it's not like I have to feel anything, I mean, in terms of the pregnancy and birth, right? You can put me to sleep or in some kind of trance, can't you?"

Marquis considered it a rhetorical question. He'd like to put her to sleep for the next century.

"And you promised a full-time nanny, so I don't really have

to bother with the kid, either, right?"

Marquis grunted, nodding his head.

"Well, then why make ourselves crazy and sick thinking about it for the next however many days, when we can just get it behind us and go on with our lives? Honestly, boss, I'd rather get it over with…if you don't mind. And you know, if you wanna use that mind control stuff to make it easier, that's cool. It's only one time; we're both adults. And you're obviously not letting me go—" She bit her tongue to stop her rambling.

Marquis ran his hands through his thick dark hair and wished he could be anywhere but where he was. "Well, that was certainly the most passionate seduction I've ever encountered."

"*Ha. Ha.*" She rolled her eyes.

"Kristina…" He spoke slowly. "I am sure you are right: If we forego invitro, then eventually, it will probably come down to just that. But as for tonight, I'm just not ready to go forward like this. Forgive me if I need a little more time to adjust to the *inevitability* of our situation."

Kristina looked surprised and mildly offended. "You don't want me, do you?" She turned away.

Marquis's head snapped to the side. What in all of creation did that have to do with anything? He was at a complete loss for words.

"Yeah," she whispered, "that's what I thought. It's cool. I understand."

Marquis cleared his throat. "Kristina, you have made it crystal clear that you would rather slide down a razor-blade into a tub of alcohol than be with me—that you despise me and this whole situation. And I can't blame you. No, I don't spend my nights pining away for you, if that's what you're asking." He tossed a rock into the river and watched it skip in perfect increments all the way to the other side. "What is it that you want from me this night, Kristina?"

Kristina stared down at the ground. A single tear crystallized in her eye, and she quickly brushed it away. "Look," she said softly, "I know this whole thing has been totally whack. And the thing with Dirk"—she held back her sniffles—"shit, Marquis, that was so messed up, how you killed him right in the front yard as if he was nothing—as if I'd never even loved him or known him."

Marquis stared at her intently. "He was dragging my mate across the front lawn *by her hair*...and threatening to kill us both. If I had been a mere human, I would have killed the man for the insult. But being a vampire *and* a warrior? Be realistic, Kristina—"

"I know. I know." She held up her hand. "Let's not go there again. *I know!*"

They sat in silence for what seemed like forever before she tried her own hand at skipping a rock, only to watch it sink like a cement block the moment it hit the water. "So much for increased power and skill." She scowled.

Marquis frowned. He picked up a smooth rock and placed it in her palm. Holding his much larger hand over hers, he drew back and demonstrated the smooth, forward motion of a throw several times in a row, working her arm in a soft, easy glide. On the last repetition, he let go, and the rock flew out of her hand, skimming across the top of the water.

Kristina threw back her head and laughed. She picked up a pair of rocks and tried again. The first one started to bounce but quickly sank. She looked back at him with interest.

Marquis demonstrated the smooth, easy toss again with his own arm, only this time, she watched carefully, imitating the movement on her own. And then she threw the second rock, skipping it all the way across the river.

"Did you see that!" She began searching the ground for more stones.

The corner of Marquis's mouth turned up, but it wasn't really a smile—perhaps a step in the right direction. Kristina was like a child. And being mated to her was going to be like raising one: a one-sided deal. If he was being honest, she reminded him a lot of Braden Bratianu, Nachari's young charge, just a little bit older and a lot more cynical. Hardened.

"Listen," she said as she continued to toss stones across the river, some skipping, some sinking, and some ricocheting off larger rocks, "I know that Dirk was bad, and I should've left him a long time ago. And I know that none of you guys were gonna let that go on forever, but I just wasn't ready...and especially not for all this." She swept her arm around the two of them, gesturing next toward the property and the house. "And I know that he would've killed me, that you saved my life the other night, even if you were an evil, *evil* monster to convert me the way you did!" She glared at him for a minute before softening her gaze. "And well, yeah, today—what you did earlier, helping me feed and letting me save face and all—yeah, that was kind of cool of you. So I guess I kind of owe you, ya know? I mean, if saving your life is that easy to do, then sure; why not?" She swallowed hard, her expression betraying her underlying anxiety.

"Thank you," Marquis said evenly, trying to be noble. "But those are all the wrong reasons, Kristina—"

"Marquis! Stop! *Just stop.*"

He swallowed his words and waited.

"Don't you see how hard I'm trying? Don't you get it?" She shook her head and dropped the handful of stones. "I'm all messed up in the head to begin with...behind Dirk...and that ain't gonna change any-time soon. You and me, we have about as much in common as a polar bear and a giraffe—"

"A polar bear and a giraffe?" The words slipped out. It was just...*gods*, where in the world did she get this stuff?

"Okay, a lion and a chimpanzee. Is that better?"

"Uh, yeah—much better. Thanks for the clarification." *Good gods.*

She huffed, indignant, but ignored the sarcasm. "And you might not like the situation anymore than I do, but at least you're not scared all the time. And at least you're not helpless."

"You're not—"

BLOOD AWAKENING

"Yes I am, Marquis!" She stomped her foot against the ground and threw up her arms in exasperation. "Damn. Don't treat me like I'm stupid! Why do you always do that? Why do you have to take away every little bit of control I might have? What do you want from me? For me to get down on my knees and admit that you're bigger, you're stronger, you're faster—and smarter—you can kill me anytime you want? Well, fine, I said it!" She was shaking from head to toe and struggling to make it stop. "At least let me say *when*. At least let me say *how*. Why can't you just let me do what I'm ready to do while I still have the courage?" Her trembling stopped, and she steadied her voice. "Maybe that's my way of handling things: Did you ever think of that? Maybe that's just how I deal." She parked her hands on her hips. "Maybe I want this behind us because it's like a dark freakin' cloud hanging over my head, and every day we wait, I just get more scared. And you just get more *powerful*."

Despite his *lack of appreciation* for the female, her words hit home.

"This time two weeks from now, I'll be incapable," she added, sounding defeated. "And I won't even care what the consequences are: your life or mine. I'm sorry, but it's the truth. That's just how messed up I am. So I'm offering this to you, *now*." She clenched her eyes shut. "At least give me that much control, Marquis."

Marquis studied Kristina carefully, and then he gently probed her thoughts: She didn't want him, not by a long shot, so what was it she was after? Because this was about a lot more than fear. As he moved silently through the recesses of her troubled mind, he saw the trepidation and confusion she spoke of—and her determination to survive. But he also saw something else....

He saw a girl who had never felt safe a single day in her life, not even when she was working at the casino under the protection of the house of Jadon. Marquis frowned. They should have taken care of Dirk much, much sooner. But her insecurity went deeper than that. There wasn't a single day in her hard, young life when she had felt *peace*. And that was something he understood.

Very well.

Staring into her deep blue eyes, he knew they would never share passion or Eros love. Theirs would be more of a brother-sister, father-daughter relationship, *if* they even achieved that—and how disgusting was that thought in light of what she was offering?

Marquis shook his head to clear his thoughts.

She couldn't give him anything—because she had absolutely nothing to give. But he could give her something. Not love, not passion, not even eroticism, but safety, security, and *peace*. And wasn't there some way to make love that wasn't about the ultimate, primal ecstasy—bite and release—but more about those deeper, more meaningful things? If there was, he needed to find it and harness it…just this once.

He sighed and held out his arm. "Kristina, come here."

As she hesitantly folded her body beneath his arm, nestling against his much larger frame, he sent her a deep sensation of warmth and security. He wrapped her from the inside out in a feeling of well-being, from her heart to her soul, down to the very toes of her feet. And then he watched as she let out a deep exhale—like someone who had been holding her breath since the day she was born.

Gently running his hands through her hair, he bathed her in unconscious images of safety and security, ensconcing her in a thick cocoon of light.

Tears escaped her eyes as she nuzzled in closer like a baby being held for the first time. It was as pitiful as it was sad, and certainly not the appropriate time for a man to seek pleasure from a woman…but this was what she had asked for. And Marquis did not see a deeper, more passionate connection ever occurring between them. No. This was all they had to exchange. She would give him twin sons, provide him with the requirements of the Blood Curse, and ultimately save his life, and he would give her one night of safety and security in exchange, with a promise to provide all of those things outside of the bedroom for the rest of their lives.

Their very, very long lives.

Marquis clenched his eyes shut. He couldn't think of that right now.

As Kristina gave into the warmth of his ministrations, she became like butter in his hands: not so much on an erotic adventure but melting, falling into a deep, spiritual trance.

Marquis made his every touch gentle, distributing ever deeper waves of security as he softly stroked her arms, her neck, and the sides of her jaw with his thumb. Until he was finally able to bend down and kiss her without resistance.

The kiss was short and soft. Just a flutter. A test.

The depth of passion he needed to deepen or sustain the kiss just wasn't there, but it still imparted trust and warmth, which in turn allowed her to relax even further as he gently laid her down on the ground.

She was definitely in a spell of sorts, just not the kind she had expected. As tears rolled down her face—tears that had nothing to do with him and everything to do with how she felt about herself—he gently kissed them away, one at a time, slowly peeling back the robe to expose her soft flesh. His hand swept gently across her narrow waist and over the small, flat expanse of her belly, willing her into even deeper serenity. He was nothing more than a conduit now, using his body to illicit the spiritual healing she had craved all of her life. Taking nothing. Making no demands. Simply giving a starving soul the sustenance it craved.

As Marquis continued to concentrate on her inner being, it became easier to touch her, caress her...kiss her. Nothing was about him.

Nothing was about them.

He would not enter her harshly or thrust away as he would a female he desired to pleasure...and be pleasured by. Rather, he would give her the experience of being cherished, of feeling worthy, until she completely surrendered for the first time in her life, and then he would gradually—*carefully*—enter her welcoming body. Careful not to hurt her with his size. Stretching her so slowly that she wouldn't even notice.

He would fill her with peace, tenderness—and seed—without a single thrust being necessary, and then he would just as gently withdraw.

The preparation might take an hour. The sex, maybe thirty seconds. As she fell off into a peaceful sleep, he would command her to conceive, awakening her only when it was time to call forth his sons to materialize from her womb.

And both of them could live with what had been done between them.

Marquis had ascended to another level entirely.

Like an artist with a canvas, or a poet with a pen, his own state of mind had elevated to semi-conscious awareness as the female beneath him parted her legs to accept him willingly. Her head tilted back, her eyes drifted shut, and warmth radiated from the core of her body like sunshine through a plate-glass window.

As Marquis subtly shifted his body in order to blanket hers, he felt an odd, uninvited stirring in the energy around them.

No. Not now! They were so close.

He placed a strong barrier around Kristina, insulating her from the disturbance, and tried to refocus.

Brother. The telepathic call slammed into his head.

He ignored it.

Brother!

Marquis tried to quiet his mind. *Ignore it, and it will go away.*

He used the massive strength of his thighs to gently push Kristina's wider so he could gain entrance. And then he began to lower his pelvis to hers.

BLOOD AWAKENING

Marquis!

Marquis pulled up, threw back his head, and grimaced. Yes, he was providing an incredible spiritual service, and yes, he was detached from any deeper, erotic relationship, but hell, he was still a man. And this close to release, his body wanted to finish!

Go away, Nachari! he demanded. *I'm busy! I will contact you in a few minutes.*

But this is important.

Later!

Very important!

Marquis slammed down a mental barrier and lowered his hips once again, the head of his shaft pressing firmly against Kristina's moist core of heat. Despite his sage-like control, a low groan escaped his throat.

Now, Marquis! Nachari pushed right through the mental barrier. *What the heck are you doing?*

Marquis felt his face flush, and anger heated his resolve. He looked down at Kristina to make sure she was still feeling the enchantment. *Brother, go away; or I swear, I will kill you!* He tried to close the telepathic bandwidth, but was met with a strong current of resistance.

And then he felt...*a mind probe.*

Had Nachari lost his mind!

Male vampires never invaded the thoughts of other male vampires. It was unheard of. Rude! *Taboo.* And rank was everything.

Nachari was his junior, barely beyond a fledgling at five-hundred years old: a recently graduated Master Wizard who was still working on his final project! Marquis, on the other hand, was an Ancient. He had been a Master for over one-thousand years, and he was the elder male of the two, not to mention the *head* of the family now that their father was gone.

This was heresy.

Marquis would throw the arrogant fool through a wall when he saw him next. He catapulted Nachari out of his mind, severed the telepathic line, and turned back to Kristina, whose eyes had now opened.

Ah hell.

He sent her a strong beacon of warmth and relaxation, and then he stroked her cheek with his hand. "Are you all right?" he drawled seductively, praying she was still with him.

Her peaceful smile told him all he needed to know.

As her arms wrapped around the steel cords of his back, her legs fell fully open. "I think I actually want this, Marquis." Her eyelashes fluttered closed, and her deep blue eyes disappeared behind heavy lids.

"No you don't!" A commanding male voice sliced through the enchantment, echoing throughout the deep expanse of mountain behind the house.

Kristina gasped in shock, and Marquis spun around so quickly he forgot he was naked. His manhood standing at full attention, he landed in an attack stance in front of his brother.

Nachari blanched and covered his eyes. "Damn! I did not need to see all that!"

Marquis growled in fury, waving his arm over Kristina to put her to sleep. He reached for his pants, using levitation to draw them into his hands, and pulled them on with preternatural speed. And then he hurled himself across the four feet of expanse between himself and Nachari, snatched the wizard up by the throat, and threw him into the air.

Dark raven and emerald wings shot out of Nachari's back as he hurled backward, flapping furiously in an attempt to stop his trajectory before he slammed into a tree. Hovering in the air, he reached for his throat to massage it.

"Have you lost your mind!" Marquis thundered. "Do you have any idea what you just interrupted?" Nachari looked down at the sleeping, naked woman lying on Marquis's robe. "Yeah, I would say I have a pretty good idea."

"You think this is funny?" Marquis picked up a stone and hurled it at his younger brother, hitting him so hard in the chest his collarbone snapped. "You have no idea!"

Nachari looked stunned. "What the hell is wrong with you?" His breath came in short pants as he released venom into his hand, packed the healing serum against the protruding bone, and waited for the fissures to fuse back into place. The moment they were sealed, he waved his arm in front of him, constructing a magical ring of fire around his body. "I'm not going to fight you, Marquis." He gestured toward the ring of fire. "I know I'm no match, but even you don't want to cross a ring of magic."

Marquis chuckled loud and sinister. He hurled his own blazing arc of fire from his fingertips, struck the magical ring dead in the center, and added to its power. And then he pulled the combined conflagration back, like a cowboy with a lasso, and bathed in the scorching heat. Looking down at his own glowing body, he smiled at Nachari.

And then he lunged.

Nachari screamed like a girl. "Stop! Brother, please!"

Marquis met Nachari in mid-air and threw him down to the ground. "You invaded my thoughts, little brother! And disobeyed a direct command!" This was the last straw. How much more could one vampire take?

Marquis had lived a long, painful life.

His twin had been sacrificed at birth, he had lost his parents to the lycans, and his cherished little brother had been indirectly murdered by his mortal enemy. And now, the only woman he had ever loved was gone as well. He glared into Nachari's petrified eyes. The unlucky bastard had just pulled the pin out of a grenade.

Apparently, Nachari realized exactly what was happening. Scrambling to his feet, he fell into formal protocol. He bowed his head, descended to one knee, and crossed his arms over his chest...waiting. His heart pounded furiously in his chest, a bead of sweat escaping his brow.

Marquis stalked around him slowly, growling in disgust, trying to calm himself down. When he finally held out his right hand, Nachari took it tentatively. He bent to the ring on Marquis's fourth finger—the one with the crest of the house of Jadon engraved in it—and kissed it with deference.

Marquis snorted. "Speak."

Nachari raised his head but kept his eyes averted. "I would humbly ask this fellow descendant of Jadon, an Ancient Master Warrior, honored elder, and esteemed son of Lord Draco—for his forgiveness. I meant no offense, my brother."

"You entered my thoughts!"

"Yes, my brother."

Marquis leaned back and crossed his arms over his chest. "In five-hundred years, you have never shown me such disrespect, Nachari. What in the world—"

"Kristina is not your true destiny." The words came out in a rush, and Nachari quickly dropped his head back down.

Marquis froze then. He cocked his head to the side as if he had heard him incorrectly. "What did you say?"

Nachari looked up but still avoided direct eye contact. "I said *Kristina is not your true destiny.* Ciopori is. Salvatore used the *Ancient Book of Black Magic* to switch them."

Marquis staggered back. "Look at me." It was a harsh command, and Nachari met his brother's stare head-on. Without pause, Marquis returned the offense and forced his way into Nachari's mind, extracting everything but the gray matter.

And then he sank to his knees, trembling.

Slowly, Nachari approached the Ancient Master Warrior—who was too stunned for words. "Is it too late?" he whispered, gesturing toward Kristina. "Did you already...have you commanded her pregnancy?"

Marquis looked up and slowly shook his head from side to side. "No." He thought about the implications and almost collapsed. "*Oh, gods,*" he exhaled slowly.

And then, without warning, he snatched his little brother up by the collar and pulled him into the strongest hug he had ever given another male. Unable to pull away, he buried his head in the wizard's shoulder and shook. "Thank you, my brother." He squeezed him even harder. "For being a wizard. For invading my thoughts. For coming here to stop me. For...for...oh hell, just thank you!"

Nachari struggled for breath, and Marquis relaxed his hug. The wizard sighed with relief. "You're welcome, warrior. And I love you, too."

twenty-two

Salvatore Nistor watched as Stefano Gervasi, the ancient Chief of Council, shook his long, bony finger at the males seated at the table and then pounded his fists into the worn, limestone tabletop, drawing his own blood. "How many dead?" he thundered, sucking the blood from the wound.

The council table remained quiet.

"Demitri, what's the final count!" Stefano demanded.

Demitri Zeclos stirred in his high-backed leather seat and took his time answering, which made Salvatore smile...*inside*: Yes, there was a time and place for insolence and a time and place for obedience. And this was the time for the latter.

"At final count, there were twelve guards, fifty children, one worthless nanny, and eighty-seven soldiers," Demitri answered respectfully

Stefano fell back into his chair, the burden of his seat clearly weighing heavily upon him. "Eighty-seven soldiers?" he repeated uselessly. "How?"

Milano Marandici, another young hopeful councilman, leaned forward. "The guards were killed by our enemies' teams. It appears they entered from both the east and the west tunnels while the colony slept. The children were slaughtered by the squad led by Marquis, and the soldiers were killed by Napolean."

"Single-handedly?" the chief asked, incredulous.

Salvatore sighed with annoyance: The chief had heard the story a dozen times. They all had. *Yes, Napolean Mondragon was far more powerful than any of them knew. And yes, he had melted a damn army of Dark Soldiers right in their own hallway by harnessing the light of the sun. Blah. Blah. Blah. Now could they just get on with it?*

"Yes, sir," Milano answered.

Stefano leaned forward, placed both elbows on the table, and glared at his second in command, Oskar Vadovsky. "Oskar, tell me you have crafted a plan in response."

Before Oskar could answer, Stefano turned back to

BLOOD AWAKENING

Salvatore, so angry that spittle shot from the corners of his cruel mouth. "And the *Ancient Book of Black Magic*—the *Blood Canon*—it's gone as well, is it not?"

Salvatore growled. Now that ticked him off, too. He had possessed that book for nearly eight-hundred years before it was stolen. Fortunately, he knew most of the contents by heart, but still, the thought that some pretty little wizard boy could have stolen it right out from under his nose made him seethe. He glared at Milano, who unfortunately shared Nachari's deep green eye color, and scowled. "Yes, Chief. I am sorry to report"—*for the millionth time*—"that Nachari Silivasi appears to have taken the tome from my lair when he exchanged my nephew."

Stefano stared at each man, one at a time, lingering a little too long over Milano, which was just plain creepy, before turning back to Oskar. "Your plan?"

Oskar cleared his throat and made a tent with his fingers. As a fourteen-hundred-year-old ancient and a dangerous adversary, he was only slightly outranked by Stefano and not someone to be toyed with...not even by their reigning chief. His eyes roamed between Stefano and Milano, and he growled with disgust.

Ah, so he had caught the strange *vibe* coming from the old geezer, too. True, Milano was rather disturbingly beautiful for a male, even with his short, disheveled hair, so typical of youth under five-hundred years old, but that was certainly not how the colony operated—males staring *like that* at other males, that is.

Oskar stood slowly. His raspy voice dropped to a low-pitched hum like a bass guitar. "The plan is simple: We restore our numbers and hit back hard by going after the king." His eyes roamed from male to male, boring holes through their skulls with the voracity of his hatred. "Fifty infants were killed, so I want two-hundred and fifty filling our nurseries within the next seventy-two hours!"

Demitri gasped and then quickly regained his cool, exchanging a knowing glance with Milano.

Salvatore laughed inwardly. Poor kid. Didn't he know that

council was exempt from colony-wide mandates, their duties being too important to group with the general population? Salvatore studied the pale wash of Demitri's skin and couldn't say he blamed him—he hadn't wanted the responsibility of a son at three-hundred years old, either. In fact, he was still yet to reproduce, but then, he had Derrian to look after now. And as for Milano, the young buck was as wild as they came, nowhere near ready to be saddled with a kid.

"Is there a problem?" Oskar demanded, glaring at Demitri.

"Not at all." The kid showed the proper respect.

"Good," Oskar flared, "because by this time tomorrow night, I want our lairs filled with the sounds of screaming, groaning women. I want the chorus of rape and the death-song of birth to be a symphony playing in my ears until every soul we lost is replaced. Is that understood?"

Demitri nodded along with Milano and Salvatore, and then he began writing on a piece of parchment.

"Now then, every male over the age of five-hundred who does not have offspring must...contribute. Those under five-hundred may choose to reproduce now or wait, and those with at least one son already may also pass on the *festivities* by choice." He began to pace around the table. "As for feeding, I do not want the males to eliminate the local food supply, but I do want them to drop enough bodies in the streets to terrify the local humans. I want pandemonium in Dark Moon Vale, enough to rile up the hidden vampire hunting societies. Let them come after our foolish brothers on the surface while we remain safely hidden away beneath the earth."

Every male at the table smiled.

"And as for the book..." Oskar glared at Salvatore and then clasped his hands behind his back. "Nachari Silivasi must be made to pay for this insult!"

Stefano, the chief of council, scowled in disgust. He stood, held out his arm to silence his second in command, and then neatly took the reins. "For *Salvatore's* foolish, foolish oversight!"

BLOOD AWAKENING

Oskar nodded and took a seat as the council chief trembled, slowly stoking the fire of his rage.

Salvatore bit his tongue and waited.

"But not before we avenge our fallen," Stefano hissed, slowly cracking his knuckles in true theatrical fashion. "I would have Napolean Mondragon broken! Humiliated! Little by little, brought to his knees in shame. I want the male ruined!"

No shit, Sherlock, Salvatore thought, *any plans on how to get there?* "And what would you have us do, your excellence?" he asked.

"Are you not our sorcerer?" the council chief thundered, striking him unexpectedly across the face with an open hand.

The force of the blow rattled Salvatore's teeth, causing his upper canines to pierce his bottom lip. He spat out the blood and glared at their leader, his body trembling with the need to strike back.

He restrained himself.

"Torture him, you fool!" Stefano shouted. "Cast a spell! Haunt his dreams! Find his weakness and exploit it!" He purred deep in his throat, an evil, rumbling hiss, and his eyes grew dark with menace. "I don't care what you have to do, just make the male suffer! For once in your miserable life, prove your reason for existence, Nistor! Or I shall have your council seat."

The room reverberated with a collective gasp.

Oskar sat forward with interest.

Salvatore cleared his throat and forced a smile. "My apologies, your excellence. I was unaware that my *service* was so lacking." His eyes shot between Demitri and Milano and then flashed quickly, two harsh red pulses, before returning to an endless void of black.

This was the opportunity they had discussed.

The chance to seize power they had each hungered for.

Ever since Valentine's death, both males had postured for his vacant council seat, each proving himself to be worthy in different ways. With the chief gone, there would be *two* standing vacancies instead of one.

Salvatore's mouth turned up in a sly grin. "Your excellence," he snarled, "you hurl such a powerful accusation, yet you stop short of corrective action. Indeed, should any male on this council fail to prove *his reason for existence*, he should be removed *at once*." And then he winked.

Demitri and Milano flew up from the table like two malevolent black tornados whipping through a barren field, gathering momentum as they approached the chief, daggers drawn, fangs bared, the adrenaline of youth coursing through their veins. The element of surprise was all that saved the bold soldiers from a certain death as Demitri's dagger sliced the chief's artery and Milano's found its way into his heart before the chief could blink.

Stefano's fangs exploded from his mouth, and he howled in rage, bringing pieces of the ceiling down upon them, but the power-thirsty males kept up their attack: swiping, biting, twisting, and attacking like madmen as the three flew around in a whirlwind at the head of the table.

When Oskar rose to go to Stefano's aid, Salvatore placed a firm hand on his shoulder. "You are our new chief now, Oskar. You do not want to do that."

Oskar looked astonished. "Are you threatening me, Salvatore?" He hissed a clear warning, his eyes narrowing in an unmistakable promise of retribution.

Salvatore bowed his head but kept his eyes focused on his quarry. "Only threatening to serve you, *your excellence*."

Oskar wasn't impressed. He leapt up on the table only to dodge the flying head of their chief as it rolled off his shoulders. Demitri and Milano had sunk their fangs into opposite sides of Stefano's neck, ripping it from his torso with their bare teeth. The males salivated like wild animals, staring at the decapitated head with a wicked blood-lust flaming in their eyes. Great lords of darkness, they looked like two possessed, rabid dogs: Blood and gore hung from their teeth, ravaged skin covered their mouths, and saliva dripped from their fangs.

BLOOD AWAKENING

Oskar growled a low, unmistakable warning: *Attack me, too, and die.*

Both males took a step back.

Salvatore turned calmly to Oskar. "What's done is done, your excellence. It would be a shame to waste this ancient one's blood when the dark lords of the Abyss—*and Napolean Mondragon*—are waiting. We should make a sacrifice, ask the dark lords for assistance in besting our enemy...while we still can."

Oskar looked as revolted as he was stunned, staring at the treacherous trio with utter disgust. He cleared his throat. "His son, Sergei, will seek vengeance."

Salvatore shook his head. "His son, Sergei, will not know. Perhaps our illustrious chief was so enraged by the attack on the colony that he attempted to go after Napolean alone. Unfortunately, Napolean was the stronger of the two. We were able to retrieve his remains for incineration and will, no doubt, need to decorate Sergei with his honors."

Oskar stepped back against the wall and ran his hands through his long, twisted hair. He glared at Milano. "Clean this mess up and move his body to the hall of sacrifice. Salvatore, prepare for an offering ceremony to the dark lords, and Demitri, you will be the one to notify Sergei once all is said and done."

The three males nodded in unison and were just about to move when their new leader held up his hand to still them. His piercing, angry eyes were the color of blood. "Stefano was caught unawares," he scowled. "In a million years, he would never have conceived of such treachery." He glared at the two young bucks. "Trust that you are only breathing because of the audacity of your coup. But know this; I will have both eyes open at all times, and from this day forward, the punishment for treason shall be eternal torture. By this new decree, one enforcer and one healer shall remain at either side of the traitor in the torture chamber—the former to inflict unimaginable suffering, the latter to ensure the traitor's survival...*for all time*. With all of the males in the house of Jaegar—and all we are about to create—each soldier need only serve one day every few years to keep the torture going *forever*. The cycle would never end."

The tips of his fingers caught fire, and he leapt across the table, decking Milano first, and then Demitri, with a scorching fist—before either male saw him coming. Both traitors hit the ground, scalps smoldering, jaws busted open, and bits of fang scattered about the floor. "Do we understand one another?"

Gulping, the two males nodded.

He then lifted Milano by the lapels of his shirt, released a sharp claw, and carved it along the left side of his face, from temple to mouth, removing his left eye in a single swipe. "If you dare to heal that scar or regenerate that eye, you will meet the fate of a traitor. Your days of beauty—and your ability to catch anyone off-guard—are both over."

Milano held his face in his hand and shook, but he nodded in submission. "Yes, your excellence."

Oskar then bent over Demitri, who was trying not to tremble. "Stand up, boy, and drop your pants!"

Demitri's eyes grew to the size of silver-dollars as he looked to the other two males for support. None was coming. They had already pressed their luck as far as it could go.

Oskar withdrew a dagger from seemingly nowhere and held it to Demitri's throat. "I won't ask you again."

Trembling, Demitri unzipped his jeans and let them fall to his ankles.

"Which do you prefer to keep? The left or the right?" Oskar spat.

Demitri gulped.

Too late.

His right testicle was sliced from his body so swiftly, a couple of seconds passed before he registered the pain and then buckled to his knees. "Cauterize the bleeding," Oskar ordered, "but do not regenerate it. *Ever*."

Salvatore winced. There was a time-limit on regeneration. After a couple of months, both males would be irreversibly *damaged*, and they'd stand out in the house of Jaegar like sore thumbs. Oh well, at least they were council.

Oskar approached Salvatore then, a look of pure contempt in his eyes, hatred dripping from his upturned lips. "I know these young fools could not have coordinated such an act of treachery on their own, sorcerer. Nor was it a moment's impulse."

Salvatore knew better than to speak.

He declined his head in reverence and waited to see what was coming. Whatever it was, it would be worth it to bring down Stefano Gervasi, to gain the dark lords' assistance in besting Napolean Mondragon—to get at the family that had killed his brother and attempted to harm his nephew. The council was as it should be: They needed Oskar's leadership and his cunning, and all actions had consequences. He would take his punishment like a man.

Incensed by his arrogant resolve, the new chief caught him by the throat and squeezed until Salvatore's eyes bulged in his head, and his body started to convulse. Salvatore refused to plead for mercy even when the elder snatched him by the hair, jerked back his head, and fed on him like a worthless human in the ultimate act of disrespect, tearing out huge chunks of his throat as he gulped.

Salvatore winced, but he didn't cry out. There was no regret for his actions. Unbidden, a small, maniacal chuckle escaped his lips.

Oskar released his throat with a disbelieving snarl. "Do you find sedition funny, sorcerer? Never in the history of our colony has such a thing been done!"

Salvatore shook his head. Despite his attempt at humility, he struggled to suppress a smile.

Their new chief was beside himself with rage. His body shook with his fury. "Demitri...Milano...stand up!"

The two gravely injured vampires struggled to their feet and braced themselves on the table. The wretched look of agony on

Demitri's face was beyond description.

"Good! Now watch—as your arrogant mastermind *learns humility.*"

Oskar threw Salvatore against the table and ruthlessly bent him over. A pair of harsh, angry hands ripped his trousers—a set of jagged claws pierced his skin at the hips.

"What the—"

"Shut up!"

Now *this* had Salvatore's attention. *You have got to be kidding!*

This just wasn't done.

This was *never, ever* done!

Salvatore's eyes scanned the council chamber door in desperation, searching for...

What?

He had no idea.

Something!

Time stood still as his trousers dropped to his ankles and he felt Oskar kick his legs apart. *Okay, fine—the new council chief has made his point. This has gone far enough!*

What the hell...

As panic began to set in, Salvatore's eyes darted around the room hysterically. He thought about fighting...resisting. *Attacking!*

Hell, dying.

But he knew he could not best the ancient one now that Oskar had drained him of so much blood. He was far too weak and disoriented. And what was it Oskar had just said? He wanted Demitri and Milano to *watch?*

If Salvatore had only seen this coming, he would have fought Oskar to the death before the crazy freak of nature could have siphoned him...but then, that was Oskar's point, wasn't it? Treachery...sedition...taking unfair advantage against one's enemy. The punishment was fitting.

As his mind struggled to comprehend the horror, Salvatore felt a hard thrust against him, and his hands instinctively gripped the table as an unspeakable pain ripped through him.

He shouted his agony.

Twisted this way and that.

Tried to mentally escape the torture.

The pain was unbearable, the humiliation beyond comprehension.

Zarek could never know.

And then he heard his own voice, as if it belonged to someone else, groaning and whimpering like a wench, his cries thrust out of him to the rhythm of Oskar's pounding.

Oh dark lords: the disgrace.

The pain.

Make it stop!

The male had made his point already! This had never been done! But then, neither had the assassination of a sitting chief of council by his own members.

Salvatore's body shook from the invasion, and then Oskar wrenched Salvatore's head back by his hair, bit out a raspy command, and *moaned with pleasure.* "Look at each other!"

Demitri and Milano were simply stunned stupid, their broken, bloody mouths hanging open, their pained faces reflecting the shame they felt—both for themselves and the ancient sorcerer being defiled before them—as they forced themselves to hold eye contact with Salvatore.

Bile rose in Salvatore's throat, and he began to dry heave—unfortunately, still to the rhythm of Oskar's gyrations—as he watched their piteous eyes fixed on his, the revulsion on their faces.

No one said a word as the vile act went on...*and on.*

And on.

At some point, Salvatore considered holding his breath in order to pass out, but he knew it wouldn't work. He gripped the edges of the table harder, instead, trying to sustain the harsh, relentless thrusts, gritting his teeth against every vile surge, biting back his own angry tears. He wanted to rip the bastard's throat out, but there was nothing he could do but take it.

This was inconceivable.

Murder was one thing. Treachery, another. *But this?*

All at once, Salvatore heard a hoarse shout and felt Oskar relax behind him. *Oh great demons of hell.* He refused to even think it. Demitri lost his dinner, and Milano followed right behind him.

As the chief backed away, Salvatore collapsed on the table, no longer able to walk. His stomach wrenched as he caught the scent of his own blood mixed with the scent of—

How did one regenerate from such a thing?

Salvatore panted from exhaustion and agony, the chief panting from something entirely different.

Oskar zipped up his pants and took a step back. "The next time we meet, boys, there will be a master at arms posted to the left and right of my seat, and a body of guards just outside the door. What you did tonight in this room will never be spoken of again. What I did tonight in this room will remain here as well. Are we clear?"

The soldiers grunted, still in shock, as Salvatore fell from the table, groveled on the ground, and tried to nod. There was little he could say—especially without an intact throat. He didn't even possess the strength to release his fangs.

"Now get yourselves together so we can get on with the offering. We have a king to destroy." With that, the furious new chief of council stalked out of the chamber.

Salvatore stared at the ground, too ashamed to look up. At least it was over. The coup had succeeded, and they had all lived through it.

Such as they were.

Yes, he thought, with profound disgrace and a new grudging respect for their leader, *Oskar Vadovsky was not one to toy with.*

twenty~three

Marquis brushed a sweat-soaked lock of Ciopori's hair away from her forehead and softened his seal on her throat, careful not to dislodge his fangs.

Dearest virgin goddess, when would the suffering end?

Trying to disguise his own trembling, he brushed her arms with his hands and held her tightly to his chest, continuing to send the life-changing venom deep into her veins.

It was two a.m., and they had been at it for twenty-four hours.

Twenty-four hours.

What amounted to an entire day of muscles stretching, joints realigning, organs failing then regenerating, blood pooling like acid in reconstructing veins, and unimaginable pain, bringing merciful bouts of unconsciousness only to jolt her awake with a new surge of agony. It had been the hardest thing he had ever done. And the hardest thing Ciopori had ever endured. Although Kristina's conversion had been difficult, it had only lasted a few hours. This was beyond comprehension.

Apparently, Ciopori's pure celestial blood, as well as the fact that she was an original female and exempt from the Blood Curse, had caused her very essence all the way down to her DNA, to fight the change like a soul invasion, as if her eternal existence depended upon it. And in all actuality, it did. There were more than a few occasions when Marquis had wondered if her body would take to the change at all.

Once Napolean and Nachari had performed the necessary ritual to reverse Salvatore's trickery, calling upon the powerful god Draco to endow Ciopori with her birthright as Marquis's true *destiny*—and to free Kristina from a fate that was never hers to begin with—Napolean had assured Marquis that he could go forward with the conversion. That the requirements of the Blood Curse remained the same as they had always been. But considering the length and hardship of Ciopori's transition,

Marquis couldn't help but wonder if they hadn't pushed fate too far.

He wanted to tell her that he loved her. To explain why he couldn't stop, no matter what: Her human body could not survive the changes that had already taken place, and her Vampyr body could not survive still being part human. No. Once a conversion began, it could not be halted, and telepathic communication was next to impossible due to the sheer amount of concentration required to circulate the venom. If Marquis had known how much the conversion would cost the woman he so dearly loved, he would have left things the way they were.

As if sensing his growing desperation, Ciopori drew in a deep breath and slowly exhaled, her rigid muscles relaxing for the first time. Marquis felt a final surge of resistance discharge from her body, and there was a tangible shift in her countenance. His incisors retracted of their own accord. He mentally scanned her composition, wanting to be absolutely sure that the transfer was complete, and then he pulled away, slowly lowering the exhausted female to the bed in his master chamber.

His tension eased with relief. "My love, how do you feel?"

It was the first time in an entire day that he'd heard his own voice.

Ciopori licked her bottom lip and ran her tongue along the top of her teeth as if she was feeling for fangs. She smiled weakly. "Like I've just been run over by a thousand chariots."

Marquis smiled. "Chariots, my love? I thought Napolean transferred our culture and language directly into your mind: Did he not?"

Ciopori laughed. "He did. But honestly, to say I feel like I've been run over by a bus just doesn't cut it. It leaves out the two-thousand pounding hooves that just stomped the life out of me."

Marquis frowned. "I cannot express how sorry—"

"My love," she whispered, holding her finger to his lips, "I'm not. Just tell me this; is it over?"

BLOOD AWAKENING

Marquis smiled then. "I believe so." He became deathly quiet, listening to the forest around them. "Tell me what you hear."

Ciopori tried to sit up a bit, and Marquis quickly placed a pillow behind her back. "I hear *the sap running through the trees behind the house*, like blood coursing through someone's veins."

Marquis smiled broadly. Dear gods, could it really be? "What else?"

She closed her eyes, and then she laughed, excited. "I hear the water rushing through the river out back—and the different tones it projects depending upon the size of the rock it is sweeping over. *Dearest Cygnus!* I can hear the flap of a hawk's wings soaring overhead." She placed her hands over her ears. "How does one keep from going mad?"

Marquis laughed and slowly removed her hands, staring down into her amazing gold and amber eyes, the sparkling diamond centers gleaming with newfound wonder. "Think of the dial on a stereo, my love, or the mute button on a remote control."

Ciopori concentrated, clearly drawing from the wide base of knowledge Napolean had imparted to her as if the memories were her own.

"Now simply turn it all down."

She giggled. "It's softer."

"Yes. Now shut it all off and enter silence."

It took her a little longer to manage his last command, but once she did, she sat straight up with excitement.

Can you hear me in your head, my beautiful wife?

The sparkle in her eyes said it all. *Yes! Oh my gods—yes!*

Now tune in again to the river, but keep all else shut out.

Her laughter was as radiant as her smile as she continued to follow Marquis's instructions, trying out her new, profound sense of hearing. One by one, he took her through exercises to introduce her to her heightened senses. He taught her how to distinguish scents so faint she could name every animal that had walked across the lawn in the past month, all the way down to the squirrels, rabbits, and mice.

He taught her how to see in multi-dimension and to sense movement at the speed of light. He taught her to move her hand through the pillow and then the mattress as if both objects were mere liquid. Now that she had the ability to rearrange her molecules at will, he began to transfer small bits of wisdom regarding the laws of physics to her, for it would be these laws that would govern not only what she could do with her newfound power, but how she would ultimately focus thought to accomplish each and every feat.

Thrilled, if not a bit overwhelmed, she rested her head against his chest and simply allowed him to hold her, both of them taking in the magic of the moment. And then she looked up at him and smiled a mischievous grin. She waved her hand elegantly above them, and the ceiling rolled back like a scroll, the full glory of the heavens shining above them in a canopy of sparkling ice. Ciopori closed her eyes and held out her hand, and then she chanted in a sing-song voice so melodious Marquis thought his heart might just stop beating in his chest:

"Behold the stars that shine so bright: the gods of time, the lords of night.

Behold their glory, strength, and grace: the makers of our fearless race.
Behold the song the goddess sings; bow down to heaven's mighty kings.
May love abound and peace arise, beneath the glory of these skies....
Within our hearts, a new wind blows; behold the beauty of the rose."

Laughing, she held out her hand and presented him with the most perfect, long-stem red rose he had ever seen. He accepted the flower, bowed his head, and offered a silent prayer of thanks to the goddess Cygnus and his lord Draco: They had not stripped away her powers as a celestial being. As an original female. Ciopori Demir—*Silivasi*—was now the living embodiment of all they had been before the Curse and all they had become after it. She had the powers of a celestial being as well as all those of a vampire. And instinctively, Marquis knew that their children would too.

If only through their offspring, the original peoples would live again.

Not wanting to disturb such a private moment, but unable to contain such an important revelation, Marquis sent a telepathic communication to Napolean. He knew the fearless leader was not going to rest until he was assured that Ciopori had come through the conversion safely anyway: He had felt the Great One's push against his mind several times over the last twenty-four hours and knew that he was waiting....

The moment the most powerful living being of their kind received the information, Marquis felt a strange void—the complete absence of the Sovereign's presence. As the keeper of the house of Jadon, Napolean carried the blood of every member in his veins—males, their *destinies,* and even their children. His pulse was the electrical current in all of their heartbeats, so even when he was far away, they felt him. Just as Napolean always felt them.

Never before had Marquis felt an absence of that pulse—not even for a fleeting moment—and he wondered if the great king's heart had failed. But then again, that simply wasn't possible. He gently pushed back against the current, hoping to sense their leader once again, and felt a barrier so powerful the gods would have trouble getting through it. And then he knew. As sure as he knew the love of the woman before him, the noble king of the house of Jadon—the only remaining male from the time of the Blood Curse—had briefly closed himself off from his people for the first time in twenty-eight centuries.

The Great One was weeping.

Ciopori reached out and stroked Marquis's face. "What is wrong, my love?"

"Nothing," he replied, taking her hand in his. He turned it over and kissed the center of her palm. "Everything is right." He cupped her face in his hands. "Do you have any idea what you mean to me? What you mean to our people?"

Ciopori smiled a wise, knowing smile. "I do, warrior." And then she leaned forward and brushed her lips against his. "But tonight, on this blessed occasion, I want to think, feel, and know nothing but you."

Marquis growled deep in his throat, his body coming instantly alive. He looked down at the beautiful woman before him, sighed with contentment, and quickly stood, sweeping her up in his arms. He carried her to the large white marble bathroom and, holding her effortlessly in one arm, turned on the 360-degree row of large shower heads in the master shower with his free hand.

Ciopori watched him, her eyes glazed over with something much deeper than love, and he felt his fangs stretch against his gums. Gods, he had waited so long to have her in his arms again. He had imagined this so many times. He had grieved the loss of her as if their love would never be again. Now, with her lying there so trusting and malleable in his arms, he could hardly restrain his desire to take her. But she deserved to be loved like the princess she was, and it would be rude to just throw her up against the wall and feed from her the way his mind was begging him to do.

Be patient, he told himself. *You have...forever.*

Testing the water once again, he stepped into the large shower, not bothering to remove their clothes. As the powerful jets washed over them, he gently set her down and grasped her by the waist, more forcefully than he intended, but hell, what did the gods expect of him?

Ciopori laughed, reading his mind. "Do you always take showers with your clothes on, warrior?"

Marquis tried to answer but snarled instead. He cleared his throat and tried again. "I don't ever want to see these clothes again—the ones you've suffered in." He reached down and grabbed the bodice of her wet silk blouse and ripped it in two. Pearl buttons flew in all directions, bounced off the shower walls, and echoed as they hit the floor.

She gasped, and his manhood jerked in response, heating his blood another few degrees. Releasing his claws, he drew a line from her beautiful, pulsing jugular all the way down to her soft, ample breasts stopping at the front clasp of her silk bra. With quickness and dexterity, he shredded it into a dozen pieces using nothing but the flick of his wrist, never nicking her flawless skin.

She shuddered and her rose-colored nipples grew hard in response. The flat, silky expanse of her stomach quivered with anticipation beneath her narrow waist. He dropped to his knees then and tugged at the soaked, ruffled skirt, pulling it deftly away from her body, along with her thin, matching panties, in one hard pull. His head fell back and he moaned as his eyes swept over the soft black triangle before him. His hands gripped her thighs hard, his fingers kneading in rough, sensuous circles, as he slowly spread her legs.

Ciopori inhaled sharply and let her head fall back, gripping the sides of the shower with two open palms, her legs quivering in his hands. "Marquis," she groaned, her voice low and seductive.

He gently brushed the back of his hand against her core, drawing out liquid heat as he repeated the motion, and then he turned his hand palm facing up, allowing his fingers to trace her inner folds. His head fell forward against her thigh, and he struggled for breath as he swept his hand over her warmth again and again, each time adding more pressure.

She fisted her hands in his wet hair and then grasped again at the shower wall as if she didn't know which one to hold onto. Marquis stood up then. He gripped her slender waist with his powerful hands and bent to claim her mouth, his kiss alternating between tasting, probing, enticing, and claiming. When he ran his tongue over the soft fullness of her bottom lip, he couldn't keep himself from nipping it gently. His tongue swept over the small droplet of blood, and he gently pulled her lip into his mouth, suckling the taste of her.

His hand found the back of her neck and held her head in place as he deepened the kiss and clutched her with a force he was fighting to restrain.

This female was his.

The gods had given her to him to keep, to pleasure, to stroke, to taste...to love.

And to claim.

The male warred with the vampire, the intellect with the instinct. One desired to gently make love to his wife; the other was desperate to claim her for all time, to mark her with his scent and his touch, to command her into full submission so that she never thought of another male again. He wanted to give her everything: his heart, his blood, and his seed. And he wanted to take everything from her.

Dear gods, he wanted to drain her of every drop of her pure, celestial blood until he passed out from the strength of it; and now that she was no longer human, there was no danger of harming her. She would simply strike him back and siphon what she needed long before she would allow herself to be harmed. Her instinct would war with his.

His shaft became so hard at the thought it felt like a spear of granite straining to push its way through his pants, and the restricting cloth grew painful against the sensitive head.

He quickly shrugged out of his shirt and ripped at his trousers, kicking them from his feet. Smiling, Ciopori removed his remaining undergarment and ran her hand back and forth over the length of him, purring as she stroked him.

Purring.

His woman had just growled *in lust.*

Marquis's fangs shot through his gums like a firecracker exploding on the fourth of July, and he dipped his head, his hands riding up her shapely curves to cup the weight of her breasts. His thumbs found the sensitive nipples and flicked, caressed, making circles before he finally bent to taste them. His sigh was so deep and primitive that the glass on the shower door rattled.

Slow down, he told himself.

Before Ciopori could move against him, which he knew would shatter his control, he fell back on his knees and pulled her velvety thighs apart. His hands grasped her at her middle, his thumbs at her hips, his palms at her buttocks, clutching and massaging the shapely curves as his head fell forward and his tongue took its first taste.

He almost lost it right then and there.

Holy Pegasus. How embarrassing would that be? He trembled, trying to regain control. He slowed his breathing, and then he dipped lower to get a deeper taste. His tongue traced every outline and curve, his lips opening to press his mouth to her warmth and suckle; he swallowed all he could like a man dying of thirst. He flicked his tongue over her cleft before taking it into his mouth and gently sucking, tracing…teasingly scraping his teeth against her core.

Ciopori cried out, fisting his hair in both hands, her body building to a rapid climax. Her hips moved in sweet, passionate circles against him, taking all he could give her and pleading for more. Her leg came up time and time again, the inside of her beautiful thigh brushing against his hair as she arched to give him better access.

Marquis was like a man possessed. The more she moved, the deeper his tongue dove. The harder she squirmed, the louder her pants and sighs. The rougher his lips became, the more she whimpered—and the fiercer he claimed her with his mouth. Sensing the inevitable, he released one of his hands and buried two fingers inside of her, careful not to lose the rhythm of his tongue, his own moans barely drowned out by the rushing water.

Ciopori thrashed against him in ecstasy, calling out his name until finally, her eyes filled with tears and she tried to pull away. "I can't take it! Marquis, stop."

Enfolding her hips with a powerful arm, he pulled her to him and held her still. As three fingers entered her, he took her cleft into his mouth and suckled hard, the thrusts of his hand demanding and urgent. She struggled to move, but he held her still as she screamed the names of the gods.

And then she went over the edge.

Trembling from head to foot, her body shook and her womb contracted over and over as powerful waves of pleasure took her. Marquis used his mental powers to send electrical currents into the sensations already overwhelming her, and he held her steady as the powerful bolts shook her body along with her orgasm. Catching it at its peak, he suspended time and held it there, allowing the primal pleasure to go on and on for well over a minute. When finally, her cries became sobs and her sobs became a pleasure so agonizing that she fought to get away, he released the peak and allowed her body to unwind.

The prolonged orgasm, along with the harsh restraint, had left her so physically and emotionally exposed that she trembled from the vulnerability. She had surrendered her control in a way that was difficult for any soul to do—for a length of time that had broken down every barrier she possessed, and tears streamed down her face. She was part of him now. He had marked her, claimed her, taken her beyond the edge and held her there with total authority while she gave herself up to his absolute command.

Marquis massaged her hips and stayed with her, taking long, lazy laps with his tongue, gently scraping his fangs along her thighs, teasing her and pleasing her gently while she came down.

BLOOD AWAKENING

When all of her tremors had finally ceased, he stood, grasped her face in his hands, and kissed her long and slow. And then his eyes heated, and he knew they were glowing feral red. A deep, primordial growl began in his chest and rose to his throat, vibrating against his tongue as he felt his fangs lengthen even farther. His shaft swelled to a heavy, painful ache.

Ciopori reached down to catch the first drops of moisture as they seeped from the weeping head, rubbing the swollen tip with her thumb. Her lips parted, and she bent to take him, to return the favor, her glorious eyes catching his with a wickedly sexy glance, but he wasn't having any of that. His need was too great. He did not possess the restraint necessary to keep from heavy thrusting.

Shaking his head, his eyes bored into hers and his lips twitched in a snarl. It was instinct not menace…passion not anger…but a warning just the same. And Ciopori took it exactly as it was intended. She stood back up. Her body became liquid compliance, her eyes begged for his touch, and she threw back her head, offering him her throat.

Marquis bent to the magnificent offering, his fangs etching soft lines into her milky skin as he drew them up and down the length of her jugular, and then he made a tiny pin-prick with the tip of a canine and tasted the blood on his tongue.

A deep moan of ecstasy escaped his throat, and he seized her by the shoulders and quickly spun her around. Clutching her waist with one arm, he pulled her hips away from the tiles and bent her slightly forward, using his free hand to place her arms high above her head, against the shower walls. Gently kicking her legs to the sides, he splayed her spread eagle. Ah, yes. Her arms and legs were exactly where he wanted them.

His erection was too large to take her with force, so he took the thickness in his hand and slowly eased the head against her, opening and caressing while testing her readiness at the same time. When she moaned and pushed back against him, he let go, gripped her hips, and slowly surged forward, filling her just

286

beyond her perimeter in one smooth stroke. He rocked slowly back and forth against her, thrusting carefully, easily, as her body stretched impossibly to try and accommodate him.

Even though she had taken him before, Ciopori stiffened with hesitation. "Marquis," she whispered, "I don't know what...what's different this time, but I can't—you're too big like this. It's too—"

Marquis bent over and suckled her neck, kissing his way up her ear then down her jaw, before reaching to turn her head back so he could kiss her. All the while, he continued to work his shaft in and out, slowly pushing deeper and deeper.

She gasped when he pulled his mouth away, panting, and there was a tinge of desperation in her voice. "Dear gods, I...I—"

"Relax, my love," he murmured, kissing the back of her neck. "Let your body stretch for me."

"I'm trying," she panted, pushing back against him with pleasure despite her protests.

Marquis held her hips down so that his body went even deeper on the next stroke, and then he held himself still, growing thicker inside her.

Ciopori whimpered.

"Ciopori," he coaxed, "relax your thighs; relax your stomach; just fall back against me and trust." Ciopori's body went lax, and like liquid butter, he felt her inner core mold and give way, making space that had never been there before as it adjusted to his size. He moaned. "That's it, baby. Oh yeah, that's exactly it."

The water washed over them both, and she looked so amazingly sexy as she laid her head to the side against the cool shower tiles, her long, thick hair falling forward, water cascading from her back. Her breasts jutted out like mounds of perfection, tantalizing his eyes as her body rocked to his rhythm, and she took all he could give her with complete surrender.

Marquis swept Ciopori's hair aside. His fangs brushed over the smooth skin where her shoulder met her neck, and he gently sank them into her flesh, forming a tight seal over the bite and locking his jaw in order to hold her in place. The whimpers that followed were crises of pure satisfaction as her body instantly splintered into another powerful orgasm.

Marquis moved faster and more deeply then, thrusting into her orgasms as she lay against the shower wall, weeping with pleasure. His own arousal grew to the point of ecstasy, and then he went over the edge with her in a cosmic explosion. He trembled, riding it out, loving her more in that moment than he had ever loved anything or anyone in his life. As he withdrew his fangs, he knew that he would kill for her, die for her.

Live for her.

And follow her to the Valley of Spirit and Light if ever she should be taken from him.

"I was dead before you came," he whispered in a deep, raspy voice, still breathing heavily. "And I was resigned to existing for all of eternity that way with Kristina." His voice grew hoarse with emotion. "I may have sired her body, but you have sired my soul. You have given me life again, Ciopori."

Ciopori reached back with one arm to encircle his neck. She turned her head to the side in order to capture his mouth. Her kiss told him all she couldn't say. When she finally pulled away, she turned to face him and gazed into his eyes. "You are my world as well, Marquis. In Romania, we lived in such fear, only shadows of our former selves. As a woman, my fate placed me in the ground, alone, with only my sister and the hope of some day finding salvation through awakening." Her smile was dripping with love. "You were that salvation, and the thought of not having you with me, beside me...*inside of me*...for the rest of my life..." She let the words trail off. "There is nothing I would not do for you, nothing I would not give you. Nothing that could ever repay you for what you have given me."

Marquis wrapped his arms around her and held her tight. After all the centuries, the wars, the losses, living so painfully alone—after a millennium, learning to shut down his heart and emotions, forcing himself into continued existence, and truly believing the gods had scorned him—he had finally been given a gift equal to his sacrifice. The restoration was greater than the loss.

Balance had come full circle.

Granted, it had taken fifteen centuries, but oh-how-sweet-it-was now that he could finally taste it. He nuzzled her hair, meditating on her words: He would never be a soft man. He would never have the easy humor, style, or wit of Nathaniel or the laid-back nature of Nachari. He would never have the gentleness of Kagen, and there would always be hard, rough edges around him—a quick fuse beneath a domineering personality—simply because of who he was and all he had been through. But somehow, this woman saw through it all. She saw the soul that he was unable to reveal. And she loved him.

She would give him anything.

To repay him?

Didn't she know that he had gotten the very best of this deal? Didn't she realize that now that he had her, he had everything? What else could a male possibly want?

And then the brutally obvious came back to him.

Of course there was something that he needed.

Desperately.

And the fact that he could have forgotten, for even a moment, spoke volumes about the peace his *destiny* had brought into his life.

Marquis Silivasi needed a son.

He needed a sacrifice of atonement for the sins of his ancestors—to be free, once and for all, from the shadow of the Blood Curse.

Gazing down into the eyes of his beautiful mate, he took her face in his hands and locked his gaze with hers. He turned his head to view the small digital clock on the bathroom sink and made note of the time: *three a.m.*

"Ciopori," he whispered, pausing to brush a soft kiss against her lips, "I would have you conceive now."

twenty-four

There was a light knock on Marquis's master bedroom door, and Ciopori turned her head and smiled. "Come in," she called, unable to shift her massive weight into a more comfortable position on the bed.

The door slowly opened and a tussled head of red hair peeked through a narrow breach. "You guys wanted to see me?" Kristina called meekly.

Marquis stirred and turned toward the hesitant female. "Kristina, come inside," he ordered, as if he were still her boss.

Ciopori placed a gentle hand on his forearm, willing him her softness—or at least hoping for a little tact. "Be gentle, my love." She flashed an endearing, welcoming smile at the female who had almost become her soul mate's partner. "Yes, please; come in, Kristina."

Kristina looked down at the floor. "Are you sure?"

"Of course," Ciopori assured, motioning the young female toward the bed.

Kristina walked in hesitantly, gazing around Marquis's bedroom as if it were the first time she had really seen it. Even though Ciopori knew Kristina and Marquis had never made love—thank the benevolence of the gods—it was still a relief to see how uncomfortable she was in his bedroom. "Have a seat," she insisted, patting the mattress beside her.

Kristina looked up then and almost recoiled at the sight of the enormous belly protruding from Ciopori's middle. "Holy shhhiiit—I mean, wow."

Ciopori didn't have to use her new mind-reading powers—which would have been an inexcusable slight to another vampire anyway—to read Kristina's mind: *That could have been me.* She laughed and rubbed her belly. "Marquis assures me this is perfectly natural and will go away the moment the babies are born." She rolled her eyes and took in a slow, deep breath. "I can only hope."

Kristina offered a disingenuous smile and fidgeted with her hands. "So, uh—why'd you guys wanna see me?"

If Ciopori didn't know better, she would have sworn she detected a hint of resentment, and maybe even jealousy, in the young girl's voice. Odd, considering how deeply Kristina had detested Marquis. But then again, he had told her that things became quite...*intimate*...beside the river, just before Nachari had stopped them from going past the point of no return. *Oh, how she loved her new brother.* Just the same, Marquis had refused any other details out of respect for the young female he had believed to be his wife, and by the looks on both of their faces, it was a lot deeper than he had revealed. Ciopori swallowed hard and briefly shut her eyes; this was a difficult situation for all of them. She needed to act with grace, not jealousy, over a female Marquis had been forced to embrace.

She reached out for Kristina's hand, but the female quickly tucked it behind her back, pretending not to notice the gesture. She sat down on the bed, as close to the edge as possible, and then she stared ahead at the wall, refusing to look at either Ciopori or Marquis, who was still protectively nestled beside his mate on the other side of the bed, holding her hand in order to block all uncomfortable sensations from her body.

"Thank you for coming," Ciopori whispered.

Kristina shrugged. "Yeah, sure. So what's up?"

Marquis appraised the petite redhead carefully then, and Ciopori knew he was reading whatever was beyond the surface quite clearly. He sighed heavily and looked directly at her, his magnificent dark eyes boring into hers. "Kristina, we felt it was important to discuss your circumstances as soon as possible. There are several things—"

"Oh yeah, well...thanks but no thanks. I'm good. I'm cool, ya know. Assuming you let me have my job back at the casino." She forced an insincere laugh. "And now that Dirk—now that the apartment is free and clear, I should be fine over there. So, like I said, thanks, but I should really be going." She shot up from the bed and rushed to the door, leaving Ciopori momentarily speechless.

Staring at her mate, Ciopori raised her eyebrows. *She's hurt, Marquis.* Her newfound psychic voice revealed her compassion.

Her pride is hurt, my love, Marquis responded. *And she is scared. You have to go after her.*

Marquis nodded. "Kristina," he called, just as she reached for the polished crystal doorknob, "wait for me in the hall. We really do need to discuss a few things."

Ciopori shut her eyes. She felt like such an ogre. How absolutely stupid and insensitive of her to think that Kristina would want to have such a personal conversation with her there. Whether or not she hated Marquis, he had irrevocably changed her life, sired her into the Vampyr race, and promised her a world far more beautiful than the one she had come from. Considering her low self-esteem, the loss had to be devastating—not to mention, humiliating. Love him or hate him, she had been cast aside for another woman.

Ciopori held her tongue out of respect.

Nothing she could say would be wanted.

Kristina nodded and quickly shuffled out the door, leaving the two of them in uncomfortable silence.

Marquis turned to face his new wife. "Do not concern yourself with Kristina right now." He patted her belly. "This is to be your only concern." The ancient male appeared to be concentrating, perhaps speaking telepathically, but if he was, it was on a bandwidth Ciopori was not familiar with.

When Nathaniel Silivasi materialized inside of their bedroom, she knew exactly who Marquis had been talking to.

"Yes, brother?" Nathaniel spoke in a smooth, satin drawl, his blue-black hair swaying gently as he sauntered across the room toward Marquis, the epitome of power and grace.

Ciopori hid her appreciation.

She knew the territorial instincts of Vampyr males, but hell's bells, she was only human, after all. Well, actually, she wasn't human anymore, was she? No matter. She was still female, and Nathaniel Silivasi was a sight to behold: Like a black panther stalking through a jungle, the male was all raw power, coiled and peacefully restrained, wrapped in a sensuous package that just screamed danger...and sex. What a family she had married into.

A low growl emanated from Marquis's throat. His lips twitched, and he turned his head to glare at her. Ciopori's eyes grew wide, and she quickly sent him a vivid image of what she intended to do with him later, once their son was safely sleeping in his bassinette. Unfortunately, Marquis didn't seem all that impressed. Instead of smiling at the decadent olive branch she had offered him, he flashed his fangs in warning. Respectfully, Nathaniel pretended not to notice any of it.

"What do you need?" Nathaniel pressed on, his arms crossed over his sculpted chest.

Marquis's eyes flashed red and he snarled at Ciopori, "Would you rather I call Braden to assist you, woman?"

Ciopori blinked. And then she laughed.

Marquis rolled his eyes and turned to regard Nathaniel. "I must deal with Kristina for a moment, but I don't want to leave Ciopori alone." He glared at her—again—his jaw set with a hint of genuine irritation.

Oh my, she teased, feigning fear—as if he were really going to do something to a hugely pregnant woman, one who happened to be carrying his sons. Not likely.

Marquis ignored the quip and kept his aggravated eyes on Nathaniel. "Since you have already been through this with Jocelyn, can you contain Ciopori's discomfort for me—keep an eye on her while I step out?"

Nathaniel smiled a relaxed, easy grin and lightly bowed his head. "It would be an honor, my brother."

Marquis stood and placed his hand on Nathaniel's shoulder, and a strong surge of energy passed between them.

What was that? Ciopori asked Marquis. *What are the two of you doing?*

Tessa Dawn

I am transferring my knowledge of your physiology to him, and yielding him my...authority...over your body. Temporarily! Do not disgrace me, woman!

Ciopori laughed aloud. *Oh, Marquis. You are so funny. I hardly think Nathaniel has eyes for anyone other than Jocelyn: I have seen her beauty, you know. And if our time in the shower did not convince you of my devotion to you—and if this enormous belly blowing up right before your eyes can't convince you—then I don't know what will.*

Then keep your eyes to yourself, he grumbled. *Must I remind you that vampires are animals—not humans—Ciopori. Territory is territory. Do not make me hurt my own brother.*

Marquis released Nathaniel's shoulder and stalked toward the door. "I'll be back shortly," he called, without turning around.

Ciopori looked up. "Wow. Did you catch any of that?"

The corner of Nathaniel's mouth turned up in a smile, but he didn't respond.

"Will he always be that *intense?*" she persisted. "Maybe it's just all the stress, but that was a bit much, don't you think?"

Nathaniel shrugged his shoulders.

"You don't agree?" Ciopori asked, noting the stark intelligence and cunning just beneath the surface of Nathaniel's eyes.

"You are his, Ciopori. You *belong* to him now. Just as Jocelyn belongs to me. He is only doing what is natural for a male of our species. In all truth, you must be careful; you almost got me bitten."

Ciopori looked away both surprised and embarrassed. "Bitten? How? You're kidding me! What would he have done?" Despite her embarrassment, her curiosity was piqued. Marquis loved his family more than his own life. These were some powerful instincts, indeed, if he could be provoked to go after one of his own brothers.

Nathaniel sighed. "He would not have tried to *kill* me, Ciopori." Then he smiled a wickedly male smile. "*Raw power, coiled and peacefully restrained?* Thank you." He laughed. "However, *wrapped in a sensuous package that just screams danger...and sex?*" He raised his eyebrows. "One more thought like that and Marquis would have leapt across the room and tried to take a pint of my blood just to show his dominance—which I am not conceding by the way."

Ciopori wilted, certain she was turning pale. "You read my thoughts?" She was positively mortified. "But I...I thought vampires were not allowed to do such a thing to each other—it's against custom, if not law!" Humiliation fueled her indignation.

Nathaniel looked at her then, like a father appraising a wayward child, far too sure of himself and far too aware of her for her comfort. "It is rude, and among warriors, it may even violate law. But I did not invade your mind; you were broadcasting your thoughts quite clearly for all to hear."

"I...I..." She didn't know what to say. Dear gods, she had a lot to learn—and quickly. "Well, you must know I wasn't serious: I didn't mean anything improper." She looked away, humiliated. "I certainly wasn't trying to flirt with you or anything."

"Of course you weren't, little sister," Nathaniel drawled. He reached for her hand and took it firmly in his own.

Immediately, Ciopori felt a surge of new male energy flow through her body. *Whoa, he was powerful.* As soon as the thought came, unbidden, she quickly clasped her free hand over her mouth, as if that might somehow shield her thoughts from his awareness. *Dear gods, what was wrong with her? She was madly in love with Marquis! About to have his children, for heaven's sake. And she had absolutely no intention of continuing to humor her already confident enough brother-in-law.*

"But that, of course, is not the point," Nathaniel said aloud.

"What is not the point?"

"Whether or not you intend to flirt with me...or humor me...is not the point. And of course you have eyes only for Marquis. *You're his true destiny.* For you, as long as he is alive, truly desiring another male is not even possible." The slight twitch of his nose was almost imperceptible. "Especially now that he has marked you the way that he has."

Ciopori reached for the covers and pulled them all the way up to her chin, her eyes growing wide with surprise. "Are you always this *forthcoming*, brother?"

Nathaniel's smile was sinful...and shameful. "If you wish, I can be as quiet as a church mouse, *sister*. What is it they say? See no evil, hear no evil, speak no evil?" His dark black eyes held a glimmer of amusement in them.

Ciopori shook her head. "Well, I would hardly call any of my thoughts—or what Marquis and I do in our own time—evil. But by all means, don't bite your tongue on my account."

His smile lit up his eyes.

"Well?"

"Well what?" he asked.

Ciopori exhaled slowly and rolled her eyes. "Well, if whether or not I intended to flirt with you isn't the point, then *what is the point?*"

"The point is…" He scooted closer to the bed. "You would be wise not to look at, touch, or even think about another male, not even in passing appraisal. And should you ever do so with a human, do not be surprised if you are the cause of his death. Marquis is not known for his mercy. Why grab a tiger by its tail, sister?" His voice was absolutely serious.

"Are you kidding me?"

Nathaniel frowned. "I would never kid about such a thing." It was obvious that he meant every word.

Ciopori was momentarily speechless, searching for a reply, when all at once a firm but gentle female energy surged in the room. *Would you shut up, knuckle-head! You're scaring the poor woman. She is too new to this family to be subjected to all that cave-man nonsense right now. For heaven's sake, she's pregnant, Nathaniel.*

No doubt, this was Nathaniel's beautiful wife, Jocelyn, and she was speaking on a public family bandwidth just to make her point.

You would do well to watch your tone, female, Nathaniel snarled in response. *Do not forget who the master of our house is.*

Jocelyn sighed loud and long. *How could I possibly? He's squirming in my arms and demanding to be fed even as we speak.*

Nathaniel's drawn-out hiss was positively frightening. His sculpted muscles contracted and released in a series of waves that started at his shoulders, moved down his arms, and ended at his torso. His dark eyes turned even darker—if that was possible.

When I return home and tie you to our bed, perhaps then, you will remember who the true *master is. Or perhaps, should you continue to try me, I might just have to teach you the difference between male and female— dominance and submission. Make no mistake, woman, I can have you calling me* master *for the next thirty days—in public—should I choose. Now tend to our son, and leave us be.*

Jocelyn's answering snarl shook the overhead lighting. *Nathaniel Jozef Silivasi!*

Nathaniel's eyes flew open wide at the mere tone of Jocelyn's psychic voice, though he tried to hide his reaction. Ciopori bit her bottom lip in an effort not to laugh.

Listen here, oh great male vampire: Do not *make me come in that room and slap you upside your head right in front of our new sister— because I will if I have to.*

Nathaniel laughed heartily then, both his sense of humor and his tenderness for his mate getting the best of him. *I'm afraid you are neither that strong nor that quick, my beautiful love, but you inspire my soul. Tonight,* colega mea de sexy, *save it for tonight.*

Jocelyn giggled then, the love in her voice apparent. *Ma asteptam, de masterat.*

Ciopori knew exactly what the words meant—*I'll be waiting, master*—and the look on Nathaniel's face was priceless. He was no longer a stern, domineering vampire, but a grinning ten-year-old boy with glazed-over eyes, looking much like he had just discovered candy.

"Yes," Ciopori said, laughing, "I can see you have things well under control at home, *my fearsome brother.*"

Nathaniel chuckled and tightened his grip on Ciopori's hand. "Ah well, a male has to try." Concentrating, he continued to absorb the full range of sensation from Ciopori's pregnancy, shielding his new sister-in-law from even the slightest tinge of discomfort.

Marquis leaned back against the sturdy railing of the back porch, his legs crossed casually at the ankles, his arms folded in front of his chest, waiting for Kristina to stop pacing.

"I still don't know what you could possibly have to say to me, but fine, I'm listening. What now, *boss*?"

Marquis raised his eyebrows and smiled. He reached into his back pocket and pulled out a black and gold rectangle of hard plastic and handed it to her.

"What's this?" She snatched it out of his hand.

"It's a credit card...with a two-hundred-fifty-thousand dollar limit on it."

Kristina's eyes grew enormous as she read the name on the bottom of the card: *Kristina Riley Silivasi.* "You're still giving me money? And you want me to keep your name? I don't get it."

Marquis shifted his weight from one foot to the other and re-crossed his legs. "Of course I'm still going to take care of you, and why wouldn't I? It's *your* name now, too. The bills for the card will come to me, and on the first business day of every calendar year, any outstanding balance will be paid in full. Then the original two-hundred-fifty thousand limit will be restored, so consider it an annual...salary of sorts."

Kristina looked stunned. "But how? When? *Why*?"

"Nathaniel took care of the details for me."

Kristina tried to suppress her excitement but failed, which pleased Marquis greatly. "Kristina, I may not be your mate, but I am still your *sire*. You will be taken care of for the rest of your life."

Her large blue eyes widened with surprise...and appreciation. "Wow, that's really cool of you, thanks."

Marquis nodded. "As for living arrangements, you will not be going back to the apartment you shared with...that human. I wish I could give you a place with more privacy, but as your safety is my utmost concern, I am having one of the executive suites at the lodge renovated as an apartment. I think you will be quite satisfied with the accommodations when they are through, and there will always be guards and security within reach. You will stay in a guest room until the suite is finished."

Kristina's lips parted like she was about to ask a question, but then she slowly pursed them back together. For the first time since he'd claimed her, the female was speechless.

Marquis chuckled. "Yes, there will be a theatre room in the suite and a large Jacuzzi as well. A wet bar should be no problem, but be careful—vampires must never lose their inhibitions...for obvious reasons."

Kristina frowned then. The news that she would no longer be mated to Marquis had clearly been a relief, but the caveat that she would never be human again must have been devastating. "So then, uh, how will I—"

"Feed?"

Kristina looked down. "Yeah."

Marquis sighed. "Kristina, you will become accustomed to your new life in time; it will not always be so difficult. I want you to understand something very important, *un pic*—little one. When I sired you, my blood became your blood, my DNA part of your DNA. You are a *true* Silivasi now—by name and blood—despite our not being together. That cannot be reversed."

Kristina tilted her head as if trying to absorb the information.

"That means that you now have four living brothers, and

trust me, as rare as females are in the house of Jadon, the idea of having a sister is an extraordinary treat. You couldn't get away now if you tried. Not to mention, as you know, vampires can be a bit *overprotective*."

Kristina sighed, finally getting it. "They wouldn't."

"Oh, they will."

She shrugged. "Well, it's not like there's anyone for me to date anyhow."

Marquis shook his head. "That is not necessarily true. There are widows in the house of Jadon just as anywhere else. Between vampire hunting societies, wars with our dark brothers, and our natural enemies, the lycans, many males have lost their *destinies* over the long centuries. The problem, however, will be getting any one of these males past your new brothers."

Kristina shook her head. "Oh, great."

"You also have two sisters by blood now as well," he offered as a consolation, "Ciopori and Jocelyn. Three, if you count Vanya. Perhaps they will assist you."

Kristina just stared at him.

"And you will soon have two nephews, so you are no longer alone in this world, *sora mea*."

"*Sora mea?*"

"My sister."

Kristina looked down at the ground.

"And all of your brothers will see to your feeding."

She looked up, a subtle flash of fear in her eyes.

Marquis shook his head. "It's okay. Your needs will not be as urgent as they were when you became ill right after the conversion. A wrist should suffice. And if that is too difficult, any one of us can siphon into a wineglass for you as long as the blood is fresh when you get it." His eyes narrowed and fixed upon hers. "You will call one of us the moment you feel hunger, understood?"

She nodded...unconvincingly.

Marquis took a step forward then. "We will keep track of

your feeding cycles, little sister. Do not think you will be left alone from this point on by any stretch. In fact, I think I already heard Jocelyn mention something to Nathaniel about your upcoming birthday—something about planning a party."

Kristina looked shocked, an odd mixture of both dread and wonder. "What if I don't want all this family?"

Marquis shrugged. "It's a little late for that."

"Yeah," she glowered, "I know." She put her hands over her neck, indicating the place he had bit her during the harsh, forced conversion. "How could I forget?"

Marquis shook his head slowly. He was extremely regretful for the harsh way he had converted her, but she had shot him after all. "Look," he said, "what is done is done. What matters now is the future." He reached into his back pocket and pulled out a set of keys. They were dangling on a custom key ring with the crest of the house of Jadon on it.

Kristina's eyes flashed with excitement, and she began jumping up and down, trying to reach the keys as Marquis held them higher and higher. "What is it, Marquis! Let me see!"

After a minute of toying with her, he finally dropped them in her hand. "You must be sure and thank Nachari. You have no idea how difficult it is to get a pink Corvette in the space of five days—even for an auto-enthusiast vampire."

Kristina's eyes teared up, and she quickly brushed the drops away. "I can't believe this…" Her voice trailed off.

"If you are still inclined to have a Hummer as well, Kagen has agreed to take you car shopping this coming weekend."

Her smile was positively radiant as she held up the keys to the Corvette. "Where is it?"

"In Nachari's garage, of course. You may claim it whenever you like."

Kristina fisted the keys and nodded her head, trying to play it cool. "Thanks, boss. You know what? You're not as bad as I thought." She looked out toward the river behind the house and immediately averted her eyes, trying to shield her face with her hair. She was battling tears—for reasons beyond the car and family—and trying like hell to hide them.

"Kristina," Marquis whispered.

"Don't go there."

"That day by the river—"

"Marquis, please...just forget it."

"I want you to know that I wasn't using you. I wasn't...pretending."

Kristina held up her hand. "Don't, Marquis. I mean, the way I see it...you know...hey, it's all good, right? You did what you had to do, and well, I'm not all that hard to manipulate...for guys, anyway...so, whatever. It's cool." She tried to force a smile.

He held out his arm and shook his head. "I will not make light of this with you, Kristina. Nor will I allow you to believe that what happened between us was a mistake."

She looked up at him then, and her blue eyes held a pain so stark that their reflection startled him. "Nah, it's okay...you know? I mean, you're with the woman you're supposed to be with." She laughed insincerely. "And lord knows—you and me—that was a disaster."

He smiled. "Then tell me why you are crying."

She rolled her eyes and looked away. "Dag, you are so pushy!"

He stood firm, staring at her without any anger or impatience—just waiting.

"I just...it's just...no big deal really."

He continued to wait, the silence absolute.

She huffed in exasperation. "It's just that, you know...no one ever treated me that special before." She turned her back to him. "Dirk never touched me like that...and neither did any of the others...but hey, it was a mind control kinda thing anyway, right? So more like a dream—nothin' that you actually *meant*."

Marquis reached out and took her by the hand. When he spun her around to pull her slight body into his own, the short female measured well below his shoulders. He wrapped his arms

303

around her and nuzzled his chin against her soft, curly hair. "You are special, Kristina. I chose to…*make love*…to you in that manner because it was the only way I could approach it that would be authentic. And I *refused* to use you or lie to you involving something so intimate. I meant every moment of it."

She shivered, her heart soaking up his words like a dry sponge dipped in the ocean.

He felt her tears against his arm. "You know…there's one thing that I wasn't able to finish, though."

She cleared her throat, and they could have both heard a pin drop from a mile away. "What?"

"There was something else I wanted to give you, but Nachari showed up before I could…finish."

She jerked away then, looking up at him with an ashen expression. "Uh, I'm pretty sure Ciopori's not havin' any of that."

Marquis laughed low in his throat. "You misread me, little one." He pulled her back into the comfort of his arms. "You are thinking of the physical aspect. I am thinking of the spiritual."

"I don't want your charity." She tried, once again, to pull away, but he wouldn't allow it.

He growled. "And I'm not very charitable, so there's no problem there." He held her until she quit struggling, and then he began to surround her body with a warm, glowing energy until she relaxed into him. Lightly stroking her hair, he placed a gentle image in her mind: that of a perfect white canvass bearing the reflection of her eternal soul.

Marquis reflected back to Kristina the spirit she had been at birth.

The perfection that had been created by her human god long before she entered the world.

He revealed her immeasurable value and beauty to her, while displaying her strength of character—her unique wit and charm, the determination she had used to survive. He presented her with her divine reflection and showered her in the light of her infinite being: a perfect woman without scars, failures, or regrets.

He showed her who she truly was beneath all of the tragedy.

Kristina twisted and turned, trying to wrench away from the overwhelming light of her being. The pure experience of self-love clashed with so many years of self-degradation, but Marquis held firm until she finally let go and began to weep. He tightened his arms and held her until the warmth had washed all of her tears...and shame...away.

He had not only shown her a side of herself she had been lost to, but in doing so, he had shared a compassionate side of himself that *no one* had ever seen. Not even his brothers or Ciopori. It was the least that he owed her—and the most powerful gift that he had to give her.

Kristina slowly pulled away and wiped her eyes. She tried to utter *thank you*, but the words stuck in her throat. Finally, collecting herself, she whispered, "You and me, I guess we've got a couple secrets of our own now, huh?"

Marquis smiled. "Most certainly." He would never betray such a private moment.

She nodded then and started to turn back toward the house.

"Kristina..."

She glanced over her shoulder.

"There will always be a special place in my heart for you."

Kristina sniffled and nodded. "Yeah...I know what you mean." She let out a deep breath. "So there's no hard feelings...about...anything...then?"

Marquis smiled a mischievous grin. "*S'all good*," he said, emphasizing her typical vernacular.

Kristina's smile was absolutely glowing, her soul shining through. "Indeed, warrior. *Indeed.*"

The two of them laughed out loud.

twenty-five

Marquis checked the time on his black, Corum, stainless steel watch: *three a.m.* Exactly forty-eight hours since he had commanded Ciopori's conception. "Are you ready, my love?" he asked, hardly able to contain his excitement.

Ciopori looked down at the unsightly monstrosity that had become her midsection over the last two days and nodded decisively. "Yes! Because if this keeps on growing, I'm going to explode."

Marquis bent down and nuzzled her cheek, stopping to place a soft kiss on her lips. *His very own wife. His very own soul-mate. His destiny.* And now, it was time to meet *his son.* How had life gone from so barren to so full in the blink of an eye? How could he have believed the gods had forgotten him, when all along they had been preparing such a rare and beautiful gift?

He sighed, and then he began to gather his energy into a focused stream of light, connecting it to the two beating hearts in Ciopori's womb. With an eloquent prayer, spoken in the ancient language, he called his sons from the cramped chamber they had so briefly shared to the full breadth of the world, commanding them to come to their father.

Small prisms of light filled the bedroom like a thousand shimmering rainbows, the interconnected colors hovering in a radiant arc until a distinct halo formed above the bed, and then a rhythmic, hypnotic sound filled the room: white water rushing in a river, the steady drumbeat of life humming in harmonic, expanding waves. From beneath the crest of the halo, gold dust began to gather, swirling in soft circles above Ciopori's pregnant belly, turning like a soft funnel, the ether connecting above, below, and within.

Ciopori propped herself up on her arms and stared in rapt wonder at the phenomenon occurring before them, while Marquis held his concentration steady, gently urging the children from their slumber with his will, intending them into the world with his power.

The first of the two infants began to crystallize. The clear outline of a child appeared in gradual waves of light directly above the protruding belly, and then steadily, the outline began to fill in. The rushing sound of water increased, and the heartbeat grew louder, more insistent, as light became tissue and ether became flesh.

Instinctively, Ciopori reached toward the child, her eyes filled with tears of wonderment, but a stern growl from Marquis forced her retreat. The midnight black hair was as familiar as his own, but the blood-red bands running through it left no question as to which child had chosen to emerge first: It was the Dark One—the one who would remain nameless.

"Look away, my love," Marquis commanded. His voice was as steady and calm as the night.

Ciopori blanched, staring at him in shock. "No," she argued defiantly, "I at least want to see—"

Without hesitation, Marquis closed her eyes and gently turned her head to the side. Although she tried to resist him, her fledgling vampire skills were no match for his enormous powers. "Please, do not resist me."

The baby cried then, a loud insistent wail, his eyes glued to his mother as if he knew she was his only hope for salvation. But there was no salvation for the one born of darkness, created without a soul, the property of a curse that sought to draw its own essence back to itself in an eternal cycle of vengeance.

And there could be no compassion.

"Marquis?" Ciopori's voice was trembling with uncertainty. "This is insane. *He's a child.* A baby. How could my sisters do such a thing?" Her powerful maternal instincts pushed back against his control. Her eyes opened, and her head turned just enough to allow a side-long glance at the howling infant. "Look at him! He's beautiful. Oh Marquis, he looks like you."

Marquis reached out and took the infant into his arms before Ciopori could make the mistake of touching him. A similar thing had happened with Nathaniel when Jocelyn gave birth to Storm, and the incident had quickly escalated out of control.

Nachari, Marquis called out telepathically to his youngest brother, not wanting to involve Nathaniel, whose own memories of sacrifice were still too raw, *Ciopori is resisting; I require another set of arms.*

Nachari materialized beside the bed so quickly that Marquis had to do a double-take. The look in the wizard's eyes was all business. He glanced momentarily at Ciopori and inclined his head. "Greetings, sister." He turned to Marquis and held out his arms. "Brother."

Having been released from Marquis's restraint, Ciopori looked back and forth between the two brothers and frowned. "Marquis, let me see our son."

Marquis handed the babe to Nachari without emotion and turned to his mate. "You will see him the moment he is born, *iubirea mea.* I assure you, I will place our son in your arms immediately."

Ciopori sighed and glared at him hard. "Do not play games with me, warrior. I know full well what and who this baby is, and I repeat—*let me see our son.*"

Nachari looked questioningly at Marquis but kept a firm hold on the infant, who was now squirming, crying, and kicking his legs.

"Nachari!" Ciopori snapped. "Do not act as if you are deaf. I am not some neophyte to be coddled. Hand me the child."

Nachari's stern eyes met hers for a brief moment before turning back to Marquis. "I am sorry, little sister; I am bound by obedience to my brother."

As if understanding the dilemma, the child began to dematerialize right in Nachari's arms, pulled by the powerful intent of the Celestial Being on the bed. As his form began to take shape in Ciopori's arms, Marquis swept a hand around the body in a hasty circle, building an impenetrable holding cell around the newborn, and then he swiftly handed him back to

Nachari. *He is surprisingly powerful. You must take him from the room before he draws any further on her compassion.*

Nachari nodded. *Shall I call Napolean to take him to the chamber on your behalf?*

"Stop talking in front of me!" Ciopori's eyes flashed dark with anger. She was clearly aware that the brothers were using a private bandwidth to communicate.

No, Marquis answered, ignoring his mate's protest. *I will do my duty as soon as your nephew is born and Ciopori is at ease. Wait for me in the front room.*

Nachari frowned, appearing uneasy about spending too much time alone with the infant, but he wasn't about to argue. "As you wish," he said aloud, and then he dematerialized from the room with the infant in his arm.

"How dare you!" Ciopori shouted.

Marquis hurried to the side of the bed and placed his hand on her cheek. "Ciopori...please. I am not trying to hurt you."

"Hurt me? You insult me!"

"Never—"

"You assume I am not strong enough to handle seeing a child that I know we must relinquish. You assume that I am not in my right frame of mind to make such a request. *And you use your superior powers to force your will upon me?* Oh yes, Marquis, you insult me! How dare you think and decide for the both of us." Her eyes bored into his. "And don't you ever take control of my physical body again without my permission. Do you understand me, warrior?"

Marquis was stunned. This was not the time for an argument. This was supposed to be the second happiest day of his life.

Women.

What did she expect?

Of course his powers were superior to hers; and of course he would always use them to protect her—as was his duty as her mate and a warrior. Why would such a thing be an insult? And if

309

he ever sensed she was in danger, he would not only take control of her body, but of her mind and spirit as well, if he thought it was in her best interest. Did she not understand who she had mated?

Marquis looked away. Despite his resolve, her words cut him to the bone. He would never, ever wish to hurt her. And as for insulting her? *Dear gods, she was his superior in every way.* What was he to do with this?

Ciopori sighed and bit her bottom lip. She reached out and took his hand. "My love, I know you mean well, but we will have to...work on some of your ways. I wanted to see the child because I wanted to understand what this curse has done to our males over the years...what kind of abomination my sisters created. I needed to see the absence of his soul for myself, *to feel it*, in order to know that there was no sin in turning him over."

"But you said he was beautiful, and you didn't understand what your sisters were doing when they made such a curse. *You said that he looked like me.* I thought you might want to keep him."

Ciopori frowned. "He is beautiful, and I do not understand such a hideous thing, but I do not pretend to be a goddess or to have the power to undo an ancient curse that has stood for millennia, nor have I forgotten my time with Salvatore in the colony. I would not have asked you to spare him. I would not have risked your life. Could you not have given me one minute to reconcile what must be...within my own soul?"

Marquis shut his eyes. "I do not like this, but if you wish, I will call Nachari back." He sighed. "But before I do, I want you to understand something: In my family, I am the first-born."

She held his gaze with intensity and cleared her throat. "I'm not sure I understand."

"When my mother had Nathaniel and Kagen, she and my father celebrated both births. When she had Nachari and Shelby, the same was true. But when I was born, I shared her womb with a dark spirit, and the nameless one who was my brother—*my twin*—was taken from my mother in the same way...was taken from me. Do you think I have never wondered about him? Never wished to have at least seen his face—to at least have the memory? Do you think I have never wondered what if—what if things were different? I, too, have questioned the cruelty of such a curse, but it is imperative that my faith remains absolute. There can be no question as to what must be done now—or what my parents did then. To see you hold that child...to once again think about my own twin.... I, too, must live with this curse, Ciopori."

Ciopori closed her eyes. When she opened them, they were soft with compassion. "I'm sorry, warrior. I forget the history...the depth of this curse." She shook her head. "It is done. And you will do what is required of you with strength and honor." She placed her hand on her stomach and rubbed it. "Now then, this one is having a fit, if you haven't noticed. I think he is in there screaming. *What's the delay*! So, no, there is no reason to return to the nameless one. Let us have our son."

Marquis ran his hands through her soft hair. "Are you sure? There can be no regrets—no resentment between us."

Ciopori cupped his face in her hands. "This is a bitter-sweet moment. How could a curse be anything else? But your words have given me all the assurance I need, and there is only peace and love between us, warrior. Now call our son, Marquis."

Marquis stared into her beautiful eyes and felt the wonder of her spirit all over again. "You are my peace," he whispered, and then he tuned in to the remaining child. With a soft apology, he repeated the ancient prayer, and called him forth.

As the gold dust settled this time, and the outline began to fill in, any question or worry was replaced with reverence and awe. The male that materialized into his father's waiting arms was positively stunning. Like his mother's and his father's, his hair was the color of a raven's wing, blacker than the night, as refined as pure silk. But his eyes—his eyes were positively captivating. A mixture of both parents, they were amber and gold with swirls of blue in the centers like an exquisite painting—the color of the setting sun beneath the horizon in a clear blue sky—and his features were chiseled like his father's, with his mother's nobility. This male's beauty would one day rival even Nachari's.

Marquis smiled, suddenly unsure of what to do with the squirming entity before him. He tested his arms and legs for strength and laughed when the child kicked and flailed his arms in response to his touch. "He's strong."

Ciopori giggled. "Of course he is."

As she struggled to sit up, Marquis reached out to help her with his mind. "Does that offend you?" he asked, still unsure of the rules.

Ciopori just shook her head. "No, you silly man. Boy, do we have a ways to go—good thing we have all of eternity to get there." She reached out and made a cradle with her arms. "May I?"

Marquis nodded quickly. "Absolutely." As he placed the baby in her arms, her face lit up with pride and love. Two angels. And both belonged to him.

"We haven't chosen a name yet," she said, offering her pinky to the infant's strong grip and then nuzzling his nose. Tears streamed down her face as she laughed and smiled and made faces at the beaming little child.

Marquis placed his hand on his son's head and gently stroked his satiny hair. "While the names of today are...colorful...I much prefer those of the Middle Ages. Strong, proud, solid names."

Ciopori smiled. "And what did you have in mind?" The baby hiccupped, and they both laughed.

Marquis shrugged his shoulders. "Perhaps something with meaning: warrior or conqueror."

Ciopori sighed. "But of course. This child really doesn't have a chance at being anything else, does he? Perhaps a wizard or a justice?"

Marquis frowned. "Are you kidding me, woman? Absolutely not. By age five, he will be an expert marksman."

Ciopori tickled his tiny belly, and he squirmed. "Don't worry," she whispered in a soft voice, "I will make sure that you get to choose your own path."

Marquis snarled and the infant giggled.

Ciopori jumped back, startled. "Can they do that already?"

Marquis nodded. "Vampire babies are born at a higher level of maturity, and they progress much faster than human infants. He thinks that what you said was nonsense."

Ciopori laughed with abandon. "No, warrior, I think he thinks what *you* said was nonsense!"

The child laughed again, and Marquis frowned. "Give me that kid; you're already spoiling him."

Ciopori rolled her eyes and tightened her hold on the infant, still laughing. "A name, husband? Middle ages? Warrior...conqueror...victorious?"

"Nikolai."

"*Nikolai.*" Ciopori let the word roll off her tongue. "I like it."

Marquis nodded, pleased. "Would you like to choose his middle name?"

Ciopori shut her eyes. "There is nothing to think about: *Jadon.*"

Marquis stared at her then. Jadon. The ancient patriarch of the house of Jadon. The original male of their kind. No one had ever used his name before out of reverence, but if anyone had a right to invoke it, it was Ciopori. Jadon Demir was more than just a powerful legend to Ciopori, one who had brought mercy to his house and his descendants at the time of the Blood Curse. He was not just the father of a species, an ancient prince, or the original ruler of a new civilization and way of life: Jadon Demir was her beloved brother and Nikolai's uncle. The reality was almost too much to comprehend. "Nikolai Jadon Silivasi. It is done, then."

Ciopori pressed her forehead to the child's and whispered something private, which Marquis was careful to mute out of respect. Sighing, he placed one hand on his mate's back and gently ran the other along his son's soft cheeks. "I don't want to leave you, but I have to go now. I cannot leave Nachari with—"

"Of course not," Ciopori whispered. "Will you be okay? If you'd like, I can call Jocelyn or Vanya to take Nikolai for a moment, and we can go together."

Marquis kissed her on the forehead, his head resting against hers. "I love you for asking, but no. It would be a sacrilege: an original female bowing down to the male's curse. No, this is my punishment—my atonement—it is my life that will be forever spared as a result." He sighed. "I will return to you shortly."

The baby's eyes shot from his mother to his father, and his face warmed with the most gentle, radiant smile Marquis had ever seen.

Marquis would get through this.

Oh yes, after fifteen hundred years of endless existence, he would definitely get through this. The required sacrifice was all that stood between himself and eternity with this beautiful woman and their newborn son.

To return to them, he could get through anything.

Marquis entered the Chamber of Sacrifice and Atonement with singular focus, carrying the struggling infant in his arms. The child was no longer cooing and crying but hissing and spitting and trying to score his father's hands with the tips of his tiny fangs. Compassion was a ploy the newborns often tried with their once-human mothers, but as soon as it failed, the darkness inevitably came out. Marquis tried not to think about the fact that he had been conceived along with a similar entity—that he had existed side by side with a Dark One in his mother's womb.

The temperature in the chamber was eerily cold, and the energy of rage, mourning, and sorrow grew with every step

Marquis took beyond the neat rows of pews toward the granite altar. He stepped up on the platform and placed the squirming baby in the smooth, hollow basin at the top, careful to keep his feet from touching the dark, swirling mist at the base. And then he stepped back and knelt on the floor, prostrate, as required. But when he opened his mouth to speak, nothing came out.

The required words—and their subsequent meaning—ran through his head in an endless loop, but he couldn't seem to speak them...not in Romanian or English: *Pentru tine, care au fost drepți și fără vină; pentru tine, care au fost sacrificate fara mila: am venit pentru a rambursa datoria mea. Pentru păcatele de stramosii mei, am oferi primul nascut fiul meu și vă implor de iertare. Ai mila de pe sufletul meu și să accepte acest copil viața în schimbul meu....*

To you who were righteous and without blame; to you who were slaughtered without mercy: I come to repay my debt. For the sins of my ancestors, I offer my first-born son and beg of you forgiveness. Have mercy on my soul and accept this child's life in exchange for my own.

Marquis's head tilted to the side as if someone else was working it with puppet strings, his eyes fixated on the other side of the room—on a heavy wooden door with crossbones and an ancient warning inscribed in the Old Language on the front: *Iată de portal pentru a coridorului de morți.*

Behold the portal to the Corridor of the Dead.

He knew there was a double entry-way just beyond that door, containing two steps that led up to a hatch: the chamber of sacrifice for the males who failed to do what he was doing now. The last place his baby brother, Shelby, had stood alive.

Marquis's heart clenched and his arms trembled. Shelby had kneeled before this same altar, bowed before the swirling black mist, and repeated such similar words: *To you who were righteous and without blame; to you who were slaughtered without mercy: I come to repay my debt. For the sins of my ancestors, and because I have failed to sacrifice my first-born son, I offer my own life in atonement. Have mercy on my soul and accept this sacrifice.*

To you who were righteous and without blame?

BLOOD AWAKENING

To you who were righteous and without blame!

Marquis trembled with rage even as the baby began to scream, and the swirling mist became agitated. No one had been more righteous than Shelby. No one had led a life with less blame, and still, they had murdered him cruelly and without mercy for a crime his ancestors had committed. And they had forced him to kneel and beg for his own soul before they did it.

To call such an entity *righteous and without blame,* he couldn't get the heretical words out of his mouth.

Marquis stared back and forth between the chamber he was in and the one just beyond that door and considered his options: If he failed to sacrifice the child, he would have to enter that evil place and offer his own life, instead. In other words, he would still have to *utter the nonsense.* The only way to defy the Blood of the Slain was to refuse either, in which case, he would be slaughtered anyway, and his eternal soul would go to the Valley of Death and Shadows as opposed to the Valley of Spirit and Light. Eternity was a very long time to endure just to make a point.

Marquis lowered his head, opened his mouth, and tried once again to offer the supplication. Once again, nothing came out. By now, the swirling mist had transformed into a black, angry cloud. Taking the shape of mangled claws, it rose from the ground, perched over the altar, and reached out to claim the infant, who was now screaming at such a high pitch that it hurt Marquis's ears. Red stains, like blood, dripped down from the sharp talons, and the room began to shake as Marquis concentrated…and forced the words.

"To you who were righteous and without blame, to you who…" His voice trailed off, and the apparition exploded in anger. The dark cloud formed a dangerous funnel, swirled around the altar, and sucked the baby up into its spiraling fury: It was waiting, demanding the supplication.

Dear gods.

Marquis looked on with horror: Now he was the one

316

without mercy. Evil or not, the child was suffering between life and death, battered about, awaiting the pronouncement of his body as a sacrifice.

And then a strong hand settled on Marquis's shoulder, and he spun around to find Nathaniel standing behind him, a look of startling intensity in the warrior's eyes. "Brother, let me help you. Release your voice to my control, and let me help you."

An arc of lightning shot out from the cloud. It struck the tip of the altar, bringing a horde of snakes to life. They began to slither along the ground toward Marquis, hissing and rising up to look him in the eyes with demonic stares. When a fissure split through the ceiling, Marquis knew he was running out of time.

Nathaniel tried to reach into Marquis's mind then—to take control without his permission—but it was sealed like an iron vault. What under heaven was wrong with him? He had a mate now. A son! *Nikolai.* He couldn't die like this. Not here. Not today.

Kagen and Nachari materialized in unison; one stood before him, the other behind him.

"Brother," Kagen implored, his eyes wild with trepidation, "give Nathaniel your voice!"

Marquis stared up at his brown-eyed brother, noting the hard set of his jaw, and slowly shook his head. Kagen didn't understand. It wasn't that he was unwilling to do it; he simply could not. In that fateful moment, there was only Shelby—his beloved younger brother—and the injustice of his murder. Marquis's indignation—*his guilt*—was a living thing, and his voice would not betray him. Gods in heaven, he was going to die.

"Look after my son," he muttered as the reality began to sink in. *He could not speak those words.*

Nachari knelt before him. He began to chant a hypnotic spell, while weaving a golden aura around his throat. He intended to force Marquis's words with magic.

"No!" Marquis yelled. "*No.*"

BLOOD AWAKENING

Momentarily stunned, Nachari lost his place. He rushed to start over, but it was too late. The mangled claw came out of the cloud and grasped Marquis by the throat. Determined to pierce the golden aura, the razor-sharp talons slashed deeply, three times, tearing through Marquis's jugular like a knife through butter. The snakes began to strike, and a high-pitched shriek shook the chamber walls.

Napolean was there in an instant. He pumped his hand full of healing venom and quickly thrust the soothing balm against the ancient warrior's throat. As the king was the only male, outside of a child's father, who could make the Blood Sacrifice, he hastily began the Supplication: *"Pentru tine, care au fost drepți și fără—"*

"Cease!" A thunderous voice rang out in the chamber, halting the king in his tracks. "His heart will not yield. Your supplication will not be accepted!" A bolt of fire flew out from the cloud and struck Marquis in the heart. It melted instantly into liquid acid, launching a slow burn inside of his body. Despite his resolve, he cried out in pain; his energy waned from the steady loss of blood.

"We are only getting started!" the Blood roared. "We will bleed you out until you are helpless; we will sustain your torture for weeks! You will beg for death before we are through!" The rage shook the building, and Marquis felt his bones begin to break, one after another.

My love! What is happening! Ciopori's voice cut him deeper than the slayer's, yet he still could not find the words. *Please, warrior, do not leave me alone to raise our son. Say what must be said and come home. Please, Marquis!*

Using the last amount of energy he possessed, Marquis shoved Ciopori out of his mind. She could not witness his pain.

He could see his brothers' lips moving, and he could feel the urgency in their commands, but their words no longer registered. The Blood would not allow Nathaniel to take Marquis's voice or Nachari to use his magic, and Kagen looked...more helpless

318

than he had ever been.

Nachari grasped Marquis's face in his hands, his indescribable eyes filled with tears and pleading.

Pleading.

Marquis held his brother's gaze with a warrior's stare as he felt his liver and his kidneys begin to twist inside. Bile rose in his throat, and he pushed Nachari aside just before he vomited all over the floor. The look of terror and grief on the wizard's face was the most horrific sight Marquis had ever seen, but before he could crawl away, a slimy hand grabbed him by the arms and began to drag him along the floor.

He closed his eyes, bracing himself for the torture to come. Where were they taking him? Ah yes, of course, to the sacrificial chamber—where they could do their worst. The pain in his body was already unbearable: Days? Weeks? How could he endure such a thing? Nikolai's face flashed before his eyes, and his heart filled with regret. Yet as sure as he was a warrior, he knew that such words of contrition would never leave his lips: He was an Ancient Master, trained in the art of war, the leader and protector of his family. Honor was everything. Duty was supreme. Shelby was his brother, and to speak such words would be to dishonor Shelby's life—to once again fail to live up to his duty.

What he could not give Shelby in life, he would give him in death.

Marquis could not go back and place himself in those fateful moments: when Valentine took Dalia, when he brutally raped Shelby's *destiny* and denied the fledgling a son. He could not go back and save his brother's life, but he was here now.

And this was no longer about an ancient sacrifice, an infant soul already lost, or a baby who would surely grow up to kill him if given the chance. It was about a male from the house of Jadon who had been wrongly accused and murdered: a sibling he had vowed—and failed—to protect.

The Blood had murdered Shelby Silivasi, and it was *not*

innocent.

Marquis closed his eyes in resignation: He could feel his body being torn apart, his skin peeling back from the bone. Consumed in the delirium of his pain, he heard his brothers shouting words he could no longer understand. He was what he was, and he had been wrong to believe that he could ever stand in this place, see where Shelby had died, and dishonor him to save his own life. Not even for Nikolai. Not even for Ciopori. He held onto the knowledge that his brothers would raise his son as if he was their own. They would take care of his princess.

And then all at once a strange sense of peace overtook him, and the pain slowly abated.

Had he died...so quickly?

Despite the promise of torture, his heart felt elevated, and his insurmountable grief began to lift. Perhaps it was absolution. Perhaps he was finally to be given the forgiveness he so desperately needed—not that of a bunch of twisted, dead females, for a crime committed centuries before him, but that of one pure soul whom he had failed.

Marquis sighed, almost afraid to hope. "Can you forgive me now, Shelby?" His words were broken and pitiable. A white light surrounded him, and his clarity returned in rapid waves. Everything in the room fell into sudden, sharp focus.

The doors to the back of the chamber flew open, and Ciopori rushed in carrying Nikolai in her arms. Her face was gaunt with pain and tears, and the grief-stricken eyes of his brothers reflected the same agony...yet he felt no urgency. There was only peace.

And then he felt it: a firm, warm hand gripping his shoulder.

He slowly turned his head in the direction of the touch, only to find a radiant male standing before him. His mouth dropped open and his lips trembled, but no words escaped.

Shelby.

Flawless, luminescent features shone with pride and grace beneath a wealth of blond curls, and deep green eyes, the same shade of Nachari's, glowed with compassion. There could be no question, Marquis had to be dead. But when he looked around the room, he saw the same look of awe on the faces of the others. Even the king looked stunned.

"Brother." Marquis tested his voice, and it worked fine for a throat that had been so viciously cut.

Shelby smiled, and his radiance lit up the room like the noon-day sun. "Greetings, my eldest and most honored brother." He knelt beside the shaken warrior and grasped him by the shoulders.

The Blood roared in defiance and lunged at the ghostly visitor, but the mystical outline of a dragon suddenly appeared, blocking its path.

Marquis gasped. *"Lord Draco!"* He blinked several times, gaping at the silhouette of the blazing celestial dragon—*the sacred god of his constellation.*

The dragon spoke through a ring of fire, and the very foundation beneath them shifted to the cadence of its words. "Marquis is from my line, and as such, he is under my protection while we sort this out!" The fire became as liquid gold before transforming once again to ether and settling over Marquis's body. His peeled skin slid back in place; his broken bones fused together; his twisted organs healed, and the blood spurting from his ravaged arteries simply ceased to flow.

"You have no right!" the Blood hissed.

The dragon spun around and squared off with the ghostly entity, eyes the color of the sun glowing in its skull. "I have every right! By the laws that govern the afterlife, the Valley of Spirit and Light has jurisdiction over the Valley of Death and Shadows. And by our law, a blameless soul, one who has lived a life of innocence, may be called upon in prayer to intercede on behalf of another. Should any such prayer be accompanied by a gift of ultimate sacrifice—the willingness of one being to lay down his life for another—then the gods may hear his petition." Draco's eyes shot across the room and landed on Nachari. "The wizard prayed to his twin for the life of their brother, even as Marquis resigned to give his life for the same. Shelby has interceded on the wizard's behalf, and the gods have granted him audience." He gestured toward the altar where the battered child still lay, mercifully unconscious. "You will still have your sacrifice—or your vengeance—but not before this Blessed One has his say."

The Blood howled its rage. It screeched and released its fangs. Its gnarled, ghostly hands curled into fists.

Draco stood to his full height then. His tail slashed back and forth through the air, sharp-edged scales glowing with the threat of retribution. He laughed a menacing snarl. "Do not test me. You may be powerful, but I am a god. You will not win."

Enraged, the entity retreated.

Marquis looked up into his baby brother's face, ashamed. "Shelby," he uttered, "I am so sorry. *I am so, so sorry.*"

Shelby's grip tightened on Marquis's shoulders, and his eyes held him in an unyielding stare. "It was not your fault, brother." He looked up and one by one met Nathaniel's, Nachari's, and Kagen's eyes. "It was nobody's fault."

The brothers drew nearer, tears falling without reservation.

As if he could no longer restrain himself, Shelby stood, turned around, and embraced Nachari. "Brother," he whispered, his voice trembling with emotion, *"flesh of my flesh, blood of my blood, heart of my heart, twin of my soul,* I have heard your prayers— today and every day. You must forgive yourself for not being here...for not saying good-bye."

Nachari wept into his brother's shoulder, clinging to him like his life depended upon it. The two shared an intimate exchange of words, using a private bandwidth, and then Shelby stepped back and removed an amulet from his neck. "Take this," he implored. "I will not be able to walk with you anymore—not until you come home to the Valley of Spirit and Light—but you can call me with this amulet, and wherever I am, I will hear you. And whenever I can, I will answer you. *You are the twin of my soul;*

death will not keep us apart."

Nachari clutched the amulet, slid it around his neck, and pulled his brother back into his arms. When they finally let go, Shelby placed his hand over Nachari's heart, and a soft yellow light entered. "My peace is yours, brother. Live for both of us."

He then turned to face Nathaniel, but the Master Warrior's emotions were too intense to appease—his anger too great, his pain too raw. Shelby held out his arms, and Nathaniel stepped back, moving away from the brother he so adored.

"It's okay," Shelby whispered.

Nathaniel shook his head. His grief and regret—his *apology*—was so powerful that it leapt between them. "No." Nathaniel continued to shake his head.

"I have seen your wife and your son," Shelby said softly, holding Nathaniel's tortured gaze. "They are beautiful! And you named my nephew after Father: Keitaro Storm Silivasi. I am pleased for you."

Nathaniel put his head in his hands. "No!"

Shelby took a tentative step forward. "I forgive you—although there's nothing to forgive."

"*NO.*" Nathaniel slumped down onto his knees, and Shelby followed in one fluid motion.

"*Nathaniel...*brother..."

When Shelby wrapped his arms around the proud Master Warrior, Marquis held his breath. Like everyone else in the room, he was overwhelmed by the intensity of Nathaniel's anguish. The male's heart-wrenching sobs racked his powerful chest in endless waves of sorrow, and it seemed like an eternity before Shelby whispered in Nathaniel's ear and, once again, placed his hand over a troubled heart, imparting peace.

And then he stood and turned to Kagen. "Dr. Jekyll," he teased, "my brother, the healer." His broad smile sent waves of warmth into the ancient's heart as the two slowly approached each other and met in a warm embrace.

Kagen stroked Shelby's hair like he was holding a child,

323

gripping him like he was the most precious thing on earth. "By the gods, I have missed you, Shelby." Kagen's voice caught. "I wanted to follow you into the next life."

Shelby nodded, his deep green eyes sparkling with kindness. "I know, Kagen, I know. But you're far too important; your gift is needed here. Brother, I will wait for you in the Valley of Spirit and Light, and we will be together again one day—but not now. It is not yet time for you. Live in peace, brother. For me...live in peace."

Kagen held on until Shelby finally, gently, pried him away, and then he simply stared at him as if he were memorizing every line and detail of his face. "I love you, Shelby."

Shelby smiled, perfectly content. "And I, you, brother."

And then he turned back to Marquis.

He approached the Ancient Master Warrior slowly, calmly kneeling down on the floor. "Marquis..." His voice held the cadence and purity of a song. "I knew if any would try to follow me, it would be you. If any would stop living, it would be you. If any would lose his way, it would be you. And then I watched as events unfolded—the vengeance you and Nachari took on Valentine." He lifted his head and regarded Nachari, holding out his hand to give his twin a well-deserved fist pound. "Thank you, my brother; that was righteous justice if ever I saw any." And then he once again turned to Marquis. "But it did not ease your suffering."

Marquis just stared at him, unable to answer.

"I watched as you found the females." He gestured toward Ciopori. "Greetings sister."

"G...g...greetings," Ciopori stuttered.

"May I see my new nephew?"

Ciopori came forward and knelt before Shelby, her hands trembling. She brushed a quick kiss along Marquis's temple as she showed Shelby the baby.

"Whoa, Marquis," Shelby muttered appreciatively. "I think Nachari might finally have a contender."

Marquis wished he could answer, but his guilt simply would not allow him the reprieve.

"He is absolute...perfection," Shelby said, bending over to kiss the child on the forehead.

Marquis felt his eyes gloss over with tears, and then Shelby grabbed him firmly by the lapels of his shirt. "You absolutely cannot die here today, my brother! Do you hear me? *I forbid it.*"

Marquis grumbled, finally shaken out of his stupor. "I have no wish to die, Shelby, but I cannot dishonor you with those words."

To Marquis's amazement, Shelby laughed. "What is past is past. You cannot bring me back by dying with me. You cannot change the Curse by defying it. You cannot honor me by leaving our brothers, your nephew, your mate, and your son to suffer without you." Shelby lifted his hands from Marquis's lapel to brace him by his jaw, not caring that it was a tender act rarely displayed between males. "Do you think that I question your dedication for a moment? That I don't know you would die for me? That you would kill for me? That you would sacrifice anything—everything—*your very life for me?*" He swept his hand around the room. "For any of us?" He shook his head. "Marquis, you have been a teacher, a father, a stronghold in times of trouble, and a wise counselor since the day I was born. You have always been my refuge, *my pride,* and my honor. Do you understand?"

Marquis swallowed hard and held Shelby's gaze, even as hot, searing tears trickled down his face.

"But it is your turn to live now. Your turn to love. Your turn to receive." He gazed at Ciopori. "For the love of the gods, do you not see what they have given you?" He touched Nikolai on the head. "Would you deprive this child of all you gave to me?"

Marquis looked down at his son.

Shelby took him by the arms and shook him gently. "Brother, if you do this thing—if you die here today—then *you* will kill me all over again. What Valentine did is not your fault, and his soul pays dearly every day in the Valley of Death and Shadows. I came here, and I bowed before that altar and spoke those words because I understood that there is a debt to be paid—whether or not we see it as fair—and because I knew the love of my life, Dalia, would soon meet me in the afterlife once she had completed her own lessons. We are free now, and we are together. And eternity is far too long to give up your soul." Shelby sat back on his heels and sighed. "Marquis...*brother*...if I asked you to, would you kill for me?"

Marquis was momentarily confused. "Of course."

"If I asked the gods to allow us to change places, would you exchange your life for mine? Would you truly die for me?"

"I will—"

"Then be of greater courage and give me the last thing I will ever ask of you: *Live for me*. Marquis, I am begging you. *Live for me*, my beloved brother. *Live pentru mine!*"

Marquis placed his hands over Shelby's and fought to remain stoic. As blood-red diamonds, fashioned from their tears, covered their linked hands, Marquis considered Shelby's words: Since the day he was born, his brothers had followed his commands, as was the way of the house of Jadon. But this time, he would do as he was bid. His brother had come back from the grave to save him, and it broke his heart that it could not have been the other way around.

Shelby placed his hand over Marquis's heart and infused it with peace. "Let it go, great warrior. Let it go."

Marquis slowly stood and approached the altar, kneeling once again before the damaged platform. Taking in a long, deep breath, he slowly exhaled and bowed his head:

"To you who were righteous and without blame; *pentru tine, care au fost sacrificate fără milă: Am venit pentru a rambursa datoria mea. Pentru păcatele de stramosii mei, și pentru că eu nu au reușit să-și sacrifice primul nascut fiul meu, am oferi propria mea viata în ispășire.* Have mercy on my soul and accept this child's life in exchange for my own."

With an angry scowl, the entity hovered over the altar and snatched up the now sleeping baby, retreating with a long drawn-out cry.

It mattered not. It was over.

"Shelby," the dragon god's voice cut through the silence like thunder piercing a clear blue sky, "you have done what you came to do. It is time to go."

"Wait!" A desperate female voice echoed through the chamber as Nathaniel's wife, Jocelyn, shimmered into view holding a now plump and growing baby in her arms. "Your nephew," she panted.

Shelby stared at the beautiful woman, no doubt taking in her magnificent multi-colored eyes, and then he looked down at the child—his entire countenance glowing with pride and joy. "Greetings, Storm," he whispered, brushing his hand over the smiling infant's cheek. He leaned over to kiss Jocelyn on the temple. "And to you as well, my sister. Thank you for this treasure."

Jocelyn exchanged a knowing glance with Nathaniel. "You're welcome."

For a fleeting moment, Shelby's features reflected a deep sorrow, though he tried gallantly to hide it. He nodded as he looked around the room, forcing a smile that didn't reach his eyes. "I will watch over you all." He turned to Nachari. "My twin, call out to me; our souls cannot be separated. I need the communion."

Nachari nodded and clutched the amulet.

And then he addressed Napolean. "Milord, thank you for staying with me at the hour of my death." His voice became barely audible. "I cannot imagine what that took out of you— what you have given to our people over the years in such sacrifice."

Napolean simply nodded his head. "You are deeply missed, Shelby. Go with honor and peace, my son."

Shelby nodded, walked over to Marquis, and embraced him

one last time. *"Live, pentru mine. Live!"*

Marquis wiped a tear from his cheek and placed his hand over his heart. He swept his arm around Ciopori and looked down at his newborn son. Truly, he was blessed beyond measure and had much to live for.

Peace was a balm Shelby was offering, if he was only willing to take it.

Love was a gift he had waited a lifetime to receive, and now it stood loyally at his side in the heart of a princess.

The future was alive in the bright amber-blue eyes of his son: Nikolai Jadon Silivasi, heir to the house of Jadon, divined of the god Perseus, nephew of a prince, grandson of a king, and the embodiment of two worlds—celestial and Vampyr.

He looked around the room at the faces of his brothers. Life with him might not be easy, but they had come to his aid so quickly, pleaded so mightily...

They loved him deeply.

Yes, he was a blessed male with much to live for.

He scooped up a handful of crimson diamonds, his own blood tears, and placed them in Shelby's hand. "Until we meet again, beloved brother, I will live."

Epilogue

800 BC

"Napolean, run!"

The ten-year-old child stumbled backward, his eyes wide with fright. His father's commanding voice shook him to his core.

"Run son, go quickly!"

"No, Father. I don't want to leave you! Father, please—"

"Go now!" Sebastian Mondragon clutched his stomach and fell to the ground. His hands and fingers curled into two twisted balls, and his body contorted in an agonizing spasm. The transformation had begun. Writhing in pain, the once-fearless warrior panted the warning a third time. "Napolean...son...please, run! Hide!"

Napolean heard his father's words as if from a distance. He wanted to flee, but he was frozen in place. Mesmerized by the horror that surrounded him, he swallowed hard and simply watched as the thick, inky fog swirled around his father's writhing body. Long, skeletal fingers with hooked claws and knobby knuckles clutched at his father's throat, raked deep gashes along his chest, and dug mercilessly toward his innards. Blood seeped from Sebastian's mouth as, inexplicably, his canine teeth began to grow, assuming the shape of—

Fangs.

But it was his father's unrelenting cries of agony that finally forced Napolean's retreat.

Napolean ran like he had never run before, his little heart beating furiously in his chest, the need for air burning his lungs. He weaved through the morbid courtyard, dodging fallen bodies and clasping his hands to his ears to block out the endless wails. All around him, males fell to the ground, cursed, and moaned. Some died immediately from the shock...or pain. Others drew their swords from their scabbards and took their own lives. Still others succumbed to the brutal torture, helpless as the darkness embodied them.

They were being punished.

Changed.

Transformed into an aberration of nature by the ghostly spirits of their victims.

The Blood Curse was upon them.

Napolean focused his eyes straight ahead, never losing sight of his destination: the imperial castle, a would-be fortress. He and his friends had hidden there so many times in the past, playing hide-and-seek, avoiding angry parents, hoping to catch a glimpse of a member of the royal family. Napolean knew the grounds like the back of his hands, and so he pressed on, desperate yet determined to get there, resigned to hide as his father had bid him.

At last, he arrived at the familiar gray castle gate.

He scurried into a small hole beneath the fortified wall and drew himself into a tight little ball. He tried to become invisible. Although he could no longer see the carnage in the village, the haunting cries continued to batter his ears like thunder against a stormy sky.

Napolean shook, remembering the moment Prince Jadon had emerged from the castle, his dark onyx eyes glazed with fear. He had gathered his loyalists to his side to explain the pronouncement—their punishment—what was soon to become a new way of life.

With so little time to prepare his men, Jadon had tried the best he could. Napolean had understood none of it, save one thing: The followers of Jadon needed to pledge their loyalty to the twin monarch as quickly as possible, before the transformation began, or they would meet a much worse fate.

Though Napolean's father had served for years in the royal one's secret guard, fighting to defeat the ever growing armies of Prince Jaegar, Napolean had been too young to join. Consequently, it had been imperative that he formally align himself with the right twin— for those who followed Jaegar were to receive no mercy.

And so, like all of the others, Napolean had knelt to kiss Prince Jadon's ring, recited the sacred pledge of loyalty—before it was too late—and braced himself against what was to come....

Napolean shivered, bringing his attention back to the present moment.

He wanted to be brave, but fearful tears stung his eyes.

Then all at once, he heard cruel, disembodied laughter, the sound coming closer and closer, assaulting his ears.

"No. No. No," he whimpered, drawing further into the hollow cavity for protection, quivering so hard his bones rattled in his skin.

The fog swirled into a miniature cyclone, rose up from the ground, and dipped low as if it had eyes that could see...

Him.

Hiding.

"You think to escape, child?" the ghostly aberration hissed, laughter ricocheting through the small cavity. Flames exploded from the center of the darkness. "Die, little one! And be reborn the monster that you are!"

Napolean screamed so loud the sound became a cosmic explosion in his ears, yet the fog kept coming. It wrapped itself around his meager body, entered his mouth, and descended into his chest.

And then the pain began.

The excruciating, unrelenting, unbearable pain.

Acid flowed freely through his veins. Fire consumed his internal organs. Bones reshaped. Cells exploded. His entire composition changed, transformed...died.

He heard his own shouting as if it belonged to someone else, someone wretched and pitiable. He clawed at his skin, hoping to tear it from his body. He bit through his hand and pounded the ground. He writhed, thrashed, and tried to crawl away, but nothing stopped the assault.

Dear Celestial Gods!

He prayed for death, but it wouldn't come.

How much time had passed before the agony had subsided, he had no idea. Had it been minutes? Hours? Perhaps days? It could have been a lifetime for all he'd endured before it had ceased...and the craving had begun.

A gnawing, all-consuming, primal thirst.

For blood.

It was the craving that had brought him out of the hole, crawling along the ground like an animal, stumbling through the darkness, searching for his father.

Now, as bitter tears stung his eyes, he absently wiped them away only to find smears of blood on his hand.

Great goddess Andromeda, what had he become?

Finally reaching the village square, he staggered to a halt beside an aged stone well. As his vision adjusted to the darkness, he caught a shadow out of the corner of his eye: No, it couldn't be.

Please gods, no!

The grisly scene unfolded in slow motion as Jaegar Demir, the evil prince, hunkered over his father's body. The prince's eyes were wild with insanity as he bent to Sebastian's throat, tore into the flesh—as if it were mere parchment—and drank his fill of...blood. Napolean could neither move nor turn away as the macabre scene unfolded before him. As the evil prince drained his father's already-gored-and-tattered body of life.

And then...

Horrified, trembling, and defeated, Napolean watched like a coward as Prince Jaegar withdrew his sword and took his father's head.

When at last the terror released him, he fisted his hands and howled at the heavens.

"Noooooooo!"

He shouted until his throat bled: "Father! Father! Father! Father..."

Buzzzzzz.

Napolean Mondragon hit the button on the alarm clock hard. He sat up and wiped the sweat from his brow. *Great gods, not again.* He swung his feet over the edge of the large canopy bed and rested his elbows on his knees, his face in his hands.

This was the third time this week he'd had the nightmare.

As the sovereign lord of the house of Jadon, the only remaining male living from the time of the Blood Curse, the memories occasionally plagued his sleep, but never this often. *Hades*, the nightmares must have been provoked by the sight of the male he had seen in the shadows just a few weeks back: the one who, impossibly, looked just like his murdered father.

The father who had been dead for twenty-eight hundred years.

Napolean rubbed his eyes and wrinkled his brow. *Gods*, he could use the sweet affection of the princess right now—the touch of her gentle hand, the gaze of her compassionate eyes, the warmth of her soft lips against his.

"Ah hell, Napolean. Why torture yourself?" He wrung his hands together and shook his head. Vanya Demir had been a bright light in an otherwise dark, unending life. Her presence in the mansion had brought song and laughter and joy to a heart that had known nothing but duty and solitude for twenty-eight hundred years. The attraction between them had been magnetic, undeniable. She had become the best reason he'd had for rising in the morning in centuries.

And that was part of why she had left.

That, and the invitation she'd received to go live with Marquis, her sister, and their newborn baby. Family was everything to Vanya, and she was not about to pass up the chance to help raise her nephew...or to be with her sister. In addition, Napolean had begun to mean far too much to the female, and she had been afraid that she might fall in love with a male she couldn't have—a male who was destined to only one woman in an eternal lifetime.

A woman that wasn't her.

Vanya was not Napolean's true *destiny*, and she had lost too much in her life already to risk losing once again.

Napolean shrugged, forcing his thoughts elsewhere. What difference did it make—why Vanya had left? She was gone. She wasn't coming back. And that was that.

Rising from the bed, he headed toward the shower and turned on the water. No, he would not obsess over the princess again. He had far too many pressing concerns with the recent discovery of the Dark Ones' colony. With the recent string of dead—no, *murdered and drained*—human bodies showing up all over the place in Dark Moon Vale.

And hell and brimstone, if that damnable nightmare was not beginning to unnerve him. Why now, after all these years, would his memories come back to haunt him so? Would he never be free of the guilt? Would he always feel ashamed of the day his father died?

And just who was that male he had seen in the shadows?

Books in the Blood Curse Series

Blood Destiny
Blood Awakening
Blood Possession (Coming Soon…)

To receive notice of future releases, go to
www.tessadawn.com

About The Author

Tessa Dawn grew up in Colorado where she developed a deep affinity for the Rocky Mountains. After graduating with a degree in psychology, she worked for several years in criminal justice and mental health before returning to get her Masters Degree in Nonprofit Management.

Tessa began writing as a child and composed her first full-length novel at the age of eleven. By the time she graduated high-school, she had a banker's box full of short-stories and books. Since then, she has published works as diverse as poetry, greeting cards, workbooks for kids with autism, and academic curricula. The Blood Curse Series marks her long-desired return to her creative-writing roots and her first foray into the Dark Fantasy world of vampire fiction.

Tessa currently lives in the suburbs with her two children and "one very crazy cat" but hopes to someday move to the country where she can own horses and a German Shepherd.

Writing is her bliss.

CPSIA information can be obtained at www.ICGtesting.com
Printed in the USA
BVOW05s0522130116

432632BV00003B/69/P

Healing the Mind
the Natural Way

Healing the Mind the Natural Way

Nutritional Solutions to Psychological Problems

Pat Lazarus

A JEREMY P. TARCHER/PUTNAM BOOK

PUBLISHED BY G. P. PUTNAM'S SONS
NEW YORK

Note to Readers

This book is a unique source of information, guidance, inspiration, and hope for people who wish to fight mental problems without the toxic effects of drugs and without long-term, expensive psychotherapy—as well as for those who have already tried those therapies without success. The information in this book should not be used for self-diagnosis or self-treatment. While correctly chosen nutritional therapy is nontoxic, the author stresses that only trained, licensed physicians in the field of orthomolecular medicine are capable of correctly prescribing safe and effective nutritional therapy tailored to your individual body chemistry. Please use the information in this book under the supervision of such a physician. The author and the publisher expressly disclaim responsibility for any adverse consequences resulting directly or indirectly from the use of this book.

A Jeremy P. Tarcher/Putnam Book
Published by G. P. Putnam's Sons
Publishers Since 1838
200 Madison Avenue
New York, NY 10016

Library of Congress Cataloging-in-Publication Data
Lazarus, Pat.
    Healing the mind the natural way : nutritional solutions to
psychological problems / Pat Lazarus.
        p. cm.
    Includes bibliographical references and index.
    ISBN 0-87477-752-6
    1. Mental illness—Nutritional aspects. 2. Orthomolecular
therapy. 3. Mental illness—Diet therapy. I. Title.
RC455.4.N8L39 1995
616.89′1—dc20   95-11787 CIP

Book design by Jaime Robles

Cover design by Lee Fukui

Printed in the United States of America

10 9 8 7 6 5 4 3 2 1

This book is printed on acid-free paper. ∞

Dedication

To the memory of my parents, who suffered and died—needlessly early, I think—because the new field of orthomolecular (nutritional) medicine, covered in this book, was not known to us.

To my loved ones who have made "miraculous" recoveries because they were lucky enough to know of orthomolecular medicine and approached it with an open mind.

To the pioneering doctors who developed orthomolecular medicine, and continue to refine it, often fighting strong odds created by skeptics who have not investigated this field with an open mind, if at all.

And perhaps most important, to those for whom I wrote this book: Those who do not know that nontoxic orthomolecular therapies offer hope for those with mental disorders, even when mainstream therapies may have failed. In the words of Marshall Mandell, M.D., who pioneered one major branch of orthomolecular therapy, this book is dedicated to "those who have suffered without hope, and need suffer no longer."

Acknowledgments

Although I spent several years researching, compiling, and writing this book in a style that might interest and engage the public, I do not consider it *my* book. The actual medical information comes from doctors who have been creating and refining the field of orthomolecular (nutritional) medicine since the 1950s.

In particular, I must thank the leading doctors who spent many hours giving me information on the phone, in person, and through the mail; reviewing the manuscript to guard against possible inaccuracies or misleading statements; sending me studies; alerting me to information not yet out in print; putting me in contact with doctors who had the most expertise with a given mental disorder or orthomolecular technique; and offering words of encouragement.

I would also like to thank my husband, Joe, for his uncomplaining support. His recovery from two illnesses, many years apart, that mainstream doctors told us he could not recover from served as an initial and continuing inspiration for my work in helping to disseminate information about orthomolecular medicine.

Contents

Foreword

On February 15, 1992, I received a letter from Ms. Pat Lazarus. She said she was planning to write a book on orthomolecular psychiatry: ". . . a compilation of orthomolecular approaches for various disorders, drawing on the expertise of a number of doctors." She would send the text to the authors and speakers who were quoted so that this material would be accurate. She requested my cooperation in dealing with the sections of the book that would describe what I had done or said. She added, "Please feel free to comment— positively or negatively—on what the other doctors have to say and on the statements I made without citing specific doctors because I believe the statements to be relatively well accepted within the orthomolecular field."

In 1992 the vitamin-as-treatment paradigm was just beginning to engulf medicine, and I thought that any book as carefully researched and written as this one proposed to be should be encouraged. The more lay people read about this exciting new field, the greater the chance they would find physicians willing to help them explore orthomolecular medicine.

Since then, I have read and commented on many chapters of this book. I am pleased to state that Ms. Lazarus has been true to her word, and I do recommend this book to physicians as well as to all others who wish to become well and stay well by the use of optimum diet, and the optimum use of various individual nutrients—vitamins, minerals, amino acids, and other factors. Several years ago I was asked on a TV program whether everyone should follow this type of program. I replied "No," and then added, "Only those people who wish to become well."

Many books have appeared within the past few years that deal with aspects of orthomolecular medicine, such as the effect of foods, whether or not one is intolerant (allergic) to them, the use of minerals, the use of megadoses of vitamins, and the impact of chemicals within our environment on health.

This is one of the few books which deals with all these aspects as they are interrelated. Clinical ecologists (doctors specializing in the effects of food, chemical, and inhalant intolerances) at one time disdained the use of vitamins. But this kind of jealous guarding of one's turf is probably past, and orthomolecular physicians are, or should be, aware of all these developments. This book will help them get started.

The first comprehensive book on orthomolecular psychiatry, edited by Dr. David Hawkins and Dr. Linus Pauling, contained major chapters from most of the early developers of this new branch of medicine. That book has been widely read, except by psychiatrists.

This book, twenty-two years later, updates and widens the discussion about orthomolecular treatment, and will accelerate the flight from the vitamin-as-prevention paradigm to the modern vitamin-as-treatment paradigm.

Few medical schools, if any, teach the history of medicine adequately. If they did, their graduates would know that the history of medicine is a history of conflict. Knowing this, they would be more willing to accept new ideas. The conflict has been between old and well-established paradigms, and the new ones which eventually replace them.

Almost every major medical discovery was finally accepted by a reluctant profession only after about forty years of controversy. In physics this gap is about twenty years. This is because once a paradigm (a closed system of beliefs and ideas) has won the field, it resists any further change as stoutly as did the one it replaced. It is supported by a corps of devoted, even bigoted, scientists or physicians, who would give up their lives rather than admit they had been wrong for so long.

All paradigms carry within them the seeds of their own destruction, for no paradigm is perfect. Eventually they are replaced by newer ones, which account for the newly accumulated data better than did the old ones.

The vitamin concept was introduced to medicine about one hundred years ago. It, too, required the dedicated effort of some of the great medical scientists. But they had a rough time of it and had to appeal to the public rather than to the medical profession. When the concept was developed, following the discovery that a diet of only white rice would cause beriberi but eating only brown rice would not, the most famous European pathologist declared that no disease was ever caused by the absence of anything. This was the heyday of bacteriological discovery, and it seemed as if every disease had some bacterial origin. But eventually the vitamin-as-prevention paradigm was accepted. This includes the belief that: (1) Vitamins are needed in very small amounts, such as is normally present in food, to prevent the classical vitamin-deficiency diseases such as beriberi, scurvy, and pellagra. (2) From which it followed that vitamins are not needed, even contraindicated, for diseases not recognized to be vitamin-deficiency diseases, or in quantities larger than those normally found in food.

This concept was enshrined in RDAs by governments searching for guidelines with respect to feeding large populations, i.e., Recommended Daily Allowances. These were probably very helpful at first when it came to advising healthy people, but have been totally useless and even harmful for advising people under stress from many causes including disease.

It took about sixty years before the vitamin-as-prevention paradigm was fully accepted, and it has ruled supreme since about 1950. At the same time as it was being established, clinicians observed certain facts which could not be accounted for by this paradigm. In the mid-1930s American pellagrologists found that chronic pellagrins did not remain free of symptoms unless they took 600 mg of vitamin B3 daily. This was an enormous dose since 20 mg or less would keep most people free of pellagra. This finding was ignored.

In 1955 two colleagues and I reported that niacin, a form of vitamin B3, lowered cholesterol levels when 1.5 g per day or more was taken. About a year later I spent a few days in Rochester, Minnesota, speaking to the Mayo Clinic, and I told them about this finding. They took it seriously, and Dr. William B. Parsons, Jr., soon confirmed our findings. This brought this new use of niacin to the attention of the medical world.

This finding totally destroyed the vitamin-as-prevention paradigm since high blood cholesterol is not a vitamin-deficiency disease, and since 3,000 mg of niacin and more were used in most cases, a dose at least 1,000 times as great as the RDA. In fact, this 1955 report is credited as the beginning of the vitamin-as-treatment paradigm. This paradigm accepts that vitamins may be useful for many conditions not recognized as vitamin deficiencies and that optimum doses should be used. Often these are large, and have been called megadoses after my friend, Dr. Irwin Stone, began to use the term. Niacin was the first vitamin to be accepted by the FDA, which considered it a drug.

The forty-year, or two-generation, gap between discovery and its application seems to be embedded in our genes. Perhaps it is a defense against too-rapid change. In the Bible, Moses took forty years to cross over from Egypt to the Promised Land. Why so long? Any competent walker can do this in two weeks. Moses realized that people brought up in the slavery paradigm could not overcome the native peoples already living in the Promised Land. He decided to march them about in circles until two generations had died. Their offspring brought up in the freedom paradigm were able to take over the Promised Land.

Why does it still take two generations for new medical ideas to become established? It took thirty-five years for niacin to become

known as the best and cheapest substance for lowering total cholesterol and elevating high density cholesterol. For another vitamin,
folic acid, acceptance of its use for preventing spina bifida has taken
only about 15 years. But the costs of this inertia are fantastic. For
example, there are about 250,000 children born with spina bifida
every ten years in the U.S.A. Each such child, in Canada, will cost
the health-care system $40,000 by age fourteen.

About fifteen years ago it was shown in Scotland that giving
pregnant women extra folic acid would decrease the incidence of
this condition by about two-thirds. The original finding was condemned and criticized. In one issue of *The Lancet* there were over
six violent letters to the editor attacking the concept. This delayed
the introduction of this simple preventive measure by about fifteen
years. Only after expensive, large-scale therapeutic controlled trials
was the original finding finally accepted.

At a cost of pennies per day, and assuming that the decrease in
incidence would be 75 percent, 262,500 fewer spina bifida babies
would have been born in the U.S.A. over a fourteen-year period had
folic acid been used routinely. Using the Canadian estimated costs,
and ignoring costs which will accumulate after age fourteen, and ignoring any deaths, the total saving would have been $105 billion or
$7.5 billion per year. This is the cost of delay. What would have been
the harm in giving an innocuous product like folic acid to pregnant
women, even before the pure scientists were satisfied? Then, if it
turned out the original finding was wrong, no harm would have
been done.

This explains why I think this book is so valuable. It will accelerate the final acceptance of a much more useful vitamin paradigm
and help put to rest forever the old one. It discusses the gamut of
orthomolecular psychiatric practice. This includes the role played by
inho]tolerances, by toxic metals, by drugs, by nutritional deficiencies
and dependencies. These factors are involved in every diagnostic
group.

The main problem with modern psychiatry is that it has not begun to use diagnostic categories which are meaningful for indicating

what treatment should be used. Whether patients are diagnosed as having schizophrenia, character disorder, or depression, they will receive one or more of the current fashionable drugs. The depressives mostly recover. The schizophrenics mostly do not.

Orthomolecular psychiatry depends more on determining the cause behind the disorder label. Thus, it has been clearly established that the schizophrenic syndrome may be caused by intolerances, by vitamin deficiencies (B3 and B6), by deficiencies of minerals, e.g., zinc, and by excess of other toxic metals, e.g., copper. A schizophrenic who is ill because he is intolerant to milk will not get well until the dairy products are eliminated. A patient who needs extra B3 will not recover without the use of this vitamin in optimum doses, no matter what else is used.

The chapter on schizophrenia provides useful definitions of this condition by underlying causes, and provides much more hope by indicating what can be accomplished. The same applies to the addictions, to children with learning and/or behavioral disorders, and to many other conditions.

I think patients should educate their doctors. I recommend that they get this book and also buy one for their favorite doctor and insist that he or she read it. In this way, they will be helping themselves, their sick relatives, and society, and will help to decrease health costs. If you cannot find a favorite doctor who will read the book, study it yourself and consult with an orthomolecular physician. You are, after all, responsible for your own health. Take charge.

—Abram Hoffer, M.D., Ph.D.
3/20/95

ALL OUR PROVISIONAL ideas in psychology will someday be based on organic structure. This makes it probable that special substances and special chemicals control the operation.

SIGMUND FREUD, father of psychoanalysis

FREUD'S PREDICTION WAS certainly correct. And when the day finally comes that his prediction is generally accepted, a principal key to psychological health will be found in the currently neglected chemistry of nutrition.

Psychiatrist H. L. NEWBOLD, M.D., *Mega-Nutrients for Your Nerves* (Berkley Books, New York, 1975, p. 21)

BASIC BIOLOGY TEXTS tell us that vitamins and minerals are absolutely necessary to create our body's basic metabolic functions. . . . If any one of the essential nutrients is deficient, we end up with brain impairment.

STEPHEN I. SCHOENTHALER, PH.D. (personal interview)

Introduction

Are you or is someone you care about prone to bursts of uncontrollable anger? Or are you "always sad," or "always nervous"? You may think these are basic personality traits that can't be changed, but they may well be your brain's biochemical reaction to nutritional habits that you *can* control. The many nutritionally oriented (orthomolecular) psychiatrists who worked with me on this book give details that can help you control your moods and energy level with your choice of foods.

If your child learns well in morning classes and seems to lose much of his intelligence in the afternoon, is something mysterious going on psychologically? Or is he eating foods at lunch that cause cerebral reactions that dull his mind?

Does your usually docile child (or your child diagnosed with childhood schizophrenia or autism) suddenly throw his glass of milk against the wall and go on a rampage? Are you to blame for not having adequately nurtured him psychologically? Does the child need psychotherapy, drugs, institutionalization? Or is the problem actually that the milk (sometimes a cause of violent behavior in those intolerant to it) has set up a biochemical reaction in his brain that causes the behavior?

If you are prone to fits of depression while cooking, cleaning house, or driving the children to school, you may have been told by an orthodox doctor that you need psychotherapy: you unconsciously resent your family and your role as homemaker. Orthomolecular psychiatrists, instead of delving into your subconscious mind, would arrange for tests to determine, among other things, if you are intolerant to coal tar or petroleum-derived products present in gas stoves, many household cleaning products, and car emissions. Consider this case history, from the files of Marshall M. Mandell, M.D.: The young man's symptoms had been diagnosed as stemming from a "deep-seated psychiatric conflict with his mother." This was "obvious" to his orthodox psychiatrist because the symptoms occurred mainly in the kitchen, his mother's domain. They disappeared when the kitchen's gas stove was replaced by an electric one.

Maybe you fear developing mental illness because it runs in your family. You have heard that some mental disorders are hereditary and that little if anything can be done to prevent your inheriting such a problem if you have a genetic predisposition. Orthomolecular psychiatrists believe that in some cases, what actually "runs in the family" are intolerances to certain foods or chemicals; an overall unhealthy diet shared through family habit; or tendencies to develop specific vitamin deficiencies or dependencies. (For instance, in Chapter 8 we discuss that Carl C. Pfeiffer, Ph.D., M.D., identified one form of schizophrenia as a familial double deficiency of zinc and vitamin B6.) Well-chosen nutritional changes can help you to change these factors before mental illness strikes, or to prevent a recurrence if you have already had episodes.

Some doctors express the orthomolecular view on preventing hereditary mental problems this way: Heredity predetermines our potential for developing an illness, but many factors can modify the *expression* of this potential. Our behavior can be modified because the *expression* of genes (that is, the molecules they produce) can be changed, greatly in part by nutritional intervention. Indeed, the word orthomolecular, which nutritionally oriented psychiatrists use to define themselves, comes from the Greek word for "straight," or "correct" (ortho), plus molecular, for molecules.

Much of what you have read so far may seem wildly improbable if you don't know much about this newer field of psychiatry. However, these statements are backed up in detail in this book by research studies, biochemical rationales, and actual results achieved by orthomolecular doctors. For now, I will point out simply that nutrients are crucial for every chemical reaction in the body. Without adequate nutrition, no organ—including the brain—can do its job well. When a brain that is ill is given optimal nutrition, it can become well again.

It might seem a new idea to think of psychological health as linked to the *physical* health of the brain, but this is far from a new concept. The statement "It is impossible to conceive of the existence of an insane mind in a healthy brain" occurred in the *Encyclopaedia Britannica*—in 1881. It was the generally accepted idea that mental disease could not exist in a brain that had no physical disorder. In the early twentieth century, that belief began to be supplanted by the idea that much of mental illness was "psychological" or due to "psychic trauma." Now, the pendulum has swung partially back as a result of previously unavailable information on the physiology of the brain. Orthodox psychiatry's response to this new knowledge is to attempt to correct impaired chemical balances of the brain with drugs. Orthomolecular psychiatry uses nutrients instead. Nutrients are the substances that *naturally* produce the healthy brain chemicals that drugs attempt to produce unnaturally. As you might expect, nutrients don't carry the potential for harmful side effects that drugs do.

This book compiles the work of a number of orthomolecular doctors specializing in various mental problems and various orthomolecular therapies. Other books on nutritional medicine tend to be narrower in scope, detailing basically one doctor's more limited views and expertise, one therapeutic approach, or therapies for only one disorder. I hope that this book therefore will be of help to an unusually broad spectrum of people.

Traditional Psychiatry and Orthomolecular Psychiatry

Like orthodox psychiatrists, orthomolecular psychiatrists graduate from orthodox medical schools, are trained in approved psychiatric residency training programs, and hold state licenses to practice. However, orthomolecular psychiatrists have chosen to *add* knowledge of nutritional medicine to their practices, often because they were unsatisfied with the success rate of traditional psychiatry. They have not completely abandoned their earlier training, and will use drugs and/or psychotherapy as adjuncts when these will best help their individual patient. Some doctors specialize in *clinical ecology:* diagnosis and treatment of food and chemical intolerances that may adversely affect an individual's brain and therefore cause mental or emotional illness. Some orthomolecular psychiatrists are also expert in the use of other alternative, nontoxic therapies such as homeopathy or biofeedback. Thus, orthomolecular psychiatry can be thought of as *starting with* orthodox therapies and going on from there to add many additional weapons to fight emotional and mental problems.

Case histories in this book are sometimes very dramatic. One reason is that people often do not go to an orthomolecular doctor until their traditional doctors say they cannot be helped, or until they themselves feel they have reached an impasse. Consequently many case histories in the files of orthomolecular doctors reflect the drama of the recovery of people whose cases were previously considered hopeless, or virtually so.

How I Came to Write This Book

The road that brought me to compiling this book began when I was 16. At that time I first learned that people's lives can hang by as thin a thread as whether their doctor happens to have read, and remembered, a relevant study in a medical journal. As almost everybody did at the time—and, I'm afraid, many people still do—I used to assume that all doctors, particularly specialists, knew everything. But one day when I was sitting in my (orthodox) specialist's office, he took a phone call from another doctor. He apologized for keeping me waiting, but "I owe him. I had a patient two years ago who was surely dying. I happened to run into this doctor, and happened to mention my patient. He happened to have read of a new treatment in a medical journal, and told me about it. So, she's alive and well now . . ."

I was dumbfounded, to phrase it mildly. The doctor's repetitions of the phrase "happened to" indicated that the woman was alive only because of a series of lucky coincidences. How many other people, I wondered, are alive only because a doctor learned of something new by accident? And how many have died because a doctor *didn't* learn something by accident?

The fact I learned that day—that valid knowledge can be "lost" in the medical literature—served me years later, when several of this country's top neurologists scolded me to "stop looking for miracles." My question that disturbed them was: isn't there somewhere, anywhere an alternative treatment for the terminal disorder they had diagnosed that was going to kill my husband, probably within three years? In part buoyed on by remembering that lady saved by the medical journal article decades earlier—and in part driven on by sheer desperation—I spent months in medical libraries, although I had had no training yet in medical-literature research. (If there were any orthomolecular doctors around then, I did not know about them.) I found hope in studies buried deep in the literature, and I took my findings to a nutritionist, who devised a treatment from the research he knew about, combined with the research I had found. The therapy consisted of large amounts of nutritional supplements that the little-known studies had found helpful, and removal of foods that commonly produce intolerances. Later, acupuncture was added.

I had not found the miracle the neurologists thought I was looking for, at least not if you define the word as I do: a wonderful happening for which there is no *known* cause. I had simply found medical research that the orthodox neurologists didn't know about. Or maybe they did know of some of it, but had rejected it because it didn't fit their philosophy of drugs or surgery.

So far, my husband has outlived his death sentence by over two decades.

Several years after his diagnosis, X-rays showed I had three pinched nerves in my spine. I bypassed pain-killing drugs and possible hospitalizations thanks to 10 inexpensive trips to an osteopathic doctor. Around that time, my little black poodle, Shiki, recovered from diagnosed "hopeless" arthritis at the age of one year through a simple change in diet. When elderly she was diagnosed by the same orthodox animal medical center (one of the nation's most esteemed) with "terminal" cancer. She not only beat her death sentence but returned to robust health through a complex therapy of nutritional supplements and homeopathy prescribed by a holistic veterinarian. This detailed therapy, while certainly not free, was very much less expensive than chemotherapy or radiation—neither of which would have worked anyway, according to the orthodox center. The only "side effect" Shiki suffered from all her alternative medicines was an intense hatred for the taste of the homeopathic preparation.

Early in my husband's "post-death years," I began to think that perhaps I had a debt to repay: to help disseminate new research. When I was given the chance to use my college journalism and science backgrounds as a writer for technical publications for orthodox doctors, I jumped at it. But I soon realized I was doing what a number of my colleagues complain they are often asked to do: "help medicine reinvent the wheel." I was often reporting on new studies that proved exactly what studies from the 30s and 40s—sometimes even earlier—had already proved.

So I decided to try to let the people who are actually doing the suffering know what little-known help might be available to them. I had an intellectual bias toward nutritional therapies. It made a great deal of sense to try to prevent and treat illness with the same substances that give us life and health in the first place. I don't want to be misunderstood: I don't believe that drugs and surgery are *never* needed. They save lives, for instance, in emergency situations in which nutritional therapy cannot work quickly enough.

To balance my personal history, I must add that I also attribute antibiotics to saving my life from pneumonia; and other drugs recently saved my husband's life from a massive hemorrhage caused by a bleeding ulcer. To balance *that*, in turn, I must report that once he was over the emergency, an orthomolecular doctor cured the ulcer without the major abdominal surgery orthodox physicians thought was absolutely necessary to "get rid of it." The cure was confirmed by endoscopy performed by the same doctor who had previously tested and seen the extremely large ulcer. The doctor easily pronounced this a "miracle," but became uncomfortable when my husband said that *he* thought the cure might be due to the orthomolecular therapy.

I have been a medical writer for over 20 years now, but have spent the last 15 years writing for the public about natural therapies. It is likely that your orthodox doctor will know little of this book's information, since medical schools teach little about nutrition.

Today much of the public seems to be more aware of alternative therapies for arthritis, multiple sclerosis, even cancer, than are many traditional doctors. But in recent years it became evident to me that many of these knowledgeable people were unaware that nutritional therapy could help problems generally considered emotional, psychological, or psychiatric. Perhaps one reason is the misconception that the brain is somehow separate from the body, when it is actually one of the body's organs just like the heart, liver, or kidneys. Thus, the thinking sometimes goes, a healthy or unhealthy body cannot make the brain (or mind) healthy or unhealthy. Actually, orthomolecular medicine had its first successes treating brain disorders before its scope was enlarged to treat illnesses of other organs. The physician generally called the father of orthomolecular medicine, Abram Hoffer, M.D., Ph.D., is a psychiatrist.

My articles on mental problems drew uncharacteristic responses. Besides hearing from people fighting the disorders discussed, I received letters from people fighting *other* mental problems. "I was surprised to read that there is help for autism. Do you know of anyone, anywhere who uses nutritional therapy for Down's syndrome?" Or "My neighbor told me in very excited terms what you wrote about Alzheimer's because her mother has it. My little girl is diagnosed as hyperactive and also with a learning disorder. I realize these have nothing to do with Alzheimer's, but do you know of any doctor who might have some new means of help?"

Perhaps the final motivation for writing this book came in a conversation with a friend, Brendan, who is highly knowledgeable about alternative medicine, has known me for as long as I have been writing on orthomolecular medicine, and has read much of my work. He said, "Everybody's given up on my brother, an alcoholic. My family has kicked him out; the medical doctors say nothing has worked; the psychotherapist says he's not responding; he long ago dropped out of A.A."

Knowing the high success rate orthomolecular doctors report for treating addiction, I was surprised that Bren's brother could not be helped. "Nutritional therapy failed, too?" I asked.

Bren looked at me blankly. "Nutritional therapy? How can there be nutritional therapy for a *psychological* problem?"

It was time for me to hit the research trail for another book.

What This Book Is, and What It Is Not

I give detailed basic information on several orthomolecular approaches for a number of emotional and mental problems. I include the oldest, most well-proven therapies as well as some of the most cutting-edge. Some of the latter are so new that even some orthomolecular psychiatrists have not studied them well. The newest therapies are described clearly as such, so you will know they have not yet withstood the test of time. You will also be aware that if you want to pursue them, the pioneering doctors I cite must be consulted by you or your doctor if he is not familiar with the approaches.

If you want more in-depth details on any disorder or therapy than I can give in this compilation, you will find them by consulting one or more of the books cited in the sections that interest you. Since these authors attempted a narrower scope than I have, they had space for more detail. If a book is not available at your bookstores or libraries, ask the store to order for you, or write the publisher yourself.

I have tried to make information for each disorder as self-contained as possible. Many books arrange chapters by nutritional approaches rather than disorders. Hopefully, my arrangement will prevent you from flipping back and forth through the book trying to assemble a cogent idea of available help.

The doctors who have worked with me on this book give suggestions for as much *safe* self-help as possible. But orthomolecular therapy often involves complex interactions among nutrients and self-help should be used mainly to lessen suffering while you wait to consult an orthomolecular doctor. Occasionally, though, very simple nutritional therapy, even for people gravely ill, can surprise everyone—including the doctors—by quickly bringing about recovery. Thus, you may find that, say, cutting out sugar or a food to which you're intolerant rids you of symptoms. It would still be important to have orthomolecular testing, to make sure there aren't other biochemical factors at work that can cause problems again in the near future.

I try to give enough studies and technical rationales to let you know something of the scientific bases for orthomolecular work. However, since this is not basically a book for doctors, more space is devoted to practical information on disorders. The case histories are actual histories from the files of orthomolecular doctors and are not, as is sometimes done, composites created to make a point. The histories are representative of countless others.

The discussion of different types of therapies should help you understand the treatment your orthomolecular doctor prescribes and also enable you to work with him or her to ensure that you get the best treatment: so that you provide the necessary information, ask the right questions, and offer suggestions of your own.

A major purpose of this book is to help you decide whether orthomolecular therapy might offer more help than your orthodox treatment. The "Resources" section at the back of the book will help you to locate an orthomolecular doctor in your area.

How to Get the Most out of This Book

Regardless of which particular disorder you are fighting, please first read Chapter 1, which will give you a framework to better understand and use information in the other chapters.

If, after reading about a specific disorder, you want further details on therapies, or if you are skeptical about any of them, read the relevant chapter in Part V of this book. These chapters present major debates regarding orthodox vs. orthomolecular medicine, and explain in technical details the main diagnostic tools and therapies used by nutritional medicine. However, this information is not directly practical in nature, and you may want to refer to it only after having read the chapter on the disorder that concerns you.

The best way to get full desired information out of *any* medical book is to refer to the Index at the back. The book might contain scattered mentions of disorders that will be listed in the Index, but that you would otherwise not know about unless you read the entire book.

The idea that all doctors know everything is passing, and with it the idea that patients should play a passive role in their treatments. Not all orthomolecular psychiatrists practice all therapies within their field, any more than all orthodox psychiatrists practice all therapies within *their* field. In practical terms this means that if an approach does not seem to help optimally, discuss with your doctor the possibility of using another therapy outlined for your problem— just as patients should discuss trying another drug or another form of psychotherapy if an orthodox approach doesn't seem to work. Find out whether your doctor has real reason to believe that the other approach is not relevant for your particular biochemical imbalance. Perhaps your physician does not know about the other approach, does not believe in it, or is inexperienced with it. If so, ask the doctor to consult about your problem with an orthomolecular doctor who has substantial experience with the approach. Doctors mentioned in this book as practicing a specific treatment will be able to refer you to physicians near you who are also knowledgeable in that therapy. The organizations listed in the "Resources" section may be of help.

If you are helping someone else, who is so incapacitated that he or she is institutionalized, it would be unwise to remove the person from the institution's care to consult an orthomolecular doctor. However, orthomolecular help is not necessarily out of reach. First, initiate any steps you can from the self-help section in the chapter relevant to the disorder. Try working with an orthodox doctor at the institution by having her read sections of this book and asking her to consult with an orthomolecular physician. Particularly helpful will be: the chapter on the disorder, the sections in Chapter 1 on orthomolecular medicine's answers to traditional medicine's arguments, and Chapters 14 to 19. Ask the doctor to read the studies cited. Point out that a large proportion appeared in highly respected *orthodox* medical journals.

That approach may not work with a *close-minded* orthodox doctor. In this case, try calling orthomolecular doctors in your area and tell them your problem. See if they have any additional safe self-help steps you might try. Would it be helpful if you sent them a blood sample to run tests on? These steps might at least give improvement—perhaps enough that your loved one can temporarily leave the institution for in-person orthomolecular testing.

The "Resources" section gives places to contact for lists not only of orthomolecular psychiatrists, but also of orthomolecular doctors who are not psychiatrists, in case you do not live near a specialist. It might seem strange in this age of specialization to read that you can get help for a mental problem from doctors other than psychiatrists. Unlike orthodox doctors, however, orthomolecular physicians deal less with diagnosed disease labels or with isolated symptoms than with correcting whatever is wrong in the individual's body. Any good orthomolecular doctor is capable of doing that as well as a good orthomolecular psychiatrist. True, the psychiatrist has more practical experience with nuances of mental conditions, but a conscientious orthomolecular doctor will consult freely with a psychiatrist colleague about the particulars of a patient's mental problem.

Incidentally, orthodox medicine has its own critics *because* of its increasing specialization. One argument is that heart specialists look for diseases of the heart, kidney specialists for diseases of the kidney, and so on—while patients are left with no one to consider diseases of the body as a whole. It is as if each organ functions independently in the body—and as if there is no integrated, whole person who is the sum total of all these organs. Long ago, I read a joke about medical specialization that I never forgot: Doctors are learning more and more about less and less, until someday all doctors will know everything there is to know—about nothing.

I hope for the day when all physicians use the best techniques for each patient without concern about whether they were originally orthodox or orthomolecular techniques. Perhaps we are moving toward that day. As Chapter 1 details, most orthomolecular doctors do try to use "the best of both worlds," and orthodox physicians already employ a number of nutritional therapies, although they may not think of them as actually nutritional.

Perhaps this book will bring at least a few orthodox psychiatrists to investigate orthomolecular therapy in true scientific fashion—that is, with an open mind—and to consider using it when it might best help their patients, especially those for whom traditional medicine offers little hope.

And it has been my dream through many years of work that this book will be a starting point for many of you to pursue orthomolecular therapy. To use a phrase of Dr. Mandell's, my thoughts have been with "those who have suffered without hope, and need wait no longer."

PART I

Introducing Orthomolecular Psychiatry

LET THY FOOD be thy medicine and thy medicine be thy food. . . . Leave your drugs in the chemist's pot if you can heal the patient with food.

—HIPPOCRATES, the father of medicine

TRYING TO TREAT an emotional or mental problem with a thinking-talking technique while the brain's chemistry is not being treated is like trying to redecorate the kitchen while the house is on fire.

—Orthomolecular psychiatrist WILLIAM H. PHILPOTT, M.D.

THE BOTTOM LINE is that a patient in psychotherapy will find that it starts to work better and faster once the person's brain has been normalized through nutritional therapy.

—Orthomolecular psychiatrist KARL E. HUMISTON, M.D.

Chapter 1

New Hope for Emotional and Mental Problems: Without Drug Side Effects, Psychoanalysis, or Shock Therapy

This chapter's title promises a lot. If you have already studied nutritional therapy—particularly if you have also had personal experience with it—the promise will probably not seem far-fetched. If you have not done research, academic or empirical, the words may smack of "quackery." Why not make this chapter the beginning of your personal exploration into a field that often offers so much hope that it is easy to assume that it's "too good to be true"? (You will find it helpful to read the Introduction first.)

What Is Orthomolecular Psychiatry? How Does It Differ From Orthodox, and How Is It Similar?

BASICS OF THIS FIELD

- Uses, basically, nontoxic nutritional therapies to restore emotional and mental health.

- Is an approach practiced by psychiatrists with the same medical degrees and licenses as traditional psychiatrists. Orthomolecular psychiatrists, however, have gone on to make a specialized study of how natural substances can make the brain (mind) healthy again.

- Is a comprehensive approach that often can successfully treat people who have failed to respond to traditional therapies.

- Usually does not require drugs or extensive psychotherapy. When drugs do have to be used, the additional nutritional therapy protects against harmful side effects.

- Places heavy emphasis on physical factors that can be scientifically evaluated, as opposed to more nebulous concepts such as the ego and the id, unconscious motivations, and repressed childhood traumas.

- Attempts to rebuild the health of the total body-mind by investigating *underlying* biochemical problems specific to the individual patient. (Drugs tend to attack, and often only cover up, isolated mental symptoms.)

- Is often substantially less expensive than traditional psychiatry.

In orthomolecular psychiatry, diet and nutritional supplementation are the basic approach and are often the only therapy needed. However, orthomolecular psychiatrists use the therapies that are most needed to make each individual patient well, whether they reflect the doctors' conventional training or the further study of nutritional medicine.

Orthomolecular doctors do not claim 100 percent success. But their combined knowledge of traditional techniques and newer, more natural therapies does allow them to help many people who have not been helped by traditional techniques alone. When drugs, psychotherapy, and electroconvulsive therapy don't work, an orthodox psychiatrist generally does not know where else to turn and may deem your case hopeless. An orthomolecular doctor's much broader outlook gives many more avenues to explore. You will see in this book that whereas traditional psychiatrists use *drugs* to affect various chemicals in the brain, orthomolecular psychiatrists focus on using *nutritional substances* that affect those chemicals the same way, naturally, every day in healthy people.

Orthomolecular doctors never treat the mind as if it were separate from the body. They will test for physical problems of the rest of the body that may cause mental symptoms. Thus, orthomolecular therapy will often restore physical, as well as mental, health, as shown by many case histories in this book.

Previously undiagnosed physical disorders often do turn out to be a major culprit behind mental symptoms. People often bypass primary physicians and go directly to psychiatrists, believing that their *mental* problems cannot be caused by a *physical* disorder. Even when they go to a primary physician first, the doctor often makes the same assumption and refers them to a psychiatrist. The psychiatrist may compound this error by starting right in to treat the patient within the psychiatric specialty. Bernard Rimland, Ph.D., director of the Autism Research Institute in San Diego, California, states, "It is extremely likely that some people reading this book are being treated for a mental problem when they really should be receiving treatment for a physical disorder."

One relevant study was reported by Richard C. W. Hall, M.D., in the orthodox publication the *American Journal of Psychiatry* (May 1981, p. 5). One hundred persons admitted to the hospital with psychiatric problems were thoroughly screened for physical illness. It was found that almost half had previously undiagnosed physical illness that either *caused* or worsened their psychiatric symptoms—despite the fact that the patients had previously been checked out and cleared by the usual methods.

Orthodox psychiatrists strive to arrive at a correct diagnosis: for instance, does the patient have schizophrenia or manic depression, two disorders often hard to differentiate by observing symptoms. The orthomolecular philosophy of seeking underlying causes of mental symptoms—rather than covering up the symptoms with drugs—leads some orthomolecular doctors to say that the "disease label"—diagnosing a specific syndrome—is not so important as pinpointing the biochemical imbalance in the individual's body. An orthomolecular psychiatrist will concentrate more on what can be done to restore a healthy balance. As one nutritional psychiatrist stated at a medical conference, "For the orthomolecular doctor, diagnostic labels have no real meaning in terms of deciding the most successful treatment."

Orthomolecular psychiatrists follow earlier training by recommending psychotherapy in addition to nutritional changes, when it is felt to be in the patient's best interests. However, psychotherapy often is found to be unnecessary when proper nutritional therapy is followed. Recommended psychotherapy is often action-oriented, such as behavior therapy, rather than the more lengthy and expensive thinking-talking techniques.

Psychoanalysis, the most costly and time-consuming traditional technique, is seldom if ever recommended by orthomolecular psychiatrists. (Psychiatrist Abram Hoffer, M.D., Ph.D., generally referred to as the father of orthomolecular medicine, says that "some of our best orthomolecular therapists were originally psychoanalysts who gave [psychoanalysis] up because of the better results with orthomolecular therapy" [personal communication].) This practice might be considered in line with traditional psychiatry, which has been moving away from psychoanalysis to search for drugs and psychotherapy techniques that are faster and less expensive. Even while Freud, the father of psychoanalysis, was alive, a doctor began stating publicly that psychoanalysis had little to offer psychiatry and that it should not become part of psychiatric therapy. The upstart who had the effrontery to dismiss Freud's psychoanalysis in this way was— Dr. Sigmund Freud. He predicted that someday tests would be developed that would show much mental illness to be biochemical in nature. It seems that Freud's prediction is coming true.

Orthomolecular psychiatry is often substantially less expensive than traditional psychiatry. Is this because nutritionally oriented doctors charge a lot less for their time? Not that I know of. But consider that nutritional supplementation is less expensive than drugs, and some people can recover through simply changing what they eat. With orthomolecular therapy, you have much less of a chance of requiring institutionalization. Expensive psychoanalysis is not needed, and psychotherapy is needed much less often than with traditional treatment. If you are treated with drugs, you have to visit your doctor every time the prescription must be renewed, but you may buy more nutritional supplements at a store. The lack of side effects so common with drugs cuts down on lost work time, as well as on the need for medical treatment for the side effects.

There is another factor that makes orthomolecular treatment less expensive. One orthomolecular psychiatrist, lamenting that he had been much richer when he practiced orthodox psychiatry, told me: "As is true of other orthomolecular doctors—who treat underlying causes instead of just masking symptoms—most of my patients get well and don't need me anymore."

What Is the Basic Rationale Behind Orthomolecular Psychiatry?

You may find it a new idea to think of mental problems as connected to faulty nutrition. Every chemical that our body organs, including the brain, need to function is produced by reactions started by nutrients. While the medical world throughout history has been riddled with debate, no one has questioned the fact that when the body doesn't receive food for a length of time, it dies. It is also undebated that when the rest of the body dies from lack of nutrition, so does the brain. Conversely, optimal nutrition can make the brain and other body organs optimally healthy.

Marshall Mandell, M.D., nicely expresses the importance of nutrients on the development of life itself: "I remind my patients that a tiny single cell—the fertilized egg that became them—was transformed into a wonderful, complex human being by the actions of genes on the nutrients brought to this cell by their mother's bloodstream. Thus we are formed from, and owe our existence to, our mothers' nutrition" (personal communication).

In the following chapters, we weave specifics of how nutrients regulate the brain chemicals that affect our minds. (See especially Chapter 3 and Chapter 18.) The main point to be made here is that *nutrients* produce these chemicals naturally every day; not the drugs that traditional psychiatrists use to change the same chemicals. Here is an example of how nutrients can be used to affect brain chemicals, in this case dopamine, in the treatment of the problem of cocaine addiction. When dopamine is present in the brain in a balanced amount, one tends to have a sense of well-being and pleasure. When cocaine is taken, there is at first a large *rush* of dopamine to the brain, leading to the initial "high." But once the unnatural rush of dopamine ends, the brain is depleted of the chemical, causing the absolute misery (withdrawal symptoms) the person is left feeling. Repeatedly taking cocaine—addiction—is thus an attempt not only to repeat the high but also to hold at bay the misery caused by the depletion of dopamine when the drug loses effect.

Dopamine is naturally produced in the body from the amino acids L-phenylalanine and L-tyrosine, working with vitamins C and B6 and the minerals iron and magnesium. Thus, these nutrients help the patient to maintain a stable sense of happiness and well-being. Ensuring a rich supply of these nutrients diminishes a person's need for the high of cocaine, and he is helped to get off the drug without the misery of withdrawal symptoms.

GUILT, BLAME, STIGMA

The orthomolecular approach tends not to include issues of guilt and blame. (This exclusion is in keeping with some of the newer thinking in orthodox psychiatry.) It is difficult to blame the sufferer for having an unbalanced chemistry, and difficult to blame parents for having caused it through inadequate psychological caring.

Previously, some patients undergoing various traditional types of psychotherapy techniques have been left with a deep resentment toward their parents, believing them to have caused their mental problem; for their part, parents have been left with a deep feeling of guilt. The resentment and guilt have done nothing to solve the mental problem of the sufferer. Indeed, the tendency has been to make patients feel anger toward the very people who could be their best allies.

The orthomolecular approach also tends to avoid the stigma inherent in diagnoses such as schizophrenia, autism, manic depression, etc. (although certainly orthodox psychiatrists don't attempt to stigmatize their patients). Orthomolecular psychiatrists—in their attempt to deal with what is *causing* the symptoms rather than with what the disorder label should be—prefer to call their patients not "schizophrenics" or "depressives," but people with a deficiency of certain nutrients or with an intolerance to certain foods or chemicals. Someone who has delusions of persecution whenever he eats wheat may be referred to as suffering from an intolerance to wheat rather than from "paranoid schizophrenia."

A SHORT HISTORY

While orthomolecular medicine is generally considered a "new" field, its basic tenets can be traced to Hippocrates, approximately 2,500 years ago. Generally called the father of medicine, he is still honored today with the taking of the Hippocratic oath, called "the ethical guide of the medical profession." Much later, in the twelfth century, the great physician Moses Maimonides echoed Hippocrates' ideas: "No illness which can be treated by diet should be treated by any other means." It would seem, then, that nutritional medicine as the therapy of choice is definitely not a new idea.

In more modern times, serious individual disorders were successfully fought with nutrition as long ago as the late 1500s, when some sailors used foods high in vitamin C to prevent and reverse the dread disease scurvy. Today, orthodox doctors use diet and/or nutritional supplementation not only for scurvy, but for a number of other disorders once considered virtually hopeless.

Solid, modern scientific research in nutritional medicine as a specialized field began in earnest about forty years ago, and it began in the field of psychiatry. Orthomolecular medicine is generally traced back to the early fifties, when psychiatrists Abram Hoffer and Hum-phry Osmond successfully used a therapy based on vitamin B3 to treat some patients with acute schizophrenia. Drs. Hoffer and Osmond ran a series of double-blind controlled studies, to confirm their success; they are considered the first doctors in the world to run such stringent studies for a psychiatric disorder.

However, at around the same time, various tranquilizers were developed and were helping many who had been without hope. Since doctors had graduated from medical school with a strong belief in drugs, and little knowledge of nutrition, it was much easier to place their faith in the new tranquilizers, rather than believing that something as "simple" as nutrients could have a profound effect on moods and behavior. Also, it was often difficult to have nutritional studies legitimatized through publication in major medical journals, which were dependent on drug advertisers for their revenues.

Nevertheless, the handful of orthomolecular psychiatrists persisted, continuing to develop nutritional therapies for other neuroses and psychoses. Since these doctors were rebalancing the biochemistry of the entire body, rather than attacking individual symptoms, orthomolecular medicine soon branched off into treating physical disorders that did not produce mental symptoms.

ORTHOMOLECULAR PSYCHIATRY: NOT A "UNIFIED FIELD"

For the sake of clarity, I have written as if orthomolecular psychiatry were a cohesively integrated whole. However, the field is not completely integrated, just as one might say that the field of orthodox psychiatry is not completely integrated. Individual orthodox psychiatrists will specialize in psychoanalysis, drug therapy, or one or more disorders; and so will many orthomolecular psychiatrists have their areas of expertise. This is why I did not simply find one orthomolecular psychiatrist to work with me on this book. I didn't want it to contain, as so many books do, basically the knowledge, practical experience, or bias of only one doctor.

Some orthomolecular physicians do have knowledge and experience in most approaches covered in this book, and they often refer to themselves as "general practitioners within the specialization of orthomolecular psychiatry." Others focus primarily on nutritional therapy, and when they feel that food and chemical intolerances may be a factor, they refer the patient to a clinical ecologist, a doctor who specializes in diagnosing and treating intolerances. Others are orthomolecular psychiatrists as well as clinical ecologists. One physician may deal largely with schizophrenia, while another may treat very few with this disorder.

A few psychiatrists consider themselves orthomolecular because they add several vitamins and minerals to the orthodox array of drugs, "talk" therapies, and electroconvulsive therapy. They never treat cases basically with vitamins and minerals; know little of therapies with other nutrients; and do not believe in clinical ecology. Be aware that such psychiatrists don't fit the definition of orthomolecular as used in this book.

INTOLERANCES (SENSITIVITIES) VS. ALLERGIES

I have referred to food and chemical *intolerances*. You may have heard them called allergies. Some orthomolecular doctors do call any abnormal reaction to a food, chemical, or inhalant an allergy—using the word with the meaning it originally had. However, orthodox allergists now do not consider a reaction allergic unless it is connected with a specific immunological response (IgE-mediated). Thus, they consider allergies to produce mainly respiratory, skin, and gastrointestinal symptoms. Clinical ecologists, testing for and treating intolerances within the broad definition of any abnormal reaction, report high success with mental (and physical) problems that have not yielded to orthodox treatment. Chapter 14 contains more detailed information on food and chemical intolerances.

WHY IS THIS FIELD NOT CALLED HOLISTIC PSYCHIATRY?

The term orthomolecular psychiatry was first coined by Dr. Linus Pauling, Ph.D., two-time Nobel Prize winner. "Ortho" is the Greek word for straight, and "molecular" refers, not surprisingly, to molecules. Thus, the orthomolecular concept is to provide the best molecular environment for the body, especially optimum concentrations of substances normally present. The word "orthomolecular," therefore, connotes a heavy reliance on physical factors that can be dealt with scientifically.

However, "holistic" is sometimes used as an umbrella term for a wide variety of alternative approaches (not all of them well proven). Also, "holistic" is often used to stress the mind's ability to heal the body. While I know of no orthomolecular psychiatrists who argue that ability, their therapies focus more on the reverse fact: that the body can heal the mind. And although orthomolecular doctors do not disagree with the idea, held by both holistic and orthodox physicians, that stress can result in emotional problems, they feel that many emotional problems "caused by" stress are actually the result of nutritional drain produced by that stress. The most simple examples of how such a drain can occur are when a person in a crisis does not eat, or binges on sugar or chocolate, and thus deprives the body of nutrition or introduces toxic substances. Nutritional doctors also believe that, when the environment cannot be made less stressful, optimal nutrition can help give the physical and mental strength to cope better.

The issue of terminology gets confused because some orthomolecular doctors do refer to themselves as "holistic" when dealing with the public and use "orthomolecular" only when dealing with other health professionals, probably because the latter term is not yet widely known to the public. A quick way to ascertain whether a doctor is orthomolecular or holistic according to this book's definition is to ask whether her bias is more toward mind over body, or body over mind.

Orthomolecular medicine shares one goal held by many holistic approaches: that of treating the patient as a whole human being, rather than as a set of symptoms located in one or more organs. You may know someone (yourself perhaps) who was sent to specialist after specialist, each of whom ran tests on a different organ—

and none of whom could find any reason for the symptoms. ("Hypochondria" is a common diagnosis for this phenomenon.) As psychiatrist Melvyn R. Werbach, M.D., points out, the pursuit of specialization can result in everyone's forgetting "the fact that the characteristics of an organism which has been torn apart into simple units may bear little resemblance to those of the functioning whole."

How Well Does Orthomolecular Psychiatry Work?

There is no simple answer to the question of how well orthomolecular therapy works, any more than there is a simple answer to how well orthodox therapy works. I can, however, give some "ballpark" ideas.

Many people do not go to an orthomolecular doctor until they feel that the usual techniques have failed them—or until they are told by their doctors that nothing can be done. Despite the fact that orthomolecular doctors so often work with the "untreatables" of orthodox medicine, the reported recovery rates for orthomolecular therapy are extremely high. I give some statistics for individual disorders in the following chapters. (By "recovery" I don't necessarily mean "cure." Although medical dictionaries often list "any attempted treatment" as one definition of the word cure—which would certainly allow for a wide use of the word—I use it only in its strict sense: that therapy can be stopped without return of symptoms. For some who recover through orthomolecular therapy, a lifetime attention to diet must be continued, just as orthodox therapy sometimes requires a lifetime on drugs—or, indeed, a lifetime attention to diet, as with diabetes.)

For some disorders—for instance, addiction—orthomolecular medicine reports much more success than does orthodox. For several disorders often considered untreatable, such as mental retardation and autism, orthomolecular treatment sometimes can offer remarkable improvement.

HOW SIMPLE IS ORTHOMOLECULAR TREATMENT?

In many instances, orthomolecular therapy is sublimely easy. Complexity depends on how unbalanced the individual's chemistry is, and for what reasons. (Oddly enough, complexity of therapy does not always correlate with severity of symptoms. An individual may suffer grave symptoms of, say, schizophrenia because of intolerance to a few foods. Removing those foods may for that person be a successful treatment. I know of cases of severe anxiety attacks disappearing when sugar was removed from the diet, and recoveries from psychoses that were achieved so simply that they amazed even the orthomolecular doctors treating the patients.)

However, some people have the misconception, often fostered by overly simplistic publications, that there is one vitamin for each disorder, or that one mineral can "fix" a number of problems. Actually, the view of "one cause and one therapy" is closer to that sometimes held by orthodox doctors than it is to the view held by nutritional physicians. Orthodox doctors do tend to search earnestly for one set of drugs, or one surgical technique, that offers the most help for a disorder. Orthomolecular psychiatrists, on the other hand, work closely with nature, attempting to rebalance brain chemistry by using the same complex of substances in the same balance that our bodies have evolved to need for complete health. This is not always a simple job.

A further complication is that the same imbalance of nutrients may give different people different symptoms; thus, orthomolecular psychiatrists cannot say that because a person suffers from, say, depression, they know automatically what nutrients are needed to correct the problem for that individual. While specific disorders do respond most often to specific therapies, as indicated in the following chapters, only scientific testing can completely tell what is off-balance in each person's biochemistry.

Sometimes the orthomolecular approach can be complex because a conscientious doctor is aware that there may be more than *one* physical problem behind the symptoms and will not "give up" on the patient if treating the first problem doesn't help. This philosophy is a factor in orthomolecular medicine's reported success rate with orthodox medicine's "untreatables." It is also a reason that ortho-molecular doctors seldom give a diagnosis of hypochondria, or psychosomatic disorder—that is, symptoms coming from a psycho-logical, rather than a physical, or "real," cause. Psychiatrist William H. Philpott, M.D., one of the earliest orthomolecular specialists in problems related to low blood sugar, tells of a woman who had been diagnosed with depression. Her previous doctor had found that she had low blood sugar, which can underlie depression in some people, and had put her on the standard high-protein diet for low blood sugar. However, the diet made her depression worse. The doctor was so puzzled that he urged her to travel from New York to Oklahoma to see Dr. Philpott, who recounts,

> I decided we had better investigate if there weren't something *be-hind* the low blood sugar that seemed to be behind the depres-sion. I put her on a fast, and her depression cleared up. Then I tested her with various foods, searching for intolerances. Within minutes after she took some chicken, there she was, depressed all over again. Chicken had been a mainstay of her high-protein diet for low blood sugar. She stopped eating chicken and the other foods she tested out to be intolerant to, and her depression went away. So, by the way, did her blood-sugar disorder.

Most likely, any complexities in orthomolecular treatment will be considered by most people to be better than drugs and their side effects, hospitalization, electroshock therapy, or trying to live a life-time with the symptoms.

WHAT ABOUT DRUGS?

One very important factor orthomolecular psychiatry offers is pro-tection from drug side effects. For many patients, drugs are never needed—for instance, when symptoms are tied to food or chemical intolerances. Most people requiring drugs are those who pose a threat to themselves or others: drugs, when they work, can cover up symptoms more quickly than natural substances—which require some time to rebalance biochemistry and more truly banish the symptoms. Obviously, orthomolecular doctors will not ask violent or suicidal people to wait for this to happen. However, even when drugs are used, the additional nutritional therapy may allow people to use lower dosages of the drugs and to cut them out completely after a while, and it will definitely cut down on the risk of side effects. In fact, some drug side effects arise from nutritional imbalances that drugs themselves cause.

One common side effect of some antipsychosis drugs is tardive dyskinesia, whose bizarre neurological symptoms, involuntary muscle movements, have ironically been themselves misdiagnosed as a psychosis. Statistics, as usual, vary; but it has been reported that up to 55 percent of patients on neuroleptic drugs develop this disorder. In Chapter 8 we discuss a study of more than 61,000 patients over two decades who were given neuroleptics *and* nutritional therapy; only 0.05 percent developed the disorder. (Briefly, neuroleptics are those anti-psychosis drugs that tend to produce reduced movement and indifference to surroundings.)

The basic problem with drugs (of all kinds, not just those used for mental problems) is that they tend to be composed of substances normally not found in the human body. Thus, the body can get "lost" trying, all on its own, to learn suddenly how to deal with these new, foreign, substances. Nutrients are substances that the body has long ago learned to use successfully—indeed, to *need*—for good health. As Carl C. Pfeiffer, Ph.D., M.D., has said, "Nutrients at their best can be smart drugs that know exactly where to go and what to do." Orthomolecular doctors often point out that the worst that well-chosen nutrients can do is to have no success in treating the disorder.

In his book *Brain Allergies* (page 96) Dr. Philpott says in reference to tranquilizers, "Patients on drugs often have to pay a high price for their symptomatic relief by running the statistically high risk of becoming permanently incarcerated in their chemical straitjackets. The result . . . can vary from such severe side effects as silent coronary death, tardive dyskinesia, parkinsonism and an increase in the possibility of developing clinical diabetes to a zombielike, miserable life of social incompetence."

If Orthomolecular Therapy Works So Well, Why Don't All Doctors Use It?

In recent years, a number of books have been devoted exclusively to the question of why orthomolecular medicine, which seems to offer so much more hope, is not used by more doctors. Some writers attack practitioners of orthodox medicine as "close-minded," "unscientific," "motivated by greed," or even of actively withholding the truth. This book's purpose is to help people who suffer, not to explore all areas of why a field of medicine that seems to offer so much is opposed or ignored by so many conventional doctors. Here, however, are a few basic answers.

MEDICAL SKEPTICISM

One prime "function" of the scientific mind is to be skeptical. Skepticism has hopefully saved many from forsaking proven medical care for "quack" therapies. However, historically, it also has resulted in uncountable deaths and sufferings that were unnecessary, while doctors expressing new ideas were attacked simply *because* they expressed new ideas. Dr. Hoffer has pointed out that there is a "big difference between healthy skepticism—which allows you to examine something you're not convinced of—and closed-mindedness," which *prevents* you from examining something you don't already believe in (personal communication).

I offer just a few examples of worthwhile new concepts put forth by supposed "quacks." Doctor William Harvey was denigrated by the medical profession for a full century, because of his "notion" that blood circulates through the body. Louis Pasteur's work enraged the medical profession and provoked violent attacks against him; one criticism was that Pasteur was a chemist, not a physician, and had no business "fooling around" with disease. His work resulted in the fields of bacteriology and virology. (Imagine what medicine might be like today if it didn't treat bacteria and viruses.) Dr. William Morton was criticized for developing useful anesthesia; one argument was that pain was a natural occurrence, and doctors who were "afraid" to inflict pain in patients were to be scorned.

Ignaz Semmelweis was a nineteenth-century Hungarian doctor whose unpopular notion was that doctors should wash their hands between performing autopsies and delivering babies. He couldn't persuade colleagues that handwashing might prevent deadly childbirth fever, which, he was convinced, was due to bacteria transmitted from the dead bodies. His peers ridiculed him, destroyed his medical career, and according to Carlton Fredericks, Ph.D., "ultimately drove him insane. But few know that he used his suicide in a last, despairing effort to convince doctors" of the validity of his idea about the spread of bacteria *(Nutrition Guide for the Prevention and Cure of Common Ailments and Diseases,* page xviii). How did Dr. Semmelweis choose to kill himself? He took a scalpel that had been used in an autopsy, plunged it into his hand, and died of the ensuing infection. (Dr. Fredericks points out a recent ironic sidelight to this already ironic story: In 1981, the prestigious medical journal *The New England Journal of Medicine,* "scolded physicians for going from one patient to another without washing their hands.")

A more recent "charlatan" was laughed at by doctors for a decade because he claimed he had found a cure for not just one but a number of deadly diseases. His unlikely "miracle cure" was a substance derived from molds. The charlatan was Sir Alexander Fleming, and the substance was penicillin.

Sometimes natural therapies have been used for centuries by the public before medical skepticism allowed these "old wives' remedies" into professional practice. Today, every medical student knows that scurvy can be prevented and treated with vitamin C, but this knowledge took about two centuries to "get through" from the public to the medical profession. Foods high in vitamin C were used by some sailors to fight scurvy for almost 150 years before one doctor took this fact seriously. (A John Smith, for instance, wrote an advice to ships' captains, detailing what "victuals" they should have on board. The victuals included "the juice of lemons for the scurvy." The wording would seem to indicate that Smith thought lemons were such a well-known aid for scurvy that no explanation was needed. Yet he wrote his advice in 1626, more than 120 years before the first doctor looked into the subject.)

It was Dr. James Lind who finally, in 1747, ran a controlled scientific study. He concluded that sailors should drink lemon or lime juice to prevent the scurvy that was a major hazard of long sea voyages. (Both fruits were found to be high in vitamin C, when this vitamin was discovered much later.) Navy officials attacked Lind. The medical community attacked him. After all, how could a devastating, "mysterious" disorder be prevented or cured simply by sipping juice?

It was nearly another fifty years before Dr. Lind's suggestions were accepted, and citrus juice was made part of the regulation diet for British sailors, who are still nicknamed "limeys." Thereafter, the mysterious disorder scurvy virtually disappeared.

However, before the juice became part of regulation diet, scurvy wiped out 50 percent or more of the sailors at sea. It has been estimated that just in the decades between Dr. Lind's findings and their acceptance by the British navy, 100,000 seamen died from scurvy—needlessly.

We might ask why the medical profession reacted so negatively to Dr. Lind's suggestion. Even if drinking a little lemon or lime juice had had no effect on scurvy, would it have harmed anybody?

The traditional skepticism and slow acceptance of new ideas leads to a very human motivation behind some doctors' refusal to investigate orthomolecular medicine: the fear of being laughed at or ostracized by their colleagues. I have given examples of why that fear is well-based. It even keeps some doctors from using nutritional therapy when they have investigated it and *do* believe in it. A number of doctors have told me they have successfully used alternative therapies, for themselves or family, for problems deemed hopeless by standard medicine, but they would not buck the tide to treat their similarly hopeless patients with the same techniques.

THE INFORMATION GAP

Another reason for the often very extensive lag between a valid discovery and its general application is the sheer mass of medical literature appearing every year. No doctor can read all of it, let alone commit it to memory. Thus, there is always a chance that valid new work will get lost in the literature unless it makes a big "splash" at a medical convention or gets picked up by mass media. Some doctors have estimated that the *average* amount of time that valid knowledge lies in limbo, lost in this information gap, is forty years.

Actually, much of the work on which orthomolecular medicine is based does happen to be in the *orthodox* medical literature—and some of it has been there since the 1920s. Orthomolecular doctors know of this work because, in researching their specialty, they have made it a point to dig it up.

A study conducted several years ago nicely sums up what I have said about the information gap and about skepticism. It concluded that hospital patients don't like to use bedpans. Leaving aside the question of why time and money had to be spent to discover something that the average person on the street already knows, the point here is that the researchers expressed concern that their results might meet with skepticism. They wrote that they hoped their findings would be seriously considered because they were "backed up" by similar results of previous research—conducted in the 1930s.

INADEQUATE KNOWLEDGE OF NUTRITIONAL MEDICINE

You might assume that all doctors thoroughly study nutrition before they receive their degrees. Actually, many medical schools do not require courses in this subject, unless you would consider a total of three hours of training a "course." A report published in 1985 by the Academy of Sciences Press in Washington, D.C., also found that the *greatest* number of hours required for the study of nutrition in the medical schools surveyed was 56. (This might seem a surprising lack in medical education, since nutrients are crucially needed for every chemical reaction in our bodies.) Dr. Hoffer adds that even when nutrition courses are required, "Much of the nutrition they teach is wrong. They indoctrinate graduates with ideas that were avant garde in 1950."

Thus, it is little wonder that many doctors do not understand what nutritional physicians are doing. Also, since it is easy to assume that something not taught in medical schools has no validity, it is not surprising that many doctors do not take time from their busy practices to investigate the scientific validity of nutritional medicine.

Actually, though, orthodox doctors often *do* use nutritional medicine, although they may not think of it as such. Orthodox doctors sometimes argue that the vitamins they prescribe for certain disorders are not nutrients but *drugs,* "because I'm using them as therapy." Nutritional medicine is used every time a doctor prescribes a specific diet for diabetes, heart disease, high blood pressure, or hypoglycemia; every time she uses vitamin B1 for complications of alcoholism, B6 for premenstrual syndrome, iron for iron-deficiency anemia, etc. Recently, proper diet has been recommended by the establishment to prevent some types of cancer; similar recommendations were offered many years earlier by doctors specializing in nutrition.

MISTAKEN IDEAS AND INADEQUATE STUDIES

Your doctor may mention reading work disproving certain nutritional studies, and indeed such studies do exist—just as studies exist that disprove research on drugs and surgical techniques. However, refutations of nutrition studies are often simply not accurate. Inaccurate refutations can be attributed to a misunderstanding of nutritional facts and also to methodological flaws in the way the refuting studies were run.

True Nutritional Facts. A basic nutritional fact is that one nutrient seldom acts alone in the body; usually, nutrients are fully effective only in balanced combination with others. Yet the common orthodox approach to determining effectiveness of a substance is to test it in isolation. This practice is based on the belief that you cannot really test how helpful one drug is if patients are taking another drug at the same time. Such thinking can be quite true—for drugs. But the reverse is often true for nutrients: You cannot scientifically test how effective a nutrient is unless you accompany it with the others on its natural synergistic team. Studying effectiveness of one nutrient used alone can be like taking away all of a baseball pitcher's teammates, and then seeing if he can win the ball game.

Another basic nutritional fact sometimes overlooked by researchers who are not specialists in this field is the concept of bioindividuality. This means simply that individual people have individual nutritional requirements. It is thus often inadequate to run studies giving the same amount of a nutrient to all participants for the same length of time.

A further often overlooked aspect of bioindividuality is that the *same* disorder can occur in *different* people because of deficiencies of *different* nutrients. Thus, a study showing that only a few people with a disorder respond to the nutrient tested does not necessarily mean it is useless for that disorder. It may mean that the nutrient *is* a valid therapy—but only for the relatively few who are deficient in that nutrient, or who have a higher-than-normal requirement. Others with the same disorder may respond to different nutrients than the one tested. Nutritional doctors deal with this phenomenon by running scientific tests to determine nutritional deficiencies of the individual patient.

Methodological Flaws. Methodological flaws are errors made in conducting an experiment or study. Some typical methodological flaws have included "invalidating" the results of a nutritional study by using smaller amounts of a nutrient than did the original researchers, using it in a different biological form, using it for a shorter time, or not using the complete nutritional therapy that is supposedly being tested for replication.

One study, currently upheld as disproving the reliability of hair analysis, which is used by nutritional doctors to indicate body mineral levels, has been used by Stephen J. Schoenthaler, Ph.D., to show his students how *not* to conduct scientific research. Dr. Schoenthaler is with the Department of Sociology at California State University–Stanislaus, and one of the courses he teaches on the graduate level is scientific methodology. Dr. Schoenthaler, who does not consider himself an orthomolecular or orthodox doctor, has found a number of methodological flaws in this study (*Journal of the American Medical Association*, 1985, pp. 1041–45), including the fact that the researcher did not collect the hair samples according to the guidelines followed by doctors who use hair analysis and by laboratories that analyze hair samples. Dr. Schoenthaler said in an interview,

> What made this study more particularly embarrassing was that the author ignored his own conclusions. Despite the fact that he had weighted things so that hair analysis might be proven unreliable, the only conclusion one could draw from his *own* statistical results was that hair analysis is very, very reliable. Anything correlated at .7 is considered [scientifically] a great predictor. . . . Most of his tests came out *above* .7. However, he just apparently decided to ignore the fact that he *himself* had proved that hair analyses were excellent diagnostic predictors.
>
> In less than five pages, he violated about 15 of the approximately 20 major methodological 'no-no's' that researchers occasionally make. In short, this study that 'proved definitively' that hair analysis is not to be relied upon is a marvelous example of a political hatchet job with no substance.

While that study is currently upheld as disproving the value of hair analysis, Joseph D. Campbell, Ph.D., has written that "by 1983

there [had] been over 1,500 citations in the world's scientific literature to attest to the usefulness of hair analysis as a screening diagnostic tool" (*Journal of Orthomolecular Psychiatry*, vol. 14, No. 4,
1985, p. 276).

Negative Preconceptions. Numerous other examples of "refutations" of orthomolecular medicine might be viewed as originating
from a preconceived bias rather than a scientific desire to discover
the truth. For instance, panels have been set up to investigate a nutritional question, or to consider revoking an orthomolecular doctor's license; and only professionals who are already known *not* to
believe in nutritional therapy, and *not* to have experience with it,
are allowed on the panel.

Bernard Rimland, Ph.D., sent me a copy of a letter he wrote in
1986 to the commissioner of the Food and Drug Administration in
which he protested one such panel that had sounded an alarm about
the harmfulness of vitamin and mineral supplements:

> The "scientific panel" referred to . . . in the press releases [is-
> sued by the American Dietetic Association] included several indi-
> viduals who have achieved national notoriety for their repeated,
> shrill, and unmeritorious outcries about the supposed harm done
> by vitamin/mineral consumption. . . . It is hard to see how a
> panel which totally excludes opposing views can be called scien-
> tific.
>
> When one considers that the 100,000,000 Americans who
> consume vitamins include hundreds of thousands who are psy-
> chotic or suicidal [people who might be considered at risk to
> overdose either because of a tenuous hold on reality or on pur-
> pose], it is indeed impressive that there has never been, to my
> knowledge, a death in the U.S. attributable to vitamin supple-
> ments except a few instances in which physicians made errors in
> overdosing with vitamins A (one case) and D (several cases).
> [These two vitamins are considered easiest to overdose with, be-
> cause they can accumulate, or "stockpile," in the body.]

Great alarm is expressed about the many thousands of reports to poison control centers concerning vitamin-mineral overdosing.

Yet such reports typically consist, Dr. Rimland says, of a parent asking if anything should be done about a handful or bottleful of vitamins a child has eaten. "As the press release says . . . there were 24,092 such 'exposures' in 1984. Yet all those 'exposures' produced not a single death or serious illness!"

Accusing those who wrote the press releases of trying "to horrify the public," Dr. Rimland pointed out that they

> cite the unique case wherein a manufacturer by mistake made tablets containing 27,000 micrograms of selenium instead of the 150 [micrograms] intended. A woman who consumed the tablets, we are told, suffered nausea, fatigue and hair loss and "could have died." In fact, the woman recovered completely, despite taking nearly 200 times as much supposedly toxic selenium as she intended. Again, this is evidence for the extraordinary *safety* of the supplement.

Other Mistaken Ideas. Another charge unfairly leveled at orthomolecular therapies is that some patients improve only because they expected to get better, a response known as the "placebo effect." Since many patients try orthodox methods before they even consider orthomolecular treatment, one might logically assume that they really *expected* to recover through traditional therapies. Indeed, by the time patients come to orthomolecular doctors, often their attitude is "I know I can't be helped, but I'm trying you now because I have nothing to lose."

Many case histories in this book tell of people who firmly did not believe this approach could help them—until it did. Even *then* some patients cannot believe the therapy has helped, and they go off it to show everybody that their improvement just happened to coincide with nutritional treatment. Some patients go through several rounds of "coincidental" recovery with the therapy and a return to symptoms as a result of abandoning the therapy, before they decide they had better stay with the "coincidence" that keeps them mentally healthy. At a recent convention, an orthomolecular psychiatrist told of a woman with schizophrenia who gladly believed her orthodox psychiatrist, who said that the idea was "bunk" that the disappearance of her symptoms came from cutting out chocolate. Only after two separate chocolate desserts were followed immediately by an attack of catatonia and an episode of hallucinations did she tell her orthomolecular psychiatrist, "You win."

There have even been cases when people with "hopeless" states of psychoses returned to normal through nutritional therapy—without even knowing they were *taking* any therapy. (The supplements were ground up and added every day to their food by family members.) And one might wonder how my little poodle (see the Introduction) twice recovered from diagnosed "hopeless" medical problems; she had an intense psychological belief in nutritional therapy? And do all the other diagnosed "hopelessly ill" dogs and cats who get well under the care of nutritional veterinarians recover because they think they will? Or are their bodies responding in a very real way to the therapy?

Another mistaken argument often leveled at orthomolecular therapy, when it results in a seemingly amazing recovery, is that the diagnosis was wrong in the first place: The patient couldn't really have had *that* disorder, because "everybody knows" that it cannot be helped nutritionally. Sometimes orthodox doctors are more comfortable in saying they grossly misdiagnosed a patient than in considering that nutritional treatment worked when traditional treatment didn't. At other times, it is assumed that the diagnosis was made incorrectly by the orthomolecular doctor—sometimes "just to rob the patient of his money"—although very often the grim diagnosis is made by orthodox doctors before the patient despairs enough to try nutritional therapy. You will see that this is true of many patients whose case histories appear in this book. (I have known of a few "quacks" using nutritional therapy for cancer who insisted that all tests—the original ones for diagnosis, and later tests checking progress of the disease—be conducted by strictly orthodox institutions. When these tests showed that the tumors shrank and eventually disappeared, did this help establish the validity of the nutritional therapy? No.)

In this chapter, I have tried to give a cogent overview of what orthomolecular psychiatry is, and what it is not. I have also attempted to explain some of the reasons your orthodox doctor may not "believe in" orthomolecular medicine even though he has never investigated it. But the goal I consider most important has been to give a new source of hope—and with it, a new course of action—for those of you suffering emotionally, and for those enduring pain because a loved one suffers emotionally. Please let this chapter's overview of information and hope serve as a background as you go on to read the chapter pertaining to the disorder you are fighting.

THE BULK OF illness today is not a medical problem,
but one of life-style and nutrition, something you
yourself must—and can—take charge of.

—DONALD O. RUDIN, M.D., *The Omega-3 Phenomenon*

MY DECADES OF work tell me that there are many
thousands of people who will become psychotic, with
life passing them by, if they continue to frequently eat
foods that give them symptoms. If they will only stop
eating these foods to which they are intolerant—or
even just space them out properly—these same people
can become socially and professionally efficient,
honored, and successful.

—WILLIAM H. PHILPOTT, M.D., orthomolecular
psychiatrist and clinical ecologist (personal
correspondence)

. . . SUCROSE, THE COMMON table sugar . . . is the
cause of a large number of physical diseases . . . and
a large number of depressions, anxiety states,
alcoholism and other addictions.

—Psychiatrist ABRAM HOFFER, M.D., PH.D.,
Orthomolecular Medicine for Physicians

Chapter 2

Prevention of Mental (and Physical)
Problems

Unlike their orthodox counterparts, orthomolecular physicians believe strongly that it is possible to prevent mental as well as physical problems, even if these problems run in your family—and even if you have already had episodes of the inherited disorder. Their view is that these disorders are often prevalent in families because of one or more of the following factors: an inherited predisposition to develop food and chemical intolerances; genetic deficiencies in absorbing certain nutrients; shared bad dietary habits. All these factors can be controlled or overcome with proper orthomolecular measures.

While this chapter offers much self-help, it's important for you to take responsibility for the prevention of illness through reasonable measures; and an evaluation by an orthomolecular doctor offers the best assurance that you will be doing all you can for prevention according to your *individual* biochemistry. This is especially true if there is a background of mental illness in your family, or if you have already had an episode—which indicates that you may have an inherited or acquired disturbed biochemistry, such as an abnormal need for certain nutrients. (See "Resources" at the end of the book for help in locating an orthomolecular physician in your area.)

Quotes on the facing page for this chapter indicate orthomolecu-

MAJOR STEPS YOU CAN TAKE TO PREVENT MENTAL AND
PHYSICAL PROBLEMS

Basic Diet	Eat a balance of amino acids, the raw materials for brain chemicals. Eliminate artificial additives. Eat unprocessed foods. Get sufficient fiber. Get sufficient essential fatty acids.
Water	Eliminate bacteria, viruses, and harmful heavy metals that can adversely affect the brain.
Food and Chemical Intolerances	Test yourself for unsuspected sensitivities that can lead to mental disorders, and eliminate substances your body doesn't tolerate.
Multivitamin/Mineral Supplement	Give your brain and mind optimal nutrition.
Exercise	Releases endorphins, the "feel-good" brain chemicals.

lar psychiatry's tenet that mental disease can be prevented. Carlton Fredericks, Ph.D., in *Eat Well, Get Well, Stay Well* (p. 51), reports a case history illustrating how a family's shared food intolerance can result in shared symptoms of psychosis. The schizophrenic mother's two children both showed "ominous" symptoms of the disorder, Dr. Fredericks says. He points out that a geneticist would find this to be due to "aberrant chromosomes," and a behavioral psychiatrist would believe it due to environmental influences. "A bioecological allergist came up with the real answer," Dr. Fredericks says, "when he insisted that wheat be withdrawn from the family diet; it was, and the symptoms swiftly disappeared."

Writing in the *Journal of Orthomolecular Medicine* (Vol. 1, No.

2, pp. 13–19) in 1986, Christopher M. Reading, B.Sc., Dip. Ag. Sc., stated, "Hereditary food allergies cause most of the major illnesses known to mankind because . . . they severely damage the digestive system and result in malabsorption of essential vitamins and minerals and amino acids." He stresses that "orthomolecular genetics is definitely of help with *prevention* of such serious illnesses as cancer, dementia, Down's syndrome, . . . heart attacks, thrombosis strokes, schizophrenia/psychoses, depressive illness, chronic lassitude/weakness, arthritic conditions and a host of other conditions so commonly running in most families."

Orthomolecular psychiatrist and clinical ecologist William H. Philpott, M.D., gives a case history of autistic twins who had been diagnosed at Albert Einstein School of Medicine in New York and were considered prime examples of the genetic factor in autism. Dr. Philpott found the twins to be remarkably alike in nutritional problems: Both were deficient in a number of nutrients, in virtually the same degree, and were intolerant to six foods. When these problems were treated, the twins' hyperactivity disappeared and they became able to communicate with themselves, their parents, and their teachers.

In contrast to the orthomolecular belief that mental illness can often be prevented even if it runs in families, let us investigate material sent out in 1987 by the Anxiety Disorders Resource Center in New York City, by Joaquim Puig-Antich, M.D., Professor of Psychiatry, Chief of Child and Adolescent Psychiatry, University of Pittsburgh School of Medicine: "At the present time, effective primary prevention of schizophrenia is limited to genetic counseling. . . . In other words, some individuals with a family history of schizophrenia may opt not to have children. . . . Children with a depressed parent have a 30 percent chance of developing major depression themselves. And there is no proven way to prevent depression in children born of these parents." He also states that depression in people over 45 may be related to biochemical changes connected with aging, but "at the present time, no way is known to prevent these cases."

The psychiatrist concludes: "[Some] believe it is now possible, albeit difficult, to eliminate or reduce certain factors that contribute to mental disorders—such as lead in paint or social and environmental stress. . . . Others believe there is little proof that primary prevention can reduce mental illness and that not enough is known to justify spending large amounts of money trying to reduce the incidence of emotional problems."

As I have stressed, there is a lot you can do to prevent mental illness, and these measures will be described in this chapter. They are summarized in the table on page 46.

In this chapter, to avoid repetition with other parts of the book, I give little in terms of studies or biochemical rationales to back up the information. If you are skeptical, or don't understand something—for instance, how can an intolerance to a few foods result in mental symptoms?—see Part V. Chapter 1, the chapter covering the disorder that concerns you, and the Index will also be helpful.

VERY IMPORTANT: This chapter is meant for those who are presently healthy mentally and physically, and want to remain so. If your doctor has prescribed a diet for any reason whatsoever, DO NOT USE THE INFORMATION IN THIS CHAPTER TO CHANGE THAT DIET. Maintain the diet until you consult an orthomolecular doctor, whose knowledge of orthodox medicine, combined with specialized knowledge of nutrition, should help you find the optimal diet to prevent mental problems *and* to control the condition you are presently being treated for.

Protecting Your Child

If you are planning on becoming pregnant, you have a good chance of preventing mental and physical problems in your baby. As Laraine C. Abbey, R.N., M.S., stated in the 1982 *Journal of Orthomolecular Psychiatry* (Vol. 11, No. 4, p. 252): "The value and importance of orthomolecular therapy lies in minimizing the effects of genetic or biochemical damage, but perhaps more important and far more exciting is the prevention of hereditary damage to offspring." As an example, she cites a 1977 study of mice born with a congenital defect of manganese transport into the brain that results in congenital ataxia (inability to coordinate movement). The ataxia could be prevented in the mice by giving them "much larger than normal dietary levels of manganese." She notes also that pregnant mice supplemented in the same way "gave birth to completely normal offspring, free of the genetic defect!!"

Chapter 9 contains specific suggestions on preventing retardation for your unborn child. Following suggestions in this present chapter will of course also be helpful.

YOUR BABY'S FIRST MONTHS

You can start your baby on the way to a healthy mental and physical life after birth by breast-feeding. Breast milk will pass on some of your immunities, allowing your baby to fight off diseases that her own undeveloped immune system could not. Also, breast milk is a good source of essential fatty acids. Psychiatrist Michael Lesser, M.D., said at a medical convention I attended, "It's been shown that if you don't get these essential fatty acids as an infant, when your brain is developing, you can develop permanent learning defects."

Marshall Mandell, M.D., a major pioneer of clinical ecology, states, "Even though many babies will be able to tolerate various foods at an early age, a baby's gastrointestinal tract and physiology were really designed for him to be fed milk exclusively for the first year or two of his life" *(Dr. Mandell's 5-Day Allergy Relief System,* p. 178). He points out that nature has designed ewe's milk for optimal nutrition for lambs, goat's milk for kids, cow's milk for calves —and a human mother's milk as the perfect food for a human infant. Thus, the milk you buy in stores is nature's perfect food for a baby cow, not for a baby human. (Veterinarians specializing in nutrition are also against milk for *their* patients unless it is mama dogs' or cats' milk. One objection: cow's milk contains growth hormones that serve to take a 40-pound calf and build it into a 700- to 1,000-pound cow or bull. "This is great for a cow," one veterinarian pointed out, "but not for a kitten." Obviously, these hormones are not good for our children, either.)

Dr. Mandell states that in a series of food tests on infants with sensitivities, "50% were found to be allergic to cow's milk and 48% were found to be allergic to corn. . . . Since most formulas with an evaporated milk base contain cow's milk and corn-derived products, you can see why many babies react to them." He also points out that formulas that do not contain cow's milk or corn products may contain other food products, such as soy, to which an infant may become sensitive.

If you are medically unable to breast-feed, consult a nutritional doctor, who will be able to guide you in feeding your infant the nutrients closest to natural mother's milk.

Overall, the best thing you can do if you are planning to become pregnant or are pregnant already is to consult an orthomolecular doctor, who will work out an individualized nutrition plan that will go far to ensure the physical and mental health of both you and your baby during your pregnancy and after the baby's birth.

Basic Diet

Please remember the admonition to consult a nutritional physician before changing a diet prescribed for an existing condition.

It is well known that the typical American diet is unhealthy. Traditional doctors warn that we eat too little fiber and too much fat. Doctors specializing in nutrition go further: They strongly criticize the fact that sugar and other additives such as dyes, bleaches, preservatives, and a host of others are added to our foods without any controlled studies. Donald O. Rudin, M.D., the author of *The Omega-3 Phenomenon: The Nutrition Breakthrough of the Eighties,* states, "We can realistically call the average everyday diet 'the Great

American Experimental Diet.'" We are the guinea pigs in this experiment.

Bear in mind the basic tenet of orthomolecular psychiatry, that anything that can harm us physically can harm us mentally, for the brain is an organ of the body, just like the lungs, heart, and liver. See the therapy chapters for details on how brain/mind disorders come basically from physical problems.

CUT DOWN ON ADDITIVES

Much has been written on the harmfulness of chemicals added to our foods. It has been stated that twenty to thirty thousand different *drugs* are given to animals, and that four thousand of these may be transferred to us by way of meat, milk, and eggs. According to nutritionist Gary Null, "A congressional subcommittee has found that 90 percent of all the drugs given to animals do not have the approval of the FDA" *(Natural Living Newsletter* 40, page 1).

Chemical additives include artificial preservatives, colorings, and flavorings, many of which have been implicated in certain cases of hyperactivity. If the product's label does not specify that these additives are "missing," assume they're in there. And don't be fooled into thinking that "no artificial preservatives" means that there are also no artificial colorings or flavors.

Until recently, purer foods were available only in health-food stores, but public awareness has made them available to some extent in supermarkets. Even in health-food stores, you must read labels; it might surprise you to see how many foods with artificial additives are sold in these stores. Still scarce in other than health-food stores are meats from animals not given antibiotics and hormones, and fruits and vegetables raised without chemical pesticides and in nondepleted soils.

EAT UNPROCESSED FOODS

When it was found that modern steel roller milling of wheat, corn, rice, and other grains contributed to the serious disorders pellagra and beriberi—and that certain forms of these illnesses could be cured by supplements of specific B vitamins—authorities said it was okay to continue this milling practice. They asked, though, that millers add back the specific protective B vitamins that the milling process robbed from the foods. Apparently little if any thought was given to the possibility that the same milling process could destroy other essential nutrients that were unknown at the time. Today it is known that the germ removed by the milling also contains other essential B vitamins, most of the essential minerals, and nearly all the essential fatty acids. Milling also destroys dietary fiber. Nutritional doctors suggest that other as-yet-undiscovered nutrients might also be being milled out.

For more information on balancing amino acids, see Chapter 3.

EAT SUFFICIENT FIBER

Fiber helps the colon to eliminate wastes from the body, a process easily understood as crucial to health. Michael Schachter, M.D., an orthomolecular psychiatrist in private practice in Suffern, New York, points out that in cultures whose diet contains ample fiber, food usually leaves the body in 24 to 48 hours. In cultures such as ours, where the diet is low in fiber and high in refined carbohydrates, it usually takes 48 to 96 hours—or longer—for food to leave the body.

High-fiber foods include whole (unprocessed) grains, raw fruits, and raw vegetables. Increasing these should help you automatically toward the goal of cutting down on meat and other high-fat foods, because fiber calories, which quickly give a "full" feeling, will be replacing fat calories.

Cooking destroys vitamins and minerals, another reason that the diet should be high in raw fruits and vegetables. Meat, however, should be cooked to destroy bacteria. We also should cook grains and beans, which are not digestible raw; and since grains grow naturally in hot climates, the heat of cooking does not tend to rob them of nutrients.

GET A BALANCE OF AMINO ACIDS

Amino acids are of great importance for mental health because they are the raw materials for our brain chemicals. Mental problems can develop when these chemicals are present in too low—or too high—amounts. For prevention, then, the goal should be to keep these brain chemicals balanced. Foods containing the full range of essential amino acids in relatively balanced amounts are fish, fowl, red meats, eggs, milk, cheese, sesame seeds, and pumpkin seeds. To keep fat intake down, try low-fat milk and cheese, and don't fry foods. Concentrate on fish and *skinned* fowl for entrees.

For more information on balancing amino acids, see chapter 3.

DON'T NEGLECT ESSENTIAL FATTY ACIDS

Essential fatty acids (EFAs) are called *essential* for two reasons: Our bodies cannot do without them, and they must be obtained from foods or supplements, because they cannot be produced independently in our bodies. As mentioned earlier, these nutrients are milled out of our grains. EFAs are also now stolen from us by hydrogenation of cooking oils. Writing of the Omega-3 family of fatty acids. Donald O. Rudin, M.D., states in *The Omega-3 Phenomenon* (p. 3): "[the Omega-3 family] started to disappear from our diet about 75 years ago and now it is almost gone. Only about 20 percent of the amount needed for human health and well-being remains."

Dr. Rudin estimates that "the average healthy person requires about 1 to 2 percent of his calories daily as Omega-3 EFA and 6 to 8 percent as Omega-6 EFA." He states that the best way to get these oils is from food. Fish (freshwater and saltwater) are good dietary sources of Omega-3 EFAs, as are northern cereal grains, walnuts, wheat germ, chestnuts, and northern beans. Dr. Rudin recommends linseed oil as the ideal Omega-3 oil (one teaspoon a day). (Linseed oil has an Omega-3 percentage of 60; salmon oil 30; walnut and wheat germ 10.)

Dr. Rudin states that oils having the highest percentages of the Omega-6 EFA are safflower (58–75), corn (40–57), and soybean (50).

In the years when orthodox medicine espoused a diet high in meat—which it no longer does—a friend argued vehemently that nutritional doctors' antimeat statements were quackery. She had read that Eskimos were relatively free of our high-incidence diseases, and, like many people, she believed that "they eat practically nothing *but* meat." Actually, their diet is extremely high in *fish*, and therefore high in essential fatty acids. It is true, though, that the fish-eating Eskimos—and, as Dr. Rudin points out, other societies eating traditional diets—have lower incidences of heart disease, arthritis, irritable bowel syndrome, schizophrenia, and "in fact, less of just about every modern malady."

Prostaglandins. Medical interest in prostaglandins has been growing only in the last 20 years. Prostaglandins are hormonelike substances that, as Dr. Rudin says, help regulate nearly every body function—including those of neural circuits in the brain. Prostaglandins are made in the body from EFAs, so if you follow the recommendations in the previous section, your prostaglandin requirements should be taken care of automatically.

WHEN TO EAT

Try to eat six to eight smaller meals a day rather than the traditional three larger ones. This practice will keep your digestive apparatus operating on an even keel rather than three daily bursts of sudden activity. Your blood-sugar level will not be subject to sudden rises and sharp dips. Doctors detail throughout this book the negative effect that low blood sugar can have on mental processes. You have heard that "breakfast is the most important meal of the day."

A biochemical reason for that statement is that blood sugar can dip quite low overnight, when the body is not taking in nutrients. If the body then does not get nutrients for several more hours, until lunch, the result can be foggy thinking, inability to concentrate, irritability—and even psychiatric symptoms. (Have you been accused of being an "emotional mess" some mornings before breakfast? Try keeping something to nibble by the bed, to give your blood sugar an upward tug as soon as you wake up.)

While eating numerous small meals may be a new idea for some, Abram Hoffer, M.D., Ph.D., points out in *Orthomolecular Medicine for Physicians* (p. 94) that that's exactly what our long-ago ancestors did. They would nibble on foods as they found them while foraging and hunting. "Our gatherer/hunter ancestors usually had some nutritious food in their stomach at all times."

Be aware, though, of a serious potential danger in eating frequent meals. Dr. Schachter, a psychiatrist and clinical ecologist, warns of the possibility of developing food intolerances if the same foods are eaten often. The more frequently you choose to eat, then, the more you should be sure to vary foods. For more on this subject, see Chapter 14.

These suggestions are intended to help prevent "psychological episodes" for those who experience an occasional "normal" dip in blood sugar from not eating for an extended time. If you suffer from the actual disorder of low (unstable) blood sugar, you can read more about the problem in Chapter 15.

ELIMINATE SMOKING, CAFFEINE, SUGAR, ALCOHOL,
AND OTHER ADDICTIVE SUBSTANCES

If you feel that giving up one or more addictive substances is beyond your power—maybe because you have tried many times and failed—read Chapter 5, on addiction. You will find ways orthomolecular medicine can help you become nondependent, without your suffering withdrawal symptoms.

The detrimental effects of these substances on mental health are discussed throughout the book: for instance, caffeine as an underlying factor in anxiety disorders, cigarettes as a factor in schizophrenia, and sugar as a problem in some cases of virtually every mental problem.

You may be ingesting some of these substances often without knowing it. For instance, caffeine occurs not only in coffee but also in teas and sodas—unless the label states that they are caffeine-free—and in some medicines. Sugar is added to many processed foods. White-flour products such as pasta, pancakes, waffles, and white bread break down in the body in much the same way table sugar does.

If the word "sugar" isn't on a label, that doesn't mean it isn't in the product. Hidden sugars on labels include molasses, corn sweetener, corn syrup, dextrose, maltose, lactose, sucrose, fructose. As Moke W. Williams, M.D., has pointed out, "Dried fruits, such as raisins, dates, and prunes, are concentrated sugar and stimulate an excessive insulin response." Dried fruits were once considered very healthy foods; and so were honey and brown sugar, now considered almost as harmful as white table sugar.

Water

It is important to drink enough water, and it is important to drink *pure* water. Often the only reason given for the importance of drinking sufficient water is that it carries wastes out of the body. But as Karl E. Humiston, M.D., pointed out in an interview, "The two hydrogen atoms and one oxygen atom that make up water are necessary for a number of chemical reactions in the body." Water helps regulate body temperature and is crucial for the absorption and transportation of nutrients. A person denied both food and water for the same length of time will die of dehydration, not starvation.

The rule of thumb often given is that we should drink six to eight glasses of water a day. A pregnant woman should drink perhaps ten. The elderly should be particularly careful to drink enough, because as we get older, the desire to drink diminishes. Lack of water causes salt levels to rise, which can result in excitability and confusion, mood changes sometimes thought to be "unavoidable" as we grow old, and sometimes interpreted as signs of Alzheimer's disease.

IS YOUR WATER POISONING YOU?

Drinking *pure* water is, unfortunately, a lot harder than just turning on your faucet and filling a clean glass. The water may contain disease-causing microorganisms, harmful heavy metals, cancer-causing chemicals—or all three. The most common microbial contaminants in U.S. waters, according to a 1991 report from the Environmental Associates of the Academy of Natural Sciences in Philadelphia, are bacteria, viruses, and parasitic protozoa—and the primary source of these microbes is human and animal feces *(Know Your Environment* newsletter, July 1991).

A September 1992 issue of the same newsletter stated, "In agricultural parts of the country, pesticides and excess nitrogen fertilizer seep into shallow groundwater wells. The excess nitrogen threatens more than 60,000 infants with an anemia-like disease, according to the U.S. EPA."

Chlorine was introduced in the early 1900s to disinfect water supplies. Since pollution keeps getting worse, authorities have been increasing chlorine amounts. High levels have been linked with genetic damage, bladder cancer, and gastrointestinal cancer.

When harmful substances don't get into our drinking glass by accident, negligence, inadequate or unmet safety standards, they can get in there by way of our pipes. Many plumbing pipes are made partially of the heavy metals cadmium, copper, or lead. Running water can carry bits of these metals out with it. The harm heavy metals can do to our mental processes is discussed in Chapters 4 and 17.

HOW TO GET PURER WATER

The simplest, least expensive step toward getting purer water is to let the faucet run for five or more minutes before using the water. This will allow time for particles of eroded heavy metals from pipes to be carried down the drain. However, this maneuver won't do anything for the estimated three hundred other contaminants that might be found in the water itself.

A more effective step would be to invest a relatively small sum for a water filter that you can put semipermanently over the faucet. Investigate before you buy; some filters screen out more contaminants than others. In his book *Nutrition and Mental Illness* (p. 93), Carl C. Pfeiffer, Ph.D., M.D., warns that "brass activated-carbon filters may actually add more copper to the drinking water."

Another solution is to buy spring or distilled water. There is debate among nutritional doctors about which is best. Some doctors vote for spring water, but only if you can research the spring source and make sure it is not contaminated. Just reading the label won't do; after all, no distributor is going to state on the label: "Bottled exclusively from contaminated sources."

The problem that some doctors find with distilled water is that it not only does not contain minerals but can leach minerals out of the body. Distilled-water advocates respond that the minerals leached out are inorganic and therefore undesirable. Distilled water, they argue, can also leach out other morbid wastes.

The latest "vote" I had on this issue came in a note from Dr. Schachter, who argued that the minerals leached out by distilled water may after all be organic and thus desirable, since "so-called inorganic minerals can chelate [bind] with some organic compounds, making them organic." He added, "I'd be concerned about mineral deficiencies if someone drank only distilled water unless whole foods and fresh vegetable juices were high in the diet."

Buy water in glass bottles. Dr. Mandell warns, "Plastic bottles may contaminate the water by gassing out petroleum byproducts."

Food and Chemical Intolerances

Although the diet outlined earlier contains only foods that are normally health-giving, any (or many) of them can be harmful if you are intolerant to them.

Rotating foods is a good way to prevent an addictive intolerance —thought by clinical ecologists to be a major form of food sensitivity. Simply put, that means don't eat eggs every day, bread every day, chicken every day, and so on. More accurately put, clinical ecologists recommend rotating foods on a four-day basis (see Chapter 14).

FINDING YOUR INTOLERANCES

Chapter 14 details tests used by clinical ecologists. If you are already ill, please get one of those tests.

Dr. Humiston, a clinical ecologist as well as an orthomolecular psychiatrist, points out that exposures to chemicals are often intermittent—a fact that may allow people to deduce sensitivities to them empirically. Do you get depressed when you clean house? Consider intolerance to chemicals in your cleaning materials. Do you have insomnia at home but sleep "like a baby" while traveling? Consider sensitivity to something in your bedroom. Tend to unprovoked tantrums while cooking or while stalled in a traffic jam? Consider intolerance to petroleum chemicals.

Orthomolecular doctors sometimes have accurate, inexpensive test kits that you can use to test your home and work environments for lead, pesticides, dust mites, airborne molds, and other common environmental allergens. They will probably also be able to recommend air filters that can effectively *trap* numerous airborne chemicals. Magazines sold in health food stores carry ads for some of these products.

As Dr. Humiston points out, empirical, immediate cause-and-effect observation will often not work for discovering *food* sensitivities. With an addictive food intolerance, "We feel *relieved* when we eat the food, we get the *symptom* much later."

Pulse Test. The Coca pulse test is completely safe and, according to the orthomolecular psychiatrists and clinical ecologists I consulted, "reasonably" to "very" accurate. (Since it was devised over fifty years ago, we might say it has passed the test of time.) The technique was discovered, in dramatic fashion, by Dr. Arthur Coca, whose wife had been hospitalized because of an attack of heart pain (angina pectoris). She had been incapacitated for three years, and two heart specialists predicted she now had little time left to live. Dr. Coca noted that an extremely high pulse rate (180 beats per minute) had been recorded on her hospital chart. Since each pulse beat matches a beat of the heart, this meant that her heart had been racing pell-mell. He questioned her, and found she had noticed that her pulse raced—sometimes—after meals. Dr. Coca suggested that she eat only one food at a time and have her pulse checked after every meal. Potatoes were found to be the culprits that shot her pulse up to 180 beats per minute; some other foods raised it also, although not as high.

Over twenty years later, the doctor's wife was not only alive and free from heart pain (as long as she avoided the foods that increased her pulse rate), but other chronic problems had disappeared: colitis, migraines, attacks of dizziness and fainting, and indigestion.

You might begin by testing substances you suspect are problems for you, and the foods that have been found to be the most common offenders. Dr. Mandell wrote in his 1988 book that in the previous twenty-five years he and his clinical ecology colleagues had found the following to be prominent in causing reactions: wheat, corn, coffee, cane sugar, milk, eggs, beef, potatoes, pork, oranges, carrots, yeast, apples, chicken, lettuce, soy products, peanuts, green beans, oats, and chocolate.

David Sheinkin, M.D., and Michael Schachter, M.D., report in their 1980 book *Food, Mind, & Mood* (pp. 105–111) that, according to Dr. Coca, you must stop smoking before and during testing, because tobacco, a major source of sensitivities, can distort results. Record your pulse rate for two or three days before testing substances. Time your pulse for a full minute. Take your pulse when you first wake up and before getting out of bed; immediately before each meal; three times after each meal, at half-hour intervals; and just before going to bed. Write down every food you eat at the meals. All this tells you your individual characteristic pulse rates. (If your lowest rate of the day doesn't occur when you wake up, suspect sensitivity to a substance in your bedroom or in the food you ate the night before.)

During the testing period, record your pulse when you wake up. Then eat a small amount of a different food every hour; count your pulse immediately before and thirty minutes after eating. If your pulse speeds up, wait until it is back to normal for at least an hour before testing another food. If you haven't eaten a food for several weeks, you may get a "false negative" result; test it again a few days later. Test also for sensitivities to your mouthwash, cleaning products, headache tablet, and—yes—vitamin pill. If you cook with gas, stand in front of the stove with the burners on and breathe normally for about five minutes. (A number of case histories in this book tell of people whose "neurosis" or "psychosis" disappeared after removing their gas stove.)

When testing for chemicals and inhalants, record your pulse immediately before, immediately after, and a half hour after the test. Note also if any symptoms develop during or shortly after the test.

Here is how to interpret your results:

- If a food makes your pulse increase six or more beats above your normal high rate, you are most likely intolerant to it.

- A rate over 84 beats per minute not accounted for by other known factors usually indicates sensitivity either to the material tested or to something in the environment.

- If your pulse differential (the difference between your daily high and low pulse rates) stays high no matter what you eat, you are intolerant either to almost all the tested foods or to a substance you are constantly inhaling. Does someone in your house smoke? Is there a garage attached to your home? Residual exhaust fumes can slip through a house all day from a car engine that runs only several minutes in the garage.

- To help differentiate between a reaction to a food and to something inhaled, consider that pulse speedups due to inhalants usually do not last so long and are not so severe as speedups from foods. Also, a rate increase of less than six beats a minute is usually due to something inhaled.

Although this testing may inconvenience you soundly for several days, it may free you from chronic "nothing-can-be-done-about-them" symptoms. Also, consider how much you may accomplish toward preventing future physical and mental problems.

Vitamin/Mineral Supplementation

Some orthodox doctors believe supplementation is a waste of money because a good balanced diet provides adequate vitamins and minerals. This view overlooks the fact that many Americans don't *eat* a good balanced diet. Also, voicing concerns of every orthomolecular doctor I know of, Dr. Humiston says, "I'm sure it was true about 50 years ago, that you could get sufficient nutrition from a good diet. But today our soil has been seriously depleted of minerals; processing of our foods has taken out more nutrients. As if that weren't bad enough," he says, "we're being exposed to more and more chemicals, and we need more and more vitamins and minerals to handle these exposures."

The table on page 63 lists a few signs of deficiencies. The list is by no means complete; nor are the signs definitive diagnostic indications, but they have the advantage of being signs you can look for yourself. If you notice any of them, point this out to a nutritional doctor. While it might seem common sense to make sure you get a very large amount of the nutrient that the sign seems to indicate you are deficient in, only a nutritionist professional can ascertain that the suspected deficiency exists and that you get a proper balance of synergistic nutrients.

NUTRITIONAL DEFICIENCIES:
SOME PHYSICAL SIGNS YOU CAN LOOK FOR YOURSELF

Vitamin A	Dry, rough elbows
	Dry nasal mucous membranes
	Dry eyes
	Dry, lusterless hair
	Night blindness
	Discomfort on exposure to bright light
	Poor vision, especially at night with low light levels
Vitamin B2	Magenta color to tongue
	Soreness and redness at corner of the mouth
	Scales and cracks on lips and in mouth
Vitamin B6	Tongue appears smooth, except for scattering of broad, mushroom-shaped papillae
	Edema of the tongue
	Difficulty in recalling dreams
Vitamin C	Gingivitis and loose teeth
	Easy bruising
	Poor wound healing
Zinc	White spots on fingernails
	Acne
	Body odor
	Impaired wound healing
Calcium	Thin or brittle nails

CHOOSING A VITAMIN/MINERAL SUPPLEMENT

Avoid any supplement that could itself cause you problems. Choose a supplement whose label states that it is free of yeast, sugar, wheat, milk, soy, corn, and artificial preservatives, colorings, and flavorings.

Psychiatrist Priscilla Slagle, M.D., recommends supplements in capsule, liquid, or powder form. Tablets, she states, can sometimes pass through the body without being digested at all. (You can tell if your body is not digesting tablets if they appear in the feces still whole, or nearly so.)

Take the supplement with a meal, so the nutrients in both can work together. Make sure the meal contains some fat, since certain nutrients need fat for absorption.

Don't worry if a supplement has several times the recommended daily allowance (RDA). Nutritional doctors state that the RDAs are too low for optimal health.

When you look at the labels for B vitamins, be aware that some vitamin distributors interpret the information that the B-vitamin complex should be balanced to mean that B-vitamins should be present in equal amounts. According to several nutritional organizations, a correctly *balanced* B-complex supplement contains the B vitamins in specific *unequal* amounts. Distrust a supplement that has equal amounts of B1, B2, B3, and B6.

Dr. Schachter warns against a supplement with high doses of zinc and little or no copper, which can result in copper deficiencies. "The ratio of zinc to copper should be 7:1, up to 14:1," with zinc being the higher amount.

Dr. Pfeiffer, while saying in his 1987 book (p. 94) that every adult "needs a dietary zinc supplement daily of about 15 mg," adds that *too much* zinc can produce a manganese deficiency. Dr. Schachter adds that one recent strong study indicates that an overload of zinc may sometimes contribute to symptoms of Alzheimer's disease.

You may have heard warnings about the danger of overdosing

with self-prescribed supplements. Nutritional doctors state that overdosage is unlikely. Much more likely, and potentially quite dangerous, is the possibility of *unbalancing*. As just mentioned, the balance between zinc and copper, and between zinc and manganese, must be considered. Likewise, taking one B-vitamin without the entire B-complex can create a deficiency of one or more of the B-vitamins not taken. Many other vitamins and minerals work in balances with each other, and this is one reason this book recommends that you take a balanced supplement, rather than trying to build your own program from pills of individual nutrients. This recommendation should also save you substantial money.

Dr. Pfeiffer suggests that adults need daily (along with other vitamins and minerals) 2 grams of vitamin C, 50 mg B6, 15 mgm of beta-carotene (or one carrot), and 400 IU of vitamin E. Requirements differ, of course, for the elderly, babies, children, teenagers, and pregnant women.

Please remember that the suggestions in this chapter are for basic preventive self-help, intended for those who are quite healthy mentally and physically. For *therapy*, a nutritional doctor might prescribe a given nutrient in a larger ratio to one of its "companions" than is normally okay—if you have a deficiency or dependency (greater than normal need) for the prescribed mineral.

Heavy Metals

Heavy-metal toxicity is often a strong factor in mental and physical symptoms. Problems associated with heavy-metal ingestion are discussed in detail in Chapters 4 and 17, which also contain information on common sources of these metals. Avoiding these metals as much as possible is an important aspect of preventive medicine. Try also to make your diet high in the foods that naturally help the body to excrete heavy metals. Cookware is often made with the heavy metals aluminum, lead, or copper. Traces of these metals can come off into food. The safest cookware is glass or stainless steel.

If you follow these suggestions, plus those earlier in this chapter for keeping water free of heavy metals, you will be going a long way to preventing these substances from creating illness in you and your family.

Exercise

Exercise is generally recommended as an aid to physical health. It also has an important positive effect on mental health. It is well-known that exercise can lift a healthy person's spirits from a "down mood." (It does this because of its effect on endorphins, brain chemicals that produce feelings of pleasure.) Orthomolecular psychiatrist Melvyn R. Werbach, M.D., goes further, pointing out in *Third Line Medicine* (p. 113) how exercise may help an already existing mental disorder. Dr. Werbach cites an experiment in which researchers at the University of Wisconsin studied a group of psychiatric patients diagnosed as depressed. Patients were randomly assigned to a program of either 1) running, or 2) one of two types of individual psychotherapy. After 10 weeks, six of the eight who ran instead of receiving psychotherapy "had recovered from their depressions, a result comparable to the best outcomes obtained by psychotherapy for patients in their clinic."

Summary

Several suggestions in this chapter—for instance, buying a water filter, replacing heavy-metal cookware, and being tested by an orthomolecular doctor—will cost some money. Ultimately, though, this information is geared toward saving you substantial money: in doctors' bills, drugs, perhaps even long-term institutionalization.

I would like to conclude with words of hope for those of you who may feel it is too late to prevent illness, because you have been eating a poor or inappropriate diet for many years. Dr. Pfeiffer says:

"Remember and be assured that one does not live this year with last year's body! All body tissues permeated by the circulation of blood and lymph can be and will be influenced by better nutrition. Bones, muscles, and even the mind are constantly being replaced and made more efficient as proper nutrients and energy are supplied" *(Nutrition and Mental Illness,* p. 105).

PART 2

Nutritional Solutions for Common Psychological Problems

ALL OUR EMOTIONS are influenced by our brain
chemistry. Nutrition is a safer way to change that
chemistry than drugs.

> —Psychiatrist PRISCILLA SLAGLE, associate clinical
> professor at the University of California, Los Angeles
> (private communication)

BRAIN SENSITIVITY [to certain foods or chemicals] . . .
affects almost all of us, whether we are sufferers
ourselves or are close to someone who is suffering. It
affects millions who have been attributing their feelings
of being rundown, irritable, or tired to "just one of
those things."

> —Psychiatrists DAVID SHEINKIN and MICHAEL
> SCHACHTER, *Food, Mind, and Mood*

I HAVE FOUND that in a surprising number of broken
marriages, spouses suffered from a blood-sugar
imbalance. Many of these husbands and wives showed
symptoms of irritability, violent temper, abnormal
sensitivity, and extreme fatigue. . . . Corrective
nutritional guidance dispelled these unpleasant
symptoms for many spouses—and, in the process, often
bolstered their crumbling marriages.

> —DR. CECILIA ROSENFELD, *New Medical Materia* 51:
> no. 8, 51–52, August 1962.

Chapter 3

Everyday Moods

The idea that we can directly affect our moods by what we choose to eat is generally thought to be a new concept. However, only the recent scientific proof and biochemical rationales backing up this idea are new. The ability to regulate moods through nutrition was known empirically thousands of years ago. One civilization instructed warriors to eat a high-meat diet to enhance aggression. The ethereal sensibilities of the spiritual caste were nurtured with a high-carbohydrate diet. Diets high in flour and sugar were frowned upon because they made people tired and lazy.

In very recent years, science has found those food/mood prescriptions to be quite effective. They were recommended in Sanskrit writings—thirty centuries ago.

Recent research shows that we "feel" the way we do because of chemicals that transmit messages in our brains, and these brain chemicals are produced by the foods we eat.

Specific brain chemicals regulate specific moods. A proper balance between the calming chemicals and the alertness chemicals should keep you emotionally on an even keel. A relatively small imbalance can make you "lazy" or tense, according to which chemicals are present in too little or too high amounts. A larger imbalance can result in depression or mania.

SOME FOOD-MOOD CONNECTIONS

Moods	Foods
Aggressive, alert, quick	High-protein foods
Calm, relaxed, "feeling good"	High-complex-carbohydrate foods
Tired, lazy, "down," "blue"	Refined flour and sugar
Jittery, tense, irritable, anxious, hyperactive, manic-like, confused, tired, "down"	Caffeine
Bouts of fury, violence, depression, hyperactivity, etc.	Foods and chemicals to which one is intolerant

Dr. Richard Wurtman, who has run groundbreaking studies on nutrition and the brain at the Massachusetts Institute of Technology, has an amusing history of stating he can sometimes hardly believe the results of his own research. Relevant to this chapter, he has been quoted as saying, "It remains peculiar to me that the brain should [be] subject to having its function and chemistry depend on whether you had lunch and what you ate. I would not have designed the brain that way myself."

When particular moods "take us over" often enough, they may become known to others—and to ourselves—as part of our basic personalities: "She's a very sad person"; "I was just born with this terrible temper"; "He's so nervous I can't stand to be around him." Looked at from one viewpoint, the information in this chapter may be taken to mean that our personalities are little more than "reactions to a bunch of chemicals resulting from what we eat." But drawn to its logical conclusion, this knowledge can be an extremely positive force. It means that we have to a considerable degree the ability to reshape our personalities along lines more pleasing to others—and to ourselves.

Although the food-mood connections described in this chapter are those generally recognized, one must keep the orthomolecular concept of bioindividuality in mind. As psychiatrist Priscilla Slagle, M.D., wrote me, some of her patients are "calmed by protein, agitated by carbohydrates"—opposite reactions than would be expected. An individual's food intolerances, for instance, may alter responses. The table on page 72 gives an idea of some common effects of different types of foods.

In treating neuroses and psychoses, traditional psychiatrists use drugs to regulate the chemicals that shape moods and emotions. Orthomolecular doctors prefer to balance brain chemicals by regulating the nutrients that *naturally* produce the chemicals. This can be a very complex task, and serious mental disorders often do not render themselves much more easily to self-help with nutrients than they do with drugs. But self-help for healthy people's everyday moods can be a different matter, and there are many types of self-help that you should know about.

You may feel that the idea that nutrients regulate moods overlooks the fact that emotions can be caused by very real circumstances. If one feels anxiety after losing a job, doesn't that emotion come directly from the lost job? Of course it is true that stress itself can influence emotions. But you might strengthen the anxiety by turning for solace to treats that upset the balance between calming and excitatory brain chemicals, or you may be too nervous to eat. Furthermore, one of the ways that stress influences emotions is by directly robbing our bodies of nutrients and thus upsetting the balance of brain chemicals that these nutrients synthesize. As Dr. Slagle said, speaking about depression, "Emotional influences and environment are important, as they cause stress which can change the brain chemistry. Nutrition can change that chemistry back to where it should be." She points out that one person may commit suicide as the result of an emotional stress that would hardly bother another, and this may sometimes be due simply to the fact that the first person may have had extremely poor nutrition at the time of stress.

Dietary Choices

The choices you make in the kitchen can go a long way toward giving you power over your everyday moods.

CAFFEINE

The common perception is that too much caffeine can cause insomnia and a little nervousness. Actually, excess caffeine can trigger irritability, hyperactivity, anxiety states, manic-like behavior, fatigue, mood fluctuations with depression, and even delirium.

In her book *The Way Up from Down*, Dr. Slagle notes that "psychiatrists are seeing the toxic effects of caffeine enough to have included a diagnosis of caffeine intoxication" in the diagnostic manual of psychiatry.

The psychiatrist recommends that daily intake of caffeine not exceed 150–200 mg. An eight-ounce cup of brewed coffee contains 120–240 mg, of instant coffee 104–160 mg, and of tea, 16–80 mg. A twelve-ounce soda with caffeine contains from 29 to 50 mg.

Excess caffeine biochemically affects moods by depleting some of the brain chemicals, Dr. Slagle says. It interferes with vitamin B1 absorption and has been implicated in depleting the body of several minerals that intimately affect moods.

Dr. Slagle always asks patients about caffeine use. She tells of a woman who complained of depression, withdrawal, insomnia, fatigue, weakness, muscle tension, irritability, and racing thoughts. An orthodox psychiatrist might well have started this woman on a drug for depression and recommended long-term, expensive psychotherapy. Dr. Slagle says, "I learned that this woman operated a gourmet coffee shop and drank about 15 cups of brewed coffee daily." The primary treatment this psychiatrist recommended was simply that the woman discontinue the coffee and add B-vitamin supplements. "All her symptoms cleared in several weeks," Dr. Slagle states.

SUGAR

Dr. Slagle says in her book that evidence is "overwhelming" that "sugar is one of the most powerful common foods capable of affecting our minds and our moods." Some orthomolecular doctors refer to sugar as "the anger food," and it is so often the cause of "unexplainable" sadness that many use the phrase "the sugar blues."

You may have heard that sugar gives a quick boost of energy; and it does do that for a short while, before dulling effects take over. Karl E. Humiston, M.D., points out that the initial "up" may be behind a child's restlessness and inattentiveness in class after lunch. In such a case, he says, "You should look for candy bars and soda [as causes] before looking for a deeply hidden psychological problem."

Dr. Slagle adds that sugar deprives our bodies of some of the vitamins and minerals needed to synthesize the brain chemicals that affect our moods—and that it may also contribute directly to deficiencies of amino acids, the raw materials for these brain chemicals.

In her book, Dr. Slagle tells of a 12-year-old girl who was brought to her because of severe depression and attacks of anger during which she verbally assaulted her parents and physically abused her sister. "As time passed," Dr. Slagle says, "it became clear that this behavior occurred whenever she ate sugar." For six years the girl has been free of the mood swings and attacks of anger except for occasional relapses—all precipitated by her returning to her sugar habit.

HIGH-CARBOHYDRATE MEALS

High-carbohydrate meals set in motion biochemical reactions that tend to reduce stress and anxiety and make one calm, relaxed, and feeling good. This mood state is appropriate for people involved in spiritual pursuits; the ancient civilization mentioned earlier prescribed a high-carbohydrate diet for such people.

However, meals too high in carbohydrates and too low in protein can cause postmeal drowsiness and lack of concentration. One writer noted that whereas most people know that a "three-martini lunch" dulls the mind all afternoon, few know that a "three-carbohydrate lunch" can have the same effect.

Thus, the rule of thumb is to eat a meal high in complex carbohydrates when it is important to be relaxed and emotionally calm afterward. Doctors stress *complex* carbohydrates because refined carbohydrates, such as sugar and white flour, are metabolized like sugar and lead to the sugar reactions mentioned earlier. When you feel edgy or nervous, try a meal basically of, say, brown rice and beans. And if you believe that nervousness is an integral part of your "personality" that you can do nothing about, consider revamping your overall diet to include more complex carbohydrates.

HIGH-PROTEIN MEALS

High-protein foods promote production of two brain chemicals, dopamine and norepinephrine, which, Dr. Slagle points out, elevate mood and increase motivation and physical and mental performance under stress. The high-meat diet prescribed thirty centuries ago for warriors promoted emotions and "personality traits" valuable to any soldier.

So if you need energy for the evening, for homework or going out, eat a high-protein dinner. But have a complex-carbohydrate snack before bedtime to calm you for sleep.

FATTY FOODS

Fat and cholesterol are digested slowly. During this slow digestion process they divert blood from the brain and thus reduce mental sharpness. As we have just seen, high-protein meals can do the opposite: increase energy and alertness. Yet high-protein meals often are also high in fat and cholesterol. To minimize fat in protein-rich foods and concentrate on the brain-food benefits of protein, choose fish, chicken, and turkey without their fatty skin, and low-fat meats and cheeses. Also, don't fry foods. Lowering fat intake is also, of course, important for overall health.

BALANCING THE DIET

We have discussed how you might choose at which times of day you are "in" which basic moods. However, an overall balance of neurotransmitters is necessary for overall mental health. Stuart Berger, M.D., wrote in the *New York Post* (January 16, 1992, p. 35), "Ideally, sufficient protein in the form of lean meat, fish, chicken, or turkey, and complex carbohydrates such as brown rice, whole grain breads, baked potatoes, and legumes should be eaten each day. This will help to balance the production of the neurotransmitters, which will help to regulate behavior."

Dr. Slagle in her book specifies further that "the full range of essential amino acids must be eaten at the same time, not part at one time of day and the rest at another time." She lists fish, fowl, red meats, eggs, milk, cheese, sesame seeds, and pumpkin seeds as foods that contain all the essential amino acids. When some amino acids are low in a consumed food, it must be combined with a protein food that makes up for the deficiency.

HOW OFTEN YOU EAT

Eating six to eight small meals a day, rather than three large ones, can keep your metabolism operating at a more steady pace. Blood-sugar level is kept more stable, resulting in a steady, even flow of glucose (the sugar that is the brain's major fuel) to the brain. This in turn should help keep moods and energy balanced. (If you follow this route, however, be sure to vary foods. See Chapter 14.)

Some of us may be "bears" before breakfast because many hours of not eating have left our brains low on fuel. Possibly this "personality trait" can be changed simply by keeping something by the bed to eat when you wake up, before you face anyone else—or yourself.

If you are prone to late-afternoon, midmorning, or midevening blues, a snack may lift your mood. But don't make the common mistake of eating sweets for a quick lift. Remember that sugar will soon leave you further down than you were to start with.

Food and Chemical Intolerances

Throughout this book, case histories from orthomolecular doctors indicate how not only *moods* can be dramatically changed when people are exposed to foods and chemicals to which they are intolerant, but also how diagnosed *psychoses* can "come and go" when such substances are given and withdrawn. Nutritional doctors believe that, according to the bioindividuality of the patient, just about any food or chemical may result in just about any mood change. (For a detailed explanation of how food and chemical intolerances affect the brain, see Chapter 14.)

Recently I kept my husband company while he was tested for intolerances. Those of us in the waiting room were enchanted for a couple of hours by a little-girl patient, maybe eight years old, whose most endearing personality trait was a radiant happiness. One woman asked, "Why are you here, sweetheart?" The girl answered, "Everybody's worried about me because I get these, like, really awful fits of depression, or whatever. And nobody knows why, though." When the girl was tested with an extract of wheat for possible intolerance, she came out of the doctor's office, sat down, and began to cry piteously. By this time we all loved her, so we offered her sympathy, hugs, handkerchiefs, and asked her why she was crying. "Because I'm so sad!" she wailed. "Oh, BOY, am I sad." Why was she so sad? "I don't KNOW. I just AM. Oh, BOY."

Shortly after, the doctor gave her a neutralizing dose of wheat. (See Chapter 14 for an explanation of neutralizing doses.) Soon she was back in her chair, in possession again of her radiant smile. She apologized to us all. "Wasn't that STUPID of me? BOY!"

Marshall Mandell, M.D., who pioneered the field of intolerances, tells in *Dr. Mandell's 5-day Allergy Relief System* of Wendy, age 38, who went to him for help with an irritable stomach and exhaustion. She also had a history of frightening, unpredictable states of intense fury that she admitted had no provocation. She had never sought help for these bouts of rage, apparently assuming that rage was just a part of her personality that she (and people around her) was stuck with. Dr. Mandell helped with her physical problems; and he also traced her "unexplained" bursts of rage to sensitivity to the large amounts of beef she ate.

Dr. Mandell says, "My clinical experience has taught me that unprovoked aggression, hyperirritability, and different types of antisocial behavior frequently are unrecognized sensitivity manifestations." He adds that cerebral sensitivities can destroy marriages. (Dr. Humiston once quipped in an interview, "It was very dramatic how my wife stopped behaving in an irritating way when I cut out wheat.")

Dr. Mandell adds that sensitivities can trigger child abuse. Denise R. came to him because she was horrified by her violence toward her children. She reported that she would hit her children for "nothing, nothing at all." Recently, incensed at her preschooler's "stupidity" when he forgot how to tie his shoelaces, she "slammed him and knocked him right across the room."

Dr. Mandell's tests uncovered many "severe allergies that would trigger sudden allergic rage and violence. . . . All she had to do was avoid the foods and chemicals that seriously affected her brain and she was fine."

One dramatic indication of the *array* of moods that sensitivities can produce is given by William H. Philpott, M.D., an orthomolecular psychiatrist and a pioneer in clinical ecology. "A woman in her mid-30's came to me who had been diagnosed as psychoneurotic. I tested her with pineapple, which made her irritable and blocked her thoughts; it also made her dizzy and gave her a big headache. Oranges made her violently angry, and her mind functioned so badly that she could hardly carry on a conversation. Rice gave her uncontrollable giggles, which turned into uncontrollable crying."

Vitamin and Mineral Deficiencies

This section covers only a partial discussion of how nutritional deficiencies can affect moods; complete exploration would require a full book in itself. (See also Chapter 18.)

Chapter 2 gives information on an overall good diet and supplementation plan. In spite of a good all-around diet, vitamin deficiencies may occur, and they could affect your moods. For example, you may take in enough nutrients, but your body may not be able to utilize them adequately. An orthomolecular physician has noninvasive tests to reveal precisely what nutrients you individually need. An understanding of the possible effects of a nutritional deficiency will at least help you work with a nutritional doctor.

B-VITAMIN COMPLEX

The B-vitamin family helps provide sustained energy because it unlocks nutrients in fats, carbohydrates, and proteins, making them available as energy. Members of the B complex help produce the brain's mood-controlling chemicals.

Vitamin B1. Deficiency in vitamin B1 can result in degeneration of the insulating sheath (myelin) that covers and protects nerve cells. Nerves then become extra sensitive, making one irritable, apathetic, and forgetful. In her book, Dr. Slagle mentions other symptoms of

B1 deficiency, including depression, confusion, and personality changes such as aggression, emotional instability, restlessness, and anxiety.

Vitamin B2 (Riboflavin). B2 deficiency causes increased sensitivity to tension because riboflavin is needed for the adrenal glands to produce antistress hormones. Dr. Slagle lists depression, insomnia, and mental sluggishness—as well as many physical signs—as symptoms of B2 deficiency.

Vitamin B3. According to a study published in the *Canadian Journal of Physiology and Pharmacology* in March 1983, B3 deficiency may result in depression, emotional instability, and loss of recent memory, even long before physical evidence of deficiency exists. Dr. Slagle lists additional symptoms including poor concentration, anxiety, and suspicion.

Vitamin B5 (Pantothenic Acid). Vitamin B5 supports the adrenal gland, whose job it is to handle physical and mental stress via hormone regulation. Nutritionist Adelle Davis in her 1972 book *Let's Get Well* (pp. 25, 26), cited studies from 1952 and 1953 showing that giving animals and humans large dosages of pantothenic acid allowed them to withstand more stress.

Davis also cited a 1954 study by physicians at the Iowa State University College of Medicine in which healthy volunteers were given a diet adequate except for pantothenic acid. "Urine analyses quickly showed a decrease in adrenal hormones, which fell progressively lower as the experiment continued," Davis writes. "The men became quarrelsome, hot-tempered, and were easily upset." They also developed low blood pressure, dizziness, muscle weakness, extreme fatigue, stomach distress, and continuous respiratory infections. Davis stated that all these symptoms are "typical of adrenal exhaustion." After 25 days the volunteers were so ill that the investigators, fearing that permanent damage might have been done, instigated a therapy of cortisone and a very high amount of pantothenic acid daily.

Vitamin B6. Vitamin B6, working with the mineral magnesium, is intimately involved in producing the brain chemicals dopamine, phenylethylamine, serotonin, and gamma-aminobutyric acid. Thus, B6 is intimately involved with the production of moods and emotions. Symptoms of deficiency include depression, insomnia, nervousness, premenstrual tension, and slow learning.

A 1990 study from Purdue University published in the June issue of the *American Journal of Clinical Nutrition* indicated that mothers' low intake of B6 during pregnancy or while nursing can even affect the moods of babies. Researcher Avanelle Kirskey stated that previous animal studies had "led us to believe that the lack of B6 caused improper development of the brain and the central nervous system. . . . It wasn't until we did the human studies on mothers who were marginally B6-deficient that we found behavior and mood also were negatively influenced." Note that these mothers were *marginally* deficient; and that marginal nutritional deficiencies are often overlooked by orthodox medicine, as covered in chapter 19.

Kirskey says that babies of B6-deficient mothers cried more often and for longer periods. The infants were measured by a standardized measure of infant development, which also revealed disorders in their vocalization progress, alertness, and general irritability.

The mother-to-baby relationship was also adversely affected. "Mothers deficient in the vitamin often would just ignore their baby's distress signals. . . . Many times they would simply let the infant's older brother or sister take care of the baby." The researcher adds: "We can't say how much of the mothers' lack of action . . . was due to the low B6 intake and how much was due to sheer frustration over the persistent crying."

Vitamin B12. Problems associated with deficiency of B12 include fatigue, depression, impaired memory, apathy, nervousness, mood swings, and confusion. Low intake has been linked with impaired production of the brain chemical acetylcholine. Nutritionist Gary Null cited the orthodox *British Medical Journal* as stating—back in March, 1966—that many "mental disturbances may be the first manifestation of B12 deficiency." By now, psychiatrist Melvyn Werbach writes me, this fact is "well proven but not usually known" by orthodox doctors.

Folic Acid. Folic acid helps produce the brain chemicals acetylcholine, norepinephrine, and serotonin. A deficiency of folic acid has been found to trigger irritability and forgetfulness, not surprising considering that serotonin is calming and acetylcholine is helpful for memory. Other mood problems of deficiency include depression, withdrawal, and mental lethargy.

Choline. Choline aids in building and maintaining steady nerves. As the raw material for the neurotransmitter acetylcholine, choline is considered helpful for memory. "Fish is brain food" is an old saying. Since fish is now known to be high in choline, this statement may be considered another example of the public's empirically knowing something long before medical science "discovers" and explains it. Judith Wurtman, Ph.D., part of the M.I.T. team that has done so much pioneering research on nutrition and the mind, reportedly had the following recommendation for her daughter when she was studying for her bar exam: eat tuna.

VITAMIN C

Vitamin C helps produce the brain chemicals dopamine, norepinephrine, and serotonin. It also plays a role in the formation of the hormone adrenaline, which (like dopamine and norepinephrine) regulates our fight-or-flight response to danger. Symptoms of vitamin C deficiency include fatigue, listlessness, confusion, and depression.

VITAMIN E

Vitamin E has been called "the energy vitamin." Since it supplies energy to the cells the way nature intended energy to be supplied, it can pick you up without letting you down hard, as sugar does.

CALCIUM

Calcium is best known for its importance for healthy bones (as in preventing osteoporosis). In addition, many nutritional experts call calcium "nature's tranquilizer." Without enough calcium, we can become irritable, quarrelsome, nervous, or depressed. Hormones (adrenaline and noradrenaline) in the adrenal cortex that are crucial to nervous-system health cannot be released without calcium.

CHROMIUM

If the body's chromium stores are inadequate, the insulin supply cannot be used properly, and the brain becomes deficient in glucose, its major fuel. Symptoms of chromium deficiency include anxiety, insomnia, fatigue, craving for alcohol, phobias, panic, jitters, and a tendency to suicide.

MAGNESIUM

When extremely nervous or irritable, you may have said you suffered from "ragged nerves." Magnesium deficiency can make nerves *literally* ragged: We need sufficient magnesium to synthesize the myelin sheaths that serve as protective insulating material for nerves.

Symptoms of deficiency include insomnia, confusion, hyperactivity, disorientation, anger, learning disability, and depression.

Amino Acids

As mentioned, some amino acids are raw materials for the brain chemicals crucial to our moods. Following are additional details; see also Chapter 18.

Essential amino acids can be obtained only through foods or supplements. Nonessential amino acids can be manufactured in the body—*if* dietary intake of essential amino acids and other synthesizing nutrients is sufficient.

TYROSINE

Tyrosine can alleviate stress by boosting production of norepinephrine, thyroid, and adrenaline in the body. It is used to treat depression.

PHENYLALANINE

Phenylalanine, Dr. Slagle points out, is the raw material for the brain chemicals norepinephrine, epinephrine, dopamine, and phenylethylamine. It also makes endorphins more available in our bodies. Endorphins help relieve pain and can produce a feeling of well-being or even euphoria. One theory holds that some addicts have a brain deficiency of endorphins.

TRYPTOPHAN

Tryptophan is the raw material for the neurotransmitter serotonin, whose function is to calm us. Thus, tryptophan can help relieve anxiety, tension, and insomnia.

HISTIDINE

Histidine is the parent molecule of the chemical histamine, which strengthens the brain's *relaxing* (alpha-wave) activity, making it easier to take problems in stride and helping to protect us from anxiety and stress. A deficiency of histidine may allow the brain's *excitatory* (beta-wave) activity to dominate, which can lead to anger and tension.

What You Can Do

As you review this chapter, note particularly which foods give high energy and which have a more calming effect; the negative effects of sugar and caffeine; the importance of frequent, small meals to give a steady supply of the brain's major fuel. See Chapter 2 for overall self-help suggestions for good mental and physical health, and for how you can test yourself for food and chemical intolerances.

If you think you may be deficient in an amino acid, vitamin, or mineral, ask an orthomolecular doctor to run the noninvasive, relatively inexpensive, tests that analyze for such deficiencies. Remember that nutrients work in cooperation with each other; thus, it may not be a deficiency of the amino acid precursor, but a deficiency of one of its vitamin helpers, that causes a deficiency of a neurotransmitter. Also, the brain's chemistry works in a delicate balance: Too much of one chemical can cause a shortage of another. For instance, large amounts of tyrosine can reduce the tryptophan available to the brain, resulting in too much of an excitatory brain chemical and too little of a calming one to balance it.

Dr. Slagle's book, *The Way Up from Down,* gives extensive detail on how to use amino acid supplementation to help yourself, and when you must consult a nutritional physician. If you feel you must supplement on your own, read that book thoroughly for the details that cannot be given here because this book has a much broader scope. Be especially aware of the dangers of self-prescribed supplementation. Robert Erdmann, Ph.D., warns in his book *The Amino Revolution* that anyone who is on a phenylalanine-restricted diet, has high blood pressure, is schizophrenic, or is taking antidepressants "should not embark upon a program of amino acid supplementation without a doctor's consent and monitoring." (It might be added that your orthodox doctor may not have the nutritional expertise to prescribe amino acids.) He also gives warnings for pregnant women and children.

IN MY EXPERIENCE, 60–70 percent of so-called "psychosomatic" reactions are basically undiagnosed food and chemical sensitivities. Many doctors have not been taught how to test for such sensitivities; thus, the causes of these reactions have remained a mystery to them.

—MARSHALL MANDELL, M.D., clinical ecologist

KERRI HAD SUFFERED since she was 10 months old from a large variety of symptoms. When she was brought to me, various doctors had diagnosed the little girl as having epilepsy, something wrong with her psyche, hyperactivity, cerebral palsy, Tourette's syndrome, and learning disability. After testing her for possible food intolerances, my diagnosis was: food intolerances. Soon after she was taken off the foods that had tested out to be problems for her, the "cerebral palsy," "epilepsy," and all her other "medical disorders" disappeared.

—WILLIAM H. PHILPOTT, M.D., orthomolecular psychiatrist and clinical ecologist

Chapter 4

*Psychosomatic Symptoms,
Hypochondria, and Other Mysterious
Problems*

Orthomolecular physicians believe you have a chance for recovery even if you have been told by one, two, or ten doctors:

- "The tests show there is nothing wrong with you; it's all in your head. See a psychiatrist."
- "You're making up your symptoms; they don't fit any known disease."
- "You're not responding to any known treatment. You'll just have to learn to live with your symptoms."

A basic concept behind orthomolecular psychiatry is that the body very often rules the mind; that is, that physical problems are very often responsible for mental problems. Thus, if you consult an orthomolecular doctor after being told your physical symptoms are psychological in origin—that is, that your mind has taken control of your body—the physician probably will suspect that you suffer from a *physical* problem that hasn't yet been diagnosed, and will run tests that many traditional doctors often do not.

Karl E. Humiston, M.D., says: "The issue is whether you're going to believe the standard lab tests, with all their limitations, or the patient." If standard tests have not revealed anything wrong, orthomolecular doctors will test for nutritional deficiencies and overloads, candidiasis, blood-sugar disorders, and several other physical disorders often not included in standard testing.

Complete orthomolecular evaluation will also include tests to discover if the patient's individual biochemistry is disordered by food or chemical intolerances. If you already have been tested by an orthodox allergist, see Chapter 14 for details of the clinical ecologist's quite different approach.

Pioneering clinical ecologist Marshall Mandell, M.D., gives a relevant case history in his book, *Dr. Mandell's 5-Day Allergy Relief System.* Bill had been regarded as having great potential to be an Olympic swimmer. Suddenly, at 18, he could barely find the energy to get out of bed, let alone swim competitively. Also, when he entered the kitchen, his personality changed; he felt dizzy, lightheaded, and usually developed a mild attack of bronchial asthma.

A medical center in the Southeast was certain he had hypoglycemia; a major national clinic stated he had a deep-rooted psychiatric problem involving his relationship with his mother. After all, Bill developed symptoms in the kitchen, and the "dominating" personality in the kitchen was his mother.

Testing by Dr. Mandell with synthetic petroleum-derived ethyl alcohol (ethanol) revealed that Bill had a severe chemical susceptibility, and that the "dominating personality" in the kitchen was the eight-burner gas stove. Also, the "attacks of hypoglycemia" he often had while driving came from a crack by the stick shift that allowed fumes from the engine into his car.

Dr. Mandell found that a food intolerance also was an important factor. In following the high-protein diet prescribed for his diagnosed hypoglycemia, Bill had been eating chicken between meals. When Dr. Mandell's technician tested Bill with an allergenic extract prepared from chicken—without Bill's knowing what he was being tested with—she reproduced all the "hypoglycemic" symptoms for which Bill was eating the chicken in the first place.

Orthomolecular doctors will recommend psychotherapy if they feel it is needed to aid their patient's recovery: for instance, if years of suffering have left behavior patterns of dependency or self-pity.

Emphasis is on behavioral, or experiential, techniques, rather than on thinking-talking therapies such as psychoanalysis.

Remember that orthomolecular psychiatrists tend to believe that psychotherapy, in whatever form, can help only minimally if the patient's body/mind is malfunctioning because of intolerances, heavy-metal toxicities, unmet nutritional needs, or other physical causes.

Symptoms

Virtually any symptoms whose cause is unknown to a traditional doctor can lead to a diagnosis of hypochondria, psychosomatic disorder, "just nerves," and the like. If you, or someone you know, suffers any symptoms whatsoever labeled as having "no organic (physical) cause," this chapter may be of considerable help.

Major Treatable Factors Behind "Nondiseases"

Following are some factors often overlooked in a traditional medical evaluation that may be responsible for unexplained symptoms.

DRUG SIDE EFFECTS

Orthomolecular doctors find that some patients diagnosed as hypochondriacs or as having psychosomatic illnesses because their symptoms are not easily categorized are actually suffering from the side effects of medications. The orthomolecular physician will try to substitute a more natural therapy to relieve or eliminate the *causes* of the symptoms the drugs were originally prescribed for. In this way, the person may be relieved of the original problem, as well as the new symptoms created by the drugs. Sometimes side effects come from the fact that the drug has knocked the body's nutritional balance "out of whack." Thus, nutritional therapy can often eliminate the side effects even when a patient cannot safely be taken entirely off the drug.

Carl C. Pfeiffer, Ph.D., M.D., in his book *Mental and Elemental Nutrients* reports the case of a man whose symptoms confounded many doctors for over half a decade. It is an example of how potentially deadly drug side effects can be. For this man, the coma he eventually slipped into was, ironically, probably the only thing that saved his life.

Dr. Pfeiffer printed a letter in which the patient wrote of his bizarre experiences. The man had a colostomy operation and was sent home with a medication, bismuth subgallate, to reduce fecal odor and to regulate elimination. He was told that in five weeks he would be able to return to work. But it was six months before he felt well enough to go back. After another year of trying to work while feeling "rotten," he resigned. At this point, he could have been diagnosed as a malingerer, or someone who hopes to avoid working while fraudulently collecting money from the government for a nonexistent disorder.

He tried another line of work requiring less mental ability, because he felt his mind deteriorating. But this manual work became increasingly difficult when he started to have new symptoms: twitching all over and peculiar breathing problems. Furthermore, he had become incontinent. His memory, ability to read and write, and eyesight were deteriorating.

After three years, he quit his new work because "I could not hold a tool steady. I lost my balance and was continually falling over . . . and sight all went out of order.

"I lost my ability to laugh or smile. I could not work the muscles of my face." Buttoning his shirt, too, was now an insurmountable neurological challenge.

Still, this man's agony had a way to go. "I became a great sufferer from insomnia [because] I twitched so much. . . . I was put on various drugs but none really helped. . . . In the day time, however, I could not keep awake. . . . My wife tried everything to keep me awake in the day time so I might sleep at night. . . . I dreaded each day time as I could not do anything up about the house or rest in bed at night. . . . I was very disoriented and mentally could not remember things and did strange things at times, and my wife had to watch me very carefully."

The man had progressed to having symptoms of Alzheimer's disease and other neurological disorders. He also obviously had been having to "learn to live with his symptoms" because drugs had not helped.

The diagnosis given at this point for all his incapacitating symptoms was "a nervous [condition] and possibly of psychological origin."

"Finally," the man goes on, "after five and a half years, I fell over in the garden in a coma." He was hospitalized for six weeks, "violent and strapped to my bed. The doctors told my wife that all the tests showed that my brain was dying rapidly." Then "One afternoon I opened my eyes suddenly and saw my wife at my bedside and spoke rationally with her. She hurried away and told the doctor, and he came and did various simple brain tests and then took my wife away and told her they would have to reassess my case."

Eventually he returned home and, over two years, "all my symptoms have disappeared slowly."

What "miracle" cured this man with the rapidly dying brain? None. While he was hospitalized, almost surely dying, no one bothered to give him the prescribed drug he'd been taking for over five years.

HEAVY-METAL TOXICITY

The medicine that seems to have been behind all the havoc for that unfortunate man was bismuth subgallate. Bismuth is a heavy metal. Other heavy metals include copper, mercury, cadmium, and lead. Each of these can cause numerous bizarre symptoms.

If you develop "peculiar" symptoms and work in an industrial environment where it is known that danger of heavy-metal exposure exists, chances are you will be tested for toxicity before you are told "it's all in your head." But if you develop strange symptoms from copper in your home's water pipes, or mercury in the fillings in your teeth, or lead from the air because you live near a highway, there is a good chance you won't be tested for heavy-metal toxicity before being told your symptoms have no organic cause "according to all the tests."

Melvyn R. Werbach, M.D., of the clinical faculty of the Department of Psychiatry at the UCLA School of Medicine, cites a relevant case history in his book *Third Line Medicine* (pp. 149–50). Soon after Jennifer and her husband moved into an old mansion, she developed irregular heartbeat, headaches, tiredness, and "a cloud over my head." Later, she developed recurrent diarrhea. Her doctor gave her various medications, but her symptoms worsened. Then she began to be plagued by sudden panic attacks.

She was hospitalized for intensive testing that included a stomach biopsy. The tests failed to find anything wrong, so her doctor decided that her problems must be psychological and sent her for marital counseling. Her condition continued to deteriorate.

One day she saw a blue-green ring developing in her puppy's water bowl. The little canine also had suffered diarrhea since entering the old mansion, but Jennifer had never suspected a connection: After all, how can an animal "catch" its owner's "mental" illness?

Jennifer had the state laboratory test the water from the old pipes after it had been sitting all night. It contained over seven times the amount of copper considered acceptable.

Armed with this result, Jennifer got a doctor to test her for high tissue levels of copper. Once therapy was started to remove the copper overload, she improved steadily from her "psychological" illness.

The table "Heavy-Metal Toxicity" on page 95 gives an overview of sources of heavy metals and of symptoms they can produce. Try to use this information as a self-help step to removing the sources as much as possible from your environment. Bear in mind that the table gives symptoms of rather severe heavy-metal poisoning. With low-level toxicity, symptoms may not be so dramatic, but may still impinge on the quality of your life.

HEAVY-METAL TOXICITY

Heavy Metal	Sources	Symptoms
Lead	Pollution from auto exhaust	Convulsions
	Cigarettes	Hyperactivity
	Coal burning	Anemia
	Water from lead plumbing systems	Colic
		Fatigue
	Lead-based paints	Mental retardation at birth
	Lead-containing pottery glazes	Psychotic behavior sometimes diagnosed as schizophrenia
	Organ meats (liver, sausage, liverwurst, kidney)	
	Foods from lead-soldered cans	
Mercury	Pesticides	Psychotic behavior sometimes diagnosed as schizophrenia
	Large fish	
	Cracked or broken batteries or thermometers	Birth defects
		Excess salivation
	Some laxatives	Loss of teeth
	Silver amalgam fillings in teeth	Gross tremor
		Kidney damage
	Coal burning	Blindness
	Over-the-counter preparations containing mercurous chloride (calomel)	Inability to speak
		Trouble walking
		Convulsions
	Industrial waste	Paralysis
		Coma
		Death

Cadmium	Water from pipes in soft-water areas	High blood pressure
		Cardiovascular disease
	Coal burning	Kidney damage
	Cigarette smoke	Emphysema
	Acid foods prepared and stored in cadmium-lined containers	Increased sensitivity to pain
		Vomiting
Copper	Lamb and calf liver	Hyperactivity
	Soybeans	Vomiting
	Water from copper plumbing	Toxemia of pregnancy
		Postpartum psychosis
	Hemodialysis	Depression
	Vitamin-mineral pills containing more copper than zinc	Dementia dialytica
		Anemia
		Schizophrenia (possibly)
	Tea bags	Hypertension
	Copper cooking utensils	Stuttering
		Autism (possibly)
		Premenstrual tension
		Insomnia
		Senility
		Death
Bismuth	Some rectal suppositories for pain	Sore tongue
		Metallic taste
	Some antidiarrhea medicines	Burning in the mouth
		Staggering
		Difficulty with memory
		Tremor
		Troubles in seeing and hearing
		Hallucinations

Dr. Werbach adds that bismuth subsalicylate (Pepto-Bismol) is a source of bismuth, "especially as it is recently being recommended in the treatment of ulcer (to eradicate *H. pylori* infection) along with antibiotics" (personal communication).

Dr. Pfeiffer offers another example of heavy-metal toxicity in his book (pp. 332–33). This might be called a "mass" case history. During World War II, suddenly some submarines aborted their combat missions and returned to Pearl Harbor. Many of the crew reported they were too sick to stand up, let alone fight a war, because of prolonged intense bouts of vomiting. Apparently this symptom was not accompanied by other signs of any known disease, so the Navy, suspecting some sort of mass plot to get out of war duty by feigning sickness, started a court-martial inquiry.

It was Dr. Pfeiffer's job to investigate such inquiries. Luckily for the sailors, even then Dr. Pfeiffer knew even then more about the effects of heavy metals than do many doctors today. Loath to accept "nondisease" as a valid diagnosis, he searched until he found the answer: All the involved submarines featured recently installed soda fountains with cadmium-plated syrup containers. The violently ill sailors had cadmium poisoning.

The sailors not affected by the mysterious symptom ate chocolate sundaes, whereas the ill sailors preferred raspberry. Raspberry is acidic, and acid substances will break cadmium into little pieces and carry the pieces around with them. Hence the raspberry sundaes had a secret topping of poisonous cadmium "sprinkles."

The phrase "the mad hatter" came into use in the 1930s because some industrial workers making hats became overexposed to mercury salts used for sizing, and suffered severe mental symptoms. There are many potential sources of mercury overloads, as the table shows, but I will focus here on one source because it is so common: If you have had a tooth filled with the usual silver amalgam, you have a constant source of mercury implanted in your body. The orthomolecular view is that the mercury in amalgam fillings can be released into the body.

This view is not unchallenged. In the May 5, 1991, New York *Daily News* it was stated that the American Dental Association, among other organizations, disagreed with consumer groups led by World Health Organization consultant and researcher Dr. Murray Vimy, that amalgams should no longer be used and that those already in place should be removed. The article quoted a dentist from a respected school of dentistry: "I have them [amalgam fillings] in my mouth, my wife and children have them, and that's about the best testimony a dentist can give."

Neither side seems to disagree with the definition of "mercury poisoning": "A serious condition caused by swallowing or breathing mercury or a mercury compound. A long-term form results from . . . repeated swallowings of very small amounts" *(Signet/Mosby Medical Encyclopedia)*. But an orthodox dentist might argue that mercury "stays put" in fillings; you cannot breathe or swallow it. Actually, though, evidence that mercury-containing fillings can be harmful has been accruing since 1926. In his book *Third Line Medicine* (page 147), Dr. Werbach cites relevant studies, including a few from orthodox journals, that seem to refute orthodox dentistry's claim that mercury isn't inhaled or swallowed from fillings.

Further evidence that mercury does not remain stable in fillings is offered by Abram Hoffer, M.D., Ph.D., in his 1989 book, *Orthomolecular Medicine for Physicians* (page 175): "Examination of fillings which have been drilled out show empty spaces where mercury once existed."

Because your traditional doctor may not check for mercury poisoning, I will give a list of classic symptoms that Dr. Werbach provides in his book (p. 148). (See the accompanying table also.) If you then suspect mercury may be behind your mysterious symptoms, or your diagnosed "psychosis," insist that your doctor test for mercury poisoning.

Early symptoms of chronic mercury poisoning may be tenderness or bleeding of the gums when you brush. There also may be excessive salivation and a metallic taste in your mouth.

The second group of symptoms are neuromuscular: shaking, jerky movements, deteriorating coordination, and increasing fatigue.

The last set of typical symptoms includes shyness, nervousness, and irritability. Later, the person withdraws from family and friends and becomes increasingly depressed. These symptoms may lead to, as Dr. Werbach calls it, "a prolonged course of inappropriate psychiatric treatment."

Other symptoms reportedly associated with amalgam fillings include headaches, facial pains, dizziness, nausea.

According to Dr. Werbach, "As soon as the last amalgam is removed, there is a rapid recovery." Whether or not you currently have symptoms of mercury poisoning, consider getting mercury amalgam fillings replaced with less toxic substances such as gold or porcelain, so that you do not risk future toxicity. Dr. Hoffer warns that "the process of drilling out mercury amalgams releases a lot of mercury particles and vapor. . . . Extra ascorbic acid should be taken before and after visiting the dentist," since this nutrient will bind with mercury and increase excretion.

FOOD AND CHEMICAL INTOLERANCES ("ALLERGIES")

Intolerances are another major factor behind mysterious symptoms, and are seldom investigated thoroughly by doctors not specializing in orthomolecular medicine. While certain foods and chemicals are especially likely to cause symptoms in susceptible people, it is possible to be intolerant to any food or chemical. The symptoms resulting from intolerance are also uniquely tied to the individual's biochemistry.

The following story was written in a letter by a patient of Dr. Humiston's, a clinical ecologist and orthomolecular psychiatrist, who was the doctor who finally made the diagnosis leading to successful treatment.

In 1979, Sylvia was playing a leading role on Broadway in an award-winning play. One night, while she was waiting in the wings for her cue, "the tiny twinge of pain came again." It gradually increased in intensity, "and a few months later my doctor referred me to a radiologist . . .

"X-rays showed that I had a gallstone or two . . . and they removed my gallbladder, and my appendix for good measure." Despite this major surgery, within months, the pain and duration of the attacks increased "considerably."

Sylvia was led into over two years more of "endless tests, innumerable x-rays, bafflement and tentative diagnoses from seven different medical men, all specialists in their own fields."

She was further hospitalized for cystoscopic examination of the urinary tract, which revealed nothing wrong; and for an operation to investigate for folding of the colon. "This operation also turned up nothing wrong."

Several months later, "I was rushed to another hospital during my most severe attack to that date of pain and vomiting." She remained hospitalized for a week "while, as it seemed to me, every test ever devised was performed on me." Yet no cause could be found for the mysterious attacks.

By now, Sylvia had had to give up her acting career.

After even more tests, and more doctors, "At last a new guess at a diagnosis: spastic colon." That doctor suggested she consult a gastroenterologist, which was the type of specializing doctor she had started with and had gone back to several times over the years.

Then a nutritionist M.D., hearing the latest diagnosis, told her that "spastic colon has been found in certain cases to be linked to food allergy."

After all her years of suffering and frustration, this particular medical suggestion "made me hit the ceiling. . . . Even if I believed in the existence of food allergies, *which I did not,* I certainly could not envision any allergy capable of causing the violent pain and endless vomiting I had been suffering for so long." (Dr. Humiston eventually treated her for food *intolerances,* which do not necessarily fit the strict technical definition of allergies.)

Finally she "grudgingly consented" to the new tests for intolerances, brooding that this "quack" testing would be a waste of money. (Chapter 14 shows the simplicity of these tests compared to the expense and invasiveness of many of her previous evaluations.) Ironically, she tested out to be rather *classically* food-sensitive; that is, she was reactive to the same foods that many persons are: beef, milk, sugar, chocolate, coffee, egg yolk, and wheat.

Thus, if Sylvia had read, with an open mind, even basic information on food intolerances at any time during her years of suffering, she herself could have quickly controlled her "mysterious" condition.

Sylvia's letter ends: "With the simple removal of the allergens from my diet, the attacks have completely disappeared." (Dr. Mandell pointed out, in a personal communication, that readers should not be misled into thinking that cutting out Sylvia's multiple "offenders" is as easy as cutting out table sugar, milk, bread, eggs, and chocolate bars. "People must read labels to see if food *mixtures* contain the substances that give them problems.")

Dr. Mandell's 5-Day Allergy Relief System tells of Vivian, the mother of three children, who became severely ill while doing household chores and while shopping downtown, suffering abdominal cramps, parched throat, burning and itching of the eyes, dizziness, and disorientation.

When extensive laboratory tests and examinations by many doctors found nothing organically wrong, it was concluded that Vivian had a "serious emotional problem." She was advised to take a long vacation away from her husband, children, and household chores— and then undergo in-depth psychoanalysis.

Dr. Mandell tested for sensitivities and found her to be highly susceptible to the gas in her kitchen stove; odors from various household cleansers and polishes; and gasoline combustion products in automobile emissions, which bothered her when she went downtown to shop. Instead of undergoing a lengthy, expensive ("and useless," Dr. Mandell added in reviewing this chapter) course of psychoanalysis, Vivian removed the gas stove, eliminated the odorous house-cleaning products she had been using, and avoided shopping during heavy-traffic times of the day. With these three steps, Dr. Mandell reports, "her nonexistent 'psychiatric disturbance with serious emotional problems' disappeared."

VITAMIN DEFICIENCIES

Vitamin deficiencies can be unrecognized culprits behind mysterious symptoms. Mainstream medicine tends to look only for *gross* vitamin deficiencies, such as those resulting in rickets, scurvy, or beriberi. Orthomolecular physicians test for and treat *marginal* deficiencies as well. They find that what might be adequate vitamin levels to ward off gross "textbook" *disease* often may not be enough to maintain a high level of *health*.

This belief is backed up by scientific studies. Dr. Werbach states in *Third Line Medicine* (pp. 141–142): "Marginal vitamin deficiencies . . . have been found to produce a variety of non-specific symptoms including fatigue, lack of appetite, depression, irritability, headaches, palpitations, difficulty concentrating, aches and pains." The people showed no generally accepted signs of vitamin deficiencies, so their symptoms would not be attributed by most doctors to such a lack. "When the vitamins lacking in their diet were replaced, the symptoms abated."

Nutritionist Adelle Davis's classic books detailed studies showing how vitamin deficiencies could cause vague symptoms, as well as diagnosed disorders. She drew on research by doctors in the 1930s to the 1960s.

What You Can Do

The surest way to get help is to enlist the aid of a good orthomolecular doctor. To find one near you, see "Resources." Following are steps the doctors working with me on this book say you can safely take on your own—as well as warnings against some steps you cannot safely take—while you wait for your appointment with an orthomolecular physician.

The first factor we mentioned as being one culprit behind mysterious symptoms was reactions to medications. However, you should *not* take yourself off any drugs your doctor has prescribed, even if you are convinced that they may be causing your symptoms. Instead, get as quickly as possible to an orthomolecular doctor; he or she will know when and how to *safely* wean you from those drugs and replace them with nutritional therapy.

You can safely take some steps on your own regarding heavy-metal toxicity. Cut down heavy-metal intake by following the suggestions in Chapter 2 for getting heavy metals out of your drinking water and by eliminating any sources of heavy metals in your environment (see table, page 95). Cook only with pots and pans made of stainless steel or glass.

Once you have cut down heavy-metal intake, optimally you should get rid of any overload remaining in your body. Robert C. Atkins, M.D., an orthomolecular doctor with many years' experience in removing heavy metals from the body, points out that you want to *chelate* them. A chelating agent combines with an undesirable metal and carries it out of the body.

Some drugs are effective chelating agents, but Dr. Atkins says, "We don't want to use them, except on the more severe or acute cases." He suggests trying a high-lentil diet "because many lentils will chelate. So will methionine and cystine, the sulfur-containing amino acids." He also recommends vitamin C and kyolic, a Japanese garlic.

Dr. Hoffer states that another good way to "eliminate these metals fast enough so they will not accumulate" is to eat a diet high in fiber, since heavy metals will bind to fiber in the feces and be passed out of the body.

Dr. Werbach suggests that readers wishing further information on chelation write the American College for Advancement in Medicine, P.O. Box 3427, Laguna Hills, California 92654.

If you suffer severe or acute heavy-metal toxicity, and therefore need chelation therapy using drugs, you should know that these drugs sometimes produce negative side effects because they remove desirable minerals as well as undesirable heavy metals from the body. Orthomolecular doctors know how to replace the desirable nutrients as necessary.

Further details on heavy-metal toxicity can be found in Chapter 17.

See Chapters 2 and 14 for more information on *intolerances*.

Marginal vitamin deficiencies can best be discovered and treated by orthomolecular doctors. On your own, you can safely take one potent multivitamin-mineral supplement daily; Chapter 2 contains information on how to choose a good one. If you already take a potent supplement, don't increase that dosage without talking to an orthomolecular doctor.

Another step you can take to increase vitamin and mineral levels in your body is to improve the quality of your diet, as described in Chapter 2.

However, being careful to take in adequate amounts of vitamins and minerals does not guarantee that your body is *using* adequate amounts. Sometimes people can take, say, 2 grams of a vitamin, but their body may be able to utilize only ½ gram (malabsorption syndrome). A nutritional doctor can tell you whether malabsorption is a factor in your case and what can be done to increase your ability to absorb nutrients.

Another nontoxic therapy someone who has mysterious symptoms might explore is biofeedback. Basically, this is a modern physical discipline that teaches how to control certain body functions previously considered beyond conscious control, such as blood pressure, muscle tension, heart beat, and brain waves. While you can ultimately use this discipline on your own, you must first be trained on biofeedback equipment. In his book, Dr. Werbach, who is the director of the Biofeedback Medical Clinic in Tarzana, California, tells of successfully diagnosing and treating a man suffering intense headaches and blackouts. Greg had seen specialists for over three years before coming to Dr. Werbach, including four other psychiatrists. Greg had collected the following diagnoses: migraine, sprained neck muscles, pinched nerve, malingerer, psychosomatic, post-traumatic psychoneurosis, and a passive-aggressive personality with repressed hostility. Biofeedback led to immediate improvement: Greg had only one fainting spell during the week after his first biofeedback session, and then had no spells for the next six weeks. Another fainting spell, however, led to Dr. Werbach's working with him for another three months, during which time he reported no problems except for an occasional headache.

ADDICTS TO ALCOHOL or drugs will frequently remark
that they've been through "detox" a dozen times. The
need for repeated treatment points to the failure to
rehabilitate the addict to the point where he no longer
has the craving. . . . Yet, given an escape from the
cultural lag in which nutrition has long been captive,
there is a great deal more that can be done for addicts.
That "great deal more" consists not only of freeing
them from the habit.

—CARLTON FREDERICKS, PH.D., *Nutrition Guide for the
Prevention and Cure of Common Ailments and
Diseases*

THE COMPULSIVE DRINKER *must* find out if the
underlying cause of his addiction is actually an
addiction to any of the food substances from which
alcoholic beverages are derived. Because if it is, and he
gives up the alcoholic beverages that contain the foods
to which he is addicted, but does not eliminate those
foods from his diet . . . he will always live in risk of
sliding back into alcoholism.

—MARSHALL MANDELL, M.D., clinical ecologist (personal
communication)

Chapter 5

Addiction to Alcohol, Drugs, Cigarettes, Caffeine, and Sugar

Orthodox and orthomolecular approaches to addiction differ markedly both in philosophy and in treatment. These differences lead directly to the higher recovery rate claimed by orthomolecular doctors. Statistics reported for orthodox therapy include a failure rate of 75 percent for alcoholism and a relapse rate of close to 85 percent for crack addiction. In contrast, doctors using *individual* alternative therapies report a 71–82 percent success rate with alcoholism and 50–60 percent success rate with crack addiction. Doctors using *comprehensive* orthomolecular therapy have reported an overall recovery rate of 85 percent as a "rule of thumb" from addiction to all substances.

Since orthomolecular doctors believe that addictions are *biochemically* based, the addict is not stigmatized as "bad" or "weak-willed." Treatment is aimed at correcting the faulty biochemistry, and this can be done directly by nutritional means, since every chemical reaction in our bodies is dependent on nutrients.

Since successful orthomolecular treatment gets at the *physical root* of addiction, the person no longer craves the addictive substance and thus does not have to use constant *psychological willpower* to stay away from it.

Readers will not find headings about "alcoholism," "heroin addiction," "cocaine addiction," etc. While orthodox doctors tend to treat different addictions in different ways, believing that a major part of the problem is in the substance being abused, orthomolecular doctors believe that the underlying problem is in the individual biochemistry of the addict. Thus, the therapy section's headings reflect the philosophy that vitamin B3, low blood sugar, food intolerances, etc., are the factors to be considered, not the substances to which the person is addicted.

Who Should Seek Help?

Years ago, I was associate editor of *Alcoholism Update,* which disseminated the work of orthodox doctors specializing in treating alcoholism to other orthodox doctors. There seemed no clear consensus as to how to arrive at a diagnosis of alcoholism: How many "yes" answers to a list of symptoms constituted a positive diagnosis? Which symptoms bore more weight? Finally one specialist said, "I don't know what all the arguing is about. If the person's use of any amount of any substance interferes in any way with his optimal happiness and functioning, then he needs help—whether you call it addiction or not." I believe orthomolecular doctors are comfortable with this loose definition, which conforms with their beliefs that people should not put any toxic substances into their body and that they should be helped to optimal health regardless of diagnostic labels.

Janice Keller Phelps, M.D., gives an illustrative anecdote about caffeine addiction in her 1986 book *The Hidden Addiction—and How to Get Free.* She was one of several physicians asked to speak to fifty doctors at a morning meeting to discuss addictive behavior. The organizers had eliminated the coffee urns prevalent at most doctors' conventions and had substituted noncaffeine items.

Dr. Phelps says, "The doctors were furious. Some of the most virulent reactions came from three of the speakers." These three "flatly refused to start the program until they had their morning cup of coffee. They couldn't possibly go on, they insisted. The sponsors had to order up an urn of coffee, and we all had to sit around and wait" until the doctors had their caffeine. "The scene we had just witnessed said more about addiction than I could have if I had talked all day." Dr. Phelps concludes: "That's the classical way that an addiction controls our lives: It always has to be satisfied first, before we can get on with what we want to do." (Dr. Phelps was herself an alcoholic for thirty years before trying orthomolecular therapy.)

Basic Differences Between Orthodox and Orthomolecular Approaches to Addiction

I have recently heard orthomolecular psychiatrists say, "Conquering addiction is at the dawn of a whole new era," and "Addiction is now one of the most treatable of all chronic diseases," and similar phrases. This optimism contrasts with the pessimistic view of orthodox medicine, which freely admits its low success rate. Sadly, some doctors using traditional techniques have gone back to the old belief that addiction is not a disease; it's a fault of character or willpower. Several orthomolecular psychiatrists state that this idea may come from the fact that orthodox therapies so often do not work: "If the treatment for the disease doesn't work, the disease must not be a disease."

Expressing the view of those orthodox doctors who have gone back to the belief that addiction is all "in the hands of" the addicted, Matthew Conolly, M.D., and Michael Orme, M.D., state in their 1988 book *The Patients' Desk Reference*, "Most experts believe that alcoholism is a social habit out of control. By contrast, many drinkers think of alcoholism as a disease—which conveniently releases them from responsibility." And in their section on drug abuse, they give what they call "a typical doctor's experience": "I can't trust drug takers at all. They're very difficult to help. I believe that if they want to stop they have to do it themselves."

Why orthodox doctors are so pessimistic about being able to help the addicted can be seen, for example, in the reported success rate for treating alcoholism: an estimated national rehabilitation success rate of 25 percent, as reported by the National Institute on Alcoholism and Alcohol Abuse (cited by Alexander Schauss, Ph.D., in *Diet, Crime and Delinquency*, p. 66). *CNS NewsTips* reported a follow-up study from the 1985 issue of the orthodox medical journal the *New England Journal of Medicine* (John E. Helzer, M.D., et al., June 27, pp. 1678–1682): after treatment, 66.5 percent of the study's subjects were still alcoholics and 12.2 percent were "heavy but nonproblem drinkers." (That last phrase begs the issue that heavy drinking is not a problem.) "Occasional drinkers" accounted for 4.6 percent of the 1,289 patients studied, and 1.6 percent were moderate drinkers. As was pointed out in *CNS NewsTips*, "Moderate drinking was defined very generously in the study—up to six drinks a day." If one were strict about what constitutes a drinking problem, one could say this study showed that only 4.6 percent of the drinkers had been rehabilitated, and 95.4 percent had not.

In contrast, a study run on alcoholics that shows what can be done using only a rather primitive nutritional therapy was published in 1983 in the *International Journal of Biosocial Research* 4(1): pp. 5–18). The patients had averaged 13 ounces of alcohol every day for 15 to 20 years. The control group received a standard hospital diet while the experimental group followed a more nutritional diet and were placed on a multivitamin supplement. They were asked to continue this supplement for six months after discharge.

After that time, both groups were reevaluated. Only 33–38 percent of those who had received the standard hospital diet were still sober whereas 81 percent of the experimental group were still sober.

Other studies have yielded similar statistical results.

Despite the strongly worded statements earlier from Drs. Connolly and Orme, many orthodox doctors are convinced of the genetic (biochemical) basis for some alcoholics—but for those without a family history of alcoholism, the addiction is thought to be due to psychology. The underlying factor in drug addiction is also often thought to be nonbiochemical. *The Patients' Desk Reference* passes off the causes of drug abuse as "either 'accidental' (a young person is introduced to drugs by a 'pusher') or an underlying psychological problem."

Proof that addiction is due to biochemistry rather than psychological problems comes in part from studies conducted with monkeys. These animals, hooked up intravenously, will inject themselves with cocaine repeatedly all day and all night, rejecting food, sex, and sleep—until they die. Have these animals become addicted because of an unresolved psychological conflict, because they fell in with the wrong crowd, or because they are morally weak? "They have become addicted," orthomolecular doctors say, "the same way people become addicted: biochemically." When first taken, cocaine releases to the brain a tremendous rush of dopamine, a natural brain chemical connected with feelings of pleasure. This abnormally high amount of dopamine results in an intense feeling of pleasure, a "high." But once the rush of dopamine is depleted, there is an abnormally *low* amount of dopamine left in the brain, and the person "crashes" and feels absolutely miserable. So he has a strong desire for more cocaine—not so much to recreate the initial feeling of pleasure, but to get out of the awful misery resulting from the secondary loss of dopamine from the brain. Dopamine is also believed to be involved with addiction to alcohol, morphine, heroin, and other narcotics. (Dopamine, as well as other brain chemicals, is formed from various nutrients; a proper balance of these nutrients can result in a proper balance of brain chemicals.)

Another difference between orthodox and orthomolecular approaches is that orthodox doctors sometimes try to treat an addiction to one drug by using another drug. Antabuse may be prescribed for alcoholism. This drug does not curb craving for alcohol, but it does make the person sick if he drinks after taking it. So an alcoholic who wants to drink on any given day may simply not take the Antabuse.

A standard treatment for heroin addiction is the drug metha-done. Actually, methadone is even more addictive than heroin, but its "high" at usual doses is mild and people can live normally on it —if you consider long-term dependence on a drug living normally.

Some Orthomolecular Therapies for Addiction

Orthomolecular doctors do not think in terms of a "magic bullet" for any disorder. They seek to determine where the individual's body chemistry is imbalanced, and to do whatever is necessary to get it back into healthy balance. Still, with addiction, as with most disorders, certain biochemical factors are more likely than others to play a role. Thus, certain nutritional approaches are most likely to help.

VITAMIN B3

In 1981, Dr. Schauss noted in *Diet, Crime and Delinquency* (p. 65) that Guest House, a treatment center for rehabilitating alcoholic priests in Michigan, was reporting an 82 percent recovery rate over several years of follow-up of their patients. Doctors there were using niacin (vitamin B3) and a diet that controls low blood sugar. This statistic is close to the 71–75 percent sobriety rate reported earlier, in 1974, by Dr. Russell F. Smith when daily dosages of niacin were given to 507 hard-core alcoholics.

Another Dr. Smith recovered after many years of seemingly hopeless multiple addictions with the help of Vitamin B3. Dr. Smith was a professor of pathology at a prestigious medical school, and had three offices. In 1953 he started drinking a fifth of whiskey a night. He became increasingly tired and hung over the next day, so he began to use stimulants. As Dr. Smith has been quoted, he was soon using "all kinds of amphetamines, uppers, diet pills, stimu-lants. You name it."

He went through Freudian analysis for three years, but it didn't help his addiction. He "went to 12 other doctors, and they didn't know what to do." He read advertisements in medical journals "saying how this or that new drug could cure me of my latest addiction, and how of course it was totally nonaddictive. But I just kept taking more.

"I saw some articles about LSD curing alcoholics." He overdosed on it—and was unconscious for two weeks."

Fourteen years after starting his first addiction, Dr. Smith "hit bottom," in his words. That year he lost his medical license, his home, and his wife, who took their children with her.

A year later, "A friend sent me a pamphlet on niacin—vitamin B3—and how it had been shown to help in rehabilitation from addiction." As stated earlier, B3 led to Dr. Smith's recovery. Eventually, Dr. Smith got an unrestricted license to practice medicine again. He remarried, became staff psychiatrist at a state hospital, and medical associations began referring addicted doctors to him for help. Dr. Smith uses for his patients a more complex nutritional therapy than B3 alone, as reported by Martin Zucker in the June 1980 issue of *Let's Live.*

In researching, I came across several booklets put out by Bill Wilson. This was the full name of the late "Bill W.," who started Alcoholics Anonymous (A.A.). These booklets were devoted to disseminating information on the use of vitamin B3. As his widow wrote in the 1971 booklet *The Vitamin B-3 Therapy: A Third Communication to A.A.'s Physicians:* "Bill's last years were mainly devoted to the spread of this information among alcoholics and other ill persons." Abram Hoffer, M.D., Ph.D., in *Orthomolecular Medicine for Physicians* (page 38) states that Bill W.'s interest stemmed from the fact that "he had observed its beneficial effect on himself and on 30 of his associates in AA."

Biochemical Rationale. A biochemical rationale for how B3 works in the body to relieve addiction is given by John P. Cleary, M.D., in a 1986 issue of the *Journal of Orthomolecular Medicine* (vol. 1, No. 3, pp. 149–57). Niacin (B3) makes the coenzymes NAD and NADP, which are essential for many enzyme reactions in the energy production systems of all cells. As he puts it simply, "Low cell energy levels cause disease." While there are other causes of low cell energy, "Several diseases can be cured at their early stages by raising NAD levels. These diseases include what [is] now diagnosed as alcoholism. . . ."

Dr. Cleary explains an interesting hypothesis called the predator response mechanism. "Man is a predator. . . . Built into the primitive part of the brain is a simple mechanism to regulate the behavior of the predator." This trigger is activated when levels of NAD become low; and "the predator seeks niacin at this point. One could say the need is a purely chemical one." Dr. Cleary writes that when man began to abandon predator habits, and to eat less meat (an abundant source of B3), "the early agriculturalists quickly found a means of subduing the unwanted predator response, with alcohol, which forms [hydroisoquinone], a substance which binds to opiate receptors in the brain."

Stating that the predator response mechanism includes restlessness and irritability, Dr. Cleary points out how visibly alcoholics or drug addicts exhibit this response when unable to obtain their addictive substances. Dr. Cleary also notes that "nicotine in tobacco is a vaso-constrictor that relieves the pangs of niacin deficiency."

Citing research from the 1970s and 1980s, Dr. Cleary states that ethanol, the active ingredient in alcohol, causes elevation of acetaldehyde, which condenses with dopamine in the brain to form a morphinelike substance (tetrahydropapaveroline). "I believe alcohol addiction is caused by morphinelike substances believed to be generated from acetaldehyde and dopamine in the brain. . . . Niacin will displace the condensation products of alcohol (acetaldehyde and dopamine) and can thus relieve the addiction by supplying the normal binding substance to the brain receptors, namely NAD."

Dr. Cleary points out that back in 1961 Paul O'Holleran published "to an unreceptive medical audience" his results of a study reporting that he was able to treat alcoholism and other addictions with NAD, which you will recall is a coenzyme which the body makes out of vitamin B3. "His study was on 100 patients addicted to heroin, pantopone, morphine, dihydromorphine, meperidine, codeine, cocaine, amphetamines, barbiturates, and tranquilizers," Dr. Cleary specifies.

Dr. Cleary believes that the results of Drs. Smith, O'Holleran, and others were ignored "due to the extreme prejudice that exists in the medical community toward the use of nutritional therapy for the cure of disease. Apparently no one could believe these favorable results were possible."

VITAMIN C

Orthomolecular doctors often consider vitamin C the most essential ingredient in treatment of addiction to all substances. Not only can it eliminate or modify many withdrawal symptoms, but it is also perhaps the best and safest detoxifier known, helping to clear the body of any residual addicting substance as rapidly as possible.

Positive results using vitamin C in treating addiction to alcohol, heroin, and methadone were reported at least as long ago as 1972.

AMINO ACIDS

In 1981, when cocaine was still officially classified as psychologically, but not physically, addictive, psychiatrist Jeffrey Rosecan studied the literature and found overlooked animal studies clearly indicating that cocaine was physically addictive. Cocaine use brought about changes in the brain chemicals dopamine, serotonin, and norepinephrine. Since these three chemicals are also involved in depression, he prescribed the antidepressant drug imipramine for all his chronic cocaine-using patients. He added two nutrients, the amino acids L-tryptophan and L-tyrosine. The first is the raw material for the production of serotonin; the second is the raw material for dopamine and norepinephrine. Dr. Rosecan presented his findings at the World Congress of Psychiatry in Vienna in July 1983: Of twelve patients treated for ten weeks, seven stopped using cocaine entirely; the other five cut their use by more than half. All reported that cocaine no longer produced euphoria, and that they had reduced craving. Although his findings were met with skepticism, he soon became director of the Cocaine Treatment and Research Service at Columbia-Presbyterian in New York. Reportedly, 80 percent of his patients stopped using cocaine.

Orthomolecular doctors report that the amino acid l-glutamine helps curb craving for alcohol, drugs, sugar, and caffeine. Writing in 1975, H. L. Newbold, M.D., in *Mega-Nutrients for Your Nerves* (p. 131), stated that "glutamine . . . constitutes, along with glucose, the bulk of nourishment used by the nervous system. . . . When glutamine is given to alcoholic rats and hamsters, they lose their desire for alcohol, or greatly diminish their intake." In humans, he says, "Some spectacular results have been documented." He mentions the case of an alcoholic given glutamine without his knowledge (it is tasteless). "Abruptly and for no apparent reason, the man gave up drinking, got a job, and in a follow-up two years later reported that he no longer had any desire to drink."

L-glutamine is the raw material for the brain chemical GABA (gamma-aminobutyric acid).

Supplements of another amino acid, phenylalanine, can increase the net available levels of three brain chemicals, dopamine, phenyethylamine, and endorphins. Increased levels of any of these tend to improve mood and relieve withdrawal symptoms.

GOOD OVERALL DIET

It is well known that an addict is often malnourished. General thinking is that malnourishment is a *result* of the addiction: An alcoholic may substitute drink for nutritious foods, and drugs rob the body of nutrients that are taken in. Nutritional doctors believe that malnourishment may also *create* addiction. In a study published in the 1972 *Journal of the American Dietetic Association* (Register et al., vol. 61, pp. 159–62), one group of rats was given a typical junk-food diet. The longer the rats ate this diet, the more they increased their alcohol consumption. Another (control) group of rats was also offered alcohol but was given a well-balanced diet. This group started off choosing a low amount of alcohol and never increased it. When given either caffeine or coffee, both groups chose to increase alcohol intake. When the junk-food diet plus coffee was supplemented with vitamins and minerals, there was a significant reduction in alcohol intake.

An interesting unexpected result came from a study apparently intended to discover the effects of a raw-food diet on hypertension and obesity. Raw food has no refined carbohydrates and is generally higher in vitamins, minerals, and enzymes than cooked food. In this study, published in the 1985 *Southern Medical Journal* (vol. 78, p. 841), 32 persons with hypertension ate an average of 62 percent of their calories as uncooked food for a mean of 6.7 months. During this time 80 percent of those who smoked or drank alcohol simply stopped of their own accord.

DIET FOR LOW BLOOD SUGAR

The typical American junk-food diet used in the above study with rats can cause low blood sugar, which in turn can result in addiction. Caffeine and tobacco can also contribute to low blood sugar. It has been estimated that 70–90 percent of alcoholics have low blood sugar. One study of two hundred alcoholics reported a 97 percent incidence of low blood sugar.

Carlton Fredericks, Ph.D., often pointed out that orthodox doctors know that low blood sugar is common in alcoholics, but they believe the disorder is a *result* of alcoholism, since blood sugar always drops when alcohol is substituted for food. Dr. Fredericks stressed that orthomolecular doctors realize that "in a sizable percentage of the cases, the low blood sugar *precedes* the alcoholism, and actually causes it." In his 1980 book, *Eat Well, Get Well, Stay Well* (p. 25), he said: "The distinction is important, for controlling a low blood sugar which has led to alcoholism will *cure* the alcoholism."

Dr. Fredericks told of a man who conquered alcoholism using a diet for low blood sugar. The man wrote Dr. Fredericks that he had heard him lecture and had received Dr. Fredericks's remarks on alcoholism "skeptically." He reported: "I have been an alcoholic since I was sixteen years old. I have had every treatment ever mentioned in the literature, including hypnosis, psychotherapy, shock treatment, Antabuse, AA, tranquilizers." He decided to try the diet for low blood sugar because he had a number of the *other* symptoms, in addition to alcoholism, that Dr. Fredericks had mentioned as precipitated by low blood sugar.

"It was two months later when I suddenly stopped drinking," the man wrote. "I took no vows. I made no promises. I simply stopped."

Dr. Fredericks met the man at another lecture three years later. "He was still on the wagon."

Low blood sugar is, in a seeming paradox, often caused by too high an intake of sugar (see Chapter 15); and doctors point out that people with low blood sugar who develop alcoholism pervert their sugar craving into a craving for alcohol. (The body uses alcohol in much the same way as it uses sugar.) Dr. Fredericks often decried the common practice of encouraging alcoholics to substitute a "sugar and coffee habit" for their "alcohol habit," stating that if someone was driven to alcohol addiction by low blood sugar, "the doughnuts and coffee will stimulate the process that made him an alcoholic."

THE SUGAR CONNECTION

We have mentioned that sugar may be intimately connected with addiction by contributing to low blood sugar. Here is a biochemical explanation of how sugar can cause a drug craving by affecting the brain chemicals that directly influence behavior. A breakfast with sugar and other refined carbohydrates—for instance, cereal containing sugar, white bread, sugar in a cup of coffee—is generally considered "okay." But do our bodies know about this assumption? The first biochemical event in the body is that insulin gets secreted; this in turn makes the amino acid tryptophan more available in the body. Tryptophan is the raw material for the brain chemical serotonin, so serotonin synthesis increases. This brain chemical is calming and soothing, and it is a good chemical to have in our brains in the *right* amount. But too much of this calming brain chemical robs us of energy and concentration and makes us feel "low," and our moods "crash." (One orthomolecular psychiatrist at a conference charted these reactions on a graph that ended with a drawing of a car crashing down a mountain.) This "crash" may make us so desperate to get a "lift" that we crave cocaine. Or maybe we will attempt to get our lift from caffeine, which can in turn make us jittery, tense, and irritable—and this may in turn make us crave alcohol to "unwind."

Dr. Hoffer has said that "withdrawal from sugar can lead to as many 'cold turkey' symptoms as withdrawal from heroin." Sugar can be such a powerful controller of behavior that it has been called "the mother of addictions." Studies with animals and humans show that the higher the amount of sweetener ingested, the more avid behavior becomes in its pursuit. One study attempted to wean rats from ethanol, alcohol's active ingredient. When they were offered 3 percent dextrose (a form of sugar) and 5 percent ethanol, the rats still preferred the alcohol. But when the concentration of dextrose was increased to 5 percent, the rats switched their preference to the sugar—and drank so much sugared water that they suffered convulsions. (Reported by E. Cheraskin, M.D., D.M.D., and W. M.

Ringsdorf, Jr., D.M.D., *Journal of Orthomolecular Psychiatry,* vol. 9, 1980, p. 162).

A comprehensive nutritional therapy is as helpful for sugar addiction as it is for addiction to other harmful substances. Particularly helpful may be the diet to correct low blood sugar: often the craving for a "fix" of sugar or other refined carbohydrates is the result of sinking blood-sugar levels.

INTOLERANCES

Another factor in some cases of alcoholism is intolerance ("allergy") and addiction to foods. Yes, it is possible to be addicted to certain foods, and they are often the foods to which one is intolerant. For details, see Chapter 14. Alcoholic beverages are often derived from foods that many persons are sensitive to. For instance, bourbon is distilled from the fermentation product of corn, barley (malt), rye, and yeast. Domestic vodka has corn, barley, rye, wheat, potato, and yeast.

Basically, the food-addicted alcoholic is driven to compulsive drinking to relieve the symptoms that are a result of withdrawal from the food substance in the alcoholic beverage.

Marshall Mandell, M.D., in 1979 published a case history (in *Dr. Mandell's 5-day Allergy Relief System,* pp. 120, 121) of a 17-year-old man whose family was concerned that he might be afflicted with "genetic alcoholism" because he was often drunk, and there were a number of alcoholics in the family.

The man told Dr. Mandell that he could not resist drinking beer. The physician gave him an extract of brewer's yeast, used in the manufacture of almost every brand of beer, to test for intolerance to the yeast. The first reaction was that the man could not stay awake.

Dr. Mandell writes: "A few minutes after he awoke, he telephoned his mother, but he was in such a confused mental state and his voice was so altered that [she] did not recognize his voice. . . . 'But I'm your son,' her son kept insisting"—only he could not remember his name. When the mother finally realized that the "crank caller" was indeed her son, she assumed he was drunk because of his confusion and the change in his voice. The yeast reaction was indistinguishable from his frequent "drunk" attacks from beer.

ACUPUNCTURE

Acupuncture is another alternative approach to treating addiction. Pioneering this therapy in America was a clinic founded by Michael Smith, M.D., at Lincoln Hospital in the Bronx, New York. In the November 20, 1986, New York Times (p. B1) it was reported that "thousands of drug and alcohol addicts have already been treated with acupuncture in the last dozen years" under Dr. Smith's program. "Now, the technique . . . has become the primary treatment . . . to cope with crack-induced psychiatric cases" at Lincoln, another hospital in the Bronx, and one in Brooklyn. Two years later, the program had expanded to other clinics nationwide. The article noted, "When the acupuncture treatment succeeds, feelings of agitation, and paranoia—and the craving for more crack—are reported gone."

The article quoted Dr. Bernard Bihari, former commissioner of the city's drug abuse services and then head of Kings County Hospital's addiction unit, as saying that on the basis of his findings, which included random urine tests of the acupuncture patients, "at least half of crack users will probably stay drug free." He added that the relapse rate for most addiction therapies was close to 85 percent.

In 1991 the New York Daily News (December 15, p. 7) reported that up to two hundred patients a day were now entering the Lincoln Hospital acupuncture clinic for treatment—and "one in five is sent to the clinic by probation or parole officers as a condition for staying out of jail. About half are pregnant women or crack mothers, whom child-welfare officials have ordered to get treatment so they can regain child custody or avoid foster care for their children."

Also by 1991, the Lincoln clinic was able to report that "at least 60% of the unscreened drug users referred by court-related agencies each year remain drug-free after two months." And dozens of clinics modeled after Lincoln's had sprung up around the world, as far away as Nepal and Saudi Arabia.

The 1991 article also stated that the director of the state Division of Substance Abuse Services had recently written in a paper, "Studies clearly demonstrate success, especially in those cases involving cocaine and alcohol addiction." Acupuncture has also been helpful in getting patients off methadone, the drug often given to heroin addicts.

Acupuncture does not require medication, has no known side effects, and carries another benefit of prime importance in this age of rising medical costs: high cost-efficiency. The state-certified acupuncturists at Kings County Hospital were physician's assistants, and each could treat forty patients a day. The treatment cost about $15 a visit and has been credited with relieving symptoms of drug dependence and withdrawal in as little as ten days.

In acupuncture treatment for alcoholism, thin, short needles carrying a mild electrical current are inserted into the cartilage ridge next to the outer rim of each ear. The relationship between needles stuck in the ear and lost desire for an addictive drug may seem, at first, tenuous; but studies show that the needles can trigger the release of endorphins in the brain. Endorphins, chemicals known to enhance moods, have been called "natural opiates."

One patient at the Lincoln Hospital clinic was Ron, thirty-four, who stated that he had been addicted to various drugs for seventeen years. "I had a $400-a-day crack habit, and when I walked into the clinic I was high. After the first time I was treated, I never smoked crack again."

Ron was by then working as a welder and said that he had been free from crack and other drugs for eight months as a result of his acupuncture treatments (New York *Daily News,* October 13, 1988, BXL).

RESTORING THE BODY TO CORRECT MAGNETIC ENERGY

Williams H. Philpott, M.D., a psychiatrist who has been a major pioneer in clinical ecology and low blood sugar, two fields basic to orthomolecular therapy, is now pioneering the use of magnets to restore the body to correct magnetic energy. He points out that this energy must be properly balanced before the biochemistry can be properly balanced. Dr. Philpott says: "A narcotic, food, or chemical addiction reactive state can lead to a biologically evoked positive magnetic energy overload. All addictions are due to this positive magnetic field overdrive. Replacing this overdrive with negative magnetic energy exposure can stop the addictive symptoms, as well as the addictive withdrawal symptoms." This therapy is discussed further in Chapter 8, "Schizophrenia."

What You Can Do

As with any disorder, the surest, safest way to get help is to consult an orthomolecular physician. See "Resources" to find a practitioner near you.

Orthomolecular doctors warn that you must work with a physician if you're trying to withdraw cold turkey from alcohol, sleeping pills, or tranquilizers, because withdrawal symptoms from these substances can be life-threatening.

The following self-help steps may be tried for drugs other than those mentioned above, and for sugar, caffeine, and nicotine. You can safely take a multivitamin-mineral pill (see Chapter 2). Indeed, you definitely should, since all addictions rob the body of nutrients. Although an orthomolecular doctor may use vitamin C intravenously, you may get some help with detoxification, and reduced craving and withdrawal symptoms, by taking the vitamin orally. The sodium ascorbate form, powdered, has been recommended: 4,000 mg (4 grams) every two to four hours while awake for a week. If diarrhea occurs, cut back to 2,000-mg dosages.

Large dosages of any vitamin, including niacin (vitamin B3), should always be chosen and monitored by a health professional highly knowledgeable in nutrition. And remember, even when taking small amounts of any of the B vitamins, they must be accompanied by the entire B-complex.

See Chapter 15 for self-help suggestions to combat low blood sugar.

Daily exercise is recommended, since exercise raises levels of endorphins, brain chemicals that help create a feeling of well-being. This can act as a strong antidote to the depression many recovering addicts experience.

While the above recommendations will be of more help than no nutritional therapy at all, you may need a comprehensive therapy to lick your addiction.

Many orthomolecular doctors strongly recommend the 12-step programs such as Alcoholics Anonymous, Al-Anon, and Narcotics Anonymous as additional support.

Karl E. Humiston, M.D., an orthomolecular psychiatrist, shares a self-help technique he developed that "people can use pretty much anytime they want to. It is a simple, easy technique—and yet I have for many years seen it give dramatic help." He adds, though, that this technique will be of minimal value to one whose nutrition and biochemistry are wrong, since "with bad chemistry, the first thing one loses is the finer level of the focus of attention," which is needed for this exercise.

The objective of the technique "is to help yourself *experience* the addictive substance without actually *taking* it." (One major problem recovering addicts face is that they are "constantly thinking, thinking of not taking the addictive substance.") According to Dr. Humiston, "You can use the exercise for any substance, including mainline drugs," simply by substituting a few specifics from the following example of cigarette smoking. "Close your eyes. Imagine—*as clearly and in as much detail as you can*—the preparation stage: getting the pack of cigarettes, the lighter; getting the cigarette out of the pack, lighting it. Imagine *feeling* the cigarette between your lips, the smoke going into your body. If you want to, you can finish 'smoking' the whole 'cigarette' in this way."

Dr. Humiston states that it may take several tries before this technique begins to work well, but that eventually, "Even many hard-core drug addicts have told me they felt just as satisfied with their imaginary drug as they ever did with the real one."

ANXIETY ATTACKS ARE one of the symptoms of low blood sugar. When nutritional measures are used, low blood sugar is one of the most easily treatable disorders.

—Psychiatrist KARL E. HUMISTON, M.D., personal communication.

[ANXIETY IS] A product of most forms of malnutrition. The two most common forms of malnutrition that cause anxiety relate to some of the B vitamins and to the excessive consumption of processed and refined foods.

—Psychiatrist ABRAM HOFFER, M.D., PH.D., *Orthomolecular Medicine for Physicians*

Chapter 6

Anxiety Disorders: Generalized Anxiety Disorder—Panic Disorder— Phobias—Obsessive-Compulsive Disorder

If you suffer from an intense fear (phobia) of heights, you may vividly remember the first time you were "struck" with a panic attack. Perhaps you were standing on a mountain, maybe only a hill, or perhaps only at the top of a flight of stairs. Suddenly you were trembling, or sweating, feeling dizzy, having trouble breathing. Ever since, you have gone to great lengths to avoid heights. You probably know your fear is irrational, but the attack was so frightening that you'll do anything to avoid its ever happening again. Orthomolecular doctors believe that the symptoms you suffered may have been the physical reactions of a sudden dip in blood sugar (brought on, perhaps, by something so "mundane" as having recently eaten a hefty dose of ice cream, or by having been exposed to a food or chemical to which you are intolerant).

Or perhaps you are "always anxious," almost constantly on guard against a feeling of impending doom. Orthomolecular doctors will consider the possibility of an imbalance between the calming and excitatory brain chemicals and will accordingly prescribe the nutrients that naturally regulate those chemicals. (Orthodox doctors use drugs—substances unnatural to the body—that regulate the same chemicals, often with toxic side effects.)

Anxiety Disorders—An Overview

In the 1980s, the National Institute of Mental Health conducted the largest study ever done of the incidence of mental disorders; researchers were surprised at the number of people found to suffer anxiety disorders. For instance, obsessive-compulsive disorder turned out to be 25 to 60 times more prevalent than previously thought. A recent statistic on anxiety disorders in general lists them as the second most common mental health problem (with alcohol/drug abuse the most common).

Discussions of anxiety disorders generally refer to "adults over 18." Are people under 18 being overlooked? Subhash C. Inamdar, M.D., professor of psychiatry at New York University School of Medicine and director of outpatient adolescent psychiatry at NYU/Bellevue Medical Center, has said he believes that adolescents are *more* apt to suffer anxiety than any other segment of the population, but they are the least likely to be diagnosed and treated. One reason is given by The Anxiety Disorders Resource Center: Unlike adults, adolescents may exhibit all sorts of "unacceptable" behavior dismissed as just another stage: "Among the more serious consequences of untreated anxiety in this age group may be drug and alcohol abuse, eating disorders and a continuum of violent behavior encompassing accidents and both suicides and homicides," a communication from the center states. While the overall U.S. death rate dropped 20 percent for all ages in the 1970s and 1980s it increased 11 percent for ages 15 to 24. The increase was due to a doubling of homicides and tripling of suicides. "Many doctors believe that underlying anxiety may be the common thread in such behavior."

As shown throughout this book, orthomolecular doctors believe that often the thread linking alcohol and drug abuse, violent behavior, eating disorders—and anxiety—is a nutritional one.

There is an overall shocking deficiency in diagnosing anxiety disorders. A publication of the Phobia Society of America refers to studies showing that it has taken an *average of eight years* for people with phobic and panic disorders to get a correct diagnosis and appropriate help. A massive study conducted in the 1980s revealed that only 23 percent of people with these disorders *were ever treated,* despite the fact that most of the affected people visited doctors frequently. The diagnostic focus tended to be on the physical symptoms, such as chest pains, rather than on the phobic or panic disorder that was the source of the symptoms.

The deficiency in diagnosis is particularly disheartening because reported success rates for anxiety disorders—using either orthodox or orthomolecular treatment—are particularly high. While statistics vary according to the source and the disorder, an 85 percent success rate is often given.

As mentioned throughout this book, orthomolecular doctors tend to be more concerned with what is unhealthy in each patient's biochemistry than in diagnosing the correct disorder "label." Thus, the diagnostic conundrum should not affect you if you work with an orthomolecular doctor. Whether your symptoms were actually due to a heart problem or an anxiety disorder, a competent nutritional physician would treat the underlying *biochemical* cause of the symptoms. A successful natural therapy will rid you of the symptoms, whether they originated from a heart problem or from anxiety.

One reason orthodox medicine worries so much about sorting out diagnoses is that it can be dangerous to give the wrong drug for the wrong disorder. (Orthodox medicine treats primary depression, primary anxiety, and anxiety mixed with depression with different drugs.)

Laraine C. Abbey, R.N., M.S., tells of a patient with severe depression, severe obsessive-compulsive disorder, and such a strong case of agoraphobia that sometimes she would not leave her chair. Since nutritional therapy was used, matching the right drug with the right diagnosis was not a problem. Abbey reports that in three months, 44 of the woman's 48 symptoms vanished. And her depression score on the Hoffer-Osmond psychological test, initially a high 13 out of a possible 18, had dropped to 1.

Concerning the role of psychotherapy, the Phobia Society released a statement in 1988 that "data gathered to date suggest that traditional psychotherapy used alone has met with little success in treating phobias and panic disorder. Nevertheless, psychotherapy can augment cognitive/behavioral therapy." Although orthomolecular doctors tend to agree that cognitive/behavioral therapy can be extremely helpful, they think of it mainly as a support treatment, and many report that often their patients do not need this therapy.

Types of Anxiety Disorders

If this information on symptoms leads you to suspect you have an anxiety disorder, insist that your doctor consider this diagnosis.

GENERALIZED ANXIETY DISORDER

People with generalized anxiety disorder suffer a generalized *persistent* feeling of anxiety as opposed to the acute attacks of fear characteristic of phobias and panic disorder. They are plagued with apprehension that something bad is going to happen, and are constantly "on sentry duty" to prevent it. They feel jittery, tense, and irritable; complain of sweating, fast heartbeat, cold and clammy hands, tingling sensations, upset stomach, flushing. Insomnia and difficulty in concentrating are common.

PANIC DISORDER

Those who suffer panic disorder are afflicted with episodes of thoughts, emotions, and physical sensations that typically accompany confrontation with immediate, extreme danger. However, these attacks occur when there is no danger.

During panic attacks, people often believe they are dying, losing control, going crazy. Breathing is labored, rapid, shallow; the heart races; there may be trembling, chest pain, sweating, dizziness, nausea, weakness or tingling in the limbs, feelings of faintness or disorientation. Arthur Rifkin, M.D., professor of psychiatry at Mount Sinai Medical Center, New York, offers a vivid image of a panic attack: "tidal waves of inexplicable fear." The experience is so intense that many who have one or more panic attacks avoid settings associated with the attacks. Thus, phobias are born.

PHOBIAS

Phobias have been described as "the fear of fear itself." Someone who had a panic attack while in a small, closed room, for instance, may associate the attack with the setting and develop claustrophobia, fear of closed or small spaces. The anticipation of terror can actually produce the physical sensation of terror the next time the person is in a small room, setting up a pattern of self-fulfilling prophecy.

Agoraphobia. Agoraphobia is a fear of being "trapped" in a public setting, away from a safe person or place. Sufferers may gradually confine themselves more and more to their safe place or person, and may eventually be unable to leave their house at all. "Some victims stay at home for decades on end," Dr. Rifkin points out.

Social Phobia. A social phobia is a consuming preoccupation that one will suffer humiliation in a social encounter. The afflicted person may be too terrified to speak before coworkers, answer questions in class, or even eat in restaurants. To make himself feel "loose and calm," he may take to drinking before and during social contacts. Doctors state that the significant role of social phobia in alcoholism is largely unrecognized.

Simple Phobias. Simple phobias are irrational fears of a *specific* type of object or situation, such as thunder, heights, or elevators.

Since literature for the public often confines itself to a small group of specific phobias, you may suffer from a phobia without recognizing it as such. You may think you have a "weird reaction" that no one has ever heard of, and so it cannot be treated. In fact, medical dictionaries for doctors give long lists of phobias, including the fear of sitting down, standing up, one's own voice, walking, one's own home, opening one's eyes, clothing, words, and food. Some people feel fear of objects on the left side, or right side, of the body; or of books, flutes, flowers, happiness. Some persons suffer from arachibutyrophobia: fear of peanut butter sticking to the roof of the mouth. While it might be easy to function without having to confront the latter phobia, consider how some of the others can limit, even destroy, lives. Or how about people who suffer from autophobia (fear of oneself); phosophobia (fear of being afraid)—or pantophobia, described, simply, as "fear of everything."

Medical dictionaries also list fear of the number 13 as a phobia. This phobia is so "respected" that many tall buildings have no 13th story; the floor above the 12th is numbered the 14th.

You may know that a fear of dogs is very common; but phobias are so widespread that dogs themselves suffer from them. A recent article told of the police dog, Lord, who had just been fired from his "job" because he suffered claustrophobia. Seems he performed his work just fine most of the time, "but if you got him in a small place he just couldn't function."

OBSESSIVE-COMPULSIVE DISORDER

Obsessive-compulsive disorder traps people in a nightmare world populated by thoughts about dirt, germs, lucky and unlucky numbers, symmetry and exactness, violence, and death *(obsessions)*— and repetitive behaviors *(compulsions)* that the sufferer performs attempting to alleviate the anxiety caused by the obsessive thoughts.

It is estimated that four to seven million Americans suffer from this disorder. A third of the victims are children and adolescents. Some are as young as three.

Like people with phobias, those with obsessive-compulsive disorder are aware of the irrationality of their behavior and may feel foolish and ashamed. Psychiatrists point out that if they ask a patient during, say, his eighth consecutive handwashing, if he believes his hands still have dirt on them, he will say that he believes they are clean. "But *just in case they're not*—I could die from the germs."

I offer a personal case history from inside the mind of a sufferer. The obsessive-compulsiveness I once experienced is a rather "classical case." My father died when I was 11. It became clear to me that he might not have died if I had done certain things "right." Fast on the heels of that idea was the knowledge that my mother might die, and maybe me, too, if I continued not to do those things "right." My list of the right things to do got crushingly long after awhile: I had to brush my hair 156 times every night, had to check 86 times to make sure the front door was locked; potentially lethal germs were everywhere (I had just learned in school that you couldn't *see* germs), and hand-washing took over a significant portion of my time. I decided that my particular lucky number was four, so most actions had to be repeated four times. Later I became fearful that four was not a high enough number to ward off the ever-impending doom; four *times* four would be safer. So it came about that even if I stopped for a sip of water in the school hallway, I had to take 16 sips—although I never allowed myself to think of them as 16: I was drinking "four-times-four" sips. If something prevented me from my "right" number of sips, I lived in terror until I got home and saw that my mother had somehow managed to live through my transgression.

My mental problem could easily be traced to causes cited by classical psychiatry. (A psychiatrist who was a personal friend once told me that the age of 11 was the worst time for a girl to lose her father, because of the stage of the Electra complex at that age.) Orthomolecular psychiatrists agree that the death of a loved one can precipitate mental illness; but they will investigate the nutritional deficiencies that the stress may have caused. In my case, my obsessions and compulsions disappeared when my mother read an article in a popular magazine and cut out the huge amounts of sugar we had been consuming in an attempt to console ourselves. An orthodox psychiatrist might have said I had a "spontaneous" recovery, that my disorder went away all on its own. An orthomolecular psychiatrist would have considered the removal of sugar of possible significance. (See the later section on sugar.)

A recent article told of someone with an elaborate set of rituals to be observed if someone passes by on his right while he is at the dining room table. He himself must perform certain acts to negate this "wrong passage," such as putting all items on the table in a neat row to the left. The other person involved must go out into the hall, knock three times, reenter, and pass the table on the left. People taunt him for his "silly ideas." But I can empathize only too well with the enormity of his task, which, he says, is to "prevent the devil from getting at me—*just in case.*"

Biochemical Changes During an Anxiety Episode

It is tempting for people who do not suffer an anxiety disorder to believe that someone who does should be able to "talk herself out of it by just thinking right." After all, it's "just a psychological problem"; it's "all in the head." And many sufferers themselves feel ashamed that they cannot talk themselves out of it. Sometimes this shame makes them hide their problem even from their family, which can lead to more problems. One woman grew up resenting her mother because she didn't attend her school plays. Only when the girl was an adult did she learn that her mother had a phobia about being in large auditoriums with the lights out.

While no one would label a person in an elevator plummeting 20 stories neurotic for feeling fear, we say that someone who refuses a top-level job because getting to his office would require taking an elevator is "weird." In other words, we have difficulty empathizing with fear when the threat seems exaggerated or imaginary. Yet the underlying biological changes accompanying terror from both real and imagined dangers are similar, as pointed out by Steven M. Paul, M.D., chief of the Clinical Neuroscience Branch of the National Institute of Mental Health. Dr. Paul describes these changes, which we know as the fight-or-flight response: "In times of danger or stress the brain needs to tell the body that something alarming is happening or is about to happen. So it sends out 'excitatory' messages . . . prime receivers are the adrenal glands." Having got the "message" that the body is in danger, these glands produce and release the hormone adrenaline. "A sudden release of adrenaline and cortisol from the adrenal glands will produce many of the bodily symptoms associated with anxiety: increased heart rate, cardiac arrhythmia, rapid breathing, and elevated blood pressure." Eating sugar can also cause a sudden release of adrenaline, one reason it can trigger anxiety.

Drugs Used in the Treatment of Anxiety Disorders

Surveys show that orthodox doctors are concerned about the side effects of anti-anxiety drugs. Benzodiazepines (commonly called minor tranquilizers) are often used. Common side effects are drowsiness and lethargy during the first two weeks of taking the drugs. Concentration and memory may also be affected, making it unwise to perform important tasks or make "big" decisions—and perilous to drive, or to work with dangerous machinery. As Matthew Conolly, M.D., and Michael Orme, M.D., point out (*The Patients' Desk Reference*, pp. 84, 85), the most serious risk is "dependency bordering on true addiction. One in every three people who take tranquilizers continuously for more than six months will experience unpleasant withdrawal symptoms when the pills are stopped." Ironically, the doctors point out that these symptoms include anxiety and panic attacks. Withdrawal symptoms, the doctors say, can disappear within a month, but may persist for up to a year.

Some clinical symptoms of anxiety are thought to be connected with overactivity in a part of the brain that produces the brain chemical norepinephrine. Dr. Paul points out that benzodiazepine drugs help inhibit that overactivity by augmenting the effects of GABA, an inhibitory brain chemical (Paper of the Anxiety Disorders

Resource Center, New York City, July 1988). As mentioned in the therapy section, orthomolecular doctors use nutrients that regulate GABA.

Orthodox doctors may also use beta blockers, because they can suppress the rapid heartbeat, flushing, and other signs of anxiety that are so alarming to sufferers. Drs. Conolly and Orme point out, however, that these drugs "are of no value in anxiety except where patients are excessively concerned about tremor or rapid heart beat." Possible side effects include cold hands and feet, aching muscles, feelings of mental and physical slowness, and vivid dreams. Occasionally these drugs can cause asthma, a side effect particularly counterproductive for anxiety sufferers who have trouble breathing.

The antidepressant clomipramine is used for obsessive-compulsive disorder because it helps to regulate levels of the calming brain chemical serotonin. (Serotonin can be kept in balance by proper nutritional measures.) Clomipramine doesn't help everybody, however. One statistic indicated that the drug "improved" more than half the patients, but half of *those* relapsed when they stopped taking it. (While in some cases those on nutritional therapy also relapse when they go off the therapy, many do not. Also, nutritional therapy, being nontoxic, can be safely continued indefinitely, if need be. The same cannot be said for drugs that cause the patient toxic side effects.)

Recently, Prozac, which also helps regulate serotonin levels, has been used in the treatment of obsessive-compulsive disorder. Harold M. Silverman, Pharm.D., in his 1989 book, *The Pill Book,* lists over one hundred possible side effects of this drug, including convulsions, delusions, coma, paralysis, deafness, upper respiratory infections, breathing difficulty, vomiting, and changes in sex drive. Some of these occur rarely; but ironically one *common* side effect is anxiety.

Orthomolecular Treatment of Anxiety Disorders

Not surprisingly, orthomolecular doctors treating a patient for an anxiety disorder will include tests for imbalances of the nutrients known to be involved in the chemical reactions that cause calming and "exciting" physical and emotional results.

MAGNESIUM, MANGANESE, AND CALCIUM

The minerals magnesium and manganese are powerful central nervous system depressants. Calcium helps regulate the balance between excitatory and inhibitory functions in the brain. In 1986, Derek Bryce-Smith, D.Sc., Ph.D., pointed out in *The International Journal of Biosocial Research* (vol. 8, No. 2, p. 136) that early symptoms of low blood calcium "are identical with those of anxiety neurosis . . ." He adds that when the availability of calcium in the blood is artificially lowered (by injection of sodium lactate), "serious symptoms of anxiety neurosis [arise] in persons prone to that condition." Dr. Bryce-Smith adds that these symptoms can be prevented by supplying extra calcium. He cites work published in 1967 in the leading orthodox journal *New England Journal of Medicine* (F. N. Pitts and J. M. McClure, 277:1329).

In the 1970s, Drs. E. Cheraskin and W. M. Ringsdorf, Jr., stated *(Psychodietetics,* pp. 87–89) that "Patients with [anxiety neurosis] may have exceptionally high levels of lactic acid (or lactate) in their blood. . . . Lactic acid binds the calcium, effectively imprisoning it," thus resulting in a calcium deficiency.

Published research linking high blood lactate levels with anxiety goes back at least to 1950. Writing in 1982, Abbey stated that this research appears "to have been undiscovered or disregarded by the many clinicians who accept the premise that anxiety reactions are . . . born of personality factors rather than . . . deriving from biochemical factors" *(Journal of Orthomolecular Psychiatry* 11, No. 4, pp. 243–259).

Sudden emotional stress or heavy physical exertion can raise lactate levels and thus deplete circulating calcium in otherwise healthy people. Drs. Cheraskin and Ringsdorf point out that you can help protect against "nervous attacks" at times of emotional or physical stress by making sure to keep your calcium reserves high.

B VITAMINS

It is thought that vitamins B1, B3, and B6 help decrease anxiety by increasing the body's ratio of pyruvate to lactate. Abram Hoffer, M.D., Ph.D., says that recently it has been shown that the natural vitamin B3 receptors in the brain also attract the benzodiazepine drugs commonly used to treat anxiety disorders. He says that although this does not prove that B3 and the drugs have similar action, it suggests that they do, and in fact both are sedative when measured in test animals (private communication). Dr. Hoffer, a psychiatrist who has worked extensively since the early 1950s with vitamin B3, adds that this nutrient increases the effectiveness of diazepine compounds and many other tranquilizers. If these drugs must be used, giving B3 will allow for a lower dosage.

In her article cited earlier, Abbey reports on a 1982 study she conducted. Of 12 patients with agoraphobia, seven were deficient in vitamin B1, six in B6, three in B3, three in B12, two in folic acid, and one in B2. These 12 people plus 11 others with agoraphobia were given broad-spectrum nutritional supplementation and additional megavitamin supplementation for deficiencies found by means of laboratory testing. After three months, 19 of the 23 showed vast improvement, with seven totally recovered; and 11 who had suffered panic attacks were completely free of them. None of the 23 fell into the "no improvement" category.

In addition to increasing the body's ratio of pyruvate to lactate, vitamin B6 can be helpful for curbing anxiety because it is necessary for the synthesis of the inhibitory brain chemical GABA (gamma-aminobutyric acid), which has been linked in the literature with anxiety reduction at least as far back as 1979. As mentioned earlier, it is thought that benzodiazepines work by enhancing the effects of the GABA neurotransmitter system.

REMOVING CAFFEINE

Noting that people who drink five to 10 cups of coffee daily may have symptoms of generalized anxiety disorder, Dr. Paul states that caffeine produces these symptoms by antagonizing the brain chemical adenosine, a potent central nervous system depressant.

An article in the October 1974 issue of the *American Journal of Psychiatry* that reviewed numerous past studies in the literature concluded that caffeine is so intimately connected with symptoms of anxiety that differentiating between anxiety and "caffeinism" was "a diagnostic dilemma."

Dr. Rifkin points out that a study by Yale University psychiatrists found that caffeine produced panic-like symptoms in 71 percent of panic-disorder patients.

Abbey, noting that most agoraphobics she has encountered have been heavy caffeine consumers, tells of one sufferer who had been unable to leave the house and who was completely cured by eliminating a habit of 10 cups of coffee a day.

CUTTING OUT SUGAR

Chapter 15 covers what happens in the body when sugar is eaten, including how sugar intake can result in the seeming paradox of low blood sugar. Symptoms of low blood sugar can be identical to those of an anxiety attack. Indeed, orthomolecular doctors list anxiety attacks as a *symptom* of low blood sugar. That is, they consider that low blood sugar is often the underlying disorder, and thus the disorder to be treated, with panic attacks or phobias merely manifestations of the blood-sugar problem. Psychiatrist Harvey M. Ross, M.D., has pointed out that an "anxiety attack" suffered while in an elevator, say, that results in a phobia about taking elevators may in reality have been an attack of low blood sugar. Thus, rather than blaming the elevator (or a traumatic incident from childhood), perhaps what should be blamed is a previously eaten candy bar.

One 1984 study backing up the above ideas found that lower values of blood sugar are indeed associated with anxiety for some people, and that glucose (sugar) infusion can produce panic attacks in susceptible individuals *(Psychopharmaceutical Bulletin,* vol. 20, No. 1, pp. 45–49).

Researchers have also shown that during the glucose-tolerance test, in which blood-sugar levels are measured after the person takes sugar, patients prone to anxiety had a high production of lactate in relation to pyruvate. We previously mentioned a high lactate/pyruvate ratio's connection with anxiety.

In an interview, orthomolecular psychiatrist Karl E. Humiston, M.D., told of a young man who came to him one morning at three A.M., complaining of an "asthma attack." "He was certainly having a lot of trouble breathing, but I didn't hear any wheezing in his chest. He didn't have a typical asthma history, either. Yet he said he'd been having these 'asthma attacks' since he was a child." Further questioning revealed that the attacks almost always came around three A.M. "I told him that this sounded more like low blood sugar than asthma." Not eating for a length of time can lower blood sugar. "I asked him what had helped these attacks in the past, and he said that his mother had always relieved them by giving him something to eat."

The man was a jail prisoner at the time, and Dr. Humiston was the night-shift psychiatrist. "I questioned him some more and found that he was being seen in the daytime by the mental health people because he suffered from severe anxiety." Another question gave a not surprising answer: "His anxiety was always relieved by eating— just as his 'asthma attacks,' had always been relieved."

Dr. Humiston's treatment plan for the "asthma" and "anxiety attacks": The man should stop eating sugar, and he should eat snacks between meals and before going to bed. As Dr. Humiston pointed out, this is not a full therapy for low blood sugar, but it is "the first line, and it almost always gives a dramatic improvement."

Several weeks later, Dr. Humiston happened to be in the mental health clinic in the daytime. Since the patient kept referring to Dr. Humiston as "my doctor," the prisoner's therapist told him he might be pleased and surprised to know that the prisoner's asthma and anxiety had both "just simply stopped." Dr. Humiston adds that while such information always pleases orthomolecular doctors, "it doesn't surprise them."

FOOD AND CHEMICAL INTOLERANCES

Clinical ecologists point out that food intolerances may have the same effect on blood sugar as sugar does. Thus, intolerances can produce the same symptoms, including panic attacks that lead to phobias.

Pioneering clinical ecologist Marshall Mandell, M.D., gives a relevant case history in his book *Dr. Mandell's 5-Day Allergy Relief System*, which also illustrates a fact shown by many histories in this book: that people who have "tried everything" with orthodox doctors without help often find a common solution to many seemingly unrelated medical and psychological problems through orthomolecular therapy. The 25-year-old woman had a history of anxiety, depression, and claustrophobia—as well as fatigue, painful menstruation and intercourse, chronic nasal symptoms, hives, and frequent episodes of laryngitis. "Several doctors had suggested that she might benefit from psychiatric treatment, but she rejected this advice," Dr. Mandell writes. "She insisted on a hysterectomy for the relief of pain. . . . By the time she came to my office, she was a terribly distraught young woman with a floundering marriage, abdominal pain that persisted despite [the] hysterectomy, frequent episodes of acute depression, and periods of claustrophobia that occurred when she was in the kitchen."

Testing revealed that the woman was intolerant to a number of household products, fumes from gas stoves, and many foods. (You may see here a logical explanation of why her claustrophobia seemed "mysteriously" limited to the kitchen.) She removed the offending household products, replaced her kitchen gas stove with an electric stove, and went on a diet "that eliminated all of the food to which she had reacted with her familiar symptoms on testing." Dr. Mandell writes that "in less than a month, all of her complaints cleared up. The low-abdominal pains that she and her doctors formerly thought were located in her uterus were actually due to allergic spasms of her lower bowel." As covered in Chapter 14, orthodox doctors today would still not be likely to test this woman for intolerances. Dr. Mandell treated her in 1967.

What You Can Do

There is much you can safely do on your own for anxiety disorders. These steps may also improve overall physical health. However, these recommendations may not address the root causes of *your* individual anxiety disorder; only a doctor can run the tests necessary for that. Professional medical help is strongly urged, since anxiety disorders can seriously impair, even endanger, life. Also, problems such as heart disease that have symptoms similar to anxiety should be tested for. Suggestions in this section are meant only as temporary aids before your appointment with a physician. To find an orthomolecular doctor near you, see the "Resources" section.

Certainly it would be to the betterment of your overall health to cut out alcohol, caffeine, and sugar. Chapter 5 offers help in overcoming addictions to these substances.

See Chapter 2 for self-help information on food and chemical intolerances. Chapter 14 may also help. See Chapter 15 for self-help on low blood sugar, and Chapters 3 and 18 for further information on regulating brain chemicals.

Make sure the possibility of anxiety disorders is considered. Remember the very high record of missed diagnoses. You shouldn't have to worry about this if working with a nutritional doctor, who will be testing your underlying biochemistry.

If you want to help someone else with an anxiety disorder, bear in mind that the sufferer experiences terror that is *physically* real. Threats, ridicule, or exposing the person to the thing that prompts his fear only make things worse. The latter is a particularly dangerous "solution" often tried by well-meaning people who do not understand phobias. The Phobia Society of America reports the case of a Navy recruit with a phobia of being pulled underwater. During a water training exercise, he was abruptly forced to confront his fear. In his desperate attempt to get out of the water, he drowned. Dr. Hoffer points out that in obsessive-compulsive disorder, the compulsive behavior alleviates anxiety, and if the behavior is prevented, the anxiety mounts.

Progress in overcoming an anxiety disorder may upset the equilibrium of a relationship. You might read up on what is called "codependency." Sometimes a spouse or friend, missing the importance he once had in a phobic person's life, will unwittingly hamper recovery. That hampering may be something as seemingly well-meaning and innocent as proposing that the person has been so "good" in sticking to his new diet that he deserves a sugar treat.

Evidence suggests that behavioral therapy for anxiety disorders is much more successful if the person is accompanied at the sessions by a loved one. This is another solid way you can help.

PART 3

Nutritional Help for More Severe Conditions

WE MUST ASK . . . what part the molecular environment of each mind plays in establishing the singularity of each individual's personality.

—LINUS PAULING, PH.D., Nobel Prize–winning chemist

AT THE PRESENT day . . . it is universally accepted that the brain is the organ through which mental phenomena are manifested, and therefore it is impossible to conceive of the existence of an insane mind in a healthy brain.

—J. BATTY TUKE, M.D., lecturer, School of Medicine, Edinburgh

PATIENTS WITH DEPRESSION, particularly when it is
suicidal, should be tested for low blood sugar. . . .
The symptoms disappear almost magically when
hypoglycemia is corrected.

—CARLTON FREDERICKS, PH.D., in *Carlton Fredericks'*
Nutrition Guide for the Prevention and Cure of
Common Ailments and Diseases, p. 45

MOST OF THE patients who come to the Brain Bio
Center with a diagnosis of manic-depressive illness and
have weekly swings in mood are merely pyroluric.
They are easily treated with adequate zinc and B6.

—CARL C. PFEIFFER, PH.D., M.D., in *Nutrition and*
Mental Illness, p. 67

Chapter 7

Depression and Manic Depression

While orthodox medicine reports relatively high success in treating depression and manic depression, orthomolecular doctors report as high or higher rates. Since nutritionally oriented doctors attempt to rebalance body chemistry for total health, rather than using drugs to cover up isolated symptoms, a patient treated successfully by nutritional means is less likely to have the recurrences common with orthodox therapy that is considered successful. Competently chosen nutritional therapy also will have no adverse side effects.

Depression

In its July 6, 1992, issue, *Time* magazine reported that "ordinary depression . . . accounts for at least half the nation's suicides." About one in seven who experience a major depression commits suicide. Another 15 percent make unsuccessful attempts to take their own lives.

Why does depression wreak such havoc if successful treatment is available? Because two out of three persons with clinical depression, it has been estimated, never *receive* any treatment. This means that vast numbers remain untreated, since recent estimates are that one

COMMON SYMPTOMS OF DEPRESSION

Insomnia	Guilt
Sleeping too much	Loss of interest in people and
Loss of energy	activities previously considered
Inability to make decisions	important
Loss of appetite	Unusual impatience, anger, hostility
Excessive eating	Social withdrawal
Lack of interest in sex	Physical symptoms, often interpreted
Anxiety	as due to a dreadful disease
Phobias	Thoughts of suicide
Feeling of helplessness	Delusions or hallucinations
Hopelessness	

out of five American adults suffers clinical depression within his or her lifetime; and that the disorder strikes 12 million Americans yearly.

Lack of treatment is considered to be due often to the fact that doctors miss the diagnosis. A 1989 study found that in 50 percent of patients with depression who were seen by general practitioners, the illness was not recognized. Also, many with symptoms never *seek* help. In 1993 Dr. Michael Freedman was quoted in the New York *Daily News* (February 4) as saying that "recent surveys by the National Institute of Mental Health found that as many as 70% of people suffering depression fail to seek treatment." This may be partly due to the fact that sufferers are still caught in the outdated view that depression is somehow their fault, and they wish to avoid the stigma of mental illness. Or, since it is their fault, they should be able to will themselves out of it.

Psychiatrist Priscilla Slagle, M.D., adds, "Many persons suffer all their lives from depression and never seek help because, since they have never felt anything but depression, they don't know there is any other way to feel. Some may be quite aware that other people are somehow happier than they are, but they believe that it is just not in their own 'nature' to feel this elusive happiness."

Dr. Slagle, who is associate clinical professor at the University of California at Los Angeles and is in private practice in Encino and in Palm Springs, California, treats depression with nutritional therapy. She herself suffered from the disorder for 20 years before investigating orthomolecular therapy. Dr. Slagle says, "I haven't been depressed since then, despite a lot of stress and loss."

SYMPTOMS

Orthomolecular doctors are less prone to worry over disease labels, and more prone to investigate the specific underlying biochemical problems of their patients than are orthodox doctors. Thus, if you have a comprehensive series of tests supervised by a nutritional doctor, these tests should pick up the physical factors *behind* your symptoms—and point to a successful nutritional therapy—whether those symptoms fit the "classical" symptoms of depression, or whether they don't. As Dr. Slagle says, "Any mood discomfort is not optimal health. Why suffer at all if you don't have to?"

The table on page 148 gives common symptoms of clinical depression. Generally speaking, it is considered that you might have the actual illness of depression if you have a combination of any four symptoms for two or more weeks.

Psychiatrist Karl E. Humiston, M.D., suggests that valid sadness over a real-life situation may sometimes be confused with clinical depression. He says, "When you are experiencing sadness, you are feeling *more;* when you are suffering depression, you are feeling *less.* A sad person might feel that he or she may simply burst from emotion; a person with depression will usually say things like 'I don't care' or 'I don't feel like doing anything' or 'What does it matter?' "

Dr. Humiston says that some depressives initially argue with him: "What do you mean, I'm feeling less? I'm feeling terrible." He agrees that "they *are* feeling terrible; but what's making them feel that way is often their severe lack of feeling. I have usually found that a person with depression will eventually describe his overall 'emotion' as tight, strained, and *empty,* rather than as sadness."

A normal reaction to a recent traumatic event should not be misconstrued as clinical depression. The rule of thumb is that if symptoms gradually clear up after being triggered by trauma, you've probably had an ordinary "adjustment disorder." If they do not, you may have clinical depression. Nutritional physicians add that anyone suffering recent trauma would do well to get nutritional support to help maintain physical and mental health through the time of stress.

ORTHOMOLECULAR THERAPY COMPARED TO ORTHODOX

As mentioned, both orthodox and orthomolecular doctors report high success rates in treating depression. But the high rate reported by nutritional doctors includes many patients who come to them only after they have already tried orthodox therapy without success. In addition, since nutritional therapy does not carry the risk of side effects that drugs do, it can safely be followed indefinitely, if necessary, to prevent the relapses so common with drug therapy. It is less expensive than psychotherapy.

Recent statistics for the reported success of drug therapy are approximately 70 percent. But let's look more closely at this statistic. While drugs and psychotherapy help most people's symptoms, they do not make the underlying cause go away. Once treatment stops, depression is likely to recur; even just cutting the dosage of drugs can lead to relapse. The relapse rate is reported by various sources as 50–90 percent within two years of stopping treatment.

A 1993 *New York Newsday* article (February 23, p. 60) followed up on a much-publicized national study, run five years previously, of over two hundred people with mild to moderate depression. The original researchers, funded by the National Institute of Mental Health, had reported that half the patients got better after four months, no matter what therapy was administered: the standard antidepressant drug imipramine, two forms of talk therapy, or a placebo medication and 30 minutes a week of supportive conversation with a doctor. According to the article, "It took another year of followup for the true, more somber, picture to emerge. As finally reported in the October 1992 issue of the *Archives of General Psychiatry,* the researchers said that a large number of those who looked well at four months relapsed, and that only 20 to 30 percent of all patients had fully recovered after 18 months." Dr. Morris Parloff, a Maryland psychiatrist, is quoted: "What the studies are showing is that the beneficial effects of drugs and therapy are surprisingly low."

In contrast, Dr. Slagle, many of whose patients had previously tried orthodox therapies without being helped, reported in her 1992 book, *The Way up from Down* (p. 6) that nutritional therapy "has proven to be 70 to 80 percent effective . . . both for patients in real trouble and for those with temporary mood swings." In a 1995 personal communication, Dr. Slagle wrote me that she still found that statistic to be true, but updated her book's statement to read that she'd now been getting those results after 18 years of prescribing nutritional therapy. (Note that the above study, which found that only 20 to 30 percent had fully recovered, referred only to patients with mild to moderate depression, not those "in real trouble.") Dr. Slagle adds that for the majority of people, who suffer only brief mood swings that are not overwhelming, "this program can be almost 100 percent effective."

Drugs used to counter depression—including tricyclic antidepressants and maprotiline, Trazodone, fluoxetine (Prozac), and MAO inhibitors—are used because they affect the brain chemicals norepinephrine and/or serotonin. As stressed throughout this book, every biochemical reaction in our bodies depends on nutrients, and this holds true for brain chemicals. Orthomolecular doctors treat depression with the nutrients that *naturally* affect the brain chemicals that antidepressant drugs affect unnaturally. Since nutrients are substances that the body is not only biochemically equipped to handle but actually *requires,* a competently chosen nutritional regimen produces no side effects.

If you are taking an antidepressant, you may have checked a reference book and been surprised to read that side effects of the drug include symptoms of depression. You may also have noted that possible (although not common) effects include seizures, hallucinations, heart failure, and paralysis. Harold M. Silverman, Pharm. D., in *The Pill Book,* gave the following warning for all classes of antidepressants: Be particularly cautious when operating machinery or driving a car. One might wonder how people who make their living working machines or driving can be safe on the job.

Dr. Slagle reports that in her many years of using nutritional therapy for depression, "I have never had to discontinue treatment because of side effects." She adds that the toxic nature of antidepressant drugs ironically leads to some patients overdosing on them to commit suicide.

Along with drugs, psychotherapy is used by traditional doctors to treat depression. Orthomolecular psychiatrists don't dismiss psychotherapy, although their bias is often away from the "thinking-talking" techniques and toward more practical, cognitive therapies in which one is taught such skills as restructuring habits of negative thinking. (Orthodox doctors often have the same bias for treating depression.) Orthomolecular doctors also commonly believe that psychotherapy will work minimally, when it works at all, for people whose brain chemistry is out of balance.

SOME FACETS OF ORTHOMOLECULAR THERAPY

While some people may be lifted from depression by very simple dietary changes, others may need more comprehensive therapy. Nutritional doctors have an array of noninvasive, relatively inexpensive tests that tell them the specific biochemical problems in the individual's body.

Amino Acid Therapy. People suffering depression tend to have low amounts of the brain chemicals norepinephrine and serotonin. As noted earlier, orthodox doctors use antidepressant drugs because they affect these chemicals. Amino acids are the natural raw materials for the production of these brain chemicals and are used in orthomolecular therapy as a nontoxic way of accomplishing what the drugs attempt. In addition, as Dr. Slagle points out, when the amino acids tyrosine and tryptophan are taken, *both* norepinephrine and serotonin are increased, whereas most antidepressant prescription medicines increase only one or the other. Thus, she says, "Valuable time can be lost giving a drug that, for example, increases serotonin, when low norepinephrine is the problem." In that lost time, people may suffer needlessly or may be driven to suicide.

Tyrosine is the raw material for norepinephrine. This brain chemical, Dr. Slagle explains, influences the centers of the brain having to do with reward-and-punishment behavior, "specifically helping one to feel purpose, pleasure and gratification. . . . Norepinephrine is also important in promoting drive, ambition, alert mental functioning and memory." A low amount of this chemical, then, results in the *reduction* of those attributes—that is, in common symptoms of depression.

In addition, tyrosine is the raw material for dopamine, a low amount of which has also been implicated in some depressions. And L-tyrosine is involved in producing adrenaline, the fight-or-flight hormone. Robert Erdmann, Ph.D., states in his 1989 book *The Amino Revolution,* that levels of adrenaline "are nearly always negligible in depression patients."

One double-blind case study, published in 1980 in the *American Journal of Psychiatry* (137, pp. 622–23) involved a 30-year-old woman suffering depression. After two weeks of receiving tyrosine, her depression had disappeared. When tyrosine was replaced by a placebo, she rapidly deteriorated. When she was switched back to tyrosine, her depression once again was completely alleviated.

A letter published in *Lancet* in 1980 (2, p. 364) recounted that tyrosine was given to two depressed patients, both of whom had failed to respond to tricyclic drugs, MAO inhibitors, and ECT (electroconvulsive therapy). Both were amphetamine-dependent (amphetamines can give a feeling of "pep" and well-being). After taking tyrosine, one patient was able to eliminate amphetamines completely; the other was able to decrease the dosage by two thirds.

The brain chemicals norepinephrine and dopamine can be derived from the amino acid phenylalanine. In her book, Dr. Slagle points out that another biochemical effect of L-phenylalanine is the formation of the neurotransmitter (brain chemical) 2-phenylethylamine. The amphetamines, the stimulant Ritalin, and the antidepressant Tofranil cause an increase of that neurotransmitter, which is one of the reasons for their excitatory effects. Some depressed people have insufficient 2-phenylethylamine, "and when this is so, phenylalanine may be necessary," Dr. Slagle says. In her experience, this amino acid needs to be added in only about 10 percent of cases.

In a 1979 double-blind study published in a German journal (H. Beckmann et al., *Archiv Psychiatrischer Nervenkrankheiten* 227, pp. 49–58), 14 depressed patients were given D,L-phenylalanine and 13 received the antidepressant drug imipramine in the same amounts. After 30 days, no significant difference was found between the two groups. In a 1977 study of 20 patients receiving D,L-phenylalanine, eight completely recovered, four had a good response, and four with partially untypical depressions had a mild-moderate response—after 20 days (H. Beckmann et al., *Journal of Neural Transmitters* 41, pp. 123–34).

The amino acid tryptophan is the raw material for the neurotransmitter serotonin, a low level of which is one of the major "culprits" in depression. Dr. Slagle points out that autopsies on many suicides show a low level of serotonin in the brain. She says, "A recent study also found a 44 percent increase in the number of serotonin receptors in . . . the brain of suicide victims. . . . It's as if the brain is hungry for this particular brain food and develops many extra receptors to try to gobble it up."

Dr. Slagle points out in her book that supplementation with pyridoxal-5-phosphate, a form of vitamin B6, "will enable optimal production of serotonin from trytophan taken naturally as part of your diet."

Vitamin and Mineral Therapy. Dr. Slagle points out that "deficiencies of almost any of the B vitamins can cause depression, so their importance cannot be overemphasized." Vitamin B6, for instance (along with the mineral magnesium), is needed by precursor amino acids for the synthesis of the brain chemicals serotonin, norepinephrine, dopamine, phenylethylamine, and gamma-aminobutyric acid.

An excess of copper in the body is implicated as a factor in depression, not only in clinical depression as discussed here but also in women with PMS and postpartum depression. Excess copper can be counteracted by elevating amounts of zinc (a copper antagonist) and by other nontoxic means. See Chapter 17 for more information on heavy-metal toxicity.

Cutting Out Caffeine. Caffeine can for some persons play such a strong role in depression that, Dr. Slagle reports, "a number of my patients get well quickly just by cutting out caffeine and adding the B-vitamin complex and magnesium." Ironically, some people suffering depression douse themselves with caffeine in an attempt to lift themselves "up." Dr. Slagle states that "small amounts of caffeine daily can enhance the mood of people prone to depression. Beyond that, trouble sets in." In her book, she recommends that daily intake should not exceed 150–200 mg, depending on body weight and health conditions. An eight-ounce cup of brewed coffee has 120–240 mg of caffeine, an eight-ounce cup of tea has 16–80 mg, and 12-ounce bottles of some popular sodas have 29–50 mg.

Cutting Out Sugar. Sugar depletes the body of B vitamins and magnesium, which are crucial to the production of adequate amounts of brain chemicals. Eating too much sugar or other refined carbohydrates is considered a major factor in low blood sugar (hypoglycemia). For an explanation of how too much sugar can result in *low* blood sugar, and for other details on this disorder, see Chapter 15. Dr. Slagle points out that sophisticated brain X-ray tests that measure glucose (sugar) utilization in the brain show that depressed patients have an overall reduction in glucose metabolism. Glucose is the major food that the brain requires to operate correctly.

Treating Food and Chemical Intolerances (Sensitivities, "Allergies"). The role that intolerances can play in various mental problems is covered throughout this book. A fuller examination, including orthomolecular therapies for intolerances, is in Chapter 14.

A study published in 1976 in *Compre. Psychiat.* (17, p. 335) reported that of 109 depressed children and adults, 85 percent were allergic.

The following case history, from the early files of Marshall Mandell, M.D., is recounted in *Dr. Mandell's 5-Day Allergy Relief System* (p. 82). Dr. Mandell was at the time pioneering a new field of medicine, clinical ecology, and his patient was one of the first to demonstrate, in a doctor's office, a mental symptom as an instantaneous reaction to foods.

The woman had been referred to Dr. Mandell because of a sinus problem, and he was trying to discover if it were caused by a sensitivity to ketchup. (In those days, patients did not go to Dr. Mandell for mental symptoms, since it wasn't known that mental problems could be due to food sensitivities.) He suspected an addictive intolerance because the patient was a self-admitted "ketchup freak." So Dr. Mandell tested for sensitivity to tomato and onion, two major ingredients in ketchup.

Both patient and doctor were surprised when, within minutes of being tested with the extracts, the woman put her head down on the examining table and began to cry. At the time, it was assumed that symptoms of depression were almost always due to psychological problems. "I went over to her," he says, "gently lifted her head, and asked what was wrong, why she was so upset."

The woman said she didn't know. "I asked her if there were any serious problems with her children, her husband, his job, the family finances, etc." She said there was nothing bothering her in her personal life.

Finally, "out of desperation to find some possible reason for her depression," she said that maybe she was depressed because her daughters would someday leave her to get married. Her daughters were in elementary school.

Dr. Mandell reports that, in the years since that day, he has found many cases of depression and manic-depression to be due at least partly to food and chemical sensitivities.

One study, published by Emanuel Cheraskin, M.D., D.M.D., and associates in the 1985 *Journal of Orthomolecular Medicine* (14, No. 2), found 63 percent improvement in patients suffering depression who underwent dietary changes for sensitivities. The patients were tested by a respected measuring instrument for feelings and mood, from the Cornell Medical Index Health Questionnaire.

While a 63 percent improvement without drug risks or expensive psychotherapy might be considered impressive in itself, remember that this was achieved with the use of only one nutritional therapy. Since these therapies are nontoxic, several nutritional therapies may be safely used as necessary to achieve even higher results.

Other Treatment Options. Orthodox doctors agree that infections can sometimes be a major factor behind depression. But they feel that one infection that orthomolecular doctors find a frequent factor (candidiasis) is grossly overdiagnosed. Orthomolecular physicians respond that orthodox doctors don't find this disorder nearly so frequently as orthomolecular doctors because they don't *look* for it nearly so often.

While candidiasis is a disorder in which yeast overgrows in any mucous membranes, the dispute involves orthomolecular doctors' "overdiagnosis" of yeast that overgrows in the intestines and releases toxins that can affect the brain. For details, see Chapter 16.

Stuart Berger, M.D., wrote in the April 18, 1989, issue of the *New York Post* about Fran, a 40-year-old woman who had been treated by a psychiatrist for two years. "As well as receiving psychiatric treatments, she had been taking anti-depressants, tranquilizers, and other drugs. Instead of getting better, she was feeling sicker and more removed from reality."

One of her many symptoms was that she was almost always depressed; and eventually she began to think of suicide as "the only solution to the misery." Fran's family considered sending her to a mental hospital, but decided first to try orthomolecular medical help. She began responding immediately to a rather vigorous therapy for candidiasis. After a while, she recovered completely from her depression and other symptoms.

Another possible culprit in depression is intestinal parasites. Dr. Humiston states that intestinal parasites such as worms can, like a yeast overgrowth, excrete toxins into the body and brain. He believes that "these parasites are an often overlooked cause of mental problems, including depression."

Bringing the Body into Correct Electromagnetic Balance. William H. Philpott, M.D., an orthomolecular psychiatrist who pioneered work with food and chemical sensitivities and with low blood sugar, is now pioneering a new technique to bring the body into correct electromagnetic balance. (For details, see Chapter 8.) In an interview, Dr. Philpott told of Sheldon, who had headed the sociology department at a midwestern university, and who was the first person with depression whom the physician treated with this new therapy.

"He was hospitalized at the university hospital," Dr. Philpott says, "and they fed him by vein, because he absolutely wouldn't swallow food. Finally, after they had tried all the drugs, they told his wife that they had no alternative but electroconvulsive treatment. But she said, 'I want to try something else first.' "

She drove him to Dr. Philpott, who gave him 12.5 grams of vitamin C intravenously as well as B6, B5, calcium, and magnesium. "I also had him breathing oxygen, to saturate his tissues with it, and I arranged magnets around his head.

"After an hour, I said to him, 'Now you know what I want you to do? I want you to go with your wife to a restaurant, and I want you to eat a meal.' And he said, 'Okay.' And here was a fellow who hadn't eaten a bite in several weeks."

Dr. Philpott gave Sheldon several more sessions of stabilizing therapy, and soon Sheldon was back at work.

It is not uncommon for orthodox doctors to believe that improvement with alternative therapy comes from the placebo effect: that is, that patients recover simply because they expected to recover. (This argument overlooks the fact that so many patients try orthodox therapy first, because they actually expected to recover with traditional techniques.) Dr. Philpott states that Sheldon "wrote me the most beautiful letter, saying, 'Forgive me for not believing in you. I had absolutely no faith that you had anything at all that would help me.' So it had nothing to do with faith in me. It simply was the right therapy to use for him."

Dr. Philpott has since treated other depressives with the same therapy and obtained similar results.

WHAT YOU CAN DO

If you are depressed—or someone you care about is depressed—don't fall prey to thinking: "Why don't you just snap out of it? There are people worse off than you. What have *you* got to be unhappy about?" Realize that depression is a biochemical disorder, with unbalanced brain chemicals distorting moods, thinking, and behavior.

Safe self-help for depression is limited. Before we cover steps you can safely take until you can consult an orthomolecular doctor, please heed this very strong warning: Take these steps IN ADDITION TO YOUR ORTHODOX THERAPY, NOT INSTEAD OF IT. See "Resources" for how to find an orthomolecular doctor near you. Since self-help is fragmentary and not based on testing of your individual biochemistry, it may be of minimal help. Substituting these self-help steps for your orthodox therapy may very well result in an even deeper depression. Since suicide is often a very real threat, you cannot risk making yourself worse.

If you are taking any of the MAO (monoamine oxidase) inhibitors, DO NOT PRESCRIBE FOR YOURSELF ANY AMINO ACID

THERAPY WHATSOEVER. Robert Erdmann, Ph.D., in his book *The Amino Revolution*, warns strongly against taking free-form phenylalanine, tyrosine, or tryptophan if you take an MAO inhibitor. Any of these amino acids added to any of those drugs will cause a "huge surge in the circulating levels of adrenaline, noradrenalin, and serotonin, leading to a range of mood-related and psychotic problems." CHECK WITH YOUR DOCTOR TO SEE IF YOUR PRESCRIBED DRUG IS AN MAO INHIBITOR.

With the above warnings in mind, you can safely try the suggestions in Chapter 2 for diet, water, and basic vitamin-mineral supplementation. Because the B vitamins are so often helpful for depression, you might take a B-complex supplement in addition to the multivitamin-mineral supplement. Dr. Slagle stresses that if the B6 is not in the form of pyridoxal-5-phosphate, purchase it separately; take 20–120 mg twice daily between meals. (The B-complex and multivitamin-mineral supplements should be taken with a meal.) The importance of that particular form of B6 is that it will enable optimal production of serotonin from tryptophan taken naturally as part of your diet—as well as allowing optimum use of all dietary amino acids.

Caffeine, tobacco, alcohol, and sugar can be very real problems for people prone to depression. Certainly it would be a safe step for you to cut out these substances. For help, see Chapter 5.

Dr. Slagle's book gives details of a comprehensive orthomolecular therapy: amounts of amino acids for various ages, which supplements should be taken at what times of day, etc.

High vanadium levels have been implicated in some cases of depression. Vanadium occurs in high concentrations in fats and vegetable oils. While it is not healthy to cut out fats and oils entirely, cut down on them if your diet is very high in them. High amounts of vitamin C may also help remove excess vanadium from the body.

Chapters 2 and 14 offer self-help with food and chemical sensitivities. Chapter 15 gives a diet for low blood sugar.

Physical tension is considered a major problem in depression.

Biofeedback training gives a relaxation technique that you can safely use on your own as needed, but initially you must be trained on special equipment. Cost-free relaxation exercises might be of some help.

The effect of light on depression has been well studied by orthodox medicine. One form of depression has been named seasonal affective disorder (SAD), which occurs in the winter, when there are fewer hours of light. Dr. Humiston gives two recommendations for getting healthy light radiation. The simplest is to get outdoors as much as possible in daylight. Also consider replacing your indoor lighting with full-spectrum fluorescent lights. "Don't confuse these with the usual fluorescent lights, which are actually the least healthy source of light," Dr. Humiston says.

Exercise is thought to raise levels of endorphins, brain chemicals that help produce a good mood. Some research also indicates that exercise causes a 200 percent increase in norepinephrine, one of the brain chemicals so often low in depression. Psychiatrist Melvyn R. Werbach, M.D., in *Third Line Medicine* (p. 113) notes that "people who are essentially healthy but score in the depressed range on questionnaires note improved moods after exercise programs." He cites a study conducted "to see if depressed psychiatric patients would also feel better after exercise" (John H. Griest et al., *Behavioral Medicine*, June 1978). The patients were randomly assigned either to a program of running, or to one of two kinds of individual psychotherapy. "At the end of ten weeks, six of the eight patients who ran had recovered from their depressions, a result comparable to the best outcomes obtained by psychotherapy for patients in [the researchers'] clinic."

Manic Depression (Bipolar Disorder)

Manic depression is thought to affect two to three million Americans, and wreaks much more havoc than it should, given its relative treatability. A 1993 study by the National Depressive and Manic-Depressive Association found that it took an *average* of eight years for patients to get the correct diagnosis. On average, participants said they consulted three doctors before getting a correct diagnosis. One reason for the delay is that the disorder often begins between ages 15 and 19 and may be dismissed as something the adolescent will outgrow. Compounding the problem is the fact that many sufferers don't seek professional treatment for more than a decade after symptoms first appear.

SYMPTOMS

Manic depression is characterized by extreme swings in mood between euphoria and depression. Although symptoms can be highly dramatic, sufferers and their families sometimes assume that the person is simply "very moody": That this is just a normal part of the person's personality, and nothing needs to be—or can be—done about it.

In the manic state, actions are exaggerated; thoughts are overoptimistic. For instance, the person may take on more work than any two persons could do in the time allowed. He may go long stretches of time without sleep, in a flurry of activity that is often disorganized and unproductive. He may talk too much and too fast, with a compulsion for repetition. (Karl E. Humiston, M.D., once had a patient who got hooked on the phrase "I gotta go there and see who's who in the human zoo." Dr. Humiston told me, "I heard him say that so often that to this day, I can't see or hear mention of a zoo without that sentence popping into my mind.")

In the manic stage, the person may also grossly overeat, have an exaggerated sense of his own worth, and be highly overgenerous ("to the point of literally giving the house away," as one psychiatrist expressed it).

Suddenly the person will drastically change moods. He may swerve from working feverishly day and night to lying in bed day and night. Instead of eating almost constantly, he may not eat at all. Instead of having an exaggerated sense of his own worth, he may now believe himself worth virtually nothing. In short, he may be just as excessively "down" as he is excessively "up" in manic phases. In this depressive phase, suicide is a real possibility.

ORTHOMOLECULAR THERAPY COMPARED TO ORTHODOX

There seems to be less strenuous objection among nutritional doctors to lithium carbonate, the drug commonly used for mania, than there is to many other drugs. But as usual, nutritional physicians have a wider range of therapies to choose from than drugs. This means that sometimes lithium is not needed. When it is, nutritional support may prevent adverse side effects of the drug while also increasing its usefulness in alleviating symptoms. Also, nutritional therapy—when used alone—can help some of the estimated 20–30 percent of those not helped by lithium.

Side effects of lithium can include kidney damage and excessive thirst and urination. Lithium should be used with caution in persons with kidney or heart problems. Another possible side effect is impairment of mental ability. A wrongly adjusted dose can cause convulsions.

As with other disorders, orthomolecular psychiatrists deal primarily with the physical problems *behind* manic depression: blood sugar disturbances, toxic amounts of vanadium in the body, etc. And, as with other disorders, some orthomolecular psychiatrists suggest that we might "label" the patient according to the specific physical problems behind the symptoms. Thus, the person HAS a blood sugar disorder, not the person IS a "manic-depressive."

The following shows how one woman unsuccessfully tried orthodox approaches and found help when the underlying physical causes of her illness were treated. Martha wrote of her own experiences in 1987 in the *Journal of Orthomolecular Medicine* (Vol. 4, No. 3, pp. 154–57). In 1977 she was diagnosed as manic-depressive. She was given shock therapy and "I was forced to take drugs that caused many unpleasant side effects, including parkinsonism. . . . Subjectively, all the drugs including lithium made me feel worse." She was told that she would have to be on lithium for the rest of her life and that there was nothing her doctor could do for her if she would not take lithium. She refused this approach.

Over the years following her first hospitalization, "I developed a series of seemingly unrelated physical health problems." Diagnoses included hypoglycemia, allergies, hypothyroidism, and chronic infection—all of which might be considered by orthomolecular doctors as possible factors *behind* manic depression, rather than unrelated health problems. Eventually, "I began to notice that there was no clear separation between my moods and my physical health."

She noticed that prior to major shifts in mood, she began to have problems sleeping—and the more severe the mood swing, the more sleeping problems she had. "On Sundays, I experienced the greatest difficulties . . . After some detective work, I realized that every Sunday our bedding was changed, and the detergent scent in the freshly washed sheets was the cause of my difficulty." When she began washing the sheets in an unscented baking soda solution, "this problem sleep cycle disappeared."

Martha discovered the research of Dr. Orian Truss on candidiasis infection, which can cause some of the physical disorders she had been diagnosed as having. Martha reports: "Candida treatment, together with avoidance of substances to which I am sensitive like eggs and perfumes . . . have stabilized my energy level. . . . I generally feel happy but not high, and occasionally sad, but not depressed." (For further information on candidiasis, see Chapter 16.)

SOME ORTHOMOLECULAR APPROACHES TO MANIC DEPRESSION

Since mania is the opposite of depression in its manifestations, we might expect to find the biochemistry to be opposite—and we might expect therapies to be reversed also. To some extent this is true. For instance, psychiatrist Priscilla Slagle, M.D., points out that if you are manic-depressive, the amino acid therapy for depression can "potentially push you over into mania—as can any traditional antidepressant medication."

However, some underlying physical factors can be behind *both* the manic and depressive stages of manic depression—and treating these factors can help to successfully treat the disorder as a whole. For instance, Martha's history showed that dealing with intolerances and an underlying infection led to an overall stabilization of moods and energy levels.

Treating a Vanadium Overload. Vanadium is a nutrient needed by the body, but only in small amounts. Studies have found an overload of vanadium in the bodies of people with manic depression, in both manic and depressed stages. It has also been shown that as patients in either the manic or depressive state moved toward a normal mood, high vanadium levels also moved toward normal. It is logical, then, that steps to lower vanadium levels in manic-depressives with an overload can help toward an overall stabilization of moods.

A relevant case history was published in 1981 in *Psychological Medicine* (11, pp. 249–56). An 82-year-old woman had severe manic depression and had not been helped by lithium and other treatments. She was given a diet low in vanadium and supplemented with high vitamin C and EDTA, which help remove vanadium from the body. Within two weeks she settled into a mild hypomanic (low-level euphoric) state. She showed no depressive states while on the therapy. Only five days after being taken off the supplements, she became severely depressed. When the supplements were resumed, she returned to the much more desirable hypomanic condition. Notice not only that this woman had had no help from previous treatments, but notice also her age. While it is easy to assume that anyone not helped by traditional therapies can never be helped, it is even easier to assume this about an elderly person.

The authors reported in the above article on a double-blind crossover study in which seven of the 10 with depression were rated "better" during the period of low vanadium intake; and 10 of the 11 with mania were rated "better."

Treating Blood-Sugar Disturbances. Carl C. Pfeiffer, Ph.D., M.D., reported in his 1975 book, *Mental and Elemental Nutrients* (p. 383), that Dr. Jack Ward at the Mercer Hospital in Trenton, New Jersey, had found that 80 percent of the people he counseled for manic depression had abnormal blood-sugar metabolism.

Psychiatrist William H. Philpott, M.D., told me of a woman who came to him in a deeply depressed state. "I had to hospitalize her because she was suicidal." Dr. Philpott ran a six-hour glucose-tolerance test for hypoglycemia.

"One hour after giving her glucose, I checked on her. Her blood sugar was high—180—and her mood had drastically changed to euphoria. Two hours later, her blood sugar had dropped to 40, and her mood had dropped right down with it. There she was in the depths of depression again." Stabilizing her blood sugar also stabilized her moods. (For more on orthomolecular treatment of unstable blood-sugar levels, see Chapter 15.)

Treating Food and Chemical Intolerances. It is not uncommon to become addicted to foods to which one is intolerant. The addictive food may initially trigger a "high," just as an addictive drug does, and withdrawal from the food may trigger a low mood. For some with manic depression, a manic phase may be precipitated by an addictive food or foods. As mentioned previously, in the manic phase a person may tend to grossly overeat, which may perpetuate the phase. Withdrawal from the offending food(s) may precipitate the swing into depression.

WHAT YOU CAN DO

The only safe and sure way to get the kind of help described in this book is to consult an orthomolecular physician. For aid in contacting one near you, see the "Resources" section.

There are, however, steps you can take that may alleviate symptoms before you can meet with the doctor. Of particular help might be modifying physical factors implicated in both depression and mania: high vanadium, candidiasis, food and chemical intolerances, and blood-sugar disturbances. If your diet is high in fats and vegetable oils, it may contribute to an excess of vanadium in the body. Cut down on the fats and oils, but do not cut them out entirely, since they are necessary for health. Vitamin C may also help remove excess vanadium from the body.

For safe self-help tips on candidiasis, see Chapter 16. Chapters 2 and 14 give suggestions for self-help with intolerances. Chapter 15 gives suggestions for maintaining an even blood-sugar level.

Also, please review the What You Can Do section on depression.

In a 1995 private communication, Dr. Slagle suggests that you also cut out sugar, alcohol, and caffeine (for help, see the chapter on Addiction); eat healthfully (see Chapter 2); and start supplements as detailed in her book, *The Way up from Down*. For those with severe mood disorder, however, amino acid therapy should not be undertaken except under a doctor's strict supervision.

Above all, don't let yourself or your loved one become an addition to the high statistic of people who suffer needlessly with manic depression. Help is available.

MY DIARY RECORDS the story of a schizophrenic mother
with elaborate delusions of persecution, both of whose
children showed ominous symptoms of the disorder.
The smaller boy heard voices addressing him from the
clouds, and his older brother talked each night with his
grandfather, long deceased, who appeared . . . as a
"purple cloud." A geneticist would have had a field
day with a family that so beautifully illustrated the
power of a few aberrant chromosomes. A behavioral
psychiatrist would have made it a strong case for
environmental influences. . . . A bioecological allergist
came up with the real answer when he insisted that
wheat be withdrawn from the family diet; it was, and
the symptoms swiftly disappeared.

—CARLTON FREDERICKS, PH.D., *Eat Well, Get Well, Stay
Well*, p. 51

I DO NOT believe there is such a disease as
schizophrenia. A patient may have multiple vitamin
and mineral deficiencies and multiple intolerances and
other physical problems that produce the symptoms
that are *labeled* schizophrenia. Getting rid of the
physical problems clears up the symptoms—whether
you call them schizophrenia or not.

—WILLIAM H. PHILPOTT, M.D., psychiatrist and clinical
ecologist

Chapter 8

Schizophrenia

The following tells of someone who lost contact with reality—showing symptoms including those of schizophrenia—while in an orthomolecular doctor's office. Yet she did not leave that office with a diagnosis of schizophrenia—or of any psychosis. Marshall Mandell, M.D., in his book *Dr. Mandell's 5-day Allergy Relief System* (pp. 192–195), tells of Nancy, a 10-year-old, who told Dr. Mandell she felt she was on a cloud and everything around was much too bright to look at. She said she was thirsty; but when the doctor gave her cool water, she complained that she had been given hot cola and was very angry.

Suddenly Nancy began performing somersaults. She believed she was going backward when she was going forward; she thought she was going forward when she was going backward. While somersaulting, she struck her elbow against a wall and complained about hitting her knee.

When asked to describe the person sitting next to her—her mother—Nancy insisted that the "man" was a teacher she had had two years previously. She stated that Dr. Mandell's face was yellow with purple spots moving across it.

She looked out the window at the sunny day and commented on how hard it was raining. She tore off a piece of paper towel, started

---

SOME PHYSICAL FACTORS BEHIND SCHIZOPHRENIA

Intolerance to various foods and/or chemicals
(Common culprits: milk, gluten, cigarette smoke, and gasoline)
Nutritional deficiencies and/or dependencies (abnormal needs)—often, B3 or
B6 and zinc
Deficiency or excess of certain fatty acids
Infections (current or developed during gestation)
Abnormal carbohydrate metabolism

---

chewing it, and announced that it was lettuce and it was delicious. Then she began chewing another piece of paper; this morsel was a hot dog.

The cause of the girl's loss of contact with reality was no mystery to Dr. Mandell. This "psychosis" had been brought on in his office when he gave her a symptom-duplicating allergy test with a solution prepared from petroleum. The test confirmed what Dr. Mandell had suspected from her medical history, which included such bizarre actions as walking smack into a car waiting for a traffic light, with its engine running: She was chemically intolerant to the combustion products present in the exhaust fumes.

"When Nancy's parents replaced their gas appliances with electric ones, and threw out household products derived from petroleum fractions," Dr. Mandell wrote in a personal communication, "there was a remarkable and immediate improvement in her condition."

Estimates of the prevalence of schizophrenia go as high as 3.4 cases for every 100 persons.

Sigmund Freud, the father of psychoanalysis, admitted that psychoanalysis could not help schizophrenia, predicting that someday we would find it to be a problem of disordered biochemistry. In recent decades, orthodox psychiatry has turned more and more to using drugs to change the brain chemistry of people with schizophrenia.

In the same time period, orthomolecular psychiatry has developed ways of restoring normal biochemistry with nutritional methods. Orthomolecular psychiatrists also will use standard drugs if that is best for the individual patient. Drugs will sometimes be used initially in addition to nutritional therapy, to control symptoms while the more natural therapy has time to balance the out-of-kilter biochemistry *behind* the symptoms. Used in this way, drugs do not tend to have the side effects they do when used without nutritional therapy.

Some orthomolecular psychiatrists suggest that we stop referring to people as having schizophrenia, and refer to them as having the physical problems behind their symptoms. This might be considered a matter of semantics—but if this idea were carried out, sufferers and their families could be relieved of an unnecessary social stigma and could clearly see how unmysterious, and potentially treatable, schizophrenia can be when viewed from the orthomolecular perspective.

In *Nutrition and Mental Illness* (p. 11), Carl C. Pfeiffer, Ph.D., M.D., breaks down what is generally called schizophrenia into very distinct and treatable *physical* problems behind the mental symptoms. For instance, one form of schizophrenia is, in his lexicon, "pyroluria—a familial double deficiency of zinc and vitamin B6." So if one has developed schizophrenia because it "runs in the family," what really may have been inherited is a tendency toward a deficiency of zinc and B6. Of course, there is a vast difference between being told, "Your sister is psychotic; she has schizophrenia," and being told, "Your sister has these symptoms because she is deficient in zinc and B6; I will prescribe some supplements."

Psychiatrist Abram Hoffer, M.D., Ph.D., writes me that he agrees that the "something that has been called schizophrenia . . . ought to be considered a syndrome, i.e., a condition which can be caused by a variety of factors, such as the ones you describe in this chapter. It would be advisable to not use that word . . . , but I think we are some time away from that." (Dr. Hoffer, known as the father of orthomolecular medicine because of his work with Hum-phry Osmond, M.D., Ph.D., in the 1950s with vitamin B3 and schizophrenia, estimates he has treated over 5,000 patients with schizophrenia.)

Dr. Pfeiffer also observes that problems with one or more of the following body chemicals can be behind symptoms of schizophrenia: prostaglandins, dopamine, endorphins, serine, prolactin, serotonin imbalance, leucine, histidine imbalance, and platelets deficient in monoamine oxidase. Nutritional maneuvers that orthomolecular doctors use are chosen in an attempt to bring such chemicals into the proper balance as they occur in a healthy person—and as they occurred in the patient before schizophrenia developed. Remember that all body chemicals are produced by reactions set in motion by nutrients.

Symptoms of Schizophrenia

In *catatonic schizophrenia*, the person is at times extremely withdrawn and at times extremely agitated. She may sit in a corner for days, staring into space, muscles locked into one position. This will be followed by a period of aimless, constant actions and sometimes violence.

Disorganized schizophrenia begins usually at puberty. Symptoms include inappropriate laughter and silliness, talking and gesturing to oneself, bizarre and often obscene behavior, and extreme social withdrawal. The person may hear, see, smell things that are not there (hallucinations). He may have delusions of a religious, paranoid, or sexual nature. ("I am God"; "The people upstairs have a machine sending out rays to kill me"; "The devil ordered me to rape the first virgin I see.")

Paranoid schizophrenia is marked by preoccupation with absurd and sometimes changeable delusions, usually of persecution or jealousy. Extreme anxiety, suspicion, anger, and violence are typical.

So-called *simple schizophrenia* develops slowly, and is characterized by lack of feeling, lack of concern for others, no energy, and no wish to be around other people.

There are other recognized forms, with symptoms that sometimes criss-cross each other, leading to confusion in diagnosis.

Oddly enough, what the public often thinks of as schizophrenia definitely is *not* schizophrenia: "split personality" (multiple personality disorder). This myth pops up in movies and books, in public speeches by learned people, and even on tee shirts ("I am schizophrenic, and so am I").

Comparing Orthomolecular and Orthodox Therapies

The therapy section gives statistics of the high success rate reported by orthomolecular medicine, even for people who have failed to respond to everything that orthodox psychiatry has to offer.

Another statistic comes from Dr. Pfeiffer, the head of the Princeton Brain Bio Center, which had by 1987 treated over five thousand patients who had been labeled schizophrenic. He reports in his book (pp. 10–11) that 95 percent of those patients fit into five categories of physical problems and "when the exact biotype guides the appropriate treatment, 90% of these patients will attain social rehabilitation." The five biotypes, Dr. Pfeiffer says, are

- Histapenia: low blood histamine with excess copper (50 percent of the schizophrenias)
- Histadelia: high blood histamine with low copper (20 percent)
- Pyroluria: familial double deficiency of zinc and B6 (30 percent)
- Cerebral allergy (10 percent)
- Nutritional hypoglycemia, or low blood sugar (20 percent)

This adds up to more than 100 percent because, as Dr. Pfeiffer said, "many patients have more than one disorder."

Note that when Dr. Pfeiffer discusses the success of treatment he uses the word "rehabilitation." To rehabilitate a patient means to restore the person to normal or nearly normal functioning. In contrast, Dr. Hoffer wrote in 1984 in the *Journal of Orthomolecular Psychiatry* (Vol. 13, No.1, p. 4), "Full recovery on drugs alone is rare, probably at a rate less than the natural recovery rate." In a personal communication, he wrote that by "natural recovery rate," he meant "spontaneous recovery—that is, with no treatment whatever."

Drugs often can cover up symptoms of schizophrenia; and their use has accounted for many responses that would have been considered "miracles" before the drugs were developed. (Orthomolecular doctors are dissatisfied with just covering up symptoms. Some call tranquilizers "chemical straitjackets" because they can keep the person quiet—making things easier for those around him—while the person continues to suffer with the illness.) However, recent statistics—from orthodox sources—estimate that 200,000 patients are not helped by, or cannot tolerate, present drug therapy. In 1992, Claudia Wallis and James Willwerth, writing in *Time* magazine (July 6, p. 55), reported that Thorazine and related drugs provide only "limited . . . recovery for just 40% of patients; 30% have flare-ups of madness and must be periodically hospitalized, while the remaining 30% are considered to be 'treatment resistant' and are largely confined to mental institutions." (Compare those statistics with those given in this chapter for nutritional therapy.) A new drug (Clozaril) helps a significant number who are nonresponsive to standard drugs. However, it is recommended *only* for those not helped by other drugs, because Clozaril can cause a potentially fatal blood disorder (agranulocytosis) in "about 1–2% of the patients"; it "can cause seizures in 1–2% at low doses, 3–4% at moderate doses, and 5% at high doses"; rapid heartbeat has been observed in 25 percent; and "in clinical trials, several patients experienced significant cardiac events, including myocardial infarction . . . and sudden unexplained death." Those facts were sent me by the public relations firm helping to sell the drug.

Clozaril poses another problem: As the 1992 *Time* article reported, it costs $4,000 annually, and doctor-monitored treatment costs up to $9,000 more.

Side effects of chronic use of neuroleptic drugs can include, psychiatrist William H. Philpott points out, "permanent injury to the liver, skin, cornea, bone marrow, heart, and central nervous system." One possible side effect is Parkinson's syndrome, which is treated by anti-Parkinsonian drugs that have their own potential side effects.

Another common side effect of neuroleptic drugs, tardive dyskinesia, is a neurological disorder with bizarre symptoms that, ironically, have sometimes been misdiagnosed as a psychosis. In 1986, David R. Hawkins, M.D., stated that evidence of tardive dyskinesia was reported at a rate of up to 50 percent and that "in general, the incidence is reported to be on the average of between 10 and 25% of patients on neuroleptics" (*Journal of Orthomolecular Medicine* Vol. 1, No. 1). In contrast, Dr. Hoffer writes in his 1989 book *Orthomolecular Medicine for Physicians* (p. 165), "Orthomolecular physicians are unfamiliar with tardive dyskinesia because it does not appear in their patients. . . . In my own practice, since 1955, I have not seen cases unless they had already developed by previous treatment."

A large-scale study run by Dr. Hawkins found almost 100 percent prevention of tardive dyskinesia. In 1989, this physician published results of a study involving 80 psychiatrists who used vitamins (B3, B6, C, and E) in addition to neuroleptics (*Journal of Orthomolecular Medicine*, Vol. 4, No. 1). The study followed 61,508 patients for two decades, 1967 to 1987. Only 34 (0.05%) developed tardive dyskinesia; Dr. Hawkins stated that an average incidence would occur in 25 to 50 percent of patients on the same drugs without nutritional support.

In orthodox therapy the treatment of choice for tardive dyskinesia is to discontinue the drug, raising the question: what then do you do to cover up the symptoms of the psychosis? Even when the drug is withdrawn, the symptoms of tardive dyskinesia, according to Dr. Hawkins in his 1986 article, are reportedly irreversible in 50 percent of patients. Orthomolecular doctors, following research begun in the 1970s at the Massachusetts Institute of Technology (see *Science* 113), treat the disorder with the nutrient choline, the raw material for the brain chemical acetylcholine. They may also use manganese, because tranquilizers can cause deficiency of this nutrient, which helps the body utilize several other nutrients. The vitamins shown to help *prevent* tardive dyskinesia—B3, B6, C and E—may also be used for therapy.

Some Orthomolecular Approaches to Therapy

Results of scientific tests of the individual's body chemistry will determine which and how many approaches are needed.

NUTRITIONAL SUPPLEMENTATION

Vitamin B3.   Dr. Hoffer describes the day he first tried vitamin B3 for treating catatonic schizophrenia:

> In 1953, when deaths from catatonia were still fairly common, we encountered this catatonic young man who had been given only hours to live by his psychiatrists. I must say I agreed with that prognosis. However, unlike his other psychiatrists, I'd had very vivid experiences dealing with vitamin B3 and psychosis. At the time, I was not aware of any references in the medical literature of more than 1 gram ever having been used. I knew that 1 gram would not be enough to pull this man from his grave. I gave him 10 grams. He did not die that day. As a matter of fact, he was still alive 15 years later, when we last encountered him. And he had been free of catatonia for those 15 years.

The man, Dr. Hoffer adds, was maintained on 10 grams of vitamin E daily for 30 days until his discharge, and "As far as I know, he never went back onto it." The psychiatrist states that it is not all that unusual for patients given adequate amounts of vitamin E to make a complete recovery and maintain it without continuing the vitamin.

Estimates state that schizophrenics have a suicide rate 22 times higher than the general public, and that 10 out of 100 commit suicide. E. Cheraskin, M.D., D.M.D., and W. M. Ringsdorf, Jr., D.M.D., report in *Psychodietetics* (p. 62) that schizophrenics treated with adequate B3 have a near zero suicide rate.

If this therapy works so well, why don't orthodox psychiatrists use it? Bernard Rimland, Ph.D., points out that Drs. Hoffer and Osmond

> demonstrated clearly in the early 1950's, in a series of carefully executed double-blind studies (the first double-blind studies in psychiatry), that multigram doses of vitamins B3 and C exert a profound ameliorative effect on a large percentage of acute schizophrenics. Most follow-up studies confirmed their findings. By the early 1970's, the Hoffer/Osmond work was receiving so much attention that the American Psychiatric Association set up a Task Force on Megavitamin Therapy.

According to Dr. Rimland, *all* members of the Task Force were already known to believe that megavitamin therapy could not work. One member had stated publicly that even if every psychiatrist in the United States believed megavitamin therapy helped schizophrenics, he still would not believe it. According to Dr. Rimland, the Task Force's report

> was riddled with inaccuracies. For example, negative findings of studies on chronic schizophrenics were cited as disproving the Hoffer/Osmond findings—despite the fact that Hoffer and Osmond themselves had pointed out that their therapy did not help chronic schizophrenics. Positive results were consistently ignored.

While it is true that the early B3-based therapy made no claim to help chronic schizophrenics, only the acute, the therapy has now been substantially refined. Dr. Hoffer reports in his 1989 book *Or-*

thomolecular Medicine for Physicians (p. 38) that it can be expected that 75 percent of chronic schizophrenics who are ambulant when B3-based therapy is begun will recover within two to three years, and 50 percent of chronic schizophrenics who are institutionalized will recover within two to five years. None will be worse. For patients with acute or subacute schizophrenia, Dr. Hoffer reports 90 percent recovery within two years, none worse. He points out that by 1989 the newer B3-based therapy had been used on 100,000 schizophrenics in North America.

Dr. Hoffer recently wrote me about several of his patients who'd had chronic schizophrenia for an average of seven years, without responding to standard treatment, before he saw them. At this point they have been under his care for 10 years. One man with paranoid schizophrenia had been divorced by his wife and disowned by his family because of the severity of his illness, and lived on the streets for three months. "About three years ago," Dr. Hoffer writes, "he graduated from the University of Victoria with a B.A. in Science. He has also been able to reestablish connections with his family. Several of my female patients are happy homemakers, some are single moms looking after their children." One woman, who once set fire to her apartment "in a psychotic frenzy" has been well for about six years and has her own business, supervising more than 12 employees.

Biochemically, how can B3 help schizophrenia? First, let us investigate briefly the adrenochrome theory, which proposes that this abnormal chemical produced in the body can lead to schizophrenia. When Drs. Hoffer and Osmond started their work, it was known that aged adrenaline turned pink, and that when it was administered to patients, they would briefly react with sensory distortions and thinking resembling schizophrenia. Drs. Hoffer and Osmond proposed that adrenaline produced in the body of people with schizophrenia was metabolized abnormally into the pink adrenaline, the active ingredient of which is adrenochrome. Drs. Hoffer and Osmond studied the chemical reactions that convert the helpful adrenaline to the abnormal adrenochrome, and found that large doses of vitamins B3 and C would slow down the conversion—and that the small amount of adrenochrome produced would be neutralized.

Vitamin B3 also can restore activity of the brain chemical acetylcholine; and it can raise levels of serotonin, a brain chemical that naturally helps calm us—or, if you will, acts as a natural tranquilizer.

Vitamin B12, Calcium, Methionine, Zinc, and Manganese. In *Nutrition and Mental Illness* Dr. Pfeiffer discusses therapy for histadelia (high histamine levels), which he identified as the true cause of an estimated 20 percent of schizophrenic cases. "The undiagnosed histadelic patient is treated as a schizophrenic, but the patient does not respond to any of the usual drug therapies or to electroshock or insulin coma therapy." He mentions that histadelia usually runs in families, so we might assume that this disorder may account for a number of cases of familial schizophrenia.

Dr. Pfeiffer and other workers at the Brain Bio Center in Princeton had treated over a thousand of these patients. Therapy included "calcium supplementation, which releases some of the body's stores of histamine, and the natural amino acid methionine, which helps to detoxify histamine by methylation—the usual mode of detoxification of histamine. . . ." He also recommended the minerals zinc and manganese and a diet low in protein and high in complex carbohydrates. He warned that if folic acid is given, "the patient definitely gets worse."

Vitamin B6 and Zinc. Back in 1982, Carlton Fredericks, Ph.D., writing of B6 and zinc, reported in *Eat Well, Get Well, Stay Well* (p. 52) that patients "by the thousands have been treated successfully with this simple therapy . . . at some twenty clinics and three brain bio centers." He added that the mineral manganese was part of this therapy. When zinc is supplemented, it can create a decrease in blood manganese. In 1983, Dr. Pfeiffer pointed out that manganese had been reported in the medical literature since 1927 to help schizophrenia (*Journal of Orthomolecular Psychiatry* Vol. 12, No. 3, p. 216).

Chapter 18 contains information on the important role of vitamin B6 in the production of many brain chemicals.

LOWERING BODY LEVELS OF ANIMAL PROTEIN

The late Allan Cott, M.D., a leading orthomolecular psychiatrist, told me in an interview, "People with schizophrenia tend to have a higher protein level in their bodies than people who do not suffer schizophrenia. We use carefully regulated fasting therapy to get the protein level down to normal. Once that is accomplished, we recommend that the patients fast a few days a month to keep that protein level down." Note that Dr. Cott said *carefully regulated* fasting. It is definitely not advisable to fast without the supervision of a physician experienced in prescribing fasting. For some, unsupervised fasting can be tantamount to suicide.

Dr. Yuri Nicolayev of the Moscow Psychiatric Institute fasted more than 10,000 mentally ill patients over many years, starting in 1945. Most suffered from schizophrenia. In addition to the initial fast, he prescribed a maintenance diet excluding all animal-protein foods. With this regimen, the Soviet psychiatrist reported, 65 percent of patients who had previously not responded to any traditional therapy were returned to *normal functioning*. He continued to examine his normal "incurables" for six years after therapy was started. The only patients who had relapses were those who strayed from therapy by eating animal protein.

Dr. Cott used the same therapy in a study on a smaller number of patients, all of whom had had schizophrenia for five years or more, and all of whom had had no relief from any form of traditional therapy. Dr. Cott achieved even a slightly higher success rate than Dr. Nicolayev, and not one of Dr. Cott's recovered patients had a relapse. Why were there no relapses? "Quite simply because none of my patients cheated by eating animal protein." For more details, see Dr. Cott's book *Fasting as a Way of Life*, pp. 74, 75.

Dr. Mandell points out that some patients in these studies "may have had brain allergies to these high-protein foods," a belief that was shared by Dr. Cott.

TREATING FOOD AND CHEMICAL INTOLERANCES ("ALLERGIES")

Orthomolecular doctors specializing in intolerances, called clinical ecologists, believe that intolerances are at least one factor in many cases of schizophrenia. A study presented by Dr. Mandell to the International Congress of Social Psychiatry in August 1969 in London investigated hospitalized schizophrenics who had not been helped by orthodox therapies. It was found that 88 percent had cerebral (brain) reactions to wheat, 50 percent to corn, and 60 percent to milk.

A number of other studies, published in orthodox journals, suggest that foods, especially wheat and milk, may contribute to symptoms of schizophrenia. Psychiatrist Melvyn R. Werbach, M.D., cites some of these studies in his book *Third Line Medicine*. As long ago as 1973, Drs. Dohan and Grasberger reported in the *American Journal of Psychiatry* (130, pp. 685–88) that some acute schizophrenics improve more rapidly when placed on a diet free of milk and cereal. In 1978, Dr. Karl Verebey et al. suggested in the *Archives of General Psychiatry* (35, pp. 877–88) that the brain requires a certain level of endorphins to function normally. In 1979, Dr. W. Domschke et al. reported in *Lancet* (May 12, p. 1024), that schizophrenics have endorphin levels ten times those of people with normal mental functioning. (Endorphins are naturally produced substances with effects similar to those of morphine.) Recently it has been found that fractions of milk (casein) and wheat (gluten) also have morphinelike activity—hardly needed by people who already have 10 times too much of this activity in their bodies.

Probably every orthomolecular psychiatrist has many case histories of people who were successfully treated when foods or chemicals to which they were intolerant were removed—and who became "schizophrenic" again when reexposed to them. In fact, a basic empirical rationale of clinical ecologists is that they can repeatedly turn symptoms on or off by introducing or withdrawing substances to which the person has tested sensitive.

Karl E. Humiston, M.D., tells of Janice, "a young lady who had suffered years from schizophrenia until I took over her care and got her off the foods she tested out to be intolerant to. Her spirit had been severely damaged by her years of 'schizophrenia' (that is, food intolerance)." Dr. Humiston and his wife, a psychotherapist and registered nurse, took her into their home as a foster child.

> In this way we could give her the around-the-clock emotional support that one's doctor or psychotherapist can never give.
>
> Janice was for the most part a model foster child. But occasionally she would suddenly start hearing voices again and throwing furniture around. If my wife and I had been average foster parents, we might have immediately packed her off to the nearest agency that would take her off our hands.
>
> But I had known that Janice's "schizophrenia" came basically from intolerance to certain foods, principally chicken. Sure enough, I could always trace her attacks to the fact that someone in an apartment nearby was cooking chicken. The odor was wafting into the hall; and, because of her intolerance, she could smell it. I would do whatever was necessary to remove Janice from the odor. Invariably, soon she would again be a very sweet, loving human being—whom any psychiatrist might meet and never connect her with the word "psychosis."

Smelling odors that "aren't there" has been considered one of the mental symptoms of schizophrenia. Clinical ecologists consider that the odors are there in low concentrations, and that other people don't smell them because they are not especially sensitive to them. Dr. Philpott, a pioneer in clinical ecology as well as in orthomolecular psychiatry, tells an early case history:

> Karl was a paranoid schizophrenic whom I hospitalized for fasting prior to testing for food and chemical sensitivities. On the

first morning in the hospital, Karl complained of "the gas smell." My orthodox psychiatric training would have led me to conclude that this nonexistent odor was just another one of Karl's schizophrenic hallucinations. But my newer understanding of chemical intolerance led me to look for a possible real source of "the gas smell." Around the corner from Karl's room, I found a door leading to a stairway. I opened the door and to my surprise I smelled gas, too. The stairway led to the hospital kitchen, which used gas for cooking. I placed the boy in another room, far from the gas smell. After several days of fasting, Karl's paranoid-schizophrenic symptoms had disappeared. I then tested Karl by giving him auto-exhaust-fume extract—without telling him what he was being tested with. In about two minutes, he announced to me that he was Jesus Christ.

Smoking is another common factor behind symptoms of schizophrenia. Just as the toxic substances in tobacco can cause disorders of the heart, lungs, etc., they can cause disorders of the brain. Dr. Philpott, in an interview, referred to an early study run by Dr. Mandell and himself at Fuller Memorial Sanitarium in South Attleboro, Massachusetts. "We were able to show that 75 percent of the schizophrenics who smoked had important mental symptoms when we tested them with a solution of tobacco smoke." Drs. Philpott and Mandell agree that "We were astounded" when 10 percent of this group became acutely psychotic all over again when permitted to smoke after stopping for a few weeks.

TREATING INFECTIONS

In an interview, Dr. Philpott gave a case history of very early work with infection as a factor behind schizophrenia. "In 1972 a girl had been admitted with catatonic schizophrenia, just standing and staring like a statue. When we fasted her, the catatonia cleared up. In those days, that was considered good proof that her problem was basically due to food intolerances. But the girl had another complaint: vaginal discharge." Dr. Mandell suggested testing her for sensitivity to candida, which often causes vaginal yeast infections that produce vaginal discharge. Dr. Philpott continued: "He put extract of candida under her tongue, and within a couple of minutes, there she was again, standing and staring and catatonic. Well, that was very impressive; and ever since, I have tested very carefully for every infection, bacteria, and fungi. I have found infection to be a factor in a significant number of my psychotic patients."

Dr. Philpott points out that recently the National Institutes of Health decided, after thousands of CT scans were done of the brains of schizophrenic patients, that infection during gestation is a prime cause of schizophrenia's eruption years later.

OTHER APPROACHES

Other orthomolecular maneuvers include checking metabolism of tryptophan (an amino acid that is the raw material for the brain chemical serotonin) and testing for deficiency and excess of omega-6 fatty acids, which are nutritional precursors to hormonelike substances called prostaglandins. Testing for abnormal carbohydrate metabolism is also part of the orthomolecular diagnostic arsenal; estimates are that 50–77 percent of persons with schizophrenia have this abnormal metabolism—which can be corrected by diet. (See Chapter 15.)

ON THE HORIZON

Dr. Philpott, an early pioneer in blood-sugar disturbances (abnormal carbohydrate metabolism) and in food and chemical intolerances, is presently pioneering another therapy. He employs the same knowledge of electric current that is behind the use of electroconvulsive therapy. However, Dr. Philpott's technique does not have the side effects of electroconvulsive therapy: convulsions and memory loss.

Basing his therapy on accepted scientific knowledge, Dr. Philpott uses magnets to bring the ill brain back into normal magnetic balance. This will in turn produce a balanced biochemistry, because all biological life and activity depend upon the energy of a magnetic field. For instance, one of the basics of our body chemistry is the acid/alkaline balance. When this balance is out of whack, we tend to get ill. The negative (north) pole of a magnet has an alkalinizing effect; the positive (south) pole has an acidifying effect. Schizophrenia and virtually all disease states result from more positive energy than negative energy.

Dr. Philpott points out that getting the body into correct polarity also stops viruses from multiplying and rebuilds the immune system so that it can destroy them—thus combatting the infectious causes of schizophrenia.

Since using this technique for schizophrenia and other mental disorders, Dr. Philpott says he is "having very good success, more than I ever had before. And the beautiful thing is that [this therapy] is completely nontoxic." When this technique has become more sophisticated than it is as this book is written, Dr. Philott dreams of a future in which "a person suffering a neurosis or psychosis could walk into any psychiatrist's office, be treated for an hour, and leave in complete mental health." He also hopes for a future in which electromagnetic therapy "has completely wiped shock treatment off the map."

What You Can Do

The underlying causes of the symptoms of schizophrenia as well as the potentially successful treatments are too complex to make home treatment feasible. The following steps may ease the misery while you find an orthomolecular physician and wait for your appointment. For how to find a doctor in your area, see the "Resources" section. More tips are in the Introduction.

Sometimes one or two simple dietary steps give immediate and startling improvement. But if that should happen, please do not believe that tests by an orthomolecular doctor are not needed. There may well be other factors that can lead to dire trouble "down the road."

All household members might consider using these ideas; they are good proposals for the physical and mental health of all of us. Also, if the person is not given a special diet not eaten by the rest of the family, he may feel less "strange."

Follow the suggestions in Chapter 2 for diet, water, and vitamin-mineral supplementation. Use the self-testing technique detailed there for intolerances. Completely cut out all substances that give a "positive" reaction. If that technique seems too cumbersome, at least eliminate milk and gluten (contained in all grains except rice), since so many with symptoms of schizophrenia are intolerant to these.

Try to cut out smoking. For help, see Chapter 5.

Try to cut out caffeine. Read labels carefully. Caffeine occurs in products other than coffees, teas, and colas not labeled "decaffeinated." Animal studies suggest that caffeine can upset the normal balance of three chemicals crucial to the health of our brains: norepinephrine, serotonin, and dopamine.

Dr. Humiston contributes what he calls "a simple exercise that can sometimes work small wonders." You might try it with the person you know who has schizophrenia. Dr. Humiston and his psychotherapist wife, Bonnie, have developed this exercise, which is based on established psychotherapy techniques. This work has not been previously published. Dr. Humiston says:

> Basically, this exercise helps to get the person's mind back in touch with the body. I think you can see that the separation of mind and body is a major factor in schizophrenia: The person's mind hears things that his ears are not really hearing; his mind sees things that his eyes do not really see. One thing that has always amazed me is how often I can look at the chest of a person

with schizophrenia and see no movement. Obviously, the person is breathing, but is managing to do so without the usual involvement of the body that is so instinctive to others.

I'll explain how the exercise works and give an example of how *well* it can work at the same time. While Bonnie was working at a state hospital, she asked the ward staffs to let her work a little with the most hopeless schizophrenics, those who had made the least progress in the last decade. She was given a group of patients who were called the "sit-and-stare-at-the-floor" patients: the schizophrenics who wouldn't talk, wouldn't join other patients for a walk, wouldn't do much of anything except—sit and stare at the floor. Medically, most of these patients had been diagnosed as "chronic undifferentiated schizophrenics."

She would gather these souls together, and she would say, for instance, "Turn your heads to the right. Can you do that?" Some could only make the tiniest turn of their heads; but at least they were beginning to connect their minds to their bodies. For others, turning their heads even a fraction of an inch was beyond their capabilities; but the idea of doing that was nevertheless going into their consciousness.

When they no longer found it difficult to turn their heads when asked, she led them to more sophisticated connections with their bodies, such as "Wiggle your toes. How do they feel moving around inside your shoes?" Then, "Touch your first finger to your thumb, your second finger, your third. What does it *feel* like?"

After only a few weeks, these "sit-and-stare-at-the-floor" schizophrenics were looking up at people, walking toward them, even smiling at them. They were *talking*. And when the staff asked, "Who wants to go outside for a walk?" they went. The only thing that had changed in their therapy was Bonnie's twice-a-week sessions.

[THERE IS] IN the mentally retarded a potential that often is never achieved; and I prefer, as do some fine medical nutritionists, to look upon the mentally retarded as being mentally dormant, awaiting awakening. The philosophy is not based on wishful thinking. Dr. Henry Turkel, unrecognized, unsung, has been upgrading Down's syndrome children successfully for many decades . . . Under your doctor's eye, there is a wide range of supplements that, added to good diet, may stimulate cerebral function. . . .

—CARLTON FREDERICKS, PH.D., *Carlton Fredericks' Nutrition Guide for the Prevention and Cure of Common Ailments & Diseases* (pp. 119–121)

RETARDATION IS A particularly bad [word], for it takes the child away from medical treatment and into a pedagogical stream. . . . There certainly are children who cannot learn due to a number of metabolic factors. . . . Once these are treated, what appeared to be retardation disappears.

—ABRAM HOFFER, M.D., PH.D., *Orthomolecular Medicine for Physicians* (p. 205)

Chapter 9

Mental Retardation

Orthomolecular doctors state that in some cases, mental retardation is really "pseudoretardation," stemming from undiagnosed nutritional problems.

Improvement for many patients with Down syndrome, the disorder most commonly related to retardation, has been reported for several decades by a clinic here in America and doctors in Japan and other countries.

Prevention of mental retardation and other birth defects is highly possible. Roger J. Williams, Ph.D., a world-famous nutrition researcher who discovered the B vitamin pantothenic acid, said in 1971: "If all prospective human mothers could be fed as expertly as prospective animal mothers in the laboratory . . . the birth of deformed and mentally retarded babies would be largely a thing of the past" *(Nutrition Against Disease)*. This chapter covers some of the knowledge discovered in the years since 1971 that makes his words even more true today.

Orthomolecular Therapy for Mental Retardation

As long ago as 1964, Carlton Fredericks, Ph.D., in his book *Nutrition: Your Key to Good Health* (pp. 54–56) advised against totally accepting a diagnosis of mental retardation because "this attitude implies complete and abject surrender to the inevitable, *which may not be inevitable.*" He expressed "concern and wonderment . . . that the subject of nutrition is largely neglected in scientific discussions on the problems of the retarded child or adult, especially in the light of knowledge that the basis of thinking is in part biochemical." As detailed throughout this book, all biochemical reactions in the brain and the rest of the body are dependent upon nutrients.

VITAMINS AND MINERALS

Carl C. Pfeiffer, Ph.D., M.D., states in his 1987 book *Nutrition and Mental Illness* (p. 44) that mental retardation can stem from chronic deficiency of zinc and vitamin B6. "We have examined and treated children in the age range of 3 to 15 years who were labeled as having 'mental retardation' or 'minimal brain dysfunction' or 'learning disability.' When the young patient has a high level of pyrroles in the urine, a low serum immunoglobulin A, and facial swelling with a history of frequent colds and middle ear infections, pyroluria should be suspected." Pyroluria is an abnormal production of chemicals called pyrroles. This condition, Dr. Pfeiffer states, robs the body of vitamin B6 and zinc. Treatment, of course, involves restoring adequate body levels of these nutrients.

A study using vitamins and minerals with 16 mentally retarded children (IQs 17–70) ultimately resulted in four children (25%) showing an IQ gain of 30–40 points. This jump in IQ (from the mid-60s to mid-90s and over 100) meant that they were no longer mentally retarded, and they were transferred to regular school classes. (These four children, as reported in the *Brain Mind Bulletin* Theme Pack, 1981, had continued to take the supplements after the formal study had ended.) All 16 of the children studied had a gain in IQ (R. F. Harrell, et al., *Proceedings of the National Academy of Sciences*, 1981, 78, 574–78).

The study included four children with Down syndrome. Three of these four had recorded IQ gains of 11 to 24 points and lost some of the accumulation of facial fluids that contributes to the characteristically swollen features of children with Down syndrome.

The children achieved these results basically by taking six pills daily containing 11 vitamins and eight minerals. Their diet, schooling, and socialization were unchanged. No child had a significant rise in IQ while taking a placebo.

A sad sidelight reported by the *Brain Mind Bulletin:* One 15-year-old, who had achieved normal grade-level performance by following the regimen after the study had ended, was taken off the supplements at the insistence of the family physician, who suspected that this treatment was quackery. The teenager's newly acquired higher IQ level deteriorated to under 50.

As this book is written, the above study is not generally accepted, because follow-up studies by other scientists have not found the same results. Donald R. Davis, Ph.D., research associate at the University of Texas at Austin, points out, however, that most if not all the studies testing out Dr. Harrell's have not truly replicated her research protocol, and that this may well be why they have not got the same results. (While many of the quotes attributed in this chapter to Dr. Davis originated from a 1989 speech at the Nutritional Conference of the Princeton Bio Center, he covers similar material in a book chapter that is a good source of references, particularly for health professionals: Nutrition in the Prevention and Reversal of Mental Retardation, in *Preventive and Curative Intervention in Mental Retardation.*)

I mention Dr. Harrell's work so you can make your own decisions about pursuing its implications further with a nutritional doctor. A more recent study on the subject of raising IQ with vitamins and minerals appeared in *Lancet,* a highly respected orthodox peer review medical journal, by David Benton and Gwilym Roberts (No. 8578, pp. 140–43). The study showed a significant increase in nonverbal IQ scores for children taking a daily multivitamin-mineral supplement.

There are also indications that certain vitamins, used alone, can be helpful for a few mentally retarded who have inborn errors of metabolism. For instance, folic acid has been found to help some whose retardation is connected with fragile-X syndrome. This syndrome is a major inherited disorder of males, and it is second only to Down syndrome as an identified cause of mental retardation. Usually retardation is moderate to severe. Behavior problems include poor ability for self-expression, hyperactivity, and autisticlike symptoms. Many reports since 1981 have confirmed that folic acid supplements reduce, or eliminate, the fragility of X chromosomes in tissue culture. (See Chapter 13 for more on autism and folic acid.)

Studies indicate that folic acid sometimes results in little or no improvement in IQ or behavior, but at other times gives rather dramatic improvements in both. It appears to "work" best when given to boys before puberty.

GLUTAMIC ACID

Use of glutamic acid is another approach not yet fully accepted. One of this amino acid's functions is to serve as a fuel, or stimulant, for the brain. In the 1940s, it was reported that children treated with glutamic acid for petit mal seizures of epilepsy showed improved personality and mental acuity. These reports prompted a flurry of studies in which either glutamic acid or a salt such as sodium glutamate was given to retarded children. These studies were reviewed by one pair of researchers in 1960 and by several other researchers in 1966. Dr. Davis points out that the first doctors reviewed only about half the available literature (and did so without noting that fact). They concluded that no benefit had been convincingly demonstrated. It is this viewpoint that currently prevails.

However, the researchers who reviewed the literature in 1966 disputed the earlier review. For instance, they found many more positive studies than the doctors did in 1960, and noted that the positive studies tended to use glutamic acid, rather than a glutamate salt, and tended to vary the dosage levels for individuals.

Nutritionist Lelord Kordel in his book *Health Through Nutrition* (pp. 49–50) recounts case histories from a study that *did* use glutamic acid and used it in varying dosages. When Marie was five, her attempts at speech were so unintelligible that even her mother could not understand her. At nine, her speech had "progressed" to the point where she could manage a few understandable words. She would sit all day, "like a living soul in a dead body," staring out the window watching other children at play.

Marie was enrolled in a study at Columbia University, along with 43 other mentally retarded children, 11 epileptics, and 14 normal children. "For six months Marie and her fellow patients (ranging in age from 16 months to 17 years) were fed pure glutamic acid three times daily. The dose for each child ranged from 6 to 24 grams."

Before starting in the study, Marie had tested out to have an IQ of 69 (technically within the "moron" range). After six months of glutamic acid therapy, Marie took the same type of test and scored 87. Instead of sitting all day staring out the window at the other children at play, Marie was now down on the sidewalk with them, "as eager for her turn as her playmates who had never been handicapped by a subnormal mentality." And she had another new interest to engage in when she wasn't enjoying herself with her new playmates: reading.

Kordel states that results with the other 43 mentally retarded children were "equally as promising," mentioning a 17-year-old boy who, before taking glutamic acid, scored 107 (normal) on the IQ test. After six months of taking glutamic acid, "the boy scored 120 on a similar test, thereby being elevated to the 'superior intelligence' class."

Since Kordel reported on that study, nutritionally oriented doctors such as Carlton Fredericks and Richard A. Passwater, Ph.D., have reported that L-glutamine is even more effective than glutamic acid.

TREATING INTOLERANCES ("ALLERGIES")

As mentioned throughout this book, clinical ecologists report that intolerances to foods, chemicals, and/or inhalants can result in virtually any symptom in individual patients, including impaired mental performance. Marshall Mandell, M.D., a pioneering clinical ecologist, recently wrote me of an early (1965) case history that was the first to alert him to the fact that intolerances could cause symptoms of what he calls "allergic pseudoretardation." He was testing an eight-year-old boy only for possible allergies that might be causing his nasal and bronchial symptoms. The child was also "hyperactive physically and sluggish mentally with a slow groping-for-words type of speech. And he had poor spelling and very poor handwriting." When Dr. Mandell tested him for possible intolerances to beef and milk, to see if these intolerances were behind his nasal and bronchial problems, the boy became withdrawn, confused, and his speech became even slower and more slurred.

> I felt sorry for him as he pathetically struggled to find the right words to communicate with me. He also became a little pale, and I wondered if his pale face might be associated with a "pale brain" that was reacting to a decreased oxygen supply from allergically contracted cerebral arteries that added to the allergic reaction in the neurons of his brain. I was struck by the thought that I had just made a mildly retarded child more retarded with a provocative test for food allergy!

As the boy's intolerances were treated "he became bright-eyed and alert, was no longer hyperactive, and spoke in a clear voice free of stammering or hesitation." Only a few weeks after treatment was started, Dr. Mandell met a neighbor of his patient, "who asked me what drugs I had prescribed, because he was such a different child." In addition, the child's mother, a teacher, reported "a great change in his spelling and handwriting" after only four days of therapy.

Dr. Mandell adds that it became obvious that the boy had lived under "an allergic cloud" that had interfered with his life by bringing on not only respiratory, but mental, symptoms. Still obviously affected by this first-of-its-kind case history from 30 years ago, Dr. Mandell ended his letter to me: "He was not retarded! He had brain allergies!"

THE "U" SERIES FOR DOWN (DOWN'S) SYNDROME

The late Henry Turkel, M.D., observed that Down syndrome ("mongolism") has never actually been as devastating as doctors thought. Dr. Turkel, who for several decades pioneered a treatment for Down syndrome, stated in 1986 in the *Journal of Orthomolecular Medicine* (Vol. 1, No. 4, pp. 219–29):

> Forty years ago, parents were advised to institutionalize their "mongoloid" infants at birth because, their doctors predicted, they would never learn to walk, talk, or be toilet trained, and their presence would destroy the family. Twenty years ago, when the majority of doctors were still warning parents that their children with Down syndrome would be severely retarded, our testing indicated that of those brought to this clinic, most functioned at or near the level of mild retardation before treatment.

The clinic Dr. Turkel referred to was the Turkel Clinic for Down Syndrome in Southfield, Michigan.

Using the therapy he pioneered (the "U" Series, a rather complicated combination of vitamins, minerals, enzymes, hormones, and drugs), Dr. Turkel, later of Jerusalem, Israel, reported significant improvement in 80–90 percent of 600 children with Down syndrome. As mentioned later in this section, another doctor, although using an abbreviated version of Dr. Turkel's therapy, has reported both physical and mental improvement in many patients—including almost normal mentation. Since 1964 physicians in Japan have announced good results in over three thousand patients, although using a restricted version of the "U" Series.

Dr. Turkel also reported that "all adults with Down syndrome above the age of 30 or 35 are believed to have the neuropathologic and biochemical changes diagnostic of Alzheimer's disease. . . . To date, reports indicate that no patient treated with the 'U' Series has developed Alzheimer's disease. . . . Some of these patients are now in their 40's and 50's."

Dr. Turkel stated that there is even "a 70–80% probability that the untreated person with Down syndrome will not experience the devastating behavioral changes of Alzheimer's disease by age 40." Dr. Turkel wrote with compassion of the unnecessary pain felt by parents who cope bravely with retardation in their children, and who then read that their children will develop Alzheimer's disease almost as soon as they have developed a semi-independent lifestyle.

Dr. Turkel described some patients who had been treated with the "U" Series and who were then in their thirties and forties.

> Janie L. lives in Arizona in her own apartment. She walks to work, keeps her checkbook balanced, pays her rent, and treats her friends to meals at her home or at a restaurant. . . . Jonathan lives with his wife in an apartment in Chicago. He supports the family as an employee of the post office. Patient S., whose father had Alzheimer's disease, was an "old man" of 40 when he started treatment. He became more vivacious, worked as a farm hand for his uncle, and took up horseback riding.

Dr. Turkel gave a technical rationale for how the "U" Series works to help those with Down syndrome. To summarize: Trisomy 21 is the physical abnormality that results in the disorder. Trisomy means a birth defect resulting from the presence of three copies of a chromosome, rather than the normal two copies. Trisomy 21, then, is the presence of three copies of chromosome 21. Dr. Turkel stated, "Trisomy 21 results in excessive gene products that interfere with nutrition prenatally and postnatally, retard development of all organs and their functions, and produce the anomalies of Down syndrome. Wastes accumulate in all tissues because organs of waste elimination are inefficient." It is the accumulation of wastes that gives the distorted, "puffed-up" look to the face and body.

According to Dr. Turkel, "The 'U' Series . . . synergistically reduces accumulated wastes and provides nutrients. The patient's entire body develops more normally in structure and function."

Although Dr. Turkel's basic therapy has been used in Japan since 1964, is accepted as alternative therapy in Norway, and is available in many other countries, Dr. Davis states that studies done on the "U" Series have not been scientifically controlled, or reported, in such a way as to satisfy this country's academic community. Thus, questions remain "such as what are the *individual* contributions (if any) of the various nutrients and drugs; and how much is lost by omitting the drugs, as Dr. Tanino did?"

Dr. Davis refers to Y. Tanino, a physician at Kyoto University. Dr. Tanino, noting the complexity of Dr. Turkel's regimen, tried large doses of 11 vitamins alone in about 60 children with Down syndrome. He reported his results in 1966 in *Annales Paediatrici Japonici* (12, pp. 31–45): both physical and mental improvements— including almost normal level of mentation—in many subjects, particularly in young boys treated for five years or longer.

Prevention

A warning was issued in 1978 by the U.S. Occupational Safety and Health Administration concerning occupational exposure to lead. According to Derek Bryce-Smith, D.Sc., Ph.D., writing in the 1986 *International Journal of Biosocial Research* (8(2), pp. 126–27), this warning "noted that children born of parents, either of whom had been exposed to lead, are at increased risk of birth defects, early death, mental retardation, and behavioral disorders." Although it has been traditional to think that only what the mother is exposed to can harm the unborn child, research in the last two decades indicates that a number of agents can also adversely affect children by affecting the father's genetic material or quality of sperm.

Proper nutritional steps, prescribed by a doctor specializing in nutrition, can help prevent birth defects or mental impairment that would otherwise be caused by lead or other toxic metals. You can find more details on metal toxicity in Chapters 4 and 17.

It is well known that alcohol and hard drugs such as crack cocaine can produce birth defects. So can some prescribed or even over-the-counter medicines. You may know of the tragic birth defects (for instance, babies born with half-formed legs or arms) caused by the drug thalidomide, once used as a sedative. Even aspirin, commonly taken by women during pregnancy, is now suspected of causing birth defects, and pain-reliever packaging carries warnings to seek medical advice before using the products. Drug side effects are often the result of nutritional deficiencies or imbalances caused by the drugs; proper nutritional measures may ward off the side effects.

METABOLIC ERRORS

Mainstream medicine is well aware that for many inborn errors of metabolism that result in mental retardation, the retardation can be prevented by proper nutritional measures early in the child's life. These disorders include phenylketonuria, urea cycle defects, and galactosemia. Phenylketonuria is a defect in metabolism of the amino acid phenylalanine; most types of this disorder respond well to diets low in this nutrient. Urea cycle defects involve toxic accumulation of ammonia in the blood because of impaired metabolism of all amino acids. "When the impairment is not too severe," Dr. Davis says, "restriction of dietary protein can prevent retardation if treatment is begun early, usually within a few days or weeks of age." Galactosemia stems from faulty metabolism of galactose, found in lactose from milk; restricting galactose can prevent retardation.

PREECLAMPSIA AND ECLAMPSIA

Preeclampsia (formerly called toxenia of pregnancy) is a complication of late pregnancy that occurs in about 5 percent of pregnancies in this country. It kills over 35,000 babies every year and leaves many thousands more mentally retarded or crippled. Severe preeclampsia may strike the mother-to-be with seizures (eclampsia), stroke, blindness, and death. Dr. Davis states that at this time medical textbooks almost without exception state that the etiology is unknown. Of course, if the factors behind a disorder are "unknown," one can do little or nothing to try to prevent it.

However, Dr. Davis says that "the time seems near when medical texts will no longer say that the factors involved in the development of preeclampsia and eclampsia are unknown. We already know enough empirically to hope that basic nutritional improvements to commonly marginal U.S. diets can greatly reduce the incidence of this major crippler of children."

An impressive study on preventing preeclampsia and eclampsia was published back in 1952 in the orthodox medical journal *Lancet* (1, pp. 64–68). When Dr. R. H. J. Hamlin became medical supervisor of an Australian women's hospital, the rate of eclampsia was one case in 350 pregnancies, a rate that had remained constant for 11 years (1936–47). After three years of a diet-centered prevention program, this rate dropped dramatically, reaching zero convulsions (episodes of eclampsia) in five thousand patients the third year. Other symptoms of severe preeclampsia also dropped sharply.

In 1963 Dr. T. H. Brewer began a diet-oriented prevention program at his county prenatal clinics for women of low socioeconomic class in California. The diet emphasized high protein and whole foods. Over half the patients belonged to ethnic minorities, and two thirds of those having their first babies were teenagers. Usually these groups of poor women have high rates of preeclampsia—up to 30 percent. Yet in over seven thousand pregnancies during the 12 years of this program, Dr. Brewer reported preeclampsia in only 0.5 percent. This is not only far below the 30 percent often cited for poor women, but is also far below the national average of 5 percent. Also, Dr. Brewer reported not one case of eclampsia. You can read more about Dr. Brewer's work in *Metabolic Toxemia of Late Pregnancy: A Disease of Malnutrition* (Charles C. Thomas, 1966) and

G. S. Brewer and T. Brewer, *What Every Pregnant Woman Should Know: The Truth About Drugs and Diet in Pregnancy* (Random House, 1977).

Dr. Davis echoes sentiments stated in Chapter 1 about medicine's information gap, when he says, "I find it astounding that these studies [by Drs. Hamlin and Brewer] have been so neglected."

Dr. Davis points out that recent studies have found that "small or moderate amounts of magnesium supplementation during pregnancy help to prevent preeclampsia. For over 60 years, magnesium injected in large doses has been considered by obstetricians to be the preferred 'anticonvulsant drug' in severe preeclampsia or eclampsia. Yet it has taken all this time for researchers to consider magnesium for *prevention.*" Dr. Davis is concerned that "this new blossoming of interest in the academic world for magnesium may result in too much attention to using magnesium as an isolated nutrient. If a woman's body is deficient in magnesium, it may likely be deficient in other nutrients, too."

NEURAL TUBE DEFECTS

Neural tube defects are malformations of the brain and spine, including spina bifida and anencephaly. In some babies the defects can be relatively minor, but others are born with their brains outside of their skulls, or their spinal cords outside of their spines—and some have no brain or spinal cord at all. In this country, there are about five thousand live births every year with serious neural tube defects. About fifteen thousand more babies with this disorder are miscarried or spontaneously aborted every year. Roughly half of those who manage to "make it" to birth die shortly afterward.

In his 1989 speech, Dr. Davis stated, "The overall evidence is so strong that proper nutrition, particularly with folic acid, can dramatically help prevent neural tube defects that most persons consider it unethical as well as impractical to do any more double-blind studies" (studies in which some members do not receive treatment).

It was over three years later that the U.S. Public Health Service recommended that all women who are capable of becoming pregnant "consume 0.4 mg of folic acid per day for the purpose of reducing their risk of having a pregnancy affected with spina bifida or other NTDs [neural tube defects]."

Dr. Davis points to an important factor in the discovery that neural tube defects can be prevented nutritionally: "This finding promises to be the first unquestionable proof in humans that a *congenital* defect is related to inadequate nutrition." He mentions that "research has been clearly showing since 1933 that faulty nutrition can cause congenital malformations in mammals, and that proper nutrition can prevent such malformations. Many have been reluctant to accept the implications of this research."

What You Can Do

If you are planning on having a baby, it is important to cut out drugs, alcohol, and smoking. (The chapter on addiction may help.) Remember that drugs not considered addictive, such as aspirin, also may harm the unborn baby. Do your best to avoid them, or consult a nutritional doctor for ways to offset possible negative effects.

While the chapter on prevention can be of help, it is not geared toward a pregnant woman, who needs proper nutrition not only for herself but for her unborn child. An orthomolecular physician will run tests to decide exactly what diet and nutrients you and your developing baby need for optimal health. Remember that research increasingly shows certain factors in the father's health can harm an unborn child; make sure the father-to-be is not left out of your doctor's visit. The "Resources" section will help you find an orthomolecular physician near you.

It is important that you do not wait until you are pregnant before taking these steps. Neural tube defects, for instance, occur during spinal development in the first weeks after conception, when many women do not realize they are pregnant.

Do not assume your doctor knows all there is to know about

preventing birth defects through nutrition, especially if the physician is not an orthomolecular specialist. For instance, a survey of New York area obstetricians and gynecologists found that the majority interviewed were not familiar with what was then the latest research about neural tube defects. Barbara Levine, Ph.D., R.D., director of the Nutritional Information Center at New York Hospital–Cornell University Medical Center, conducted the survey, which also found that most doctors "do not recommend vitamin supplementation to those who are considering or trying to conceive," and "the majority of physicians interviewed assume that if a woman is at her ideal body weight she is eating a balanced diet."

By taking the steps recommended above, you will guard your child not only against possible retardation, but against other birth defects as well. And you will be optimizing your own health.

If you are trying to help someone who already has mental retardation, you have seen from this chapter that nutritional therapy can be too complex and variable to lend itself to self-help. You must work with an orthomolecular doctor.

You can safely take a few steps on your own while waiting to see the physician. Read Chapter 2 and put your loved one on a good basic diet and vitamin-mineral supplement. *(Dr. Fredericks has warned that supplements should not be chosen by lay people for someone with Down syndrome. For instance, one form of vitamin D is toxic for people with this disorder.)* Follow the other suggestions in Chapters 2 and 14 to protect your loved one and yourself from the harmful effects of food and chemical intolerances. Chapters 4 and 17 give self-help tips on heavy-metal toxicity.

Orthomolecular psychiatrist Karl E. Humiston, M.D., tells of an emotional awareness he gained about retarded people, an awareness that, he says, is not taught to psychiatrists in their academic training:

> At the time, all my personal upbringing and all my academic training as an orthodox psychiatrist had led me to believe that the only thing that was really valuable or important about hu-

man beings was their IQ. Then I was asked by leaders in my church to teach a Sunday-school class to a group of mentally retarded people. On the first day, as the class assembled, I was dismayed. How was I going to teach anything to these people with the vacant eyes? Some of them couldn't talk; they would try mightily, but only strange sounds like "Uh rrrr rrr kkk" would come out. How could I ever teach them to sing a hymn?

However, it was *I* who was to learn something that day. Those who couldn't talk could sing with much more clarity. My personal opinion is that this was because singing is more from the spirit, and less from the mind. What hit me with great force that day was the *spirits* of these people. Their minds were damaged; for many of them, their bodies were severely damaged also. Yet they all retained a spirit that was undiminished and undamaged. I ended up teaching my class much more successfully than I had thought possible—by trying my best to relate to the intact human spirit that was behind those vacant eyes.

Dr. Humiston's experience is reminiscent of a statement made by Dr. Pfeiffer: "Perhaps if doctors would treat these children as being only 'mentally dormant,' their prognoses for recovery would be greatly improved."

EVERY PENAL INSTITUTION that has used the low-sugar
diet reports a decrease in antisocial activity of about 48
percent.

—STEPHEN J. SCHOENTHALER, PH.D, associate professor of
sociology and criminal justice, California State
University–Stanislaus, personal interview

IF A PERSON with criminal or violent tendencies is
hypoglycemic, I don't believe there can be any
successful management unless the person stays away
from sugar. If they don't, nothing else is going to
work.

—KARL E. HUMISTON, M.D. (personal interview)

Chapter 10

Criminal Behavior and Violence

The following true occurrences may seem implausible if it is assumed that criminal behavior and violence are matters of deep-rooted psychology, "bad" personality, or unfortunate socioeconomic background. Viewed from the orthomolecular belief that criminal behavior and violence may be due to directly treatable biochemical problems, these occurrences will make perfect sense.

Occurrence No. 1: In 1978 a study devised in Fulton County, Georgia, public schools gave three pairs of rats to schoolchildren who were instructed to feed each pair a different diet. They fed one pair a prescribed healthy diet, another a diet typically eaten by humans in this country, and the third a diet consisting only of refined carbohydrates and milk. The first pair fared as happy, calm, and healthy, and the children often made pets of them. The rats fed the typical American diet became fat, lazy, and unalert. The children were afraid to pick them up, because the animals became skittish, frightened, and agitated at the slightest touch. The rats fed the refined carbohydrate–milk diet were nervous, skinny, and—even when left untouched in their cages—wild. If the youngsters attempted to touch them, they were often bitten. It was not uncommon for the children to beg their teachers to let them feed "our vicious and sick" rats the same diet they had been feeding the first pair.

Occurrence No. 2: Occasionally, when offenders have learned of research showing that dietary changes might stem their antisocial behavior, they have legally petitioned for such a change. And they have done what they could on their own, such as refusing sugary foods. Interestingly, some of those attempting a self-cure had been considered "incorrigibles": criminals who delighted in violence, or were compulsively driven to repeatedly commit crimes. Psychologist Alexander Schauss, Ph.D., in his book *Diet, Crime, and Delinquency* (pp. 8–10) tells of a group of over 40 inmates at the U.S. penitentiary at McNeil Island, Washington, who in the late 1970s appealed to the Federal Bureau of Prisons to alter their diet and to increase the availability of nutritional supplements. The Bureau denied the request.

Occurrence No. 3: Researchers are scientifically investigating hair samples of criminals and nonoffenders. With high accuracy, they can tell which hair samples are those of criminals and which aren't. They do this by evaluating the levels of certain minerals in the hair samples (and thus in the bodies and brains) of the unknown subjects.

William H. Philpott, M.D., a major pioneering orthomolecular psychiatrist and clinical ecologist, gives the following case history. It shows graphically a fact detailed later in this chapter: that milk can, in some persons, set in motion chemical reactions that end in violence. (Remember that the schoolchildren's most vicious rats were fed a diet high in milk.)

The young man's mother brought him to Dr. Philpott because the boy had developed the habit of grabbing young girls and choking them. He had also physically attacked his school principal. The tests Dr. Philpott administered gave him scientific reason to believe that the young man's basic problem came from his body's biochemical reaction to the extremely large amount of milk he was drinking: "With his mother sitting beside him in my office, I fed him an average-sized glass of milk. For 15 minutes, the three of us sat around calmly, talking of this-and-that. Suddenly, for no discernible psychological or sociological reason, the boy jumped up and began to choke his mother. I grabbed him; but his intent to kill her was so strong that I practically had to choke *him* before I could force him to release her."

If Dr. Philpott had not been around when the young man reacted to that glass of milk, would the local headlines the next day have read: "Son kills mother. No motive known"? How many actual headlines like this could have been prevented simply by not eating a food to which one was intolerant?

Basic Orthomolecular Approaches to Violent Behavior

In this section, you will read a statistic of 45–54 percent decrease in antisocial behavior for one dietary approach. While this statistic might seem high compared to the relative lack of success we have come to expect from traditional treatment of criminals, bear in mind that there are a number of other approaches in the arsenal of orthomolecular medicine. According to individual biochemical problems, many people who could not be included in the above high statistic might be helped by a treatment that uses two or more orthomolecular approaches.

LOW-SUGAR DIET

Recent success with treating criminal behavior by means of diet owes much to the research of Stephen J. Schoenthaler, Ph.D., associate professor of sociology and criminal justice at California State University–Stanislaus. In an interview, Dr. Schoenthaler told a behind-the-scenes story of the first of his series of studies, which show that a low-sugar diet can cut antisocial behavior by up to 54 percent. (The study was run in 1981 at Tidewater Detention Center in Virginia.) A double-blind study, in which neither staff nor subjects know who is receiving the tested material and who is not, is considered especially reputable because it reduces the possibility of misperceived results due to expectations. Dr. Schoenthaler points out, "Actually, this study was *completely* blind, because neither the staff nor the subjects even knew there was a study going *on*."

This unique circumstance led to an unusual meeting after the study had run four months. "The unit chief—the only one who knew a study was taking place—asked the staff if anyone had noticed any changes in the last several months. We knew that the antisocial behavior had fallen off 48%; we just hadn't told them."

The staff agreed that "things have become a lot calmer around here; there's a lot less trouble." The supervisor asked if anyone had any ideas as to what might have caused the sudden change. Dr. Schoenthaler says, "There was a dead silence." Finally, "to fill the silence," someone joked that the answer must be astrological, pointing out that there had been a shift in the stars at about the time the new peaceful period had begun.

"So it was rather obvious that the staff had not guessed that any sort of a study had been going on, let alone that the study had involved a change in diet. Thus, there was virtually no possibility that they had noticed a lessening of tension because they psychologically expected this study to work. What was also telling," Dr. Schoenthaler concludes, "was that even when the staff was finally told about the study, about half of them still protested that they couldn't believe that a change in diet could have any effect on antisocial behavior."

In 1994, Dr. Schauss wrote me that very few penal institutions have inculcated low-sugar diets. "I know of a number of institutions that showed a decline in antisocial behavior because of studies but went back to the old diet anyway, usually from pressure from dietitians, physicians, administrators, etc."

Dr. Schoenthaler does not believe that it was primarily sugar itself that had caused the antisocial behavior. "What we found was that the people who responded to the low-sugar diet had been marginally malnourished. This malnourishment came from the fact that they were consuming a high portion of their diet in the form of sugar. Sugar has no nutrients; thus, these people were eating a diet deficient in nutrients. When the brain is deficient in even one nutrient, it cannot function optimally."

Occasionally it is pointed out that Dr. Schoenthaler's diet also tends to be low in fat. Dr. Schauss says that fat, like sugar, "accounts for many calories in the diet but contains no essential vitamins and minerals."

In Dr. Schoenthaler's studies, the low-sugar diet had little or no effect on females. Yet, when orange juice was added at meals and as an evening snack, both males and females showed decreased antisocial behavior. At present, Dr. Schoenthaler says, it is not clear whether the juice was helpful because it is high in several nutrients (including vitamins B1 and C) that are often low in people with antisocial behavior—or whether some other factor was involved. For instance, the subjects may have substituted the juice for quantities of milk.

(Information on Dr. Schoenthaler's work was obtained basically in private interviews. Details are published in *Nutrition and Brain Function*, W. Essman, editor, Karger Publishing Company, Basel, Switzerland, 1986; in *Nutrition Today*, 1985, 20(3):16–25; and in numerous issues of *The International Journal of Biosocial Research*, including 3(1):1–9, 1982; 4(1):25–39, 1983; 5(2):79–87, 88–98, and 99–106, 1983; 7(2):108–131, 1985; and 9(2):161–181, 1987.)

BLOOD-SUGAR PROBLEMS

Testing for problems such as unstable or low blood sugar ("hypoglycemia") may be considered tied in with the previous approach, since cutting out sugar and refined flour products is part of the therapy for blood-sugar disorders. (See Chapter 15.)

Dr. Schauss refers in his book, *Diet, Crime, and Delinquency* (pp. 19, 24), to "a vast medical literature suggesting the role blood sugar disorders can play in antisocial behavior" and cites studies as far back as 1921 and appearing in prestigious orthodox publications. Yet although "repeated studies have demonstrated an unusually high rate of hypoglycemia (averaging 80–85%) among offenders . . . most correctional facility medical personnel still treat the problem as nonexistent."

Dr. Schoenthaler states, "The role of low blood sugar in aggressive behavior has been so well proven that even the A.M.A. officially announced in 1984 that low blood sugar is linked to aggressive behavior."

Dr. Schauss (p. 20) cites a case history from orthomolecular psychiatrist Abram Hoffer, M.D., Ph.D. The man had been in jail seven times in 10 years, usually "because he liked to attack policemen." When he was examined, "he began to perspire profusely and suddenly he pulled out a two-pound jug full of sugar which he began to consume in large quantities. He told the doctor, 'This is the only thing that keeps me well.' He was tested and it was found he had severe [reactive] hypoglycemia. He was placed on a diet and over the next ten-year period did not have any more difficulty."

Karl E. Humiston, M.D., gives another case history.

> I was medical director and psychiatrist for the mental health unit inside the Idaho State Penitentiary. The men in my unit were too dangerous to be outside prison and too mentally disturbed to be inside prison. I performed a standard five-hour glucose tolerance test on them, which showed that all 12 had unstable blood-sugar levels. The two who were the most explosive and violent—they had been convicted of rape and murder—had the most unstable blood sugar curves. Both walked around most of the time with coffee, candy, or soft drinks and rarely ate breakfast.

Not eating for a length of time is another cause of dips in blood-sugar levels.

> They were so explosive and edgy that they could not sit through a card game without throwing cards on the floor, shoving the table over, or trying to hit someone. I managed to get them to stop the sugar and caffeine and to eat all three meals. In less than a week, they were changed men; it was a really dramatic improve-

ment. They were able to sit pleasantly through conversations and card games. I was even able to walk in and say good morning without receiving the usual two-word epithet in return.

Dr. Humiston's superiors ordered him not to talk about the improvement in the two men; when he did, he was fired.

One area of Dr. Humiston's specialized training is in family therapy. He says:

I wish all parents could realize how often their child's naughty behavior is due to the fact that the child has undiagnosed hypoglycemia and eats sugar. Such a child will break his favorite toy, do anything he can to hurt his parents and siblings, refuse to do the things he most wants to do, will be absolutely driven to completely negative behavior. What a blessing it might be for parents if they knew that such seemingly unexplainable behavior was due to very concrete dietary causes that can be treated.

He adds that a child with unstable blood sugar may misbehave so frequently that his own misbehavior "punches his self-esteem full of holes. This in turn adds a *psychological* reason for further spiraling of bad behavior."

Summing up the effects of low blood sugar on "bad behavior," Lendon H. Smith, M.D., suggested in his 1976 book, *Improving Your Child's Behavior Chemistry* (p. 57) that all criminals should have their blood-sugar levels thoroughly tested. He also gave this "medical" hint for pediatricians: They "should walk into schools and ax down the candy machines."

ABNORMAL AMOUNTS OF MINERALS IN THE BODY

Dr. Schauss, who is the director of the American Institute for Biosocial Research in Tacoma, Washington, wrote me recently discussing the "solid science in the treatment and prevention of violence" relating to the "discovery of manganese as a possible marker of the tendency toward violence." He refers to the discovery of "the unusual prevalence of more than 0.7 ppm of manganese in the hair of violent offenders. 70% of offenders have it. By comparison, the incidence is about 3% in matched non-offenders." Dr. Schauss states that "these findings have been confirmed in two studies involving more than five juvenile and adult institutions by the University of California."

Dr. Schauss tells of a violent nine-year-old child who had a high ratio of copper to zinc. The child had attempted to kill another student in a playground. He was given proper mineral therapy, and when last seen—four years after treatment—"he was a B-average student with an outstanding record for classroom behavior. And this was a boy whom school officials once described as the most violent elementary pupil they had ever had to contend with."

FOOD AND CHEMICAL INTOLERANCES

In 1985 in a leading medical journal, the *Lancet* (March 9, p. 540), Dr. Egger reported testing 72 persons for intolerances, 31 of whom showed antisocial behavior. Out of 48 foods investigated, the food generally considered "good" that provoked the most symptoms was milk. And many of the antisocial problems improved when milk was removed from the diet.

Dr. Schauss cited even earlier research in *Diet, Crime, and Delinquency* (p. 14), in which testing of juvenile offenders revealed that 88 percent had evidence of an intolerant reaction to milk. This was reported by a branch of the U.S. Department of Justice in the March 1981 *Journal of Behavioral Ecology*. Also, a number of studies have found that many juvenile offenders drink extremely high quantities of milk as compared to nonoffenders. Some offenders were found to get 50 percent of their calories from this one food.

Of course, milk does not turn everyone into criminals, not even everyone who is intolerant to it. Also, milk is not the only food that can result in violent behavior. Marshall Mandell, M.D., reports the following case history in *Dr. Mandell's 5-Day Allergy Relief System* (pp. 89, 90). The man was a 19-year-old schizophrenic prone to violence. Dr. Mandell writes that "despite psychiatric treatment, he continued to have violent outbursts including physical assaults that terrorized and injured his widowed mother. In a state of desperation, Mrs. W. came to me with the hope that Michael could be helped sufficiently for him to remain at home without her living in constant fear that he would cause her severe bodily injury.

"When I saw him in my office, Michael . . . walked about in a heavy mental fog like a zombie as a result of the large doses of medication that were being used to control him. . . . Mrs. W. told me of her constant fear that her son was destined for a state hospital for dangerously ill mental patients. She referred to him as 'my beautiful and deeply troubled son.'" Dr. Mandell could see that the mother's fear was a very real one: "Michael would have been condemned to a tranquilizer/sedative–induced near vegetative existence in a state mental institution if we could not clear his mind sufficiently in order to reach him and free him."

Because of Michael's unpredictable and extreme outbursts of violence, testing for food intolerances was not performed in Dr. Mandell's office, as it usually was. Michael was placed in a maximum-security psychiatric unit, where he was fasted under careful supervision.

> At the end of the five-day fast, our patient was gentle and clearthinking. Fasting [had] stopped the harmful allergic-biochemical effects of all offending foods on his nervous system at the same time. And with this simple, safe, and inexpensive diagnostic and therapeutic measure, we were able to reach Mrs. W.'s "beautiful son," the real person inside this troubled being. His illness was reversible and there was real hope!

> A series of feeding tests was begun to see which foods played a role in his schizophrenia and violent behavior.

> Within a half hour of eating several eggs, this now pleasant, cooperative young man was transformed into a raging, uncontrollable wild animal. . . . It took five members of the psychiatric

staff to prevent him from harming others and himself as he was placed in a straitjacket for several hours until his egg-provoked allergic violence subsided.

Sometimes I personally experience results of orthomolecular approaches only after having researched and written about them. It always surprises me how much more vivid one actual experience can be than pages of statistics and scientific studies. I was editing this chapter when I accompanied my husband to his appointment with a clinical ecologist. A boy about nine was in the office, being tested to see if intolerances were contributing to his mysterious bursts of violence. The violence occurred regularly after lunch and had been attributed by a psychologist as coming from an unconscious psychological reaction to someone or something at school. Long-term psychotherapy would probably be needed to sort things out.

We shared the waiting room for over two hours during which the boy was tested for reactions to various foods. Each time he used his "reaction-waiting" time to play gentle games with his father, sit quietly reading, or to talk in a gentlemanly manner with the grown-ups in the room. It was hard to believe any parents could be blessed with a more well-behaved child. The doctor called him in for about the sixth time, and within minutes a loud racket came from the office. The boy raced out, with his parents and the physician in hot pursuit. His father tried to hold him; the boy scratched and kicked his father with obvious intent to hurt him, and ran screaming into another waiting room where he scattered furniture left and right. I was torn between a desire to see what happened in the other room and a desire to find a safe spot in case the child came rampaging back in my direction. An office aide literally tackled the boy; and his father and the doctor were able to grab ahold of him. I saw the boy's face as he grappled furiously with the three adults. Had this been a scene in a movie (which is what this seemed like), the boy would probably have been playing the role of someone suddenly possessed by the devil.

It turned out that the sweet-natured boy had been "possessed" by a test sample of apple. It also turned out that his lunch regularly included an apple for dessert.

What You Can Do

Clearly it would be unwise to attempt to balance the biochemistry of a hard-core criminal all on your own. See the "Resources" section for how to contact an orthomolecular doctor near you if you feel violent tendencies or have a family member prone to violence.

The doctors working on this book have offered steps you can *safely* take on your own, but only as helpful stopgap measures while you wait to see an orthomolecular physician.

Studies have shown that a daily multivitamin-mineral pill can be helpful in cutting down antisocial behavior in some people. Make sure that the pill is hypoallergenic; there is evidence in the literature that supplements with certain additives make some people's antisocial behavior even worse. Chapters 2 and 14 give further safe self-help information.

You can safely cut out sugar and other refined carbohydrates. These are generally considered not only to serve no useful function in the body, but to be actively harmful.

Not eating all night, between dinner and breakfast, can lead to violence and other antisocial behavior in those whose low blood sugar triggers such behavior. (Remember that fasting for a number of hours can make blood sugar dip.) Snack before bedtime and keep something to eat by the bed for possible awakenings during the night or for taking upon arising. For more information, see Chapter 15.

Since so many crimes are committed by people under the influence of alcohol and other drugs, and by women suffering from premenstrual syndrome, the chapters on addiction and women's problems might also be helpful.

PART 4

Nutritional Solutions for Special Problems of Women, the Elderly, and Children

THE SYMPTOM-BASED APPROACH to treating PMS with drugs has simply not been effective. The vast majority of PMS cases stem from biochemical imbalances that can be managed and reversed through nutritional therapy.

—STUART M. BERGER, M.D., *New York Post*, August 6, 1985, p. 26.

ANOREXIA NERVOSA . . . now appears to be easily curable . . . in the majority of cases where zinc deficiency is diagnosed as a factor. . . . Improvement is often apparent within days or sometimes hours even in patients where the illness has been of long standing.

—DEREK BRYCE-SMITH, D.SC., PH.D., *The International Journal of Biosocial Research,* Vol 8(2):115–150, 1986

ADDING LARGE AMOUNTS of *natural* progesterone to the body postpartum can be *very* helpful to prevent postpartum psychosis or depression.

—CHRISTIANE NORTHRUP, M.D. (personal correspondence, 1993)

Chapter 11

Women's Psychological Problems:
PMS—Painful Periods—Postpartum
Depression and Psychosis—Anorexia
and Bulimia

Traditionally, women have been told that problems like premenstrual syndrome and painful periods were "all in their heads" or just part of being a woman. One might expect those ideas to be outmoded by now; but as Lois Halstead, Ph.D., R.N., pointed out in 1992 (Rush-Presbyterian–St. Luke's Medical Center *Insights,* Vol. 15, No.2, p. 2), they are still widely pervasive among many healthcare professionals. She headed a study of 100 women with advanced endometriosis, a *physical* condition that can cause severe menstrual cramps. (The uterine lining grows outside the uterus.) Thirty-seven of the women said they had visited as many as seven physicians before being diagnosed, and that many of them had said the pain was "in their heads" and they were overreacting.

As mentioned throughout this book, orthomolecular doctors have an overall distaste for a diagnosis that a patient's symptoms are "all in the head," rather than physically based.

One major factor behind some "women's problems" is hormonal imbalances—a fact not disputed by orthodox medicine. Hormones, like all chemicals necessary to our bodies, are formed by nutrients. If nutritional imbalances are taken care of, hormonal imbalances can be corrected as a natural result.

COMMONLY REPORTED SYMPTOMS OF PREMENSTRUAL TENSION

Depression	Bloating
Irritability	Fatigue
Anxiety	Insomnia
Mood swings	Breast tenderness
Nervousness	Dizziness or fainting
Food cravings	Heart pounding
Headache	

Premenstrual Syndrome (PMS, Premenstrual Tension)

It is estimated that as many as 60 percent of American women have noticeable symptoms of premenstrual syndrome (PMS), and that one out of three of these women ends up in hospital wards, psychiatric institutions, or prisons. In addition, Guy E. Abraham, M.D., a pioneer in work with PMS, stated that it is a "major unrecognized cause of social problems such as divorce and juvenile delinquency."

Despite these grim facts, PMS, first described in the medical literature in 1931, was neglected for so long that it was called "a newly recognized problem" 54 years later in a Factsheet put out by the Neurosciences Information Center. Commenting on how women with PMS symptoms were usually diagnosed during those years, Stuart M. Berger, M.D., wrote in a 1985 *New York Post* article (August 6, p. 26): "Until recently the chauvinistic attitude of medicine assumed the condition was a sign of 'female hysteria,' the predictable lot in the lives of a majority of women resulting from 'unfulfilled desires.' "

Christiane Northrup, M.D., an obstetrician/gynecologist practicing in Yarmouth, Maine, who is president of the American Holistic Medical Association, told me in an interview that it was an article in *Family Circle* that finally brought PMS to the medical community's attention. Suddenly, within a year or two, "PMS was the big topic at almost every ob gyn conference. That was truly a case of the tail wagging the dog."

PMS can have a bewildering variety of symptoms; some sources put the number of possible symptoms at 150. A few of the more common are listed in the table on page 220. The basic clue for suspecting PMS is if negative physical or mental changes occur almost every month within two weeks preceding the start of menstrual flow —and if they regularly disappear or greatly lessen after menstruation starts.

ORTHOMOLECULAR THERAPY FOR PMS

Some of the drugs that have been used to treat PMS are tranquilizers, antidepressants, diuretics, progesterone, oral contraceptive pills, and amphetamines. "None of these have had the clear-cut positive results we would hope for," says psychiatrist Priscilla Slagle, M.D., in *The Way Up from Down* (p. 160).

Dr. Northrup, using nutritional and holistic techniques, reports "approximately a 70% rate of significant improvement" in her patients. She adds that many of her patients had been given up on by orthodox medicine. Dr. Berger writes of Marie, "a classic PMS patient" *(New York Post*, October 7, 1986, p. 27). Before treatment, "she could count on one good week a month. . . . Ten days before her period, her whole body would swell up; she had to wear a larger dress size." Other symptoms included clumsiness and irritability. Then "her mood would plunge into depression." The first month Marie was on nutritional therapy, "her symptoms were already better; and by the second month they had completely disappeared." Dr. Berger points out that Marie "couldn't believe that anything as easy as a diet could make that much difference in her life," a common reaction of people who try nutritional therapy for various disorders.

Dietary Changes. Dr. Northrup finds that for a few patients, "simple things like stopping caffeine and refined sugars will be unbelievably beneficial; and that's all they need do. For a few others, a simple multivitamin-mineral will clear up the symptoms.

"One thing I recommend across the board to my PMS patients," she says, "is that they cut down on fat. Almost all women who come to me with this disorder have been on diets with about 40 percent fat, as is the average American. I recommend that they decrease to 20 percent." Animal fats can contribute to the high estrogen levels that may exacerbate PMS. (PMS symptoms are sometimes due to the wrong balance between the hormones estrogen and progesterone.) However, Dr. Northrup says, "All women need good sources of essential fatty acids for optimal hormone functioning." She recommends capsules of flaxseed oil, black currant seed oil, or oil of evening primrose (500 mg four times a day). Other recommendations from nutritional doctors are that safflower and sesame oils be substituted for animal fat.

Dr. Northrup also says that "stopping dairy foods is *very* important. The cattle we're now raising are pumped full of antibiotics and hormones so that they'll be efficient milk suppliers, and this can interfere with a woman's hormone balance. So for a while it's crucial that she cut dairy out of her diet completely; for many women, that makes a big difference."

Dr. Northrup recommends that her patients stay away from red meat unless they can get it from a reliable organic source. Commercial red meat, again, contains high levels of hormones and antibiotics.

Vitamins and Minerals. In 1980, Dr. Abraham published a double-blind crossover study that followed women from all four PMS subgroups (that is, women with a large variety of symptoms) and found that 21 of the 25 responded better to vitamin B6 than to the placebo (*Infertility* 3, pp. 155–65). It has been reported that a major problem in studying *drugs* for PMS is that often patients receiving the placebo report as great or greater improvement as those receiving the drug.

Five years later, investigators reported in the orthodox journal *Lancet* (1985, 1, p. 1339) that 70–80 percent of 630 women taking small amounts of B6 daily reported "significant improvement" in their symptoms.

One way in which B6 helps is in combatting premenstrual fluid retention, which can cause swelling of tissues in the stomach, breasts, legs—and brain. Orthodox doctors may suggest diuretics to combat water retention, but nutritional physicians warn that diuretics may draw the minerals magnesium and potassium out of the body along with water. Dr. Berger pointed out in his 1985 *New York Post* article that Dr. Abraham has reported a widespread deficiency of magnesium among women with PMS, and while diuretics may help in the short term, they "can set up a vicious cycle which contributes to the problem."

The orthomolecular approach considers the possibility of too much copper relative to zinc. Carl C. Pfeiffer, Ph.D., M.D., wrote in *Nutrition and Mental Illness* (p. 67) that "it is not generally known that [premenstrual] tension occurs when blood copper is highest and blood zinc is lowest. Copper is a stimulant to the brain, while zinc has an antianxiety effect." This copper-zinc imbalance "reverses at the onset of menstruation, often coinciding with relief of tension and other symptoms."

Additional Approaches. Dr. Berger in his 1986 article points out that in the second part of the menstrual cycle, blood sugar tends to drop. Some doctors think that this may account for the strong craving for sugar reported by many PMS sufferers. One easy step recommended to help maintain an even blood-sugar level is to eat small meals several times daily, rather than three large meals. (For more on nutritional therapy for unstable blood sugar, see Chapter 15.) A strong sugar craving can also be a sign of a *Candida albicans* infection (candidiasis), which nutritional doctors believe is a factor in PMS for some women. Antibiotics often set the stage for candidiasis, one reason Dr. Northrup asks her patients to cut out dairy and red-meat products high in antibiotics. For more on candidiasis, see Chapter 16.

Dr. Northrup reports that aerobic exercise helps many women, because it increases production of endorphins, brain chemicals that improve mood and decrease pain perception. She warns, however, that too-high endorphin levels can contribute to anorexia, so exercise should not be carried to an extreme.

PMS strikes some women so hard that they are virtually incapacitated. When such patients first come to Dr. Northrup, "They're usually just too strung out to do exercises and alter their diet." So she will start them on the hormone progesterone, either orally or applied to the skin. "For many women, just a little bit of this skin cream in the last two weeks of the cycle is all the progesterone they need." Orthodox doctors also use progesterone, but the kind used by Dr. Northrup is a natural one, made from wild Mexican yams. The physician states that synthetic progesterones "are associated with all sorts of side effects, such as depression, moodiness, bloating, headache." Ironically, those side effects are also common symptoms of PMS. "Natural progesterone is almost entirely free from side effects."

Dr. Northrup finds that orthomolecular therapy works best if patients combine it with a technique to gain insight into their lives, "whether that be psychotherapy, a 12-step program, or merely keeping a personal journal of feelings and events."

The vast majority of women with severe PMS come from quite dysfunctional homes, or have in other ways undergone an extreme amount of stress. . . . By and large, these women have spent their whole lives adapting to what was expected of them; and they don't know who *they* are. So with the physical changes that accompany premenstruation, all their bottled-up rage or sadness tends to come forth. It may come forth in a non-diplomatic, or an inappropriately violent, way; but this rage is based on the *truth* of the feelings they have kept bottled up.

So when a woman comes to me with "unexplained" rage as one of her symptoms, I try to help her explore how her rage might be totally valid. In this way, she can be relieved of the idea that her anger is a symptom of a sort of insanity. At the same time, I help her explore how this awful anger can be resolved by taking simple, constructive actions.

WHAT YOU CAN DO

If symptoms are severe enough that they lead to suicidal thoughts or violence, or are damaging your marriage or career, you require immediate help from a doctor. For how to find an orthomolecular physician near you, see the "Resources" section.

However, many facets of orthomolecular therapy lend themselves easily to safe self-help for those with milder symptoms. The preceding section refers to specific chapters in Part V which offer details of self-help. In his 1993 book, *Healing through Nutrition*, Melvyn Werbach, M.D., tracing additional nutritional therapies from the medical literature, gives safe self-help suggestions according to the basic symptoms you suffer.

Take a good vitamin-mineral supplement, as discussed in Chapter 2. Dr. Northrup recommends that the supplement contain at least 100 mg of vitamin B6. (Dr. Werbach's book recommends 40 mg daily.) Never take one B vitamin alone; take the full B complex.

The overall diet Dr. Northrup recommends is 20 percent fat, 50 percent complex carbohydrates (whole grains, fresh fruits, vegetables), and 30 percent protein (beans, seeds, nuts, organic meats, eggs). Avoid refined sugar, including refined white-flour products (white bread, pancakes, waffles, pasta. Whole-grain products are fine). Drs. Northrup and Werbach point out that these recommendations are similar to those newly recommended by the establishment for maintenance of overall health.

You may be concerned about getting enough calcium if you cut out dairy products. Karl E. Humiston, M.D., states that "while it's true that dairy products contain the highest calcium concentration of any foods, it's also true that we may *get* more calcium from other foods, because our bodies do not absorb cow's milk calcium very well." Dr. Northrup points out that dark green leafy vegetables are "loaded with calcium," with one cup of broccoli, kale, or collards containing 300 mg, as much as a cup of milk. "Many herbs are rich in calcium, as are some mineral waters." Dr. Werbach, however, writes me that "if dairy products are eliminated, calcium supplementation is probably necessary. Calcium-citrate-malate is one of the most absorbable" forms. Dr. Northrup adds that magnesium intake should be two thirds the amount of calcium. Calcium/magnesium balance is one of those crucial balances mentioned often in this book.

She also states that women should stop at least all *high-fat* dairy foods for a while. "No-fat dairy works for some women but not all." She suggests that a woman with PMS symptoms try eliminating dairy for two months—"then add low-fat dairy to see how you feel."

Cutting out caffeine requires reading labels, because caffeine is in many products, including some non-prescription medications and even some herbal teas.

For exercise, Dr. Northrup recommends a brisk 20-minute walk three times a week.

Since, as Dr. Northrup points out, "any amount of stress will increase susceptibility to PMS," it is important to avoid as much stress during the two weeks prior to menstruation as you can. Ask your family to take some of the "load" off you at these times. Also, find relaxation exercises that you like and practice them as needed.

The idea that stress can increase susceptibility to PMS does not bring us back to the old-fashioned idea that it's "all psychological."

A major way that physical and emotional stress harms is that it causes the body to use up nutrients faster, upsetting the body's chemistry.

The natural progesterone Dr. Northrup uses, except in very mild or severe cases, is Pro-Gest body cream. For information, or to order directly, contact the Pro-Gest Co., Professional and Technical Services Ltd., Portland, Oregon 97232; tel. 800-648-8211. "Use one-fourth teaspoon on soft areas of the skin two times a day from ovulation to onset of menses," Dr. Northrup recommends. "This small amount, in my opinion, is completely safe; and over time, it can be decreased." The cream, she adds, "can make a big difference." For severe cases, Dr. Northrup prescribes a natural progesterone taken orally. This form is available only by prescription, and "women on this should be under a doctor's care."

Dysmenorrhea

Dysmenorrhea is the medical name for painful periods. Traditionally, as has been common with "women's disorders," dysmenorrhea was thought to be psychological, not physical. For example, one theory was that a woman suffering from period pain unconsciously resented being a woman. However, studies have shown that dysmenorrhea, like other "women's problems," is often due to hormonal imbalances. Specifically, high levels of a substance known as prostaglandin F_2 alpha are present in the uterus, and this is believed to cause uterine contractions and cramps. Period pain may also be caused by other physical problems, such as pelvic infection or endometriosis.

ORTHOMOLECULAR THERAPY

Orthodox treatment of dysmenorrhea includes antispasmodic drugs, prostaglandin inhibitors, and painkillers.

Orthomolecular treatment includes the use of prostaglandin,

which can be regulated by regulating the balance of essential fatty acids in the diet. These are the nutrients, Dr. Northrup points out, that naturally help the body to form the right balance of prostaglandins.

Dr. Werbach, writing in the *International Journal of Alternative and Complementary Medicine* (July 1992, p. 10), cited a study that found that magnesium reduces the menstrual blood level of prostaglandin F_2 alpha. That double-blind study reported improvement in 21 of 25 women receiving magnesium. A 1990 study found magnesium, compared to placebo, to have "therapeutic effect on both back and lower abdominal pain," and "the women on magnesium markedly reduced their absences from work due to dysmenorrhea." Dr. Werbach points out that magnesium is both a muscle relaxant and vasodilator.

The psychiatrist states that "there are other nutritional treatments for dysmenorrhea and each appears to have a different mechanism of action, which suggests that they could be combined for maximal benefits." He cites a study published in *Lancet* back in 1955 (1: pp. 844–47) in which one hundred women received either 50 mg of vitamin E (alpha-tocopherol) three times daily, or a placebo for 10 days prior to menstruation and for the next four days. "After two cycles 68% of the women receiving supplementation improved, compared with only 18% of those receiving placebo."

Acupuncture, used extensively by acupuncturists to control various types of pain, may be used. Dr. Northrup mentions that a 1986 review article by Joe Helms, M.D., in the *American Journal of Obstetrics and Gynecology* found that acupuncture works well for dysmenorrhea.

WHAT YOU CAN DO

As a safe self-help regimen of essential fatty acids to balance prostaglandins, Dr. Northrup recommends oil of evening primrose, OR flaxseed oil, OR black currant seed oil, 500 mg four times a day.

She recommends that all hydrogenated fats be avoided, and that you take a daily multivitamin-mineral capsule. She notes that one or two tablets a month of the painkillers Advil, Motrin, or Anaprox can be very helpful as well as safe. (Note that her recommended dosage is very much below that recommended by these drugs' labels.)

For relaxation exercises, she notes that "Transcendental Meditation has been shown to be a very good stress-reducer."

Acupressure, a cousin of acupuncture, uses finger pressure at the body points where needles are applied in acupuncture. Some health-food stores have charts showing acupuncture points. Apply pressure to the areas of your feet and legs that correspond to acupuncture points spleen 4, 6, 9, and 10. Or lie on your back with your feet on a chair, place your fists under your back in the lumbar region, and lift up in the pelvic area. This creates pressure in the lower back, thereby releasing tension in the abdominal area. Move your fists around to create more pressure. Further details can be found in my 1980 article in *Pain Topics* (Vol. 3, No. 2, April, p. 8).

Postpartum Depression and Postpartum Psychosis

Symptoms of postpartum depression, which begin usually two to six weeks after a woman gives birth, include fatigue, feelings of help-lessness, irritability, disinterest in previously enjoyed activities, changes in sleep or eating patterns, fears about the baby's safety, or disquieting hostile thoughts toward the infant.

Don't confuse postpartum depression with "baby blues," de-scribed as weepiness occurring three to 10 days after giving birth. This affects up to 80 percent of new mothers and goes away, with-out treatment, usually within a few days. Be aware that postpartum depression has at times been misdiagnosed by doctors as the more simple "baby blues." If you feel your symptoms are more those of depression than of a few days of "weepiness," don't accept a diag-nosis of "It'll pass in time all on its own."

Postpartum *psychosis* also occurs after giving birth, but the woman loses contact with reality, may have hallucinations, and is prone to violence. Suicide is a distinct possibility.

Postpartum depression and psychosis are triggered by hormonal changes a woman undergoes after childbirth.

Postpartum depression is often estimated to affect 10–15 percent of new mothers, although some estimates state that 50 percent suffer some degree of the disorder. Statistics for postpartum psychosis also vary: from one in every 1,000, 2,000, or 3,000 pregnancies to two in every 1,000. It has been stated that each year, at least 40,000 women in America are hospitalized for psychiatric illnesses related to childbirth.

If left untreated, postpartum disorders may persist for months, even years. And they often *are* left untreated—despite the reported 40,000 hospitalizations yearly. One reason is that many women "do not recognize their symptoms as an illness," says psychiatrist Madelaine M. Wohlreich, M.D., director of the Postpartum Disorders Project at Pennsylvania Hospital in Philadelphia. "They think they are bad mothers or that they are affected by something that is supposed to happen."

The diagnosis may be missed by health professionals, too. Diane Semprevivo, M.S., M.N., R.N., a childbirth education coordinator in Maternal-Child Nursing at Rush-Presbyterian–St. Luke's Medical Center, has written *(Insights,* Vol. 14, No. 4, 1991): "People in health care say they don't see many women with these disorders. But where are you going to see them? We let new mothers out of the hospital 24 to 48 hours after they've delivered their babies. Most women don't begin to develop symptoms before the third day after delivery."

Traditionally, violence stemming from postpartum psychosis has been thought to be usually self-inflicted. But in 1988 in New York City a woman was acquitted of legal guilt in murdering two of her babies, and attempting to murder a third, because of insanity: specifically, postpartum psychosis. Less than four years later, the *New*

York Post reported (May 18, 1992, p. 14) that postpartum disorders had been blamed "for dozens of murders in the past few years as the mental-health community begins to take seriously the effects of hormones on a woman's mind after she gives birth." While some doctors continue to state that violence against the baby is rare, I have wondered how many cases of new mothers who "inexplicably" throw their babies down an incinerator, or "for no reason" jump off buildings holding their newborns in their arms, might be explained if postpartum psychosis were considered. And I have wondered how many of these tragedies might have been *prevented* if the diagnosis had been considered.

One medical worker sharing that concern is Semprevivo. "I'm convinced," she has said, "that many of the babies found in garbage cans or abandoned in the street had mothers suffering some form of postpartum psychiatric illness." Studying 20 women hospitalized for postpartum psychosis or depression, she found a common thread: they felt resentment toward family and health-care providers for not taking them seriously when they first complained that something was wrong. "People often forget that if you ignore these women's cries for help, babies may die."

ORTHOMOLECULAR THERAPY FOR POSTPARTUM DISORDERS

Orthodox treatment for postpartum depression uses psychotherapy, medication, group therapy, and marital counseling. Antipsychotic drugs are used for postpartum psychosis.

Chapters 4 and 17 cover how an overload of heavy metals can cause brain symptoms. As far back as 1975 Carl C. Pfeiffer, M.D., Ph.D., wrote about the relationship of rising estrogen levels, which occur in pregnancy, and the rising of the heavy metal copper *(Mental and Elemental Nutrients,* p. 327): "Copper, and particularly ceruloplasmin (a copper-containing protein) is elevated by estrogens; therefore, the levels of copper and ceruloplasmin rise progressively during pregnancy. Serum copper is approximately

115 mcg percent at conception, and reaches a mean of 260 mcg percent at term." Thus, copper level more than doubles during pregnancy. "After delivery, a period of two to three months is required before the original serum copper level is reached. This high postpartum copper level may be a factor in causing postpartum depression and psychosis."

He also stated that a common factor in depression in general was more copper than zinc in the body. Following these two leads, doctors such as Derek Bryce-Smith, D.Sc., Ph.D., of the University of Reading in England have used zinc therapy. Dr. Bryce-Smith reported in 1986 that postnatal depression "now appears to be easily curable . . . in the majority of cases where zinc deficiency is diagnosed as a factor" (International Journal of Biosocial Research, Vol. 8(27), p. 140).

Emotional stresses can contribute to postpartum depression, Christiane Northrup, M.D., points out, by setting up negative biochemical changes. While hormone levels always change to some degree after a birth, "I believe that emotional stresses at this time can cause even *more* fluctuation in estrogen and progesterone, as well as increased nutritional needs."

An absent or non-supportive husband might come readily to mind as a cause of emotional stress for a woman who has recently given birth. Interestingly, Dr. Northrup's first thought is of a missing or non-supportive *mother*. "One of the things that happens when you have a baby," she says, "is that, for some reason that seems to go back generation after generation, you want your mother present. If she was never present, not even when you were a baby—and she is still not here now, when you yourself have given birth—this can bring back all the loss you felt as a child and redouble it." Dr. Northrup notes that postpartum depression is common in women whose mothers physically abused them or were alcoholics.

WHAT YOU CAN DO

You can help *prevent* both postpartum depression and psychosis by consulting an orthomolecular doctor before and during pregnancy. She or he will conduct scientific tests that show exactly what is going on with your individual body chemistry. Remember that hormone fluctuations are considered by both orthodox and orthomolecular doctors to be culprits in postpartum depression and psychosis. A correct balance of nutrients can create a correct balance of hormones.

In this way, you will also be going a long way toward preventing disorders in your baby that orthodox doctors often consider unpreventable, such as mental retardation. (See also Chapters 2 and 9.)

Dr. Northrup notes that women with PMS also often suffer postpartum depression; "I believe the two disorders are intimately related." She recommends natural progesterone as *"very* helpful in preventing postpartum depression and psychosis." (See What You Can Do in the section on PMS.) The physician adds, "I would start immediately postpartum. Don't wait until symptoms occur."

Dr. Northrup adds that postpartum depression sometimes "runs in families." As with all disorders that run in families, orthomolecular doctors believe the cause may be shared poor dietary habits, genetically transmitted intolerances to certain foods or chemicals, or genetic inability to properly absorb certain nutrients. Thus, a family predisposition can often be short-circuited by means of preventive orthomolecular treatment.

Since more copper than zinc may be a crucial factor in postpartum depression and psychosis, make sure that your nutritional supplement contains more zinc than copper. Other tips on reducing copper are in Chapters 4 and 17.

Anorexia (Anorexia Nervosa)

Anorexia nervosa has been called "the dying-to-be-beautiful disorder" because it usually starts with dieting to improve appearance, and it often ends in death. A recurring statement in the literature is that "Of all mental illness in Canada and the United States, anorexia nervosa is the leading cause of death." This is not surprising in light of the fact that the anorectic's excessive dieting creates severe malnutrition. (As stated repeatedly in this book, nutrients are necessary for every biochemical reaction in the body.) Up to 10 percent of anorectics are male.

Among anorectics who undergo traditional therapy, it is estimated that half will fight it for the rest of their lives, and about a fifth will die. This is a tragically unnecessary waste of life, since successful nutritional therapy may be as simple as zinc supplementation.

ORTHOMOLECULAR THERAPY FOR ANOREXIA NERVOSA

Orthomolecular doctors basically look for the very tangible and very treatable physiological factors in anorexia. Orthodox doctors often blame sociological factors, particularly stresses on women to be thin. Also often blamed by orthodox psychiatrists are very complex (and therefore difficult-to-treat) psychological issues, for example: "unresolved problems in the oral incorporation stage, which impede separation-individualism"; "adolescent anorexics perceive their bodies to be the last vestige of their infantile archaic grandiosity." Obviously, trying to uncover and then resolve such problems is not a very quick or direct therapy for someone who is literally starving to death.

Actually, many psychoanalysts agree that classical psychoanalytic techniques should be avoided. When a patient's life is threatened, she will be hospitalized with a forced feeding of about 3,000 calories a day. This will put weight on the emaciated body and prevent death by starvation—for the duration of the woman's hospital stay.

However, this technique doesn't address the biochemical imbalances that may have *caused* the anorexia, and that may continue it once she leaves the hospital.

Psychotherapy is the mainstay of the orthodox approach. Drugs may be used to help the depression that often accompanies anorexia. Therapy can take several years. Some orthomolecular doctors argue that if you treat the biochemical basis of anorexia, all forms of psychotherapy become unnecessary. Others say that sometimes psychotherapy is needed in addition to orthomolecular therapy.

A biochemical rationale given as a cause of anorexia is that dieting elevates levels of opioids, and the patient may become addicted to them. (Opioids are naturally occurring compounds in the brain that act like heroin or morphine.) Thus, even if dieting was begun for social or psychological reasons, it may turn into a *biological* addiction.

One study, conducted at the University of Minnesota, whose results support the idea that dieting can lead to anorexia was covered in a 1991 article in the New York *Daily News* (June 9). Thirty-six mentally and physically healthy volunteers were placed on a six-month diet that cut their food intake by half—a common reduction for women dieters. "After losing 25% or more of their body weight, the volunteers experienced most, if not all, of the 'classic' symptoms of an eating disorder." All the volunteers were men.

Another biochemical cause of some cases of anorexia was put forth by Derek Bryce-Smith D.Sc., Ph.D., in his 1986 article cited in the previous section: While it is probable that initial food reduction springs mainly from social factors, what keeps the diet going beyond rational boundaries is often primarily a *zinc deficiency*, which is a natural result of very little food intake. Furthermore, doctors have found that some people who become anorectic didn't absorb zinc properly in the first place (zinc *dependency*); in this case, a zinc dependency, rather than social factors, may actually be the *initial* factor in anorexia.

Symptoms of zinc deficiency include loss of appetite and impaired sense of taste and smell, which could be expected to further reduce desire for food. Another symptom is depression, which often accompanies anorexia. Dr. Bryce-Smith states, "We reasoned that the vicious cycle would be broken by providing extra zinc: the other inevitable dietary deficiencies would normally be automatically remedied as soon as the patients started eating normally and their mental depression abated. This new approach has proved gratifyingly successful."

Many other workers have reported good results with zinc supplementation. For instance, psychotherapist Alexander G. Schauss, Ph.D., writes of "the rapid increase in weight consistently seen by us and numerous other independent observers in Canada, the United States, England, Denmark, Sweden, the Netherlands, and West Germany."

Dr. Bryce-Smith published a case history of a 13-year-old girl in *Lancet* in 1984 (2: p. 350). After two weeks of zinc supplementation, the girl's appetite and mood improved. After four months of supplementation, she gained 13 kg., and her depression lifted. Ten months after she *stopped* taking zinc, however, she had returned to her original state. When zinc was reintroduced, she again improved.

Nutritional therapy makes no "magic bullet" claims, and zinc is not an exception. Orthomolecular doctors, believing strongly in the uniqueness of each individual's biochemical problems, consider other possible underlying factors, including food intolerances and yeast infection (candidiasis).

What You Can Do

Obstetrician/gynecologist Christiane Northrup, M.D., stresses that you might easily prevent anorexia by never putting yourself on a stringent reducing diet.

Consultation with a nutritional doctor is particularly important, because anorexia propels its victims into serious multiple nutritional deficiencies. However, if an anorectic suffers from serious malnutrition, and orthomolecular help is not *immediately* available, the orthodox treatment of hospitalization with forced feeding is very much preferable to any delay. This treatment might well be what the nutritional physician would start with, anyway. Orthomolecular doctors tend to rely heavily on their orthodox training in emergency situations.

There are, however, some steps you can safely take in a nonemergency situation before you can consult an orthomolecular physician. Chapters 14 and 16 give suggestions for safe self-help with intolerances and candidiasis.

I realize it will be tempting for some readers to try using zinc on their own. "Since it's natural, it can't do any harm" is a common misconception. (While that statement is true of nutritional therapy prescribed by a competent nutritional doctor, it is by no means always true of self-prescribed therapy.) Thus, I feel compelled to give details of the proper zinc therapy, lest you try to create your own. Even with this information, please use zinc on your own only for a short time, until you have consulted an orthomolecular doctor.

The form of zinc used is zinc sulfate. It has been given in amounts of 50 mg three times daily with meals (150 mg daily). Taking more than that can cause a decrease in the body of HDL cholesterol, which is important for a healthy heart, and can impair immune responses. Side effects reported from excessive zinc supplementation include nausea and transient worsening of depression or hallucinations. Zinc supplementation may increase grand mal seizures in epileptics.

Also, realize that most if not all anorectics mentioned in this chapter as helped by zinc had first tested out scientifically as deficient, or as having a greater than normal need.

Bulimia

A person suffering from bulimia goes on binges of eating enormous quantities of food. To rid herself of the calories, she follows with forced vomiting, excessive exercising, laxative purging, and/or fasting.

It is estimated that one out of every five young women develops bulimia. Despite emphasis in the literature on *young* women bulimics, Dr. Northrup states that she knows women of all ages who are bulimic. This disorder, like anorexia, is often mistakenly thought to be entirely a "woman's problem." Donald R. Durham, Ph.D., pointed out in an article in *Total Health* (June 1991, p. 37) that "men in sports and professions that require rapid weight changes, or the achievement of specific weight classes, are quite prone today to use bulimia . . . as a weight control technique."

Like the anorectic, the bulimic may get started down her road with a reducing diet. However, she takes a different turn when she decides she can enjoy her favorite foods and still lose weight by the combination of stuffing and purging.

Bulimics may eat at one sitting as much as 55 *times* what an average woman eats daily. The cost of this food can be astronomical, and some become thieves or prostitutes to support their disorder.

Physical problems that bulimia causes include adrenal exhaustion, irregular menstruation, pernicious anemia, heart attack—and death. These come about because, like the anorectic, the bulimic develops malnutrition. (Despite the high amount of nutrients ingested, the body has very little time to *use* them.) Dr. Northrup adds that excessive self-induced vomiting can cause rupture of the stomach.

ORTHOMOLECULAR THERAPY FOR BULIMIA

Bulimia, like anorexia, has often been thought to stem from sex-role or parent-child conflicts. Psychotherapy is a mainstay of orthodox treatment, and antidepressant drugs are also used.

Orthomolecular doctors point out that psychotherapies don't address either the *physical* damage caused by repeated bingeing/purging or the biochemical problems that may have caused bulimia initially. However, once the underlying physical factors are remedied, an orthomolecular physician may recommend the type of psychotherapy known as behavior modification for some women, to help them from falling back into bulimic behavior habits.

One biochemical factor in bulimia was found by researchers at both the National Institute of Mental Health and Duke University. A March 1989 article (by Judy Folkenberg, *American Health*, p. 60) reported that these scientists had found much lower amounts of a hormone in bulimics after eating than in normal women. The hormone (cholecystokinin) helps control appetite satisfaction. The article pointed out that antidepressants decrease bulimic symptoms for some patients, and that one effect of the drugs is to boost the amount of that hormone. (More simply put, the drugs result in a feeling of satisfied appetite after eating less food.) "Someday we're going to regulate appetite with drugs," said one researcher. Perhaps it would be better to produce the appetite-regulationg hormone the way hormones are naturally produced: by nutrients.

The article states it is unknown whether the hormone malfunction is the *cause* or *result* of the repeated bingeing and purging. This cause-or-effect question is a recurring one with bulimia and anorexia, since both result in malnutrition, which interferes with all body processes. Orthomolecular doctors argue that nutritional treatment can remedy the biochemical problems, whether they are the cause *or* effect of bulimia.

Orthomolecular doctors find that bulimia is often a form of addiction, with the addictive substance being food, rather than cocaine or alcohol. When a bulimic for a time doesn't eat foods to which she is addicted, she suffers withdrawal symptoms. To overcome these symptoms, she binges on those foods for her "fix." If she worries about her weight, the obvious solution is to purge herself of the enormous amount of calories consumed.

Usually the bulimic binges on refined carbohydrates, which can result in unstable blood sugar. And since refined carbohydrates are a good "feeding" ground for the yeast organism *Candida albicans,* the bingeing can also lead to the disorder candidiasis, which harms the immune system and perpetuates the bulimic problem.

A 1986 article in the *Journal of Orthomolecular Medicine* (Vol. 1, No. 4, p. 246) points out that orthodox doctors place some patients on MAOI drugs for their accompanying depression. Since these drugs cause negative reactions when taken with certain foods, patients are prescribed restrictive diets. "It is significant," the article states, that these diets are known to "promote stable blood-sugar levels and a yeast-free environment." Since patients treated nutritionally may recover *without* antidepressants, those who are helped by them "may be benefiting as much from the diet as the medicine."

Karl E. Humiston, M.D., gave a case history in the 1984 *Journal of Orthomolecular Psychiatry* (Vol. 13, No. 1, p. 1) of a 42-year-old housewife who had begun bulimic episodes a decade previously. They "occurred during her premenstrual two weeks, and after consuming coffee or sweets. She had always suffered premenstrual tension and repeated vaginal yeast infections." The patient was placed on an anticandida program, including a sugar-free, yeast-free diet. "A month later she reported 'incredible' improvement," including freedom from premenstrual tension. After subsequently being treated for food intolerances, often coexisting with a yeast problem, a variety of "lesser symptoms . . . cleared up." This history shows, as do so many from orthomolecular doctors, that getting at the actual physical cause of one diagnosed problem can also clear up "unrelated" diagnosed problems.

WHAT YOU CAN DO

Self-prescribed nutritional help is limited and may carry dangers. To find an orthomolecular doctor near you, see the "Resources" section.

Chapters 14–16 offer suggestions from nutritional doctors for safe self-help for addictive allergies, unstable blood sugar, and candidiasis. The chapter on depression may also help. See the suggestions in Chapter 2, including those for a multivitamin-mineral pill.

WITH OPTIMUM NUTRITION, I believe senility and
memory deterioration will become a thing of the past.

—CARL C. PFEIFFER, PH.D., M.D., *Nutrition and
Mental Illness*

IN MANY INSTANCES, Alzheimer's is a misdiagnosed
multiple-symptom form of a partially or completely
reversible cerebral malfunctioning that has nutritional
and allergic components.

—MARSHALL MANDELL, M.D. (personal communication)

Chapter 12

Alzheimer's Disease and Senile Dementia ("Senility")

Robert C. Atkins, M.D., once told me, "If geriatric specialists would make nutrition part of their specialty, very many people could leave nursing homes and get back to their lives." Dr. Atkins is an ortho-molecular physician in private practice in New York City and is well-known as the author of several successful books on nutritional medicine.

Another doctor who worked nutritionally with senile dementia was the late Carlton Fredericks, Ph.D. In his 1980 book *Eat Well, Get Well, Stay Well* (pp. 55, 56), he speaks of "institutions for the senile aged. There," he says, "the emphasis is on the purely custodial, and *rehabilitation* is an empty word." He tells of a 94-year-old retired lawyer he encountered in a nursing home. The man was "silent, obviously listening to the beat of a distant drum. . . . He was seated in a chair facing the doorway, his eyes unfocused, oblivious to his surroundings." Dr. Fredericks suggested that the man be given supplements of glutamine, vitamin E, and vitamin B complex by injection. When he returned to the home about six months later, the 94-year-old man was, as before, seated in the same chair and facing the door. However, this time he was reading *The New York Times*.

Dr. Fredericks adds: "Many of the older people who are relegated to the scrap heap of senility display symptoms, readily apparent to the trained eye, of nutritional deficiencies."

In a personal communication, Marshall Mandell, M.D., added that when senile dementia is due to nutritional causes, and when these are comprehensively treated, patients can be "significantly improved—or restored to normal."

Alzheimer's and senile dementia are virtually the same disorder, both in terms of symptoms and in terms of treatment approaches an orthomolecular physician will pursue. Technically, however, senile dementia is the term used for a breakdown of mental functions (dementia) in the *elderly*. The strict definition of Alzheimer's is senile dementia when the symptoms occur in a person under 60 ("presenile dementia"), but some doctors use the terms "senile dementia," "Alzheimer's," and "senility" interchangeably. I quote doctors and literature sources with the label they have used, whether it fits the strict definitions or not.

Symptoms

Although stages of deterioration are not always clear-cut and linear, they follow more or less the following sequence: Early on, initiative, drive, and energy decrease. The first clear clinical stage is marked by forgetting recent events; the person may be unable to remember what he did yesterday, but may reminisce happily, and in accurate detail, over a high school prom or a college triumph. (Eventually, even these long-ago memories will fade from the person's mind.) The victim will lose his "word-finding" ability. He will be aware that he can't find the word he wants, and may begin to use many words to describe something. He may forget where he puts things, show impaired job performance, and undergo personality changes, becoming inflexible, suspicious, and hostile, for example.

Confusion and disorientation later strike the sufferer. He may occasionally ask plaintively where he is, who you are, and even who he is. In a frantic attempt to "hold on" to words, he may put labels on lamps, chairs, and tables so he can read the names for these things; he may carry a slip of paper around with his wife's name on it, so he can refer to it when he "loses" her name.

In the last stage, all intellectual activity is gone; and the person needs constant care. He becomes mute and unable to dress himself. He loses interest in eating. He may lose all recognition of family members and may cease to recognize himself in the mirror. The labels and notes he made earlier for himself are useless, because he can no longer read them. The only remotely merciful fact about this stage is that, presumably, the person is totally unaware of what he has become.

When examined after death, the brain of someone who suffered from Alzheimer's disease has an abnormally high number of plaques (starchlike protein deposits). There are also "tangles," masses of fine filaments, in the brain cells. These tangled filaments are believed to be the remains of collapsed cell structures that the brain has been unable to break down and remove. There is noticeable cell death in strategic areas; and the brain has lost its ability to produce vital chemicals necessary for physical and psychological functioning.

Diagnosing and Misdiagnosing Alzheimer's and Senile Dementia

If someone you care about has been diagnosed with Alzheimer's or senile dementia, please realize that the diagnosis may not be accurate. Currently there is no definitive test for these disorders except at autopsy. While the person is alive, the diagnosis can be at best only an educated guess. Doctors from all fields agree that very often, symptoms diagnosed as Alzheimer's or senile dementia are really signs of much more treatable diseases.

So uncertain is a diagnosis without postmortem confirmation that the National Institutes of Health's consensus criteria for diagnosing Alzheimer's while the patient is alive include only the categories "possible" and "probable."

There is so much room for error in diagnosis that the literature often refers to *pseudosenility* ("fake" senility) as if it were a disorder itself. The *Brain Mind Bulletin* reported in 1981 that the President's Commission on Mental Health stated that there are more than 100 reversible (i.e., capable of being successfully treated) syndromes which mimic senile dementia. Thus, before a doctor can make even a possible or probable diagnosis of senile dementia, the physician must first rule out over one hundred other possible causes. This practice is not always carried out.

NUTRITIONAL FACTORS AS THE TRUE SOURCES OF SYMPTOMS

Sometimes the real cause of diagnosed Alzheimer's or senile dementia can be as simple as overall poor diet. An orthodox specialist in geriatrics told me some twenty years ago, "Very often, if we can get these 'senile' people back onto a good diet, they won't be senile anymore, just as they were not senile before they started the poor diet." I specified that this was an orthodox doctor, because orthodox physicians do not tend to believe poor nutrition can play a major role in many diseases, especially ones generally considered "hopeless."

There are many reasons for the decline in the quality of elderly people's nutrition, this doctor pointed out. "Elderly people often have no one to cook for and no real desire to cook just for themselves. Often they have physical problems making it difficult to shop for groceries, or financial problems making it difficult to buy wholesome food." Also, when today's elderly were young, there were popular conceptions about good nutrition that have now been disproved—for instance, "sugar is good for you," and "tea and toast make a wholesome meal."

Harold M. Silverman, Pharm.D., in *The Pill Book,* lists several specific nutritional causes for symptoms of dementia: reduced levels of sodium in the body; too much calcium in the blood; and severe deficiency of niacin, folic acid, or vitamin B12. He states that appropriate treatment "will take care of the dementia."

As this book went to press, psychiatrist Michael Schachter,

M.D., alerted me to the fact that one recent study indicating that an overload of zinc might contribute to Alzheimer's disease "was powerful enough to get people's eyebrows raised." As with all new research, check that your doctor is aware of it.

It may seem strange that something as simple as a deficiency of a nutrient—and therapy with that nutrient—can trigger and reverse symptoms of a disorder as complex and devastating as senile dementia. However, as discussed throughout this book, nutrients are necessary for every chemical reaction in the body—including the production of the brain chemicals whose proper balance is crucial to the healthy functioning of our brains.

OTHER TREATABLE FACTORS THAT PRODUCE SYMPTOMS

It has been estimated that 10 percent of reversible dementias are caused by alcohol and drug side effects or overdose. Dr. Silverman states, "Medications should always be considered a possible source of dementia."

He also points out that dementia symptoms can develop in people with heart failure, abnormal heart rhythms, or high blood pressure. These disorders can result in a lessened supply of blood to brain cells; this in turn results in loss of functioning of these brain cells. Other causes of dementia symptoms include poor thyroid function; diseases of kidneys, liver, and lungs; underactive pituitary or overactive adrenal gland; severe infection; tumor; anemia; and depression.

Charles Herrera, M.D., director of the sleep disorders program for the older adult at Mount Sinai Center, New York City, has pointed out that older insomniacs may display disruptive behavior or may become withdrawn and sink into despondency. Such behavior, he says, can propel the unfortunate person into an institution, especially when these symptoms are mistaken for signs of Alzheimer's or other psychiatric or neurological problems.

EXPECTATION OF ALZHEIMER'S AS A FACTOR IN OVERDIAGNOSING

Elderly people are often assumed to have senile dementia simply because of the myth that most elderly people develop this disorder. As it is not uncommon for doctors to misdiagnose simpler problems as senile dementia, it is even more common for medically untrained people to fear, mistakenly, that this disorder has taken hold of themselves or someone they love. Behavior that might be assumed to be senile dementia in an elderly person will be assumed normal when a younger person does the same thing. Even a teenager suffering chronic insomnia might exhibit the symptoms Dr. Herrera mentioned above; but no one would consider putting a teenager into an institution with a diagnosis of Alzheimer's. Relevant to this, psychiatrist Karl E. Humiston, M.D., told me: "One of my own loved ones goes streaking frantically through the house at least twice a week proclaiming loudly that he has lost something; it has totally, mysteriously disappeared; and it will surely never be found. In an elderly person, the combination of the lost object with the extreme agitation might lead to the fear of senile dementia. But my loved one in question is my son; he is 11 years old; and what he has usually lost is, perhaps conveniently, his homework."

Diagnosed Alzheimer's and senile dementia are not nearly so prevalent as you may have been led to think. (And remember that by no means all persons *diagnosed* as having these disorders have them.) Six statistics from different sources are as follows: 10 percent of the elderly get Alzheimer's; 6 percent of persons over age 65 suffer from Alzheimer's, with the percentage rising to over 20 percent after age 85; according to two sources, only 5 percent of the elderly suffer from dementia; according to another two, of the people now living in the United States, only 2–3 percent will ever get Alzheimer's.

The Self-Fulfilling Prophecy of Senility

Gerontologist Alex Comfort gives the dramatic estimate that 75 percent of the "aging" that occurs in this country is a self-fulfilling prophecy that "our folklore, prejudices and misconceptions about age impose on 'the old.' . . . If we insist that there is a group of people who, on a fixed calendar basis, cease to be people and become unintelligent, asexual, unemployable and crazy, the people so designated will be under pressure to be unintelligent, asexual, unemployable and crazy" (quoted in the *Brain Mind Bulletin* Vol. VI Theme Pack, 1981).

It is almost axiomatic that people who keep actively engaged with life tend not to manifest the mental and physical degeneration often found in those who, for instance, have been led to believe that retirement is a time when all one can do is to sit idly around the house. The brain is like a muscle: if you don't use it, it may atrophy. A study reported in the *Journal of Gerontology* (42, p. 82) found that older adults showed improved performance on both mental and reflex tasks after only a few weeks of playing computer video games.

Other research suggests how inactivity and social isolation might play a role in senile dementia. Some researchers over the years had found that rats' brains degenerated between maturity and old age, but other researchers had found no brain degeneration. In the late 1970s, Dr. Marian Diamond at the University of California–Berkeley reported a study that may explain the observed differences. "In many of the studies showing losses of neurons, the animals were in isolation." But they had the company of their "peers" in Dr. Diamond's investigation, and in the previous studies that also had shown no loss of brain cells as the animals aged.

Dr. Diamond pointed out that if the animal studies are correlated to human aging, the isolation of elderly patients in mental wards may be a factor in the abnormal decrease of brain cells seen in postmortem investigations. "If you have a clear cardiovascular system and keep active," she stated, "the nerve cells seem to have endless potential" (quoted in the *Brain Mind Bulletin* Theme Pack from Vol. III, 1977, 1978).

Some Orthomolecular Approaches to Therapy

A thorough evaluation by an orthomolecular doctor will rule out the numerous disorders that can cause symptoms that mimic senile dementia. An orthomolecular physician, as compared to orthodox colleagues, will have a higher degree of suspicion about nutritional problems that may be behind the symptoms and will order laboratory tests to identify those problems. "When unmet nutritional needs have been corrected," Dr. Mandell says, "the mental symptoms will be reversed, and the misdiagnosis of senile dementia can be discarded."

A comprehensive regimen using all the nutrients that have been shown, when studied separately, to help might include vitamins B6, B12, B15, and E; and folic acid, choline, and lecithin. Trace minerals, particularly zinc, manganese, and chromium, might also be included.

CHOLINE AND LECITHIN

In 1977, the *Lancet* (October 1, p. 711) published a study by W. D. Boyd and associates on the effect of choline in seven patients with severe Alzheimer-type senile dementia. Choline is a nutrient that the body uses to produce the brain chemical acetylcholine. One month's treatment with choline chloride resulted in noticeable improvement in cognition.

In 1979, M. Marsel Mesulam, M.D., and Sandra Weintraub, Ph.D., from Beth Israel Hospital in Boston reported on their use of choline chloride and lecithin on six patients with Alzheimer's in a paper they presented at the International Study Group on Memory Disorders, in Zurich. Two of the six showed improvement in memory, language functions, and daily living ability. One patient who had deteriorated so badly that she could not safely be left home alone was now able to go on errands. The other, who had suffered much slowing of thought, speech, and movement, "has shown a great increase in fluency so that she is more alert and effective in social interaction."

There has been considerable research on the role of choline in memory, the loss of which is the earliest and most pervasive symptom of senility. In one study, led by Dr. Raymond Bartus and reported in 1980 in *Science* (209, pp. 301–3), a group of elderly breeder mice were fed a choline-enriched diet, and another group the same age were given a diet deficient in this nutrient. After several months on the diets, all the mice were taught a new task. Later, they were tested for their memory of how to do the task. The mice on the choline-rich diet remembered the task as well as three-month-old mice reared on a normal diet who had been taught the task. In sharp contrast, the choline-deficient mice remembered the task as poorly as 23-month-old mice on a normal diet. They were prematurely senile.

This study measured not just memory in a general sense, but specifically the ability to learn and remember *new* things—that is, short-term memory. As mentioned earlier, this is the aspect of memory that is first lost in senile dementia and Alzheimer's.

As I write this book, researchers at the University of Texas at Dallas are preparing to test several new drugs on Alzheimer's patients. One is being tested because it has been shown "to improve memory by prolonging the action of acetylcholine, a brain chemical progressively lost in Alzheimer's patients." Orthomolecular doctors use the nutrient choline because it is the raw material for the production of acetylcholine.

Abram Hoffer, M.D., Ph.D., wrote me a last-minute update, as this book went to press, indicating his belief that orthomolecular doctors in general no longer find choline to be extremely useful. "There are, however, studies beginning using the higher, long-chain, Omega-3 fatty acids, and these might be more valuable."

B VITAMINS

One study, conducted by William and Bonnie Thornton, found that nine of 26 older psychiatric patients at a University of Illinois center showed extremely low blood serum levels of folic acid. Three of these patients had been diagnosed with senile dementia; their condition was so advanced that they suffered hallucinations. Two of these three improved when given supplementary folic acid *(Brain Mind Theme Pack* from Vol. III, 1977, 1978).

One reason vitamin B6 is used to treat symptoms of senile dementia is that it (along with magnesium) plays a crucial role in converting dietary choline to the brain chemical acetylcholine, mentioned above. Research has also shown a connection between a deficiency of B6 and damage to receptors for another important brain chemical, dopamine.

OTHER NUTRIENTS

Impressive improvement of many symptoms of senility with the use of vitamin E and the mineral selenium was reported by Matti Tolonen, M.D., of the University of Helsinki. For one year, 15 residents of a Finnish nursing home took these two nutrients daily, while another 15 received placebo. Neither the participants nor the supervising nurses knew which patients were getting nutritional supplements and which were getting the inactive placebo. After only two months, the nurses said they had observed so much mental and emotional improvement in some of the patients that they could guess who was getting the nutrients and who wasn't. They were right 80 percent of the time. Psychological evaluations confirmed what the nurses had noticed in the elderly residents taking the supplements: They were more alert, open to change, willing to take care of themselves, and more interested in their environment. They were also less depressed, anxious, hostile, and tired. This study is described by Roger Yepsen, Jr., in *Your Guide to Lifetime Memory Improvement* (Rodale Press, 1986).

Pioneering doctor Carl C. Pfeiffer, Ph.D., M.D., reported back in 1975 on the importance of manganese in senility. He found that levels of the simple chemical spermine could be elevated in the body by supplementation with zinc and, more importantly, manganese. He reported also that spermine levels were found in high concentration in patients and normal individuals with adequate memory for recent events—and low in patients with Alzheimer's and senile dementia. In his 1987 book *Nutrition and Mental Illness* (p. 74), he pointed out that "the brain badly needs [spermine] to make more RNA."

ALUMINUM AND ALZHEIMER'S

Orthomolecular doctors will probably test for an aluminum overload. There seems at present no agreement as to exactly what role aluminum plays in dementia, but many researchers agree that there is some connection. Orthomolecular doctors do not tend to wait until a finding is accepted by all doctors before applying it for the benefit of their patients, as long as the treatment can do no harm. Dr. Pfeiffer was one of many orthomolecular doctors convinced that aluminum plays a leading role in these disorders. In *Nutrition and Mental Illness* (p. 104) he wrote, "Alzheimer's disease labels frequently disguise simple aluminum poisoning."

Brains of deceased Alzheimer's patients have been found to contain four to six times the amount of aluminum found in normal brain cells. As long ago as 1973, Dr. D. R. Crupper and associates at the University of Toronto injected aluminum into cats and found that they became slower learners in a simple avoidance task. Dr. Pfeiffer refers to this work in *Mental and Elemental Nutrients* (p. 306).

The following letter, which was printed in the *New York Times* on November 26, 1989, was written by Michael A. Weiner, President of the Alzheimer's Research Institute in Tiburon, California. "Aluminum has been known as a neurotoxic substance for nearly a century. . . . It is the only element noted to accumulate in the tangle-bearing neurons characteristic of [Alzheimer's] disease and is also found in elevated amounts in four regions of the brain of Alzheimer's patients. . . .

Weiner asks:

> What is wrong with recommending low aluminum intake as part of an Alzheimer's risk-reduction program? It is a neurotoxic metal of no known use in the human body and is implicated in several other disease states. There is no need to continue using aluminum in antacids, analgesics and other medications.

> Before the 20th century, aluminum was not used in any foods or pharmaceuticals, and there is no evidence that Alzheimer's disease existed before this century. We are well past the stage of needing to wait for the last double-blinded study before we can recommend preventive steps.

You will note that Weiner commented that there is no evidence that Alzheimer's existed before the 1900s. You may know that symptoms of dementia in some aged people were well-known long before then. However, *Alzheimer's*—when the word is used in its strict definition of "*pre*-senile dementia"—was not known until the 1900s. Orthomolecular doctors point out that this new disease, Alzheimer's, began appearing at the same time as the deterioration of our national diet and the increased use of aluminum.

Removal of aluminum and other heavy metals from the body involves chelation. Some nutritional substances act as chelators; but for heavy toxicity, orthomolecular doctors use intravenous EDTA (ethylenediaminetetraacetic acid), a synthetic amino acid. (See Chapter 17.)

Psychiatrist Hoffer, in his 1989 book *Orthomolecular Medicine for Physicians* (p. 155), tells of an elderly man he interviewed one month after the last of 20 chelation treatments. "He had had Alzheimer's disease," Dr. Hoffer writes. "According to his wife he had deteriorated to such a degree he could no longer speak intelligently, was disoriented in space, and could not be left alone in a city for even a few seconds, as he wandered away and became lost." An avid golfer, his handicap had gone up from seven to 27. Dr. Hoffer reports that the man had "no memory of the condition he had been in" before chelation, but he remembered that sometime during the treatments he had "awakened." The psychiatrist states that when he interviewed the man, he "showed no evidence of any Alzheimer's speech disorder." The patient's golf handicap went back down to his original seven.

What You Can Do

You can do much to *prevent* Alzheimer's and senile dementia symptoms by decreasing intake of aluminum, increasing intake of substances that are natural chelators, and by making sure you have adequate intake of the nutrients used by orthomolecular doctors in treatment.

Sources of choline include lecithin, wheat germ, whole grains, green leafy vegetables, seeds, nuts, fish, eggs, and soy beans.

As with every disorder covered in this book, the surest, simplest, and safest way to get help, for prevention and treatment, is to consult an orthomolecular physician. See the "Resources" section for how to find one near you. The Introduction gives further information on how to work with a nutritional doctor, including what you can do if your loved one is institutionalized and cannot go in person to a physician specializing in this field.

Make certain all other possible causes of symptoms mimicking Alzheimer's and senile dementia have been ruled out before you accept one of the latter diagnoses. If your doctor is an orthodox physician, you may have to insist that nutritional causes and an overload of aluminum be considered.

Before your appointment with the orthomolecular doctor, the following steps, suggested by doctors, can be taken on your own, to help alleviate symptoms.

Try to get your loved one on a healthy diet and give a daily multivitamin-mineral pill (see Chapter 2).

Try to see that your loved one drinks plenty of water. Dr. Humiston says, "People who are already a bit confused often don't drink enough water, partly because they don't notice the subtle feeling of thirst that used to impel them to drink. Many think that water's only role in good health is to flush toxins out of the system, but water is also an essential nutrient. The two hydrogen atoms and the oxygen atom in water combine over and over with numerous other chemicals in the body to make substances necessary for all sorts of internal chemical reactions."

DO NOT DISCONTINUE ANY PRESCRIBED MEDICATIONS ON YOUR OWN, but check with a doctor to determine any possible side effects, since some side effects can be mistaken for symptoms of dementia. Two or more drugs can interact with each other and cause symptoms that won't be listed *anywhere* as side effects of any of the individual drugs. Mention the drugs to your orthomolecular doctor, who may be able to substitute nutritional therapy for the disorders for which the drugs were prescribed.

Avoid adding more aluminum to a possible already existing overload (see Chapter 2 for information on how to get aluminum out of your water). If you are cooking with aluminum cookware, replace it with stainless steel, glass, or Corning ware. Other sources of aluminum are baking powder, buffered aspirin, underarm antiperspirants (some, but not all, brands found mainly in health-food stores are aluminum-free), aluminum foil, and antacids. Dr. Mandell suggests that aluminum cans containing soft drinks may be culprits. Check with your pharmacist to see if prescription medications contain aluminum. Again, do not discontinue prescription drugs before consulting your physician.

Pay attention to the idea of the self-fulfilling prophecy for Alzheimer's and senile dementia. I will give a few specific suggestions as to how you can prevent that prophecy from "fulfilling itself." For example, your concern may be with your mother, who lives alone and seems to be showing signs of senile dementia.

If she is safely able to get out of her house, encourage her to do so. Let her know that her strength and mind may be deteriorating at least partly because she is not using them. Find a social or church group for her to join. Maybe while your mother was raising you, or working full time, she looked forward to having time to pursue certain activities. Remind her now of those past dreams and do whatever you can to get her started on fulfilling them.

Make sure your mother has objects around her to occupy her time actively while she's alone. (Remember the study about those video games!) Did your mother, when she was "totally herself," love flowers and plants? Why not give her some to care for? Consider jigsaw puzzles and other games that use the mind and can be played alone. But don't frustrate her by choosing games obviously beyond her present capacity. If she is capable of taking good care of a dog or cat, getting her one might be a great help. Numerous studies show how beneficial a pet can be to a human's physical and mental health. Pets are excellent companions: They are available for "their person" 24 hours a day, and are noncritical, even if their person is a bit "slow" or "strange." Some enlightened nursing homes have arrangements with animal shelters whereby a "mascot" is brought in once a week to the elderly, who pet the animal, hold it in their laps, etc. That day of the week is when most patients in the nursing home perk up. (It is also the day of the week when the orphaned or abandoned animal tends to perk up.) Again, be careful not to "overburden" your mother beyond her present capability: Caring for a young puppy or kitten can be too much for many who already have problems of their own; consider a mature dog or cat. (If you adopt one from the ASPCA, for instance, you will have the added pleasure of possibly saving that animal's life.) If you feel that even a mature dog or cat will overburden your mother, consider a bird or goldfish. While these may not be as strong a companion, they still will be living entities around her to keep her constant company—and they will give her something active to DO while she takes care of them.

Visit your mother whenever you can. Explain to other family members the importance of visiting her. Ask her neighbors to drop in, maybe just for a few minutes a day.

AUTISM IS OFTEN a symptom of vitamin-B6 dependency. . . . All studies known to me in which vitamin B6 has been evaluated have shown positive results.

—BERNARD RIMLAND, PH.D., Founder and Director of the Autism Research Institute; Founder of the Autism Society of America (personal communication)

WE CANNOT OVERLOOK the fact that so many children diagnosed with "hyperactivity," "learning disorder," "dyslexia," "behavior disorder," and "minimal brain dysfunction" suffer from reversible allergic and nutritional disorders whose causes can be eliminated or controlled.

—MARSHALL MANDELL, M.D., clinical ecologist (personal communication)

Chapter 13

Children's Mental Problems: Autism—
Childhood Schizophrenia—
Hyperactivity—Learning/Behavior
Disorders

Orthomolecular psychiatrists view autism, childhood schizophrenia, and the diagnostic variations of learning and behavior disorders as usually being linked to distinct biochemical factors that can be treated nutritionally. This view takes away both the mystery and the stigma of these disorders, and works against the old belief that parents were at fault for their children's disorders because they did not give proper psychological nurturing.

Autism and Childhood Schizophrenia

What are some of the biochemical factors that orthomolecular doctors work with in treating autism and childhood schizophrenia? Bernard Rimland, Ph.D., is the founder and director of the Autism Research Institute—previously called the Institute for Child Behavior Research—in San Diego, and the founder of the Autism Society of America. He has for many years reported solid results in treating many cases of autism as a manifestation of vitamin-B6 dependency. (A nutritional dependency is an abnormal need for the nutrient. Chapter 18 discusses the vital role B6 plays in producing many of our brain chemicals.)

Another relevant biochemical factor is food intolerance. Carl C. Pfeiffer, Ph.D., M.D., points out in *Nutrition and Mental Illness* (pp. 53–54) that "recent studies have indicated that celiac disease [sensitivity to gluten, a protein in wheat, rye, barley, and oats] may be responsible for many cases of 'schizophrenia.' " This chapter discusses these and other nutritional deficiencies and food and chemical intolerances that have been implicated in both autism and schizophrenia.

Obviously, there is an enormous difference between thinking of your child as having the dreaded disorder called autism, and thinking of him as needing supplements of vitamin B6; an enormous difference between thinking of your child as having the psychosis called childhood schizophrenia, and thinking of her as having to cut certain foods out of her diet.

Childhood schizophrenia and autism are considered closely related. Indeed, it wasn't until 1943 that psychiatrist Leo Kanner, M.D., identified autism as a separate disorder; until then, autism had been thought to *be* childhood schizophrenia. I discuss autism largely in reference to children because most persons seeking help are the parents of those who suffer—even though their child may have reached adulthood. However, bear in mind that studies showing improvement sometimes include in their statistics adult autistics who have, in fact, shown the most improvement. For instance, in one study evaluating mostly children, it was a woman of 55 who responded most dramatically.

HOW WELL DOES ORTHOMOLECULAR THERAPY WORK?

Orthomolecular psychiatrists do not guarantee that your child will completely recover with nutritional approaches, but he has a good chance of becoming a functional child, and then a functional adult. And it is possible that he can blossom into a human being who for all intents and purposes never had suffered a psychosis.

Dr. Rimland tells of an 18-year-old autistic man who was about to be "evicted" from the third mental hospital in his city. Massive amounts of drugs had had no effect; he was considered too violent to be kept in the hospital. (While the usual "picture" of an autistic is that of a withdrawn, non-emotional person, some are prone to violence.) As a last resort, his orthodox psychiatrist tried the vitamin B6 and magnesium therapy pioneered by Dr. Rimland. "The young man calmed down very quickly," Dr. Rimland says. "The psychiatrist later visited the family and reported that she found the young man now to be a pleasant and easy-going autistic person who sang and played his guitar for her."

One can imagine his family's quandary before the nutritional therapy. He was too violent to be cared for at home, and too violent to be treated even in an institution. Who was to take care of him?

To give a hint, for now, of the success your child may have using orthomolecular approaches, let us consider a few of the studies that have been done on only one nutritional therapy, that using B6 and magnesium. (Remember that some patients in these studies, because of their individual biochemical needs, might have responded better to another orthomolecular approach, or to a combination of two or more.) Back in 1968 in Germany, V. E. Bonisch *(Praxis der Kinderpsychologie,* 8, pp. 308–10) published results of an open trial using vitamin B6 on 16 autistic children: 12 of the 16 improved, and three spoke for the first time. In 1973, Dr. Rimland reported (in *Orthomolecular Psychiatry,* edited by D. R. Hawkins and L. Pauling, New York: W. H. Freeman, pp. 513–39) that of 190 autistic children given large doses of several vitamins, including B6, 45 percent showed "definite improvement." And in 1978 a team headed by Dr. Rimland reported in the *American Journal of Psychiatry* (35 pp. 472–75) that 11 of 15 autistic children improved when given B6. This was a double-blind placebo cross-over study, considered to provide a very high level of scientific accuracy.

Dr. Rimland states that in his studies, all children who improved did so "significantly—and in some cases, the improvement was remarkable. There was better eye contact, less self-stimulatory behavior, more interest in the world around them, fewer tantrums, more speech." Furthermore, he says,

> Other studies from this country and abroad have demonstrated very clearly that 30–60% of autistic children show significant behavioral and other benefits [from a nutritional therapy based on B6].
>
> As a matter of fact, all studies known to me in which vitamin B6 has been evaluated for autistic children have shown positive results. This is a rather remarkable record, since the many drugs that have been evaluated for autism have shown very inconsistent results. If a drug shows positive results in about half of the evaluation studies, it is considered a success and is then advocated for use with autistic patients.

While drugs tend to mask symptoms without solving the problems underlying the symptoms, studies have shown B6 to help normalize brain waves and urine chemistry, in addition to improving behavior and increasing speech. For instance, studies with B6 alone and with B6 plus magnesium lactate showed lowering of urinary homovanillic acid, the principal derivative of the brain chemical dopamine. B6 is involved not only in the production of dopamine but of other important transmitters of brain signals, including serotonin. A current popular hypothesis as to the cause of autism is an imbalance in the latter chemical.

SOME ORTHOMOLECULAR APPROACHES TO AUTISM AND CHILDHOOD SCHIZOPHRENIA

As is usual with orthomolecular medicine, doctors will base their choice of therapies on the individual biochemical problems of the patient.

Food and Chemical Intolerances ("Allergies"). William H. Philpott, M.D., a leading orthomolecular psychiatrist and clinical ecologist, gives this case history:

> The twins were diagnosed as autistic by a neurologist at a leading school of medicine in New York. They could not talk, could not be educated, and were quite hyperactive. I found them to be deficient in a number of nutrients—in virtually the same degree. I found them both intolerant to six foods. Just as they had virtually identical symptoms of autism, they had virtually identical biochemical problems behind those symptoms. We treated their nutritional deficiencies and withdrew them from the foods that touched off their brain reactions.

Later, the neurologist who had diagnosed the twins called the mother and asked her to bring them to a medical conference. Dr. Philpott says, "As identical twins with identical autism, they were prime examples of 'the genetic factor' in autism. The mother told the neurologist that the boys were no longer hyperactive, were communicating, and were now capable of being educated."

The link between one food intolerance and childhood schizophrenia was suspected by Dr. Lauretta Bender back in 1953, when she noted that schizophrenic children were extraordinarily subject to gluten intolerance (celiac disease). Her observation was picked up on throughout the years by other researchers, and in his 1987 book Dr. Pfeiffer stated that "the psychiatric picture of the celiac child is not unlike that of the schizophrenic child."

The two children described below were treated for intolerances, and both were also treated nutritionally for diagnosed low blood sugar, which is sometimes closely linked to food intolerances in the orthomolecular view.

When nine-year-old Jack came to Full Circle, a residential research center in the San Francisco Bay Area, he tripped over his own feet, his longest sentences were three words, and he would respond to questions with "I dunno." He had psychotic episodes in the morning. He could not find his way out of his room and down to breakfast. Once at the table, he couldn't get the food onto his fork, let alone into his mouth. Jack and his family had been in traditional therapy for years. The therapist informed the parents that they were responsible for the boy's schizophrenia, and that Jack would probably commit suicide by age 14.

Doctors at Full Circle found that Jack was extremely intolerant to many foods and chemicals, and that he had severe low blood sugar. In this disorder, blood-sugar level can fall dramatically when frequent meals are not taken; Jack's level would go down so low overnight that by morning he was out of touch with physical reality —because glucose (sugar) is the brain's main "fuel." The staff put him on a diet for low blood sugar, a maneuver that entirely ended his morning "psychosis."

Also, tests showed dramatic psychological and behavioral responses to wheat, egg, yeast, chlorine, and several food dyes. Removing these foods and chemicals resulted in further improvement.

After a year, staff members reported that "Jack now speaks long, complex sentences and is in continuous touch with physical reality. He is still a strange child in a world of his own, but he will not have to spend his life in an institution." And, presumably, he will not be fulfilling his former therapist's prophecy of suicide by age 14 (reported in *Commonweal,* undated).

Dr. Philpott includes the following case history in *Brain Allergies* (pp. 136–46). The writer is Angela's mother, who sent letters as progress reports to Dr. Philpott. She speaks eloquently of the pain felt by parents of autistic children; she also speaks eloquently of the help parents may find if they work with an orthomolecular doctor.

Angela's mother first wrote in February of 1976, after Angela had been on Dr. Philpott's prescribed therapy for six months. "It's hard to believe Angela is the same little girl as six months ago. . . . I watch with a mother's joy how my four-year-old daughter is exploring her world for the first time. And best of all, her affection is growing for those around her."

Angela's mother summarized the child's history before Dr. Philpott's treatment. "Angela had not learned any words by her first birthday, not even 'mama.' " She rarely noticed her parents' presence. When she did, "I was a stranger and an intruder."

In Angela's second year she grew worse, throwing tantrums for no reason. "She began spending hours in her open closet, picking up little toys and watching them drop over and over. . . . If I interfered with what she was doing by picking her up, she would just stiffen and scream. It was as though she preferred objects to people."

When Angela was three, doctors in a UCLA autism project diagnosed her autistic. Luckily, someone gave the mother a brochure on the upcoming 1975 National Autistic Conference, which both parents attended. "One presentation in particular impressed us. It was on allergies that affect the brain and central nervous system, and megavitamin therapy. I had suspected some foods were affecting Angela adversely. Here were professionals who thought the same way."

Angela's parents took her to Dr. Philpott, who tested for food and chemical intolerances. After five weeks of the psychiatrist's prescribed regimen, Angela was toilet-trained, a milestone that her mother described as "a miracle. . . . Most of all, she had become so much calmer and happier in those five weeks."

Soon, Angela "began to notice things in the house and explored as if she had been blind and could suddenly see. . . . It's as if she is slowly waking from a deep sleep. For the first time she is taking interest in what people are doing around her. Her eye contact with her family is good . . . and she has lost much of her repetitive mannerisms. . . . She will come into whatever room we happen to be sitting in and climb up into her dad's lap. . . . For the first time we really feel like a family. . . .

"She started school a little over a month ago, and she is doing fine." This was a special-education class at a public school. "Life is no longer treading water for Angela. She is swimming for home."

Angela's mother wrote again less than eight months later. "Angela began talking about a year after she went through the initial [phase] for Dr. Philpott's food allergy testing. . . . Angela enjoys verbalizing and realizes that a magic barrier that separated her from other people has disappeared, which has helped her surge forward in spontaneous social contact. She is very affectionate . . ."

The mother concludes: "Angela was a confirmed case of autism . . . by Dr. Ivar Lovaas and Dr. Simmons of UCLA in 1974. She was a completely incoherent, hyperactive mess then. We went another year with no help and no progress in Angela. Dr. Philpott took her on as a patient in July 1975. Now, one year later, Angela is a different child, as if she was never that bad and all the heartache was a collective nightmare for our family."

Dr. Rimland adds a postscript. He was speaking at a conference on autism in May 1976—a few months before the mother wrote (above) of even further improvement. Dr. Rimland says,

At intermission, Mrs. Calvera brought Angela to me; she was a beautiful and well-behaved little girl. When I delivered my talk on autism and nutrition, I asked Mrs. Calvera and her daughter to come to the podium. Mrs. Calvera spoke about her experience; and the audience listened with great interest. But actually, all eyes were riveted on Angela. She was sitting—quietly but alertly—at the speaker's table, confronted with several long-stemmed and very fragile water glasses. Angela picked one up very carefully, took a little sip of water, and placed the glass back down very carefully.

Dr. Rimland ends:

You couldn't have asked to see a more normal-appearing and well-behaved child. Angela demonstrated to that audience much more eloquently than I could have that the methods of clinical ecology . . . are indeed effective and can often bring about behavioral improvements that border on the incredible.

Vitamin B6 and Magnesium. Earlier, we touched on studies investigating this therapy. Dr. Rimland investigated this approach from another angle: He asked parents to record their empirical observations on how the 12 most commonly used drugs helped their autistic children, in comparison with vitamin B6 and magnesium. The treatment reported as having the highest ratio of favorable to unfavorable effects was B6/magnesium: 43 percent of the parents reported these nutrients made their children better, while 5 percent reported worsening of symptoms. Deanol (a combination of two forms of the nutrient choline) was reported as second best, seeming to help 29 percent of the children while 16 percent of the parents said it appeared to make their children worse.

The drug rated most favorably was fenfluramine. It was reported as helping 29 percent of the children (the same percentage as the second-rated nutritional therapy), but it appeared to make 19 percent worse. The drugs phenobarbital, Ritalin, and amphetamines were reported to make 40–51 percent of the children worse.

Remember that these statistics represent the subjective findings of parents. It is always possible in such cases that people may "see" results because they expect to see them. (It may also be argued that parents know their child more intimately than the physician, and can observe the child's behavior around the clock.)

Folic Acid. Another approach that helps some autistic children is supplementation with folic acid, a B vitamin. Dr. Rimland tells of a scientist who was working on another problem and who placed a fragile X chromosome in a test tube. "This fragile X chromosome had been identified six years earlier as a cause of some cases of autism. The scientist also placed some folic acid in the culture medium. When he went back to check things out, he couldn't find the fragile X chromosome. The folic acid had improved the chromosome so that it was no longer fragile."

Dr. Rimland tells of an autistic child whose major compulsive behavior had been: Take three steps, make a 360-degree turn; take three steps, make a 360-degree turn; take three steps, etc. When the child was given folic acid, "He walked in a straight line." To test whether folic acid had indeed been the reason for the improvement, the nutrient was withdrawn for a while. When the child was brought back to Dr. Rimland for reevaluation, "He came into the office, took three steps, made a 360-degree turn; took three steps, made a 360-degree turn, etc. We again put him on folic acid; he again walked in a straight line. We again removed the folic acid; he again reverted to his three-step, one-circle compulsive behavior."

Treating Yeast Overgrowth (Candidiasis). Dr. Rimland tells of another factor behind some cases of autism: the taking of antibiotics. That might seem an outrageous statement to some, so here is a brief medical rationale. It is known that antibiotics destroy the bacteria in the intestines that normally prevent an overgrowth of yeast. Overgrowth of the yeast *Candida albicans* in the intestines can spread toxins throughout the body. Since the brain is part of the body, these poisons can attack the brain and make it diseased.

Dr. Rimland says he'll "never forget" the time he published a case history of a child who had been

> perfectly normal until he suffered an ear infection and was given antibiotics. Suddenly, he became an autistic child; just one of his symptoms was that he had lost speech. My Institute got absolutely flooded with letters from parents who had had the same experience: their children had been perfectly normal at an age past that in which autism is supposed to show up if it ever does —and had suddenly been diagnosed as having autism after taking antibiotics.

According to many orthomolecular doctors, candidiasis is often what actually underlies the food sensitivities that seem to be the primary source of distressing symptoms. Thus, treating candidiasis can be helpful for autism and childhood schizophrenia by clearing up troublesome intolerances as well as by getting rid of the candida overgrowth itself.

Other Nutritional Approaches. The late orthomolecular psychiatrist, Allan Cott, M.D., told me in an interview that "The child with schizophrenia can often be improved by using the basic hypoglyce-

mic diet of high protein, low refined carbohydrate, and no sugar."
Dr. Cott was the founder of the Allan Cott School for Seriously Disturbed Children in Birmingham, where, he said, the children did not
have to take drugs "except infrequently for the most seriously ill."
The diet for low blood sugar (hypoglycemia) can be so important,
Dr. Cott stated, that "all of us working in this field have seen cases
where a patient has not altered the vitamin, mineral, or even drug
regimen and has had a relapse simply by wandering off this diet."

A typical therapy may also include removing salicylates, and artificial colors and flavors from the diet, since many children test out
to react unfavorably to these. (See p. 274)

Dr. Cott used vitamin B3 for childhood schizophrenia partly because it is a powerful natural sedative (some studies have shown it
to be as effective as Valium) and because it can help the child to
sleep better. Dr. John Smythies in 1977 headed a team at the University of Alabama Department of Neurosciences that found that B3
increases REM sleep by 40 percent in humans. (Chapter 8, on adult
schizophrenia, discusses how successful B3, even when used virtually alone, can sometimes be in treating schizophrenia.)

"Typically," said Dr. Cott, "children with childhood schizophrenia test out to be low in manganese, calcium, magnesium, and
zinc." Calcium and magnesium are well known to have a calming
effect, and they can be helpful with schizophrenic children, who
tend to be hyperactive.

For the autistic child, vitamin B15 may be used in large amounts;
like B6, it can stimulate speech, as Dr. Cott was the first to show.
Zinc may also be given; Dr. Cott was credited with noticing that
some symptoms of autism are similar to symptoms of zinc deficiency.

Behavior Therapy. Another approach recommended by orthomolecular doctors for childhood schizophrenia and autism is behavior
therapy. Actually, Dr. Rimland states that "behavior modification is
the single most effective therapy." (Don't confuse this action-
oriented technique with the analyzing-talking therapies.)

Dr. Rimland asked parents to compare behavior modification, psychotherapy, several other techniques, and removing three dietary factors to which people are commonly intolerant. An overwhelming 83 percent felt behavior modification helped their child. The second-highest rated step was removing sugar: 52 percent felt it helped. Next was removing milk, with 46 percent reporting that this was helpful. Fourth was removing wheat: 44 percent improvement. Eighth on a list of nine was psychotherapy, with 35 percent of parents reporting that it helped their child, and 6 percent reporting that it seemed to make the child worse.

A Structured Environment. Dr. Rimland's work over the years has led him to "the conclusion that it is extremely important that the children be in a structured, demanding educational setting." This can be at home, in a school, or when possible ideally a combination of both. But it is of prime importance that these children be given an ordered existence, and that it be simply *expected* of them that they can do their very best in every activity. For instance, Dr. Carl Fenichel of the League for Emotionally Disturbed Children in Brooklyn, New York, told the meeting of the National Society for Autistic Children in 1969 that he had entered the field of educating "so-called emotionally disturbed children with the conviction that what the children needed was love, affection, and a permissive approach. . . . Our children taught us otherwise. We learned that disorganized children need someone to organize their worlds for them . . . that what they needed was teachers who knew how to limit as well as accept them" (quoted by Dr. Rimland).

WHAT YOU CAN DO

Obviously, if you are to help your child to full potential, you cannot expect to do this using self-help alone. For how to find an orthomolecular physician near you, see the "Resources" section. The Introduction may be of further help.

Re-reading this chapter will give some clues as to steps you can safely take on your own before you can get together with the physician. For instance, if you have been conscientiously trying to provide a permissive environment for your troubled child, consider what has been said about the benefits of bringing order into your child's *dis*ordered world. If you have been trying traditional psychotherapy, and it has not helped, consider behavior therapy.

Read labels carefully for artificial flavors and dyes and eliminate foods that contain them. For details of what you can safely do about intolerances, see Chapter 2 and Chapter 14. Chapters 15 and 16 give self-help suggestions for low blood sugar and candidiasis.

Dr. Rimland has developed a safe, effective way you can use vitamin B6–magnesium therapy on your own. I MOST STRONGLY URGE YOU NOT TO TRY THIS THERAPY WITHOUT READING DR. RIMLAND'S DETAILS. You can obtain these by writing the Autism Research Institute; the address is in the Resources section.

Holding your autistic child may be helpful. Although one of the common symptoms of autism is that the child appears to dislike being touched, there is enough mention in the literature that this might help, that it is worth your trying.

Several relatively new techniques help autistic children to communicate without speaking. Discuss with your doctor which one might be most helpful; remember, though, that nutritional therapy can stimulate *actual* speech. One technique, called *facilitated communication*, involves teaching the autistic to express in typing what others would normally express orally. Like other techniques, it has revealed that there is much more of an aware person "inside" the autistic than has previously been thought. One child typed, "I am not autistic at the typewriter"; another stated that without facilitation, "I would be helpless once again and it would be like a naked death"; another, when asked to name two causes of high blood pressure, quipped through his keyboard, "Cholesterol and tests." Since the technique allows communication between the autistic and the world, it can allow the child to learn to read and do schoolwork.

Although the following technique has not to my knowledge been subjected to studies, those who wish to try every possible avenue may want to consider it. A family ran a desperate "experiment" on their severely autistic son. Basically, since he could not join their world, they joined *his*. For instance, they sat with him hour after hour and copied whatever compulsive behavior he chose for himself. Their approach was long and tedious, but apparently it resulted in their severely autistic child's becoming capable of normal speech, normal schooling, and bright, caring human relationships. The family's experiences are recounted in detail in the book *Son Rise* by Barry N. Kaufman (Warner Books, 1977).

Orthomolecular psychiatrist Karl E. Humiston, M.D., comments:

> What that family did seems to be very close to a technique used by the famous psychotherapist Dr. Milton Ericson. He would record his psychotic patients as they talked, then would go home and practice their way of speaking until he could imitate them perfectly. The next week, when the patient had stopped talking, Dr. Ericson would start speaking in exactly the same tone, rhythm, cadence, and use the same facial expressions, gestures, posture. This technique seemed to give Dr. Ericson a way to *connect* with the patient in a therapeutic way that others could not match.

Learning and Behavior Disorders, Minimal Brain Damage, Hyperactivity (Hyperkinesis), etc.

As Abram Hoffer, M.D., Ph.D., says in his book *Orthomolecular Medicine for Physicians* (p. 205), he once counted up to a hundred different diagnostic terms in use to describe children with learning and behavior disorders. "Most of them have little significance, more often reflecting the diagnostic bias and interest of the diagnostician than a true syndrome." He points out that orthomolecular physicians prefer to work not with diagnostic labels for symptoms, but with the *causes* of the symptoms, "such as cerebral allergy, vitamin deficiency or dependency, or mineral problems."

Orthomolecular psychiatrists object to labeling a child as, say, learning/behavior-disordered because such labels stigmatize him, not only to others but to himself, whereas referring to him as being deficient in certain nutrients, or intolerant to specific foods, does not.

Orthomolecular doctors do not negate the effects that pshychological problems may have. Dr. Hoffer states that "a small group suffers from a variety of psychosocial factors including broken homes, parental brutality or pathology," and that it is as wrong to treat these children with vitamins "as it is to treat children suffering from nutritional problems by psychotherapy or family counseling. Unfortunately, the second error has been, and still is, the more common one."

While so-called learning and behavior disorders and hyperactivity make the child a problem for parents and teachers, it is important to keep in mind that the child is also a perpetual "problem" for himself. If we believe in a biological basis for these disorders, we should realize that these children often cannot control their emotions, tempers, or hostile and aggressive behavior. It has been pointed out that they are often virtually incapable of responding to either punishment or reward. The child may have a healthy drive toward a positive identity but—because of the above incapabilities —he is faced with failure day after day. Further complicating his world is the fact that his peers, reacting to his more infantile organization, make him the butt of ridicule. Thus, learning and behavior problems, although biologically based, often set in motion a psychological spiral: The child decides that as long as he continues to try to be good, he will continue to fail miserably. He may reason that it is far better to ally himself with children who share his problems. Perhaps he can become a "good guy" with *them,* maybe even a leader—the "best at being bad" as one psychiatrist phrased it.

Some children with these disorders may not immediately seem to fit the profile drawn above of a child who cannot control negative behavior. Perhaps the child can learn well, or behave well—sometimes. Traditionally, it has been assumed that such a child is merely being "lazy" or "spiteful" by not learning or behaving well most of the time. But an erratic pattern of "bad" behavior does not at all rule out the possibility that the problem is biochemically based: The child's "good times" may come when he has been free, for a while, of a food or chemical to which he is intolerant, or when he has had less than his usual amount of sugar.

ORTHOMOLECULAR THERAPY

As is common with orthomolecular therapy, treatment will be chosen to the *individual's* biochemical imbalances that may be affecting his brain. Thus, while I discuss approaches "piece-meal," for easier readability, you will see that some case histories combine one or more therapies for success.

SOME ORTHOMOLECULAR TREATMENTS FOR HYPERACTIVITY AND LEARNING
AND BEHAVIOR DISORDERS

Eliminate salicylates and artificial colors, flavors, and preservatives from diet.

Treat toxicity from lead and other heavy metals.

Treat food and chemical intolerances.

Remove sugar from diet.

Treat nutritional deficiencies and dependencies.

The Feingold Diet for Learning and Behavior Impairments and Hyperactivity. In the 1970s, Benjamin Feingold, M.D., a pediatrician and allergist, developed a diet for treating children with learning and behavior impairments and hyperactivity. Dr. Feingold's diet eliminates artificial colors, artificial flavors, salicylates, and the preservatives BHA and BHT. Salicylates are naturally occurring chemical compounds thought to interfere with the production of several brain chemicals, including norepinephrine, acetylcholine, and dopamine. Foods containing salicylates include apples, apricots, berries, oranges, nectarines, grapes, peaches, plums, cucumbers, tea, and tomatoes. (The regimen also advocates cutting out aspirin-containing compounds and perfumes. Salt and soda should be substituted for toothpaste.)

Back in 1948 Dr. Stephen Lockey, a Pennsylvania allergist, reported that the behavior of many of his patients improved when they eliminated food dyes from their diets. In the early 1970s Dr. Feingold reported to a meeting of the American Medical Association that food additives were responsible for the hyperactivity in many of the hyperactive children he had seen in his practice. According to psychologist Alexander Schauss, Ph.D., the director of the American Institute for Biosocial Research, the American and Canadian medical establishments initially dismissed Dr. Feingold as "senile," or "a quack," or "disputed by all authorities"—while in Sweden and Norway, authorities responded by banning all artificial food colors.

In the following years, some studies confirmed Dr. Feingold's findings; others did not. In 1984, Bernard Rimland, Ph.D., director of the Institute for Child Behavior Research (now the Autism Research Institute), wrote an article in the *Journal of Orthomolecular Psychiatry* (Vol. 13, No. 1, pp. 45–49) in which he questioned the results of the negative studies: "How researchers can claim they have tested 'the Feingold diet,' which eliminates over 3,000 additives, by conducting experiments on fewer than 10 dyes, is beyond me. . . . By and large, the studies used doses of 1.6 to 26 milligrams of colorings per day." Yet the FDA, in a "more objective analysis," found actual daily consumption of colorings to be 59–76 mg. Some of the younger children took in 121 mg daily, and some of the older, 146 mg daily.

Dr. Rimland discusses other serious faults in the negative studies, adding that despite being heavily weighted against finding the Feingold diet effective, "All studies, without exception, do concede that some children do respond to the diet."

Echoing several of Dr. Rimland's statements, Dr. Schauss refers to a double-blind study by Swanson and Kinsbourne, published in *Science* in 1980, which Schauss notes, "found that 17 of every 20 children challenged with the [artificial] dyes displayed the symptoms and signs associated with the hyperkinetic syndrome." Dr. Schauss points out that this study challenged the children each day with an amount of dye approximating the FDA's estimate of children's actual daily intake of these dyes.

Dr. Schauss wrote me in 1994: "Feingold's diet still is disputed, although it is indisputable that many thousands of children are well today because of his diet."

Treating Heavy-Metal Toxicity. Orthodox and orthomolecular physicians agree that too much lead in the body can result in behavior and learning problems. High lead levels were also linked to hyperactivity in studies published in American journals as far back as 1943 and confirmed in Switzerland, Sweden, and England.

In his book *Diet, Crime and Delinquency,* Dr. Schauss tells of a West Coast family, all four of whom suffered fatigue and depression. Also, the children's schoolwork became poor and they suffered sharp mood swings. "Their family doctor found no apparent physical base for the problems, and referred them to a psychiatrist. After spending several thousand dollars, they saw no improvement."

After reading about lead poisoning in a popular magazine, the family visited a nutritionist, who found that they had lead poisoning, a condition for which the family doctor had not tested.

In 1977 *Science* (198, pp. 204–6) published a study in which researchers tested the hair of 31 learning-disabled and 22 normal children for levels of 14 elements. On the basis of levels of cadmium, cobalt, manganese, and chromium the researchers were able to predict with 98 percent accuracy which children belonged in which group. Studies have also linked copper and aluminum to learning difficulties in some children.

Treating Food and Chemical Intolerances ("Allergies"). Dr. Hoffer, called the father of orthomolecular medicine because of his work in the 1950s with schizophrenia and vitamin B3, states in *Orthomolecular Medicine for Physicians* that for many years he was puzzled because some children with learning and behavioral disorders responded to vitamin treatment, while others—whose symptoms appeared to be the same—did not. "The mystery cleared," he writes, "when the concept of cerebral allergy became part of orthomolecular psychiatric treatment, for then a large proportion of children who had failed to respond to vitamins recovered when the foods to which they were allergic were identified and removed from their diet."

Marshall Mandell, M.D., one of the major pioneers who introduced the concept of cerebral allergy, pointed out in an interview that symptoms that "come and go" may very well be due to intolerances to foods or chemicals: When the offending substance is acting on the brain, symptoms flourish. When the person's body is free from the substance, symptoms fade. In *Dr. Mandell's 5-Day Allergy Relief System* (pp. 149–50), he objects to the diagnosis "minimal brain dysfunction" and to the belief that the symptoms are caused by permanent brain damage. He argues that children diagnosed with this disorder do turn in good performances sometimes, and that this offers proof that the brain dysfunction is reversible and not due to *permanent* brain damage.

In a speech before the 1969 Annual Congress of the American College of Allergists, Dr. Mandell told of a child's behavior during the three hours after a test for ethanol intolerance. Her actions became infantile, and she was alternately withdrawn and belligerent. Her speech varied from confused and slurred to intense screaming. She was unable to read, write, or spell. Indeed, her thinking power had so deserted her that she did not know her age or even her name —and her mother was an unknown stranger.

Dr. Mandell has found that milk is the number one problem food for children, and wheat is the number two offender. This is true not only of the disorders discussed here. These two foods are, he says, "the cause of many mental, physical, and 'psychosomatic' ailments in children." We might consider: How many of our children are making us suffer—and are suffering themselves—needlessly because of the old belief that milk and wheat products are good for all children?

Removing Sugar from the Diet. In late 1979 the New York City Board of Education began what might be termed a "mass experiment" on the effects of sugar and other dietary factors on learning ability. The board ordered a reduction of sugar in the school lunch and breakfast program and banned two artificial food colorings. Six months later, the city's scores on the standardized California Achievement Test, a nationalized test of academic achievement, rose to the 47th percentile nationally. A year before, New York City had ranked in the 39th percentile, virtually the same ranking it had held throughout the 1970s.

The following year the school system banned foods containing synthetic colorings or flavorings. This maneuver was followed by a rise in the test scores to the 51st percentile rank nationwide. In the fall of 1982, the food preservatives BHA and BHT were banned— and in the spring of 1983 the city's test scores rose to the 55th percentile rank. Stephen J. Schoenthaler, Ph.D., et al. reported that "no other school district could be located which had reported such a large gain above the rest of the nation so quickly in a large population."

Dr. Schoenthaler and his colleagues explored possibilities other than diet for the higher score results: placebo effects, student-to-teacher ratios, increased breakfast consumption, changes in racial and ethnic composition, etc. The authors stated: "Until such time that a rival theory can be generated which can explain the gain in national academic rank . . . the conclusion must stand that the primary cause of the academic gains was the dietary changes" *(International Journal of Biosocial Research* Vol. 8, No. 2, 1986, pp. 196–203).

Remember that the rise in test performances occurred without restrictions on sugar or any of the other banned substances in the children's diets away from school. One can speculate that the results might have been even better if the pupils had eliminated these substances from their diets entirely.

In *Improving Your Child's Behavior Chemistry* (p. 164), Lendon H. Smith, M.D., suggests this simple home test of the effects of sugar on children's behavior: "Notice how an insignificant stress . . . will put the child on the floor if timed two hours after a doughnut, a dish of ice cream, or even a piece of gum. The same stress . . . two hours after an ounce of protein will be met with calmness or a shrug."

Karl E. Humiston, M.D., has stated that "hyperactivity is first and foremost due to sugar, secondarily to food and chemical intolerances." In an interview, he gave the example of a seemingly "hopeless" hyperactive young man. "From age 13 to 18, he had been incarcerated in a maximum security building for the mentally retarded. He wasn't retarded—in fact, he was very bright—but he was so hyperactive, irritable, abusive, and hostile that it was felt that a tight-security environment was necessary to control his behavior. In his early 20s, he was hospitalized in a psychiatric ward, and he often 'amused' himself by pushing the button that the staff used to call for help. The bells would go off, and many of the staff would appear to help, and he would jump up and down, like a little kid, and say 'Look at 'em come! Look at 'em come!' "

At one point, Dr. Humiston visited him in another psychiatric hospital, "and they had him in a locked room with just a bare mattress in it, because he threw everything around in his hyperactive rages."

Dr. Humiston and his wife, Bonnie, a psychotherapist, took him into their home "because my wife saw that we probably knew how to save him. If he didn't get nutritional help, he would be 'down the tubes' for good." Dr. Humiston admits to a few frightening incidents when the young man would sneak sugar. "One time, in a sugar rage, he started waving a kitchen knife around and cut my stepdaughter in the hand when she tried to take it away. Another time, after eating a candy bar, he ran out into the street and started yelling obscenities to the whole neighborhood."

Eventually the young man was turned around as a result, Dr. Humiston reports, of his being taken off sugar and foods to which he was intolerant and being given suitable vitamin supplementation and a stable family environment. "Now," Dr. Humiston says, "he is leading a decent and responsible life—not only supporting himself and keeping himself out of trouble, but also doing a lot of good community service to help others."

Treating Nutritional Deficiencies and Dependencies. An experiment in 1957 with rats deficient in vitamin B1 found that they persisted stubbornly in previously learned responses, despite punishment. This is a behavior pattern common in children with learning and behavior disorders. The study also found that B1-deficient rats became aggressive and showed exaggerated reactions to conflict situations. The researchers reported "behavior irrelevant to the situation, such as attacking the test apparatus and biting it repeatedly."

A 1980 report by Derrick Lonsdale, M.D., in the *American Journal of Clinical Nutrition* (Vol. 33, No. 2, pp. 205–11) stated that behaviors common with behavior disorders consistently appeared in teenagers who were deficient in B1: poor impulse control, frequent irritability, hostile behavior, and sensitivity to criticism.

In 1982, Dr. Arnold Brenner reported in the *Journal of Learning Disabilities* (Vol. 15, No. 5, pp. 258–64) on 100 hyperactive children given B1 supplements. Eleven responded dramatically but relapsed when given placebo.

Back in 1970, in *Schizophrenia* (2, pp. 70–79), R. G. Green reported success in treating learning disorders with niacin (vitamin B3) and suggested that many children with this problem may actually have *subclinical* pellagra. Pellagra is a disorder well accepted by orthodox medicine as due to deficiency of B3; the behavior symptoms of pellagra are thought to include perceptual changes, learning disorders, hyperactive hehavior, and an inability to respond in an accepted way to social sanctions.

Dr. Hoffer, a major authority in the use of B3 for mental problems, stresses that the *amount* given may be crucial: "A child who will recover on three grams daily may be totally unresponsive to two grams daily." While it might seem common-sense to assume that if one's diet is sufficient in a vitamin, one is "getting enough" of it, Dr. Hoffer states *(Orthomolecular Medicine for Physicians,*

p. 208) that about half the children he sees with diagnosed learning and behavior disorders fall into the vitamin-*dependency* group; that is, they need more of a vitamin or several vitamins than do most people to achieve the same biochemical results.

Research suggests that vitamin B6 can greatly benefit hyperactive children who have low blood levels of this nutrient. The vitamin increases levels of serotonin, a brain chemical that helps keep us calm. One study found B6 to be more effective than Ritalin in decreasing hyperactivity and B6, in contrast to the drug, continued to have a beneficial effect into the following placebo period. (M. Coleman et al., *Journal of Biological Psychology* (Vol. 14, No. 5, pp. 741–51, 1979.)

Depending on what biochemical problems are factors in the individual case of hyperactivity or learning and behavior disorder, giving extra amounts of other nutrients, such as iron or zinc, may help. An *overload* of the mineral manganese, however, may be a causative factor in learning disabilities. (It has been pointed out that infant formulas contain three to 100 times the manganese content of breast milk.)

WHAT YOU CAN DO

If your child has any of the problems discussed in this chapter, the most important step you can take is to have her tested by an ortho-molecular doctor. (See "Resources.") Chapters 2, 14, 15, and 17 offer steps you can take until you meet with the physician.

Read labels carefully for artificial flavors and colors. You can receive detailed information on the Feingold diet by contacting the Feingold Association, P.O. Box 6550, Alexandria, Virginia 22306; telephone: 703-768-3287.

To prevent morning low blood-sugar level, give your child a bit of food before bedtime. (Make sure there is no sugar in the snack.) Try to get the youngster to eat breakfast, so that lack of food does not allow for a dip in blood sugar before lunch. In his book (pp.

187, 188), Dr. Smith also recommends supplying the child with protein to munch on during the day. Some teachers have been successful in "activating their pupils' brains" by acting on the information that children's brains have "two to three times the energy requirements of an adult's; it is impossible for them to function from breakfast to lunch without nibbling on some protein."

PART 5

A More Detailed Look at Major Nutritional and Physical Factors Affecting Mental Well-Being

Chapter 14

Food and Chemical Intolerances (Sensitivities, "Allergies")

Although the medical field historically has been riddled with debate, perhaps no argument is more rife than that between mainstream allergists and their alternative counterparts, clinical ecologists. Doctors in these fields have been throwing verbal punches at each other for some seven decades.

Basic Debates

Mainstream allergy specialists believe that allergies cause mainly gastrointestinal, respiratory, and skin problems. They generally do not believe that allergies cause mental symptoms. Yet as H. L. Newbold, M.D., observed, "In this country reports of psychological reactions caused by allergies began to proliferate in the 1870's, and they continue to this day" *(Mega-Nutrients for Your Nerves,* page 43). Orthomolecular doctors claim a high percentage of success with psychological and psychiatric problems—even with a number of cases deemed hopeless by orthodox psychiatry—as a result of testing for and treating "allergies."

The debate centers partly on the definition of the word "allergy." Clinical ecologists traditionally have referred to an allergy as *any* altered reaction to a normally harmless substance. This was the original definition when the concept of allergy was introduced in 1906. But by 1926, research had indicated that *some* of these altered reactions came from specific immunological changes (mediated by IgE antibodies). The proposal was then made that the word "allergy" be restricted to refer to reactions that could be shown to reflect these changes. Medical schools quickly accepted this new definition, in part, as psychiatrist Melvyn R. Werbach, M.D., explains in *Third Line Medicine* (pp. 150, 151), because the identification of the mechanism of the reactions "gave the field a more scientific base —which, in turn, elevated their [allergists'] stature in the medical community." Some allergists resisted the new definition, however, because many of their patients who suffered symptoms when exposed to certain substances had no known immunological abnormalities, yet their symptoms responded to treatment. These doctors eventually renamed themselves clinical ecologists. Recently some clinical ecologists, board-certified in Environmental Medicine, have been referring to themselves as environmental physicians.

Michael Schachter, M.D., reports that during the 1980s, evidence accumulated linking most food sensitivities to *IgG* antibodies, which would explain why they could not be linked to *IgE* antibodies, the antibodies that orthodox allergists looked for to confirm diagnosis of allergy. It would also explain why allergists have believed that food allergies are rare, while clinical ecologists have found them to be very common. The identifiable IgG-mediated response would also seem to give the proof of immunopathology that was previously lacking.

Meanwhile, some orthomolecular doctors have been using alternative terms—"intolerances," "sensitivities," or "allergylike reactions"—although others continue to speak of "allergies." They agree, however, that if a reaction to a food, chemical, or inhalant causes suffering, and if treating for that reaction helps the patient, then the reaction should be treated—no matter what you call it. This book refers to sensitivities and intolerances, using "allergies" only when quoting a doctor. When a clinical ecologist uses the word "allergies," though, remember that the reference is to problems that *include*—but are *not limited to*—those treated by orthodox allergists.

The media have helped disseminate orthodox allergists' views against clinical ecology. Not long ago an investigative television program and a long article in a respected mainstream magazine implied that just about all patients of clinical ecologists end up in isolated, sterile communes, where visitors are seldom allowed because the smells of cleaning fluid on their clothes, and shampoo on their hair, are feared by the commune members. Mainstream psychiatrists were quoted as feeling sincere concern that these patients' "hypochondria" and "psychosomatic problems" were being pandered to, while they were being led away from traditional psychiatric techniques "that could help them."

As you will see throughout this book, the above "isolated commune therapy" is definitely not the usual treatment prescribed by clinical ecologists—and many people who go to clinical ecologists have already *tried* traditional techniques without help.

Similar misconceptions have appeared in such prestigious official papers as the Position Statement on Clinical Ecology, approved by the Executive Committee of the mainstream American Academy of Allergy and Immunology. It was published in the *Journal of Allergy and Clinical Immunology* in August 1986 (pp. 269–71). It states: "Treatment usually [*sic*] requires major changes in the home environment and life-style. . . . Home and working environments are restricted with recommendations for . . . special isolation rooms where the air is filtered and from which all synthetic materials have been removed. Social lives are often markedly restricted, since most environments away from home are 'unsafe.' " Although that paragraph begins by stating that it is about the usual *treatment,* it contains the following: "At times, the patient is hospitalized in a comprehensive environmental control unit. . . ." Someone who does not know much about clinical ecology might assume that hospitalization in a sterile environment is also part of the usual treatment. In fact, this procedure is done for several days for initial *testing,* and then only in extreme cases.

The Position Statement also cites a 1983 article in *Psychosomatics* (24, page 731): Clinical ecology "neither promise[s] nor give[s] hope of eliminating the offending condition, and the patients do not seem to expect it. . . . Patients seem content with their condition and the reassurance that their symptoms have a physical cause." This assertion overlooks the countless people who have recovered and contradicts the promises that doctors using clinical ecology do, indeed, make. For instance, consider these statements: From psychiatrist Abram Hoffer, M.D., Ph.D., "Once the allergies and sensitivities are established, treatment is relatively simple" *(Orthomolecular Medicine for Physicians,* page 179); from Dr. Michael Schachter, psychiatrist and clinical ecologist: "The simple use of sound principles of nutrition, exercise, and stress reduction . . . is often enough to relieve the symptoms of sensitivities." William H. Philpott, M.D., psychiatrist and clinical ecologist, has said, "When we give patients with chemical sensitivities enough vitamin C and balance out their nutrition, a great [many] of the chemical allergies disappear."

The Position Statement's summary includes the objection that clinical ecology is "time-consuming" and again that it "places severe restrictions on the individual's life style." Yet immunotherapy, a major treatment of mainstream allergists, "usually continues until the patient shows no allergic response for two to five years" *(Signet/ Mosby Medical Encyclopedia).* And clinical ecologists believe that their treatments place far fewer restrictions on lifestyle than do the often serious diagnosed disorders, such as schizophrenia, that they help. They add that their techniques are less time-consuming and less expensive than, as Dr. Newbold phrased it, "going to a psychiatrist several times a week for years on end, with little or no result."

Often, when mainstream doctors learn that one of their "untreatable" patients has recovered under the care of a nutritional doctor, they assume that the recovery was due to a placebo effect, in which the results seem to be caused by the patient's belief in the efficacy of a treatment, not by the treatment itself. Dr. Philpott—who, like most clinical ecologists, has seen numerous "hard-core" schizophrenics snap out of their world of nightmares when offending substances were removed—points out that "schizophrenics . . . are not really very suggestible."

Mainstream allergists also have decried the lack of "properly controlled studies" in clinical ecology. The Position Statement states, "Anecdotal articles do not constitute sufficient evidence of a cause-and-effect relationship between symptoms and environmental exposure." These "anecdotes" (presumably, case histories) reach into the many thousands; and Dr. Werbach as long ago as 1986 cited some 13 double-blind studies (as opposed to anecdotal articles) backing up the basic tenets of clinical ecology. All but two were published in staunchly orthodox medical publications (see *Third Line Medicine,* pp. 153–54).

Those are not the only studies (a few of the others are mentioned elsewhere in this chapter). However, some clinical ecologists themselves lament that medical literature has relatively few hard scientific studies proving their work. One factor has been that orthodox journals often have not wanted to print studies run by clinical ecologists. (There is sometimes a catch-22 in getting nutritional studies printed in these journals: "Nutrition cannot possibly help, so why bother to investigate if nutrition can help?") Another factor in the relative paucity of published studies is that some clinical ecologists have considered empirical evidence to be of prime importance, their viewpoint being that it works because they all see it working repeatedly. Many have expressed that view along these lines: "When people who have been sick for years have unsuccessfully tried every other therapy, and get well and remain well simply when their sensitivities have been treated—and when we can repeatedly turn those symptoms on or off by reintroducing or removing the substances to which they are sensitive—this is proof."

Symptoms

Dr. Philpott expresses the view of clinical ecologists, which is in stark contrast to that of traditional allergists: "Symptoms of sensitivity can be any symptom that the body is capable of producing, physically or mentally." (This does not mean that all symptoms are caused by sensitivities.) Case histories in this book give specific examples of this statement.

A sensitivity that affects the brain is "an accomplished mimic," David Sheinkin, M.D., and Dr. Schachter point out in *Food, Mind and Mood* (pp. 37–38). In medicine, mimics are disorders that have symptoms similar to other disorders and thus may be easily misdiagnosed. For instance, Dr. Sheinkin and Schachter point out that syphilis was nicknamed "the great imitator" because a patient with syphilis could go to the doctor's office complaining of anything from body sores to pains in his liver, from arthritis to hallucinations. Similarly, "Because brain sensitivities can affect different portions of the brain, they mimic many psychiatric, neurological, and physical syndromes."

How Can Sensitivities Affect the Brain?

Pioneering clinical ecologist Marshall Mandell, M.D., says, "If your skin, eyes, ears, nose, throat, sinuses, lungs, stomach, colon . . . can be sites of allergic reactions [as traditional allergists agree], it should not surprise you that there is no reason why your brain cannot be allergic . . . The brain is . . . supplied with blood from the same kind of allergen-transporting arteries that supply all the other potentially allergic tissues in an allergic individual" *(Dr. Mandell's 5-Day Allergy Relief System,* pp. 81–82).

In *Nutrition and Mental Illness* (p. 48), Carl C. Pfeiffer, Ph.D., M.D., states that it should be "no surprise" that food sensitivities can affect the mind, "since the brain is perhaps the most delicate organ of the body" and uses "sometimes as much as 30% of all the energy we derive from food. . . . Allergies to foods can upset levels of hormones and other key chemicals in the brain."

Prevalence of Sensitivities That Affect the Brain

As mentioned, clinical ecologists report very high statistics of brain sensitivities in their practices. They argue that traditional doctors refute these statistics because, disbelieving that brain sensitivities exist, traditional doctors do not test for them—and therefore do not find them. In his book (p. 85), Dr. Mandell tells of a study he and Dr. Philpott conducted at Fuller Memorial Sanitarium in South Attleboro, Massachusetts, in the early 1970s: "We showed that 90% of the patients . . . had a significant degree of cerebral [brain] allergy. Furthermore, we were able to demonstrate that the symptoms that had made it necessary to admit these patients to a mental hospital could be duplicated by tests for allergy." Dr. Mandell mentions that Dr. Hoffer, who pioneered the field of orthomolecular medicine with his work with vitamin B3 and schizophrenia, reported after a year of testing for sensitivities, that 50 percent of the cases of schizophrenia that had not been helped by nutritional therapy and medications had been cases of food intolerance. Theron G. Randolph, M.D., has said that people with untreated "allergies make up the single largest group of unsatisfactorily treated patients today" (quoted by Dr. Mandell, p. xi). He has also been quoted as saying that 60–70 percent of symptoms diagnosed as psychosomatic are actually undiagnosed maladaptive reactions to foods, chemicals, and inhalants.

Types of Sensitivities

Clinical ecologists recognize three basic types of intolerances: fixed sensitivity, cyclic sensitivity, and addictive sensitivity.

FIXED SENSITIVITY

People with a fixed food intolerance react the same way every time they eat a troublesome food; an example is someone who breaks out in hives whenever she eats shellfish. Since the reaction is immediate and unvarying, this type of intolerance is easily recognized. It is what most people think of when they hear the word "allergy," and it is the only type of food allergy that most traditional allergists recognize. In contrast, clinical ecologists believe that fixed food sensitivities comprise a very small proportion of food intolerances; some put the amount as low as 5 percent.

CYCLIC SENSITIVITY

A person with a cyclic sensitivity, unlike someone with a fixed intolerance, may react differently at different times; sometimes he may not react at all. Whether or not a reaction occurs depends upon how often the food is consumed and on other factors, such as environment, stress, and overall state of the immune system. In particular, if a person with a cyclic food sensitivity eats an offending food once within a five-day period, he will get no reaction, since the food has had a chance to clear the system before more of the same food is reintroduced.

ADDICTIVE SENSITIVITY

With an addictive intolerance, the person craves the foods or chemicals (such as those in cigarettes) he is sensitive to and suffers withdrawal symptoms if he abstains from the substance. In order not to suffer these symptoms, he keeps himself on a maintenance level of the substance. This continual bombardment of the body can cause chronic physical or mental problems.

An addictive intolerance is extremely difficult for the person to suspect. After all, *not* smoking the cigarette (or *not* eating the addic-

tive food) gives symptoms; taking in the addictive substance alleviates them. Also, the substance makes the person feel "up."

Tests

Tests used by clinical ecologists differ in terms of convenience, expense, and accuracy for various sensitivities. Discuss with your doctor why a specific technique is chosen for you.

INTRADERMAL PROVOCATIVE TESTING

Extracts of foods are injected under the skin. (A modification of this
method tests for sensitivities to certain chemicals and inhalants.) A
problem food will create a whealing response (patch of "itchiness")
on the skin; sometimes it also will reproduce the symptoms which
have been bothering the patient. See Treatment section for further
usefulness of this method.

SUBLINGUAL PROVOCATIVE TESTING

Soluble extracts of foods are placed under the tongue. (A variation
of this technique tests for sensitivities to some chemicals and inhalants.) Any substance that evokes symptoms is considered a substance to which the patient is intolerant. See Treatment section for
further usefulness of this test.

RAST (RADIO-ALLERGO-SORBENT TEST)

Although the RAST blood test was developed to help diagnose inhalant allergies as understood by traditional allergists (that is, allergies
produced by antibody protein molecules called IgE), its newer use is
to find the presence of another type of antibody, IgG. The RAST
works by a technique that labels the IgG and IgE antibodies in the

blood with a radioactive substance; the quantities of the antibodies can then be measured with a Geiger-counter type device.

FASTING FOLLOWED BY CHALLENGING

This procedure is based on the fact that it generally takes three to five days for all foods to metabolize and eliminate from the body. Once the body is clear of all foods, they are reintroduced one at a time. Since the fast has made the body clean of toxins, offending foods will cause an immediate reaction. (We all know the scenario in which a nonsmoker takes a puff of a cigarette, or a nondrinker takes a gulp of alcohol, and has an intense reaction.)

While this procedure is mentioned often in case histories in this book, by the time you read this, it will probably be in much less frequent use. For instance, Dr. Philpott, who helped pioneer the technique, recently stated that he has now dropped it in favor of one that "is less bothersome for patients: five days of feeding them [only] foods that they don't eat ordinarily. This clears out the system as well as if we fasted them." Dr. Schachter agrees that this technique works as well as fasting, adding that fasting can be extremely dangerous for some people.

CYTOTOXIC TEST

In the cytotoxic test, live white blood cells from the patient's blood are mixed with a food extract. If the extract is from an offending food, the blood cells react; they remain normal if the food is safe.

Dr. Schachter in 1987 pointed to new evidence that "the RAST will largely be able to do what the cytotoxic test has done in the past, in a more reproducible manner." In private communications in 1993 and 1994, two clinical ecologists warned that the cytotoxic test has to be done "perfectly" to be valid. Dr. Mandell wrote of a 50 percent margin of error. So if your doctor orders this test, ask questions.

Treatments

Orthodox allergists and clinical ecologists both attempt to identify and remove offending substances. Allergists may use antihistamines, steroids, and other drugs. Clinical ecologists, like all nutritionally oriented doctors, prefer to stay clear of drugs because they tend to cover up symptoms without getting at the cause, and because—being substances unnatural to the body—they may create side effects. Allergists may use immunotherapy, a technique dating back to 1911. Dr. Werbach comments: "Immunotherapy has limited value; it requires a patient to have a series of sometimes uncomfortable injections weekly, often for years, in the hope of producing a decrease in the severity of the allergic reactions."

ELIMINATION OF OFFENDING SUBSTANCES

Elimination of offending substances can be very simple and works well in many cases. For instance, this book tells of people who have recovered from serious mental symptoms simply by substituting an electric stove for their gas stove. But Drs. Sheinkin and Schachter ask (p. 182), "What happens if you have discovered sensitivities to wheat, corn, and milk? Eliminating these three basic foods . . . could place enormous restrictions on what you could eat." One alternative is the rotation diet, discussed below.

ROTATION DIET

With the rotation diet, you abstain from troublesome foods for a period of time that leaves you free of symptoms. (Dr. Philpott specifies that foods that give minor reactions should be avoided for at least six weeks; foods that give major reactions, for at least three months.) Then you may be able to reintroduce the foods without problems—provided you don't eat them more than once every four to five days. (More severely sensitive people may need to follow a seven-day rotation diet.)

Clinical ecologists warn that if you are sensitive to a number of foods, you probably have the tendency to develop sensitivities to foods you eat often. If you rotate only the foods you are presently sensitive to, you may compensate by eating certain nonrotated foods more often—and possibly develop sensitivities to *them*. You can prevent this by rotating all your foods.

NEUTRALIZING REACTIONS

For every food to which a person is sensitive, there is a specific concentration that will not cause a reaction, but will instead temporarily block the usual symptoms the food triggers. An individual's specific neutralizing dose can be determined during sublingual and intradermal provocative testing, by trying different dilutions of the offending substance until a dilution is found that produces no symptoms. For treatment, neutralizing doses of a number of substances can be mixed together and taken all at once by placing a prescribed number of drops under the tongue daily.

Drs. Sheinkin and Schachter give a recent theory as to how the neutralizing dose works: it "stimulates T suppressor cells [of the immune system] to put brakes on the B cells that produce the antibodies" to the offending substance. Thus, over a period of time the frequent, small neutralizing doses will condition the immune system to stop reacting inappropriately to larger quantities of the substance.

The doctors state that long-term use of neutralizing doses apparently produces no ill side effects.

ENZYME POTENTIATED DESENSITIZATION

The term enzyme potentiated desensitization refers to a technique that allows one to lose intolerances (be desensitized) partly through the use of an enzyme, β-glucuronidase. Although the technique was developed in the 1960s (in England, by physician Leonard McEwen), it has been in use in the United States for only a short time. W. A. Shrader, M.D., one of the first to bring the technique into this country, said in an interview that the reason for its lack of use has simply been that it has not been very well known: "It is not commercially produced by any drug company."

Basically, the technique uses "incredibly small doses of multiple allergens—foods, inhalants, and/or chemicals." Mixes can be made to "cover pretty much the whole spectrum of antigens to which people can become sensitized," says Dr. Shrader. The enzyme is added to the individualized mix just before it is given.

To start, the injection is given every two to three months, then the intervals are stretched out. Generally, "people can stop forever, or for very long periods of time, after about sixteen to eighteen injections."

Dr. Shrader reports that this technique offers no danger to patients, and it allows people to be exposed without problems to foods, chemicals, and inhalants to which they were intolerant before the therapy. He adds that "across the board, the technique is about 80% successful. There's about a 7–10% failure rate." The study reporting these rates, he says, currently consists of over 1,200 people.

To simplify Dr. Shrader's explanation of the biochemical rationale for this technique: The enzyme transmits the signals of the allergens in the injected mix into the epidermal layer of the skin. The signals (or "messages") are then transmitted into the lymph nodes, which in turn produce cytotoxic cells (CD8$^+$ lymphocytes) "that go around and actually shut off the helper cells that are primarily causing the problem" of intolerance. "We used to think there was just suppressor activity, but now we find there's actually cytotoxic activity as well." A cytotoxin is an agent that can kill abnormal cells without harming normal ones.

BLOCKING REACTIONS

Vitamins C and B6 are sometimes used intravenously to give an almost instantaneous effect to people in the midst of severe sensitivity attacks. (In similar situations, orthodox allergists may give steroids intravenously.)

The vitamins can be taken by mouth to *prevent* a reaction, one to one and a half hours ahead of the offending food, so they can be absorbed and "ready for action when the food strikes." Drs. Sheinkin and Schachter note that oral doses of C and B6 should be determined under medical supervision.

One 1981 double-blind study found that eight of nine patients who had symptoms when challenged with monosodium glutamate showed no response to MSG after 12 weeks on B6. Similarly, a 1985 study showed that vitamin C protected animals against adverse effects of monosodium glutamate *(Food and Nutrition Bulletin 7, pp. 51–53).*

Another blocking measure is a combination of sodium bicarbonate (baking soda) and potassium bicarbonate. This will make the pH of the body more alkaline. Generally, when sensitivity reactions occur, the pH shifts toward acidic. Again, a physician should be consulted.

OTHER TREATMENTS

Clinical ecologists, like other nutritionally oriented doctors, attempt to make sure they are getting at the *root* of the problem and treating that, rather than covering up symptoms with drugs. As Drs. Sheinkin and Schachter note in *Food, Mind and Mood* (p. 102), clinical evidence shows that many people with sensitivities have digestive problems, and that correcting these problems may do away with the sensitivities. For instance, "Offending foods or chemicals may shock the pancreas into not functioning properly; as a result, digestion is impaired and the sensitivities worsen, which further inhibits the functioning of the pancreas. To overcome the problem . . . tablets of pancreatic enzymes can be taken." A doctor should decide frequency, dose, and type of enzymes.

Hormonal problems will also be treated if necessary; much clinical evidence indicates that such problems predispose people to brain sensitivities. A full evaluation will also address overall nutrition, exercise patterns, and stress. As Drs. Sheinkin and Schachter say, "Inadequate nutrition and poor physical conditioning give sensitivities a chance to flourish, while excessive stress allows them to practically walk into your life."

An orthomolecular doctor will also test for chronic viral, parasitic, or fungal infections believed to affect sensitivity by their actions on the immune system. "Often when the infections are cleared, the sensitivities are diminished or disappear," Drs. Sheinkin and Schacter state. Karl E. Humiston, M.D., specifies that the "presence of parasites should be suspected particularly when a patient is 'allergic to everything.'"

Dr. Randolph, a pioneer in clinical ecology, has recommended that physicians consider the Hubbard method of detoxification for chemically sensitive patients who do not respond completely to standard techniques. If you fall into this category, suggest this method to your orthomolecular doctor. The Hubbard method includes exercise, vitamin B3, a variety of other nutrients supplied in proportion to gradually increasing doses of B3, and coldpressed polyunsaturated oils.

What You Can Do

The preceding sections give some measures you can take on your own, such as the rotation diet. Chapter 2, on prevention, contains other self-help ideas, not only in the section on sensitivities, but throughout: Remember that clinical ecologists report a healthy diet and environment will sometimes do away with intolerances as a "side effect."

The books *Food, Mind, and Mood,* by Dr. David Sheinkin and Dr. Michael Schachter, and Dr. Marshall Mandell's *Dr. Mandell's 5-Day Allergy Relief System* give numerous self-help hints. If you use these books, please read all information carefully several times before starting any steps other than those covered here. While both books give details for fasting—after strong warnings about who should not fast—I agree with physicians who state that *no one* should fast without being under the care of a doctor who understands this technique. I recommend instead Dr. Philpott's suggestion for eating seldom-used foods instead of fasting. "These foods should be of the same food family as those the person commonly eats," he says. The book by Drs. Sheinkin and Schachter details which foods belong to which families.

Chapter 15

Low Blood Sugar (Functional Hypoglycemia)

Low blood sugar involves the release of too much insulin by the pancreas. You may be more familiar with the "flip side" of low blood sugar, diabetes, which involves too *little* release of insulin and a *high* blood-sugar level.

Low blood sugar is one of the disorders that orthodox doctors believe is highly overdiagnosed by orthomolecular physicians. The latter respond that this so-called overdiagnosis allows them to help many patients who have not been helped by orthodox physicians.

Orthomolecular doctors report an extremely high success rate in treating low blood sugar. For instance, Robert C. Atkins, M.D., in his 1990 book (*Dr. Atkins' Health Revolution*, p. 108) says that when a standard diet for the disorder is followed, "a good 95% of the patients will . . . experience a steady, uncomplicated improvement, with all the symptoms vanishing within a few weeks." He adds that most of the other 5 percent respond when fruit and milk sugar are eliminated.

Basic Debate

Orthodox doctors maintain that patients do not have hypoglycemia unless their blood sugar reading goes below a certain number during testing. (There seems to be debate among orthodox doctors as to exactly what that number should be.) Orthomolecular doctors maintain that if the patient shows any *symptoms* during testing for hypoglycemia, these should be taken at least as seriously as any numbers reading. As Carlton Fredericks, Ph.D., stated: "The symptoms provoked by the test are meaningful; the numbers are not." He adds that on the basis of such arbitrary numbers, "thousands of hypoglycemics . . . have been told their tests were normal and their troubles 'all in the mind' " *(Eat Well, Get Well, Stay Well)*. He tells (pp. 29–41) of a college professor suffering for three years from worsening seizures, blackouts, dizziness, and anxiety. Several physicians diagnosed these as "nervous reactions" and "anxiety attacks." Eventually he insisted on a glucose-tolerance test. Used by both orthodox and orthomolecular doctors to test for hypoglycemia, this test involves fasting for twelve hours, then drinking a glass of glucose (sugar). At intervals for the next several hours, blood samples are tested for glucose levels.

One hour after drinking the glucose, the patient had a massive seizure that required two men to hold him in a chair; then he became unconscious for some 20 minutes. There followed two hours of frequent episodes of stuttering, shakiness, and inability to concentrate. Next were dizziness and a bizarre visual symptom: everything was white. The lab report did not indicate hypoglycemia, because, Dr. Fredericks says, "At no time were his sugar levels low enough to be called 'hypoglycemic' by any of the 'magic number' standards."

Shortly afterward, he was taken to the hospital with a severe attack of vertigo and was given a battery of tests, which revealed no physical problems. During the 10 days at the hospital, he was fed normal hospital fare, including much sugar. (Later we discuss how sugar is the major factor behind low blood sugar, contradictory as that might sound.) He had seizures, fell out of his wheelchair, cried, shook, staggered around his room, and complained incessantly that the room was moving in one direction while he was moving in another. His physicians sent him to a psychiatrist to be treated for their diagnosis: psychosomatic illness.

The professor wrote his physician that after his hospital release, he started B-complex supplementation and a hypoglycemia diet, and that now he had "remained free" of most symptoms for five months. "Especially, I have had no seizures or blackouts."

Symptoms

Symptoms accepted by orthodox medicine include tremulousness, cold sweat, hypothermia, headache, confusion, hallucinations, bizarre behavior, and convulsions. If hypoglycemia is untreated, it can result in coma and death.

To those symptoms, orthomolecular doctors add schizophrenia, alcoholism, hyperactivity, phobias, depression, insomnia, violent outbursts, suicidal tendencies, learning disorders, and problems diagnosed as psychosomatic.

Dr. Stephen Gyland wrote a paper describing the symptoms of 1,100 of his hypoglycemic patients. Dr. Gyland himself had once suffered from the disorder. It was three years before anyone gave him the glucose-tolerance test; during that time 14 specialists and three major clinics diagnosed brain tumor, diabetes, and cerebral arteriosclerosis.

A partial listing of Dr. Gyland's patients' complaints, and the percentage complaining of them, includes:

- nervousness, 94 percent
- depression, 77 percent
- forgetfulness, 67 percent
- mental confusion, 57 percent
- unsocial, asocial, antisocial behavior, 47 percent

- phobias, fears, 23 percent

- suicidal intent, 20 percent

- nervous breakdown, 17 percent

The diagnoses they had received before Dr. Gyland gave them the glucose-tolerance test included, but were not limited to, mental retardation, psychoneuroticism, rheumatoid arthritis, alcoholism, and Parkinson's syndrome.

How Can Low Blood Sugar Affect the Brain?

Carl C. Pfeiffer, Ph.D., M.D., likens blood sugar's role in running the body to gasoline's role in running a car engine. "Sugar (glucose), manufactured from various foods and transported in the blood, is the fuel from which the body cells obtain the energy for all cellular activities. When the supply of gasoline diminishes, the engine begins to sputter erratically until replenished with fuel. Similarly, body cells can no longer produce adequate energy when blood glucose and mineral stores become depleted." He adds that "Of all the organs . . . the brain is the most dependent on the minute-by-minute supply of glucose from the blood. . . ." Thus, "It is no surprise to find that hypoglycemia . . . can result in the signs and symptoms of mental imbalance" *(Nutrition and Mental Illness, p. 57).*

Stephen J. Schoenthaler, Ph.D., states the brain's dependence on glucose vividly: "You know that without oxygen to the brain, we die within minutes. Without glucose to the brain, we would also die within a matter of minutes."

Types of Hypoglycemia

There are two basic types of this disorder. One is *organic,* meaning that it comes from such physical problems as tumors, damage to the liver, or Addison's disease. Orthodox and orthomolecular doctors agree that this form is rare.

The other type is called *functional* (nutritional, reactive) hypoglycemia because symptoms develop as a reaction to something taken into the body. In most cases, the culprits are foods containing sugar (glucose). You may think: "Shouldn't sugar be *good* for low blood sugar; don't we want a higher level?" While sugar indeed does raise blood sugar, it does so at high speed, setting off a seesaw reaction in which blood glucose drops. When blood glucose dips too suddenly or to too low a level, symptoms such as fatigue, faintness, confusion develop because the brain is deprived of its fuel, glucose. Additional symptoms may develop from the body's attempt to "brake" the quick fall by the sudden release of counterregulatory hormones, such as adrenaline. The sudden release of adrenaline can cause such symptoms as palpitations, anxiety attacks, and cold sweats.

Functional hypoglycemia is very common, according to orthomolecular doctors. Dr. Atkins estimates that it accounts for over 99 percent of hypoglycemia cases. It is this type that orthodox medicine believes is grossly overdiagnosed.

Treatment

The diet most people with low blood sugar in this country have been advised to follow has been used since 1924. It is high in animal protein and low in complex carbohydrates.

Another diet, traditionally more popular in Europe, seems to be coming into more frequent use by orthomolecular doctors in this country. (At first description, it may seem the exact opposite of the above diet, but they have several basics in common, which will be discussed shortly.) In his 1987 book *Nutrition and Mental Illness* (p. 61), Dr. Pfeiffer states: "Today we know that a diet low in animal protein, but high in complex carbohydrates, gives consistently better results. . . . These naturally occurring carbohydates help regulate blood sugar levels, thus preventing the rapid swings responsible for hypoglycemic symptoms. These whole foods also contain the trace minerals necessary for the transport and utilization of carbohydrates inside the body."

In comparing the two diets, nutritional doctors do not lose sight of the concept of bioindividuality. Michael Schachter, M.D., has said, "In my experience, both diets are effective, but some people do better with one, and some do better with the other." Dr. Fredericks, although a strong advocate of the high-protein diet, admitted that some people "need other types. . . . Our biochemical differences are greater than our similarities." Discuss with your doctor which diet might work better for you.

These diets are not so diametrically opposed as they might seem. Carbohydrates allowed in both diets are complex, such as grains, fruits, and vegetables. Both diets recommend in particular a lot of fresh vegetables. Both eliminate caffeine and alcohol. Probably most important, both diets eliminate *refined* carbohydrates, such as white flour and all forms of sugars, including fructose. In one study (1982), eight patients with reactive hypoglycemia were placed on a low-refined-carbohydrate diet. Symptoms disappeared in seven of the eight, and the other had substantial improvement. When refined carbohydrates were increased, symptoms returned (L. R. Sanders et al., *Southern Medical Journal* 75, p. 1072).

Both diets are high in foods that prevent the pancreas from the sudden release of insulin that sets in motion the seesaw effect. This need for a slow, steady release of insulin is one reason that nutritional doctors often recommend six or eight small meals a day, rather than three large ones.

Clinical ecologists point out that low blood sugar and sensitivities can be closely entwined. For instance, Dr. Schachter states, "Low blood sugar lowers the sensitivity threshold. Many symptoms connected with sensitivities clear up completely when hypoglycemia is controlled." The reverse may also be true: "Many cases of hypoglycemia are in reality examples of a *sensitivity* to sugar or to foods that can lower blood sugar."

William H. Philpott, M.D., a pioneer in treating hypoglycemia, agrees and notes, "If you cut out what the person is sensitive to, the hypoglycemia disappears, and there is no need for the hypoglycemia diet."

Dr. Schachter recently told me in an interview that "the mineral chromium has been shown to be very effective in stabilizing blood sugar—either diabetes or hypoglycemia. One basic reason for hypoglycemia is a deficiency of chromium."

What You Can Do

If you or someone you care about has symptoms of a mental disorder, or symptoms for which orthodox doctors have found no reason, make sure your physician considers the possibility of a blood-sugar disorder. If your doctor is not orthomolecular, you may have to insist on taking the glucose-tolerance test. If you are told that you "do not have hypoglycemia," but you nevertheless had symptoms during the test, see if your doctor is open-minded enough to read this chapter. If the physician cannot be convinced, consult a nutritional doctor.

On your own, you certainly can safely cut out sugar and other refined carbohydrates, alcohol, caffeine, and tobacco. You can also do sensible exercise and eat six to eight small meals daily (vary foods to prevent developing intolerances). Even if you don't have hypoglycemia, these steps will be good for your general physical and mental health.

Some orthomolecular doctors state that, if symptoms indicating probable low blood sugar are not dangerous to the patient or others, doctors might try a hypoglycemia diet without giving the costly and sometimes grueling glucose-tolerance test. If the diet is successful, this may be considered proof that the problem was hypoglycemia. Dr. Fredericks quotes Dr. Gyland (p. 40): "If hypoglycemia is the problem, improvement with the proper diet should be spectacular in one or two weeks."

While the diets may seem particularly tempting for self-help, please note that physicians say that *doctors* might sometimes prescribe the diet without giving the glucose-tolerance test. However, letters from readers over the years have indicated that some will try nutritional self-help "no matter what." If still you feel compelled to try one of the diets, remember that improvement should be very noticeable within a week or two if hypoglycemia is the problem. If there is no large improvement, another disorder may be behind your symptoms, and you need a scientific diagnosis of what that problem is. Also keep in mind that diets high in animal fat are implicated in such disorders as cancer and heart disease, and that animal protein may be a factor in some cases of schizophrenia.

Orthomolecular doctors warn that both diets, because they emphasize certain types of foods, may lead to intolerances unless foods are rotated (see Chapter 14).

Chapter 16

Yeast Infection (Candidiasis)

Candidiasis is caused by an overgrowth of the yeast fungus *Candida albicans* in the intestines. This is one of the disorders that, orthodox doctors say, orthomolecular doctors overdiagnose. And once again nutritional physicians claim that treatment of the "overdiagnosed" disorder is a factor in their successful treatment of patients who have not responded to orthodox measures.

Basic Debate

Orthodox medicine maintains that Candida infestations are usually limited to such infections as diaper rash, oral thrush, and vaginitis. Generalized, or systemic, symptoms are considered rare.

Orthomolecular doctors state that many of their patients do have generalized candidiasis. Robert C. Atkins, M.D., for instance, in *Dr. Atkins' Health Revolution,* estimates that over one-quarter of his patients suffer from this problem. Orthomolecular doctors might be faulted for "loose semantics" in referring to the form of candidiasis they so often treat, in which the *symptoms* are body-wide, as systemic. The technical definition of systemic candidiasis is a candidiasis infection that has been transmitted through the blood-

SYMPTOMS OF CANDIDIASIS COMMONLY MENTIONED BY
ORTHOMOLECULAR DOCTORS

Arthritic pains	Irritability
Food and chemical sensitivities	Nausea
Intestinal bloating	Pneumonia
Anxiety	Chronic sinusitis
Poor absorption of vitamins and	Hair loss
minerals	Memory loss
Urinary frequency, pain, burning	Depression
Bronchitis	Premenstrual syndrome
Constant colds	Emphysema
Fatigue	Postnasal drip
Diarrhea	

stream. Dr. Atkins, who admits to loosely using the term "systemic candidiasis," states that the organism candida rarely gets into the bloodstream, and that "the general candidiasis we most often see is correctly termed "mucocutaneous," that is, pertaining to the skin and mucous membrane.

Orthomolecular doctors hold that generalized symptoms arise when the overgrowth of candida in the intestines releases toxins, which are absorbed from the intestines and sent throughout the body. The immune system may be adversely affected.

Symptoms

The table above shows how easy it is to misdiagnose causes of candidiasis symptoms if this disorder is not considered. Many symptoms are identical to those of other illnesses; furthermore, a number of these symptoms can be present at the same time, and doctors are traditionally taught that someone reporting that many different symptoms "must be a hypochondriac."

Note that food and chemical sensitivities can be symptoms of candidiasis. Sometimes the best way to treat sensitivities is to treat the *underlying* candidiasis instead.

To the symptoms listed in the table, Abram Hoffer, M.D., Ph.D. *(Orthomolecular Medicine for Physicians,* pp. 170–71) adds that Dr. C. Orian Truss, a major worker with candidiasis, found that many patients with chronic illnesses such as schizophrenia and multiple sclerosis "did not get well until their yeast infection had been contained."

Dr. Atkins states that candidiasis "produces an imbalance that can affect so many people in so many ways that we can refer to it as 'the missing diagnosis.' . . . these symptoms are presented by millions of patients who will never be correctly diagnosed. Their mainstream physicians will not search for the presence of this overgrowth, and so they will not find it, because they do not believe it can cause generalized symptoms."

Factors Behind Candidiasis

Diets high in yeast and sugar are major culprits in candidiasis. The role of yeast is self-evident, but you may wonder: Why sugar? You probably know that in the making of bread, even a small amount of sugar added to the yeast-flour mixture greatly increases the rising effect of the yeast. In the same way, sugar in the intestinal tract serves as an ideal culture medium, or food, for the growth of *Candida albicans.*

Other common factors are birth control pills, steroids, and antibiotics. Antibiotics kill not only harmful bacteria, but also friendly bacteria necessary for good health. When friendly bacteria are knocked out, yeast germs multiply.

Some orthodox doctors, commenting that generalized candidiasis is an epidemic invented by orthomolecular medicine, ask where this disorder was hiding until recent years. A look at the above factors gives an answer: Sugar was much less common in our diets until it began a steady rise in the 1920s; the age of antibiotics did not begin until the forties and fifties; and the Pill didn't come along until the sixties.

Orthodox medical encyclopedias and pharmacy books confirm that some drugs, including antibiotics, can make people vulnerable to candidiasis.

Dr. Atkins states that dental fillings containing mercury, the most commonly used fillings, "may be the most important cause of all." In the May 1984 *Journal of Prosthetic Dentistry* Dr. David Eggleston published research showing that removing and/or putting in mercury-containing fillings brought about sharp changes in the level of T cells, which are critical to immune functions. Dr. Atkins comments that this impairment of the immune system "may be exactly what leads to candida overgrowth."

Dr. Atkins also points out that candida "has been shown to convert the ordinary toxic ionized mercury vapor to . . . methyl mercury, which [is] ten times more toxic than elemental mercury, and which can be retained in brain tissue for 18 to 22 years."

Tests

Until the mid-1980s there was no scientific diagnostic tool for generalized candidiasis. Orthomolecular physicians would have preferred an objective diagnostic tool but, in the absence of one, they treated their patients anyway. Diagnosis involved taking a careful history, with particular attention to common symptoms, including: bloating, particularly when aggravated by beer, bread, pasta, or sweets; general malaise; weakness; forgetfulness; hair loss; and joint pains similar to those of arthritis. Also considered important was a history of antibiotic use, taking the Pill or steroids, and recurrent athlete's foot or fungal infections of the nails. When this investigation indicated a possible candida infection, treatment for candidiasis was prescribed. If the treatment got rid of the symptoms, it was assumed that candidiasis had been the culprit.

This reliance on empirical evidence was an easy target for ortho-dox doctors. Dr. Atkins points out, as do many nutritional doctors, that they can sometimes afford to use therapeutic trials because they use mainly health enhancers, rather than drugs. Dr. Atkins states: "The worst thing that can happen is nothing."

Now, however, there is a laboratory test that provides an objec-tive basis for diagnosis. The test compares the level of candida anti-bodies in the patient's body to that of the normal population. Everyone has some candida in the intestines; the fungus does not cause symptoms unless there is an excessive amount. Antibodies are formed when the body tries to fight off an infection. Since this test is relatively new, make sure your doctor knows of it.

Treatment

Basic therapy is a specific diet (see the table on pages 313–14). Pri-mary steps are the elimination of sugar and white flour, and the re-duction or elimination of other simple carbohydrates (which are quickly metabolized into sugars) and foods associated with yeast or mold. As with all diets, orthomolecular doctors will make changes according to the individual's food sensitivities or other health problems.

Yeast is used in the production of alcoholic beverages. Dr. Hoffer describes a bizarre experience of a few people with heavy yeast infestations: They became drunk on the alcohol generated in their intestines.

BASIC DIET THERAPY FOR CANDIDIASIS

(As used at the Hoffman Center for Holistic Medicine, New York City)

ELIMINATE CERTAIN FOODS THAT ENCOURAGE CANDIDA GROWTH

1. *Sugars*—including corn, cane, beets, dates, maple, honey, molasses, fruc-tose, dextrose, maltose, lactose, and fruit juices.

2. *Artificial sweeteners*—Not recommended.

3. *Yeast*—Brewer's yeast used in beverages: beer, wine, champagne, brandy, whiskey, rum, ciders, and root beer. Baker's yeast used in breads, rolls, and pastries.

4. *Fungi*—Foods such as mushrooms and truffles, as well as fruits, vegetables, or other foods that have mold growth. Freeze foods and leftovers. (Molds can grow on refrigerated leftovers.)

5. *Fermented beverages and condiments*—Vinegars, ciders, and foods containing fermented ingredients such as mayonnaise, salad dressings, ketchup, soy sauce, pickles. Use lemon and olive oil (with spices if tolerated) as salad dressing.

6. *Cheeses*—Cheese is a high source of mold. High-moisture cheeses with a short shelf life may be tolerated. These include cottage cheese, cream cheese, and ricotta, feta, and farmer's cheese.

7. *Malt or malt-containing products*—Products such as malted milk, soybean milk, breakfast cereals. Some patients can tolerate plain, puffed rice and shredded wheat.

8. *Processed and smoked meats and fish*—Hot dogs, sausages, luncheon meats, and corned beef often contain sugar, spices, yeast, and other additives.

9. *Vitamins and minerals*—Some vitamins are derived from yeast or contain brewer's yeast or derivatives of yeast. Check labels.

10. *Canned, bottled, or frozen fruit and vegetable juices*—Juices are commonly made from overripened or damaged produce, and generally the skin of the fruit, which contains surface mold and rotten spots, is also pulverized into the juice. Freshly squeezed juices should be consumed shortly after preparation.

11. *Dried fruit, coffee, and tea*—These tend to harbor mold.

12. *Melons*—Cantaloupes tend to develop molds. Be cautious with the use of other melons.

Foods and nutritional supplements that have anticandida properties may be recommended. These include garlic, caprylic acid and other short-chain fatty acids, and yogurt or live lactobacillus acidophilus cultures. Homeopathic dilutions of candida may be used.

What You Can Do

Use the information given in this chapter as a springboard for discussing with your doctor the possibility that candidiasis may be a factor behind your symptoms. If your doctor is staunchly orthodox and close-minded, you may not have much success, and you may want to discuss your symptoms with a nutritional doctor. See "Resources" to find a doctor near you.

If your doctor has prescribed antibiotics for a medical problem, DO NOT stop taking them because you have seen here that they can precipitate a yeast overgrowth.

Consider consulting a holistic dentist to check for mercury toxicity from fillings.

Do not self-prescribe the nutritional supplements mentioned in this chapter. It is safe for you to take a daily multivitamin-mineral supplement. Make sure that the label states that the product is yeast-free and sugar-free.

Certainly, eliminating many of the substances suggested in the table—sugar, alcoholic beverages, artificial sweeteners, coffee, tea, and processed smoked meats and fish—is safe self-help. I know of no nutritional doctor who believes that these are anything but detrimental to health. Indeed, eliminating *all* foods indicated in the basic diet will not hurt you—if their elimination does not lead to such a limited diet that you don't get varied nutrients, or that you eat some foods so often that you become sensitive to them. (See Chapter 14.)

However, cutting out all the potentially harmful foods without running into the above problems of a limited diet can be extremely difficult unless you consult a nutritional expert. Also, orthomolecular doctors, while considering a diagnosis of candidiasis, are ruling out other disorders that can cause the same symptoms. While the candidiasis diet in itself may not be harmful if this disorder is not behind your symptoms, you might be endangering yourself if you waste time trying it while the actual disorder is not being treated.

Chapter 17

Heavy-Metal Toxicity

Heavy-metal toxicity is discussed in Chapter 4, "Psychosomatic Symptoms, Hypochondria, and Other Mysterious Problems" because it so often plays a role in these problems. You may find it helpful to look through that chapter before proceeding.

Basic Debates

Orthodox medicine agrees that heavy metals can cause problems: The *Signet/Mosby Medical Encyclopedia* states that "large amounts of any of them may cause poisoning." Yet orthodox and orthomolecular doctors criticize each other over several issues. Particularly contentious is the debate on silver amalgam fillings, whose major component is the heavy metal mercury. The *Encyclopedia* states that mercury poisoning is caused by "swallowing or breathing . . . small amounts" and lists some 14 symptoms listed including slurred speech, staggering, bloody diarrhea, and fatal kidney failure.

Orthomolecular doctors criticize orthodox dentistry for ignoring the possibility of harm from these fillings and treating it as a nonissue. Mentions in the literature proposing fillings as a problem go at least as far back as 1926. In that year Alfred Stock, a biochemistry professor, documented his own problems from mercury toxicity. Robert C. Atkins, M.D., points out in *Dr. Atkins' Health Revolution* (p. 150) that the American Dental Association does have concern about the dangers of mercury, but that its concern is for the dentist. "It has set strict guidelines for the disposal of mercury in dental offices. The scrap mercury that is left over from [fillings] is to be placed in a sealed container, because vapors can be released into the office. These ADA authorities recognize that mercury . . . must be stored in a safe place." Dr. Atkins suggests this as a further indication that mercury should not be "stored" in anyone's mouth.

Symptoms

Symptoms of heavy-metal toxicity can be dangerous, even lethal, for three reasons:

- They can mimic various physical and mental disorders, leading to misdiagnosis and treatment for those nonexisting disorders.

- They can seem like a hodgepodge that fits no "textbook disease" whatsoever, and you can be labeled as having hypochondria or a psychosomatic problem requiring psychotherapy. While you are undergoing unnecessary psychotherapy, the heavy-metal toxicity is not being treated.

- Orthodox medicine tends to be less suspicious of heavy-metal toxicity than orthomolecular medicine and may not test you for this problem—one reason the above two mistakes occur so often.

The following case history illustrates these points. It was given by Hal A. Huggins, D.D.S., in 1982 in the *Journal of Orthomolecular Psychiatry* (Vol. 11, No. 1, pp. 3–16). By the time he saw the 17-year-old girl, she had been investigated by 50 medical practitioners for the symptoms that had begun 20 minutes after she received several dental fillings. Following are some of the "highlights" of this case:

- Symptom: Hyperventilation. Diagnosis: Reaction to a diet pill.
- Symptom: Hyperventilation. Diagnosis: Nerves.
- Symptoms: Unable to breathe, pain in chest and back. Diagnosis (after 13 days of testing in a hospital): Nerves.
- Symptom: Very painful menstruation. Diagnosis: Possible hepatitis.
- Diagnosed with a possible gallbladder problem. (At around this time there was "much pressure to send her to a mental hospital for drug therapy." Psychotherapy and psychiatry had previously been recommended.)
- Symptom: Suicidal. Referred to a minister.
- Emergency-room trip because of intense chest pain and sensation of dying. Diagnosis: Nerves.
- Emergency room because she was fiery red from waist up, and felt like she was "burning up." Diagnosis: Nerves.

After she was tested for mercury sensitivity, her fillings were removed, and all symptoms stopped within 15 days.

Dr. Huggins mentions that most of the patient's reactions are covered in the literature as associated with mercury poisoning.

Tests

Urine and blood tests reveal amounts of heavy metals. Orthomolecular doctors also often use hair analysis, a technique criticized by orthodox doctors. (See pp. 36–37 in Chapter 1 for a refutation of this argument.) They may also test as a matter of course for mercury toxicity from dental fillings. The mercury vapor test is performed by an instrument that gives a digital readout of the mercury content in the air sample at the tip of the instrument. Placed in the mouth, it acts like "a silent Geiger counter," according to Dr. Atkins, and "locates mercury leaks in a minute."

Treatment

The basic treatment, of course, is eliminating the source of the poisoning. Chapter 4 lists some foods that naturally chelate (remove) heavy metals from the body. Orthomolecular doctors prefer to use natural chelators, but for people who are heavily toxic, they will often use the controversial EDTA, because it is a more powerful chelator. EDTA therapy is an intravenous infusion of ethylenediaminetetraacetic acid, a synthetic amino acid. The treatment is done in the doctor's office and takes about three hours, after which the patient returns to normal activity. In his book *Orthomolecular Medicine for Physicians* (p. 155), Abram Hoffer, M.D., Ph.D., says: "There are two opposing views [about this treatment]. One, held by physicians who use it, is favorable; these physicians were all persuaded to use it by learning of favorable responses and, once they began, were convinced by the responses they saw. . . . The opposite point of view is held by physicians who have never used it and are unfamiliar with the literature."

Dr. Atkins points out that the medical literature includes 1,800 clinical studies on chelation and that all but one described results favorable to chelation. Actually, since EDTA is a synthetic chemical, EDTA chelation is, Dr. Atkins states, completely within the paradigm of mainstream medicine. (It is orthodox medicine's preferred treatment for lead poisoning.)

Dr. Atkins reports that careful records are kept of all chelation patients nationwide by diplomates of the American Board of Chelation Therapy, and that as of 1988 over 500,000 patients had been treated with EDTA, and approximately 80 percent had had their symptoms improved.

The main problem with EDTA is that it rids the body not only of harmful heavy metals but also of necessary minerals, a fact that can lead to dangerous side effects. For nutritional experts, replacing these minerals is a relatively simple task. For them, EDTA therapy *includes* restoring the "good" minerals to optimum level by supplementation.

Dr. Atkins (p. 222) explains how EDTA works to rid the body of a heavy-metal overload: "Most heavy toxic minerals are divalent; that is, they carry two positive charges ready to link up with two negative ions. EDTA . . . binds or attracts those minerals in such a way that it draws the positive charges to itself. The EDTA-mineral complex thus formed remains in solution. Such a solution . . . is now capable of passing through the blood vessels to the kidneys and out of the body."

Such essential minerals as calcium, magnesium, and zinc are also divalent. That is why they, too, get "escorted" out of the body by EDTA and must be replaced.

Orthomolecular doctors also use EDTA to treat other conditions, such as cerebral vascular disease, arthritis, peripheral vascular disease, and coronary heart disease. They argue that EDTA can be an effective way to prevent bypass surgery. For more information, *Dr. Atkins' Health Revolution* would be a good starting point.

What You Can Do

First, see the What You Can Do section in Chapter 4. Consider having your fillings tested for mercury leakage. If there is a problem, have them replaced with nonmetallic filling materials. Be aware that the process of drilling out mercury amalgams releases a lot of mercury particles and vapor all at once. Dr. Hoffer recommends that you take extra ascorbic acid before and after dental visits. If you work with a holistic dentist, the doctor should know ways to prevent harm from the sudden release of mercury; discuss this ahead of time. If you work with a mainstream dentist, have the doctor consult a holistic dentist.

Chapter 18

Nutrients and Brain Chemicals

The relatively recent discovery that imbalances of brain chemicals can be behind mental disorders revolutionized psychiatry. Drugs, used because they affect the levels of these chemicals, are the greatest help mainstream psychiatry historically has devised.

But how do the necessary chemicals normally get every day into the brains of those who are never given these drugs? And how do they get produced in a sufficiently *balanced* fashion so that many never develop mental illness—and thus never need the drugs? It is nutrients that naturally produce the brain chemicals that affect our thoughts and behavior.

Brain chemicals are often called neurotransmitters because they *transmit* electrical signals between brain cells (*neurons*). If any of these chemicals is too abundant or in short supply, brain function can become disrupted, resulting in distortions of mood, perceptions, and emotions. For instance, an excess of an excitatory neurotransmitter may result in hyperactivity or mania; too much of an inhibitory neurotransmitter may result in depression.

Elsa Colby-Morley, Ed.D., Ph.D. (*Journal of Orthomolecular Psychiatry* Vol. 12, No. 1, p. 38), cites published research going back to 1974 indicating that eating large quantities of dietary constituents that are raw materials for neurotransmitters can raise blood and brain levels of the neurotransmitters themselves.

In 1980 Drs. J. H. Growdon and Richard J. Wurtman, of the Massachusetts Institute of Technology, published an article in the September *New York State Journal of Medicine* on nutrients and neurotransmitters. Of this article Dr. Colby-Morley says that Drs. Growdon and Wurtman "see the composition of the recent meal, the concentration of amino acids and choline in the blood, as affording the brain neurons the ability to make and release several of their neurotransmitters—serotonin, acetylcholine, and perhaps . . . dopamine and norepinephrine." Dr. Wurtman, referring to this research, asked, "Why does it come as a surprise that what we eat can directly influence the brain?"

A simplified discussion follows of several brain chemicals, covering some of the nutritional raw materials (precursors) and other nutrients involved in the production of these chemicals. The most common omission in this simplified discussion is of the enzymes that help in producing the brain chemicals.

Serotonin

A deficiency of serotonin has been associated with anxiety and with depression. Antidepressant drugs tend to work by increasing the brain's level of serotonin and norepinephrine. (Low levels of the latter neurotransmitter have also been implicated in depression.)

The pathway to the *natural* production of serotonin starts with the amino acid L-tryptophan. Iron, vitamins C and B6, and magnesium help convert the amino acid into serotonin.

Gamma-aminobutyric Acid (GABA)

When GABA is released from neurons in the brain, it has a calming, tranquilizing effect and thus plays an important role in our response to stress and the relief of anxiety. Orthomolecular psychiatrists point out that foreign substances such as Valium, the barbiturate drugs, and alcohol that also stimulate the GABA receptor serve as *unnatural* tranquilizers.

This is how GABA naturally comes into existence: The amino acid L-glutamine is picked up from the bloodstream by a neuron, where it is converted to L-glutamic acid. Vitamin B6 and the mineral magnesium are necessary for this conversion. The enzyme glutamic acid decarboxylase then transforms L-glutamic acid to GABA.

Dopamine

Dopamine is involved with pleasure. It is thought that too little may result in depression, and too much, in mania. Changes in dopamine level are also believed to play a role in the "highs" of taking a drug like cocaine, and the "lows" of withdrawal. Disorders of dopamine metabolism have been implicated in schizophrenia and in Parkinson's disease.

The pathway for the manufacture of dopamine starts with the amino acid phenylalanine and proceeds to the amino acid tyrosine, which is converted to L-dopa and then to dopamine with the help of enzyme and coenzyme catalysts. Other nutrients needed for these conversions include vitamins B6 and C, and the minerals iron, magnesium, manganese, copper, and zinc.

The precursor to dopamine—phenylalanine—has been used to treat depression. So has tyrosine, which, though formed from phenylalanine, as shown above, may also be obtained from the diet or from supplements. Psychiatrist Priscilla Slagle, M.D., reports in her book *The Way Up from Down* (p. 240) that she usually prescribes tyrosine rather than phenylalanine because the former is one chemical step closer to dopamine. It is also a step closer to the neurotransmitters covered in the next section.

Norepinephrine

Norepinephrine (and epinephrine) are formed basically by the same pathway as dopamine, except that another enzyme and coenzyme work to convert dopamine to these two chemicals. Deficiency of norepinephrine is considered a factor in depression, and an excess is thought to be a factor in the flip side of depression: mania.

Acetylcholine

Acetylcholine is thought to affect aggressivity and tension. In the 1986 *International Journal of Biosocial Research* (Vol. 8, No. 2, p. 135) Derek Bryce-Smith, D. Sc., Ph.D., points out that "killer" rats have raised acetylcholine levels in a structure in the brain called the diencephalon. He cites work published in 1982 indicating that killer rats can be transformed into nonkillers when acetylcholine uptake is blocked. And "killers" can be created by giving them the antiacetylcholine esterase pilocarpine.

The production of this neurotransmitter starts when the nutrient choline joins a molecule of acetylcoenzyme A in a reaction catalyzed by the enzyme choline acetyltransferase. The hard workers B6 and magnesium, again, are intimately involved in producing this brain chemical.

Phenylethylamine

The raw material for phenylethylamine is the amino acid L-phenylalanine. It is converted to the neurotransmitter with the help of B6 and magnesium.

Phenylalanine might be considered capable of a "triple play." Supplements can increase the net available levels of *three* brain chemicals. As mentioned previously, it serves as the direct precursor for dopamine, as well as phenylethylamine. It also *inhibits* the enzyme that breaks down endorphins. Endorphins are natural opium-like substances in the brain. Like morphine, endorphins alter moods and have painkilling properties. It is believed that endorphins may play a role in the moods experienced by schizophrenics. Dr. Colby-Morley reports, "It has been suggested that the endorphins may play such a major role in regulating moods that disturbances in these molecules could lead to any number of mental illnesses."

Increased levels of any of the above three brain chemicals can improve mood and relieve withdrawal symptoms. Thus, as one psychiatrist working with cocaine abusers stated, "The amino acid phenylalanine carries a big whammy in treating cocaine addicts."

Chapter 19

Nutritional Deficiencies and Other Factors

This chapter does not include studies or rationales because the information is, comparatively, well-known and undisputed by orthodox medicine. (However, much of this may not be known by your individual orthodox doctor.) See Chapter 18 for a discussion of the direct help many nutrients give in the natural production of brain chemicals.

The table on page 330, based on information in the book by psychiatrist Priscilla Slagle, M.D., *The Way Up from Down* (pp. 241–56) shows some of the symptoms, generally considered "mental," that may actually be physical reactions to vitamin or mineral deficiencies. The information is by no means complete and makes no attempt to list symptoms generally considered "physical," rather than "mental."

Vitamins cannot be synthesized in the body, nor can some of the fatty acids, amino acids, and minerals. Thus, these nutrients must be taken in foods or supplements. Even nutrients that can be made in the body depend for synthesis on those that must be taken into the body.

SOME COMMON "MENTAL" SYMPTOMS OF NUTRITIONAL DEFICIENCIES

Vitamin B1 deficiency	Depression	Memory loss
	Irritability	Confusion
	Emotional instability	Anxiety
Vitamin B3 deficiency	Depression	Anxiety
	Organic confusional state in the elderly	Irritability
Vitamin B5 deficiency	Depression	Quarrelsomeness
Vitamin B6 deficiency	Depression	Premenstrual tension
Vitamin B12 deficiency	Depression	Mood swings
	Hallucinations	Paranoia
Vitamin C deficiency	Depression	Confusion
Magnesium deficiency	Depression	Anxiety
	Hyperactivity	Disorientation
	Learning disability	Nervousness
Zinc deficiency	Depression	Apathy
Iron deficiency	Depression	Irritability

B Vitamins

B vitamins "unlock" nutrients in proteins, carbohydrates, and fats so that the brain and other organs can use them for fuel. They aid in keeping the body supplied with oxygen and in stabilizing nervous-system functions. Many B vitamins assist in manufacturing DNA-RNA nucleic acids that carry the genetic code for repair, growth, and multiplication of all cells and tissues—including, of course, cells and tissues of the brain.

Vitamin B3 can raise the level of the brain chemical serotonin and can restore activity of acetylcholine. It can act as a sedative. It has been used successfully by orthomolecular psychiatrists since the 1950s to treat schizophrenia. B6 is important in forming hormones in the central nervous system, and helps control sodium/potassium levels in body fluids. When this ratio is unbalanced, edema may occur.

Vitamin C

Vitamin C is involved in almost every biochemical reaction in the body, including synthesis of brain chemicals, and is an integral part of the vitamin B3–based therapy for schizophrenia and nutritional therapy for addiction.

Chromium

Chromium is very important in helping glucose, the brain's major fuel, to travel from the bloodstream to the cells.

Magnesium

Magnesium helps activate vitamin B6. Chapter 18 shows how crucial magnesium and B6 are in producing brain chemicals. In the chapter on children's problems, for instance, you will see B6 and magnesium often prescribed together.

Manganese

Manganese activates choline and adenosine triphosphate, key components of several of the brain's neurotransmitters. If these nerve messengers work at cross-purposes, or do not work efficiently, schizophrenic behavior may be one result. Children suffering childhood schizophrenia are often low in manganese (as well as zinc, calcium, and magnesium).

Amino Acids

As seen in Chapter 18, some amino acids, assisted by other nutrients, produce brain chemicals necessary for mental health and happiness. Amino acids also are needed because they build proteolytic
pancreatic enzymes. Chapter 14 touches on the importance of these
enzymes for mental health. Orthomolecular psychiatrist William H.
Philpott, M.D., adds that amino acid deficiency can lead also to reduced quantity and quality of hormones and antibodies, and to a
body's excessive demands for vitamins, minerals, and trace elements.

Marginal Vitamin Deficiencies

Orthodox medicine easily recognizes that *gross* vitamin deficiencies
can cause diseases: for instance, gross deficiency of vitamin C results
in scurvy, of B3, in pellagra. Traditionally, doctors have assumed
that if you show no clinical signs of gross-deficiency diseases, you
are adequately nourished.

However, as Melvyn R. Werbach, M.D., states in his book *Third
Line Medicine* (p. 143), the gross-deficiency stage may be thought of
as the fourth in five stages of vitamin deficiency. The first stage involves reduction of tissue stores of the vitamin and depression of its
excretion in the urine. In the second, enzymes dependent on the vitamin begin to have reduced activity, and the body's biochemical reactions are impaired. In stage three, symptoms such as insomnia,
irritability, and loss of appetite become apparent. But since these are
not specific symptoms of any particular vitamin deficiency, they may
still not be connected to a deficiency by a doctor not specializing in
nutrition.

These three phases are followed by the clinical stage, in which
classical symptoms of the vitamin-deficiency disease are shown. It is
this stage that is readily acknowledged by orthodox doctors. However, by this time there is only one stage remaining, "the terminal

stage," which results in death if the vitamin deficiency is not corrected.

Dr. Werbach was referring to research published back in 1979 by the Department of Health, Education, and Welfare (Myron Brin, in *Behavioral Effects of Energy and Protein Deficits,* Washington, DC, US, NIH Publication No. 79–1906).

A 1984 article in the *Journal of Orthomolecular Psychiatry* (Vol. 13, No. 1, pp. 27–33) cites government and other studies that found substantial portions of the population to have marginal vitamin and mineral deficiencies. The article also cites studies showing that marginal deficiencies can produce numerous symptoms, including but not limited to anxiety, hysteria, depression, hypochondria, psychopathic deviation, and anorexia. Some studies went on to show that behavior returned to normal shortly after nutritional therapy was undertaken.

Nutritional doctors generally consider the official recommended daily allowances (RDAs) of vitamins and minerals insufficient because they were established to prevent the development only of classical deficiency disease symptoms.

It is possible to be marginally deficient even if you take in "enough" of a nutrient. Drugs, hormones, disease, surgery, and stress may alter your body's ability to utilize nutrients normally. Or your body may lack this ability even under usual circumstances. See the next section.

Vitamin Dependencies

If you have a vitamin dependency, you need an unusually high level of the vitamin(s) in question to function normally.

In their book *Food, Mind & Mood,* David Sheinkin, M.D., and Michael Schachter, M.D. (p. 212) state that vitamin dependencies "are often due to either an inherited or acquired deficiency of an enzyme. . . . Severe enzyme deficiencies and their possible correction by large doses of vitamins is well recognized by mainstream medicine. What is not so well recognized is that these [enzyme deficiencies] may occur in milder forms."

The doctors point out that the diagnosis of enzyme deficiencies, as well as other metabolic problems, can often be accelerated by measuring amino acids in the urine and/or blood, a testing procedure that until recently was not "economically feasible." When a medical procedure is not economically feasible, it often is not easily available to the public. Make sure your doctor considers using this test.

Deficiencies of Essential Fatty Acids (EFAs)

Essential fatty acids, when present in the body with proper amounts of certain vitamins and other factors, are converted into prostaglandins. Prostaglandins are hormonelike substances with powerful effects on brain function and on all tissues of the body.

Studies, many of them in the orthodox literature, indicate that essential fatty acids can be helpful in treatments for a variety of problems. For example, Robert C. Atkins, M.D., in *Dr. Atkins' Health Revolution* (p. 344), cites, in particular, studies masterminded by Dr. David Horrobin using evening primrose oil, one of the few significant sources of gamma-linoleic acid (GLA): "Horrobin has succeeded in publishing studies of the type that orthodoxy *must* accept—double-blind, controlled, statistically significant, done at English-speaking teaching hospitals." To mention only the disorders most relevant to this book, Dr. Atkins states that these studies *"absolutely prove* that GLA is the most effective treatment yet for premenstrual syndrome. . . . They virtually prove its value in . . . aiding alcoholism. . . . It has also been tested and shown to have favorable results in hyperactive children, depression, schizophrenia."

Resources

When requesting that information be sent by mail, always supply a large self-addressed, stamped envelope.

American College for
  Advancement of Medicine
P.O. Box 3427
Laguna Hills, CA 92654
800-532-3688

American Holistic Medical
  Association
2002 Eastlake Ave. E.
Seattle, Washington 98102
919-787-5146

American Preventive Medical
  Association
459 Walker Road
Great Falls, VA 22066
703-759-0662 (Send $12.95 for
  Orthomolecular Yellow Pages)

IN CANADA:
Canadian Schizophrenia
  Foundation
16 Florence Ave.
Toronto, Ontario, Canada M2N
  1E9

FOR CHELATION THERAPISTS:
Great Lakes Association of
  Clinical Medicine
70 West Huron
Chicago, Illinois 60610
312-266-7246

FOR CLINICAL ECOLOGISTS:
American Academy of
  Environmental Medicine
303-622-9755 (phone only)

FOR DENTISTS:

Environmental Dental
  Association
9974 Scripps Ranch Blvd. - #36
San Diego, CA 92131
800-388-8124

FOR AUTISM:

Autism Research Institute
4182 Adams Ave.
San Diego, CA 92116
619-281-7165

FOR HYPERACTIVITY:

Feingold Association
P.O. Box 6550
Alexandria, VA 22306
703-768-3287

FOR ELECTROMAGNETIC THERAPY:

Philpott Medical Services
17171 S.E. 29th St.
Choctaw, OK 73020
405-390-3009

Bibliography

Atkins, Robert C., M.D. *Dr. Atkins' Health Revolution: How Complementary Medicine Can Extend Your Life.* New York: Bantam Books, 1990.

Cheraskin, E., M.D., and W. M. Ringsdorf, Jr., D.M.D. (with Arline Brecher). *Psychodietetics.* New York: Bantam Books, 1976.

Cott, Allan. *Fasting as a Way of Life.* New York: Bantam Books, 1977.

Davis, Adelle. *Let's Get Well.* New York: Signet, 1972.

Erdmann, Robert, Ph.D. (with Meirion Jones). *The Amino Revolution: The Breakthrough Program That Will Change the Way You Feel.* New York: Simon & Schuster, 1989.

Fredericks, Carlton, Ph.D. *Eat Well, Get Well, Stay Well.* New York: Grosset & Dunlap, 1980.

———. *Nutrition Guide for the Prevention and Cure of Common Ailments and Diseases.* New York: Simon & Schuster, 1982.

———. *Nutrition: Your Key to Good Health.* North Hollywood, Calif.: London Press, 1964.

Hoffer, Abram, M.D., Ph.D. *Orthomolecular Medicine for Physicians.* New Canaan, Conn.: Keats, 1989.

Hoffer, Abram, M.D., Ph.D., and Morton Walker, D.P.M. *Ortho-*

molecular Nutrition: New Lifestyle for Super Good Health. New Canaan, Conn.: Keats, 1979.

Kordel, Lelord. *Health Through Nutrition.* New York: Manor Books, 1950.

Mandell, Marshall, M.D. (and Lynne Waller Scanlon). *Dr. Mandell's 5-Day Allergy Relief System.* New York: Harper & Row, 1988.

Menolascino, Frank J., M.D., and Jack A. Stark, Ph.D., eds. *Preventive and Curative Intervention in Mental Retardation.* Baltimore: Paul H. Brookes Publishing, 1988.

Newbold, H. L., M.D. *Mega-Nutrients for Your Nerves.* New York: Berkley Books, 1978.

Pfeiffer, Carl C., Ph.D., M.D. *Mental and Elemental Nutrients: A Physician's Guide to Nutrition and Health Care.* New Canaan, Conn.: Keats, 1975.

———. *Nutrition and Mental Illness: An Orthomolecular Approach to Balancing Body Chemistry.* Rochester, Vt.: Healing Arts Press, 1987.

Phelps, Janice Keller, M.D., and Alan E. Nourse, M.D. *The Hidden Addiction: And How to Get Free.* Boston: Little, Brown, 1986.

Philpott, William H., M.D., and Dwight K. Kalita, Ph.D. *Brain Allergies: The Psychonutrient Connection.* New Canaan, Conn.: Keats, 1980.

Rudin, Donald O., M.D., Clara Felix, and Constance Schrader. *The Omega-3 Phenomenon: The Nutrition Breakthrough of the Eighties.* New York: Rawson Associates, 1987.

Schauss, Alexander, Ph.D. *Diet, Crime and Delinquency.* Rev. ed. Berkeley, Calif.: Parker House, 1981.

Sheinkin, David, M.D., Michael Schachter, M.D., and Richard Hutton. *Food, Mind and Mood.* 2nd ed. New York: Warner Books, 1987.

Silverman, Harold M., Pharm. D. *The Pill Book: Guide to Safe Drug Use.* New York: Bantam Books, 1989.

Slagle, Priscilla, M.D. *The Way Up from Down.* New York: St. Martin's Press, 1992.

Smith, Lendon H., M.D. *Improving Your Child's Behavior Chemistry*. New York: Pocket Books, 1976.

Werbach, Melvyn, M.D. *Healing Through Nutrition: A Natural Approach to Treating 50 Common Illnesses with Diet and Nutrients*. New York: HarperCollins, 1993.

———. *Third Line Medicine: Modern Treatment for Persistent Symptoms*. New York: Arkana Paperbacks, 1986.

Index

About the Author

Pat Lazarus has been a medical journalist for more than twenty-five years. She has published over four hundred articles on medicine, mostly in technical publications read by doctors to keep on top of new research. This is her second book for the lay public. Her first, *Keep Your Pet Healthy the Natural Way,* is considered the classic book on nutritional (orthomolecular) therapy for dogs and cats.

Listed in the *International Who's Who of Authors and Writers,* she is a former member of the National Association of Science Writers in the United States.

She lives in New York City.